HIDDEN IN TIME

HIDDEN IN TIME

MICHAEL PHILLIPS

Tyndale House Publishers, Inc.
WHEATON, ILLINOIS

Visit Tyndale's exciting Web site at www.tyndale.com

Interior maps and illustrations by Joan L. Grytness

Designed by Melinda Schumacher

Library of Congress Cataloging-in-Publication Data

Phillips, Michael R., date
Hidden in time / by Michael Phillips.
p. cm.
Includes bibliographical references.
ISBN 0-8423-5501-4 (pbk. : alk. paper)
I. Title.
PS3566.H492H54 1999
813'.54—dc21 98-48042

Printed in the United States of America

06 05 04 03 02 01 00
7 6 5 4 3 2 1

contents

✦ ✦ ✦

Go up and down the streets of Jerusalem . . .

search through her squares. . . .

Stand at the crossroads and look;

ask for the ancient paths,

ask where the . . . way is, and walk in it.

JEREMIAH 5:1; 6:16

✦ ✦ ✦

The Strange Fate of Six French Crusaders

Jerusalem, A.D. 1121

Six men, in two columns of three, shouldering stout poles of acacia wood, ascended a low, dark, rocky incline out of a small burial chamber beneath the ancient city of David.

Five of the six wore around their necks emblems which signified their Christian faith and crusader loyalties. The sixth and leader of the band, one Hughes de Payns, was a Frenchman of the order known as The Poor Fellow Soldiers of Christ and the Temple of Solomon. He had enlisted these crusaders for a secret assignment which, he intimated, could make them rich beyond imagination . . . if, he added solemnly, they could be discreet, and do exactly as they were told.

Their burden was of exceeding weight. Yet expressly for such a discovery had de Payns left his homeland and sojourned to this distant land. The others of his order knew nothing of today's exploration.

The air was still dusty with particles from the recent tremor which, as if by miracle, had opened the way to the priceless treasure. The footing beneath them was uneven, and every step fraught with peril.

While none would dare scoff openly at the old tales about contact with the gleaming surface, it was doubtful whether they actually believed them. Yet with difficulty they were struggling not to put the legend to the test. The way was narrow, stones cluttered the path underfoot, and one or two wondered if the earth had altogether settled beneath them.

It was a dangerous time and place to be transporting an object so heavy, and for which such delicacy and care were required.

Indeed, their way was more treacherous than they realized.

✦ ✦ ✦

It had been three weeks before when de Payns stood in another vaulted underground cavern, gazing about in wonder with a different group of companions, his eight noble friends who had come here with him from France.

Two held large torches, the others various picks and digging implements. Only moments before they had broken through stones and rubble to the spot. Dust from their work continued to settle in the tomblike air.

All at once it seemed to Hughes de Payns that perhaps the rumors cherished for two decades had basis in fact. He had come to the Holy Land and heard the unbelievable reports in 1104, and had been waiting for this revelation ever since.

"These stones under our feet appear marble," said one, a certain Godeffroi de St. Omer, de Payns' second in command. "At one time they obviously lay in the open air."

His comrades now joined in speculation.

"From the old temple ground?" suggested one.

"From Herod's temple, to be sure," rejoined St. Omer.

"The stones around us are rubble from destruction by Emperor Titus."

"And perhaps other destructions," remarked André de Montbard.

As the discussion continued, all offered various opinions concerning the origin of the surface.

"It may even be that we are standing on the stones of Zerubbabel's temple, not Herod's," said St. Omer.

"Or Solomon's," suggested Montbard.

"It doesn't matter," said de Payns. "We must get deeper."

Their leader was not at present interested in the history of the place. He had studied the site more than any other man alive. He knew every detail of what had occurred on this mount, from David's sacrifice on the threshing floor of Araunah the Jebusite in 1020 B.C. until the present. It was the secrets of what had gone on underground here that possessed him, not what had transpired above it.

"Now that we have broken through to this level," he said, "our next objective must be to find our way below the shetiyyah.[1]

"But the Dome mosque is on top of it," said his friend St. Omer.

"Yes, Godeffroi," he rejoined, "and we are under it."

As they continued to discuss their options and the best means of continuing the excavation, the conversation was not in Hebrew or any other Middle Eastern language of the region. These were not natives to this land. The fluid French tongue flowed from their lips, for all were French noblemen.

They had arrived in Jerusalem two years before on a quest far more secretive than the crusades which had originally brought such numbers of Europeans to this land.

✦ ✦ ✦

Hughes de Payns and his eight fellow Frenchmen excavated and explored for two weeks under the Muslim mosque after their discovery of the marble floor.

They had penetrated several layers lower and had come to a larger cave, off which many

[1]Literally, *stone of foundation*: the large boulder purported to be the mountaintop where Abraham offered Isaac, later said to have formed the floor of the Holy of Holies of Solomon's temple, and still later over which the Dome of the Rock was constructed.

passages spread into the blackness. Water trickled through the bottom of one. Again speculation was vigorous.

"There are so many tunnels and caverns—what are they all?"

"Tombs, hiding places, perhaps even dried-up cisterns."

"The Romans and the Hebrew King Hezekiah were geniuses at bringing water into the city from the surrounding hills."

"But Hezekiah's tunnel is to the south."

"Another canal ran from the north down to the Gihon Spring."

"Many shafts and chambers are connected with burial sites as well as water systems."

"How do we know which tunnels to follow?" asked St. Omer.

"We shall probe those that descend," said their leader. "I am convinced we will find what we seek below the temple. We will investigate the tunnels two by two. Keep your lamps strong. Do not lose your way."

Two hours later, all gathered again in the same chamber. Eagerly they discussed their explorations. Only de Payns and his partner were absent.

At length their steps were heard returning from the depths of a black corridor. De Payns emerged, followed by his comrade, stooped from the tunnel's low roof.

"Did you find anything?" asked Montbard.

"At first I thought so," replied de Payns. "We moved steadily downward. But the way led too far away from the Temple Mount, toward the northwest as it seemed to me. We went for a good distance, hoping it would turn and descend to a lower level. Eventually we were forced back. Rubble and stones barred our way."

"Why don't we break through?"

"It leads in the wrong direction," replied de Payns. "By the time we could go no farther, we were outside the city wall. There could be nothing out there. If that which we seek is in Jerusalem, it is beneath the mount, hidden in some temple crypt, or possibly south, in the direction of Hezekiah's excavations."

He paused, as if debating with himself as he reflected again on the direction of the tunnel from which he had just come.

"No one would bury so priceless a treasure outside the city among the cemeteries," he mused. "It gave life and victory to the ancient Hebrews," he added in a rare moment of prophetic unction. "No tomb is capable of that."

✦ ✦ ✦

In the intervening days, however, the conviction grew within Hughes de Payns that perhaps he had been mistaken.

He had felt strange sensations in the tunnel leading out below the hilly region of the tombs. But a peculiar forboding he could not explain kept him from speaking of it to his companions.

Instead, another plan slowly came into his mind.

Without the knowledge of his French friends, he secretly enlisted the aid of five other crusaders with whom he was acquainted. Leading them into the depths of the city in the middle of the night while his Templar colleagues slept, de Payns retraced his earlier steps from days before.

He led his small band by a different route into the tunnel outside the city gate. After several hours, at last they succeeded in breaking through the obstructions that had previously barred his way.

Climbing over stones and through rubble, they entered a maze of narrow passageways connecting several sections of tombs. The crusaders glanced about with trepidation. Many of the graves carved in walls of rock had already been put to use. But de Payns was not spooked by bones or rotting burial cloths.

He did his best to keep track of the twisting directions of their steps. An inner sense told him he was on the verge of a startling discovery. He would attempt a drawing of this burial maze when he returned to his quarters.

Suddenly he felt uncomfortable rumblings beneath his feet.

He paused and glanced back at his companions. Their wide eyes in the dim light of the two oil lamps showed they had felt it too. This was not the first occasion when the earth had shaken this region in violation of sacred decree.

De Payns gestured for them to follow and continued on. A minor tremor, he thought to himself. He had come too far to turn back now.

Ahead appeared a conflux of several passages, one to the left, another angling right at about thirty degrees, and another slanting sharply backward, nearly paralleling that by which they had come.

He stopped again, signalled for a lantern, then gazed into each of the three tunnels to see which might present itself as the logical course to follow.

Again the ground shook, more violently this time. An involuntary cry or two escaped several of the men's lips. Dust and a few pebbles fell onto their heads.

Still their leader remained unfazed. He continued to examine their surroundings.

Another jolt rocked beneath them. Then, at de Payns' side between the two angled passages, several rocks of the wall gave way and crumbled and fell at his feet. He leapt out of the way as his companions scrambled back.

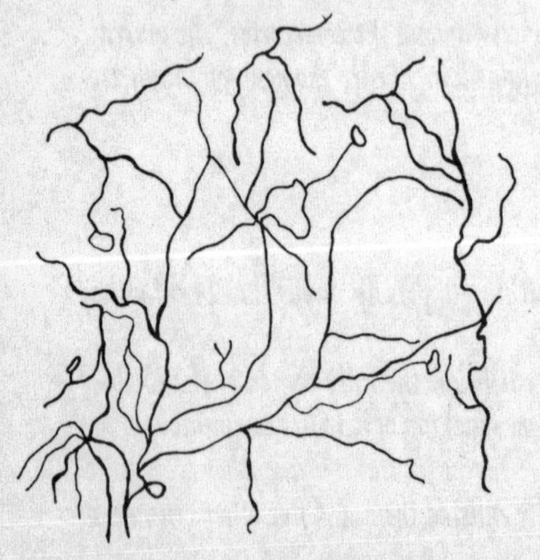

"Wait . . . come back," cried de Payns. He now held one of the lanterns and examined the portion of wall that had shaken loose. He saw what appeared a rectangular outline.

"The tunnel is secure," he said. "We are safe enough. It is only a few stones from the wall that were dislodged."

As he spoke, he began poking about, knocking away more loose stones. Suddenly his hand shot through an opening and he heard a thud of falling stones in some unseen chamber behind the wall. De Payns quickly handed the lantern to another and began knocking and pushing at more loose stones.

"It looks like a vault, perhaps a crypt sealed up behind this wall," he shouted. "The quake loosened the stones. It opens off the main passage. Help me remove these rocks."

Within five minutes the former doorway was sufficiently broken apart. De Payns climbed into the opening, then reached back through it for a lantern.

One by one the others followed.

✦ ✦ ✦

Thirty minutes later, they stood in awe and disbelief. They had found that which no man had laid eyes on in more than seventeen centuries. The acacia poles were still intact and strong enough for transport.

The six lifted their burden and squeezed their way toward the entry of the small chamber in which the unknown ancients had left the sacred box for repose.

The discovery had been made in a tiny cell down a long corridor from the main crypt into which the broken doorway had opened.

They managed to get it aloft, though there was barely enough space to press together and move out of the chamber where it had rested in darkness for so long.

"Careful," said de Payns. "Do not lay a finger on it. I must let go a moment to take the two lanterns ahead in the corridor. Hold this side steady."

He picked up first one, then the other lantern from the floor.

"Watch out!" cried a voice behind him.

"I've got it," replied another.

"Do not let the poles droop," said de Payns. "Keep them level until I rejoin you."

He walked along the corridor, set the lanterns down some distance away, then turned back to rejoin the others.

Another shout reverberated off the enclosing walls.

"I told you . . . look out—you fool, don't—"

"It's slipping!" cried another. "I can't hold—"

A shriek sounded the likes of which none who heard it would ever forget. Even as its otherworldly echo died away, he who made it collapsed in a heap on the floor of the passage.

Dread hung in the air. The four remaining, two on each side, struggled to steady the heavier weight.

De Payns grabbed one of the lanterns again and hurried to the scene.

He stooped beside the remaining four and extended a lamp toward the body.

The flickering light cast upon their fallen comrade revealed the answer to his question. That he was dead was obvious from one glance into his face. What he had beheld in the final instant before death de Payns did not know. But it was assuredly not from this world. In terror, none spoke for long seconds.

"Now you know to heed my warnings," said de Payns somberly as he stood. He himself was shaken more than he dared reveal. "I think it best we keep the weight evenly distributed on the two sides," he added. "I will hold the lantern so that no one else loses their balance. Bring it through—"

Again the ground shook. It was soon obvious that what had come before was but a precursor to this most severe quake. The entire city rumbled above them.

De Payns leapt back. The weighty treasure swayed dangerously on the shoulders of the four. But the way was too narrow and they had no means of escape, nor room to ease it back to the ground. One stumbled on the body of their dead companion. The ground was moving violently. The passage filled with falling rock and debris. The box tipped. A hand or two tried to steady the poles, but with the quake it was no use.

Muffled shouts and exclamations were followed by another scream, then a great crash. Rocks tumbled from the ceiling and fell everywhere. De Payns saw his crusader companions being buried in the very crypt in which they had discovered the treasure. But he could do nothing to save them.

Suddenly a fierce light burst into the passage. Brighter than the sun itself, it reflected off the gold even as their discovery disappeared in falling dust and stone.

De Payns cried in terror and pain. Both hands shot to his eyes against the blinding rays. The lantern crashed to the ground. The light seared his tongue as if with a hot iron of muting fire.

A great roar rang in the ears of his soul, whether with audible words or with an intuitive sense of apprehension, Hughes de Payns could never say. However it came to him, he knew the meaning of the words spoken out of the Light.

"In my time . . . ," rumbled the Voice of Light. "In MY TIME!"

Gradually the foundations of Jerusalem stilled.

The echo of earthquake and voice, and the brilliance of light, all faded into silence and darkness.

Trembling in panicked horror, de Payns knelt to the ground, thinking again of the lantern. He could see nothing. Only blackness. A more terrifying blackness than he had ever imagined.

When his groping hands finally touched it, no flame met his finger. Already he suspected the darkness deeper than the mere absence of candle flame.

De Payns regained his feet and began feeling about. He took a few steps. How could he hope to find his way? Would he ever see daylight again?

He remembered the expression he had seen on the face of the dead man earlier. It was a look that would haunt him the rest of his days. That which had been hidden in time had been sealed off yet again, its would-be discoverers with it. He alone possessed the secret of both men and sacred repository.

Whatever he may have come to Jerusalem to find, Hughes de Payns wanted no part of it now!

Trembling, he fled in the darkness. Through the tunnels he stumbled and ran like a crazed wild man, frantic and without sense of direction, hands outstretched, attempting to feel his way, bumping and colliding into walls and protruding stones.

He was buried alive under Jerusalem, but knew not where. If there existed a way out after the quake, only a miracle would lead him through it.

PART ONE

LONDON

✦ ✦ ✦

How gladly would I treat you like sons and give you a desirable land,

the most beautiful inheritance of any nation.

I thought you would call me "Father" and not turn away from following me.

But like a woman unfaithful to her husband,

so you have been unfaithful to me.

JEREMIAH 3:19-20

✦ ✦ ✦

one

Hidden Mystery of the Ages

(1)

Two eyes squinted through powerful binoculars.

"Still clear," their owner whispered. The female voice, however, betrayed anxiety.

Silence.

Two hundred yards away, a tall man, athletic of build, dressed entirely in black to match his face, crept along a stone wall in the darkness. He surveilled the same building. Though not meant for him, through a tiny speaker in his ear he also heard the words just spoken. No movement or sound came through the shadowy night.

Inside the edifice at the center of their attention, a third figure moved noiselessly through a maze of stone corridors. Surrounded by an iron railing and high fences, this structure was the centerpiece of a complex and highly secretive venture. It sat in the midst of what appeared a military compound. The gray granite block exterior was of recent construction, square and uninspired design, and from the center of its roof rose a green copper dome.

Everything culminated on this night here in the village of Aksum in the northern Ethiopian highlands.

At grave risk to his life, the daring adventurer had gained entrance to the Sanctuary from the roof. His reputation had been built with pick and shovel, digging back into the antiquity of human history. This night's exploration, however, had been affected not by holes bored through rock but rather through skylights, ventilation systems, and an elevator shaft.

It was the most ambitious quest of his life. If he were successful in at last laying eyes on this prize, he would henceforth be known as no mere archaeologist but as the greatest antiquarian of all time.

Beside the towers of Aksum's famous church, St. Mary's of Zion, the stone repository in which he crept had been built only three and a half decades earlier as permanent home for the sought-after, mysterious, and powerful wonder of the ancient world.

The building whose security the daredevil had cracked was called the Sanctuary of the Ark. His research confirmed that within its thick walls rested the ark of the covenant of the Hebrews.

The sacred relic had been lost to history since its disappearance from the temple of Solomon in Jerusalem, sometime approximately nine hundred or a thousand years before Christ. On this night he hoped at last to uncover evidence to solve once and for all the mystery of its location.

If he or his lookouts were discovered, however, any monk of the church or citizen of the town would not hesitate to kill them. They protected these holy precincts against sacrilege with vigor.

Nor were they opposed to bringing bullets to aid in such duty.

(2)

The guardian monk, whose lifetime responsibility was to preside over the Sanctuary, awoke. It was the middle of the night.

He was the only human allowed in the Holy Place of the chapel where the ark was kept. In his solitary chamber a presence disturbed his slumber.

It took but seconds for him to gather his wits. He rose instantly and made his way across the floor. His bare feet made not a sound.

Deep within the granite complex the adventurer did not realize he was no longer alone. Even had he known, he would not have turned back.

He was too close!

Before him, in the center of the room, atop a waist-high table of carved stone, sat . . . *something* . . . an object . . . a mysterious shape.

His tiny flashlight was hardly capable of illuminating the whole. Draped over with embroidered cloth, about it clung the heavy scent of incense. The covering appeared faded blue. White and purple designs were sewn into it. Tattered fringe bordered the bottom.

The uninvited guest to the sacred chamber shone the beam back and forth. As he walked forward, he thought of the passage from Numbers 4 he knew from memory: "When the camp is to move . . . take down the shielding curtain and cover the ark of the Testimony with it. Then . . . spread a cloth of solid blue over that. . . ."

The rectangular shape in front of him appeared approximately three and a half feet from end to end, and a little over two feet high and deep. The cloth draped over its top, however, was raised higher toward both ends, as if covering two pointed protrusions.

Wings . . . the shape of the angels' wings!

Heart beating wildly, he paused before the cloaked object, then stretched out his hand. Was he about to make known to the world the hidden mystery of the ages?

He took hold of one end of the fabric near its fringed edge. Just uncover it and snap a quick roll of photographs and the mystery would be solved!

Slowly he began to lift it up and back.

An inexplicable compulsion arrested his motion. The moral dilemma at the root of this enterprise, that he had broken into a church like a thief, suddenly entered the brain of his newly growing spiritual consciousness.

But he did not have leisure to consider the implications further.

(3)

Outside, the glare of two automobile headlamps lit the blackness of the streets about half a mile away.

The binoculars observing the silent building immediately turned toward the light and refocused.

"Scott . . . Scott, do you see that?"

"No. Still clear down here," replied the lookout at the wall of St. Mary's. "What is it?"

"A car—coming this way."

"Speed?"

"Fast."

"I hear it. Adam," he said into the tiny microphone next to his mouth, "we may have company."

Again silence fell. The sound of the automobile's engine could be heard through the night.

"Adam, did you hear me?"

"I copy," returned a whispered voice.

"The car is moving this way," came the woman's voice again. "Adam, get out of there!"

"I can't. I've just about—"

"Juliet's right, Adam," interrupted the archaeologist's assistant. "We're not alone. There's another car speeding from the opposite direction now. Break it off!"

"I've got to at least get a pic—"

"Adam," cried Juliet, "please!"

"I have to move!" said Scott. "My position's compromised—gotta go!"

The screech of tires ended further communication. A powerful searchlight from one of the car's windows probed the adjacent street and walls. Scott fell to his stomach. The beam passed over him by inches.

"Adam . . . hurry!" repeated Juliet as loud as she dared. Her own vantage point was safe. But she was terrified for the others. This was her first time out in the field with the team on a project she had been in on from the beginning. Now she wasn't sure she liked this new line of work!

"I heard," came back the voice in her ear. "I'm on my way!"

(4)

A second automobile raced to the scene and skidded to a stop.

Immediately it emptied of six Ethiopian soldiers. They fanned out around the grounds of St. Mary's and the Sanctuary, automatic rifles ready to fire first and make inquiries later.

Inside, the robed and bearded guardian entered the chapel, candle in hand. He glanced about. He saw and heard nothing. Everything seemed in order. The odd-shaped tabotat, nearly uncovered only seconds earlier, sat where it had rested unmoved since construction of the Sanctuary.

Far above in the upper portions of the building, the intruder whose presence had awakened guardian, soldiers, and perhaps the power of the ark itself, scrambled hastily through the same vent by which he had gained access. As carefully guarded as was official access to information concerning this place, security for the building itself was noticeably low-tech. Getting in and out had been, not exactly a piece of cake, but a relatively uncomplicated matter for one with the right contacts and know-how.

And one with daring to go along with sophisticated gadgetry.

Two minutes later he emerged onto the roof under the cover of night. He saw his danger well enough. Below him, Sanctuary and church swarmed with soldiers and monks. However they had been alerted, they had wasted no time getting here. Lights flashed about and panned corners, side streets, and alleyways.

Escape would require even more pluck than the flight in. The roof wasn't high enough to give much maneuverability. There was but a slight breeze. He would have to hit it just right. Or else crash straight down into the search party below!

"I hope you made it out of there, Scott!" he said to himself. "But I'm not waiting around to find out!"

No time to strap himself. He'd hang on to the aluminum bar for dear life. He might have to let go before he reached the ground anyway.

He hoisted to his shoulders the custom-made lightweight hang glider by which he had arrived onto the roof an hour earlier. If only he could get some distance away before one of those spotlights from below accidently panned upward through the sky!

He tested the direction of the wind one last time. He turned into the faint current, then sprinted toward the edge of the building.

With a downward dip, he glided away from the wall and into invisibility.

Shouts, running, and lights below remained focused in the two dimensions of earth's plane. As they scanned and probed doors and windows and fences and streets, none felt the sweep of a great black wing soar past them overhead.

(5)

Eight or nine hundred yards away, beyond several high fences and alongside a run-down row of dwellings whose occupants all slept, another automobile sat next to an empty town square, its lights turned off, its engine silent.

Beside the car stood a diminutive young woman. Her long blonde hair was conspicuously out of place in this region of the world. She had tucked it up under a canvas hat of the African safari type so as to attract no attention.

Nervously she glanced about for her companions.

She had seen and heard the activity in the distance. Something must have gone wrong.

Behind her, footsteps ran up.

"Scott!" she exclaimed, spinning around. "Am I glad to see you. What happened?"

"Don't know. All of a sudden Juliet saw lights. She barely had time to warn us. I just got away."

"Is Adam . . . ?"

"Don't know that either. I took off. I didn't have the luxury of his means of transport. I had fences to climb!"

"And Juliet?"

"She'll be fine. She was near enough the hotel to walk back without being caught in the commotion."

Both glanced about. They were thinking the same thing—how long should they wait before giving thought to their own safety? The soldiers would no doubt soon widen their search.

Jen Swaner, the blonde Swede, and Scott Jordan, the black American, continued to probe the night for the Englishman who was their leader. No sound could be heard other than an occasional shout from the direction of the church.

Two or three minutes passed.

A great winged rush swept overhead.

They spun around and looked up as Adam Livingstone's feet landed at a run several yards away. They hurried toward him with quiet exclamations and greetings.

"I don't believe you made it this far!" said Scott. "How did you do it?"

"I hit a little updraft as I sailed over those fellows' heads," said Adam, grinning. "Help me get this thing dismantled and folded up."

"Leave it. Let's get out of here."

"I invested too much in this design to scrap it. Besides," Adam added, "after what I saw in there, nothing's going to keep me from coming back! Drat, I wish I'd pulled the camera out sooner and hadn't wasted so much time! Jen, get the motor going."

Jen ran for the car and jumped behind the wheel.

Scott and Adam stuffed the collapsed glider into the trunk. The tall men squeezed into the tiny rented Toyota. Jen shifted the car into gear. As carefully as she dared, Swaner sped toward the hotel where Adam's team, not to mention his fiancée, Juliet Halsay, was booked.

This trio had been together on some daring escapades. But if they got through tonight in one piece and safely out of Aksum, this might prove their closest brush yet.

"Given the hornet's nest we aroused," said Adam as they approached the hotel a few minutes later along a side street, "I think we ought to retrieve Figg and Crystal immediately. Where's Juliet?"

"On her way back to the hotel."

"Good. We need to head south in both cars tonight. I have the feeling they'll be searching every accommodation for miles by morning. I'm not sure it would be healthy for us to hang around."

two

Private Opportunities

(1)

The ambitious eyes staring at the microfiche photograph thought for a moment, then enlarged it for closer inspection.

At first glance the face was not especially stunning. Yet it possessed an intriguing expression. One that might be worth looking into further, and, if handled cleverly, just might provide one reporter a doorway into journalistic possibilities.

It would have to be handled skillfully. It couldn't seem crass. Something more than the typical interview or story. A fresh angle.

Get the public interested in the girl.

A follow-up or two. Lots of pictures. Let interest build of itself. It was certainly worth a try to help jump-start a career that was at present going no place.

And there was the helpful element of sadness to go with the subtle enchantment of mouth and eyes . . . the fatal bombing that had taken the lives of half her family. Sympathy always helped. And, with the business of Scotland Yard's subsequent investigation, the merest suggestion of mystery. The sad face brought a slight bite of conscience. But there was no time for that. This was the news business.

Plus the American private investigator snooping about, ingratiating himself into the household, making a nuisance of himself with the Yard's detectives. What was a retired, overweight PI doing in London anyway? All in all, this little entourage surrounding Adam Livingstone had lots of interesting angles.

This might prove the journalistic coup of a lifetime.

(2)

Five hours west, in the small town of Peterborough, New Hampshire, the sun was rising.

Rocky McCondy, former policeman and widower, and current private investigator, groggily closed his massive fist around the impertinent alarm clock on his nightstand as if he would crush it to powder. His goal, however, was merely to squeeze the lever back to the *off* position and silence the thing. After some fumbling the objective was achieved. He lay back onto his pillow and exhaled.

McCondy had a long day ahead of him.

He would not quite be able to enjoy his full morning routine—an icy shower, several strong cups of Starbucks, and a leisurely perusal of the morning's *Boston Globe.* The dousing of cold water would not take long. That morning ablution he performed wherever he happened to be. But the paper would not arrive on his porch today. He had cancelled delivery indefinitely. And the Yukon Blend he would drink on the road.

He would be on his way to New York within the hour. He had an afternoon flight to Yerevan, Armenia, just across Turkey's northeastern border. Two packed suitcases sat by the front door in readiness.

He was not a man prone to exaggeration. Realism and practicality had made him a good investigator, a second career he had practiced since leaving Boston's police force. The last two years had been the most exciting, working with, and at present *for,* English archaeologist Adam Livingstone. But Rocky McCondy knew well enough that he was bound on this day toward nothing short of making history. If they actually pulled Adam's crazy, harebrained scheme off, everyone connected with the project, including him, could well be famous before summer was out.

But he wasn't in it for that, but because it was an adventure. One of the greatest adventures of his life.

After a minute or two the big man swung his feet around, climbed out of bed, and headed for the bathroom. He found himself sustained by the aroma coming from his automatic coffeemaker, took another deep lungful of the morning, and continued toward his daily wake-up appointment under the cold showerhead.

Six minutes later, dressed and shaved, though with his rumpled graying hair no more combed than it was on any other morning, he made his way into the kitchen. There he poured himself a tall mug of the steaming black invigorating brew and probed its edges.

Fifty minutes later Rocky locked his two-story house and was on his way.

He made a brief stop for a final good-bye and word of prayer with Pastor Mark Stafford and his wife, Laurene, then headed west to Keene toward I-91.

(3)

The English reporter rose from the computer screen. It was time to do more research into this Livingstone group. A door, an opening, was always necessary to get the inside scoop, the story behind the story . . . the real goods.

"Hey, Prentiss–what do you have on that fellow Livingstone and his organization?"

"The archaeologist?"

"Right."

"I didn't know he had an organization."

"I mean his staff, his family, his research team."

"Ah, right–yeah, we've a pretty decent file. I'll put something together."

"Photos, too–I want lots of photos."

"Can do. What do you want it for, Shayne?"

"Just a little background research."

"Check with Glendenning. He did double duty out at Sevenoaks back during the Noah's ark flap. Got some decent stuff."

"Does he know Livingstone?"

"I think they're on good terms. What has Livingstone got going these days? All that wandering around in Africa last year with nothing to show for it. Then the Turks pulling his plug on Ararat three months ago–not much of a story there."

"I wouldn't be so sure. I've heard there are new developments on that front."

"You got something, Shayne?"

"I heard a rumor that the Turkish authorities may OK his plan about bringing the ark down after all."

"That would be huge news. In the meantime, if I were interested in old bones, I'd go see Sir Gilbert Bowles. There's a colorful bloke."

"Colorful, but boring," the journalist rejoined, then returned to the computer desk.

"Hey, Shayne," called out Prentiss a minute later. "I just remembered something I saw on the wire. *Society World*'s scheduled to run a story on Livingstone's mother in a few weeks. She found her higher consciousness off in Tibet somewhere."

"Found her what?"

"You know–the rich woman's adventure in the Himalayas with a religious twist. Might be something for you there."

"Thanks, Prentiss. *Society World* is hardly my cup of tea, but I'll be sure to get a copy."

(4)

The journalists at the offices of the BBC were not the only ones probing the news accounts of the famous English archaeologist.

His colleague and fellow scientist Sir Gilbert Bowles sat back the following afternoon perusing an advance copy he had previewed off the Internet of the article soon to be released on Livingstone's mother. What he read irked him.

Everything about Livingstone annoyed him.

The man was in the news everywhere! Whatever the man did seemed newsworthy to some overeager reporter. You couldn't pick up a magazine or newspaper without seeing his name or picture someplace. Now even his mother was getting in on the act.

Bowles hated it. He hated Livingstone!

He himself had been Britain's leading archaeological authority, knighted by the queen, author of a best-selling apologetic for evolution . . . until Livingstone's absurd discovery on Ararat last year. He bitterly resented how the man had turned the public tables on him.

In many ways Sir Gilbert Bowles perfectly represented the classic image of the archaeologist, with the single exception, perhaps, of his massive physical bulk. At six feet four inches and two hundred and seventy pounds, he might have been mistaken for a defensive end for the Pittsburgh Steelers, for he could move with astonishing agility when he had to. But his trademark gray panama hat, hiking boots, and khaki shirt and pants immediately turned any observer's thoughts to Australia's outback, the African bush, or another exotic locale where adventurers traipsed around in their perpetual search for the unusual and the ancient.

Another singular Bowlesian trademark, his wit, he used to make Christianity and Christians everywhere the favorite target for his sarcasm. He relished nothing more than keeping an audience of modernists in stitches with his characterizations of fundamentalists as unsophisticated buffoons.

He was good at it too. Conservative Protestants couldn't stand him. His ponytailed, sandy gray hair added to his offbeat image, which was completed by a silver serpent dangling from a fleshy left earlobe. The authority and humor with which he expounded his popular brand of atheism, bolstered by wide scientific expertise, seemingly incontrovertible, and the delight he took in debunking every religious myth he could get his hands on, convinced his detractors that the ornament of jewelry bore high significance in illuminating the nature of his deepest allegiances.

His best-selling book only increased the animosity of the religious community toward him, a fact that couldn't have pleased Bowles more. *Homopithecus: The Link Is Found,* some claimed, was the most influential apologetic for evolution and against the notion of God since *The Origin of Species.* Actually, no one had made such a claim for a couple of years other than the publicist for Bowles' publishing company. Despite the fact that Bowles was a legitimate and decently respected scientist, the scientific veneer of claims in his treatise was relatively thin. Upon that success had Bowles' reputation grown almost as rapidly as his midsection. He had become a sought-after spokesman for pseudoscientific gatherings, and had parlayed his year or two of enormous popularity into a personal fortune and one of the most recognizable faces and frames on the BBC.

Bowles tried to laugh off the whole Livingstone phenomenon. His discovery of the gigantic Old Testament craft of supposed Noachian construction, which he proposed actually to lift off the mountain, had vaulted Livingstone's reputation far above his own.

Now everything was Livingstone, Livingstone, Livingstone!

Bowles' own offers and invitations had dried to a mere trickle. He would be fifty years old in seven months. That, along with diminishing professional engagements and the increasing effort it took to hoist himself up a flight of stairs, had combined for the first time in Gilbert Bowles' life to produce a sense of his own mortality.

He did not think of it in so many words, of course. Bowles was a man who would never admit to anything remotely resembling introspection. But it could not be denied that an irritating sense of unease swept through him occasionally . . . and he didn't like the feeling.

The fact that Livingstone had apparently had a "religious experience" from his cogitations after finding Noah's ark made Bowles despise the man more. And now the fool's mother was being featured in the news for a "life-changing" conversation with some idiotic, balding Tibetan monk—the whole thing was so laughable it made him sick.

There was more than one way to skin a cat, he thought to himself. He would find a way to upstage Livingstone. Failing that, he could always leak some sleazy story to bring the blighter down a few notches.

(5)

Archaeologist Adam Livingstone breathed a sigh of relief and settled into his seat.

The night escape from Aksum through the desolate wastes of Ethiopia in two unreliable rented cars had been exhausting. Added to the fatigue was the disappointment of having to cut their mission short. His goal had been to photograph the ark and prove its existence and location. The frustration of having to rush from the sacred chapel with his camera full of unexposed film was almost too much.

They reached the Ethiopian capital of Addis Ababa two days later. After a night in the airport, they secured standby seats on an early morning Air France flight to Paris. At least it was in the general direction of home.

Adam tightened his seat belt, then laid his head back and closed his eyes. He was beat.

Minutes later the plane was aloft and banking toward the northwest.

He had begun to nod off when a voice spoke beside him. He was surprised to hear his native tongue. "I always breathe easier when we level off."

Adam opened his eyes and glanced toward the center seat. An American woman between fifty-five and sixty was looking toward him with a nervous smile. Her white knuckles still clutched the two armrests.

"I fly a great deal," he replied, returning her smile. "There's really nothing to be afraid of."

"I know what they say about airplanes being the safest mode of travel. But when I feel those powerful engines and all that speed, I can't help—"

She paused. A puzzled expression came over her face.

"Say—don't I know you?" she said. "You're . . . aren't you the explorer Adam Livingstone?"

Adam laughed lightly. "I'm not sure I would call myself an explorer. But my name does happen to be Adam Livingstone."

"I thought so!" she exclaimed. "I read about you in *Time* last year. I was so excited. It's true, isn't it—that it's really Noah's ark you discovered?"

"I think so," replied Adam. "It made a believer out of me—literally. We hope to continue our research when we get it off the mountain."

"Off the mountain!" exclaimed the lady. "You can't be serious?"

"I have a team of experts working on it. We have the technology to pull it off. I believe the only factors that can prevent it are politics and the weather."

"Now that I think about it, I did read something about your wanting to move the ark. I suppose I must have forgotten about it. But what did you mean when you said it 'literally' made a believer of you?"

"Before last year's discovery on Ararat," Adam answered, "my perspective on God could have probably been summed up with the words *apathetic agnosticism.* After that experience, however, standing on those ancient planks embedded in glacial ice, and for several months considering the consequences of what it meant—after that experience I became a believer, a Christian."

"I am happy to hear of it. I think I recall reading about that in one of the Christian periodicals."

"Yes, they have been after me rather persistently, I'm afraid," said Adam.

"How do you mean?" asked the woman.

"Ever since news of my decision leaked out, I've had the feeling they want to make me a poster boy for the faith, so to speak."

"I am fascinated with your work. Have you made any other discoveries since then?"

Adam thought it best to mention neither the Garden of Eden nor the ark of the covenant to this good-hearted woman. "Let's just say I always have a theory or two running around in my brain waiting to be tried out," he responded evasively. The smile that accompanied his words apparently proved satisfactory.

"And aren't you . . . didn't I read that you are to be married soon?" went on his inquisitive neighbor.

"Ah, yes—*there* is a subject I don't mind talking about!"

"So it is true!"

Adam nodded.

"When is the happy day?"

"In a few months. We haven't set a date."

"What is she like?" asked the woman with an eager expression. Now they were onto a topic far more interesting than archaeology!

"The most wonderful young lady possible for a man to meet," replied Adam. "Would you like to hear about her?"

"Oh, indeed I would, Mr. Livingstone!"

(6)

Several hours west, in the early predawn hours of the same morning, Sir Gilbert Bowles awoke suddenly.

His whole right side was seized with terrific pain. Knives shot through his shoulder up and down his arm.

In terror the big man struggled to rise, knocking the clock off his nightstand. Its glass shattered, though he was scarcely aware of it. The two hands read 3:17 A.M.

Clumsily he got his feet under him. He was breathing hard. His whole body was chilled with clammy sweat. He didn't need a mirror to know that his face was ashen.

Bowles groped for the light switch, then staggered toward the bathroom. A dash of cold water on his face—that's what he needed. He would kill the blasted cook! That infernal shrimp—

His legs gave way. With an awkward buckling of knees, he collapsed on the floor.

Lungs heaving, his breath came in short, labored bursts. This was more than a bad case of indigestion. Something was seriously wrong.

Bowles lay on the floor, trying to gather his wits.

The pain subsided. Momentary relief replaced terror.

He let out a sigh, then struggled to rise. Curse his stupid arm! The useless thing had gone numb. He couldn't get any leverage to push himself up.

He shifted his weight. Leaning on his other arm, he ponderously rose.

That was better, he said to himself. The spasm had passed. Now for that dash of water and maybe a good stiff belt of Scotch.

Bowles managed only two more steps. A jolting grip seized his chest. Two gigantic hands took hold of him with superhuman force and twisted his innards in opposite directions.

He sucked in a sharp breath of air. Fierce pain nearly caused him to faint, like he'd been shot in the chest with a howitzer.

Unconsciously his one good hand grabbed at his heart. He lumbered toward the phone where it sat on the table. He'd call—

Again Bowles' feet gave way.

He toppled forward, bringing phone, several books, and a teapot breaking and clattering down upon him. He collapsed on the floor with a resounding crash, and knew no more.

(7)

Three rows ahead of where the conversation between British archaeologist and American woman was taking place, a young woman of twenty-three years sat with an amused smile on her face.

She had recently opened a magazine. Now she set it aside to listen to the conversation in progress behind her. Adam's voice had risen somewhat. She could tell from the fun in his tone that he intended her to hear what he was saying.

". . . name . . . Juliet Halsay," he was saying. "But not for much longer. She is soon to be Mrs. Adam Livingstone."

In her seat, Juliet nearly melted at the words. She hardly believed everything that had happened so suddenly during the past year. First there had been the tragic London bombing that had taken her father's and brother's lives. For financial reasons her mother had moved to live with one of her sisters in Bedford. Juliet had herself gone to visit her other aunt, Andrea Graves, at the estate where she resided in Sevenoaks outside London. How could Juliet possibly have imagined that she would fall in love with her aunt's employer, the owner of the estate, who just happened to be one of the most famous and handsome bachelors in all of England!

Or that he would fall in love with her!

". . . tall and thin, dazzling figure, silky, light-brown hair, perfect white teeth, and enchanting smile."

"She must be beautiful!" interjected the woman.

"The envy of every Hollywood producer," rejoined Adam. "She is positively besieged by offers."

Oh, Adam–stop it! thought Juliet, her smile widening as her face reddened. *She might believe you! And I'm not a bit tall–I'm only five feet seven.*

What an adventure it had been–exploration in Africa, discovering what Adam thought were evidences of the original Garden of Eden, being kidnapped, Adam's daring rescue of her in Scotland, and then his romantic proposal back in Saudi Arabia at the Eden site.

Juliet still had to pinch herself to remind herself that it wasn't a dream.

Adam was the one Hollywood producers were looking at, not her–six-feet-two-inches tall, trim, strong, athletic, blue eyes, light hair, tan face, and a Robert Redford smile–his was one of the most photographed faces in all England. At first glance no one would take him for a scientist.

But Adam Livingstone's passion was antiquity. His dream was to delve into man's beginnings. Not only had he located Noah's ark embedded in glacial ice on Turkey's Mount Ararat, half a lifetime's research had culminated shortly thereafter—aided by computer models he had devised of the earth's changing geologic and weather patterns, as well as continental drift—with the discovery of what Adam was convinced was the Garden of Eden, with Mount Sinai at its center as the source of the four rivers spoken of in the book of Genesis.

The fulfillment of his research, and these astonishing finds, eventually took Adam Livingstone out of the world of mere science and into the world of faith. Man's beginnings, and the whys and purposes of those beginnings, had become to him of far greater import than ever before.

Along with beginnings, Adam Livingstone's new faith had also drawn him into a keener awareness of the future. He had come to see how intrinsically linked were the two ends of history's spectrum, the beginning of time and the end of time, the alpha and omega, the accounts of Genesis and Revelation.

Some of his new Christian friends had expressed their view privately that he, Adam Livingstone, might occupy a role of singular importance in the outworking of God's plan for the days ahead. The significance of the amazing discoveries he had made, they felt, could not be denied. Whatever God was doing, Adam Livingstone was in the middle of it. There were also those—perhaps sensing the same thing—who had done what lay in their power to stop Livingstone and silence his spiritual speculations. These dark forces, however, had not yet been successful in their attempt.

In the months that had passed since their last visit to the slopes of Jebel al Lawz in Saudi Arabia, the prolific greenery sprouting from its base had continued to luxuriate and expand. The mystery tree in its midst had slowed its vertical growth, though its trunk continued to become more massive. The region was gradually attracting more and more notice.

And along with everything else, Adam Livingstone had taken another step he would never have anticipated—he had become engaged!

Meanwhile, Juliet tried to return to the magazine on her lap. But with Adam back there talking to a stranger—about her!—it was no use.

Finally she couldn't stand it any longer. Juliet rose and made her way down the aisle toward the lavatory at the rear of the plane. She slowed as she drew alongside Adam, giving a bump to the knee that protruded into the walkway.

"Oh, excuse me, sir!" she exclaimed. "How clumsy of me."

She looked him straight in the eye with a da Vincian smile, attempting by sheer force of will to convey the unspoken message, *Stop, you're embarrassing me!*

"Don't mention it, miss," returned Adam with a broad smile and a playful wink. He turned back to his neighbor and continued, "Did I tell you how stunningly beautiful Juliet is?"

Adam, you are impossible! groaned Juliet to herself, though she was unable to prevent snickering as she continued on down the aisle. She paused as she came near Scott's and Crystal's seats.

"What's Adam up to?" asked Scott. "Looks like he's engaged in a heated conversation up there."

"The lady in the next seat recognized him," Juliet replied to Adam's best friend and coworker, Scott Jordan. "He's giving her an earful."

"About what?"

"About *me!*" said Juliet, laughing.

"You'd better get used to it," warned Scott. "You're marrying an important man. Everyone will want to know about you."

three

Sevenoaks

(1)

Adam telephoned his housekeeper from Paris. When the adventurers arrived back at Sevenoaks four hours later, Mrs. Graves was ready for them.

The most lavish homecoming tea imaginable waited in the dining room—fresh bread with jams and cheese and cold cuts, cakes and biscuits, hob nobs, scones, fruit, and water boiling and waiting to be poured into waiting teapots. Scarcely were the suitcases inside than they gathered in admiration of the housekeeper's spread. A welcome aroma of steeping tea wafted in the air.

"Ah, Mrs. Graves!" said Adam as they walked in. "I can tell you have been busy."

"I know how airline food is, Mr. Livingstone," she replied, trying as always to be practical but inwardly beaming. "By the way, where is Crystal?" she asked after greeting the others.

"Her husband met us at the airport. She went with him. They were anxious to get home."

Beeves—whom Adam jokingly referred to as his butler but who was in reality more a handyman and gardener—and his wife were summoned from their cottage behind the house to join in the homecoming. Soon questions and stories and laughter filled the room. Every detail of the Ethiopian adventure was recounted again, even though the object of their search had not actually been revealed.

"Oh, Auntie, it was such a close call getting away in the middle of the night," exclaimed Juliet. "I was afraid we were all going to be killed!"

"Not a chance," replied Adam. "What would you say, Scott—does that escape deserve being rated a close call?"

"We've had others that were pretty tight through the years," replied the American, then paused. "But I would say," he added with a grin, "that this one was right up there!"

"We almost had it, didn't we, Scott. We were so close!"

"Next time!"

"*Next* time?" repeated Mrs. Graves, turning toward her employer with teapot in hand. "You're not–"

"Going back?" interrupted Adam enthusiastically. "Of course! Just as soon as we can arrange it. Now that we know the ropes, we've got to get back before they have a chance to tighten security."

"When will that be?"

"Three weeks, perhaps, a month at the outside. We've got to get things rolling in Turkey, then we'll zip down to Ethiopia again–in and out just like that, eh, Scott? No more of this dallying around. It was stupid of me to go so slow, though everything took longer than I'd planned. Next time, I'll get in, yank off the blankets, snap the photos, and be done with it."

"You *will* be very careful handling those coverings," said Juliet. "I'm not sure I like the sound of that cavalier tone!"

Adam laughed. "I will exercise extreme caution. I want to live to tell about it!"

"And your qualms of conscience about breaking into a church?" asked Juliet.

Adam shrugged. "I'm still wrestling with it," he said. "But for now I have decided that history outweighs protocol, and that the ark *needs* to be made known. Speaking of Turkey," Adam went on, turning again in Scott's direction, "Rocky should have arrived. We'll have to give him a call."

"What exactly did you see?" asked Mrs. Graves, returning to the subject of the ark.

"The basement room in the Sanctuary building was pitch-black," replied Adam, his voice quieting, "and I didn't have much time. I was walking toward the thing and had just taken hold of the fabric covering when Juliet yelled into my ear that the jig was up."

"I wouldn't trade a hundred pictures for having you wind up in jail!" said Juliet.

"What happened next?" asked Beeves.

"I heard a sound," answered Adam. "I shut off my penlight and made a dash back to the roof. From there it was a simple matter of pointing my glider into the wind and rejoining the rest of the team half a mile away."

"Didn't they shoot at you?"

"They never saw me. We got out of Aksum that same night."

(2)

In a quiet London hospital room, a nurse stood gazing down at the bulky form which was her charge through these early morning hours.

She rarely got to know her patients. Half died without regaining consciousness. That was the disadvantage with the Cardiac Intensive Care Unit. But there could hardly be more important work, watching for any sign of life, monitoring equipment, keeping ready the instant any change became apparent. Yet all the while the unconscious patients who would never know her struggled in that precarious and mysterious world between life and death.

As she listened to the labored breathing of the huge man who had come in early yesterday, she could not help but think him of the unfortunate half who wouldn't make it. They said the surgery had gone tolerably well. And he had been sleeping soundly ever since she had come in at midnight. But his face didn't look good.

She stared at him for several minutes. There was a faint sense of recognition. But she couldn't identify why she thought she had seen him before. It was a lonely face, she thought. No one had called or come to see him. She wondered if he had any family or friends. Then she found herself wondering if he were a Christian, and how prepared he was to face eternity.

Something in the hard lines of the man's face told her, whoever he was, and whatever events of life had led up to now, that he had not made the best use of his days thus far on the earth. She could not help but think, at this moment when he was closer to eternity than he had ever been before, that he was *not* prepared for it.

She laid a gentle hand upon his clammy white forehead.

"God," she whispered, *"If this man is lost, give him another chance, so that he might know you."*

She gazed into the forlorn face another minute or two, then turned and left the room. When she returned thirty or forty seconds later, she carried an extra copy of the Gideon's Bible from the visitor's room down the hall.

She placed it beside the bed, uttered another prayer for the man she did not know, then resumed her duties, if not exactly feeling better, at least with the assurance that the big man was in God's hands.

(3)

When next Gilbert Bowles became aware of existence, it was not the sensation of light that first penetrated his consciousness, for his eyes were closed. Rather it was the stale odor of sickness and death.

Feebly his lids parted a crack. He tried to move but was incapable of it.

Light followed smell into his brain—yellow light, and long corridors, and people dressed in white.

He breathed in and out. He could not do so deeply. The first physical sense he became aware of in his body was not pain but constriction . . . heaviness . . . exhaustion. Never had he felt so weak in his life. And what were all these infernal tubes and contraptions!

Again he tried to move. He succeeded in lifting his head slightly off its pillow. It felt like it was made of lead.

Then came the pain. He could tell it originated someplace deep. Whatever the reason for his being in this place, it was serious.

The realization sobered him. Gilbert Bowles was not a man who wanted to be at anyone's mercy. But right now he was clearly not his own master.

He lay back and exhaled a long breath. Before he had time to reflect further on his predicament, a nurse entered the room. An instrument at her station had alerted her to the fact that her patient was coming awake.

"Good morning, Mr. Bowles," she said cheerily.

At this particular time, cheer and smiles did not top the list of things the large archaeologist was interested in having lavished upon him.

He attempted to speak. The only sound he succeeded in producing, however, was an irritable gurgle. It was a good thing. His words would probably not have been kind.

"You gave us quite a scare," she went on, glancing at the bedside monitors, then beginning to fuss with something about the sheets. "You were in surgery for four hours. You've been sleeping for almost twenty-four, like a baby according to the night nurse. We didn't know if you were going to make it. Now we need to get you up."

"Surgery . . . for what?" Bowles croaked.

"Bypass surgery for your heart, Mr. Bowles. You had a massive heart attack two nights ago. You were as good as gone when they brought you in here. But Dr. Potts is the best—he's the one that gave your heart a second chance."

"What . . . how . . . ?" His voice was barely audible.

"Your housekeeper, Mr. Bowles," said the nurse. "Your fall woke her up. She found you collapsed on your floor and called emergency. The ambulance rushed you here. You owe her your life, Mr. Bowles. If I were you, I'd give the lady a raise as soon as you're back on your feet."

The conversation, brief as it was, tired him. Bowles saw a water glass out of the corner of his eye. A thick black book was sitting beside it. He was thirsty but could not bring himself to summon the energy to ask for the water, and he certainly had no interest in reading. He tried to raise his hand and point to the glass, but his arm was as heavy as his head. At last he nodded noncommittally, then closed his eyes.

He was so heavily drugged that he was only halfway alert anyway. He let the nurse proceed with her affairs without benefit of his attention. She continued to chatter away, but he tuned her out and heard next to nothing.

That he had almost died and might not yet be altogether out of the woods were two thoughts it would take some getting used to. He would worry about the implications later. Right now, he just wanted to go back to sleep.

(4)

High above Amsterdam, in a secure and private penthouse suite, a white-haired Dutchman, a diminutive balding Englishman, and a tall, powerfully built Swisswoman were engaged in dialogue.

There had been no meeting of the appointed members of the Council of Twelve since the kidnapping of Adam Livingstone's fiancée had failed to disclose whatever the archaeologist's objective had been in the African desert. Their hasty helicopter escape from the Masonic stronghold outside Edinburgh had left these three, the acknowledged leadership triumvarite of the Council, noticeably shaken.

And not merely because of the failure to stop Livingstone. Most pressingly on the agenda of their collective mind was their troublesome colleague from Azerbaydzhan. Halder Zorin had grown far too independently minded.

"The other eight may have objections to ousting him," Lord Montreux was saying. "It is unprecedented."

"These are unprecedented times," rejoined their host, Rupert Vaughan-Maier. "Everything in the Dimension points toward a climax. It is hardly to be wondered at that the enemy would disrupt the unanimity of the Council. But nothing prohibits Zorin's removal. I intend to recommend it."

"And if others object?" queried the Englishman.

"If we three push for it," said the Swisswoman, Anni D'Abernon, "the others will go along. They will bow to our judgment."

The secret Council, of which these three comprised one quarter, was made up of representatives of twelve nations and surreptitious societies affiliated by bonds too ancient for its members to recognize the diverse branches and offshoots of its roots. Their charge was to implement what was loosely known as the Plan, by which the Dimension of which they were the most powerful human representatives would secretly gain control over every world system. Nothing occurred, from economics to banking to politics, around the globe that they were not aware of or had not orchestrated themselves. The governments, banks, and stock markets who did their bidding, however, knew little or nothing of this clandestine syndicate. There were those in high places, of course, who had heard of the Illuminati and the Rosicrucians, and other such societies. Most, however, considered such mere legend, little realizing how powerful indeed were the contemporary counterparts of those age-old guilds.

On the Council sat at least a half dozen whose ancestral lines extended back centuries to the beginnings of those occult movements. But even some on the Council did not realize how deeply rooted was their power in that all but forgotten brotherhood known as *the Knights Templar,* from which the Illuminati, the Society of the Rose and the Cross, as well as the Masonic Order, were founded. As the Templars had been established in secrecy, so too did the Council of its present-day descendents continue to influence world events unseen.

And now that the new age of the Third Millennium had come, to the Council had been entrusted to make the way on all global fronts ready for the ascension of their own World Leader. This was the age the Dimension of their Power had awaited, when the ultimate triumph over humankind would be realized.

"I agree," assented Vaughan-Maier to D'Abernon's previous statement. "Zorin must be removed. Whether we were mistaken originally, or whether the lust for power has infected him I do not care to inquire at this time. He was obviously not our man. Someone else must be installed in Baku."

"A Council member?" asked Lord Montreux.

"That is a decision we may leave to the eleven."

"And his replacement?" said D'Abernon.

"I have several names to put forward," replied Vaughan-Maier. "But the final decision concerns me far less than for Zorin to wander around loose. He knows too much. Not only must he be removed from the Council, we will have to change chips, codes, and private communications systems. Meanwhile, is there anything new on the Livingstone front?"

"We continue to observe him closely," replied D'Abernon.

Recent events involving the English archaeologist had sent rumblings of foreboding through the Council, threatening their origins and millennial timetable. Their enemy, long quiet on certain fronts, had infiltrated the heart and mind of Adam Livingstone, and he in turn had stirred up untoward activity in unpleasant directions. They had been warned that he was a dangerous adversary, on the verge of major discoveries that could undo much for which they had spent centuries preparing. They knew the prophecy that had come down to them—that following the day of a certain feared discovery, the veil would be lifted, and the people of the covenant would recognize their Anointed One. It was their responsibility to prevent that day. For if it came, their age of power would be at an end.

The work of Adam Livingstone had precipitated a crisis in the Dimension for exactly that reason. The Power of the Air still trembled with ancient reminders of its enemy's presence which Livingstone seemed about to unlock again. It fell to the twelve members of the Council to eradicate the threat posed by Livingstone's research.

But nothing they did had been successful at stopping him, nor discovering, even with the help of Lord Montreux's seductive daughter, Candace, what were the exact nature of Livingstone's recent hypotheses. He had been waylaid but not silenced. They had stepped up surveillance, by means of satellite and human observation. He made no move they were not aware of.

"Zorin is not involved, is he?" said Vaughan-Maier. "He nearly bungled the entire Livingstone episode last time."

"He is not involved," D'Abernon replied. "I am making use of high-level military and mafia operatives to keep tabs on Livingstone. They know nothing about us, but they are completely reliable."

"What have they learned?"

"He is displaying an unusual interest in Africa again."

"In connection with his movements of last year?"

"That we don't yet know. He was recently in Ethiopia."

"Ethiopia!" repeated Vaughan-Maier, his tone serious.

"Our recent tracking of his movements indicates that he has just returned from Aksum in Ethiopia."

"What was he doing there?"

"Apparently he broke into a small but highly secure cathedral. What he was after they could not be certain."

"That could mean—"

"I know what you are thinking, but I doubt it."

"First the ark of Noah, then his search in the African desert," Vaughan-Maier went on. "It is certainly possible such could be his objective. He is singularly intrigued by those fabled objects and places the enemy's people make so much of. If that *is* his objective, he must *not* be allowed to find it. The impact against us could be catastrophic. It could begin the enemy's timetable . . . and unravel everything."

"I too have also heard the reports about Ethiopia," said the Swisswoman. "But he will find nothing."

"He is a resourceful man."

"I tell you, there is nothing to find. Such worrying does not become you, Rupert. I have never seen you like this. Relax. It is *our* Master's timetable which will prevail in the new millennium, not the enemy's."

Irritated by her remark, Vaughan-Maier said nothing.

"What if the Ethiopian legends are true?" put in Lord Montreux.

"Then we will take action in due course," replied D'Abernon. "Thus far there is nothing to substantiate it."

It grew preternaturally chilly in the warm penthouse.

"But if it was," said the Dutchman, speaking again, "and we could get our hands on *that* . . . it would change everything." Even as he said the words, Vaughan-Maier's voice trembled slightly.

"I have no doubt that this new Ethiopian gambit is but a wild-goose chase," insisted D'Abernon.

"We cannot afford to take that chance," rejoined Vaughan-Maier. "With such a repository of the enemy's power in our grasp, or if we could destroy it, our difficulties with Livingstone would be over. I want to be kept informed of everything concerning this affair. If the legendary object still exists, we *must* have it, and get rid of it forever."

(5)

A group of fifteen or twenty men and women took seats in a comfortable and spacious New Hampshire living room. When everyone was comfortable, Mark Stafford, pastor of the small church of which everyone in the group was a member, began.

"As I told the congregation last Sunday," said Mark, "I feel strongly that we in our church should do our part to join with brothers and sisters in many congregations and prayer groups across the country to pray and fast for revival. I feel too that we should pray for a rekindling of fervor for the Word of God throughout society. God is leading thousands in what seems to be exactly the same way—to pray for a revival based on the power of his Word."

"Haven't people been praying for revival for years?" asked one of the group.

"You're right," answered Mark. "But with the coming of the new millennium, the leading in that direction has grown much stronger. God is clearly getting ready for something of major significance."

About half of those who had gathered at the Stafford home on this evening had been meeting together for some time, mostly discussing matters pertaining to biblical prophecy. The study group had grown during the past six or nine months. The genesis of the group had roots several years earlier during informal sessions of prayer and study between Mark Stafford and the man who was not with them on this evening, Rocky McCondy.

"God always seems to call his people to pray," Mark continued on, "during times of particular significance. I think we would all agree this to be such a time. The battle for minds and hearts everywhere will grow more and more intense as the end times draw near. I believe we are to pray that the truth and power of the Scriptures will be revealed in new and wonderful ways in people's lives."

"Amen!" sounded two or three voices around the room.

"As God leads, then . . . I suggest we begin to pray," said Mark, "and ask the Lord to lead us as we embark in this direction."

Heads began to bow.

"*Lord,*" began Mark after two or three minutes, "*we pray that your will would be accomplished—among us . . . in our nation . . . around the world.*"

"*We pray, as Mark said, for new revival in our land,*" said another.

"*May men and women from all walks of life,*" now prayed Mark's wife, Laurene, "*find themselves turning to your Word. May they find a power that they have not known before.*"

"*Bring the prayers of thousands together, Lord, that your word might penetrate into people's lives, making them ready for your return.*"

"*Reveal the truth of the Scriptures, heavenly Father.*"

They continued to pray for some time. After about an hour, they began informally to talk about the changing millennium in light of the scriptural prophetic timetable.

Gradually the night grew late in the Stafford home. The discussion had broken up about thirty minutes earlier. Only four or five now remained with the pastor and his wife.

"The prophetic things we were talking about earlier," Mark was saying, "are far more than an intellectual exercise. The Father truly is making ready a bride for his Son."

"How soon will these things begin to happen?" asked one of those who had stayed behind.

"I don't know," replied Mark. "I cannot say what exactly the Lord intends to do, or when. I do know we are to pray, and make our own hearts ready."

Again they bowed their heads and closed their eyes.

"*Lord,*" prayed Laurene, "*whatever are your chosen doorways leading into the next era, we pray that you will accomplish your purposes.*"

"*Make your people ready and fit for your Son's coming,*" added Mark. "*Hasten that day, Lord. Reveal the signs of the times. Show forth the mysteries that have been hidden . . . and make your people ready.*"

(6)

"Rocky!" said Adam into the telephone. "You made it in one piece."

"A long flight, and a bumpy ride down from Yerevan! But I'm here at last. What do you want me to do, Boss?"

Adam laughed. "Mainly I just want you *there*," he replied. "Until we get a break in the negotiations, which Scott and I are working on, you're our man on the scene. Start coordinating security plans with the people from NASA in particular, also Raytheon and Rockwell. We want to be ready to move the minute we can."

They spoke for several minutes. Adam filled him in on the Ethiopian excursion.

"How are the blimps coming along?" asked Rocky.

"I talked to Boeing two weeks ago. They say they'll be ready."

"And the delivery of the helium?"

"NASA is still cooperative. Keep your fingers crossed they don't change their minds. This is going to seriously deplete their supply."

"How long will it take the blimps to get here?"

"They say within a week."

"The weather can change in twenty-four hours."

"I know." Adam sighed. "The weather is the wild card in all this. But if the Lord wants it to happen, we ought to be able to trust him for that end of it. In any event . . . good to talk to you, my friend. We'll probably stop by for a day or two either on our way or coming back from Ethiopia next time around."

"You want me to go up to the site?"

"If you can without making the Turks nervous. Low-profile it."

"I'll do the bumbling American tourist number—plaid shorts, camera slung over my shoulder, straw hat . . . you know the bit."

"Sounds perfect. I'll be setting up another meeting with the Turkish officials who hold the power of the decision in this. After that we'll have a better idea where we stand."

"When do you think that will be?" asked Rocky.

"Couple . . . maybe three weeks. As soon as I can arrange for the meeting, and Scott gets the equipment we need for our next Aksum attempt, we'll be on our way. Between now and then, try to hook up with Jennings from NASA and Forrest from your State Department. They've been working with the Turkish people all winter making sure the site isn't compromised. Before you do anything, get that jet lag behind you and rest up. I'll talk to you again tomorrow."

(7)

As Anni D'Abernon flew from Amsterdam back to Zurich in her private jet, she reflected on the meeting just concluded with her two colleagues. She also revolved in her mind events of the last several months.

Adam Livingstone had been troublesome. There had been a time they had thought to recruit him to their side. But he was now solidly in the enemy's camp. That alone made him dangerous.

But in her heart she hated her onetime colleague Halder Zorin far more. The one factor she, Rupert, and Montreux had not discussed was the long-term prognosis with regard to the Zorin problem. Even if they succeeded in replacing him on the Council, and changing all their communications systems . . . in Vaughan-Maier's words, he would *still* know too much.

The clear solution was one none had actually voiced. Obviously they could not discuss it openly with the other eight. It was too coarse, too plebeian. It was not the sort of thing the Council *did* with those of its own number.

But she had made up her mind even as she was leaving Rupert's office.

She would take care of it herself. She would keep them from having to discuss it by dealing with it discreetly. It would simply be *handled.*

She pulled out her laptop. It was high time to put something together, and Ciano Bonar was the obvious choice. It would be necessary to update her dossier on Zorin more fully. In the meantime she would load in the information on Livingstone and bring those files up to date. She had a detailed tracking of his movements for the last year, except during those few occasions when he had slipped from sight in Africa. Now she would add these last two weeks of strange activities in Ethiopia. She couldn't wait for the new system's safeguards. She had to get to work on this immediately even before they changed their codes.

She would telephone for a full update from her operatives, then download from the laptop as soon as she reached Zurich.

Then notify Ciano.

She took out her satellite phone and punched in the private number. The conversation lasted five or six minutes. She hung up and returned to the computer in front of her. Soon her fingers were busy clicking across the keys.

Livingstone's discovery of the ark of Noah had been the beginning, she reflected as she went through to update his file. He had grown more and more dangerous since. But their own Master's Plan must not be thwarted or delayed. This new Livingstone activity renewed the anxiety she had felt last year in Africa. Especially if . . .

She could not bring herself to formulate the words in her brain.

He could *not* have found it! She would certainly have felt the repercussions of such a Dimensional cataclysm.

Why was she hesitating, as if the words themselves had any force?

She would not be cowed by ancient Hebrew superstitions! She closed her eyes and quickly typed in the words. Her file must be complete.

But she could not prevent a brief shudder coursing through her frame as the four words left her fingers.

(8)

In a lonely hotel lounge in Oak Ridge, Tennessee, a man sat on the edge of a stool, head buried in his hands, an empty glass on the bar in front of him.

How could he have allowed it to come to this? A few careless decisions . . . and suddenly he was in so far over his head he could never hope to get out.

When Lucille first got sick and had to quit working, he was sure they would be able to make it with his extra part-time job. A temporary hardship. His new boss insisted on paying half his salary in cash. He didn't question it. Lucille would be back on her feet in several months. Things would return to normal.

But how could he have foreseen meeting Kelly?

She had been so understanding at first. She admired his dedication to his wife. Yet as Lucille's condition worsened, and the doctor bills mounted, and his frustration along with them, he had confided more and more in Kelly. The evening job had increased from two days a week to three, then four, changes he willingly accepted in order to see more of Kelly. He told Lucille his hours had been increased, and that his quitting time had been moved from 8:00 P.M. to 9:00. It was the first lie, just a tiny one, to cover an extra hour several evenings a week with Kelly.

After that, one thing gradually led to another.

It always started small, he thought. A seemingly insignificant lie that would hurt no one. But the consequences of lying always increase at compound interest, and Fred Hutchins' account was about to come due.

Even the second job eventually was not able to meet the expenses of Lucille's illness. By then his credit cards were maxed out. Things had gone much too far with Kelly. He took out a new card to use when he was with her, and a secret post office box to go along with it.

The lies grew. Fred knew he was flirting with danger, yet he couldn't bring himself to give Kelly up. She was always there for him, always understood what he was going though.

Now he had missed four house payments in order to keep the new Visa paid up. He couldn't let that card get behind or questions might be asked. But every other piece of plastic in his wallet was at the limit and interest accumulating rapidly. Luckily he had been able to get to the mail to intercept the final demand notice on the house before Lucille saw it. He had twelve days left before the bank initiated foreclosure proceedings.

Quickly Fred sent off an application for a new card the same day. He had been carrying the advertisement around for a week–ten-thousand-dollar limit and instant approval. No credit check. If it came through as promised–in seven working days–it should get him healthy with the house. He could make the four back payments with the new card. At least it would get the bank off his back and give him some breathing room.

But then yesterday's nightmare burst the bubble of his temporary optimism. Notification of an IRS audit!

The news might not have been so bad except that he had filed the 1040 himself. He had fudged on Lucille's medical expenses. He had never been audited–what was the harm, he thought. Everyone did it. And he hadn't declared *quite* every penny of income from his night job.

Actually, he hadn't declared *any* of the cash he had received. Even that wouldn't be so bad if he hadn't shown the expenditures made when he was with Kelly as business deductions. He couldn't let them look too closely into those "entertainment" expenses or it would lead to questions about the nature of his job, his hours and salary structure. Pretty soon the whole thing would unravel, the affair would come out, the unreported income be discovered, and he would be facing tax evasion charges.

He knew the piling up of stress and guilt was making his work suffer. He thought he had been covering it well enough to get by. But not only had he received greetings yesterday from the IRS, his day boss had come to him at closing time with a simple enough message: Shape up or ship out.

He took Kelly dancing after work. At least he could enjoy a few minutes of happiness before the roof caved in completely. Just for an hour. Or maybe, he thought, he might squeeze it till eleven o'clock and tell Lucille he'd been asked to stay on another hour.

Tomorrow he had a day off from both jobs. He'd try to find an attorney he could talk to about the IRS problem, to see if he had any options that might keep him out of jail. Maybe he'd give the credit card company a call, too, to see if they'd finished processing his application.

What he hadn't counted on in the middle of a *very* close waltz on the dance floor adjacent to the hotel lobby–as Kelly gazed adoringly into his eyes–was to look up and see his twenty-six-year-old daughter standing not ten yards away staring at him.

Fred sucked in a gasp of air. "What is she doing here!" he whispered as his face went pale.

She wasn't supposed to be coming to town to visit until next week! Had he lost track of that too?

"What is it, Fred?" asked Kelly.

"It's . . . it's my daughter—I'm afraid she saw us. I'd better go and talk to her."

He released Kelly and stepped back, and walked hurriedly toward the lobby. Her mouth hanging open, his daughter looked at him with shock and horror. As he approached, the expression changed to one of revulsion and disgust.

"Sally . . . Sally, please," he said, "if I could just—"

Already her face was red and her eyes swimming with tears. She turned and ran from the hotel.

He sat alone in the bar two hours later, trapped by circumstances of his own making, and with no way out.

He couldn't go home. But what *could* he do?

To make matters worse, he had been feeling a strange pain in his chest since midway through the afternoon.

Finally he rose to go. He walked toward the door and out into the night. It was sometime after midnight. Unsought, tears began to fill Fred Hutchins' eyes. He had not wept since childhood. But once they were begun, he could not stop them.

four

Success!

(1)

The team left on its second trip to Ethiopia in a month.

Mrs. Andrea Graves knew it was a dangerous venture, and could not help worrying. Especially after their hair-raising stories from the first attempt! Mr. Livingstone's work used to be more scholarly. All of a sudden, she felt like housekeeper to a secret agent!

She had gradually reconciled herself to the fact that lines of station had been crossed between her master and her niece. Mrs. Graves was, after all, from the old school. It had been difficult for her to get used to the fact that her own sister's daughter, a girl from such simple beginnings, was engaged to her master, Mr. Livingstone. But she had grown accustomed to it. Her feelings for Adam and Juliet went beyond mere devotion. She loved them both with all her heart.

Such a short time ago Juliet had been an emotional recluse. But her bout with depression had led to a spiritual awakening. And now she was a happy and smiling adventurer, engaged to one of England's most popular men.

In a way she envied the young people. They had their lives ahead of them. In their eyes everything was new and exciting. But, she mused, she would not be young again. She and her late husband had had a good life together. Every stage of life had its rewards. She was enjoying this phase of hers. Besides, the last year had brought her in on the adventurous life too—a little too close for comfort at times.

She smiled every time she thought of poor Mr. McCondy and how she had treated him at first. She learned to be grateful for him quickly enough, especially after he rescued them from that horrid gunman.

Well, all that was in the past. She took a sip of tea, opened her Bible, and began to read her daily psalm, a habit she had had since childhood.

Hear me, O God, she read silently. *Hide me from the conspiracy of the wicked, . . . [who] sharpen their tongues like swords and aim their words like deadly arrows. They shoot from ambush at the innocent man. They encourage each other in evil plans. They plot injustice and say, "We have devised a perfect plan!"*

She shuddered and turned her eyes aside.

Lord, she prayed, *after what happened last year, protect us all. Especially watch over Adam and Juliet while they are away. Whoever those evil people are who were after Adam and who kidnapped Juliet, I pray that you would foil them and confuse their plans.*

(2)

When Adam and Juliet and the others left a month before, the house was so quiet at first. With no one to cook for and cleaning at a minimum, Mrs. Graves began to wonder how she would occupy her days.

After about a week, she sat down one morning and opened the day's newspaper. Even with the house empty, like many a good Britisher Andrea Graves kept to her routine. Ten o'clock tea in her private lounge was her favorite time of day. A cup of tea, her daily psalm, followed by the newspaper.

She paused as she skimmed the society page. Outside a gentle rain fell. Gradually the paper eased to her lap. Just think, she mused, Juliet would be pictured there soon too. All at once the realization came to her that there was very little Juliet really knew about Mr. Livingstone's life. Glancing absently at the photos in the paper reminded her that she had cut out dozens of articles in various newspapers and magazines over the years about her master and his family and one or another of their exploits.

An idea popped into her mind. She would make a scrapbook from the clippings! This would be an ideal time for such a project!

Mrs. Graves rose from her chair and immediately went in search of the memorabilia box she kept in her secretary. Already a vision of the finished book came into her imagination. It would be her engagement gift to Juliet—a book of photographs and articles about her husband-to-be!

In less than an hour, every table and countertop in the domain that was Andrea Graves' kitchen was strewn about with papers and articles and photographs and clippings from the box she had retrieved.

That was three weeks ago. She had put everything away when they arrived home, and the moment they left for this second trip to Ethiopia, she had taken it out again. They planned to be gone a week or less this time, and she was determined to have the scrapbook ready upon their return.

(3)

Adam's plan to penetrate the Sanctuary building beside St. Mary's of Zion cathedral in Aksum a second time within a month was essentially the same as the first.

Two factors made it more daring, and dangerous, this time around. *Two* of them would float noiselessly and invisibly out of the sky just after 3:00 A.M. onto the roof instead of one. That alone doubled the risk. Secondly, he couldn't be absolutely sure they hadn't beefed up security, which might include alarms or motion detectors on the roof.

First it was Adam's turn. He leapt into the blackness, timed his fall for about thirty seconds, then pulled the cord. There sat his target, faintly visible far below him.

Nothing had been released to the media by the Ethiopians about a break-in. Alarms had gone off outside, but no one had actually seen him. Nor, as far as he knew, had they discovered the rooftop means of entry where he had gained access to the elevator shaft leading down through the building to the underground basement, thus bypassing internal alarms.

Their security was decidedly behind the times. Adam was confident the same method would work. But he was concerned about possible changes at floor level. Thus, he determined it best on this occasion to make no contact with the floor. He would run no risk of disturbing any new pressure or motion monitors that might have been installed. That's why he needed Scott on the scene with him—to raise and lower him from above. He had to keep both his own hands free. And the operation would involve extra equipment and thus take longer.

He was nearly there. The landing was tricky, but most of the roof was flat and reasonably unobstructed by vents and equipment. Fortunately, the guards stationed around the compound had little reason to peer up toward the sky.

Adam circled once more around the onion dome of the cathedral, choosing his final landing site on the Sanctuary next to it, then eased the glider down . . . down . . . until his foam-padded shoes made contact.

Five or six quick running steps brought him to a halt. He stopped and stood, listening carefully.

"Juliet," he whispered into his microphone, "anything going on in front that you can see?"

"Nothing," replied Juliet from the same vantage point where she had watched with binoculars three weeks before.

"Have Crystal radio Scott in the plane to come on ahead. Tell him the east edge of the roof offers the widest spot. He'll see me by then. Then tell Figg to scram. We don't want anyone getting suspicious about what someone's doing flying around above Aksum at this time of night!"

In the blackness above him, Adam listened for the faint sound of the small Cessna from which Scott would soon join him.

So far so good.

(4)

Forty minutes later, after Scott's long silent glide down from eight thousand feet, and with their paragliders safely stowed, Adam and Scott entered the elevator shaft and began the downward descent. It complicated things for two remote control pulleys to operate on the rooftop, but they couldn't take time to move down and back separately.

In another twenty minutes they squeezed through the ventilation shaft and removed the return air grate and set it beside them in the cramped space.

"There it is, Scott," said Adam.

"I don't see a thing–it's pitch-black."

Adam flipped on the halogen light attached to the top of his head. A thin beam shot into the room below.

"There . . . look."

"I do see it–just like you described! The covering of blankets, and–"

"That's it–in the shape of angels' wings. Let's get to it," said Adam. "We've got to rig up a line directly above it to support me."

"It's not secure enough here," said Scott. "I'd feel more confident back in the elevator shaft."

"You're probably right–that's where the winch would be most solid."

"It would involve two or three changes of direction with the pulleys, and I wouldn't be able to see you."

"As long as you can hear me, it ought to work," said Adam.

Adam sent his light across the ceiling to the opposite side of the room.

"Look, there's our spot," he said. "The abutment of that stone column. That's where we'll tie off the supporting cable."

"Right, I see it."

"Let's put together the fishing pole and string a line across to it, then use it as a lead to string the cable over and back, tying it off securely on this end."

"It would be easier to descend to the floor like you did before."

"We can't chance it," replied Adam.

It took an hour to string the cable directly over the ark, then for Scott to secure the winch in the elevator shaft and get Adam hooked and ready.

"I think I'm set," said Adam through his microphone up to Scott at the controls, out of sight in the elevator shaft. "Ease off the tension just a bit," Adam went on, " . . . good, that's it. Perfect."

"Are you ready?"

"I think so. I'll float out into the room."

Scott relaxed the tension on the winch. The cable moved away from him.

"That's it," he heard Adam say. "OK, ease off a bit . . . good . . . a little more . . . I'm almost there. About another four feet . . . easy . . . that's it. Stop."

"Where are you?" said Scott into Adam's ear.

"I'm exactly above it . . . in the middle of the room," replied Adam. "I'm attaching the last two pulleys to the horizontal cable . . . all right, they're secure. Now attaching the two lines over them . . . good. It'll take me a minute to get my feet hooked. . . . "

Scott waited.

"Good—I'm set. I'm letting myself down . . . my feet are holding. All right, I think I'm ready to descend. Let's go take some pictures!"

Adam felt his weight being lowered inch by inch, as he descended headfirst into the eerie quiet of the room, his feet securely attached to the pulley above.

"You sure you know how to do this?" he asked into his microphone.

"If I can lower you six hundred feet through midair and hit a six-foot shaft down to Noah's ark," replied Scott, "I think I can lower you a few feet into a big open room."

"Yeah, but then I wasn't standing on my head!"

"I won't bump you on anything."

"Let's hope we're right about what awaits us at the end of this line," said Adam. "It could be an even bigger discovery than before."

"That's why you're the famous Adam Livingstone, don't you know? You find things no one else can."

"This is serious business, Scott. Don't make me laugh."

"That's why we're here, isn't it—to prove it exists?"

"Yep . . . and I'm nearly low enough. Stop for a minute."

Adam felt himself slow to a crawl, then a stop. He rotated his head about. The tiny light probed the bundled object straight below him.

"I'd say I'm about six feet above it," he said. "Let me down very, very carefully. I don't want to crash into the thing."

Again he felt himself descending.

"That's good, Scott . . . easy . . . all right, about five feet . . . four . . . three . . . slow it up . . . two feet . . . OK, I think I can reach it from here—stop."

Adam's heart pounded in anticipation. This was the moment of truth.

He stretched out his arms. Fully extended he could just touch the topmost tip of the faded blue embroidered cloths at the very point below which he dared hope sat angels' wings of pure gold. With a finger he made contact with the blanket. A tingle shot through his arm.

"Can you give me another three inches, Scott."

Again he lowered, then stopped.

"All right, this is it . . . I'm attaching the claw-teeth to the top of the blanket. . . . "

Scott waited.

"These covers are old," said Adam. "I'm glad we foam-lined the pincers or the fabric would tear . . . all right . . . pull up the blankets, Scott. Actually, to be on the safe side, hoist me up about a foot too. I don't want to accidently touch anything as you're bringing up the coverings."

Instantly he felt a tug on his feet, drawing him back into the empty space of the room. Then the second line went taut . . . the blankets began to lift, then gather together . . . then rise off the object they had been guarding and covering who could tell how long.

The expression which next filled Scott's ear where he sat at the dual controls in the elevator shaft was unlike anything he had ever heard from Adam Livingstone's lips in all the years they had been working together. What he detected was a sudden intake of air. It was a sound, for all Scott could tell, that might have been a death gasp from the lips of his friend. But then followed a faintly discernible expression of astonishment, incredulity, and disbelief.

"What . . . what is it, Adam! Is something wrong?"

Scott's earpiece was silent.

"Adam . . . Adam, what's up . . . is everything–"

At last, with great relief, Scott heard Adam's familiar voice.

"Everything is fine, Scott," said Adam. "I was just too choked up to say anything."

"Why . . . are you in pain?"

"No, nothing like that, Scott."

"What then?"

"We've done it, Scott," said Adam, " we've actually found it."

"You mean–"

"It's the ark, Scott. Believe it or not, I am staring down from a few feet above . . . on the ark of the covenant!"

(5)

Gilbert Bowles sat upright in his hospital bed.

It was strangely quiet. He glanced about. The clock on the wall showed 2:37 A.M. No wonder everything was so infernally still–it was the middle of the night.

Why couldn't he sleep all of a sudden? This was a blasted inconvenient time to get insomnia!

He sat staring straight ahead. It was no use. He was wide awake.

Without thinking of it consciously, his hand stretched out and picked up the book lying on the stand next to his bed. It hadn't occurred to him what it was until he opened it and saw the familiar double columns.

Bah! A Bible! he thought to himself. Who had put that there?

Well, there wasn't anything else to do. It might be good for a few laughs. Chalk it up to research for his next speech. He might find something choice he could use to prove the whole thing a load of nonsense.

Without turning the page, he began to read where he found himself.

For the truth about God is known to them instinctively. God has put this knowledge in their hearts. From the time the world was created, people have seen the earth and sky and all that God made. They can clearly see his invisible qualities—his eternal power and divine nature. So they have no excuse whatever for not knowing God. Yes, they knew God, but they wouldn't worship him as God or even give him thanks. And they began to think up foolish ideas of what God was like. The result was that their minds became dark and confused. Claiming to be wise, they became utter fools instead. And instead—

Humbug, Bowles said to himself, just like he always knew it was!

He slammed the book closed and set it back on the nightstand. Staring into space was better than any more of such idiocy!

(6)

As they approached the X-ray scanner in the airport of Addis Ababa, the capital of Ethiopia, Adam took the rolls of precious treasure from his pocket and clutched them tightly in his hands.

"I know they say it's safe," he said to Juliet at his side. "But I am not letting this film anywhere near that machine!"

He walked forward and spoke in confidential tones to the man in charge, then returned.

"Keep your eye on that guy," he said softly to the others as he returned. "If he bolts, after him, Scott."

"You didn't tell him why the film is so valuable?"

"Are you crazy?" Adam laughed. "I just requested that it not be put through the machines. But look at him—don't you think he has a suspicious look?"

Juliet smiled. "Adam, you're getting paranoid."

Adam looked around the airport.

"I don't know . . . don't you get the funny feeling someone's watching us?"

"Now I know you're paranoid," said Figg, Adam's technical man who had piloted the Cessna, walking up from behind. "Relax, man—the hard part is over."

"I hope you're right," said Adam. "It's just that I've had the sensation of being followed ever since we got to Aksum three days ago."

"Occupational hazard," said Jen, "always afraid someone is trying to steal your latest discovery."

Forty minutes later they boarded and settled into their seats. Juliet was thankful that she and Adam were beside one another this time. That ought to prevent any more conversations with inquisitive passengers!

"Is the film safe to your satisfaction?" she asked.

"Right here," said Adam, patting his pocket. "I don't intend to let it out of my sight till we're home!"

"Adam," said Adam's secretary, leaning across the aisle from where she sat beside Jen. "Look–they've got a copy of that article on your mum."

"I didn't know it had been released . . . what does it say?"

"I'm just going to read it," replied Crystal.

"Pass it over when you're finished. Hey, Scott, Figg, how are you two doing up there?" said Adam, leaning forward to the seat in front of him.

"No problems. Like Figg said, the hard part's behind us."

"We need to be thinking about the Turkish negotiations again, now that this is behind us," said Adam.

"I thought I'd call the State Department's liaison again as soon as we're back in London," said Scott. "Marcos is supposed to have spoken with him. Then of course get in touch with Rocky and see how he's doing. Figg and I probably ought to fly to Turkey ourselves. I'm hopeful something will break anytime."

"Right, and I'll make sure the Rockwell and GE people are on target with the helium balloons. Figg, you got any more definite timetable on the melting equipment?"

"They're supposed to be ready to ship."

"Good, we probably ought to move on that even before we get the go-ahead. We want to be able to start on that end of it immediately. And we'll want to check again on the helium delivery from NASA."

They continued to discuss plans as the plane took off. Several minutes later, Crystal handed the magazine across the aisle. Juliet opened the copy of *Society World* and began reading the article they had been talking about.

> Frances Livingstone, London philanthropist, surprises English society for no less than the dozenth time. As always, with an unexpected twist.
>
> While others of her station concern themselves with balls and flower shows, horse races and luncheons, Mrs. Livingstone heads up clothing drives, safaris to Africa, or joins a mountain-climbing team up the Matterhorn.
>
> "Society life is boring," said Mrs. Livingstone recently. "With the years I have left I want to accomplish good in the world, and have fun doing it. Who says a woman my age can't be an adventurer!"
>
> Like son, like mother, some might say.
>
> Ever since the death of her husband–late London businessman and importer Giles Livingstone–nineteen years ago, his widow has scarcely remained in any single place in the world longer than six weeks at one time. Nor has she shown the slightest inclination toward remarriage.
>
> "How could I possibly marry again?" Mrs. Livingstone exclaimed when *Society World* put the question to her. "I'm far too busy and

happy to share my life with a stuffy retired man who smokes cigars and drinks port and whose mornings are taken up with the *Times* crossword puzzle. Now that would be boring!"

In the years since her husband's passing, Mrs. Livingstone has crisscrossed the globe any number of times, exploring jungles, building orphanages, speaking and raising money for dozens of humanitarian causes, and putting in a two-year stint with the Peace Corps. Disaster relief is her deepest interest. Whenever earthquake, hurricane, flood, volcano, or other natural calamity strikes, Frances Livingstone is not far behind, pledging not only time and eager hands, but her own personal assets as well, for the aid of the suffering victims.

Mrs. Livingstone's latest adventure, however, has taken even her closest friends and associates by surprise. None were prepared for this!

Following her visit to Indian orphanages last winter, Mrs. Livingstone ventured north, returning to Britain via Tibet. She determined to add to her list of achievements a visit to a historic monastery high near the border with Nepal to request funds for her various orphanage projects.

What she hadn't bargained on was being converted by the monks in residence and remaining in the visitors' quarters three months. Mrs. Livingstone hadn't set foot inside a church in nearly two decades. But this was different, she said.

When Frances Livingstone returned to London, her face glowed with the luster of her deeply moving "religious experience." She now considers herself a pilgrim toward the light of holiness and calls herself a devoted follower of the Tibetan monk known simply as the *Holy One*.

Some wondered if her famous son, archaeologist Adam Livingstone, had been out under the African sun too long when he let slip the news last year that he had become a convert to the Christian faith. Perhaps spirituality runs in the family.

Society World attempted to reach the younger Livingstone for his perspective on his mother's newfound life. He was, however, reportedly out of the country. Though his moves have been carefully watched since last year's discovery of Noah's ark, Livingstone's plans have remained closely guarded. Several junkets out of the country have been made but their results are unknown.

And now that wedding bells are in the younger Livingstone's future, the only guessing left is the exact date and location of the ceremony.

Juliet set down the magazine and smiled.

What did Adam think of all this, she wondered. They had not seen his mother since her recent return from Tibet.

Meanwhile, a private jet took off from the same runway they had lifted off from half an hour before. It carried three men who possessed startling information, including videotape and tape recordings from four bugged hotel rooms, all of which would be of enormous interest to the woman who had hired them.

As soon as they were aloft, the pilot set his heading almost exactly northwest . . . in the direction of Zurich.

(7)

A tearful forty-three-year-old mother sat down on the couch of her living room and tried to pray. Even the birds outside her kitchen window didn't sound cheery today.

What was the use? She tried to pray every day. But her efforts always ended in tears of heartache.

She had not seen her daughter for several months. The last time the girl had screamed horrid things at her: "You don't understand me, always treating me like a child. I'm sixteen. I don't need this anymore!"

Then she had turned and slammed the door, leaving her mother in stunned shock. They had not heard a word from her since. They suspected drugs . . . or worse.

Her pastor tried to console them by saying it was normal and to be expected. "Just keep loving her and praying for her," he said. "She will come back. Everything will be fine."

But it was not fine.

Yesterday the police came to the door. At sight of the two uniformed officers her heart jumped into her throat. They wanted to ask her daughter a few questions, they said. She didn't know whether to be relieved or to fear that Brandi was mixed up in something awful. Though she didn't say it in so many words, she could tell by the look on the female officer's face that she wondered what kind of upbringing the poor girl had had to cause her to wind up like this.

She wiped her eyes and opened her Bible, then flipped absently through it. Her marker was still in Luke 15 from the last time she had read the story. It brought fresh stabs to her heart every time. But it was the only passage of Scripture that offered any hope.

Her eyes went straight to the words on the page.

> *But while he was still a long way off, his father saw him and was filled with compassion for him; he ran to his son, threw his arms around him and kissed him.*

The son said to him, "Father, I have sinned against heaven and against you. I am no longer worthy to be called your son."

She closed the Bible. She could bear to read no more. The words of homecoming were too painful right now. How could she rejoice when she didn't know if she would ever see her daughter again?

God, if your Word does have power, she prayed, *I beg you, bring this passage to life in our family. Please bring Brandi to her senses. Let her know that I love her, Lord . . . I can't bear it! Please, may she find a Bible, somewhere . . . somehow. Use it to bring her back to us.*

(8)

As soon as the Livingstone team arrived back at Sevenoaks, Adam hurried downstairs.

"Adam, where are you going?" cried Juliet, chasing him to the door downstairs. "Wait for me."

"I'm going to the lab. We've got film to develop!"

"Not now—you don't even have your coat off!"

She caught up with him and they hurried down to the basement together and into the lab.

"I'll just turn the lights and heat on," said Adam, "and get the developer and other solutions warming up."

Five minutes later they exited the lab together.

"Remember the time I was coming out of here and you chewed me out?" said Juliet.

"I didn't *exactly* chew you out, did I?" asked Adam.

"You were pretty gruff. I cried the minute you were out of sight."

Adam paused, then took her in his arms and kissed her.

"I don't ever want to make you cry again," he said. "That is, unless it is for pure happiness."

They stood a moment or two more, contented.

"A lot has changed since that day," said Adam at length. "Any regrets?"

"Are you kidding? I'm the luckiest lady in all England."

They walked upstairs and into the sitting room where everyone was chatting freely and fixing tea and plates from the food Mrs. Graves had laid out. She was in the process of pouring tea and passing around the plate of biscuits.

"Scott," said Juliet as she took a seat and began sipping at her tea, "I want to know what *you* were thinking in the Sanctuary the whole time you were at the controls."

"I was wishing I was in there with this guy," he said, laughing and nodding toward Adam, "rather than stuck in the elevator shaft! And then when I heard him exclaim, or gasp, or whatever the sound was, I was afraid something had happened, that he'd fallen, or touched it and been struck dead."

Now it was Adam's turn to laugh.

"Honestly, Adam," added Scott, "it was *really* a strange sound."

A faraway look came over Adam's face. The room quieted. They all waited, knowing Adam was reliving the remarkable discovery.

"It is like nothing I can describe," he said at length. "It was like no moment you can imagine."

He shook his head in wonder.

"When those blankets rose up off it," he went on, "and I saw that first gleam of gold reflected back from my light, and then saw the tips of those wings so close below me that I actually could have stretched down and touched them with the tip of my finger–"

"Adam, don't even think such a thing!" said Juliet.

"Don't worry, I was being extremely careful. But though it was dark, and I was hanging suspended upside down in the air, I was in such awe at what I was actually looking at . . . I don't even know what I said to Scott. It was astounding. I mean . . . what else is there to say but . . . there it actually *was* right below me. It was really *there*!"

"Did you feel anything unusual?" asked Juliet.

"Like what?"

"I don't know, like the presence of God."

"Hmm," replied Adam, "now that you mention it, I suppose I should have. But I don't remember feeling that God was there in any kind of unusual way. I mean I felt a sense of awe at seeing it, but more from the sight itself than a sense of presence."

The others listened in wonder as he continued to reflect on the amazing experience.

"But I knew we didn't have time to fool around," Adam went on. "I didn't intend to be caught short this time. So I got the camera out immediately and started snapping exposures as fast as I could."

"But hanging there like that," said Mrs. Graves. "I don't understand how you could photograph anything but the top of the mercy seat."

"I was suspended on a wire that stretched across the ceiling," said Adam. "Once I was ready, Scott was able to pull me back toward him and then lower me again alongside the ark. Then he raised me again and I manually let myself across the guide wire in the other direction past the center point, then down again, in order to photograph the other side. It was exhausting. My arms were so tired by the time we got out of there. It was a bit of crude work at times–I even set myself rocking a little back and forth above it so as to increase my vantage point of both ends. Every inch won't be perfectly visible in the photos. But it was as good as we could manage under the circumstances."

"Then what did you do?" asked Mrs. Graves.

"As soon as I'd taken three rolls of black and white, and some color digitals and we were satisfied—and by this time I'd been hanging so long my head was throbbing!—Scott lowered the cable with the coverings. I carefully spread them as they descended so they would slip back over the ark as before. I tried to make them look just like when we arrived. Then I unfastened the latch, and Scott drew me up and out. We disconnected the pulleys and wires and winched ourselves up through the elevator shaft as we had descended, and back up to the roof. I doubt they even know we had been there."

A long pause followed.

"I wish you all could have been there with me," said Adam. "But I suppose it's a little like Armstrong on the moon. Only one person can be first. Hopefully, after what we've accomplished, before too much longer the whole world will behold what my eyes have seen."

"Do you really think that will happen, Adam?"

"That's the plan. After what we've learned, and with the photographs to back it up, I hope the Ethiopians will bow to public pressure and make the ark public. It's the whole world's treasure."

"Not to mention that it would prove the Bible," said Juliet.

"I thought of that!"

"*If* it can be authenticated as the real Old Testament ark," said Scott.

"That's another reason it needs to be made public—for research."

"We need to call Rocky and tell him the news."

"Let's wait until we have the photographs. An investigator like him will want proof."

(9)

"Oh, Juliet!" exclaimed the housekeeper, momentarily forgetting what she'd just been listening to. "With the excitement of your coming home, it slipped my mind. I have something to show you!"

Mrs. Graves set down her cup, stood, then hurried from the room. She returned a minute or two later carrying a wrapped package. She handed it to Juliet.

"I made it while you were gone," she said, smiling like a proud child bringing home a school project. "It's an engagement gift."

"Thank you, Auntie," said Juliet. She took it with wide eyes of question, glancing at Adam as if to ask if he knew anything about it. He shrugged.

Juliet tore back the colorful wrapping to reveal the book.

"It's a scrapbook about Mr. Livingstone," beamed Mrs. Graves.

Juliet flipped through it. "Thank you, Auntie Andrea," she said, "it's wonderful!"

Already Jen and Scott were crowding around, looking over Juliet's shoulder.

"Hey, look—there's Adam swooping down toward the house after we got back from Turkey!"

"I've never seen that photograph," said Adam. "That's the one that put my mum in such a dither when she was in Alaska."

"And my first introduction to Adam Livingstone, the day he flew toward the grounds on a multicolored paraglider in front of the whole London press," put in Juliet, "though I was down in the lab at the time. I didn't actually see it until it was run on the telly that night on the BBC."

"Always the publicity hound," said Scott.

"How else was I going to get through that crowd at the gate?"

"Hey, look," said Jen, pointing excitedly to a page. "There are you and me and Scott at the South African dig."

"There's a good one," said Adam chuckling. "Sir Gilbert and me side by side after receiving those awards at the British Archaeological Society banquet. It was all the poor man could do to stand there beside me and keep a smile on his face."

Unaware of the mortal danger which had recently come to Adam's occasional adversary, the conversation about him continued in spirited fashion.

"Bowles is just jealous of you," said Jen.

"Don't sell him too short, Jen. He's a decent research man, even if he doesn't have a clue who's behind the world's science. Give him time—he may come around yet."

"Gilbert Bowles!" she exclaimed. "You've got to be kidding."

"No one's out of God's reach, Jen, not even a confirmed atheist like Sir Gilbert."

Swaner said no more, but wasn't convinced. She still didn't like the man, even if Adam insisted on giving him the benefit of the doubt.

"Mrs. Graves, you sly woman," said Adam in loving jest, now turning toward his housekeeper. "I didn't know you were collecting all this."

"Wait," insisted Scott, growing frustrated with the two girls. "Start at the beginning—yeah, there's a picture of Adam and me with Marcos at school."

"Who is Marcos, sir?" asked Beeves.

"An old college buddy of mine from the University of Colorado," answered Scott. "He and I came over here to Cambridge together to study for a year. That's where I met this Livingstone chap."

"Scott's friend is an important man, Beeves," added Adam. "You always said he would be, didn't you, Scott?"

"He's in your House of Commons, is that it?" said Mrs. Graves.

"Almost," Scott replied. "He's in what we call the Senate. There are those who say his political career isn't going to stop there either."

"Look," said Jen, as she and Juliet continued to thumb through the new scrapbook, "there we are up in the tundra on that mammoth expedition. Look at you, Scott, in the old dirty parka that Russian fellow lent you."

"It smelled so bad," Scott said, chuckling, "that I thought the wolves would catch my scent and come down out of the woods after me!"

". . . and the dig in Israel . . . there we are posing on the top of Masada."

"I wish I could have seen that!" said Juliet.

"You may get your chance, my dear," said Adam. "You know what they say—no one goes to Israel just once. Your first visit gets you hooked, and you return time and again."

"Remember the Mediterranean tour you took us on that summer, Adam?" said Scott, pointing to the picture as Juliet turned the page.

"How could I forget? The women lounging about the ship, while you and I were going crazy for some earth to dig our fingers in!"

"There's Crystal and her husband alongside the rail . . . and Jen with that Italian fellow who wouldn't leave her alone."

"Don't remind me!" groaned Swaner.

"Oh—the Celtic digs in Switzerland and Scotland!" said Adam, now showing as much enthusiasm as the others for a new page of photos and clippings. "I think those were among my favorites of all the places we have been. Juliet—you and I will go to Switzerland and Scotland together one day. I promise."

"Even though this is a photograph, not a clipping," said the housekeeper, flipping ahead to the end of the book, "I had to find something with Juliet to put in."

"It's the picture I took of the two of you in Africa last year," said Jen.

"Oh, I look like such a ninny!" exclaimed Juliet. "It's no wonder . . . I was in such a daze just to be there."

"You couldn't have been too much of a ninny," said Adam. "I was already starting to fall in love with you."

(10)

Twenty-five hundred miles east and slightly south, in an expansive villa overlooking the Caspian Sea, two eyes of deep gray probed the image coming onto his computer screen. The features of the man's handsome Slavic face betrayed a serious expression. The thick lips of his wide mouth pursed themselves while he watched, and black eyebrows gathered like a storm cloud.

He recognized the lithe features and olive Mediterranean complexion. She certainly did not look as dangerous as he knew she was. His colleague from Zurich had grown careless to allow him to penetrate the heart of her encoded E-mail message system and private files.

Of course she had always underestimated him. He had been monitoring D'Abernon's little back-and-forth Internet games with her former lackey Mitch Cutter for years. He'd known about Cutter's final assignment almost the moment the fool booked passage to Baku. Now Cutter was dead. And from the looks of it, D'Abernon was sending her new underling to finish the job.

There wasn't a code in existence that couldn't be broken eventually. And he was as good at it as anyone.

In his younger years, even before the breakup of the Soviet empire, he had hacked his way into British and U.S. banks and made off with untraceable funds that were still listed on unexplained debit accounts. Chase Manhattan, Visa, and AT&T had all joined—though none of them knew it!—to finance his villa. Just for fun, he had even penetrated NATO defense systems and broken Israeli missile launch codes, though he'd never done anything with the information.

With sufficient time, wherever a telephone line went, he could trace through it as if it were a tunnel he was invisibly walking through. Give him a telephone number anywhere in the world, and he could uncover whatever information was attached to the other end of it. If he wanted to, he could steal every byte and megabyte and gigabyte of information on any computer to which it was linked. And now the Internet had made that invisible tunneling easier, providing him access to every computer in the world hooked to the world's mass of communications systems.

There were no more secrets left in the world.

What was *this* little tidbit, he said to himself, leaning forward and squinting at his screen . . . something about new codes to be initiated among—

What!

—new codes to be initiated . . . among the *eleven*!

They were planning to squeeze him out!

Well, he thought, with a cunning smile, they had not initiated them quite soon enough.

As the rest of the Swisswoman's private file on Ciano Bonar came through, Halder Zorin clicked the print command, then rose and strode toward the large picture window that looked out upon the bay and harbor.

He had to watch himself. As much as he despised her, he knew that Anni D'Abernon was as skilled, powerful, and ruthless as he himself. Now it appeared she was determined to be rid of him. He would have to turn the tables on her.

Not that it would reinstate him in the Council's good graces. It was probably too late for that. According to this information, the eleven had recently met without him. But if they thought they could be done with him so easily, they were mistaken. He had invested too much in Baku to step aside. He was the one the Council had selected to lead the new order headquartered here. He would not let them change their minds. They could not oust him. It was his destiny to rise yet higher on the world stage.

He would take them out one by one if he had to. Secretly and by stealth. They would never know nor supect who was behind it.

And D'Abernon, the devious amazon—she would be first! He would ultimately claim her place of leadership on the Twelve, and gradually turn it into a Council of *One*.

His fury with his former colleagues mounting, Zorin returned to his computer. He still had access to the highly secretive codes by which the Council conducted its private business. They scarcely imagined how vast was his computer genius. Almost anything that could be done on a computer, he was capable of doing himself. Their private codes were mere child's play.

D'Abernon had recently downloaded a series of files that provided him opportunity to sneak through an unguarded electronic back door into her own system within the network. Once he was into her private file cabinet, he could move about inside it at will.

What was this!

The *ark of the covenant!* What was she–

And if it wasn't Adam Livingstone right there in the middle of it!

So, my old friend . . . we meet again! What are you doing in her computer? I see you have been nosing around in Ethiopia . . . what are you up to?

Zorin's brows wrinkled. The ark of the covenant–this was big . . . a major development. Were these mere speculations . . . or was there possibly something to it?

Zorin thought, then returned to his mouse and keyboard. Now that he had penetrated D'Abernon's system, there was one more file he needed to see.

He typed in a few commands, then waited.

The next file to appear on the screen was his own. Quickly followed D'Abernon's complete dossier on him. As he read it, if possible, his wrath increased yet more. She had indeed done her homework. Unfortunately for her, not quite well enough.

He spun around, not waiting to print the information, and strode with heavy step to a locked cabinet. He opened it hastily, reached in, and took out a Makarov 9 mm automatic pistol. In another minute or two it was loaded with a fresh fifteen-round magazine and tucked securely in a shoulder holster under his arm. From now on it would never leave him. When Bonar showed up, he would be ready for her.

In the meantime, he would plan a more proactive strategy to exact revenge on the Council.

(11)

Juliet Halsay had recently rekindled her childhood love of swings.

Several months ago she had begun exploring the environs outside the Livingstone estate by foot. She had discovered a small park with a perfectly delightful set of swings. It was empty. The row of swings dangling from their chains had proved irresistible.

The childhood passion had returned. Since then, when the team was not off somewhere she had fallen into the habit of slipping out the back gate of the estate by herself every day or two before evening tea and walking to the park.

She made her first return to the park the day after their return from Ethiopia.

The distance was only about a ten-minute walk from the estate. Something about the thrill of soaring through the air released a girlish lightheartedness in her spirit. She felt free, even if momentarily, in a way that nothing in her adult world could quite equal.

Little did she realize, however, that someone had been observing her routine, noting the route of her walk, and had been waiting for her appearance at the park again.

As she swung back and forth on this day, Adam's words continued to sound in her mind as they had for the last several days—*I was already starting to fall in love with you.*

How could she be so lucky, thought Juliet contentedly. Adam Livingstone . . . in love with her.

There were still times she could hardly believe it!

✦ ✦ ✦

The time will surely come when I will punish the idols of Babylon . . .

"Days are coming," declares the LORD, *"when I will punish her idols . . .*

the LORD *will destroy Babylon . . .*

or the LORD *is a God of retribution; he will repay in full.*

JEREMIAH 51:47–56

✦ ✦ ✦

The Knights Templar

Jerusalem, A.D. 1121

When Hughes de Payns wandered miraculously out of the depths of Jerusalem and was led back to the Temple Mount, first by some children who found him, then by one who knew him by sight, his comrades knew immediately that something was wrong. That he was blind was obvious the moment they saw him, though why would forever remain a mystery. No external injuries on his body or head were apparent.

He did not speak for three months. His sight began to return after six. Never to human soul, however, did he divulge what he had seen beneath the great city, nor why the earthquake had affected him so. He carried the secret with him to the grave.

This had not been how he envisioned the holy pilgrimage when first he heard what lay hidden in the land of the Christ. Back then David's city and its wealth of the ages had possessed him.

✦ ✦ ✦

Jerusalem, no stranger to invasion, first fell into the hands of Islam in the seventh century, in what amounted to the twenty-third siege of the city. Pilgrimages by devout Christians continued after that time as before, largely undisturbed, until shortly after the beginning of the second millennium A.D. At that time, however, persecution against westerners began to increase noticeably.

A clash became inevitable when the Church of the Holy Sepulchre was desecrated in 1009 by the Fatimite caliph Hakim. Relations with the West deteriorated further when Jerusalem passed out of tolerant Egyptian hands and came under the control of the Seljuk Turks in 1021. Throughout the remainder of the eleventh century, talk grew in Rome and Constantinople of a holy war against the Muslim infidels.

The First Crusade to rescue the Holy Land out of Muslim hands was launched in 1096 under the French leadership of Godfrey of Bouillon and Robert, Duke of Normandy. The sacred city was wrested from the hands of the Muslims in 1099 by an army of approximately twelve thousand. Godfrey was named "Protector of the Holy Sepulchre." His successor and brother,

Baldwin of Bouillon, became Jerusalem's first Christian king. Baldwin I made the Muslim mosque on the Temple Mount, at the very site of previous Jewish temples, his personal headquarters.

Young crusader Hughes de Payns, a knight of the lower nobility of the region of Champagne, arrived in Jerusalem seeking adventure in 1104, along with thousands of other European knights.

What the young Frenchman found, however, was not what he had expected. Hughes de Payns discovered a mystery. A secret of fabulous wealth and power untold.

There were rumors.

"It's still here, you know," an aging Jew who had survived the Muslim years whispered to him after de Payns had managed to get him drunk on a large quantity of local wine.

"What's still here?" asked the young Frenchman.

"The source of our power. What the angels carried off. It's been here all along. They didn't destroy it. They hid it. Nebuchadnezzar never laid eyes on it. It's solid gold, you know."

"What are you talking about?"

"Haven't you read the account in Exodus 37? I thought you Christians revered our Torah."

"We do. But—"

"You young fool," rasped the old Jew, "I'm talking about the place where God dwells."

"You don't mean . . . the ark?"

"Keep your voice down," said the Jerusalemite. "It's a secret, the mystery of the ancients."

As he spoke, the words burned themselves into de Payns' soul.

"Only a few know," added the old man.

"And you are one of them?"

The wizened face nodded with cunning smile.

"Why don't you go get it?" asked de Payns.

"I am no adventurer. I am only an old man who knows the secret of Baruch. It is a mystery of power and wealth."

"Baruch—what is the secret of Baruch?"

"Study the Prophet, young man."

"What prophet?"

"The Prophet who was here at the time. Baruch wrote the words, not the Prophet. He wrote the words and hid the clues. He was one of the four."

"What four?" asked de Payns, more and more perplexed at the cryptic words.

"The angels, you fool . . . the four angels."

As he listened, the young Frenchman was already being seduced by a power of which he knew not.

"The secret? You mean . . . the ark?" he said again.

"The ark, and many mysteries besides," replied the Jew. "It lies buried beneath the Dome. The Muslims would kill anyone who came near."

"Not now. We've taken control of the mosque."

"The mysteries of that place are lost for all time."

"Why?"

"Anyone who touches it dies. No man can possess it. It is a secret to be known, not possessed. The angels knew, but they are gone . . . disappeared, ascended to the heavens."

The man broke into an ironic laugh. De Payns could get nothing more out of him.

That was seventeen years ago.

De Payns returned to Jerusalem again in 1113, this time with his friend the Count of Champagne. They searched high and low for the old man, but never laid eyes on him again. They made discreet inquiries. No one professed the slightest knowledge of the ark or its whereabouts.

De Payns began to wonder if the cryptic conversation had been a dream. Perhaps he had drunk too much of that foul wine. Yet he could not dislodge the man's words from his brain.

He remembered the words—secret . . . mystery. Henceforth would the life of Hughes de Payns and all who followed in his footsteps be shrouded in mystical obscurity. From darkness would they derive their power. For ultimately it would be the Great Darkness they would serve.

It was during that second sojourn to Jerusalem that de Payns' plan had come to him.

✦ ✦ ✦

Hughes de Payns' third journey to Jerusalem would prove his most eventful. From it he would become known to posterity for all time, and would spawn the most secretive occult organization in the history of man.

When de Payns returned to the Holy City in 1119, eight other French knights accompanied him, all from the region of Champagne and Orléanais, several from in and around the city of Chartres. André de Montbard was uncle to the venerable abbot, Bernard of Clairvaux, an influential Christian leader in Europe. De Payns himself was Bernard's cousin.

Though such was not their original intent, the curiosities and obsessions of these nine led to sorcerous consequences. All power in the spiritual realms has two sides, that which can be used to bring light and that which can succumb to darkness. By now de Payns' fascination for the ark had turned to a lust that would send roots throughout the world to oppose the very purpose for which God had commanded the ark originally be built.

The nine had come on a sacred mission, they claimed. They sought immediate audience with Jerusalem's Christian leader, fellow Frenchman King Baldwin II, veteran of the First Crusade, who had been elected to succeed his cousin a year before.

"We have come," de Payns told the king, "to present ourselves to you and to the holy land of our faith, in poverty, chastity, and obedience. We pledge ourselves to the service of Christian pilgrims throughout this land, to patrol the roads and byways, keeping them safe from marauders and bandits. To such we dedicate our lives and our service to our Lord, and to you."

Baldwin was hardly in a position to turn down such a vow. The success of the First Crusade had made Jerusalem a primary source of revenue for the Church, whose instrument Baldwin was. With Palestine in the hands of the pope, increasingly were penitents ordered to make pilgrimage to Jerusalem, there to place lucrative gifts on the various altars and shrines of the Christian faith. However, it suffered considerable loss of revenue at the hands of Muslim robbers and highwaymen. The roads through deserts and rocky hills teemed with Arabs and Egyptians on the lookout for easy western plunder. Much western wealth too often found its way into the hands of Bedouin and Arab sheiks rather than the coffers of Rome.

Here appeared a group of stalwart young warriors, fully armed and battle ready, saying they would fight any enemy to protect pilgrims journeying to the holy places of Jesus Christ.

De Payns, of course, said nothing of his primary objective. The less anyone knew about that, the better. It was a secret the nine—and only they—shared. Secretiveness early became the creed of this select fraternity.

Baldwin eagerly accepted the service of these brave fighting knights. "Where will you billet yourselves?" he asked.

"We have left all to serve you, worthy King," replied de Payns. "We have come with only the clothes on our backs and the swords in our hands . . . to serve you, worthy King."

"You will need quarters," mused Baldwin. "As long as you are here," he added, "you might as well protect me as well as the streets and roads."

"Your wish is our command, worthy King," replied de Payns humbly.

The young Frenchman paused, as if the idea had just come to him. "Perhaps," he said, "there might be a corner of your own palace that would be suitable."

"Of course!" rejoined Baldwin enthusiastically. "The entire mosque has been ours since we ran the infidels out twenty years ago. I use but little of it for my needs. You shall take up quarters on the Temple Mount with me."

"You are more generous than we deserve, worthy King. We are your humble and obedient servants."

"You shall have your own portion of Al-Aqsa," said Baldwin. "I shall myself supply everything you require."

Thus did the Knights of the Temple come into being.

Within a short time of their arrival in Jerusalem, their true purpose—excavating below the temple grounds—was secretly under way. Two years after their arrival, at last they broke through onto the marbled stones of the former temple, though whether that of Herod, Zerubbabel, or Solomon, none of them knew.

Three weeks later came the earthquake which would alter de Payns' destiny forever, and seal away for another nine hundred years that which he and his companions had come to this land to find.

History would never know that indeed he discovered that which he sought.

But only for moments before it was buried again. He was never allowed to possess it, only see it for a blinding instant.

When he emerged from the crypts and tunnels and later continued to roam those underground regions, it was to ancient knowledge he was led, instead of holy containers plated in gold.

PART TWO

TURKEY

✦ ✦ ✦

"Woe to the shepherds who are destroying and scattering the sheep of my pasture!" declares the LORD*. . . . This is what the* LORD *Almighty says: "Do not listen to what the prophets are prophesying to you; they fill you with false hopes. They speak visions from their own minds, not from the mouth of the* LORD*. . . . I have heard what the prophets say who prophesy lies in my name. . . . I am against the prophets who wag their own tongues, and yet declare, 'the* LORD *declares.'. . . I did not send or appoint them."*

JEREMIAH 23:1, 16, 26, 31-32

✦ ✦ ✦

five

Going Public

(1)

The scene in the basement photo lab of the Livingstone estate the day following their return from Ethiopia was of uncontainable excitement.

With shuffling feet and wide eyes, even Mrs. Graves and Mr. and Mrs. Beeves clustered around along with Crystal, Jen, Juliet, Scott, and Figg. At the eye of the storm Adam sat calmly at the tray of developer, swishing the solution over a half-dozen 8 x 10 sheets of black-and-white photographic paper. Silence filled the darkroom, where overhead a small photographic bulb gave off a thin red light.

As they squeezed over Adam's shoulders for the first hints of an image coming into focus through the developer, whispered comments and questions began to buzz among them.

A shape began to show the first stages of definition on the top sheet.

A few exclamations sounded. It was exactly what they expected, yet hardly could believe they would actually see.

Slowly it darkened. The form gathered detail. The other sheets also started to reveal their mysteries.

Adam grabbed some tongs and picked up the first print, doused it in stop bath, then held the wet picture dripping aloft toward the light.

Exclamations now burst from every mouth in earnest. Then a hubbub erupted, with everyone talking at once in amazement. The rest of the prints followed in quick succession, revealing different angles of the image of the ark and mercy seat.

"I must admit," said Adam, "I can hardly believe it myself!"

"Congratulations, Adam!" said Juliet exuberantly.

"Seeing it right side up," he rejoined, examining one of the photographs again and shaking his head in wonder at how well they had turned out, "it is a whole different view than when I was there hanging upside down in the darkness."

"The photographs are stunning," said Crystal.

"Perfect," added Scott. "I am very impressed—so clear in every detail."

"Well, let's get the rest developed and dried," said Adam. "Juliet, you go back to the print machine and print up the other two rolls. And we'll get to work on the color digitals in the computer. Then we'll get all the pictures out into the light where we can really look at them."

(2)

An hour later, seated in the front living room, Adam's team and household staff were all talking at once as they passed around more than thirty 8 x 10 brilliant images of Adam's discovery in the Sanctuary next to St. Mary's in Aksum.

Mrs. Graves, however, examining one of the photographs with a curious expression, was not saying anything. During a brief lull, Juliet heard her mumbling something to herself.

"I wonder . . . "

"You wonder what, Auntie Andrea?" asked Juliet.

Gradually some of the others glanced in her direction.

"As beautiful as it is," said Juliet's aunt, "I can't help but wonder what is *inside* . . . and whether the tablets of Moses, and Aaron's rod, still exist. Imagine, tablets written by God's own hand."

"We won't know those things until the Ethiopians make the ark public and allow Levites from Israel to open the ark," said Adam. "I am hopeful such a day may not be too far away, and that what we have done here may hasten its coming."

"Why Levites?" asked Scott.

"According to Old Testament law, only levitical priests can touch the ark without dying."

A few nods went around the room and the mood grew more serious.

"What are you going to do now, Adam?" asked Jen.

Adam paused thoughtfully.

"I have been thinking about contacting Sir Daniel Snow to see if he wants to do a live interview . . . and then making these photos public."

A low whistle escaped Scott's lips. "Whoa—that would blow the lid off the thing!" he said. "With Snow's prestige, and spreading these photos out on live TV . . . the whole world would be talking about it!"

"Why Daniel Snow?" asked Crystal.

"I'm not altogether certain," replied Adam. "I have a feeling he might be the right man to do it. But I'm still thinking over what is the best way to proceed."

(3)

Within the week, however, Adam's Ethiopian photographs were not the only ones circulating through the Livingstone estate. Where this latest picture had come from no one in the Livingstone household could imagine.

But there it was on the second page of the *Daily Mail*—Juliet leaving the back gate of the estate—with the caption in bold type: "Livingstone Mystery Houseguest."

It was followed two days later by a similar photograph, this time a close-up of Juliet's face.

"But when was it taken?" Mrs. Graves questioned her niece.

"I don't know, Auntie," replied Juliet. "Obviously some time when I was out walking. But I never saw anyone with a camera."

"I don't like it," remarked Adam. "I know what it's like to be hounded by the press, and I do *not* want them pestering you. Somebody's trying to manufacture a story here—for what purpose I'm not sure."

"How can we prevent it?"

"You could stay inside," replied Adam. "But then I have never believed in allowing the paparazzi to hold me hostage, so I couldn't blame you for not taking my advice. But somehow or another, we're going to put a stop to it."

The photographs in the paper, however, continued. The accompanying captions became more and more daring and suggestive. From "Lady in Adam Livingstone's Life" to "Mystery Woman: Relative or Mistress?" they had taken to running a brief story alongside the pictures, creating impressions and illusions out of thin air.

"The identity of the unknown young lady," read Juliet one morning, upon opening the paper to yet another surprise photo, "who moves in and out of the home of Adam Livingstone at will remains a mystery today as much as when the story first broke a week ago—"

"There is no story!" she exclaimed, throwing the paper down in exasperation.

"There is now," rejoined Adam. "And newspeople are starting to hang around outside by the gate again. The *Mail*'s creating a story from nothing."

"Well, I hate it," said Juliet. "I'm going out for a walk."

"What—are you crazy . . . after all this?" Adam laughed.

"I'll dare whoever it is to try it again! I'll walk right out past the front gate. Then I'll watch for *them.*"

"I'm not sure I like the sound of that—I'll go out front to distract them . . . you sneak out back."

"I'll be fine. What was that you were just saying," Juliet responded playfully, "about letting the paparazzi hold you hostage?"

"OK, but be careful. Someone with a telephoto lens is watching you."

(4)

Juliet reached the park. She'd seen no one as she walked. She began to feel less edgy. She removed her scarf and approached the swings. One was already occupied with a young lady who looked not much older than herself. Juliet was glad she was not the only adult enjoying the playground.

She nodded a greeting to the newcomer, then sat down and began to move back and forth. For a few minutes, only the creak of the chains broke the silence.

"There's nothing quite like a good swing," the other young woman said. Juliet turned toward her and smiled.

"I loved swings when I was a girl," Juliet replied.

"I've never lost my love of playgrounds," said the other girl with a light, sparkling laugh.

"When I'm on a swing I feel so carefree and peaceful."

"It's a sort of freedom, isn't it? The wind on your face, your hair flying back, always seeing if you can get just a little higher."

"That's it exactly!" Juliet said.

"Do you come here often?" asked the other.

"Almost every afternoon. How about you?"

"This is my first time. Whenever I'm in a new place I always try to find a park where I can swing."

"Are you new in Sevenoaks?"

"Only a few days. I'm learning my way around."

"Then let me welcome you, though I'm still a newcomer too. I've lived here less than a year myself. My name is Juliet Halsay."

"I'm happy to meet you, Juliet. I'm Kimberly Banbrigge."

"Good to meet you too." As she spoke, Juliet glanced at the sky. It had darkened since her arrival. Suddenly great drops of rain began to fall.

"Uh oh," said Juliet, jumping down to the ground and starting to run. "I didn't bring an umbrella!"

"Look's like we're in for a drenching!" said Kimberly.

"Maybe I'll see you again sometime," called Juliet over her shoulder as she hurried from the park and along the street by which she had come.

(5)

In the tiny room of a managed care retirement community, an eighty-seven-year-old lady who had walked with the Lord more than seventy years bent two creaky knees to the floor and knelt beside her bed.

Hers was an extensive prayer list. It had grown throughout those seventy years. Names were dropped from time to time, as circumstances altered the prayer needs of those whose cares she lifted to the throne of grace. But through the years more names were added than deleted.

Her mission in life was prayer. Her name would never be known. She would not accomplish much this world would find noteworthy. But she could pray. And she had done so energetically for more than half her long life. The world she hoped to influence was that unseen realm where many would greet her one day with gratefulness for the strengthening role her prayers had invisibly played in the development of their faith and spiritual maturity.

To her friends and acquaintances at Bellevue, she appeared like all the rest—aged, stooped, and feeble. Osteoporosis had long since claimed her spine. But Another claimed her spirit. Little would observers know that the frail body which was nearing the end of its earthly sojourn was home to the soul of a battle-tested soldier in an army of which they were but faintly aware.

But like many of God's warriors in these times when darkness was seen as light, she had lost dear members of her own family to the enemy. Temporarily, she believed. But that did not ease the pain to see them serving the false idols of the age. Those warriors battling strenuously against the onslaught of the many and various guises of modernism were the very saints, it seemed, whose families were most severely attacked. Her own family had been torn apart on several fronts. She even wondered if the enemy's attacks against her family were *because* of her prayers, as well they might be. With end-times cunning, Satan was seducing God's people away from the imperative of Paul's words to the Romans concerning conformity to the world. Those who apprehended the battle line and perceived the Church's peril at this point of its blindness, were those, like her, vigorously attacked and discredited. But her personal suffering would not stop her from praying. She was under orders. She must obey.

Her prayers on this day had gathered about her granddaughter, from whom she had only an hour before received a letter. Included was a copy of a feature article on the girl, who had recently turned thirty-seven, in one of the glossy women's magazines, in which she was acclaimed as a rising star in a new generation of "intelligent feminists." Her granddaughter, in fact, was already a full professor of philosophy at a prestigious East Coast university, and a leader in cutting edge modernist thought.

She had written one book, entitled *Women With Brains: The Women's Movement Asserts the Power of the Intellect,* and was reportedly working on another. Obviously she thought her grandmother would be proud of her. But instead the article brought tears to the prayer warrior's eyes. The girl had discarded the Christian upbringing of her childhood. It was obvious from one look in her face, and everything in the article confirmed it. She considered herself so mature at thirty-seven, so enlightened, so avant-garde and in step with the times, so confident and self-assured.

Her blindness was heartbreaking to the old woman. In truth her granddaughter knew so little of the only thing worth knowing, that the last shall be first and the first last. The girl's open ridicule of what the article referred to as the "failed leadership of the masculine model," flaunted values the old woman held sacred.

"Oh, God," she prayed quietly, *"the poor girl is so caught up in a world that will one day evaporate. The world worships its ideas, its intellect, its philosophies, but they are mere vanity, as poor old Solomon found out soon enough. Wake up my dear Oriel, Lord. Awaken her from this love affair with her own mind. Lord, I pray that you would bring something into her life . . . give her a reason to want to read the Bible. When that time comes, Lord, may she be struck as with a bolt of fire to realize that it is true . . . and may that lead her to realize that you are true, most of all, and that until she faces your claim upon her intellect, the rest is but wood, hay, and stubble destined for the furnace."*

(6)

Several evenings later, Adam and Juliet sat side by side in Adam's private sitting room on the second floor of the house. They had been reading, and now Juliet casually flipped on the television.

There was the renowned journalist Sir Daniel Snow, whose name had come up between them several times, in the middle of one of his famous interviews. At the sound of Snow's voice on the television, Adam glanced up from his book and found himself staring at Snow's face. As he watched, Adam began to nod to himself as if in confirmation of what he had been thinking.

"You know," he said to Juliet at length, "I think Snow's our man."

"Our man for what?" she asked.

"For making the Aksum discovery public," replied Adam. "I have the feeling he's a reliable journalist who would give the story the respect it deserves."

He paused briefly.

"And what would you think," he then went on, "about going public with the Jebel al Lawz findings at the same time?"

"I think the time may be right," said Juliet.

"So do I," rejoined Adam. "I think I will give Snow a call."

The following morning Adam was on the phone to the London offices of the well-known journalist. After identifying himself, he was quickly put through.

"Sir Daniel," he said when Snow came on the line, "Adam Livingstone here . . . how are you?"

"Very well, Mr. Livingstone. What a surprise to hear from you."

"Call me Adam, please, Sir Daniel," replied Adam.

After a few pleasantries were exchanged, Adam got straight to the point.

"What I am calling about, Sir Daniel," he said straightforwardly, "is to ask if you would like the journalistic scoop of the millennium."

"That's quite a statement," replied Snow. "What's it about–Noah's ark?"

"I'm sorry," answered Adam. "That I cannot divulge."

"You expect me to go on the air without knowing what you're going to say?"

"I know it is an unusual requirement."

"We would have to tape it of course."

"I'm sorry again, but it would have to be live."

"That's a tall order, Adam. I doubt my producers would OK it."

"I think they will," replied Adam. "You tell them that I have an astounding discovery to make public which will be unlike anything the world has ever seen. I think I can guarantee you that a rerun of the interview, once the news breaks, will eclipse anything shown on television to date–Super Bowls, World Cups, moon landings . . . anything."

"You sound extremely confident!"

"It's huge, Sir Daniel . . . huge. I assure you this is no stunt."

"Well, I must say, I am intrigued."

"It is absolutely on the level. I would like you to conduct the interview. You may name the time and place. But it must be live. And I don't intend for anyone, other than my staff of course, to know about it before I make public my findings on camera. I hope you can trust me enough to go with it on that basis."

"You have made your terms plain enough, Adam," said Snow. "I appreciate your calling me. I'll see what I can arrange."

six

Intertwined Thoughts

(1)

Lady Candace Montreux followed the society pages of the London *Times* with keener interest than was good for any woman.

It wasn't that she looked to find a flattering tidbit about herself. Even the daughter of Lord Harriman Montreux wasn't quite *that* shameless. Mostly it was to keep up on the latest gossip concerning her social peers. If her name came up every so often, so much the better.

Lately, however, the exercise had been more irritating than fruitful. She was sick of the photos and articles about Adam Livingstone's so-called "mystery girl." There was no mystery about it. The wealthy heiress to the Montreux fortune knew well enough who it was. And the young intruder was not worth all the fuss!

Now here today appeared yet another photograph. And beside it, one of Adam Livingstone.

The normally pale face turned ashen. She could not believe the words staring back at her from the page.

Adam Livingstone engaged!

All at once Candace Montreux felt sick. The feeling lasted only a second or two. Anger rose quickly to replace nausea. As it did, crimson flooded her cheeks—the color of unabated fury.

How dare he! thought Candace. How *dare* Adam do such a thing to her! She had been waiting for him to get over this ridiculous fetish. The girl was a common nobody. It was but a silly infatuation!

Candace threw the paper to the floor in disgust. She rose tempestuously, lit a cigarette, and paced the room like an angry caged tiger. The motion inflamed her passion the more—a passion, not of love for Adam, but hatred of being spurned.

Everyone would see this and think immediately of her. Everyone in London knew she had been waiting for Adam to come to his senses. Had not she and Adam themselves been pictured in the *Times* upon numerous occasions?

Not exactly calming, but realizing she hadn't finished reading the entire article, Candace walked over and gathered up the paper where it lay strewn across the floor. She ought to have as many facts as she could. Something might prove useful. She needed to measure her next moves with care.

What was this—here was Gilbert Bowles in the news too. England's two foremost archaeologists sharing the spotlight again! SIR GILBERT BOWLES SURVIVES MASSIVE HEART ATTACK read the small heading. A brief biographical sketch followed, which included the location of his recuperation.

Maybe she ought to go visit him, thought Candace. He'd probably heard the news about Adam. If not, it would be good for a mutual laugh. Sir Gilbert hated Adam as much as she hated Juliet!

Candace ground her cigarette into the ashtray with a motion of disgust. *We'll see who has the last laugh!* she thought, then spun about and walked toward the door.

(2)

If the truth were known, Sir Gilbert Bowles really didn't have many friends. And not a single close friend.

That fact had never bothered him. But with mortality staring down its cruel barrels from such close range, he found himself giving more thought these days to things like friendships. And life itself.

Friendship . . . what was it all about? Perhaps he ought to—

He stopped the thought in its tracks and did his best to turn over, as if the motion would quiet his brain.

Introspection was not Gilbert Bowles' cup of tea. He had always depended on activity to occupy his attention. Lying in bed gave his body no release, nothing to *do*. So off his mind went on the explorations for which till now he had always relied on hands and feet.

Gilbert Bowles' mental sojourns of the past weeks had been nothing like what he had experienced in thirty years as an archaeologist. They had not been pleasant. He would rather be in a jungle on the remotest corner of the globe than in this infernal bed! *Anything* would be better than facing the uncharted regions of his mind. Tigers, rhinos, deadly snakes, enraged elephants—give him the tools of his trade and he feared none of those.

But this!

His middle-of-the-night wakings when all was still—they were the worst, when a vague discomfort of soul made its relentless trek across his conscience like an angel of darkness stalking him. It was probably that cursed Bible. He should never have opened it the other night.

Voices, whisperings out of the blackness . . . calling, questioning, tormenting . . . voices he did not recognize . . . voices from realms he knew not.

Indeed a new form of seed-life was attempting to come awake in the crusty, self-absorbed scientist who all his life had considered himself an atheist. In actual fact, if Paul's words to the Romans were true, there could be no such thing as an atheist—only those who *say* they believe in no God, foolish men and women who imagine they can live without a Father. Foolish *children* rather, for until they bow before their need of a Father, they cannot become the men and women they were created to be.

Some seeds have unusually thick shells and remain hardened against the divine influences that are supposed to open them. If warm suns and gentle rains are not sufficient for germination, they must be broken by more stringent means. Occasionally do spiritual hurricanes and earthquakes become necessary before the sun can break through.

For the first time in half a century, the germ of potential life lying deep within Gilbert Bowles was beginning to be reached from outside the precarious shell of so-called atheism he had built up. Faint warming hints from the sun, and moisture from spiritual rains sent invisibly through people and circumstances, aided by the sudden approach of mortality, had at last begun to crack the hard encompassing shell of independence.

Sir Gilbert Bowles had spent his entire life digging up dead things in the ground, never apprehending the seed of eternal life that lay planted within his own heart. This was no dead fossil but a sleeping reminder of a Father in heaven who had created both the fossils he dug as well as he himself. The Creator may have been an entity whose existence he denied. Nonetheless from him came every breath Sir Gilbert now labored with difficulty to draw in and out, through miraculous lungs his own evolutionary atheism could neither produce nor explain.

The morning's thoughts had been taxing. He tried to get comfortable. Maybe he could go to sleep. He didn't want to think.

Suddenly, with the strength that was slowly coming back into his frame, he reached across his bed, grabbed up the Gideon's Bible which he blamed for all this, and heaved it across the room. It fell with a crash, sending to the floor with it the glass and pitcher of water with which the nurse had been ministering to his thirst after the fashion of Matthew 25. The motion nearly ripped the IV cord out of his vein. A stab of pain shot through his arm. He winced, then turned his back to the sound of footsteps hurrying toward him.

The nurse ran in seconds later. But to her questions she received only irritable grunts of reply.

(3)

Candace Montreux glanced tentatively into number 215.

Most hospital rooms had almost a festive look from gifts brought by well-wishers. But this one contained not a single flower or card. She first thought she must be mistaken. The room appeared vacant. Then she saw a form huddled away from her, a single white sheet draped lumpily over it.

The patient had been dozing off, or at least trying to.

"Sir Gilbert . . . ," said a female voice.

The sheet moved. The man under it turned slightly and made an effort to glance behind him. It took a blank stare of a second or two to focus. It wasn't the nurse, he could tell that much.

"I read about your convalescence in the paper," the voice went on. "Immediately I said to myself that I ought to come see my old friend from Cairo."

Bowles would rather not be reminded of it, but the comment helped him get his brain working again. And seeing another human face brightened the room. He could not help returning Candace's smile with a feeble one of his own.

"Lady Montreux," he croaked softly, " . . . kind of you to come . . . I must say it is unexpected." He pushed a small remote to raise the upper portion of his bed so he could see her more clearly.

Candace was glad for the additional words. Though brief, they gave her the chance to catch her breath after seeing Sir Gilbert's pale form. His once ponderous girth had become a svelte two hundred and thirty-five. She would hardly have recognized his gaunt, sallow face. The poor man seemed to have aged ten years since she had last seen him.

"I'm . . . I'm happy you . . . are recovering so nicely," she said, though without much conviction. Candace felt distinctly uncomfortable in this role of supposed ministry. The whole place gave her the creeps. "Have you heard the latest about our friend Adam Livingstone?" she asked.

"No . . . no, I don't suppose I have."

"He's engaged."

"Ah, Candace, my dear—my congratulations."

"No, you—," Candace replied sharply, then caught herself. "Not to *me,*" she went on. "To that ridiculous schoolgirl who's been fawning all over him."

Bowles nodded nonchalantly. "Tough break, Lady Montreux," he said. "I'm sorry it didn't work out for you." His voice actually sounded sincere.

"Ha! What would I want with Adam," rejoined Candace. "Now that his true colors show themselves. Daddy always said his station was too low for us. I don't know how I could have been such a fool as to think I was in love with him. If he can be content with such a child, I would be too much of a woman for him."

If ever there was an opening for Bowles to come back with a spirited dig of his own at Adam, Candace had just offered it on a silver platter. But he seemed uninterested.

"Livingstone's not such a bad guy," he said.

Candace stared back at him in disbelief. Had she heard the man right—*not such a bad guy!*

This was no fun, she thought. Sir Gilbert had changed. She knew heart attacks sometimes did that to people. But she hadn't expected it of Bowles. He had become a positive bore!

Candace added a couple more comments, increasing her sarcasm toward Adam. But she continued disappointed in Sir Gilbert's banal replies.

With feeble words about the time getting away and many things to do and Bowles needing his rest, she backed toward the door. She didn't want to hang around this smelly hospital any longer.

(4)

Adam Livingstone sat in his study, a lukewarm cup of tea at his side.

His feet were propped on his desk. Eyes and brain were engrossed in the book resting on his lap. On the desk behind the cup of tea were stacked a dozen or more volumes on the ark of the covenant that he had read over the past six months. The history of the search for the thing was absolutely fascinating.

Adam read another ten or twenty minutes, then rose and walked to the relief map which covered one entire wall of his study.

This wall, this map, was the place upon which his entire career was documented—the planet Earth. He had been to every continent upon it, had sailed its seven seas and many others besides, and possessed visas for fifty separate countries. There were few places on this wall he could rest his eyes where his feet hadn't also walked.

Much of his work through the years had begun right here—staring at this map and allowing his imaginative brain to soar. Questions then followed: What had been . . . what *might* have been? What secrets might the earth unlock, if only he could find the hidden keys into them?

That was his life—asking questions . . . then trying to find the answers.

All his expeditions began here. His oval Eden theory had begun right in this room.

He loved the earth. He loved its science. He loved to probe meanings and beginnings. Now that he was a Christian, those meanings and beginnings contained so much *more* meaning. He may have still been thought of as a Renaissance man by the world. But in his own eyes, what he wanted now was to delve more deeply into God's plan for the ages . . . and most importantly how he himself fit into it.

His thoughts drifted again toward the ark of the covenant. As they did, his eyes focused again on the map.

Slowly they came to rest southwest of Paris.

"France," he said to himself, recalling what he had read awhile ago in the book he had been studying. "Why would France occupy such a pivotal role in the mystery of the ark's movements?"

He reflected on the conundrum another minute or two.

"Hmm . . . I'll have to look into that later . . . ," he mumbled. "It's obviously got nothing to do with Ethiopia. I've got to prepare for Sir Daniel, not get sidetracked by France."

(5)

Sir Gilbert Bowles was released from the hospital. But he found it no more mentally comfortable at home.

It was too quiet. For the first time in his life he began to dread the lonely silence. His secretary had cancelled all speaking engagements and interviews until further notice. There was nothing to do except watch the telly and grouse at his housekeeper. If he did wind up giving her the raise the nurse had suggested, it would not be immediately. He was feeling too surly for a generous gesture such as thanking her for saving his life.

And he could not stop thinking about Adam Livingstone. It only made his mood that much grumpier. He had always thought he hated his adversary, the man whose hair was always perfect, whose suit was always spotless, whom the press loved.

Then out of Bowles' own mouth had come the incredible words, *Livingstone's not such a bad guy.*

He could hardly believe he'd said it!

The very reminder of it was as confusing to the stubborn archaeologist as his crumbling atheism was disconcerting to his subconscious sense of well-being.

What was becoming of him?

I need to get away, Bowles said to himself. I need a change . . . something . . . anything.

Maybe a cruise, he thought, perusing an advertisement in his stack of mail. A Mediterranean cruise . . . that was it. The perfect diversion!

He'd have his secretary find him something right away.

If he couldn't get out in public here in London, the public would come to him. If the right sources discovered his plans, he might even get free publicity from the exposure. And he would make sure they would. He'd let word leak out that he was going abroad.

All he'd have to do would be sit in a deck chair and enjoy the sunshine and sea air. His doctor should hardly mind that. It would be the perfect physical and mental restorative.

He'd come back fit and ready for his next adventure!

seven

The Interview

(1)

The hype had been building for two weeks, ever since Sir Daniel Snow announced that he would be interviewing Adam Livingstone live on BBC television for what was billed as one of the most remarkable historical discoveries of all time. Added to the pre-event publicity, which the producers were playing for all it was worth, was the simple fact that even Daniel Snow was in the dark about the topic.

MS-NBC had been given U.S. broadcast rights in arrangement with the BBC, and was hyping it on its side of the Atlantic with equal if not greater enthusiasm. Already, per Adam's words to Snow, both networks were scheduling a simultaneous rerun seventy-two hours after the live telecast, *if* the news proved everything Adam promised. Sir Daniel himself, quoting Adam's own words, was billing it as what Mr. Livingstone claimed to be "the scoop of the millennium."

Speculation ran rampant about what might be the mysterious discovery about to be made known to the world, running the gamut from evidence of the missing evolutionary link to life on Mars. Thus far no leak from the Livingstone camp had divulged a whisper what it could be about, although Mrs. Graves had been contacted by one of the seamier tabloids and offered £100,000 for an exclusive inside story.

Recuperating at home, Sir Gilbert Bowles was sought by more than a dozen networks and journalists to give his commentary as soon as the interview was over. But under strict orders from his doctor, he had to refuse them. It took all the willpower he could summon to watch this thing unfold and be unable to play some role in it.

Having to turn down the opportunity to appear live on camera practically killed the recovering archaeologist. *Whatever* Adam Livingstone planned to say on the air, he was confident he could debunk it, and do so with flair! He was sorely tempted to ignore his doctor's orders.

But in the end he realized he had better not risk it. He would deal Livingstone's comeuppance in his own time and own way.

(2)

In order to capture the live and spontaneous feel of the event, Sir Daniel chose the expansive lobby and lounge of London's Lebensgarten Hotel for the interview.

When the eagerly anticipated afternoon finally came, the hotel was packed with journalists and camera personnel from every media organization in the U.K., the U.S., as well as many from the Continent and other parts of the world.

Half the seating was reserved for the media and various dignitaries. The atmosphere was electric, exactly as Sir Daniel had planned. It was not quite a media circus, for once the interview began, one could probably have heard, if not a pin, certainly a nail drop. But that it was a major media event there could be no doubt.

Adam and Snow took seats in front of the cameras and spotlights, while Juliet and Jen sat in the front row of those gathered to watch. Mrs. Graves and Crystal's family had chosen to remain in Sevenoaks. Scott and Figg had already left for Turkey to join Rocky. Even as the interview began, in fact, unknown to Adam, Scott had been called in for a hastily arranged meeting with high-ranking Turkish officials. As the interview got under way, Rocky and Figg watched in their hotel room in Dogubayazit wondering what had called Scott away so suddenly, and whether he would be back before the telecast was concluded.

"This is Sir Daniel Snow. I am speaking to you live from the Lebensgarten Hotel," began the journalist. "I hardly need to introduce my guest to our audience, but for the record, ladies and gentlemen, I will say that sitting beside me is renowned scientist Adam Livingstone, last year's discoverer of Noah's ark. When you contacted me, Adam," Sir Daniel went on as a dozen cameras zoomed in on the faces of the two men, "you asked me if I wanted the scoop of the millennium. That was a little over two weeks ago. Today here we are, live on camera, with the whole world watching. I am more eager to hear what you have to say now than when you first telephoned me."

The entire room silenced if possible even more in anticipation of what was coming. Adam sat calmly. Every eye and camera awaited whatever words would follow.

"All right, Adam," said Sir Daniel, turning with a smile to his guest, "the floor is yours."

"Thank you, Sir Daniel," Adam began. "You have been gracious in allowing me to reveal what I have to share with the world in this manner. Actually, I have *two* discoveries to make public at this time. No extra charge for the second," he added, turning his winning smile first toward the reporter, then briefly in the direction of the camera.

A low murmur spread through the audience.

"The first I will tell you about occurred last year, not long after our discovery of Noah's ark on Mount Ararat in Turkey."

Adam drew in a breath before launching into his remarks in earnest.

"As many of you know," he began again, "my work during the past two years has been devoted almost entirely to what might be called biblical research. Three areas have particularly interested me, one of which has been widely publicized—the search for the ark of Noah.

"Before I make public the second two areas, however, I would like to tell you what impact this research has had upon me personally. Afterward I hope to be able to explain what I think is the significance of these three discoveries—or more properly, revelations, for such I believe they are—and to what together I believe they all point."

Adam cleared his throat.

"When I began my quest to find the remains of Noah's ark," he went on, "little did I anticipate where that search would take me. And I do not mean to the mountains of Turkey! Indeed, within months I realized . . ."

Adam continued for ten minutes, first recounting his personal adventure of faith in Africa, then culminating in what he believed God had revealed to his team in the vicinity of Jebel al Lawz, showing pictures and maps he had prepared.

"I must say, Mr. Livingstone," said Snow when Adam stopped, "that is the most incredible thing I have ever heard. You truly do believe you have found the Garden of Eden?"

"That is not exactly how I phrased it," smiled Adam. "I said that I believe that God has revealed a *portion* of the original Garden—very well what was once the center of that garden—and is causing it to blossom anew."

"Why did you not make some disclosure at the time? Why this delay?"

"I did not feel at liberty to bring it to public view," replied Adam. "It was not my revelation to make. It was and is a holy site. Human life on planet Earth began in Eden. That is where God breathed his life into that first man and first woman. I believed its message to be a quiet one about life with God—for personal revelation, not public fanfare."

"You obviously feel something has changed?"

"I do. . . . I believe this discovery, and the others, signal that an event of unparalleled significance is soon coming to the earth. That is why I sense God saying that now is the time for wider revelation."

"Yes, well . . . right—but . . . but what do you think it all means . . . what kind of unparalleled event?"

"The second coming of Jesus Christ," replied Adam.

Coughing and uncomfortable hemming and hawing were immediately evident throughout the room. Chairs creaked and heads turned, many wondering if Adam Livingstone was joking. His face, however, showed clearly enough that he was in dead earnest. Sir Daniel Snow did his best to recover his equilibrium after the unexpected statement.

"This is . . . uh, positively astounding, Adam," he said, trying to get the discussion back on a scientific footing. "Of all the archaeological research done in the world, I cannot imagine anyone actually thinking that the Garden of Eden would ever be located. This is an astonishing claim. If it proves to be true, it would certainly change the way the world looks at the Bible, wouldn't you say?"

"I would say exactly that, Sir Daniel," replied Adam. "And I do not find anything so unreasonable in the discovery. In a way, I might even say we should have expected it."

"Why expected it?"

"Because everything God does has significance. Every living thing is a reflection of its Maker. So is it likely that God would plant a tree of life upon the earth, only to allow it to wither and its species become extinct and forgotten? Would God create a tree of life and then let it . . . die?

"I cannot imagine it. It is not the way God, our Father, works. The Bible never said the Garden *died,* but that it was hidden. Things of God do not just fade away into the desert. Everything has purpose. Everything God does lasts, and has eternal import."

"In other words, you would say that the Garden has remained in existence all this time, but was hidden . . . covered over?"

"Right."

"Gone dormant, so to speak?"

Adam nodded. "The *most* significant things return into God's plan a second time," he said, "elevated to a higher, more spiritual plane. God's designs are always realized. The circle of purpose always returns to close upon itself in fulfillment of what was in God's mind to accomplish. Is this not the truth of Isaiah 55—*'My word . . . will not return to me empty, but it will accomplish what I desire and achieve the purpose for which I sent it.'*

"So you see, Sir Daniel, all these things have filled me with the conviction that the closing of the Garden's door in Genesis 3:24 only represents *half* the story of Eden. The other half is yet to be told—*the reopening of that door!* And I happen to believe the time of that revelation is at hand. I believe the Garden of Eden still lives upon and within the earth. Till now we have not yet been permitted to behold it, for it has remained sealed. But what God creates does not die. The time of that revelation has come."

"Everything you say makes sense, Adam," replied Sir Daniel. "But you must know that there will be skeptics and debunkers who will look at the evidence and draw different conclusions."

"Certainly. But I am hopeful the third discovery we have made will help to alleviate those doubts."

(3)

In the privacy of his own home, the somewhat slimmed girth of Sir Gilbert Bowles shook with laughter. This almost made up for the fact that he was not able to participate.

He hadn't enjoyed anything so much in years! Watching his nemesis and adversary self-destruct on television before the whole world was a better tonic for his recovery than all the pills and dietary precautions his doctor had prescribed over the past several months.

"The fool!" exclaimed Bowles with delight. "The positive fool!"

"The Garden of Eden!" chortled Bowles to himself. "Really, Adam . . . you've outdone yourself this time! Ha, ha! And preaching about the end of the world to boot. Ha, ha, ha!"

Even for Adam Livingstone, this claim stretched credibility to the breaking point. *This couldn't be better,* thought Bowles. Livingstone had finally gone over the edge. It might even be time for him to start a new book. He could use his upcoming cruise to get a good start. A title was already coming to him: *The End of the World and Other Myths*.

Bowles continued to chuckle. British archaeology was *his* again!

(4)

Adam continued toward the main topic for which the interview had been scheduled.

"There would be all sorts of ways to beat around the bush and lead into the discovery which we have recently made," the archaeologist went on. "But I think the best way will simply be to say what you have been waiting to hear. I know these words will be difficult for many to believe, but here they are:

"My research team and I have located an object hidden from the world for twenty-five hundred years, an object removed by divine instruction from the Holy of Holies of the temple of Solomon in Jerusalem, an object which found its way at some point in its history into Africa, where it has resided, possibly for millennia or more. Of course many will know of the rumors through the years of an Ethiopian connection, but more specifically along those lines I am not prepared to divulge at this time. I hope those who possess the object will themselves make those details public. I am speaking of the ancient ark of the covenant of the nation of Israel."

At those words, the gathering of spectators and newspeople burst into an uproar of astonishment. Adam waited until the hubbub died down, then continued.

"What I have said is incredible, I know," he went on. "But I can tell you that I saw it with my own eyes."

"Is . . . is it solid gold?" asked a dumfounded Daniel Snow, barely recovering his shock at what he had just heard.

"Of course, I conducted no tests," replied Adam. "It never was of *solid* gold, but of acacia wood plated inside and out with gold. I was unable to touch it, of course. As you know, it cannot be touched except by Levitical priests. However, it appeared to be of gold as I photographed it."

"Photographed it!" exclaimed Snow.

"I knew there would be skepticism, so yes—I have photographs with me."

"Are you prepared to show us?"

"I am."

An even greater electric anticipation buzzed the large room.

Adam turned and nodded to Juliet where she sat some twenty feet away. She rose and walked forward. Cameras swung around and zeroed in on her. This was indeed great theater, more than Snow had bargained for.

Adam took the packet. Juliet returned to her seat. Cameras pivoted and swung wildly. Snow glanced back and forth between the two. Adam began to spread out on the table before them a dozen or more 8 x 10 color glossies.

Cameras zoomed on both the table and Snow's incredulous face as he leaned forward.

"I cannot believe what I am seeing!" exclaimed the journalist after another second. "Can you get a close-up?" he said, looking up toward the cameras. "Wow—this is . . . unbelievable . . . well, see for yourselves, ladies and gentlemen!"

He picked up two of the photos and held them toward the audience, continuing to shake his own head. Television cameras closed in for tight shots of the gold object, while the entire hotel lobby filled with exclamations of incredulity, disbelief, and wonder.

(5)

In her private quarters in Zurich, Anni D'Abernon smiled to herself as she watched the broadcast. What Adam Livingstone didn't know was that she *did* know the precise location he was taking such care to keep secret. She knew how he had gotten in and out and bypassed the Sanctuary's security. She knew almost everything about Livingstone's scheme.

The reports which had come in from her operatives had been remarkably detailed and useful. She would probably have to use others for the next phase of her scheme. She would talk to Rupert first.

This Livingstone interview would have worried her a year ago. Now she was able to laugh it off. It might even work to their advantage. It would make Livingstone appear the fool in the end.

It was remarkable how much better she felt knowing she had finally turned the tables and managed to get one step ahead of him.

(6)

Slowly the hubbub, if it did not exactly die down, at least subsided sufficiently to allow Snow to continue.

"This is an astonishing claim, Adam," he said. "You are certainly correct, if it proves out—it might indeed be the discovery of the millennium, or several millennia for that matter. Can you tell us *how* you took these photographs?"

Adam explained that he and a companion had gained access to the ark's repository in the middle of the night, without disturbing anything, had taken the photographs, and had left the ark unharmed, untouched, and unchanged in any way. He did not, however, reveal specifics of the break-in or location.

"The quality of these photographs isn't the best," he added. "These were taken with a small digital camera because I knew people would want to see the color. We will try to enhance them by computer to pull out more detail. But I also took two rolls of black and whites for greater detail and contrast."

"You had two cameras?"

"That's right."

"Why black and white?"

"You can't go much higher than 1600 film speed with color. I knew it would be dark and I couldn't use flash. With black and white you can go all the way up to 3200 and do quite well in extremely thin light."

"What kind of film did you use?"

"Kodak T-Max 3200. Would you like to see those photos too?"

"Yes . . . yes, I would."

Adam took three or four black and white 8 x 10s from the packet and laid them before Snow.

"Yes, I see what you mean. The color captures the gold, but the black and whites pick up more detail. But tell me, why the stealth . . . the break-in? Why did you resort to such methods? Perhaps I should also ask, why the photographs, and even finally, why this interview?"

"I tried to go through channels," replied Adam. "It was not my wish to break in as I did. But the government in question was unwilling to talk about the ark or acknowledge possession of it. In the end I had a simple decision to make: Did I want to respect that privacy—and I realize some might say those who possess it have the right to keep the ark to themselves—or did I feel there was a greater issue, a greater good to be achieved? Obviously I came down on the side of the latter."

"A greater good, you say?"

Adam nodded. "My business has always been to unearth and try to reveal what secrets the past has to tell us," he said. "I believe in revelation, not concealment. It is my conviction that this treasure ought to belong to the world. I do not dispute the claim to possession. But I say, make it public so that the world can know the truth of the Bible's claims. That is the reason I took the photographs and contacted you for this interview, so that the world could know of the ark's existence, which must truly be considered the eighth wonder of ancient civilization."

(7)

As Rocky and Figg watched the broadcast, Scott burst into the hotel room.

"I have news, Rocky, Figg," he said, "huge news."

"Can't it wait?" said Rocky. "Sit down, and watch this. Adam is really giving Daniel Snow the whole nine yards!"

"No time, Rocky. I've got to try to get through to him."

"He's on the air. It's live. You'll have to wait till the interview is over."

But already Scott was on the telephone.

(8)

Meanwhile the televised discussion in London continued.

"So you don't only believe that the Bible is true, but that it is *provably* true?" Daniel Snow had just asked. "Is that what these discoveries signify in your view as a scientist?"

"Obviously," replied Adam, "I do not see any other rationally sound position. The Bible is not merely one of many religious books from which bits and pieces of truth can be gleaned. The Bible is *the* Book of books—the *only* document which explains the universe and man's role in it. I believed in the truth of the Bible before. Yet do not these discoveries validate that fact with more force? Its historicity is irrefutable. I do not say that there will not continue to be atheists in the world, and people who continue to say the Bible is but full of myths. But they will be individuals with their heads in the sand. With the two arks in existence for all to see, the Bible's veracity can no more be in doubt."

"Be that as it may, and let us say for the sake of argument that I accept your hypothesis, so what? What difference does that make today, in this modern age?"

"All the difference in the world, Sir Daniel," replied Adam. "It is the *only* thing that makes a difference. It is *the* central fact of the universe, the very fact of life."

"I'm not sure I follow you. My life is no different now than it was ten minutes ago, before you showed us those photographs of what you say is the ark of the covenant. Perhaps the Bible is provably true, as you say. But my life is unchanged."

Adam waited a second or two before responding.

"Perhaps it *should* be, Sir Daniel," he said.

Heavy silence followed.

Sir Daniel stared back as one stunned. This day had already contained far more surprises than he had expected. And he had certainly not expected such a simple yet profound answer to his challenge.

Adam realized he had put his host in an uncomfortable position and therefore quickly went on.

"Not only is the Bible's history true," he said, "it is a book whose truth changes lives. That's another thing that separates it from other books. The Bible's truth is not ordinary truth, it is *life-changing* truth."

"*How* does it change lives?" asked Snow, recovering himself. "As I was trying to ask before, how does the ark's existence impact life today?"

"Let me see if I can explain it like this," said Adam, "by telling you what I believe to be the significance of the two arks—the ark of Noah and the ark of the covenant. If the accounts in the Bible are true, if God actually spoke to a man named Noah and said, 'It is going to rain—build a boat larger than a football field, then take animals and your family and get inside it,' then the logical truth to follow is simply this: God is a *personal* God who *speaks* to men. It's simple, yet life-changing. God is *real.* He *speaks.* And if this same God spoke to a man named Moses and told him, 'Tell your craftsmen to build a receptacle for the tablets to these specifications,' then the significance is the same. God speaks. He is real. He intends to exist in relationship with mankind. Don't you see the huge import of it—*God intends to exist in relationship with man.* That is the impact on you and me . . . right now."

"Yes . . . I begin to understand what you are getting at."

"If God speaks to men and if the Bible is true," Adam went on, "the conclusion that follows is that the life of Jesus is as historical as is this ark we see before us. He walked and spoke and was put to death on a cross. Then he rose from the grave. Truth, Sir Daniel. The resurrection is true. The claims of Jesus Christ are true."

"Are you speaking as a scientist or as a Christian?"

"Both. The fact that there has for so long been a dichotomy between the two shows how little about origins scientists really understand. Every true scientist *has* to be a Christian, otherwise he remains in the dark about the most basic fact of science underlying every other fact—where it all began. I did not become a complete scientist until I married science with faith. With your permission, I would like to explain why I believe the Bible is provably true . . . speaking as a *scientist.*"

"By all means," said Sir Daniel.

"When I said," Adam continued, "that these discoveries prove that the Bible is true, obviously I do not mean that everything in the Bible can necessarily be proven. The way science works is to examine what evidence you have, and then draw conclusions concerning those areas where no evidence exists. Proof by inference is a valid scientific process. All science works that way. We barely possess actual evidence about one tenth of one percent of reality. But from that one tenth of one percent, we draw inferences."

"Fair enough," said Sir Daniel. "But what does that have to do with the Bible?"

"Just this. If we had proof, say, that something in the Bible were absolutely and verifiably false, then even the discovery of the ark of the covenant would, in a sense, prove nothing. We would be left with some of it true and some of it false. But the fact is, Sir Daniel, *nothing* in the Bible has ever been proven categorically false. Wherever historical evidence exists, from ancient records of the Hebrew people, to Roman records about the time of Christ, those historical documents support everything in the Bible. I repeat, nothing in the Bible has ever been *proven* false. Nothing. But if suddenly the ark of Noah is found and proven legitimate, and now the ark of the covenant, these become tangible proofs that by inference can be extended over the whole."

"I'm afraid you lost me there," said Sir Daniel.

"I'm sorry," said Adam with a chuckle. "Let me try to summarize my point. We know that every point in the Bible cannot be proven. Too much time has passed. Did Jesus actually turn water into wine at a wedding in Cana? We can't know. The people are gone. The clay jars are gone. The water is gone. The wine is gone. We have no scientific evidence. Proof is impossible one way or the other."

Adam paused and became even more serious.

"But if at every point," he went on, "where evidence *does* exist, the biblical record *is* proven reliable, and at no point whatever is there evidence to disprove a single one of the Bible's claims, then scientifically the inference must follow that all the Bible is true and reliable. It is a technique scientists use all the time. Why not use it to evaluate the biblical account? And now we have these huge and astonishing pieces of irrefutable ancient evidence to strengthen that claim. Scientifically and logically, the inference is that the Bible is true. And this astounding fact has implications for us all."

"What kind of implications? I come back to my point of a few minutes ago–I do not see how all this changes anything for me–now . . . today."

"The implication of God's reality–that he is involved in our lives, that he speaks and directs men concerning how they should live. The significance of what we have been talking about is not in the ark itself. The ark of the covenant is but a symbol. It was originally built to house the presence of God. Symbolically, not in actual fact. The presence of God cannot be contained. This was a representation God gave the ancient Hebrews to enable them to begin understanding a far greater mystery. They were not yet capable of grasping the full magnificence of the truth that God desires to live in human hearts. So he gave them a symbol they *could* understand. Then he continued to reveal more and more of that mystery a little at a time throughout mankind's developing history, until finally Jesus came, God's very own Son, God himself in human form. At that point, God was ready to tell the human race plainly once and for all the resounding truth to which the ark pointed: *He lives in men's and women's hearts.* This artifact has no power in and of itself. The power is in the presence of God. That presence resides within all those who believe in him and who have invited his Spirit to dwell within them."

(9)

"Look, I don't care who you are, they're in the middle of a live television broadcast," said the BBC's assistant producer. "I can't possibly–"

For the third time he found himself interrupted by the importune caller on the other end of the line. His own assistants had already hung up on the fellow twice. Now this third and most insistent call had been passed up the line to him.

"So you say," he said at length, "but how do I know that you are–"

Again the insistent voice broke in.

"All right," said the producer, "you've got a point–you did manage to get through our security, though how you got this number in the first place is beyond me . . . all right, yes . . . I'll get a note to him . . . but if this isn't on the level–"

Again he was forced to listen.

"Yes, you've made that point . . . I just hope you know what you're doing."

(10)

"These are remarkable claims, Adam," said Sir Daniel. "So then why all the buildup with the ark of the covenant, if, as you say, it has no real significance?"

"It has tremendous significance," rejoined Adam. "It is a historical discovery of epic proportion. But its spiritual significance is even larger. It points to that greater reality that symbol was meant to represent from the beginning. And I think the reason God has allowed it to be found today, is so the world can see and know the veracity of the Bible. But even greater than the scientific or intellectual proofs of the Bible is the proof of the heart. What does this miraculous book have to say to *me*, to *my* life–that is the question these discoveries ought to prompt. If it is true, then so much at which modern man scoffs takes on new meaning. It means that God really answers prayer. What a fantastic revelation! It means that God dwells in hearts. A yet more remarkable revelation! It means that miracles occur. It means there is truly an afterlife. Where will the philosophies of modern man be after this? Don't you see–it makes the Bible's claims *true*.

"We have a very *personal* Creator, Sir Daniel. The greatest implication is that God has a claim upon our lives, a claim to our obedience. That is the glorious and astounding truth of the ark of the covenant. If he created us, then he has a claim upon us.

"Furthermore," Adam went on, picking up one of the photographs of the ark and holding it up, "this ark means that God's *presence* is with us. We are the living, breathing beings of which the ark of the covenant was made to represent."

Adam pointed first at his own chest, then at Sir Daniel's.

"*That* is the true ark of the covenant, your heart. That's where God wants to dwell. This ark, as wonderful a find as it is, and as beautiful an object as it is—means nothing alongside the astounding and astonishing truth that God wants to dwell inside us, Sir Daniel. Inside our hearts! This is what the ark *means*—that God's presence requires a dwelling place, a home. That home is within us."

(11)

"But wait," said Sir Daniel, "I am being interrupted. . . ."

One of his technical assistants walked on camera and handed Daniel Snow a piece of paper. He glanced down at it, then up at his assistant.

"But we are on the air . . . I can't possibly . . ."

"He insists that it is absolutely urgent," whispered the man.

Cameras zoomed in on the producer and journalist, trying to pick up their conversation.

"This is unheard of," insisted Sir Daniel.

The producer shrugged. "All right . . . ," said Sir Daniel, "bring us a portable phone."

The man walked off. Sir Daniel looked over at Adam, shook his head and smiled, though with a hint of annoyance.

"Well, this has been a day of surprises," he said. "I don't suppose one more can hurt. It seems, Adam . . . that you have a telephone call which simply cannot wait."

A confused expression spread over Adam's face as the interview was temporarily suspended. A moment later the assistant returned carrying a portable phone. He handed it to Adam.

Adam took it, still puzzled, wondering if it was some stunt dreamed up by Snow.

"This is Adam Livingstone," he said. Cameras again zoomed in for a close-up of his face.

"Scott!" he exclaimed, "what in the world—"

The importune voice on the other end of the line silenced him just as it had Daniel Snow's assistant producer. The call was brief. Thirty seconds later Adam handed back the phone and turned to Sir Daniel with a smile.

"It would seem our timing is fortuitous, Sir Daniel," he said. "It appears I have yet another stunning announcement to make."

"Go ahead—we're listening."

"That was my assistant Scott Jordan," said Adam. "He and a few others of my technical team are in Turkey. Scott called to tell me that he just got out of meetings with officials less than half an hour ago, and that the go-ahead has been granted for our plans to lift Noah's ark off the slopes of Ararat!"

A single loud exclamation erupted out from the audience. Adam and Sir Daniel turned to see Juliet clamping a hand over her mouth in embarrassment at the outburst.

"When will you begin?" asked Sir Daniel.

"As soon as we can," replied Adam. "I think we will begin packing as soon as this interview is over, and be on our way within twenty-four hours. This is the breakthrough we have been waiting for."

The lobby broke out in applause and noisy talk as half the journalists rushed from their seats to file stories.

The interview was clearly over.

eight

What Can It Mean?

(1)

Headlines and news bulletins throughout the world the following day proclaimed the incredible Livingstone announcement in type ranging from a quarter inch—*The Wall Street Journal*—to four inches—*The National Enquirer.* The *San Francisco Chronicle's* three-inch and the London *Times*' two-inch headlines were more the norm.

The declarations were as varied as the accompanying editorial perspectives given to the news: From ARK OF COVENANT FOUND to BIBLE PROVEN TRUE, and from GARDEN OF EDEN IN SINAI DESERT to ARK OF NOAH TO BE LIFTED FROM ARARAT to LIVINGSTONE TRIUMPHS AGAIN.

Whatever the various spins put on the events of the previous day, there could be no doubt that Adam Livingstone was at the center of the world stage.

The first rerun of the broadcast was planned, and both the BBC and MSNBC fully expected it to be like nothing the world of television had ever seen. Already every major Bible publisher was scurrying, trying to buy up whatever time was available within an hour on either side of the event, and putting together hastily prepared ads to be aired.

(2)

The manager of a Christian bookshop in a small town in northern California arrived at the store about 9:15 two mornings after the Snow interview and was surprised to see three cars already in the parking lot and several people milling about the front door.

Sales had been slumping for several years. Amazon.com, CBD, and the big box retailers had just about spelled the doom of most independent Christian bookstores, theirs included. It had been more years than she could remember since the last time customers were actually waiting before the store opened. True, yesterday had been busier than normal, with Bible sales like nothing she had ever seen. Most of the day's purchases were made by people she had never seen before. As she drove up, parked, and unlocked the store, she realized those waiting this morning were not regular customers either.

She hardly had the lights on before the people began filing in. They all wanted the same thing: Bibles.

She greeted each one warmly, and led them to the Bible alcove, where within ten minutes twelve people were browsing and comparing translations.

If this kept up, she thought, she was going to be out of Bibles within the week! She'd better place a sizeable order with Riverside and Tyndale this morning.

(3)

The day was sunny and bright on the campus of Bryn Mawr College in the suburbs of Philadelphia.

On her way to class, a young professor walked across a brick-lined pathway toward the library and several other buildings.

"Good morning, Ms. Tornay," said a voice behind her. She pivoted to see one of her students running to catch up.

"Hello, Elizabeth."

"What do *you* think about the news?" asked the girl as she fell into stride.

"What news?" asked her instructor.

"About the ark of the covenant."

"Oh, that . . . I haven't really thought about it, Elizabeth."

"But it's so exciting . . . how could you not?"

"It's not something that interests me."

"You didn't watch the interview?"

"No, I'm afraid I didn't."

"But you will watch the replay of it tomorrow evening?"

"I don't know. I hadn't thought about it."

"Oh, but it seems if anybody would watch, it would be you."

"Why do you say that?"

"Because truth is what your class is about—finding the truth. Isn't that what philosophy means?"

"I think that is an accurate statement, as long as we keep in mind that each must find what truth is for themselves."

"But just think, Ms. Tornay—if the Bible can be proved true, it would completely change the way people looked at the search for truth. All the philosophy books would have to be re-written."

"I doubt the implications are quite that significant."

"It would make the Bible the cornerstone of philosophy again, not treated as insignificant as it is now."

"I hardly think the Bible will become the cornerstone of philosophy," said the professor, laughing.

"But we will talk about it in class, won't we, Ms. Tornay?" persisted the enthusiastic student.

"We shall see, Elizabeth. I'll have to give that some thought."

"Well, I'm on my way to the gym. I'll see you in class this afternoon."

Professor Tornay paused reflectively as she watched the girl hurry on along an adjacent sidewalk. As she continued past the student union, her eyes fell upon one of the newspaper machines as she passed.

HEBREW ARK PROVES BIBLE, CLAIMS LIVINGSTONE read the headline.

She walked on, entered the building in front of her, and climbed the stairs up to her office.

Two hours later, however, she found herself back in front of the union, this time buying a copy of the paper, then quickly folding it and tucking it under her arm.

Later that evening, in the privacy of her apartment, she read through the account for a second time.

It couldn't be true, she thought to herself. It simply *couldn't* be true.

Yet as she tried to go to sleep an hour later, she couldn't shake her student's words from her mind . . . *finding the truth . . . what philosophy means . . . change the way people looked at the search for truth.*

(4)

Rupert Vaughan-Maier rolled over and looked at his clock. It was a few minutes after four in the morning.

He hadn't slept since midnight. Unsettling forces were at work. A peculiar agitation in the Dimension.

He rose, turned on a light, dressed, then went to his bedroom phone. The number he called was a private Zurich line.

Anni D'Abernon answered immediately. It was obvious from her voice that she was also wide awake.

"Something is up," said Vaughan-Maier.

"Yes, I have been expecting your call," she replied.

"It is this Livingstone business—there can be no other explanation."

"Relax. A temporary disturbance."

"How can you be so certain?"

"The people I told you about . . . they are working on it. Livingstone will be handled."

"You're not planning to kill him."

"I know better than to make a martyr of him. We will make him a laughingstock instead. Wait a minute . . . I have another call coming in."

The line went silent between them for a minute or two. When D'Abernon returned she now found herself on hold. She waited. Vaughan-Maier returned about thirty seconds later.

"While I was waiting for you," he said, "I had a call as well—Wilson Abrams. He is extremely on edge. It seems sales of the enemy's book in his country are exploding."

"A groundless fear," rejoined D'Abernon with a hint of exasperation. "It is not a *threat*. It will blow over, I assure you."

"Was your call from one of the Council?" asked Vaughan-Maier.

"De la Cruz," D'Abernon replied. "Perhaps you should contact the others, Rupert, with a prepared statement."

"You are right. I shall put something together."

Vaughan-Maier hung up the phone. Yes . . . he would calm and reassure the Council. That was his role. He was the elder statesman, after all. But he was still agitated.

(5)

Despite her insistence that there was nothing to it, especially nothing that could possibly concern her, feminist Ph.D. Oriel Tornay cleared the following evening to watch the rerun of the Livingstone-Snow interview.

Everyone on campus was talking about it. She had to stay informed, she reasoned. She would videotape it, then go over it with a fine-tooth comb at her leisure. She would bring all the logic of her training to bear on the case, find every flaw in what Livingstone said. She would use it in her classes to demonstrate the pitfalls to beware of from religious types whose hollow philosophies could not withstand the critique of modernism.

She began to look forward to it. This would give her the perfect practical opportunity to illustrate what she tried to teach—showing young women how to use their intellects to expose the myths perpetuated for centuries by men's religions.

The hour of the telecast came. With a self-satisfied smirk on her face, Oriel turned on her television and sat down. These smug Christians who loved to get themselves interviewed on TV were all alike. Dispensing with their self-righteous and ridiculous ideas was child's play.

From the moment Adam Livingstone began to talk, however, unexpected sensations began to rise up within her. An expression of curiosity and question came over her features as she stared at the face of the renowned British scientist. She didn't find it so easy to dismiss him as she had anticipated. The man did not seem like a kook. She had the feeling he could probably hold his own in a debate on almost any topic. At the same time she had the feeling he wouldn't debate at all, that he would only gaze at her with that handsome, infectious smile, as if to say, *There is no need to debate. You'll understand one day. You will see the truth too, as I did.*

And as she watched, Oriel was flooded with inexplicable reminders of her grandmother. Suddenly the article she had sent her a few weeks ago seemed remote and distant, the accolades so meaningless.

Then came an involuntary thought into her well-trained, logical, incisively philosophical and doubting brain—*What if . . . what if it really might be true?*

An unwelcome thought!

She could not deal with it. The idea was too unsettling. The pride of her feminism squirmed in its lair. She grabbed at the television remote and pushed the Mute button. She didn't have to listen to this!

She rose and walked about the apartment like a caged animal. But the question, once let loose, was after her. And there was no hope of escape.

The next day, in disbelief that she was really doing it, she found herself walking into a Bible bookstore not far from campus.

As she glanced about, she remembered going to a store like this as a child with her grandmother. The memory she had always carried of the incident, and thus her image of all Christian bookstores, was of a dumpy, stale little hole in the wall. But that was certainly not the case now. This place reminded her of a classy Hallmark shop, bright and cheerful, with pleasant upbeat music playing.

"Hello," said a sales clerk, smiling broadly. "Is there anything I can help you with, or would you like to look around?"

"I, uh . . . I would like to get a Bible," said Oriel, feeling oddly strange and out of her element. She could speak to five thousand women about exerting the power of their brains. But the simple act of asking for a Bible had thrown her sweat glands into high gear.

"Is there something special you had in mind," said the clerk, leading her across the floor, "in the way of a translation?"

"One of the modern ones, I suppose," replied Oriel nervously. "Just something inexpensive, in paperback if you have it. I want to read about the ark of the covenant."

(6)

In the meantime, Sir Gilbert Bowles didn't know what to think either.

He had guffawed his way through the interview. Yet like Oriel Tornay he had found irritating sensations rising up within him, reminding him of that idiotic passage of the Bible he had stupidly read in the hospital about God's qualities being seen from the world he made, and men being fools who didn't see it.

He had never heard such poppycock in his life. But even after a week, he couldn't get the infernal words to go away!

Well, *he* didn't see it! And he was certainly no fool!

Maybe he'd read the thing wrong. He'd been in a bad way at the time. That was surely it. His brain had twisted the phrases around and was playing tricks on him. He'd get hold of it again, now that he was thinking straight, and see what it really said.

But how would he ever locate the passage? He hadn't a clue where it might be. He'd just opened the book and there were the blasted words staring back at him.

There was some book he'd heard about once that located passages in the Bible if you knew a word or two of the verse. He'd try that, although he didn't remember what the thing was called.

But somebody would know. He would find out, and settle this thing once and for all.

(7)

Meanwhile, in the Christian bookstore in California, Bible sales continued briskly, increasing even more following the Snow rerun.

The shop's manager had placed one order, but was already putting together another before the first even arrived. Some of her Bible suppliers were beginning to run out of stock on the more popular editions. She knew she'd better plan ahead. Paperbacks were selling most of all. People didn't care that much about fancy bindings. They only wanted to get at the information inside—what the Bible *said*.

So she was ordering as many paperback editions as she could get her hands on, and others up to twenty or thirty dollars. If this run on the Scriptures subsided and she found herself overstocked on Bibles, then she would be ready for the next Christmas season. It never hurt to have plenty of—

"Excuse me," said a voice in front of her.

She glanced up from the catalog on the counter in which she had been absorbed.

"Oh, I'm sorry!" she said. "I was getting a Bible order ready and didn't see you walk up."

"That's all right." The young lady smiled. "Actually, that's why I'm here. I want to buy a Bible."

"So does everybody these days," said the manager, laughing. "Are you wanting to read about the ark of the covenant too?"

"That's what started it, I suppose—the Adam Livingstone discovery. But it's not just that. I want to read it all. I suppose I am what you would call a new Christian."

"Oh, that's wonderful—I am happy to hear it."

"I know it may sound funny, but actually I've never had a Bible of my own. I was watching the interview, and I don't know how to explain it, but right then I knew that God was real. So I prayed, right while my television was still on. I asked God into my heart, just like Adam Livingstone was saying. Do you think that makes me a Christian?"

"It certainly does. When you ask Jesus into your heart, that's the place to start."

"Good," replied the young lady. "I wasn't really sure what to do. I remember hearing people talk about repentance too, and though I've never committed a crime or any sin like that, I asked God to forgive me of my sins too."

"We all sin in our own way," said the manager. "I grew up in the church, and that's something I had to learn in my own life."

"That's what I realized. So like I said, I asked God to forgive me. And then as he was talking about God wanting to dwell in hearts, and wanting to be in relationship with men and women, I just said, 'God, I would like you to live in my heart too, so I invite you to come in and live with me and help me to be your child.'"

"That is so wonderful. Thank you for telling me about it."

"Then I thought I should have a Bible. But to tell you the truth, I don't know anything about it. What should I read?"

"Start with the Gospels," said the manager of the store. "They're the most important part of all. I'll show you where to find them when you pick out a Bible. That's where Jesus tells us how to live, what to do, how to think. Once you've invited him into your life, there's nothing so very complicated about living as a Christian. It's just doing what Jesus said, and trying to follow his example. Come over here . . . I'll show you the Bibles, and help you pick out one you like. Then I'll show you where to locate the Gospels, and a few other books you'll find helpful."

"Thank you. I'm really new at this. I appreciate what you've told me."

(8)

In Washington D.C., Senator Marcos Stuart hurried up the Capitol steps. He was late for a meeting with the Majority Leader, and he was not a man you liked to keep waiting if you wanted to move up.

Five minutes later he walked into the Leader's office. Three or four other senators were also present. The discussion in progress, however, did not pertain to the subject of the day's meeting. He shook hands with the others and took a seat.

"Hey, Stuart," said one of the men, a certain Duke Quinby, the senior senator from a key midwestern state who was being looked at seriously as a potential vice-presidential candidate, "we were just talking about the Daniel Snow interview. I understand you know the English fellow Livingstone."

Marcos nodded. "As an acquaintance," he said. "His assistant, Scott Jordan, and I went to school together."

"What do you think of all this?" asked Quinby.

"I don't quite know what to make of it," replied Stuart. "Scott was certainly never the religious type. Matter of fact, neither was Livingstone . . . that is, until a couple of years ago. Then he went wacky all the way with it."

"Talked to either of them recently?"

"About a year ago," replied Marcos, shaking his head. "Why?"

"I don't know," said Quinby. "That's what we were talking about before you came in. I'm not the religious sort either. But ever since that interview I haven't been able to get it out of my mind. I mean, if the Bible really is *provable*, like Livingstone said—wow . . ."

He glanced around at the others, as if repeating the point he had been making before Stuart's arrival.

"I don't know what to think but that it would change everything," Quinby went on. "The implications for all of us, for our country, political implications . . . *everything* would be on the table. I mean, we couldn't ignore religious issues anymore. It would impact everything from school prayer to nativity scenes in front of schools and government buildings. How could the government ban nativity scenes any more if the event is as historically reliable as Washington crossing the Delaware? If the Bible is true as a historically verifiable book, then how could the government prohibit its being read in school? I would think we would have to change the laws to *insist* that it be read. That's what I mean—this thing has really got me thinking. If Livingstone is right, how can we in government continue with business as usual?"

Again he glanced around. The other senators could see that Quinby was serious.

(9)

When the assistant manager of the Scripture Union Christian bookstore in London looked up to see the huge man with a silver serpent dangling from one ear walking toward the counter with purposeful stride and gruff expression, his first thought was that the store was about to be held up at gunpoint. The khaki-clad man looked about as unfriendly and imposing as anyone he had ever seen.

"Uh . . . good morning, sir," the man said.

"I'm looking for some kind of book that's supposed to locate verses in the Bible," said the customer, if possible in a yet more irritable tone than his expression.

"There is what's called a concordance," replied the clerk, doing his best not to stare at the earring.

"Yes, that's it . . . I knew I'd heard the word before."

"We have Strongs, Youngs, Crudens, and several others."

"I don't care which. I don't want to buy one, I'm just trying to find a particular verse . . . something about, uh . . . God's–"

This whole thing was odious enough. And this store positively made his skin crawl. But having to say the non-being's name aloud sent a repellent tingle down Gilbert Bowles' spine.

"Er . . . *God's* attributes or qualities or some such thing." He struggled to go on. "Being visible in the world . . . or maybe it's something like in the things he made–I don't know, something like that."

"Oh, well, if you only want to find that verse," said the man in a more friendly tone now that he realized he could be of help to the man in front of him, "we don't need a concordance for that. The verse you want is in the first chapter of Romans."

"Romans . . . what's that?"

"One of the books of the New Testament–Paul's letter to the Romans."

"Do you have one?" asked Bowles. "I'd like to read that verse."

"Certainly. Any particular translation?"

"No, no, I don't care," replied Bowles irritably. "I just want to see what it says."

The clerk picked up a Bible from the other side of the counter, opened it, thumbed through the pages, then set it down on the counter between them and turned it around.

"There it is," he said, pointing to the page, "the twentieth verse."

Bowles bent down and began reading. The store was silent for perhaps twenty seconds. Then he swore loudly, spun, and walked toward the door in a rage, leaving the perplexed man staring after him in shock, glad that there were no other customers in the store.

(10)

A month after the interview, in the programming offices of *Sixty/Twenty,* a television magazine, the executive producer had called a meeting of his top-level journalists.

"This Livingstone thing is hot," he began. "I've been watching to see how it develops and I think it's time we got on it."

Nods went around the room in agreement.

"Can we get Livingstone himself?" he asked. "Any of you have contacts that could be useful?"

"There's a senator who's plugged in somehow," said one of the reporters. "I could set something up with my people on the hill."

"Plugged in . . . how?"

"Knows somebody on the team, I think."

"Might be a good starting point. See what you can arrange. In the meantime, do we have a crew in Turkey filming preparations for this Ararat thing?"

"We do," replied one of the assistant producers.

"So does every other network and paper and news magazine in the world," put in one of the others. "We're covering it because it's the biggest scientific project since the space shuttle–some are comparing it with the moon landing. It has tremendous public appeal. But how to get the angle on it–that's the thing . . . a different perspective to set our story apart from a hundred others."

"Ideas?" said the executive producer, glancing around the room.

"Why don't we do a series of up close and personal interviews with someone in each of the companies involved . . . GE, Rockwell, Raytheon, Boeing, NASA?"

"Right–get them talking about how they became involved, what their company's part of it is, how they're contributing to the overall effort."

"Or along the same lines," suggested another, "but from a different angle. We could look at each of the different parts of the project itself–the melting of the glacier, the construction of the blimps to lift it, the strapping equipment to keep it all in one piece, and the accumulation of nearly the whole world's available helium supply–"

"Yeah, and I've heard they've developed a new kind of hardening foam just for this project that will keep the whole thing intact."

"The technology is supposed to be enormous. Livingstone's been working on it for a year, trying to raise money at the same time as he's been developing the systems that will have to coordinate together."

"I doubt he'll pull it off," said the resident skeptic among them.

"If he does," rejoined the producer, "it *will* be the biggest scientific story since the moon landing."

"Everybody's got good ideas," said one of the senior journalists. "But I still think we're in the area that the other programs and networks will cover. Everyone's going to be thinking the same kinds of things. Why not let our regular news department handle them? They could do all this. What *Sixty/Twenty* needs is a completely unique slant."

The room fell silent. She had a good point, and the rest knew it.

"There is an angle," said another of the reporters who had not yet spoken, "that comes at it not from a technological standpoint at all, but from perhaps what you'd call a societal or maybe even a spiritual angle."

"We're listening."

"I've been fascinated by a story that's developing–the sudden increase in Bible sales since the Livingstone interview."

Laughter immediately spread throughout the room. The staff of *Sixty/Twenty* was well known for the anti-Christian bias of its program.

"Bibles!" exclaimed one of the men. "You have got to be kidding!"

"B-o-r-i-n-g!" singsonged another.

"Big deal," added yet another. "The Bible is always the number one seller. That's hardly news."

"This is different. It's never been like this. They say stocks are already being depleted."

"I still say it's boring," insisted the singsonger.

The executive producer, however, was intrigued. The Bible was not his cup of tea, but he knew a different angle when he heard one, and he thought he may have heard one just now.

"This may be worth pursuing," he said. "I want to hear more."

"I don't have much more," said the man who had suggested it. "I'm envisioning a story behind the story kind of thing, the impact the Livingstone discovery is having in people's lives as evidenced by the surge of interest in the Bible. Obviously it's an exaggeration, but I read one quote about the run on Bibles comparing the phenomenon to bread sales prior to a famine."

"That's absurd," commented another.

"Perhaps . . . but can we afford not to look into it? Especially right now, with interest in religious things so high. I have the feeling it could be one of our biggest segments of the year."

"All right, you've sold me," said the executive producer. "The story is yours. Get started. If Livingstone pulls this thing off we'll want to run your piece as soon after it as we can. So have a proposed storyboard on my desk in forty-eight hours."

nine

Operation Noah

(1)

An attractive young woman in her mid-twenties stood on a makeshift wooden platform, microphone in hand, in front of two or three hundred reporters and journalists, and an assortment of media types, mostly standing. Some sat on the ground. There were no chairs.

Almost all of them were dressed in outdoor clothing of the backpacking or safari sort. It could have been a set for the filming of a Banana Republic ad. There wasn't a tie or three-piece suit for miles. A few of the women present, which comprised probably a third of the total, wore loose and casual dresses, though mostly jeans. The air was seasonably cool for early September, though dry. It was high enough in elevation, just over forty-five hundred feet, here on the highland slopes south of the village of Igdir, to prevent scorching late-summer heat, though it would probably rise to eighty or eighty-five degrees Fahrenheit by afternoon.

News and film crews and volunteers hoping to work on the project had been arriving in droves for a week, setting up trucks, vans, satellite relays, and tents across the barren, rocky landscape. For millennia this region had been home only to the wind, goats, sheep, shepherds, and the various wild creatures who could survive here. Suddenly it looked like an off-road and SUV convention. Hundreds of trucks had been rumbling in nonstop for weeks, carrying everything from food and water and other supplies, to technical equipment and computers, to generators and huge cats and earthmovers. Exxon and Shell had brought in enormous tanker-trucks full of diesel and gasoline to service the needs of the thousand or more small vehicles, trucks, and machinery on hand.

Behind the gathering of the press, the sounds more resembled downtown San Francisco near the construction site of a new high-rise, than a remote corner of the globe most present would never have imagined visiting only two months before.

"Hello, my name is Juliet Halsay," the young woman began. "I am standing below seventeen-thousand-foot Mount Ararat in Turkey, where behind and around me you can see and hear the massive buildup of preparation for what has been dubbed by the media *Operation Noah*. Up on the mountain itself work is also in progress. The support village where we are standing, as you can see, is multiplying in size and complexity literally every hour. Hopefully within the next few days, the many facets of this complex mission will culminate when the team led by Adam Livingstone will bring the ark of Noah down to rest not far from where we are standing."

Juliet could hardly believe she was doing this! If she stopped to think how many millions of people were watching her on television, she would shrivel up and die on the spot. So she had determined beforehand that she *wouldn't* think about it. She would just pretend that she was chatting informally with these few people in front of her and block the rest out of her mind. Although she did hope her mum and two aunts were watching!

Spread out for miles were hundreds of tents, cars, vans, buses, even airplanes and helicopters. The scene resembled a gigantic technological Woodstock more than an archaelogical dig. Indeed, the majority of the digging—or more accurately *melting*—had already been done, two years before, to locate the long-buried treasure which now sat up on the mountain at the center of the world's attention. The present assignment was to safely transfer that monument of the ancient world, so that it might be preserved for the entire human race to see up close.

The mysterious snowcapped mountain of legend called *Ararat* was the focus of the whole world's attention. For weeks intensive and highly specialized work had been in progress in preparation for the coming climax. Today's was the first scheduled press briefing by the Livingstone team's newly designated spokesperson to orient newcomers and bring listeners up to date on progress at the ark-site, and provide an idea of what could be expected in the days to come. Most television networks were broadcasting the event live, and many were also taping for replay that evening by their stations at home.

"Behind me are six large-screen monitors," Juliet went on, "where we will be able to observe work on the mountain as the week progresses. I am linked by headset directly to Adam Livingstone on the mountain and to Scott Jordan, Mr. Livingstone's assistant, and will be in constant communication with them.

"It has been eight weeks since approval was granted by the Turkish government to go ahead with this final stage of the project, for which planning and preparation has been under way a year. However, political considerations continued to leave the end result in doubt until this most recent breakthrough in negotiations. The weather has been remarkably, some would say miraculously cooperative here in the highlands of eastern Turkey. Much of the groundwork, as I say, had already been done, but two months ago everything swung into high gear. The technological hurdles have at times been monumental. But it appears we are at last ready to see if the labor will pay off in the single unifying dream of Operation Noah—lifting the recently discovered ark of the Old Testament off Mount Ararat and moving it down onto the plain here at the base of the mountain.

"Before I outline the schedule we are expecting to follow for the next few days, and then open it up for your questions, I would like to take this opportunity to say a big thank you from Mr. Livingstone and all his team, and everyone here, to all the schoolchildren around the world who are watching. We have received thousands of pounds that you have collected in your schools, and Mr. Livingstone asked me to thank you personally. He is using your money to pay for many of the tens of thousands of helium balloons that will be fitted inside the ark to help lift it. When you watch the ark rise from the mountain several days from now, you can know that your pences and pennies helped make it possible."

(2)

The scene over Mount Ararat in eastern Turkey was unlike anything this region of the world had ever seen.

Ten or twelve huge, specially designed blimps—each four times the size of a 747 jumbo jet—hung suspended over the mountain in readiness, practicing even now for the job for which they had been constructed. They appeared as surreal motorized clouds, so huge they made ordinary sporting events' television blimps look like two-seater Cessnas beside U.S. Air Force Transport C-5 behemoths.

Up and down the slopes—between the village where Juliet was speaking to the press up to the ark-site itself—equipment and machinery crawled back and forth in an unending line on a hastily constructed dirt roadway. Gigantic military helicopters buzzed about the mountain like a swarm of science fiction mechanical bees, moving people and supplies up and down in a continuous flow. Four helipads had been constructed near the ark on the glacier, within easy walking distance from the Livingstone command center—a huge tent resembling a circus big top.

Much of the transport of equipment had been carried out on military vehicles. Olive drab and camouflage were the prominent color schemes in evidence. A special road as wide as a four-lane highway had been laid to the site by the U.S. Army Corp of Engineers from Yerevan, twenty-five miles north just across the Armenian border. The traffic flowing back and forth on it already at times resembled a California rush hour.

Many of the preparations had been under way for almost two years, with starts and stops and stalls as the Turkish government had waffled and changed its mind any number of times about whether to allow the project to proceed. The "lease" agreement concluded by Adam Livingstone three years earlier, making possible his discovery of the ark's location, had been for five years. However, it was filled with so many clauses and exceptions that the Turkish government found it an easy matter to hold things up. But Adam's preparations had continued. The blimp construction maintained its schedule, orders were placed for the melting equipment, straps, helium, and ten thousand other necessary items. Experimentation continued with the new foam being perfected at DuPont. Once final go-ahead was given, the rest fell quickly into place. The blimps had arrived three days ago from their long journey from Boeing headquarters in Seattle.

The melting equipment, essentially the same sort of state-of-the-art torches as had enabled Adam to melt into the glacier when the discovery was first made, had been operational now for two weeks. Fourteen technicians had been working their way around the outside of the ark's hull, while another six were busy inside the vessel, wielding their torches as carefully as any archaeologist his shovel, screen, and broom. Inside the ark, the meltwater was pumped overboard, where it joined with the flow created by the external torches. A steady trickling stream worked its way down the mountain, giving visible evidence that the ark was indeed slowly being excavated out of its burial chamber.

As the encasing block of glacial ice disappeared, from all vantage points above and below gradually the huge ocean-worthy craft designed by the Almighty came into view. It was an astonishing sight indeed that began to capture the world's attention. More and more airplanes flew by, with the result that aerial photographs and videos began making nightly newscasts in nearly every nation on earth.

So careful were the melters that none of the ark surface itself was ever touched by flame. The burning was only carried out to within approximately a half, or if possible a quarter, of an inch from the surface. From there they allowed nature to take its course, which it did over most of the surface within another twenty-four to thirty-six hours. They had melted around the edges of the ark, as well as many of the inside portions, and were getting close to the point where the surface was exposed.

As the shape of the vessel came into view, there were reasons for both elation and disappointment. That the exterior hull was almost intact was probably the most astonishing fact of all—no doubt because of the heavy pitch content and coating of the timbers—which would allow, in theory at least, the entire vessel to be lifted off the mountain in one piece. Much of the interior had rotted away, however. Though portions of several floors and decks still existed, with traces of human and animal quarters, much of the roof and upper decking were gone.

A massive network of scaffolding had been erected to surround the structure. Anchored into the glacier itself, miles and miles of scaffolded walkway enabled workers to walk around the hull or inside the ark as needed, though nowhere actually making contact with the wood.

Meanwhile, at the valley base camp approximately eight miles away, trucks, equipment, supplies, newspeople, and volunteers continued arriving. It had, in fact, swelled within just a few short weeks to a city of more than fifteen thousand temporary inhabitants. Feeding and housing everyone in some ways logistically resembled a military invasion. That the location was so remote from sources of supply and transport lines necessitated planning and organization on a herculean scale. Food, running water, sanitation, portable bathrooms, medical supplies—about everything necessary to keep a small city functioning—had to be brought in from the outside.

Power, too, was a major consideration. Huge generators had been brought in to provide electrical power. The fuel needs to create electricity and to power equipment, cars, and trucks, would have run several Iranian oil wells dry. As it was, one of the major oil companies had brought two tankers into the Gulf of Iskenderun—one of refined gasoline, the other of diesel. From there the contents were being transported overland through Turkey by fleets of tanker-trucks.

Turkish opposition to the project had eventually given way to financial considerations. Tourism and scientific research connected with the ark would bring in millions, perhaps billions in these first years. Signs of the new permanent city that would inevitably grow up at the base of the mountain could already be seen. Indeed, Ararat City, as it was being called, might one day become one of the important cities in the region. The huge runways already laid down by the Army Engineers for the landing of the C-5s, which could be seen unloading on the ground about two miles away, would surely become the basis for a major airport within a year or two.

Two hotels were already under construction, with some rooms supposedly to be ready within a month. A dozen other buildings, several gas and diesel facilities, a water pumping station, and an electrical power plant, were all on the drawing board and plans moving quickly forward.

These developments were greeted eagerly by the Turks, and more so because much of the necessary infrastructure for Ararat City would likely be funded by American and British interests, while Turkey would reap the benefits for years to come. The companies involved were all contributing millions in order to gain the publicity of being one of the companies selected to rescue Noah's ark. Money and support, once a significant hurdle for the Livingstone team, were gushing in almost without limit.

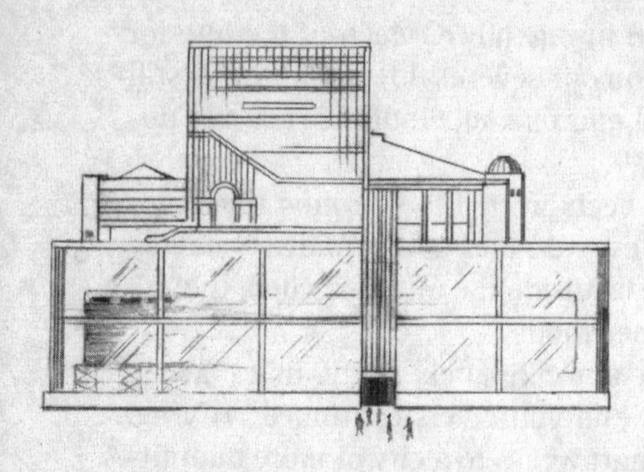

The largest and most important of the construction projects envisioned was for a gargantuan climate-controlled environmental "hangar" to act as permanent home for the ark. It was already well into the early stages of construction at the base of the mountain. It would ultimately rise several stories high, visible for miles, and would be the visual and scientific foundation stone of the new city.

Not only would the ark become one of the wonders of the world, in all likelihood if Operation Noah was successful, the ark hangar would doubtless eclipse the other seven wonders, and become the most visited historic site on the globe. The ark would be safely protected. Tourists would be able to walk around it, even inside it, through tunnel glass–walkways that would not affect the climate of the protective environment.

The immense building would not exist merely for tourism. It would house hundreds of offices and laboratories, and would, its Turkish planners hoped, become something of a scientific Mecca, acting as a base for many kinds of research, as well as a spiritual, cultural, and conference center for the world's religions. Ark research would of course continue, and possibly spawn whole new research projects.

With all this, a modern airport, and vast hotel and dining facilities, Ararat City could well become a metropolis within five years.

(3)

Meanwhile, Juliet was continuing with her press conference.

"As you can see on the monitors behind me," she was saying, "the melting is an extremely delicate process. Yet the equipment has had to be powerful enough to remove many tons of ice and water. Those preliminaries are nearly complete. Technicians have already begun to apply the special hardening foam inside those melted portions of ark, taking special care where timbers are thin and in what remains of the animal pens. No stick or fragment of frozen or fossilized animal dung is to be disturbed. Mr. Livingstone is treating every inch of the ark with the same care he would any delicate archaeological dig, since, it is hoped, the ark will provide much new historical knowledge of ancient Middle-Eastern culture. When the melting phase is completed, every inch of the ark will literally be sealed in foam, thus making shifting or damage impossible."

"The foam," called out one of the reporters, a certain David Larsen from *Architectural Review Magazine*, who was head of the design team for the new hangar building, "will it affect the ark in any way? I would think its chemicals might be damaging."

"Not at all," replied Juliet. "As you know, portions of the ark are petrified, others, apparently frozen almost immediately and kept in solid ice ever since, still retain their woody fibers. The foam being used was specially formulated to Mr. Livingstone's specifications by DuPont. It is water-based, water-soluble, biodegradable, and is absolutely harmless."

"What exactly will it do?"

"The foam will be carefully applied throughout the ark, both to protect fragile portions of planking and stairs and walls, especially the animal pens, as I said, down to the tiniest of objects. The foam will coat them, then harden, encasing even the smallest and most delicate finds and potentially breakable bits of wood in a solid protective casing. When more foam fills in large portions of the empty spaces, it will also have the effect of solidifying the entire structure and holding it rigidly together."

"That would take an enormous amount of foam."

"DuPont has manufactured and brought enough to fill the entire ark, if need be," replied Juliet. "It can expand to ten or fifteen times its original size within four hours. The beauty of it, of course, is that the foam is about as close to weightless as it is possible to be, being over 99 percent air. Thus encasing the ark in these huge quantities of foam adds almost nothing to the overall weight."

"How will it be removed once the ark is down?"

"It will gradually melt away once the ark is safely off the mountain as if it were ice itself. It will begin to disintegrate after approximately two weeks and will disappear without leaving a trace of residue, literally evaporating into the air, and the residue turning to water. Yet it is one of the strongest such foams ever developed, outperforming all petroleum-based expanding foam sealants in use today, and completely environmentally safe."

"I have a question about the blimps."

"Yes, er . . . Mr.–"

"Don Samuelson, CBS News. My question is this: Does anyone really expect them to be able to lift such an enormous object? This strikes me as a gigantic publicity stunt."

"I'm sure that same honest skepticism is shared by many, Mr. Samuelson. I don't know what I can tell you other than to wait and see. I will add that the blimps you see up there, though from this distance seem small, are actually three to four times the size of ordinary blimps. Even now, as you can see, there are enormous weights of many tons hanging from them. These weights have been computed to approximate the weight of the ark. When they are replaced with the ark, according to the calculations of the lift-potential of the helium content within each blimp, they should be capable of raising the ark.

"As you have pointed out, the weight of the ark will be enormous. No one really knows how much it will weigh. Mathematicians and engineers from

NASA have been working with Mr. Livingstone for over a year, with extremely complex computer simulations, trying to make the most accurate estimates possible and to anticipate every contingency."

"What are they doing up there now?"

"Practicing dry runs. They must not only have the power to lift, but must work in perfect unison so as to keep the ark steady."

"The ark must be incredibly fragile. One jerk and it could crumble to pieces."

"That is a serious concern," answered Juliet. "To prevent any sudden shifts or jerky movements, the straps by which the ark will be suspended in the air are flexible, like gigantic incredibly strong bungee cables. These will act as shock absorbers and keep the ark's brief ride in the sky smooth and gentle. They will absorb shifts and variations between the blimps of a hundred feet or more. Yet in their practice runs thus far the blimps have been able to keep within thirty feet in elevation with one another."

"Will Mr. Livingstone himself be in one of the blimps?"

"The blimps will be under the control of Scott Jordan. Adam himself–er, that is . . . Mr. Livingstone will ride on the ark itself."

"How will the ark finally be attached to the blimps?"

"Workers have been boring through the last of the ice beneath the hull to feed through two-foot wide thick-woven, nylon-webbed strapping. Ninety straps will be placed every three feet under the 450-foot length of the vessel, effectively encasing the hull in a grid of strapping to which will be attached the lines up to the blimps. This will mean 180 lines–ninety on each side–extending up from the ark to the blimps, or approximately fifteen lines per blimp. Thus, as they go through their practice runs, you can see fifteen lines hanging from each blimp, from each of which is suspended a weight approximating our best estimate of what will be the effect of each one of the cables up from the ark. Actually, they calculate that the ark can be lifted with nine rather than twelve blimps. The extra three give a sufficient margin for error, and allow for the constant variation in lift-capacity as the blimps bounce unpredictably on the air's currents. This is another reason for the flexible rubberized cables, much like if one engine of an airplane goes out. Even if one or two of the blimps drop unpredictably from an air pocket, the weight of the ark will still be easily supported by the other blimps, and the cables will immediately contract, keeping the ark steady and smooth."

"And they truly believe this will work?"

"Yes, Mr. Samuelson," said Juliet, smiling, "they truly believe it will work."

"What if it gets all attached and the weight is too great?" asked Bonnie Love of the BBC.

"If the calculations are that far off, then more blimps will be brought in as needed, or more helium attached to the ark itself."

"The balloons that will be placed inside the ark," said Archie Storm of the BBC, "they're not actual . . . *balloons*, are they, like children buy?"

"Not exactly, Mr. Storm, but not so far from it either. The Mylar being used is much stronger, and the balloons larger. But the principle is identical. Imagine weather balloons, which as you know are capable of carrying a significant amount of equipment. During the foaming process, actual chambers will be created inside the hollow core of the ark with the foam, that is, where there are no structural obstructions. These will be filled with helium balloons and then sealed off so they cannot float away. In the end, if you can imagine, the entire interior of the ark filled with either foam or helium. The ark itself, in a sense, from the cumulative effect of these thousands of helium balloons in all available interior space, will become something like a blimp itself. Hopefully sufficient helium will be able to be put into the ark in this way to reduce the weight of the ark by 25 or 30 percent."

"What will happen to the helium balloons when the foam melts?"

"A good question," replied Juliet. "Actually, they will eventually be released from their chambers and float away. Presumably they will come down all over the world, as souvenirs of the project. Each is stamped with the words *Operation Noah.* Perhaps one of you will find one floating down in your own garden a month or two from now."

"Who is doing all the work? In fact, who *are* all these people—there must be thousands . . . who is paying them?"

"Most are not paid," replied Juliet. "We have been literally besieged by floods of volunteers from all over the world, mostly college students, but also many professional people. More than fifty doctors have come donating their services in case of medical emergencies. Engineers, scientists, archaeologists, computer experts, secretaries, nurses, mechanics . . . once news of Operation Noah broke, people began coming from every walk of life. We literally have more people offering to donate their services than we know what to do with. In fact, an entire tent with staff of five—themselves among the first volunteers to arrive—has been set up simply to handle the flood of volunteer requests. I would venture to say that 50 percent of the world's college and university students of archaeology have changed their summer plans and are making the trek here instead. As you can see, Volkswagen buses of eager students are pouring in."

"Is this causing more problems than it is solving?"

"If it continues, crowd control will become a problem. Yet everyone understands the nature of what is going on and seems very cooperative. The last thing these people want is to cause difficulty which could jeopardize the project. On the positive side, it seems that whenever a new need arises, there is someone to fill it. Even with such a simple thing as refuse collection, yesterday a group of students took it upon themselves to begin going around and gathering burnables. A day later, they have organized a team to collect all sorts of garbage, which they are taking outside the tent city and either burning or collecting for later disposal.

"Of course Mr. Livingstone must make certain that those actually involved with the ark itself are trained and skilled, as many who have come are. Fortunately, too, most of these volunteers are aware of the limitations of the locale and have brought much of their own food and water. You can see tents popping up for miles."

"I notice many companies and corporations . . . are they also volunteering their services?"

"There has been overwhelming corporate support. This is such a historic event, it seems everyone wants to be part of it. Companies, even the military of the United States, the United Kingdom, and Turkey have contributed far more than we expected. It's been quite a team effort. For almost every need that has presented itself, there have been a hundred volunteers eager to help. Certain aspects of the work, of course, require a level of specialized expertise that cannot be compromised. The blimps are piloted by NASA experts. The foam is being installed by technicians sent over from DuPont. And of course Mr. Livingstone is overseeing the whole thing."

"And when the ark is brought down—isn't that the most dangerous aspect of the plan?"

"You are right. The ark will be gently lowered onto the temporary foundation prepared for it, off the ground some thirty feet, and then the hangar constructed around it . . . right over there," Juliet added, pointing to one side where the hangar foundation and ark platform were being completed. "Oh, I see Adam there coming into view on one of the monitors behind me . . . Adam—Adam, can you hear me?"

"Yes—you're coming through loud and clear." As he spoke, Adam waved toward the camera.

"Is there anything you would like to say to the media?" Juliet asked.

"Tell them to pray the weather holds for another week."

"What is the latest timetable?" asked Carlisle Brady from ABC. Juliet relayed the question to Adam.

"I am hopeful we will have the foaming completed in twenty-four or thirty-six hours," replied Adam. "Then we will begin installing the tens of thousands of helium balloons which will be sealed in the inner chambers of the ark to reduce the weight once the lifting begins—"

"Yes, I've been trying to explain all that to them," said Juliet. "I know they would rather you would come down . . . you could no doubt make it more understandable."

"I'm sure you've done fine," rejoined Adam. "In any event, however much helium we are able to stuff inside the ark itself will enable the blimps to handle the load more easily. Completing the exterior melting and foaming, then stringing the poly straps beneath the hull—that will take longer, another three days perhaps. All in all, if everything goes well, we should be able to lift off the glacier in five or six days."

"And then," asked the BBC's Love, "how long will it take to get it down here?"

"We plan liftoff for dawn," said Adam, "when the wind is at a minimum. We will budget the whole day to slowly transport the ark down to the hangar foundation, and several hours for a very, *very* careful landing."

"And if you get weather between now and then?"

"We will have to make the best of it," replied Adam. "Our chief consideration is protecting the ark. We will do nothing that jeopardizes either the ark or the lives of the workers. If the weather turns severe or winds pick up, we will have to ground the blimps and wait it out, then see where we are when it blows over."

(4)

In London, a reporter who had not been assigned to Turkey watched the broadcast with interest. It was time to run another article.

It appeared the Halsay girl had scooped her own story. She was no longer a mystery, especially since the *Times* had run the engagement announcement. And here she was in front of a hundred cameras for all the world to see.

So much the better. Now they would capitalize on the ark publicity to heighten interest in her even more!

Potential captions began coming to mind—LIVINGSTONE MYSTERY GIRL JOINS TEAM, or MYSTERY GUEST'S ENGAGEMENT TO WORLD'S MOST FAMOUS MAN.

The objective was to increase public interest in the future Mrs. Livingstone, who was playing such a key role in this Ararat project. She had been vaulted out of the "mystery" role into that of celebrity. Her sudden fame, now that her face would be known to the world, would make her an instant star in the paper.

There were a few more photos available from last time. They would find one to run, and tie it into the ark extravaganza.

The reporter thought for a minute or two, then began typing a new story to again put the famous Ms. Halsay on the front pages. She would begin working into it something about the American investigator too. He was a colorful character, the kind Brits loved to read about. If she could just find out whether he carried a gun under his jacket—that alone would double readership. She'd call him LIVINGSTONE'S MODERN COWBOY.

(5)

Housing for the thousand or so professionals and corporate employees who had been part of the preparation with Adam from the beginning of Operation Noah, as well as for the Livingstone team itself, had been established in separate semi-permanent tent facilities located nearer the mountain, from which regular helicopter runs went back and forth as often as needed. Running water, electricity, and decently tolerable bathroom and shower facilities had been operational for six months.

NASA, Rockwell, Boeing, and the other companies involved had set up facilities for their own people. Adam's team had three tents—one as lounge, kitchen, dining room, and office, and two other smaller tents, one to accommodate beds for the men, another for the two women. These had been home to Scott and Rocky on and off for months, and were far more comfortable than the dusty tents they had used in the African bush.

That evening in the main Livingstone tent, the team had just finished a supper of gourmet frankfurters with Bush's baked beans and canned coleslaw. Rocky's assigned nights for cooking usually featured such basic fare, while Figg, Jen, and Juliet showed somewhat more creativity, venturing into the regions of pasta, magnificent salads, and tacos. Scott and Adam, busy on the mountain almost round the clock, were spared participation in the culinary schedule. They traded nights on duty guiding work at the ark site, or, if needed, both might remain on the mountain all night, grabbing what catnaps they could snatch.

Juliet had been moaning about her day in front of the press, and the endless questions that had followed her throughout the day.

"I was so nervous standing up there!"

"Juliet, you were fabulous," said Adam, spreading Dijonnaise on his second hot dog. "When you hailed me and then we talked back and forth, with you relaying questions from the reporters—it was great. You sounded like a seasoned professional."

"I totally concur," added Jen, helping herself to another spoonful of coleslaw. "You had those briefing papers Adam prepared for you down cold. You should have seen her, Adam—question after question . . . she had the answer to every one."

"That's my girl! I knew you could do it."

"I still hated it."

"I'm not so sure about that," rejoined Adam. "I heard that excitement in your voice. I bet you enjoyed trading barbs with Samuelson."

"I did not!" she groaned.

"You did great. I watched the whole thing and you handled yourself like a pro," said Rocky.

"Where were you?" exclaimed Juliet. "I never saw you all day."

"Prowling around out of sight, like a good security man."

"I saw you too," added Figg. "When I had the chance. He's right—you were in command, Juliet."

"Well, thank you, but it was still an ordeal," replied Juliet. "I can't imagine briefing the press and fielding their questions every day. But I suppose we all have to do our part."

"Any security problems, Rocky?" asked Adam, turning toward the private investigator.

"None. It's really remarkable with so many people that everyone's pitching in. There's a terrific spirit of camaraderie everywhere. I drove through the new tents springing up over there eastward, and all through the main conglomeration . . . everything was calm and orderly. Oh, but I forgot the most remarkable part. Can you believe it—a whole regiment from the U.S. National Guard showed up and volunteered their services. I was going about my business when there I was staring at a colonel in front of me, in army green from cap to boots, saluting me!"

"Right," said Adam, nodding.

"You knew they were coming!"

"When they arrived, they contacted the communications center. They notified me immediately and I told them to report to you."

"How did they know where to find me?"

"I told them to look for a large American wandering about looking for trouble. I said you were in charge."

Rocky roared. "That's what they said you said," he replied. "'Mr. McCondy, *Sir,*'" the colonel barked, snapping his salute, 'the President sent us to help out in any way we can.' So I've got a whole unit of guardsmen taking orders from me! And the highest I ever got was corporal! What am I going to do with those guys?"

"Let's hope it stays peaceful and you don't have to do anything with them," said Adam.

(6)

The incredible day for liftoff finally came. The weather continued to hold. The foaming was complete. More than one hundred thousand helium balloons of varying sizes were securely stored inside enclosed chambers inside the ark, containing in excess of two hundred thousand cubic feet of helium, which it was hoped would equalize fifteen to twenty tons of the ark's weight. All the thick nylon straps undergirding the ark's hull were attached by high-tensile-strength, expandable fiber cables up to the blimps. As the counterweights were released from the blimps, blimps and ark ought to simultaneously lift together.

Most of the team had risen before dawn. When Juliet walked into the main tent, the smell of brewing coffee already wafted in the air. Rocky was haunting the coffeemaker in impatient anticipation, waiting with cup in hand for the first instant when he could pour out a sampling of the rich black invigorating liquid. Figg was finishing his second bowl of oatmeal and a fourth slice of toast. Scott and Adam had both spent the night at the headquarters tent on the mountain.

"Good morning, Rocky, . . . Figg," said Juliet.

"Morning, Juliet," replied Figg. "The big day, eh?"

"I guess this is what we've been waiting for. I hope, for Adam's sake, it goes without a hitch."

Rocky glanced at his watch. "What time do you have to be out there in front of the press?"

"5:30," said Juliet. "The final countdown begins at 5:45."

"And liftoff?"

"6:15."

Figg rose. "I'm off. Gotta get to that chopper I hear revving up out there. I'm late as it is."

Jen walked in, still stretching and rubbing her eyes.

"Hey, Jen," said Rocky.

"Morning, everybody," mumbled the Swede. "That coffee of yours ready yet, Rocky?"

"Almost . . . let me check."

"Figg, I'll be up on the next flight," added Jen, "as soon as I'm awake."

"Okay . . . cross your fingers, everybody," said Figg. "See you in the history books," he added, then he hurried from the tent.

(7)

Forty minutes later, with two cups of tea and a hasty breakfast inside her, Juliet again occupied center stage at the foot of the mountain, with media attention and a hundred cameras focused on her.

"Ladies and gentlemen," she began, "the big day is here. You'll have to excuse me if I bumble over my words today. I am very nervous . . . and excited of course. But as I'm sure you've been aware all week, I am not a newsperson. Adam . . . that is, Mr. Livingstone, needed somebody to keep you off his back—"

A trickle of laughter filtered through the crowd.

"—and since I was the newest member of the team, low man on the totem pole, as it were, I received the duty."

"And you've done a great job of it, Miss Halsay!" shouted Don Samuelson from the second row.

A round of *here-heres* and light applause followed Samuelson's remark.

"You're very generous, Mr. Samuelson," said Juliet.

"You may have a future in broadcasting!"

"No thank you," replied Juliet with a smile. "Yours would be too difficult an act to follow, Mr. Samuelson."

Brief laughter accompanied her rejoinder to the outspoken American.

"You've all been extremely kind," Juliet added. "But now we have approximately forty minutes left before scheduled liftoff of the ark from Mount Ararat, so perhaps we should review for those watching on television the schedule of this morning's . . ."

As she spoke, various networks carried out their own simulations and commentary, showing drawings and computer models of what viewers should expect. CNN had constructed the largest booth, where even now a panel of experts was discussing the day. Its telecast was displayed live on its own large monitor about a hundred feet from the platform where Juliet was speaking. Crowds moved back and forth between these and several other booths where well-known news personalities were speaking live in front of their own cameras.

"The main difference between today's adventure and something of the nature of a moon shot," CNN's anchorman was saying, "is that we will all be able to actually see events as they unfold with our own eyes . . . right up there–"

As he pointed, his cameras swung around to show a panorama of Ararat, which appeared as a scene from an Indiana Jones film. Two or three helicopters flew about, and the twelve blimps hovered over the ark with their lines attached in final readiness. Most of the scaffolding which had surrounded the ark for weeks had been dismantled, and nearly all activity had come to a standstill. The convoy of trucks and equipment up the road to the site had been suspended. Much of the manpower had been transferred off the mountain down to the platform at the hangar site, where up to four thousand volunteers would gather throughout the day, in the event sheer manpower was needed to jostle the ark a few feet one way or the other with ropes as it lowered into final position.

Preparations were complete. All that remained was to wait for the answer to the question on every man, woman, and child's mind: Would the colossal operation succeed?

Or would it result in catastrophic tragedy–the ark crashing to the ground and splintering into a million pieces, plunging archaeologist Adam Livingstone to a certain death?

By day's end he would either be hailed as a hero of legendary stature, or a daredevil whose recklessness cost the world a great treasure . . . and who had paid for his foolish obsession with his life.

So confident was Livingstone, however, that he would ride the ark himself, *without* parachute or other means of escape should something go wrong. He would be strapped to the ark, and would cast the lot of his future with its success or failure–a story line seized by the media to heighten the drama and danger yet the more. Perhaps the very real chance of catastrophe–and the vision of ark and blimps plummeting to the mountain together with Livingstone with them–helped to account for the vast television audience which was reportedly watching live this very moment.

This might be history, but it also might well be disaster in the making. No one wanted to miss it.

Nor did the television cameras fail to pan every few minutes to the waiting fleet of fire, ambulance, and rescue vehicles poised at the base of the mountain access road for any sign of trouble.

Every network likewise had its resident skeptic on hand to voice the multitude of reasons why this escapade should never have been allowed in the first place. But of one fact there could be no doubt—the eyes of everyone within miles were focused on Ararat.

Everyone's, that is, except one.

No one even saw the lone van exiting the tent city as the crucial time approached, slinking away unnoticed while attention was diverted elsewhere. Its driver, an expert in both helium and de-icing technology, had actually been sent to the site for a more clandestine purpose. Though he had been a member of the de-icing team during the previous month, his work an hour before this moment had been of another nature. He had taken advantage, as his employer had planned, of the fact that he was one of the few on the mountain with clearance to move freely anywhere about the exterior of the ark, including under the hull where the final de-icing and strapping procedures had taken place. Once his deed was accomplished, he made sure no one saw him again.

None of the management team, nor any of his fellow workers had yet noticed his disappearance.

Meanwhile, with a large mug of coffee in hand, Rocky eventually took up a position behind the crowd listening to Juliet.

As the countdown began, journalists, news teams, and spectators directed their attention to the large screens. Cameras were positioned on two of the blimps looking down on the ark, and at the command tent showing various angles of the ark from below. One displayed the hull of the ark up close where it would be able to look underneath the ascending base of the craft as it rose into the air. Another was focused up on Adam where he stood on the bow.

A few questions continued. But gradually even the press quieted. Then a hush spread over the makeshift city. It was time to wait, savor the spectacular happening, and pray for the safety of those involved.

(8)

The countdown reached its final moments.

The drama could not have been more palpable had the scene been Cape Kennedy prior to a launch for the moon. It was Scott's voice, where he sat in the command blimp floating above Ararat, which boomed over loudspeakers on the mountain, and was transmitted down to echo over Ararat City. The village quieted yet more. Not one in a crowd that had now swelled to twenty-seven thousand moved a muscle. Every eye was riveted upon the mountain. Most of the spectators clustered about the giant monitoring screens or clutched binoculars.

"Ten . . . nine . . . eight . . . seven," came Scott's voice, counting down in even cadence, "disconnect final blimp weights . . . four . . . three . . . two . . . one . . . . . . a-n-d *zero*—blimps accelerate to 80 percent of upward thrust!"

Several long tense minutes followed. No one wanted to blink for fear of missing something. Only the faint whirr of the blimp engines could be heard revving up to near maximum power according to Scott's command.

Then came Adam's voice over the loudspeakers.

"The cables are stretching taut," he said. "It's getting close . . . they're about—"

His voice went silent.

"Accelerate to *90* percent," now sounded Scott's voice.

On the screen Adam could be seen glancing upward at the one hundred and fifty lines stretching to the blimps above him, then trying to peer down over the edge of the ark from where he was standing strapped to the bow.

"Scott . . . Scott, I'm feeling something," he said. "I think there may be movement . . . I'm feeling . . ."

Another ten or fifteen seconds passed by.

"Figg . . . Figg," said Adam toward the base of the hull, "what's going on down there?"

"It's jostling around," came Figg's voice over the speakers. "It's trying to do something . . . I'm not sure what."

Not only were the voices of Adam and his two assistants, one above him and one below him, being listened to by everyone standing at the base of Mount Ararat, their words were being transmitted live around the world, where estimates placed the viewing audience at an astonishing 65 percent of the world's population.

"It's definitely trying to break loose," Figg exclaimed. "I can see—wait a minute . . . yes, I see—it's lifting . . . Adam, *it's lifting from the ice!*"

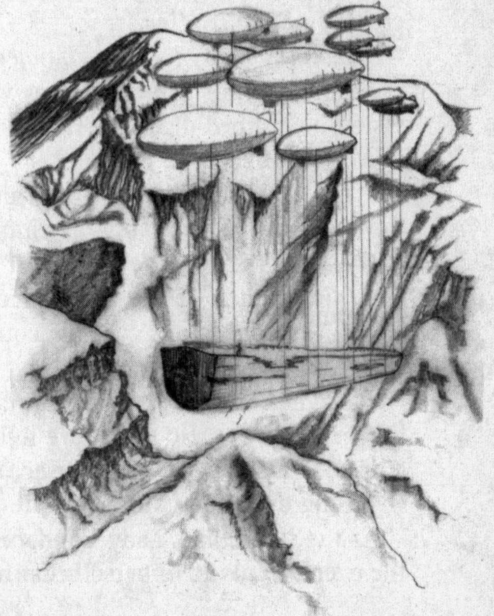

"I feel it," yelled Adam. "We're coming up . . . the ark is definitely lifting!"

A tremendous surging cheer broke through the watching throng. Those with binoculars glued to their eyes now began to yell along with Adam.

"I can see it!" they cried.

" . . . it's going up . . . it's lifting!" clamored thousands of voices.

" . . . there it goes . . . "

" . . . it's moving . . . "

" . . . it's lifting off the mountain!"

Bedlam broke loose. A huge roar of

humanity could be heard from base camp to mountain and back again. Horns blared, shouts and applause and whistles punctuated the air, while the roar continued as from a huge open sport's stadium.

If Juliet had attempted to say anything now, it would have been hopeless. She stood watching Adam's face in the monitor crying like a baby, proud and happy for him. He was smiling and shouting and laughing all at once, as the liftoff of Noah's ark became clearly visible. The ark rose ten feet, now fifteen, and finally twenty, then thirty feet above the floor of ice, and slowly pulled away from the mountain. It had indeed become a moving ship of transport again, though now a floating spaceship, and with a cargo of a mere single man who stood upon the bow as it rose into the air.

The triumphant moment had come . . . and he had done it!

(9)

In their living room in Peterborough, New Hampshire, Mark and Laurene Stafford sat in front of their television set, watching the events with hearts full of wonder and praise like millions of individuals the world over.

Spontaneously they began praying again for Adam Livingstone.

"*Lord, however you intend to make use of this spectacular moment,*" said Mark, "*I pray that you will turn people the world over to Truth, to your Word, and to you.*"

"*Instill within millions who are watching at this moment a new enthusiasm for the Bible,*" added Laurene.

"*Yes, Lord. We pray for a great revival of spiritual hunger, and a great increase in Bible reading.*"

"*And may many lives be changed as a result.*"

Meanwhile, Sir Gilbert Bowles watched the historic newscast on his television in stunned disbelief. How very different were his thoughts than those of Mark and Laurene Stafford.

What was that crazy old tub, anyway? It couldn't really be *Noah's* ark, Bowles thought. The thing was impossible.

How had Livingstone pulled off something so enormous! And with every television camera in the world focused on his face!

Yet if it was a stunt . . . how could he possibly have engineered a hoax of such grandiose proportions?

Just when he thought he was finally through with Livingstone, here he was bigger than ever. He had more lives than a cat! Sir Gilbert continued to sit staring at his television, confused, bewildered, not believing a word of it, yet watching the drama unfold before his very eyes.

At the same time, Lady Candace Montreux watched the BBC coverage of the event, thinking to herself that it could have been her standing in front of the whole world. She could be famous, her picture on the cover of fashion magazines everywhere.

Yet she hated all that field stuff!

Ugh—having to sleep in tents and eat from a can! Let the Halsay girl have it. Who wanted it?

Noah's ark or no Noah's ark—she would get her fame some other way. Adam had finally flipped this time . . . and good riddance. At least so she tried to tell herself.

A mother and a grandmother who would never know one another, separated by more than a thousand miles, whose hearts suffered the same aching love for the two young women they loved, prayed similar prayers. Their words mingled heartbreak and hope, despair and faith, as do the prayers of many of God's heartsick saints. In what a multitude of ways do the simple yet depth-probing words, *I believe, help my unbelief,* reach the heart of the heavenly Father. And how thankful must be all who pray for those earnest words of humanity spoken to our Lord so long ago.

"Dear Father," prayed the grandmother, *"may my Oriel be watching this remarkable event. May it rise up within her to question whether perhaps you are real and personal after all. Lead her to your Word, dear Lord. Make her hungry to search it to find the truth, and to realize the emptiness to which her modern philosophies have led her."*

"Oh, Lord," prayed the mother, *"I ask you to prick and probe my Brandi's heart. May some reminder of her upbringing strike root within her. May she be drawn to the Scriptures in a new way. Bless Adam Livingstone, though I will never meet him. Bless him for what he is doing for mankind. Protect him and watch over him. I pray that Brandi will be drawn to a man such as Adam Livingstone, and that seeing Noah's ark will make her think what she has allowed herself to become. Turn her heart toward home, Lord . . . turn her heart toward home."*

Back at Sevenoaks, Mrs. Andrea Graves wiped at the tears flowing from her eyes. She couldn't believe it . . . she simply couldn't believe it! Adam . . . her very own Mr. Livingstone! And dear Juliet . . . in front of the whole world!

She just couldn't believe it!

And around the globe, television audiences in homes and factories and offices and universities, and schoolchildren in thousands of classrooms, watched enthralled as the marvel no one would have believed possible unfolded before their eyes.

(10)

As they soared around the slope of the mountain, standing atop Noah's ark as it rose slowly into the sky, lifeline around his waist attached to the solid foam interior core holding the gargantuan vessel securely in one piece like a gigantic rock, Adam was reminded of just two short years ago when he was being lowered into the glacier at this precise same spot.

It had been so still on that day. He hadn't known what they were about to find, or that his whole life would be changed as a result. Now that whole monstrous section of that same glacier was gone—broken and exploded and hammered, and finally burned away inch by inch, and its treasure uncovered. And today that treasure had been miraculously lifted out of its long frozen grave.

Scott had been at the controls above him then too, like today, although two years ago he had been operating a cable from which Adam dangled from the tip of a great crane. When Scott and Figg put their heads together, thought Adam, they could do anything. On how many occasions had he put his life in Scott's hands . . . and he was still alive and kicking!

It was not so quiet today as then. Above him whirred the powerful engines of twelve blimps, lifting him away from the mountain.

Adam gazed up and around. The morning's sky was a brilliant blue. Snow still clung to both peaks of Ararat. This spot was so far from anywhere. Yet the technology of modern man's ingenuity had been transported halfway around the world in order to make this unbelievable event possible. Below him sprawled an entire city that had sprung up in just two months.

Funny, Adam thought, he knew he was at the center of the world's attention. Probably three or four billion pairs of eyes were fixed on him at this moment. Yet he was alone, gently riding through the sky on the bow of the vessel God had used to save mankind from the great flood's destruction some four and a half thousand years before. It was the oldest man-made object on the face of the earth, surely the most historic find that would ever be made.

And God had revealed it to *him*. And he had used the event to lead him to a greater discovery yet—the discovery of a personal relationship with his Creator.

Thank you, Lord, Adam whispered.

"What's that?" said Juliet in his ear. "Did you say something, Adam?"

"No . . . no, nothing," replied Adam. "Uh . . . how does it look from down there?"

"Unbelievable . . . spectacular."

Adam could scarcely feel the movement beneath him. Scott maintained such perfect control of the blimps, orchestrating the controls such that all twelve functioned as one, that Adam literally felt he was riding on air, as indeed he was.

Noah . . . Noah, Adam thought, *what were* you *feeling when you stood where I am standing, as you felt this great proud vessel made by your own hands move through the surging sea of rain? Were you afraid? Were you excited? Were you heartbroken for a world grown beyond God's power to redeem it? What did you think, old patriarch of the ages, when you felt the ground of this mountain beneath you when the waters began to recede? How long did you remain here, what did you do, where did you go after the flood?*

Adam smiled to himself.

Perhaps one day, you mighty man of old, I shall ask you myself!

(11)

On the ground below, Rocky roved amid the crowd.

Everything was proceding precisely as planned. Adam on the ark, Scott above, Figg below, Juliet with the media—all was as it should be. Everything had gone off without a hitch.

But Rocky's investigative instinct could not rest.

He thought back to his first meeting with Adam Livingstone and what had brought him to England in the first place—to warn Adam of danger. Was it likely, he thought, that the forces intent on destroying Adam's work back then would be unconcerned about them now? Rocky doubted it.

When he thought about it, maybe things had been going a little *too* smoothly.

Like those of everyone else present on this momentous occasion, Rocky's eyes were glued to the huge boat making its way toward them.

Suddenly his body tensed. He gripped his binoculars more tightly. Frantically his fingers fiddled with the focus knob.

He couldn't exactly be sure . . . but . . . there seemed to be—

Rocky squinted through the lenses.

Yes . . . something attached to the underside of the ark's hull between two of the supporting straps!

Whatever the object was, no one else in this jubilant throng had spied it. No television camera had picked it up. And neither Scott nor Adam could possibly see it from their angles.

Inch by inch the ark moved closer. Rocky continued to stare at the tiny bump which had attracted his attention. Gradually he felt a strange forboding. It was a sensation he'd come to trust.

Was it some irregularity in the wood? At this distance Rocky could not tell. But the color was wrong. In fact why was there color at all? Especially that faint hint of orange. The ark was dark brown, the foam a light tan, the straps black . . . what could—

A chill swept through Rocky's frame.

He let the binoculars fall from his hands and the next second was racing toward the media stand where their jeep was parked.

How the thing got there . . . it hardly mattered. Time for questions later.

Breathing heavily from the run of five hundred yards, Rocky ploughed into the crowd without being polite. Elbowing through, he jumped in the jeep, turned the key, revved up the engine, and blasted on the horn to clear people away, then sped off in a cloud of dust with Juliet staring bewildered after him from the platform.

Clearing the crowd on the outskirts of the tent city, he jammed his foot to the floor and went bumping and careening off across the uneven terrain with reckless speed, avoiding rocks and swerving to miss ditches. The jeep flew and bounced along as if part of an off-road obstacle race, one, sometimes two of its tires losing contact with the ground altogether. This was no time for Sunday driving!

He wouldn't be able to get far up the slope. All he needed was to get close enough for a better look. In four or five minutes Rocky had covered about a mile and a half, and had shrunk the distance between himself and the ark's shadow to about half.

Rocky slammed on the brake, skidded to an uncertain stop, and leapt from the jeep. The next second his eyes were glued to the lenses of his binoculars, staring up at a sixty-degree angle as the flotilla of blimps and its priceless cargo approached him like great ominous clouds in the sky of blue.

He stared straight up at the hull, scanning back and forth. Where was it . . . where had the thing gone–

There it was!

From where he stood, the instant it came back into view all doubt was gone.

Just as he had feared. Adam had picked up a bomb on his ship!

Rocky jammed his fist to the jeep's horn. Finally he succeeded in getting Adam's attention. He waved his arms wildly. But all Adam did was wave back!

"Adam, hey . . . Adam!" he shouted up toward the mammoth object. "Adam, you've got . . ."

But his voice was lost in the breeze and the faint drone of blimp engines high above.

This was ridiculous. Adam couldn't hear him! Even if he could manage to convey the danger, what could Adam do? He couldn't see the bomb!

Rocky leapt back into the jeep and sped back the way he had come. He would have to raise him by radio.

(12)

Rocky roared into the heart of the tent city, spewing dust and rocks in every direction.

The crowd fled before him, yelling and scurrying as it had dispersed minutes earlier. Rocky was out of the jeep and lumbering toward the media platform before the engine had idled to a stop.

Juliet was in the midst of answering a question when commotion erupted around her. She stopped in midsentence.

Rocky forced his way past reporters and journalists.

"What is–?" Juliet began.

Rocky grabbed her and pulled her aside.

"Give me your headset," he interrupted, motioning her toward him as he tried to get away from the crowd. Don Samuelson saw the look on Rocky's face. Sensing that something was up, he pushed his way through to follow them.

Juliet grabbed the headset from her head and handed it to him. Rocky began speaking immediately into the microphone.

"Adam . . . Adam, can you hear me?" he said frantically. "He's not on the loudspeakers, is he?" he asked, turning to Juliet.

"I'll switch it off," she answered.

"Adam," he said again. "It's Rocky—we've got a problem."

"You've got to put the earphone on," said Juliet. "Here—"

She struggled to attach the contraption to Rocky's head.

"Oh . . . OK—there you are . . . Adam . . . did you hear me?"

"Loud and clear, Rocky," said Adam. "What's up?"

"Unless I'm mistaken . . . I think a small explosive device is attached to the ark."

"What! I've seen no indication—"

"You couldn't. It's directly beneath you. I spotted it from down here."

Beside Rocky, Juliet's face turned white. Neither of them noticed Don Samuelson inching closer and craning to hear. Several other journalists squeezed toward them. Samuelson held up his hands to keep them back, nodding and gesturing to indicate that things had taken a serious turn and that he would keep them abreast of it as soon as he knew something.

"Adam, you're going to have to disarm it," Rocky was saying.

"Me, why . . . but how?"

"You're the only one who can get to it. I can't reach it from below. A chopper would be worse than useless. You're too high in the air for fire ladders, and besides, we don't have any. You've got to get to it immediately. It could be set to go off any second. Scott, you there?"

"Yeah, I'm listening."

Behind him, Rocky heard Scott's voice blaring over the public system.

"Switch off from loudspeaker, Scott!" he said.

"Oh yeah . . . right."

"You've got to get that thing down as quick as you can," Rocky continued. "For all we know there's been monkey business with the blimps too. I don't see anything, but it wouldn't take much."

"There's not much I can do," said Scott. "I'll angle us down a tiny bit faster, but we've got to take it slow."

"I know," said Rocky. "Just do what you can."

"What do you want me to do, Rocky?" asked Adam.

"The only way I see is for you to rappel down over the side," said Rocky. "You've got to get to the thing and tell me what you see."

"I've got no equipment, no rope."

"What about your lifeline?"

"Not long enough. It's just to keep me from falling over the side. It's not more than thirty or forty feet long. Without equipment, and with the shape of the hull curving away from me, I'd be liable to fall off."

"Yeah . . . hmm, I see the problem." Rocky thought for a moment.

"Why don't we wait until we're down," came Adam's voice again into his ear, "and deal with it then."

"Look, Adam," rejoined Rocky, "you haven't thought this thing through. Whoever did this wants *you* out of the way as much as the ark destroyed. Do you think they're going to let that boat land and you just waltz away? I'm sure it's got a timer, and I *guarantee* you it's set to blow long before you reach the ground. You've *got* to rappel over the side or it's good-bye ark, and good-bye Livingstone! Aren't there *any* other cords or ropes up there?"

Now it was Adam's turn to think for a minute. Unconsciously he glanced up.

Of course! They had a hundred and fifty cords!

"Scott . . . Scott, are you there?" he cried into his mike.

"I'm hanging on every word."

"Can we get away with cutting loose one of the cables? Will the ark still hold?"

"That's why we devised it this way," replied Scott. "My calculations give us at least twenty to spare. Losing one strap won't change the load on the others enough to notice."

"That's all I need. Have you got someone who can manage to slice one of the cables off the connection to its blimp?"

"We'll get it done."

"One of the ties toward the front," added Rocky, "so Adam doesn't have to go hunting all over for it. But, Adam, you make sure it doesn't flail and whack you silly."

"Got it," said Scott. "Stand by."

Adam and Rocky waited. Two or three minutes went by.

"OK—we can manage it," said Scott at last. "Watch out, Adam—it'll be a strap on the right side, what's that called—starboard . . . get out of the way, here it comes."

Adam looked up toward the blimps, while Rocky peered through his binoculars. Seconds later both saw one of the support lines go limp, then drop through the sky toward the ark like a dead snake, its end flailing dangerously.

A gasp went up from the crowd below. The line crashed with tremendous force onto the bow of the ark, while the strap to which it was attached beneath dropped from the ark's hull. Adam scrambled to it and grabbed and pulled it onto the center of the bow before it could unravel and disappear over the side.

"Yeah!" exclaimed Rocky.

"Got it, Scott! What does it look like?"

"Looks fine."

"I thought I felt a momentary sag."

"It'll hold."

"Get to it, Adam," came Rocky's voice. "Cut off the other end. You've got to let the strap go. All you need is a length of cable. Since you don't have equipment," Rocky went on, "we'll estimate the length and hope for the best. Tie it off, securely on the starboard side someplace, figure the width across the bow, then I'd say forty or fifty feet down to the device."

"I'll figure an extra fifty and tie it securely around my waist to prevent a free fall. I ought to be able to ease myself down by hand."

"Loop a coil or two of the slack end around your waist," added Scott. "That should help you mimic the rappelling motion."

"Right," said Adam.

"I'm driving back out," said Rocky. "I'll get underneath you so I can see what you're doing."

Rocky turned and ran for the jeep. By the time he had his hand to the key Juliet was already seated in the passenger side.

"Don't try to stop me, Rocky," she said. "I'm going with you."

By now everyone within sight of Rocky had heard what was going on. The media and crowd erupted into a frenzy as word of the bomb spread to the thousands of spectators, and was beamed around the world within a minute.

(13)

On the bow of the ark, Adam Livingstone stood stripped of the lifeline that had held him secure on this strange flight from the mountain. He peered down over the bow of the ark. He'd done some pretty daring things in his life, but he might look back on today and say this one took the cake.

He saw Rocky's jeep roaring across the floor of the plain below him. After another minute he had the new line tied off across the bow, and now awaited Rocky's final instructions.

They did not take more than another ninety seconds to reach him. Estimating the total length he would need, he tied the line snuggly around his waist. Through his headset came Rocky's voice.

"Start making your way down," said the investigator.

"Here goes."

"Adam . . . Adam," came another voice into his ear, "be careful."

"Juliet, is that you—where are you?"

"I'm here with Rocky . . . right below you. Be careful."

"Not to worry," said Adam.

The next instant, from her position on the ground Juliet saw Adam's legs dangling over the edge of the ark. His whole body came into sight, then dropped suddenly ten or fifteen feet into midair.

The gasp of terror which escaped her lips luckily did not unnerve him. She had already handed the headset back to Rocky and Adam never heard it.

"Oh, Rocky, I can't watch!" she cried.

"He's been in tighter spots than this—he'll be OK."

"Oops!" said Adam into Rocky's ear. "That first step was a humdinger!"

"Watch yourself up there," said Rocky. "You nearly gave Juliet a heart attack!"

"And about burned the skin off my hands stopping my fall," rejoined Adam. "I thought the coil around my waist would slow me down a little more. This is going to take some getting used to."

Juliet's and Rocky's weren't the only eyes riveted upon Adam Livingstone. Three-quarters of the world watched as he bounced and lowered his way—awkwardly at first, in jerky rappel-like movements, letting out increasing handfuls of rope—holding its collective breath and wondering the same thing . . . would the bomb detonate before he reached it?

As he descended and the mostly petrified hull curved gradually away from him toward the keel, Adam not only had to let himself down through the air but also had to kick against it in order to swing back and forth and keep alongside the hull. Otherwise he would not be able to reach the bomb. Rocky heard increasingly more strenuous breathing through his earpiece, indicating the difficulty of Adam's task.

"You're about two-thirds of the way down," he said at length, peering through his binoculars at Adam's progress. "You'll need to work your way about ten or fifteen feet to your right."

Adam did not reply, but gradually did as Rocky said.

"You're getting close. . . ."

"Rocky," exclaimed Adam, "there it is, I saw it on my last swing in."

"I can see you," said Rocky. "Take it easy . . . it's probably about six or seven feet more to your right."

"How am I going to do this as I'm swinging in and out, and with both hands on the rope?"

"Can't you tie off around your waist when you've got enough length? Is there anything up there you can grab onto? How about an edge of one of the straps?"

"I don't know, it's . . . they're so snug against it . . . maybe I can get hold of a bit of board that's been rotted through . . . yeah, there are some holes and rough spots in the hull . . . I'll try it."

Again it was silent. Adam continued to jostle into position, closing in closer toward the bomb.

"Careful," said Rocky, watching him swing back and forth, "I don't want you smashing into that thing."

"I think I'm close enough . . . I'm tying off for length . . ."

Rocky waited.

"I'm looking . . . I'm going to try to grab . . . there's a rough spot, a bit of a hole in the wood . . . I'll try it . . . oops, missed . . . again . . . got it! I think it's holding. I'm steady for the time being, though awkward. I don't know how long I can hold myself here . . . but I may be close enough to get to it. Now what, Rocky?"

"Is the thing all of one piece?"

"Yes, three sticks of explosive, wrapped with tape . . . metal base, timer with wires to the detonator . . . nothing fancy."

"How is it attached?"

"Uh . . . looks like putty or something like it. There's some gray goop oozed out from behind the base plate."

"Check and see if it's still pliable."

Adam extended a hand and gingerly probed at the edges of the device.

"Yeah, it's soft."

"Good—that means you might be able to pry the thing loose. Any chance that putty's some kind of plastic explosive?"

Adam probed again, then drew back his finger and sniffed.

"No, not a trace of it," he replied. "Just some kind of gooey stickum, I think a garden variety putty."

"All right, then *very* carefully, see if you can get a finger under one edge and pry off that faceplate and loosen the whole thing."

"Will movement set it off?"

"Don't whack it with your fist, if that's what you mean. But if you're careful it should be all right."

Gently Adam stretched out his hand again. Everything was silent. Rocky's binoculars and Juliet's eyes and every television camera in Ararat City zoomed in as tightly as possible on the delicate operation. The only persons not watching were Scott and the rest of the blimp crew, who could not see below the top of the ark. Their business continued to be bringing the ark steadily down for a careful landing.

"I feel it loosening . . . I think I'm—Rocky, I'd feel better about this if you and Juliet weren't so close underneath us."

"Consider us scramming, Boss! Let's go, Juliet," said Rocky. "You drive . . . I'll keep watching."

Five seconds later they were speeding away.

"Rocky . . . Rocky," cried Adam a minute later. "It's loose. I've got it in my hand."

"Great!"

"What now?"

"Get rid of it. Give the thing a heave!"

Adam glanced below him where the jeep was tearing across the ground ahead of a dust cloud. He waited only another few seconds to make sure they were far enough, then flung the bomb as hard as he could in the opposite direction. It sailed through the air for three or four seconds, then crashed on the rocky ground six hundred feet below the vessel it had been engineered to destroy.

The next thing the twenty-seven thousand spectators at the base of Ararat saw was a great fiery blast rising from the side of the mountain two or three miles away. An instant later the deafening sound of the explosion reached their ears. As it died away, and the smoke plume floated harmlessly into the air beside the ark, everyone remained poised anxiously to see whether the ark would survive. As the echo died away, gradually the steady drone of the blimp engines came back into hearing. They realized the flotilla and its cargo were continuing their downward descent unfazed by the close brush with disaster.

A great roar of cheering, even greater than at liftoff, again swelled up from the tent city. It grew to such a crescendo that Adam himself heard it where he dangled by the end of his makeshift lifeline.

Juliet slammed on the brake. The jeep skidded to a stop. She and Rocky jumped out and turned back to the ark.

"Great job, Livingstone!" cried Rocky. "I knew you could do it."

"I'm exhausted," said Adam. "But, Rocky, we forgot one little detail."

"What's that?"

"How do I get back up onto the bow so that I don't get squashed when we land?"

"Climb up the rope."

"But my arms are like lead!"

"You can relax later. Just get back up there!"

(14)

Two hours later, the blimps, with their incredible cargo, slowly descended toward the landing platform prepared for the ark.

Once again Adam stood atop it, the triumphant visionary of the incredible project, while above Scott instructed the pilots in this last and most difficult stage of the operation. One false move here and everything would be for naught.

The ride down from the mountain had taken four and a half hours. Except for the scare with the bomb, it had gone almost as smoothly as anyone could have hoped. As it drew close, the crowd grew restless.

Blimps and ark approached. When it was half a mile away the gargantuan size of the thing became truly a spectacle to behold. Once more Juliet was in command of the headset link with Adam, and again switched his voice back to the amplifier and loudspeaker. Rocky continued to roam and wander about, even more on his guard than before to spot any more potential foul play.

Inch by inch continued the historic descent. The ark came hovering above them in almost terrifying enormity. Gradually the crowd separated and backed from underneath its great shadow, realizing again just how dangerous this truly was.

At last they were directly above the hangar landing dock. Scott halted the horizontal movement of the blimps.

Next came the delicate phase, the lateral descent onto the waiting platform, each of whose ark-hull shaped ribs was lined with hundreds of rubber tires fastened in place. Truly this docking from the air resembled the docking of a boat approaching harbor.

"One hundred feet," came Figg's voice from ground zero into Scott's earpiece, "seventy-five . . . fifty . . . forty . . . thirty . . ."

Now the crowd got into the act. Fifteen or more thousand voices, of students and corporate magnates and journalists alike, shouting up from Ararat City, counting down, the distance they could see better than either Scott or Adam: *Twenty, nineteen, eighteen, seventeen . . . !*

"Slowly, Scott," said Figg, "I don't know if you can hear me above the noise, but we're getting close . . . seven feet, six . . . gently increase your throttle, four . . . three . . . about another foot."

Scott changed the descent to about an inch per second.

"Slow, man," said Figg. "Nine inches . . . six . . . four . . . three . . . two . . . one . . . "

At last Adam felt a slight bump.

"Noah's ark has landed," said Adam. "I repeat–*Noah's ark has landed!*"

Ararat City exploded with cheering and clapping, horns and whistles and blaring, and flares lighting the sky.

"Let's detach the cords before anything happens, and get those blimps out of here," Adam continued, trying to talk to Scott.

But now Juliet was yelling in his ear. "Adam . . . Adam," she cried. "You did it! Everyone is so excited!"

"I can hear them!" Adam said, looking down from his high perch several stories above the ground.

"I am so relieved . . . I was scared, Adam."

"So was I . . . where are you?"

"Right here . . . no, to your right," cried Juliet.

Adam looked around. At last he spotted the media platform, where Juliet was waving her arms toward him.

"When are you going to come down?" said Juliet. "I want you down on the earth!"

"As soon as I can get off this thing–by the way, how *do* I get down! Scott," he cried, "we forgot one thing–how do I get off this boat!"

"Adam," Juliet was saying in his other ear, "Daniel Snow is on my satellite phone."

Adam laughed. "And what does he want?"

"An interview, what else?"

✦ ✦ ✦

Among the prophets of Jerusalem I have seen something horrible:

They commit adultery and live a lie . . .

Do not listen to what the prophets are prophesying to you;

they speak visions from their own minds . . . They keep saying . . .

'You will have peace'. . . I did not send these prophets . . .

I did not speak to them, yet they prophesied.

But if they had stood in my council,

they would have proclaimed my words to my people.

JEREMIAH 23:14-22

✦ ✦ ✦

PROLOGUE

Discovery of Ancient Mysteries

France, A.D. 1122–1200

Crusader King Baldwin II of Jerusalem in time moved his quarters from the Muslim mosque to the Citadel. The young Frenchmen whom he had sanctioned to protect the Holy Land then virtually possessed Mount Moriah to themselves. It was the holiest site in Judaism where three temples had once existed, and the third holiest site in Islam where two mosques still stood.

After discovering the sacred rock upon which Abraham was said to have been prepared to offer Isaac—or Ishmael, depending on whether one listened to the Jewish or the Muslim version of the legend—the nine French knights stood upon it to take the sacred and secretive oath that established their order. They called themselves The Poor Fellow Soldiers of Christ and the Temple of Solomon.

The magnificent dome above the sacrificial stone they called the Templum Domini, *or the Temple of God. The adjacent Al-Aqsa Mosque they called* Templum Solomonis. *They hardly distinguished the Muslim origins of both from the ancient Jewish origins of the site, and the original Temple of Solomon.*

In the intervening months they made much progress beneath the Temple Mount, while acting out the role to which they had dedicated themselves as protectors of Jerusalem.

Rumors slowly spread. Some said these strange French knights had come to the city on business other than to protect its pilgrims. No one could deny that they were skilled warriors. But they were now rarely seen battling Christendom's enemies except in occasional twos and threes. In fact, they were little seen at all.

Nothing was known for certain. But it seemed they spent more time inside their quarters on the Temple Mount than patrolling Palestine's roads.

✦ ✦ ✦

It was a month after de Payns regained his sight and the excavations beneath the Temple Mount resumed when they made the discovery which would set the Knights of the Temple on the road toward fabulous wealth and influence.

It was not the discovery the others had come to Jerusalem hoping to make. Yet it was one which would change the civilized world.

Their excavations broke through into a chamber too small for living but appearing a vault of some kind, of six exactly equal cubical sides. It was clearly not a tomb. No passageways opened from it but that through which they entered. It seemed a storage chamber, though no valuables or gold and silver artifacts were present. The room was small, clean, and unspoiled by sign of destruction. Somehow, by its depth, it had escaped the centuries of spoilage which had passed back and forth above it under the feet of the world's armies.

They stood several minutes gazing about in silence, sending the light of their torches in all directions around them. An eerie sense stole upon them that something momentous was at hand.

"I cannot escape the feeling," said de Payns at length, "that we have arrived at the heart and center of the ancient temple, even at the foundation of a great mystery of the Hebrew people, perhaps of the wisdom of Solomon himself."

His words struck awe into his companions. All eight besides de Payns were present. The number of their company was far from accidental. Their number, nine, was that of the occult. Nine was intrinsically linked to both three and six, and was itself a factor of that significant threefold collection of sixes yet to come—666.

"This chamber feels to me like the burial crypt in the heart of an Egyptian pyramid," de Payns added at length. "Something is here . . . some great secret."

"But the ark is not here," said one. "That is what we seek."

"Perhaps not," replied de Payns, keeping his own knowledge of what happened during the quake to himself. "But perhaps there is something of even greater value."

"I see nothing but a few worthless old jars," said Montbard.

"I tell you, there is something here, André. This is a depository of some kind. Perhaps it was once used to house the temple treasury, but now. . . ."

Holding his torch in front of him, de Payns now approached a recess of stone on one of the walls, where stood a group of six or eight clay jars, approximately three feet in height, which de Montbard had noted. All were perfectly intact, of wide base and mouth, each with a round lid on top.

The others crept toward the recess behind him. De Payns handed his torch back to his friend, then carefully removed the lid from the one closest. He motioned for more light, then peered inside. With trembling hand he reached through the wide mouth. A moment later he withdrew his hand, holding a thick scroll of rolled papyrus.

He turned, knelt to the marbled floor, then with exceeding care began to unroll it. The others gathered around, staring down upon what were texts and drawings of great antiquity. The script was obviously Hebrew. But these were no mere scrolls of Jewish Scripture, which would have been valuable enough. Instead, drawings and mathematical notations and geometrical symbols also filled the sheet.

At length one of their number, a man skilled in building and architecture, brought his hand to his head in a gesture of incredulity.

"It may be," he said, "that we have stumbled on something of great import. I think we have found the original plans for Solomon's temple," said the architect.

"Here is one with a drawing of the ark of the covenant," added another, who had a second scroll unrolled on the floor in front of him. "I can make out nothing of the writing, but it appears to be a chronology of the ark and its movements—I think these represent dates."

"There are dozens of scrolls!" said another. "Look, every jar contains four or five, some six or eight."

"This one may be from the time of Jeremiah," said another, who had unrolled yet a third. "It may, in fact, be in Jeremiah's own hand."

"That would date it from the sixth century B.C. from the time of the Babylonian invasion. Do you suppose Jeremiah himself hid these records?"

"There is a great deal more here," said de Payns, who was proceeding to examine the rest of the jars.

"Here is one of Egyptian origin," said St. Omer.

One of their number was dragging out a rectangular chest from the corner which had been obscured by the jars. He removed the lid.

"We have found more than scrolls," he said. "This is an amazing discovery—look, these are manuscripts in primitive book form—written in Egyptian hieroglyphics. I had no idea the Egyptians were experimenting with this form."

"The first codex finds date from the later dynasties."

Carefully they removed the manuscripts and gingerly opened their thick papyrus pages.

"Here is a drawing of the Egyptian pyramids, with extensive mathematical computations, as well as what look to be engineering equations and other strange notations."

"Unless I am mistaken, here are scrolls of Babylonian origin. . . ."

Meanwhile another of the company was carefully scrutinizing another of the manuscripts. "I do not think I am far mistaken," he said at length, "in saying that this is a sorcerer's guide—a handbook of wizardry. These are incantations, chants, and spells."

"It is said the Egyptians possessed powerful magic."

"Here's a scroll, of sheepskin parchment, in Hebrew," said another who was poring over a scroll he had spread upon the stone floor. "It would date from two or three centuries B.C."

"There are ancient mysteries here, the source of much power," said de Payns. "We have stumbled upon a repository of wisdom and magic. These may even unlock the secrets of the Pyramids."

"Where would the Jews of Jerusalem have acquired such documents?"

"Solomon could easily have possessed such treasures. He had contact with Egypt. Much trade passed between Jerusalem and the pharaohs, as well as with Babylon."

"It could be that he received them as payment in that trade."

A lengthy silence fell.

"It may be that we have discovered something even more valuable than the ark itself," said de Payns, "the ancient science of ancient Egypt and Babylon."

He stood and gazed at the treasure trove in wonder.

"It is well known," he said, "that the Egyptians possessed knowledge that has been lost. Not only were they master builders and learned in advanced mathematical concepts, their seers and sorcerers possessed psychic powers. They must have preserved hidden secrets of their science, architectural knowledge, and other enchantments. I believe we have stumbled into a crypt that was meant to preserve those secrets, a revelation of Egypt's source of might."

Again he paused. His comrades peered up at him in the flickering light given off by their torches. On his face was a look such as they had never before seen. No one considered speaking. They waited.

"I sense power emanating from this place," de Payns said softly. "I feel it among us. I sense even now that it is being passed on to us, as from ancient worlds lost to the sight of mankind."

The hush which descended upon the nine indeed originated from regions not of the earth. The former glory of Solomon's temple had indeed departed. A dark control had replaced it. As of one accord, they knelt and gathered into a small circle in much the same manner as they had before on the sacred stone of Abraham. They clasped hands as one.

"Do each of you solemnly vow, by the force that guided us to this place and chose to make this revelation to us, to keep this day under a veil as long as you live?"

"We so swear," came eight whispered replies in the flickering light.

"To none shall we divulge what we have found or what we learn from this library of discovery, but to those who vow in like rite to maintain the secrets of the ancients which have been passed on to us. Do you all so pledge?"

"We so pledge."

"Then by these vows are we forever bound," said de Payns. "We, and those who follow in the mysteries of the temple."

✦ ✦ ✦

When de Payns returned to Europe in 1127 after eight years in Jerusalem, it was to seek an audience with the pope.

Much had changed since his clandestine pilgrimage in 1119. The nine founders of the mystical order now possessed many secrets. Indeed had the mantle of ancient Egypt and Babylon come to rest upon them.

Hughes de Payns and André de Montbard sought their mutual relative, the abbot of Clairvaux, and presented a letter from King Baldwin of Jerusalem, praising the Templars, and asking Bernard to intercede on their behalf with Pope Honorius II. Their hope was that Bernard, whom many considered the most powerful Christian in all Europe, would request papal sanction for the military order known as the Knights of the Temple.

Bernard took on the request with vigor. Upon his enthusiastic recommendation, the pope granted the request. The new order was sanctioned by papal council the following year. Bernard himself wrote the rule upon which the Templars would be based and which would henceforth outline their activities.

The original rule, the Règle du Temple, *like the rest of Templar foundations, was highly* secretive. It called for the election of a Grand Master of the temple of Jerusalem, whose authority over the brotherhood of the order was law. It set up a complex system of commanders, chaplains, and various levels of other offices, to all of which one could be admitted only on the basis of secretive oaths of lifetime obedience.

Hughes de Payns was elected the Templars' first Grand Master. Upon his seal was a likeness of the Dome of the Rock. In its very origins, therefore, already had the supposed Christian foundations of the order begun to be diluted, usurped by the great gold-domed icon of Islam.

De Payns travelled throughout Europe gaining support for the Templar mission. Grateful pilgrims blessed the order with bequests. Soon they became an avalanche of wealth. The thought of brave Christian knights fighting Muslim infidels captured the imagination of medieval Europe. Peasants and nobles alike gave according to their means in hopes of sharing vicariously in the perceived blessings. The new order grew rapidly in prestige and power at an astonishing rate, bringing in thousands of recruits and massive donations.

The continued support of Bernard of Clairvaux increased manyfold this flow of wealth. Louis VII, king of France, granted the Templars land near Paris which became the order's European headquarters. Other wealthy Frenchmen followed. Stephen of England granted to them several large estates and paved the way for de Payns to travel throughout England and Scotland, visiting wealthy nobles on behalf of his cause. Henry I granted lands in Normandy. From Spain and the rest of the continent came lavish bequests to these "poor" knights of Christ.

✦ ✦ ✦

Meanwhile, as de Payns and Montbard travelled and as the order gained respectability and wealth, the rest of the original company remained in Jerusalem to continue, in secret, those subterranean explorations and excavations which had already yielded so much. The lust to find treasures of more material splendor—gold, silver, and precious artifacts—grew stronger the wealthier the order became. Within a decade or two, tunnels and underground passageways extended in all directions from their headquarters in the former Muslim mosque.

Secrecy continued to define the Templars and their successors. Little of their findings ever became publically known. By the end of the century the Knights Templar was the most powerful order in the world—the wealthiest institution in the Church outside the papacy itself.

Their philosophy took on increasing sorcerous and mystical elements. Some said those highest in the order came together in a darkened room once yearly, at which time an object possessed of magical powers was placed in their midst. In a circle would they gather, extending their fingers until each one was lightly touching the rim of the object, said to be made of solid gold. Thus would otherworldly powers be transmitted to these select few, which they passed on to the rest of the order throughout the world.

The Neoplatonism of the Templars unified and blended all religious thought. Christianity became but one of many pathways to truth. Science, symbolism, architecture, and secret ceremony became more foundational in the passing on of Templar secrets than religion. From the eight-sided dome above the sacred stone where they had taken their oath sprang the octagonal *shape that would come to characterize Templar architecture and the Gothic style which they authored. By such means would the Templars infuse their sacred geometry and occult wisdom throughout Europe.*

What secrets had the original nine knights discovered that made this possible? What architectural mysteries made the Cathedral of Chartres one of the most intriguing in all of Europe, which ultimately spawned the Gothic design of the Renaissance?

The outside world would never know the answers to such questions. One could be initiated into the order only by an intricate system of oaths and pledges of loyalty, the most binding of which was the vow forbidding any passing on of knowledge to those on the outside concerning the order.

Such secret oaths and pledges would bind together all the fraternal orders and societies, guilds and lodges, councils and other mystic organizations, which would branch and grow from the root of these beginnings.

Part Three

ETHIOPIA

✦ ✦ ✦

A voice is heard . . . weeping for her sons. . . .

This is what the Lord says: "Cease your loud weeping, shed no more tears,

for your work will be rewarded," declares the Lord.

"They will return from the land of the enemy.

So there is hope for your future," declares the Lord.

"Your sons shall return to their own land."

JEREMIAH 31:15-17, NIV AND NEB COMBINED

✦ ✦ ✦

ten

Surprising New Best-Seller

(1)

Neither Brits nor Americans understood the other's system of government beyond a second- or third-grade level. But newspapers, networks, and other news agencies on both sides of the Atlantic did their dutiful best every few years to *seem* interested in spite of the fact that most of their viewers and readership weren't.

Now again had arrived the BBC's opportunity to transform the American political process into something at least marginally understandable to the man-on-the-street Englishman or Scot.

"Hey, Glendenning," called out the news editor after the journalist exiting his office after a discussion of his assignment, "tell Shayne I'd like to see her."

Three minutes later the young woman entered Edward Pilkington's office.

"Shayne," he said, "I want you to cover the American elections. There's a fund-raiser in Washington with a few big names, including this fellow Quinby who's been in the news. The people upstairs say he's a man to watch."

"Can't you send someone else? I'm working on another story. How about Prentiss?"

"Look, Kim," replied Pilkington, "I've been told to follow Quinby. He'll be our angle. I want you on it. So turn on the charm. Wile him with your English accent. You know how American men are—they think it makes you sound sophisticated."

"Are you saying I'm *not* sophisticated?" rejoined Shayne, a smile playing at the edges of her mouth. Already she was thinking perhaps a trip to the States wouldn't be so bad.

"You heard every word I said," Pilkington retorted playfully. "Nothing even resembling that came out of my mouth. All I'm saying is that impressionable Americans sometimes get swept off their feet by the *sound* of a Brit. So go to America, and turn on the English charm."

(2)

When Kim Shayne landed in Washington D.C., her first objective was to find her hotel, which was near the airport, take a relaxing bath, have a light room-service supper, and get to bed early.

Forty minutes later she walked into her room at the Hilton and threw herself down on the bed. Now she would take that bath, she thought, slipping off her shoes.

When she emerged from the bathroom—clean, relaxed, and warm—she flipped on the television. Then she began to dress.

" . . . whole world knows the name *Adam Livingstone,*" the television personality began.

At the words Kim Shayne's ears perked up. Now *this* was a surprise, she thought—an American television special on the countryman in whom she had reasons of her own to be interested.

"A well-known archaeologist in England for years," the commentator went on, "Livingstone burst onto the international stage two years ago with his discovery of Noah's ark in Turkey. Then followed this year his astonishing claim regarding photographs of the lost ark of the covenant, along with the supposed location of the original Garden of Eden. . . ."

As the introduction to the long-awaited segment of *Sixty/Twenty* continued, video clips showed Adam at various archaeological digs around the world, then briefly on camera with Sir Daniel Snow.

"But now Adam Livingstone has outdone even himself, pulling off what no one would have dreamed possible—excavating Noah's ark from Ararat's glacial ice, lifting it off the mountain by a flotilla of helium blimps, successfully floating it to the base of the mountain, and landing it on a special prepared platform around which will be constructed an environmental hangar at the ark's permanent home."

The series of video clips gave way to a triumphant shot of Adam standing atop the bow of Noah's ark as the powerful blimps led it through the sky, Mount Ararat in the background, toward the landing site.

"It has been a remarkable and triumphant string of successes for Adam Livingstone in a very short time. He is already considered a shoo-in for just about every Man of the Year award, and three weeks ago his face appeared simultaneously on the covers of *Time* and *Newsweek.*"

A pause followed as the camera zoomed in on Adam's smiling face.

"Who is this real-life Indiana Jones? And what impact has all this had on individual lives the world over? The answer may surprise you. It certainly did us. We'll tell you all about it . . . tonight . . . on *Sixty/Twenty.*"

As a series of commercials came onto the screen, Kim quickly finished dressing, then sat down in front of the television, perusing the room service menu.

In two or three minutes the program resumed by detailing a brief outline of Adam Livingstone's career, then moving in an unexpected direction.

"What we decided to do," the journalist was saying, "was ask people whether all these biblical discoveries have made any difference—not to the world, not to science, not to archaeology . . . but to *them*. We began by asking what they think of the claims made by Adam Livingstone. Do they believe them? If so, how their lives have been impacted. The answers astounded us.

"Everywhere we went, people said almost the same thing: *It has caused me to start reading the Bible.*"

A series of vignettes followed, impromptu on-camera interviews with six or eight people, all according to much the same pattern of response—*Yes, I think I believe it,* the people said. *I'd never thought much about the Bible before, but suddenly I find myself curious and wanting to read it. After all, if the Bible is true, I'd better find out what it has to say.*

"And this appears to be the unexpected impact of Adam Livingstone's exploits," continued the journalist. "The Bible has become a hot commodity. Everywhere, in all walks of life and among all racial and socio-economic groups, in factories and schools and offices . . . people are carrying Bibles and reading them at every opportunity. And not merely reading about the ark of the covenant or the ark of Noah, but reading the entire Bible.

"We were intrigued. What is it about this ancient book, which some would say has little relevance for our times, that people are finding so compelling? So we sent out two *Sixty/Twenty* film crews to eight cities and ten university campuses in every region of the country. At each location they spent half a day filming people and asking them about their reaction to Adam Livingstone's discoveries. An astonishing 20 percent of the people we interviewed were actually carrying Bibles at the time. We found the Bible to be the number one subject of discussion at colleges and universities everywhere.

"As a result of this interest, Bible sales have surged dramatically. Everywhere reports are coming in of record sales numbers. Warehouses at every major Bible publisher are depleting. Three of the top five titles on the *New York Times* Best-seller List last week were Bibles. The Bible is being openly talked about everywhere, from the front page of *USA Today* to editorials in the *Wall Street Journal*. Every nightly newscast on every major network, it seems, features some Bible documentary. The Internet is alive with literally tens of thousands of new Bible-based Web sites and discussion groups."

As the report progressed, film clips were shown of headlines and bookstore check-out counters and student discussion groups and individuals sitting on park benches and buses and standing on street corners reading the Bible.

"Likewise churches everywhere are reporting enormous turnouts. Everyone is clamoring for messages on one subject—the Bible. Is it really provable, as

Adam Livingstone has claimed? Is a revival under way, as many leading evangelical leaders claim? Or is this a fad which will soon pass the moment Adam Livingstone is no longer so prominently in the news?

"This huge interest in the Bible, which appears to be worldwide, has even spread to Hollywood. Following on the recent success of religious programming concerning angels, *Sixty/Twenty* has learned that no fewer than a dozen new television pilots are under consideration—three in the early phases of production—all with religious or Bible-related themes.

"Still other reports of so-called miracles and answers to prayer and changed lives are being told. We have the following story which resulted when a twenty-six-year-old terminal leukemia patient, Bianca Andretti, found in her Bible the story of . . ."

Kim Shayne rose and turned off the television. The rest of the world may suddenly be fascinated with Bibles, she thought. But she wasn't.

She had other reasons than religion for being interested in Adam Livingstone.

(3)

Fred Hutchins of Oak Ridge, Tennessee, excused himself and hurried to the bathroom. He had to be alone.

It was difficult to explain the sudden outbreaks of tears which were coming over him these days at the most awkward times.

What was happening? He hadn't cried since he was a kid. And he had no intention of starting again now. This was ridiculous. He was a grown man, for heaven's sake!

It had all started with that thing on TV about Adam Livingstone and what they were saying was Noah's ark. He hadn't cared much about it. But Lucille had wanted to see it, so they'd watched together. Ever since their daughter's visit he had been trying to show Lucille more consideration. Though she had been cold and aloof toward him, Sally said nothing about the confrontation in the hotel.

Strange sensations had stirred within him as he'd seen the huge boat lifting off the mountain—feelings he couldn't explain. He found himself blinking a little too strenuously to be accounted for by something in his eye.

Then last night's broadcast of *Sixty/Twenty* stirred him up more. All the men and women at work were talking about it today—Noah's ark . . . the truth of the Bible . . . the ark of the covenant . . . the reality of God . . . his power to change lives . . . miracles—Christians and skeptics arguing various points of view. Everyone had watched *Sixty/Twenty* and had an opinion.

Probably the lump in his throat had nothing to do with Livingstone and that Noah's ark business. What could it possibly have to do with that anyway? It was probably just the accumulated stress of his impending financial crisis. Who wouldn't be close to tears with what he was up against?

He had stalled the bank with another house payment, and managed to get a postponement of the IRS audit. But who was he trying to fool? Eventually the day of reckoning would come.

Maybe he ought to kill himself and be done with it. He had enough life insurance to take care of Lucille.

He walked into the bathroom, relieved at last to be alone, and especially relieved that none of the other workers were there. He drew in a deep breath and walked to the sink. He doused his face with cold water.

He stood up and took a long look at himself in the mirror, his face still dripping. He was a mess.

He put his hands on the bathroom counter and his head slumped down. All of a sudden the words erupted from his mouth in an unexpected gush. *"God!"* he cried. *"If your Word really is true like they say . . . if you really do work miracles in people's lives—please . . . please, God, help me!"*

(4)

Disturbing reverberations in the Dimension from which they took their orders had brought together the current scions of three of Europe's most ancient and powerful families.

The Dutchman had descended from the Germanic line of Renaissance-era bankers. The Englishman, with Rothschild blood in his veins, came likewise from direct Rosicrucian roots. The Swisswoman could trace her family's lineage back to twelfth-century France in the region of Chartres, a fact which gave her the deepest standing of all in the ancient occult fraternity. Both men were thirty-second degree Masons. The families of all three had been intertwined with the Illuminati and a dozen of its offshoots for centuries.

The room where they sat was dark except for a single candle on the table in front of them. An unknowing observer might have thought they were praying. Nothing, however, could have been further from the truth. Any man or woman who knew what true *prayer* was would have felt his or her skin crawl at the sounds emanating softly from these three mouths. In their deception, they flattered themselves that light was being given them through the otherworldly oracles whose guidance they sought.

A climax approached for which their sinister Master had prepared for centuries. Now unexpected forces threatened the success of that Plan.

. . . beware, intoned one of the men in a weird chant. *Many doors are imperiled . . . beware of the enemy's people . . . must keep his powers hidden from them. . . .*

"Your Wise One speaks of doors," said the woman in her own voice. "My Spirit Guide has spoken to me of a door where a presence has been sealed—"

Suddenly she stopped. Her body shuddered, as if being taken over by a power able to control her at will. The single word *presence* sent an invisible spiritual earthquake through the room. When next she opened her mouth, the crooning which came from it was not of her own voice.

Danger approaches, it said. *More potent than before . . . threatens all . . . that presence must not be found. When it is, he will appear . . . ?*

Again came a tremble that rocked the three at the word *he.*

. . . great mystery . . . revelation must be prevented . . . place in the universe where we are vulnerable . . . force of the blood must never be discovered. . . .

The woman slumped in her chair as one spent. These were things never spoken of. Indeed must the danger be great. The two men began conversing in low tones.

"I have never seen the Dimension in such a state," said Vaughan-Maier.

"Nor I," agreed Lord Montreux. "I am confused by the message. I understood the object had been found by your daughter's friend Livingstone."

"He must be eliminated. My Guide says he must be forever silenced and the object prevented from being made known."

"There is no other way."

"So too, I fear, must be our troublesome Council member."

Gradually the Swisswoman came to herself.

"He will not be with us much longer," she said. "The plan of which we spoke last time is in effect."

The two men nodded.

"This surge of interest in the enemy's book is our greatest threat."

"We have seen such things before," said Montreux. "They are always temporary."

"We have always ensured that people revered the book itself without delving into its secrets," said the Dutchman. "I do not think we need to be concerned."

"It is different this time," rejoined D'Abernon. "This threat is greater than ever before. My Guides say there is danger that the *power* of the book may be discovered in a widespread way. If that happens, we are undone. Livingstone's influence is formidable," she went on. "I am confident we will overcome him. As he has led us to the one, he will lead us to more of the enemy's sacred things, that we may destroy them, and put a stop to this worrisome trend."

"What about the other ark, in Turkey? It would be an easy matter to destroy it too."

"No. Now that it has been made public, our best strategy will be to make it into a tourist attraction. We must simply divert people's minds from what it *means.*"

(5)

As Kim Shayne walked toward the auditorium, a group of men stood at the door handing something to those who were entering. Before she realized it, she was holding a Gideon's New Testament in her hands. She stuffed it into her purse, then continued inside and found a seat.

The auditorium was packed. A recording of lively band music was playing as the participants in tonight's discussion made their entrance. The hubbub increased, heads turned, cameras flashed, applause rippled through the crowd. The seven men sat down and the moderator came forward to quiet the crowd and offer her introductory remarks of welcome. One by one each of the guests proceeded with a five-minute opening speech, which would be followed by what everyone hoped would be a spirited discussion, with questions from the floor.

When time for them came, comments from the audience were equally split between press and citizenry. They went on for some time. Shayne, who had not spoken yet, stood about six or eight rows back in the crowd. The moderator acknowledged her.

"Senator Quinby," she said, "Kim Shayne with the BBC. I was sent here to try to make sense out of your confusing political process for the people in my country."

"It confuses many in our country too, believe me!" interrupted Quinby.

"After tonight I can believe you!" rejoined Shayne. "What I would like to ask," she went on as the laughter subsided, "has more to do with personality than issues. Tell me about character, charisma, personality. What kind of man or woman, in your opinion, Senator Quinby, does it take to be a leader in your country?"

The pause that followed was lengthy. Then Quinby spoke.

"I'm not sure I can really answer you very well," he said in a soft and thoughtful voice. "The politics of recent times in our country would seem to indicate that charisma and personality are of far greater importance to the public in selecting politicians than character, ethics, morality, and integrity. That disturbs me. I have been thinking much of this as I ponder my own political future. The question before me is not so much what kind of man does it take to be a leader, but what kind of man do I *myself* want to be."

"And have you found an answer, Senator?" asked Shayne.

"I'm not sure, Miss Shayne," he replied. "But I have a feeling the answer may lie in the book your countryman, Mr. Livingstone, has turned the focus of the world toward, the book those men from the Gideons were handing out this evening in front of the auditorium."

"Are you saying that you are looking for the key to your political future in the Bible?"

"That's exactly it, Miss Shayne," said Quinby.

A light ripple of reaction spread through the crowd.

"For too long in this country," the senator went on, "we have prided ourselves on what we call the separation of Church and State. Whatever value that doctrine may have had when the term was first coined, I have the feeling it is in need of a serious overhaul. Speaking for myself, whatever future I have, whether in politics or anything else, I *do* intend to base it on the truths of the Bible. That's where I believe I will find what kind of man I want to be, and in a larger way, getting back to your original question, what kind of man it takes to be a leader. In short, I think it takes a man of truth. Whether men of truth and personal character will be elected . . . that I cannot say. But I *can* say that such is the kind of man I want to be."

Kim sat down and glanced at her purse, thinking of the New Testament inside it. Before she could think what it all meant, another reporter spoke up.

"Why is everyone so interested in the Bible these days, Senator?"

"I cannot speak for everyone," replied Quinby. "What I can tell you is why I happen to be interested. It is very simple, really. The moment I heard Adam Livingstone being interviewed by Sir Daniel Snow, I realized the truth in what he said—that there are implications for each one of us personally if in fact the Bible is true. I have not been able to get that out of my mind: *What does the Bible's truth mean to me?* Isn't that really the question it boils down to? Isn't that what Noah's ark and the ark of the covenant are about? If the Bible is true, what does it mean *to me?* Once I started asking that question, looking at myself more honestly than I ever had before . . . I discovered that my outlook on everything began to change. Suddenly the Bible became a very, very personal book. I tell you . . . I haven't been able to put it down since."

eleven

Plans

(1)

Adam, Scott, Figg, and Rocky remained at Ararat to coordinate the next phase of hangar development and construction.

The project was under the auspices and control of the Turkish government, working with an international scientific consortium that had grown out of the cartel which had largely funded the original exploration two years before. Adam remained intrinsically involved in its organization and would eventually be a permanent member of its Board of Directors.

Juliet flew back from Turkey with Jen. Unknown to them as they descended into London, the woman whose life was destined to intertwine with Adam's efforts more than anyone now knew, was also feeling the effects of a lengthy intercontinental flight. Minutes after Juliet and Jen landed at Gatwick, Kim Shayne's 747 from the United States touched down at Heathrow.

Jen went straight home from the airport. Juliet drove back to the house at Sevenoaks. A small crowd of journalists was waiting for her. Juliet approached the gate in bright spirits, saw the bustle of activity, then stopped and got out. After her relative success with the media at Ararat, she found herself looking forward to the exchange. The moment she stepped out of the car, however, she saw disappointment on the faces of the reporters who clamored up to the car . . . disappointment that she was alone.

The first question voiced burst the balloon of her optimism.

"When will Mr. Livingstone be back?" shouted one of the reporters.

Why did such a simple question catch her off guard? Of course they would want to see Adam. He was the toast of England, the talk of the world. The whole of Operation Noah was about Adam Livingstone . . . not her. Who else would they want to talk to?

"He . . . uh—he won't be back for a couple more weeks," Juliet answered, suddenly feeling unsure.

A few more questions followed. She fumbled through them, then excused herself and continued on through the gate and into the house.

For the rest of the week Juliet struggled with the sinking feeling that her success with the media at Ararat had been an illusion. She recognized the feeling—the sagging confidence, the creeping depression enclosing her from every side, the return of old doubts about her role in Adam Livingstone's life.

Mrs. Graves knew something was wrong as soon as Juliet walked in. She did her best to buoy up her niece's spirits, but to little avail. Juliet could not stop the downward slide of her emotions. Why would she be assailed by so many doubts after such a triumph? Knowing that when Adam returned the pressure would be on to accelerate their wedding plans only made her mounting anxiety worse.

It was a difficult two weeks. She longed to see Adam. Yet she dreaded seeing him at the same time.

She would force herself to be cheery when he returned and not let him know there was anything wrong. This would all blow over, she tried to convince herself.

(2)

Adam returned to Sevenoaks fifteen days later. Rocky flew home to New Hampshire. Scott and Figg remained in Ararat City.

Adam and Juliet walked through the expansive gardens at the back of the Livingstone estate in the late afternoon of the day of Adam's return, their first time alone together. Adam was in an expansive mood, talking excitedly about what had happened and filling Juliet in on what they had accomplished in the last two weeks.

"Will the hangar be completed by winter?" asked Juliet.

"Not completed, but at least the shell and roof up so that work will be able to continue."

"I don't suppose it really matters though, does it?"

"Why do you say that?" asked Adam.

"The ark's been out in the elements for thousands of years . . . it isn't as if one more winter is going to hurt it."

"I see what you mean," said Adam, laughing. "Good point."

"What about the foam?" asked Juliet.

"Melting is probably 60 or 70 percent complete. It's working just like DuPont said it would. The ark doesn't appear to have suffered so much as a scratch from the voyage."

"And the balloons?"

"One by one, then by the tens and hundreds, they started flying up in the air as the foam released them from their chambers."

They walked on awhile in silence.

"You know," said Adam at length, "as exciting as Ararat was, and even though we've got a lot to do there, it's time we started moving forward on the wedding. Have you talked to your mum about any of the details?"

Juliet shook her head.

"We also need to think about where to focus our efforts next. Now that the ark is off the mountain, that research will continue on without us. From here on it will be so much more than just our project. Noah's ark belongs to the whole world."

They continued to walk, but it remained quiet between them. Adam led the way to one of the garden benches. He sensed Juliet's mood.

"What is it?" he asked.

"Nothing," she replied softly.

"Come on . . . you can't fool me."

"I don't know. I suppose I've been feeling funny since Ararat."

"What—why?"

"I was so out of place."

"Out of place? No—you were great!"

Again Juliet did not reply. How could she ever make someone with Adam's self-confidence understand the kinds of self-doubts that occasionally swept over her? How could someone like him realize that no matter what anyone said, and however many compliments they lavished on her, she couldn't help at times feeling that she wasn't *really* a member of his research team.

They sat down. Adam put his arm around Juliet and drew her toward him.

"Lord," he prayed, *"we ask for your leading in the many decisions facing us during these times. Show us what you want us to do and when, both about the work and research as well as with our own plans."*

"Help us trust you," said Juliet softly. *Help me trust you,* she added to herself.

After several more minutes he rose, offered his hand, and pulled her to her feet. Hand in hand they walked back toward the house.

(3)

Dusk descended over the Azerbaydzhan capital of Baku.

A slender figure, dressed in black from head to foot, slunk silently toward the expansive villa where her quarry resided with his three servants and an occasional mistress.

From a vantage point on the hill above, Halder Zorin gazed through powerful infrared binoculars at the figure attempting to gain access to his own home.

A smile crossed his lips.

He knew his life was in danger. It made the game all the more challenging that his adversary was his former colleague, and a formidable adversary.

Did they really think they could be rid of him so easily? This was *his* city, *his* country. He had eyes and ears everywhere. Even if he hadn't intercepted D'Abernon's message, he would have been apprised of this stranger's presence in Baku before she was out of the airport.

The smile quickly faded, replaced by seething hatred. He could kill her right now if such was his desire. But the vixen might be more useful to him alive than following Mitch Cutter to the bottom of the harbor. He doubted she knew anything about the other ark. But he would keep her alive just in case.

Had the absurd display in nearby Turkey come six months earlier, it might have concerned him. He would well have arranged for an errant missile to blow the purported ark out of the air into ten million meaningless splinters. But the thing no longer concerned him. Let them have their religious toy. Let them research it and dissect it and examine every inch of it. He couldn't care less. He had larger fish to fry. Alongside the *other* ark, Noah's decaying boat represented only so many pieces of wood. Now gleamed in his eye the possibility of true power the likes of which had never been seen.

He would get his revenge on D'Abernon . . . but in his own way. He would either kill her, or take over the Council completely. Maybe both.

They couldn't toy with him. He would kill them *all* if he had to.

After he had his hands on the ark of the covenant!

(4)

Adam Livingstone sat alone in his study.

It was early in the morning. He had been home a week. He now sat with a cup of tea on the desk beside him. In his hands he held several of the photographs he had taken in Aksum.

As always, the instant one project was behind him, he was on to the next. With one ark safely at rest at the base of Mount Ararat, Adam's thoughts had returned to the other ark whose future might rest in his hands.

What to do next was the question. What to do about these photographs?

He continued slowly to turn them over, one after the other, gazing at the remarkable object with wonder.

Like the ark of Noah, he was convinced that it belonged to the whole world. Ethiopia may possess it as a material *thing*. But let the world know of it, see it, wonder at it. The truth of the Bible ought to be known.

And this priceless object before him, as much as the ark he had just left behind in Turkey, demonstrated that awesome truth with physical and historical *evidence*.

As soon as Juliet was up and Jen and Crystal were here, he'd talk it over with them, maybe get Scott and Figg on speakerphone with them from Turkey. They'd brainstorm the options and see what they could come up with.

Three hours later, when the three women of the team sat in the main office at Sevenoaks, Adam completed the call to Turkey.

"All right, I think we're all here," said Adam. "Scott, Figg . . . you both hear me OK?"

"Fine here," came Figg's voice through the speaker on Crystal's desk.

"Me too—loud and clear," said Scott. "How are you ladies doing?"

"We're fine," said Crystal. "How's the weather in Turkey?"

"Actually it's starting to cool down a bit. I'm beginning to feel autumn in the air. The construction crews are working round the clock to try to get everything in the dry before winter. It's looking more and more like a city all the time."

"And the ark?" asked Juliet.

"It's not going anywhere, believe me!" said Figg.

"Speaking of the ark," said Adam, "the reason I wanted to talk to you all is to help me decide what we ought to do about the other ark. We've got the photographs. I went on television with Daniel Snow. But the Ethiopian government still hasn't said a word. Somehow we've got to get them to make the ark public."

"Why don't you just tell everyone where you took the photos?" said Scott.

"I thought that it would be best for the Ethiopians to volunteer the information."

"But they haven't."

"Which is our predicament."

The discussion continued for perhaps another ten minutes, but without resolution to Adam's quandary. Eventually the room and telephones fell silent. Till now Juliet had contributed very little to the discussion. But it was she who next spoke.

"Why don't you film a documentary on the ark?" she said.

Adam turned toward her with the expression on his face he always wore when his brain was starting to race. He said nothing immediately, gesturing for her to continue.

"All that research we did," Juliet went on, "the list of Scriptures, the *Kebre Negast*, the historical assignments you gave all of us, looking into the history of the *Timkat*. It's fascinating. Who knows, maybe right now when Operation Noah and the Snow interview are fresh in the public's mind—it might have some impact to encourage Ethiopia to tell what they know."

"That is a fabulous idea!" exclaimed Adam finally. "I think you're onto something. What do the rest of you think?"

"I agree," said Scott's voice on the speakerphone. "Your stock is high right now, Adam. You're the natural one to do something on the ark."

"Use your prestige to pressure Ethiopia to go public," added Figg, "just like Juliet said."

"Why not tell the story of the queen and Menyelek right on camera," suggested Jen, "go through the Scriptures, then the theft, the ark's travels, where it ended up."

"It would be great," added Crystal, "if we could film the *Timkat* too."

"Right," said Adam, "show that not only does Ethiopia have the ark, they celebrate it every year. And it's only a few months away. Juliet, you've done it," he added, turning toward her again. "It's a positively brilliant idea."

"What do you want us to do, Boss?" said Crystal.

"Why don't you get in touch with Jim Lindberg at the BBC? Tell him what we have in mind. We'll have to low-profile it all the way. After the Snow interview, I don't want to go into Ethiopia with horns blaring. I'm envisioning a single cameraman and maybe one BBC interviewer to be on camera with the rest of us. We'll go in as tourists and start filming without a big hoopla."

"I'll get right on it."

"In the meantime, the rest of us will dig out our research notes from before and start putting together a preliminary schedule and script."

twelve

Ancient Land of Mystery

(1)

Filming for the BBC documentary began at the Livingstone estate.

After an introductory buildup showing replicas and artistic renditions of the ark of the covenant, the scene broke to Sevenoaks, with the Livingstone research team poring over Bibles and ancient books, Adam narrating his own interest and initial research.

"Once you found yourself fascinated with the ark," asked the interviewer, Jim Lindberg, a longtime acquaintance of Adam's, "where did you begin? How did you actually start on your search to try to find it?"

"First we had to try to trace the ark's history," replied Adam. "The ark of the covenant was constructed by one of Moses' most skilled craftsmen, a Hebrew by the name of Bezalel. . . ."

As Adam briefly related the Old Testament history of the ark, a series of paintings were shown depicting pivotal moments in the tale, such as the ark being born aloft by Levites leading the Israelites into battle, and it striking dead those who touched it.

"But you obviously felt that the ark still existed," said Lindberg. "How did you come to such a conclusion, and where did it lead you?"

"Unexpectedly, our search led us to Ethiopia."

The scene broke to Adam's team getting ready, then flying and landing in Addis Ababa, capital of Ethiopia.

(2)

Rome was as good a place to disappear as anywhere.

More importantly, it was the city where Fausto Webbe kept his clandestine basement where anyone in the world could get a new identity . . . for a price. Whether the man had indeed sold what he might have possessed as a soul to the devil before embarking on his spidery career, Zorin had no idea. But Webbe was the best. So he would pay what the scum asked.

He knew D'Abernon's stooge was still in Baku trying to get onto his trail. She was really something, with that ridiculous olive-green beret that would stand out in any crowd. Zorin smiled at the thought, then unconsciously gave his own leather cap a tug over his forehead. He had people watching the fool and her beret. He would take care of both later, and stomp his foot on that hat of hers in the end. In the meantime, he had other matters to attend to.

Zorin turned into a shadowy alleyway. Halfway along it, he descended an outdoor flight of stairs, then ducked into a recess which ended at a locked door.

He knocked twice, then again. A moment later it opened and Zorin entered a room even darker than the alley, which a lone dim bulb hanging from the ceiling was insufficient to light.

A man stood before him with grizzled thinning hair and yellow teeth.

"I have need of your services, Webbe," said Zorin in flawless Italian.

The man smiled a half-toothless grin, then turned, motioned, and led his visitor deeper into the blackness.

(3)

Two weeks passed after the initial filming at Sevenoaks. Now they were in place to continue.

"All right, then," said Lindberg toward the camera held by his colleague Bridges, then turning toward Adam as they walked along the hillside, with a flock of sheep and an Ethiopian shepherd in the background. "You began tracing the history and movements of the ark. And your research led you to this ancient land of mystery. Tell us how that happened. How did you pick up the trail of the ark? What clues did you discover?"

"Actually," replied Adam, who was dressed in casual clothing, khaki cutoffs and a white straw hat of the shape made famous by Harrison Ford, "it all began with an Ethiopian legend and a few passages in the Bible."

"You felt the answers were there?"

"The Bible always has more to reveal than at first meets the eye," replied Adam. "It is a miraculously endowed book of hidden meanings. Often its deepest truths are not revealed without great persistence. So we dug through the pertinent Scriptures as if it had been an archaeological dig—asking ourselves questions . . . always asking questions."

"I take it your efforts paid off?"

"We found some things that intrigued us," replied Adam.

"Where does Ethiopia come in to the biblical story?"

"According to Ethiopian legend the ark disappeared during Solomon's reign. Because of what happened at that time, present-day Ethiopians trace their kingship to what they call the Solomonic dynasty. They believe there is an unbroken dynasty from Solomon to Haile Selassie I, who was killed in a revolutionary coup in 1974. According to tradition, he was the two hundred twenty-sixth in a *direct* line of descent from Solomon himself. He was said to be wearing Solomon's ring at the time of his death."

"What is such a claim based on?"

"The *Kebre Negast,"* replied Adam.

"Most of our viewers will never have heard of it."

"It is the Ethiopian national epic. The English equivalent would be *Beowulf,* something like the *Iliad* and the *Odyssey,* or the Sumarian *Gilgamesh Epic."*

"What's it all about?" asked Lindberg.

Though they knew the story, Juliet, Jen, and Scott walked beside Adam listening intently as their leader explained where their research had led them. Every so often the camera zoomed in for close-ups of the other members of Adam's team. Adam himself was so at ease in front of the public eye that the sequence came off as spontaneous, relaxed, and unrehearsed.

(4)

Gilbert Bowles lay back on the bed in his first-class stateroom of the Norwegian cruise liner *Bislet.*

This was the life, he thought—so much better than enduring a bone-chilling winter in London. They would steam out of Portsmouth this afternoon, and in less than forty-eight hours the temperature would be a pleasant seventy-five degrees.

But he was exhausted. Getting aboard had taxed his weakened frame.

Some unplanned impulse caused him to roll over and open the drawer of the dresser. Staring him in the face was a Gideon Bible.

Blast it all! he thought, shoving the drawer shut. Couldn't he escape religion even here? Were those ridiculous Bibles everywhere! He had a good mind to take the infernal book up on deck and chuck it overboard! He'd had enough of that religious claptrap when he was drugged up after the heart attack.

Gradually Bowles dozed off.

A knock came to his door. Groggily the archaeologist rolled over. Another knock. He attempted a reply which came out as a lethargic grunt.

The ship's steward took the sound as a summons to enter.

"Mr. Bowles," the man said tentatively, peering through the door as he opened it a few inches. "I am sorry to disturb you before we set sail. But we have a lady upstairs who saw your name on the manifest—I suppose because her name is Bowden, and appeared just ahead of yours. Once she realized you were on board, she became extremely agitated and immediately came to find me."

"Agitated," repeated Bowles, who had by now crawled to a sitting position, "whatever in the world about?"

"Wanting to meet you, sir. It seems she is quite taken with both you and your book. She has it with her. She asked me if I could possibly get you to autograph it." He pulled out the copy of *The Link Is Found*.

"Oh . . . oh, yes . . . well, certainly," grunted Bowles, struggling to his feet. "A fan you say?"

Nothing proved more a tonic to his spirits than a fan in search of his signature!

"Perhaps the lady would like to meet me," he added, coming steadily more to himself, "and have me sign the book personally."

"I'm certain she would be overwhelmed by the gesture, Sir Gilbert. That is most kind of you."

"It is the least I can do, my good man. Tell me, how old is the lady . . . is she travelling alone?"

"Yes, actually, she is. I would say she is in her late thirties or early forties."

"Well, then, tell Miss, uh . . . Bowden that I shall be delighted. As a matter of fact—wait, I will accompany you and tell her myself."

Bowles drew up his sizeable chest and sucked in a great restorative breath. He then followed the steward from the room feeling almost like his own self again at this unexpected brightening of his prospects.

(5)

"*Kebre Negast* literally means 'The glory of the kings,'" replied Adam to the interviewer's previous question. "It is a potpourri of stories, myths, and legends of Ethiopia's ancient past, gathered in the fourteenth century by six Tigrinyan scribes. It is a prime example of period literature, probably based on facts handed down orally which, as time passes, take on a life of their own. The compilers claimed to be translating an Arabic version of an earlier Coptic work into the local Semitic language. Most of the *Kebre Negast* concerns the parentage of Ethiopian Emperor Menyelek I, who was born in the tenth century B.C. It is from him that stems the unbroken succession of emperors."

"You must have found yourself believing a good deal of this legendary account," said Lindberg.

"You're not so far wrong." Adam smiled. "I suppose I am of the view that myths and legends have to start somewhere. I believe that there were originally facts that gave rise to the traditions."

"So you must differentiate between the fact and the fiction?"

"An archaeologist has to figure out what ancient peoples and cultures were like from the tiniest of clues," Adam went on. "A bit of bone, a broken shard of pottery, an unearthed portion of some structure, a grave, perhaps. In the research we did in trying to find the location of the ark of the covenant, I felt that I was digging into historical sources in the same way we dig into the earth—trying to discover what *facts* might still be discernible."

"And you felt the Ethiopian legend to be based on truth?"

"Right off I felt the possibilities were tantalizing," replied Adam. "And supported by other evidence, literary and archaeological."

"What other kinds of other evidence?"

"To answer that question," replied Adam, "we need to travel to the mountains near Lake Tana, then to the ancient town of Aksum. On our way, I will tell you an intriguing story—a story which lies at the very root of this whole mystery."

The scene changed again. The two BBC representatives with them—Bridges and their producer—set up various sites as backdrops to Adam's continuing tour of the country to interweave with the story of the ark.

"The curious fact that has to be accounted for," Adam began at another site en route to the mountainous region of Lake Tana, "are the Jewish roots in Ethiopia. They are of extremely ancient date, originating many centuries before Christ. I call this a curious fact because we see it no place else in Africa—not Egypt, not Kenya . . . nowhere. How did the religion of the Jews find its way to *Ethiopia?* And so long ago, extending back to 1000 B.C."

"I see what you've been saying—it is a fact that has to be accounted for."

"My point exactly. For journalist and archaeologist alike, *why* is always the question. There have to be explanations. There is a connective link between the two countries right around the time when Solomon was king of Israel. Some even claim that one or more of the lost tribes of Israel exist to this day in the Simien mountains and around Lake Tana in Ethiopia, among the indigenous Jews known as *Falashas*. That is where we are headed."

"What does the *Kebre Negast* say about all this?"

"I feel it offers a plausible explanation. The epic basically tells the story of a beautiful young queen by the name of Makeda who came to the throne of Ethiopia sometime not many years after 1000 B.C."

He nodded with a significant expression.

"Here's where the story gets interesting," he went on. "This Ethiopian Queen Makeda had heard of a great king to the north. Reports said he was the wisest man in all the earth. So she decided to travel to Israel to learn what she could from this man."

"Solomon!" exclaimed Lindberg.

"Precisely, Jim. The Hebrew king was only too delighted to hear that such a woman wanted to visit him. When she arrived, he received her with great fanfare. And immediately he was overwhelmed by her beauty. Solomon listened to her request, and agreed to teach her the art of rule and statecraft.

Queen Makeda gave Solomon gifts of gold, spices, and other gems. In turn he taught her many things, including the Jewish faith. Makeda was so enthusiastic about what she learned, in fact, that she converted to Judaism."

"The connection with the Ethiopian tradition!" said Lindberg.

(6)

Anni D'Abernon stared at the computer screen filled with Halder Zorin's face as if silently commanding it to yield some secret that would enable her to gain mastery over him.

She hated him. Even the electronic likeness of his eyes possessed power. She hated him because she recognized him as her greatest threat. Had they been ordinary mortals, they might have loved each other. A passionate love it might have been. They would probably have destroyed one another in the end.

D'Abernon stared into Zorin's eyes with intensity, daring the unmoving image to come to life, that the two inheritors of the Dimensional Eye might each probe the other's depths to determine once and for all which would rule and which would be defeated. In her heart, she knew that ultimately it would come to such an encounter.

She looked across her office toward the safe. Yes, she possessed a power none of the others knew of. If only she knew more of what her father had known in the mysteries of its use. But his unexpected death had taken much of the ancient familial wisdom to the grave.

D'Abernon glanced away. Things were fraying around the edges. Her family's and the entire order's legacy now rested with her. She realized well enough that Montreux and Vaughan-Maier were concerned. They thought she had become too preoccupied with the Zorin problem. But they didn't understand the gravity of the situation. They were her closest colleagues. But they were still men. Subtleties sometimes escaped them. She knew Zorin's power. The Council had authorized it. It could not be so easily destroyed.

Before she did anything about Adam Livingstone, she *had* to put an end to Halder Zorin. Hopefully the new Ethiopian enterprise would resolve it. If they could just keep Zorin from messing it up.

Behind her the private telephone rang. She walked across the floor and picked it up without speaking.

"He is not in Baku," said Bonar's voice on the other end.

A silent curse exploded in D'Abernon's brain. But she retained her poise.

"You went to his home?"

"Vacant. Servants on indefinite holiday."

"You made . . . discreet and thorough inquiries?"

"He is said to have left the country, destination unknown."

"I see . . . then remain in the city and learn what more you can. I will investigate here. His movements have not been invisible in recent years. If I find a track that appears promising, I will have you follow it."

(7)

"Originally you said your research began with the Bible," said Lindberg, "and then you were led to the *Kebre Negast*. Does the Bible confirm these Ethiopian legends?"

"You may have heard of the Queen of Sheba," said Adam in reply.

"Ah—*now* I see the connection!"

"According to the Jewish historian Josephus," replied Adam, "Queen Makeda of Ethiopia was none other than the biblical Queen of Sheba."

Adam paused as they walked, opening the Bible he was carrying.

"The Queen of Sheba's visit to Jerusalem is recounted in 2 Chronicles 9," he went on, as he found the passage he was seeking. "It is brief, but as I say—tantalizing." Adam read the account on camera.

"I think I may be beginning to understand how the pieces fit," said Lindberg. "Is this relationship between Solomon and Queen Makeda the basis for Ethiopia's descent of kings?"

"Exactly. A son was the eventual result of the relationship—half Hebrew, half Ethiopian. The boy's name was Menyelek. Queen Makeda returned to Ethiopia, bore a son, and when he was of age, he returned to Israel, to his father Solomon."

"Why did he return?"

"Some think Solomon wanted Menyelek to succeed him as Israel's king. But the young man's future in Israel was doomed from the start. It is a very contemporary story—Menyelek was a half-breed, not a pure Jew, and there was obviously prejudice against him. In any event, after a year at Solomon's court, Menyelek returned to Ethiopia. When he did, according to the *Kebre Negast*, it was with something more priceless than all the treasures that had exchanged hands between his mother and his father."

"The ark of the covenant?" said Lindberg.

Adam nodded. "And that is how the ark wound up in Ethiopia—it was stolen from Jerusalem by Menyelek, the son of Solomon and the Queen of Sheba."

"And you believe the account?"

"I am saying that the *Kebre Negast* makes that claim," replied Adam.

They arrived at Lake Tana.

"What happened after the young man Menyelek returned to Ethiopia?" asked Lindberg.

"Legend says they brought the ark originally to the mountain which lies in the middle of Lake Tana . . . right over there," said Adam, pointing behind him across the water. "It is called *Tana Kirkos,* or *Debra Makeda,* the mountain of the queen. There it is supposed to have resided in an inauspicious tabernacle, worshiped by the ancient Jewish strain present in Ethiopia. And then, after the country was converted to Christianity, the ark was transferred to Aksum. The Ethiopians see the ark's presence as evidencing the transfer of God's covenant from Israel to Ethiopia. They see theirs as the successor to Israel's position as God's chosen nation. They guard that role with jealousy."

"That's an even more astounding claim than possession of the ark—Ethiopia as God's chosen land."

"These people believe it," replied Adam. "That is what the *Timkat* celebrates—that heritage. We will be watching the celebration three days from now."

(8)

Filming broke while the van drove into the nearby mountains above Lake Tana to visit a settlement of indigenous Falasha Jews.

"How did you come here to Ethiopia?" Adam asked one of the priests of the community. "Did your ancestors leave Israel during one of the exiles?"

"Long before that," said the man, eyeing the cameraman twenty feet away with suspicion.

"How long?" asked Adam.

"We have always been here."

"But when did you come . . . originally?"

The man nodded, as if to repeat the answer already given.

"How did the Jewish faith migrate from Israel to Ethiopia?" persisted Adam. "Have your ancestors been here since before the time of Herod's temple, even before the Hasmonaeans?"

"That is correct."

"When did your ancestors come, then?" Adam persisted.

"We came with the ark," replied the man matter-of-factly. "We are the lost tribe. That is why it has pleased God to protect the ark in our possession all these centuries."

The man ambled away. Adam thought it best not to press it further. He walked back toward the others as the camera continued to roll.

"As we researched the history of this isolated people," Adam said in a soft voice approaching the camera, "we discovered that indeed many Falasha traditions are of such antiquity as to scarcely bear resemblance to modern Judaism. Many of their traditions, in fact, resemble the Judaism existing at the time of Solomon."

"What is your explanation?" asked Lindberg, now moving on camera with Adam.

"It would seem that their roots are not linked to modern Judaism, but rather extend directly back to 1000 B.C. If indeed the ancestors of these

Falashas were transplanted to Ethiopia from Jerusalem by the small band who came in the ninth century before Christ, and in the years since this pocket of Judaism was never connected to the changes that came to the Jewish faith elsewhere . . . it would certainly seem to answer the evidence. In other words, exactly as that man told us—because the ancestors of these people came with the ark."

"That is an astounding thing," remarked Lindberg. "That in these Falashas and their customs, we may actually be touching, however faintly, some portion of the Jewish faith that existed in Jerusalem three millennia ago."

"These people are *living* reminders," said Adam, "of a very ancient past."

"And yet they possess the ark no longer?"

"After Ethiopia was Christianized in the 300s," replied Adam, "the story is that the Christians took it. They built a church to house the ark, and brought it from the mountain island in Lake Tana to Aksum."

"So that's the completion of the route," said Lindberg. "Menyelek and his comrades took the ark from Jerusalem. It travelled with them through Egypt, eventually arriving at Tana Kirkos."

"Until the 300s A.D., around the same time as the Catholic Church began enshrining biblical points of interest in Jerusalem as well," added Adam. "Legend has it that the Christians took it to St. Mary's of Zion church in Aksum, where it remains to this day. And that is our next stop."

(9)

Though it was cold back in England, the temperature in Aksum, the ancient Ethiopian city on the fourteenth parallel north of the equator, was a balmy twenty-six degrees Celsius.

Scott, Jen, Juliet, and Adam led the film crew through Aksum in preparation for the yearly processional that had been celebrated in Ethiopia for centuries. Adam explained what they would be seeing.

As the crew filmed the chapel of St. Mary's of Zion church, Adam whispered to Juliet,"There it is, behind those walls."

"I have to admit," she said softly, "I like it better in daylight with you beside me! Do you think they know you broke in . . . and about the photographs?"

"I'm not sure," replied Adam. "As far as I can tell, I don't think they even know we're back in the country. No one has looked twice at us."

"You'd think if they felt a threat they wouldn't bring the ark out for this celebration."

The brief moment was quickly over. Jim Lindberg approached again, his cameraman behind him.

"Explain to us something of the *Timkat*," he said as the camera again focused on Adam.

"It is the great yearly religious celebration in Ethiopia," replied Adam.

"*Timkat* stands for epiphany. But it has a different significance in Ethiopia than for the holy day by that name in the western Church. It represents the time once yearly when they bring out the ark of the covenant and celebrate and dance and sing as the processional proceeds through the streets of Aksum."

"They actually bring the ark out into public view? Will we see it?"

"No one actually *sees* it. Whatever object leads the processional, it remains covered. Whether it is actually the ark has always been the question. They *say* it is the ark. But to every more specific inquiry, the only answers are along the line of, 'The ark is a great mystery.' When they dance and sing, the object of the celebration remains covered with ornately decorated cloth and thick blankets. Some think it to be a replica of the ark. The Ethiopians have always been fond of making replicas of the ark. That's why in every church we visited throughout Ethiopia, large or small, icons and especially tabots of the ark, are visibly in evidence."

"What explanation is there for such replicas?"

"I don't know," answered Adam. "It has puzzled me from the beginning. I have no answer for it."

Two hours later they stood as the sacred processional approached. Brightly clad priests and followers danced and sang in celebration of David's dance before the ark. A variety of musical instruments, drums, tambourines, traditional Ethiopian music and dress and dancing accompanied solemn priests chanting and spreading incense as they went. The atmosphere blended reminders of Eastern Orthodox Christianity with the spirit of a Mardi Gras. The entire festive atmosphere could only be described as distinctly and wonderfully African.

"Do you understand any of this?" asked Lindberg as the singing, dancing processional came toward them.

"Very little," answered Adam. "It is called the dance of David. They are celebrating the ark based on 2 Samuel 6:14. Look . . . here it comes."

In the midst of the processional came four priests bearing an object aloft on poles.

"I'm sure you see what I mean," said Adam. "It *could* resemble the ark."

"The shape is roughly consistent with the traditional image, as well as the photographs you presented last month," added Lindberg. "However, it is so thickly draped with ornately embroidered cloths and fringed blankets and linens that it is impossible to tell what is beneath them."

As the crew filmed the procession continued on by them. Gradually its sounds retreated into the distance.

(10)

The next day they took a break from filming on the documentary. Adam again sought through official channels to gain permission to view the ark in the open. But the answer was the same as every official request he had made before.

Two evenings later in their suite at the hotel, he and his team discussed how to conclude the filming.

"All right," he said, "we've exhausted every avenue. If they continue to insist on secrecy, I think it is time we threw a bomb into the middle of our documentary. What do you think?"

"What are you suggesting?" asked Juliet with a worried tone.

"Nothing dangerous," replied Adam, laughing. "Just tossing a little firecracker into the hornet's nest by way of a dramatic climax to our documentary."

They stared at Adam, waiting.

"Why not go public all the way with it—alerting the media, and just saying, 'Hey, guys—we *know* you've got it.'"

"Right on, Boss!" exclaimed Scott.

"Let's go for it!" chimed in Jen.

"Then I think I shall make a few well-placed calls tonight to various news agencies in Addis Ababa," Adam went on, "and in the morning to Aksum's newspeople. We'll also get in touch with CNN and UPI tonight. I think it's time we brought this documentary onto the front page."

"Are you going to tell Jim?" asked Jen.

"We'll let him in on it tomorrow. He'll love it. We'll put word out to the media that we are filming a documentary on the *Timkat* and the ark of the covenant. We'll let it be known that we'll be shooting the final climax tomorrow afternoon . . . how does three o'clock sound? That should give everyone a chance to get here, but not give the Ethiopians enough advance warning to kick us out!"

(11)

Several minutes after two the next afternoon, Adam and his team and the BBC film crew rolled up in their van. A good-sized crowd had already gathered. Police and uniformed army officials were clearly in evidence, spread all around St. Mary's.

"What's this about, Livingstone?" said an American reporter whom Adam had known for some years.

"Wait and see, DeWald," replied Adam. "We've been filming a documentary for the BBC."

"On the ark of the covenant, according to my sources. Is it here, Livingstone?"

"Wait and see, DeWald . . . that's what I hope we will find out."

The reporter scurried off for his camera, as did several others who had overheard the exchange. A brushfire of speculation spread through the crowd. Cameras from a half-dozen networks were already rolling.

Adam waited for his own film crew to get ready. Though a palpable undercurrent of tension was present, a hush of expectancy settled over the scene. Everyone waited to see what would happen next. Another news team arrived and hurriedly ran forward, then the engine of another van could be heard racing toward them. Moments later out piled several more photographers who had only learned of the incident the previous day and had driven all night from Nairobi. When Adam judged the buildup sufficient, he walked forward to the main gate. Lindberg gave the signal to Bridges at the camera.

"We're here to speak with the Guardian of the ark," said Adam to a uniformed Ethiopian who appeared in charge.

The jitteriness of the contingent of army guards increased slightly. They glanced about at the cameras.

The man did not acknowledge Adam's statement. Instead, he turned and spoke to one of the policemen standing inside the fenced compound, who then pivoted and walked toward the church and disappeared inside. Three minutes later, a tall, robed priest, with white hair and deeply bronzed skin, came out of the building and slowly walked across the compound toward them. His gait was deliberate, his expression dispassionate.

"Are you the Guardian of the ark?" asked Adam as he came near.

"The people of God guard his priceless possessions in their hearts," came the true but evasive reply in English.

Adam smiled and nodded. "Well spoken—a shrewd answer, and true."

The man did not reply, nor acknowledge Adam's statement by the slightest twitch of facial muscle.

"But I am here to inquire about one very special possession," persisted Adam, "which in truth does belong to all God's people, but which you have been keeping to yourselves for generations. It is time for you to allow the rest of the world to participate in the knowledge of this priceless treasure."

Adam and the aging descendant of Cush stared into one another's eyes with the expression of adversaries each testing the will of the other, yet also with the subtle admiration of brotherhood.

"We know the ark is inside," said Adam at length. His voice was calm, respectful.

"The ark is a great mystery," came the soft words of reply.

"Why will you not make it public? As you yourself said, God's most priceless possessions must be guarded in the heart. I am asking you to allow God's people the world over the privilege of knowing this treasure in their hearts."

"Some mysteries must remain mysteries."

"But the ark is no longer a mystery in the way you mean. You know it is there, behind you—" Adam pointed to the Sanctuary building beside the main church. "And *we* know it," he continued.

A mysterious smile was the priest's only reply.

"The mystery you speak of is right behind those walls," said Adam again, "and I have the photographs to prove it."

Adam pulled out the folder he had been holding, and with dramatic flourish removed a handful of pictures. Cameras everywhere zoomed in as ripples of exclamation spread through the crowd.

"Look, Mr. Guardian . . . look at these. These photographs were taken *inside* the Sanctuary behind you. In the name of the whole world, I am asking that you let the world see the ark."

By now police were arriving in increasing numbers. The scene showed signs of becoming ugly. The crowd began to chant. "Open the Sanctuary, let out the ark!"

The chief guard to whom Adam had first spoken stepped forward. Before Adam realized what was happening, the man had grabbed the photographs from him.

"We will have to confiscate these," he said.

"But wait . . . those are—" Adam began to protest.

He took a step toward the man with his hand outstretched.

Suddenly a dozen or more army guards, still as statues till that moment, sprang into action. They brought rifles off their shoulders and approached the scene. Instantly Adam stopped in his tracks.

"Relax . . . relax, everyone," said Scott Jordan's voice behind Adam. "Come on, Adam . . . back away, and we'll just fade into the sunset. These guys are a little too nervous to suit me."

Adam lowered his hand and took a step or two back. The crowd was silent, the tension thick. Neither priest nor head guard showed hint of expression on their dark faces. The standoff only lasted a few seconds.

Then noises and shouts erupted from the Sanctuary behind them.

Two or three guards came running out, waving their arms and yelling frantically. The Guardian had sent someone to check the basement security before coming out to the main gate. And the result of that brief probe was now shouted out for every major news service in the world to capture live on film.

(12)

"It's gone . . . the ark is gone!" they shouted. "The ark of the covenant has been stolen!"

Pandemonium broke out.

Everyone was shouting and yelling. Policemen and soldiers were running about. Cameras tried to capture the bedlam on film. Journalists were speaking into cameras and microphones and tape recorders.

Adam found himself at the center of shouts and scuffling and commotion, all cameras attempting to find him in the middle of the commotion.

He felt hands tugging him away.

"Come on," said Scott's voice.

"But we can't . . . we have to find out. . . ."

"Let them sort it out," insisted Scott. "We'll find out what happened later. Right now we've got to get you out of here. If we hang around, you'll end up in some Ethiopian jail. Jim," he yelled over his shoulder to Lindberg, "load up your people. Juliet, Jen . . . into the van. We've got to split."

In the hubbub of movement, sirens began to sound. Army guards and police ran everywhere. The Guardian of the ark had disappeared.

In a daze, Adam felt himself pulled away, then surrounded in a sea of faces of many colors, then a coat or blanket thrown over his head. He was shoved into the open door of a vehicle and pushed to the floor. A door slammed, an engine roared.

The vehicle bounded away, and soon the sounds of the crowd and sirens receded out of his hearing behind him.

✦ ✦ ✦

The word of the Lord came to me . . . :

". . . go now . . . and hide it there in a crevice in the rocks."

So I went and hid it . . . as the Lord told me.

JEREMIAH 13:3-5

✦ ✦ ✦

PROLOGUE

Jeremiah's Secret

Jerusalem, 586 B.C.

Flames lit the summer night sky. Though smoke billowing from Lachish, Azekah, and Jericho could not be seen through the night, the bitter stench of conquest lay over Judah like a black cloud. The year-long siege had reached its inevitable climax. The city's food supply was exhausted. The Babylonian army had breached Jerusalem's walls two hours before. Its warriors now poured in. Destruction would be complete when the sun rose again.

Each of the three figures moving with stealth among the shadows knew that before morning their bodies could lie among the toppled stones of these ancient walls. Yet before such a fate overtook them, perhaps they might preserve the most precious reminder of their nation's sacred heritage . . . if not for themselves, for a generation who would follow. For surely God's people would return after the days of their impending captivity.

They hastened through the streets to the appointed rendezvous. Waiting with torch in hand, the Prophet greeted each with solemn nod, then proceeded into a narrow alleyway between two buildings. The three followed.

Shouts, screams, mayhem, and confusion erupted randomly about them. The tramping feet of Nebuchadnezzar's soldiers echoed in the distance. They had already set fire to the outlying portions of the city. King Zedekiah had fled toward the Jordan. There was no doubt the end had come to the kingdom of Judah.

They must make haste. What they were about to do, if discovered by their Levitical peers, would cost them not only their priestly robes, but their lives. Even if not discovered, it could cost them their lives. By the hand of God, not men.

Baruch, son of Neriah, of noble birth, brother of King Zedekiah's chamberlain, trembled at the idea. Would they be struck dead, as tradition had it, for entering the sacred place and tampering with its contents? If so, he prayed Yahweh would be merciful to their souls.

Jerusalem's prophet had foretold this day for years. Baruch had stood in the city's streets, listening to the man of God shouting to passersby: "O Jerusalem, wash the evil from your heart. A besieging army is coming, raising a war cry against the cities of Judah. They surround her like men guarding a field, because she has rebelled against me, declares the Lord. The whole land will be ruined. Flee from Jerusalem!"

Few paid him heed.

Baruch was one of those who listened. Many said he threw away what would have been a life of high position by casting his lot with such a fanatic. But the Prophet's words stirred him. He had become the Prophet's friend and disciple, and in time, his scribe. With his own hand, Baruch wrote down the oracles and prophecies. Thus when the Prophet came to him by night two days ago, as he had Nuri and Mishael, Baruch obeyed. Dire were the straits to which Judah had been reduced. Baruch knew the Prophet's worst fears had come to pass.

They came alongside one of Solomon's ancient walls.

The Prophet paused and glanced about. Gesturing for the three to follow, he ducked into the shadowy recess of an adjacent building, opened a door, then disappeared. A moment later they stood inside a chamber scarcely large enough for four men. The door locked behind them. They saw only blackness.

A scraping sound, stone against stone . . . then a chink of light shone up from below. It widened, coming from an opening in the floor. Again their eyes could make out forms in the dark. They now bent to the task of assisting their leader in removing the heavy floor stone. A minute later they were following the Prophet down steep narrow stairs into the underground passageway where a flickering wick awaited them. He took the lamp from its wall stand, then proceeded through the tunnel that yawned ahead of them.

The four walked single file as rapidly as the confined walls of dirt and stone allowed, turning right, then left, and at many angles. All sense of direction soon left the three shuffling in the shadows behind the lamp. All was quiet, save breathing and muffled footsteps.

At last the corridor widened. The Prophet stopped, then turned to face the three he had chosen for this important errand.

The thin light from the lamp he held flickered upon his face. The features were rugged, worn by the sorrow of his eyes. At sixty-four, Jeremiah ben Hilkiah of priestly lineage was Judah's most reviled and persecuted prophetic spokesman. He had foretold destruction for forty years. Though the events of this night confirmed the divine inspiration of his predictions and would ensure his legacy as one of humankind's great prophets, no joy was on his face. Only tearstained ridges of grief and heartache.

He loved this city, this land, and its people. Had he not spoken the poignant words being fulfilled before his very eyes? "Take warning, O Jerusalem . . . put on sackcloth and roll in ashes, for suddenly the destroyer will come. An army is coming from the land of the north. They come to attack you, O Daughter of Zion."

But the season for prophecies was past. He had been faithful to speak what God had given him. His warnings had not been heeded. Now God had given him something else to do. If this secret mission were ever known, it might be centuries, even millennia, before what he did this night came to light.

"What you are about to see has been known but to few," said the Prophet. His voice sounded as ancient as the gaze in his eyes. "Certain of the caves and passageways under the city are well known. But these catacombs under the temple, even below the great foundation stone itself and extending far below and northwestward beneath the ridge of the holy mount, have been unknown

but to a very few since our father David's time. What you will see in the Holy Place above where we now stand, even my eyes have never beheld. Where we will venture deep into the earth, no one alive knows of but myself. I must put into the earth what the Lord has commanded me. It may be said in some future time that angels came to the Holy City to rescue its sacred objects, and that the earth opened before them. But we are only God's men doing as he bids us. Knowledge of what we do this night will remain a sacred trust for us to carry forth to our people if the Lord wills us to survive this night."

He glanced earnestly at each one. "Do you solemnly pledge to the Lord your faithfulness to this trust?"

"We so pledge," answered each of the three.

"Then come," said Jeremiah. "Have no fear. The Lord our God is with us."

He turned, opened a door in the stone face of wall, which moved, though with some sound, with apparent ease, then led upward back up out of the tunnel.

✦ ✦ ✦

Ten minutes later, the four emerged again into the fateful night.

The three who followed knew nothing about the secret passageway, but saw that they now stood within the temple walls. The sounds of the Babylonian army and its destruction came again to their ears, closer now. More flames illuminated the sky. Smoke filled their nostrils.

Only a few moments did they remain in the night air. The edges of the Prophet's robe flew behind him as he hastened across the white stones of the temple courtyard. He began to fear they had delayed too long.

The three quickened their pace to match his long stride. Up the stairs they hurried, across the porch, and toward the Holy Place. No other soul was about. If the presence of the Most High was still here, his was the only presence. Judah's priests had fled with the king.

The Prophet hesitated, pausing on the final step. He turned back and allowed his eyes to take in one final gaze over the city. In a fleeting second his whole life passed through his brain.

Jeremiah recalled the Lord's first words to him. He had resisted at first, claiming youthfulness and an inability to speak. But his objections carried no more weight with the Most High than had those of Moses almost a thousand years before him. God commanded him to speak, and therefore he had spoken.

"O Jerusalem!" Jeremiah prayed as his eyes passed over the silhouettes of its buildings. "You wonderful, foolish, stubborn city–how I love you. Yet how you have squandered your sacred inheritance. Oh, but Lord God," he added, lifting his voice to heaven, "raise this city again, even from the rubble of this heathen army. Go with your people as they are scattered this night. Bring them back, Lord, to the holy mount, to the city of David."

He exhaled a deep sigh of grief, then hastened on. Baruch and his comrades followed.

✦ ✦ ✦

A minute later they were inside the Holy Place and approaching the Holy of Holies. The Prophet strode without hesitation across the floor toward the doors of entry. He had long been on intimate terms with him whose presence dwelt in this innermost room of the temple. He knew him well enough to fear him without being afraid.

Not so confident were his companions. As he placed his hands on the olive-wood doors into the Holy of Holies, their steps faltered.

The Prophet felt their hesitation and turned. Even in the dark he saw that the color had drained from their faces.

"Come," he urged. "I cannot carry the ark alone. It must be removed."

"But . . ."

"You need have no fear, Baruch," said Jeremiah. "He is with us. He will protect us."

"Are you not afraid?" asked the young scribe and disciple.

"Even I have never ventured here," replied the Prophet. "For years God has been speaking to me, sometimes in mysterious ways. He has often told me to hide things. His commands have puzzled me. He told me to hide a linen belt and later to take it out of its hiding place. He told me to hide large stones and bury them in the pavement before Pharaoh's palace. He told me to buy a field and to hide the documents and deeds in clay vessels so they would last for many years, even as the sacred tablets were hidden in the ark. He has even hidden me away—in prison, in a cistern. Now he has shown me that these were all but signs to prepare me for this night, to ready me for what he would give me to do—hide away the Lord's presence until the day of his appearing. The prophecies of the linen belt and the stones hidden in clay and documents hidden in jars are now to be fulfilled. Come . . . see, I have no fear."

Jeremiah opened the doors and walked inside past the veil. Still timid, Baruch followed. He trusted the Prophet, yet traditions of the ark's power went deep. Every young Hebrew was taught the command of Numbers 4:15: They must not touch the holy things, or they will die. Well they knew the story of Uzzah, who steadied the ark when the oxen pulling it stumbled, and who had been struck down dead on the spot.

Light from the Prophet's torch illuminated the holy chamber.

A hush descended. All sounds of the siege faded. The four men about the business of angels stopped. There rested the ark upon its table, with its gold mercy seat and two gold-wrought cherubim. Jeremiah approached and put his hand to one of the carrying acacia poles. His three companions watched in astonishment. He motioned to Baruch to take hold of the other end. The young man came forward with tentative step and wide eyes. Fearfully he grasped the end of the pole. A tingle of awe surged through his arm at the touch. The others likewise took hold of the ends of the other pole.

A series of hasty instructions followed. A few moments later each of the four lifted the sacred burden, then began to make their way slowly across the stone floor. Carefully they left the room and retraced their steps the way they had come. Outside the Holy Place, shouts and fire grew closer.

With hurried step they hastened through the night without words.

Again came the return descent into the tunnel. Managing it was tight work. Reaching the bottom, they set down their load and briefly relaxed. The Prophet ran back up the stairway to secure the door of stone above them. No one must know of their movements.

Jeremiah rejoined his comrades and now led them deeper and deeper below the bowels of the city. Thirty minutes later, none of the three accompanying the Prophet had an idea where they had come. There were other sacred vaults beneath the temple that the Prophet knew about, but they were not of concern now. They too contained secrets, but of other kinds than this. On this night he led his companions away from the temple precincts, traversing beneath the city walls toward the northwest. They had generally walked along a parallel to the ridge of Mount Moriah above them toward its northwesternmost point. They were not far from Solomon's quarries, in the same labyrinth of hiding places where David had once sought refuge from his enemies and escaped from Jerusalem by night. Now, four centuries later, these of David's sons had come through many twisting passageways, circling, turning, descending. They stood in remote caverns where no human foot had trod since the great king's.

Again they paused with their holy burden at the junction of three passages. Fatigue replaced anxiety.

"We have nearly reached our destination," said Jeremiah. "Baruch, help me roll aside this stone in the wall. Mishael, take my torch."

Both did as instructed. In a second another passageway was revealed behind the wall.

"These regions are unknown to our people," said the Prophet. "When our task is accomplished, we will seal off this passage with smaller stones. This section of the tombs will be closed off from communication with the outside world. It will not be discovered until such day as the Lord himself reveals it. Here will the ark be safe, with the cherubim to watch over it, until such time as Yahweh decrees an end to the captivity of his people."

The three listened with awe.

"To us is entrusted the secret of this hiding place," Jeremiah continued. "The Lord will see to it that one of us survives what has come upon the city, whether here or carried away to Babylon. Now come. We must take it into the cavern that will be the final resting place of God's salvation."

Again they followed, making tight work of their burden. Beyond the opening the way again became easier through the large cave. Then again a narrow passageway, down a slope, and at length they arrived at the final grotto. With care they eased the sacred object into its hiding place.

The Prophet's voice was soft, but in it they felt the ageless authority of Yahweh's anointed spokesman. "To none must you divulge what you know," he said, "and what we do here this night."

Jeremiah eyed his companions earnestly.

"Do each of you so pledge your faithfulness before the Lord to preserve the secret of our heritage?"

"We pledge," they said.

"When the season of captivity ends, a new day of revelation will draw nigh," said Jeremiah. "Then shall our descendents make known the secret of this night. The law and Atonement will be one. Then will come the day when the power of God will be revealed to all the earth."

"Praise be to the Lord," said Baruch, son of Neriah.

"Praise be to the Most High," said Nuri, son of Gurion.

"Praise be to Yahweh," said Mishael Ben-aryeh.

"Praise his name," said Jeremiah, son of Hilkiah.

Part Four

AMSTERDAM

✦ ✦ ✦

In those days . . . men shall speak no more

of the Ark of the Covenant of the Lord;

they shall not think of it nor remember it;

it will not be missed.

JEREMIAH 3:16, NEB, NIV

✦ ✦ ✦

thirteen

Clues and Catastrophe

(1)

Adam walked though the Amsterdam airport. As he passed a news kiosk featuring daily papers from around Europe, his eyes fell on one of the English editions.

ADAM LIVINGSTONE SOUGHT IN ARK THEFT read the headlines. A photograph below showed a drawing of the ark of the covenant. As Adam slowed for a closer look, he saw that under the photo were the words, "English archaeologist disappears. Ethiopian officials enraged."

He walked on. He hadn't exactly disappeared. Scott had thrown a coat over his head to get him out of sight, shoved him onto the floor of the van, and whisked him away before anyone had the chance to arrest him. But he would have to sort that out later. Soon after arriving back in England a mysterious delivery had arrived at Sevenoaks which sent him out of the country again.

The message was cryptic: "If you want to see the ark again, be in front of the Amsterdam Opera House at 8:50 on the morning of . . . It is your only hope of clearing yourself. Come alone."

He obviously had to comply. So here he was on the way to what sounded like a very peculiar meeting. He had taken the 6:40 flight from Gatwick, landed in Amsterdam twenty minutes ago, and was booked on a return flight at 3:15 this afternoon. By then he would know what was going on, and have something to take to Inspector Thurlow at Scotland Yard. If it meant temporarily giving himself up in order to convince the Ethiopian authorities that he had nothing to do with the burglary, he was willing to go that far. He just wanted some concrete information to bring to the table. Hopefully this bizarre junket to the continent would provide it.

Suddenly Adam realized he had been surrounded as he walked by several men in business suits. Not a word was spoken. It was clear that from now on he was with them.

They led him to a waiting limousine. He was ushered into the backseat. His escorts disappeared after slamming the door shut. The driver sped out of the airport. Adam knew questions would be pointless. They left the city, drove for perhaps twenty minutes, and came eventually to a lightly wooded region where few houses were visible.

(2)

The car slowed.

Through mechanized gates they entered a large country estate. A winding paved drive went on for approximately three-quarters of a mile. The car stopped in front of a sprawling, two-story brick house of nineteenth-century modern Dutch design.

The car door at his side opened. Adam stepped out. He was met and led inside by a butler who could have stepped out of a P. G. Wodehouse novel and no doubt likewise had some set of double letters in his name. Moments later he found himself standing in a book-lined but sparsely furnished library. The room was obviously not intended as a haven for reading and relaxation, but rather a place to wait and be impressed by the facade of intellectualism.

Six or seven minutes passed.

A door opened behind him. Adam turned. A distinguished gentleman he faintly recognized entered. He was impeccably dressed and appeared in his mid-sixties. He was followed by a tall, imposing woman of obvious breeding, reminiscent of the Amazon sort, whom he recognized instantly from Cairo. Hers was neither a face nor a demeanor he would easily forget. Immediately he stiffened. He knew he was in the presence of adversarial forces.

"Mr. Livingstone," said the white-haired man, "I am glad you are able to join us. My name is Rupert Vaughan-Maier."

"I could hardly refuse," replied Adam a little stiffly. "Where is the ark of the covenant?"

"All in good time, Mr. Livingstone. Perhaps it has not escaped your attention that it is *we* who are in the position to ask the questions. Patience and cooperation on your part will be rewarded in due course."

Out of the corner of his eye Adam detected the hint of a smile on the woman's lips, almost as if she were amused by her colleague's affable manner toward the enemy. In that instant Adam realized that ultimately this contest would come down to a battle of wills between himself and her.

"We are aware," continued Vaughan-Maier when Adam did not reply to his previous statement, "of your difficulties with the Ethiopian authorities. . . ."

Adam continued silent.

"We have it in our power to see that you are cleared of the charges, *if* you cooperate with us . . . or to make your life, shall we say, difficult, should you chose any other option."

"Your message said you had information on the ark's whereabouts," now said Adam.

"We do." Vaughan-Maier nodded. "All we ask from you is information."

"What kind of information?"

"We are desirous of learning of the location of other sacred items."

Memories and snatches of images came back to Adam, most vividly the reminder of these same two faces staring at him from an escaping helicopter in Scotland. Whatever else they were, they had certainly been involved in Juliet's kidnapping. He found himself filled with both anger and heightened wariness.

"From our brief previous associations," he said cautiously, "I would not have been led to expect that you had an interest in sacred history."

"All things are not as they may appear, Mr. Livingstone. We have many interests."

"What do they have to do with me?"

"You seem knowledgeable in such areas. You have developed a knack for finding objects of a religious nature. You knew of the ark and somehow managed to photograph it. You claim knowledge of the fabled Garden. And there is obviously the matter of the large vessel in Turkey. All we want to know is what else you have access to."

Adam thought of the attempted sabotage in Turkey and wondered how much they knew of *that.*

"What makes you think I am aware of anything else?" he asked, even more on his guard.

"Tut, tut, Livingstone, it is useless to play games with us. We are realists—we will pay you handsomely, as well as removing this blot from your reputation. It may be that some sort of joint venture might be arranged for your future projects."

"I hardly think—"

"We have vast resources, Livingstone," interrupted Vaughan-Maier, trying to remain congenial. His patience, however, was wearing thin. "We may be able to help with your quest to make sacred artifacts more widely known. There are rumors of a grail, a bloodstained shroud, a certain robe of ancient date and Hebrew origin, old manuscripts of the book you people revere, a skull with purported connections to the Galilean prophet, pieces of wood from a Roman cross . . . perhaps other things."

"I know nothing of any of these."

"I do not know whether to believe you or not," said Vaughan-Maier.

"That is your choice," rejoined Adam. "I am telling the truth."

"You are lying," said the woman. "Enough of this, Rupert. He will not listen to reason. He will have to be coerced. You *will* tell us what we want to know," she said, fixing her powerful gaze intently upon Adam. "If you do not—"

She stopped. "It is useless," she said, speaking these first words to herself rather than either of the two men. "We are wasting our time. You will see soon enough."

She exited the room. Vaughan-Maier gestured with his arm, indicating that Adam was to follow.

(3)

Mrs. Andrea Graves had been agitated all morning.

To be more accurate, she had hardly slept a wink the previous night. That fact, however, she would never admit to a human soul. What had thrown her into such a turmoil was the simple statement from her employer that a guest was expected at Sevenoaks.

"By the by, Mrs. Graves," Adam said after dinner the previous evening, as if the fact were the merest detail of insignificance, "we shall be having a houseguest in a day or two."

The housekeeper nodded. Adam's next words, however, fell upon her ears like an unexpected bombshell.

"Mr. McCondy will be returning from America," he said. "I will be off early before you are up. But by the time I am back from Amsterdam, he should be on his way. He will be arriving sometime day after tomorrow. Have his room ready, will you please? Mrs. Beeves can help you if need be."

"Uh . . . oh, yes . . . yes, of course, Mr. Livingstone," replied the housekeeper. She was struggling to hide the fact that she had lost the capacity to breathe.

Just a houseguest!

The poor woman could hardly wait to excuse herself. She would begin preparations immediately!

What exactly about the American she liked even she couldn't have said. Things just seemed more *right* when he was around. He was part of the family. She had secretly hoped he would lay over in England a few days after returning from Turkey. But there had been no mention of it. Since then she had heard nothing to indicate when and if she would ever see him again.

Now he was coming back! She must have everything ready. She would go out later in the morning and get her shopping completed before Mr. Livingstone returned. At the top of her list would be to pick up a pound of fresh-ground coffee at a specialty shop she had located since Mr. McCondy's last visit.

(4)

Adam was led from the library outside behind the house where an enormous lawned park spread out for acres.

Straight ahead walked the woman. He followed.

In the distance, at the top of a small hill in the middle of unlandscaped but cleanly mown grass, Adam saw a plain white gazebo. Under the rising morning's sun, something gleamed from beneath it. As they drew closer, Adam's heart began to pound.

The bright reflection was . . . yes . . . definitely he could see the color of gold!

The woman stopped and turned to him. Adam's dumfounded gaze was riveted on the object sitting on a plain wooden table without poles some fifty feet in front of him.

"I see you recognize the artifact," she said with a smile, obviously enjoying the irony of the moment. "It was good of you to lead us to it."

The words slammed against Adam's spinning brain with the force of a wrecking ball.

"But . . . but I–"

"Come, Mr. Livingstone, we have been watching your every move for years."

"But . . . but how did you . . . where did–"

The amused chuckling of the Dutchman met his incredulous ears.

"Do you think you are the only one with connections and high-tech devices?" he said, drawing alongside the other two.

"We followed you, Mr. Livingstone," added the woman, "and you took us straight to it. I presume it may begin to dawn on you why it is pointless to play games with us. We will have what we want. You *will* tell us what you know, otherwise the consequences will be swift and irrevocable. Cooperate and you may leave here and take the object with you. If you will but trust us, all will be well."

She gestured almost disdainfully toward the gazebo with her hand. "Go . . . have a closer look, Mr. Livingstone. I am sure you will find it fascinating."

Adam half-staggered toward it, then stopped fifteen feet away, staring at it, then turning back with a look of incredulity and confusion.

"You see, Mr. Livingstone," said Vaughan-Maier, walking forward with the woman, "we brought you to Amsterdam in order to return it to you."

"But refuse, and we will destroy it before your eyes," added D'Abernon. "And the world will blame *you* for its loss."

"You cannot . . . *destroy* it," said Adam, incredulous at the idea.

"Ha! You think you possess the power to prevent us?"

"Of course I don't," said Adam. "It is the power of God which is not to be taken lightly."

"Bah–the power of God!" she spat back. "A cowardly being with no capacity to prevent us doing whatever we like. I might have thought better from an intelligent man like you, Mr. Livingstone."

She strode forward. Hesitantly Adam followed. She walked straight toward the box of apparent pure gold gleaming in the sun and stretched her hand toward it.

"Wait!" yelled Adam. "Don't touch it!"

She stopped, withdrew her hand, then faced Adam with a scornful smile.

"Why do you stop me, Mr. Livingstone. Would you save *my* life? You would save the life of your enemy?"

"Yes . . . yes, of course! You must not touch it, or–"

"Or I will die? You really are too amusing, Mr. Livingstone. All the more so that you actually believe the ancient fairy tale."

"It is true, I tell you," said Adam. "You must not–"

(5)

From behind a clump of trees a man now appeared and slowly approached across the lawn.

"Zorin, what in the–" began the Dutchman.

"What are you doing here?" exclaimed D'Abernon.

The newcomer continued forward, smiling disdainfully at their obvious annoyance. "I didn't want to miss out on the fun," he said.

"This is none of your concern."

"I am making it my concern."

"How did you get past–"

Zorin waved off the rest of the question with his hand. "You do not actually think you can keep secrets from me," he said. "Don't be so naive. But what have we here?" he went on, glancing toward the gazebo. "Ah, my Swiss friend," he said with affected significance, "I did not realize you were the superstitious sort. Some kind of religious ceremony, is it? Thinking of converting, are we? Is the good Mr. Livingstone witnessing, as I believe they call it, to you about the many benefits of following his God–"

"Silence, Zorin," said D'Abernon in a commanding voice. "I don't know where you have been hiding, but now that you are here, there is nothing I can do to prevent it."

As Adam watched the curious display, he was at first incredulous to see this conflict between the minions of evil. He recognized the new arrival too. But their petty argument encouraged him not to lose heart.

Silently he began to pray.

Zorin and D'Abernon continued to exchange venomous words in subdued tones. Adam's prayers increased in vigor and boldness.

Then the conversation between the two stopped. D'Abernon turned toward Adam. His eyes were open and he stared at her calmly, but his lips were moving imperceptibly. She had sensed prayer coming against her. She was both unnerved by it and, if possible, filled with yet greater hatred.

She left Zorin and approached Adam again. As she drew near she saw that he was speaking, though to none of them.

"*. . . hedge of protection, Lord, Jesus, around your ark . . . may your will and plan be accomplished,*" Adam whispered. After another moment he began quoting words from Psalm 91: *"He who dwells in the shelter of the Almighty . . ."*

She bore into him with her eyes for several long seconds but was unable to silence him.

(6)

The shocking words came off the page with such force it felt like the blast of a verbal shotgun at close range.

And if I have cheated anybody . . . I will pay him back four times the amount.

Larry Slate was nobody's fool. He knew a policy like that was a sure road to bankruptcy. He didn't know how it might have affected the economic standing of first-century tax collectors who liked to climb trees, but in today's economy it would be suicide.

Four times! It was the craziest thing he had ever heard of.

Yet there were the words on the page. What had possessed him to pick up the silly book in the first place? And who was this fellow Zacchaeus, or however you said his name? He must have been a sandwich short of a picnic in the brains department.

Actually, the account made Zacchaeus out as a crook. So maybe he deserved it.

But *he* was no crook! He was an honest businessman. He published a magazine. What was so wrong about that? He gave people what they paid for.

He slammed the idiotic book shut, jumped from the chair, and walked outside, trying to put the whole thing out of his mind. But it wasn't so easy. The single word kept peppering him with silent accusation.

Cheated . . . cheated . . . cheated . . .

No, he was no crook. But maybe something just as bad. An *honest* cheat . . . someone who had amassed a fortune cheating the truth.

His magazine empire, while operating within the law, was certainly no bastion of virtue. He had become worth millions playing on men's loneliness and lust. He had always tried to convince himself that he provided a legitimate service. But it was pornography, plain and simple. Who was he trying to kid? He was nothing more than a porn publisher.

How many people had he ever helped? On the other hand, how many marriages and young lives had he helped ruin? He was a multimillionaire many times over. Yet after reading those few words in the Testament a local pastor had had the courage to give him . . . suddenly it all seemed so empty, meaningless . . . even wrong.

He had contributed to the debasement of society, and lined his own pockets by preying on people's weaknesses. He had cheated the truth.

He was fifty-six. Was it too late to change all that?

But how could *he* possibly apply these words? If he really intended to take them to heart, what conclusion was there but that he had wronged *every* person who had ever bought one of his magazines?

There was no way to apply these words to *his* situation. It would take hundreds of million dollars to give everyone who had ever bought one of his magazines four times the cover price.

What was he thinking . . . the idea was ridiculous!

(7)

"You see, Mr. Livingstone," now said the white-haired Dutchman, "we are determined to stop the reading of the book. We will do whatever we have to. As my colleague said, we are prepared to destroy the object before you if necessary. It is really up to you."

"And you imagine that destroying it will stop people from seeking the truth?" said Adam. "I should think you would know better."

"Truth—bah!" exploded D'Abernon, finding her voice again. She was in no more mood to put up with Livingstone's stalling. "What is truth but an illusion of small minds? People are easily swayed. If the artifacts are destroyed, they will lose interest. The followers of the one you call your god have always been easily distracted to revere objects. By destroying the artifacts, we will destroy his power in their minds."

"You are seriously mistaken," rejoined Adam.

"I do not care to mince words with you. We will do what we have to do. I fear it is you who will find yourself mistaken."

Zorin had withdrawn several yards and now stood watching, amused. He was content to bide his time.

D'Abernon again approached the gazebo. This time no appearance of unwelcome guest stopped her from making the point she had begun earlier. Adam was shocked by her brazenness.

"You and what you call your god . . . Look, what kind of power does he have?" she taunted. "See, I can touch it without the consequences your fables speak of."

She reached out, paused melodramatically, then placed her hand on one of the golden angels and held it there.

A heavy silence followed. Adam's face registered stunned disbelief.

With her hand still clamped firmly on top of the lid, the Swisswoman threw back her head and laughed.

"Where is the power of your god, Livingstone?" she said with disdain. "You stand there praying like the fool you are, praying to this . . . ha, ha—a powerless box of gold!"

With both hands she grasped the edge and lifted the lid. "You pray to an empty box . . . a nothing! His presence, they say . . . ha, ha! Look . . . look inside, Livingstone—there is no presence here, no bones, no budding staff, no ridiculous tablets of stone."

"But . . . God's power—"

"Nothing can harm me. Nothing can harm any of us. Come, Rupert—show him."

Tentatively Vaughan-Maier appoached, and with a slight hesitation placed his hand on one of the gold sides.

"Power!" D'Abernon cried. "I will tell you of power. *We* possess the power of the new age. We are filled with *true* power, Livingstone. You are a fool if you think this box or your prayers or words from your book of fairy tales can stand against us. Now I ask you again, will you cooperate and tell us what we want to know? Will you tell us of the other artifacts?"

"The power of God is not in objects or artifacts," said Adam softly.

"Enough! He will listen to nothing," she said. "Come, Livingstone, come here. I am not asking you, I am *telling* you—look inside!"

Tentatively Adam approached. He felt a shove behind him. It was Zorin. The woman held open the lid with one arm.

"Look inside, Livingstone," she commanded again.

At last he peered into the box.

"But . . . that is—" he began.

"Yes." She laughed. "Exactly! A certain highly effective explosive. I see you recognize it. And do you see this?" she added, pulling a small electronic device from a pocket. "Right again—the detonator! Now do you see why you must tell us what we want to know? If you do not, I think you know what the result will be. You are a greater fool than I took you for if you imagine I will not use it."

"But I am telling you the truth," said Adam, shaking his head in horror. "I do not know of the objects you have mentioned."

"If you did, would you tell us?"

Adam did not reply. He did not know what he might do to save the ark.

Suddenly he felt himself pulled rudely away from the gazebo. D'Abernon still stood behind the table.

"We will get what we want, Livingstone," she said. "This means nothing to me. See—I fear nothing from your so-called god." She pounded on it with her clenched fist. "His power is nothing. This object is nothing. I mock it, I mock you . . . and I mock him! We will stop this interest in spiritual things," she cried. "We will stop it if we have to seek out all your idiotic sacred artifacts and destroy them one at a time."

"The power of God is not in the objects," said Adam. "You can destroy them all. You can kill me. But you will never stop God's power. The artifacts have no power in themselves. His power is in his Word—in his very being."

"You are a fool for worshiping such a one, Livingstone. Tell us what we want to know. This is your last chance before I give the order!"

The woman waited but a few seconds, then headed out of the gazebo. Adam staggered back. She walked but far enough to make sure she was out of danger. When they were a hundred feet from it, she again removed the object from her pocket, turned, and pointed it toward the gazebo.

"No!" cried Adam, breaking loose from Zorin's clutches.

But it was too late.

A great blast exploded in the morning air. A blinding light swallowed ark and gazebo together in a ball of orange fire.

The force and heat of the blast met Adam as he ran, jolting him to a standstill. In horror he stood gaping as fifty thousand shattered bits of wood and glass and metal dropped across the lawn like an evil rain, tinkling and crashing onto the scorched slab of concrete where only moments before the gazebo had stood.

Gradually the explosive echo died away. The residue of smoke from its fireball dissipated into the sky. Behind him the cruel laugh of the Swisswoman sliced like a tormenting knife into his soul.

"Go, Livingstone," said D'Abernon. "You are free to return to England. We are through with you, with your ark . . . and with your god."

From behind Adam felt arms gripping him. He did not resist. A cloth drenched in chloroform clamped harshly over his mouth and nose.

The light faded, his knees buckled, and he knew no more.

fourteen

Despondency

(1)

When Adam next became aware of existence, he was sitting on an airplane in midflight. How he got here or how long he had been onboard he hadn't an idea. It was late in the day, and he was on a different flight than scheduled. It took a few minutes for his head to clear. Finally memory returned. His first thought was that he had dozed into a bad dream. He must still be on the morning shuttle for Amsterdam.

He shook himself further awake and glanced out the window. There was the channel below him.

It had *not* been a dream, he thought. He was bound *toward* England!

A feeling of sickness and revulsion swept over him. What had he done? All his research and investigation had . . . led to this!

It was all his fault. He had not been careful enough. He had led them to Aksum and the ark. They had followed him, maybe even used his own techniques to break in and steal it.

His own obsession to find the ark had led to its destruction!

How could he have been so deceived as to think he was doing mankind such good, when it had come to this in the end? What if Operation Noah was the same? If they could destroy the ark of the covenant so easily, what might they be planning in Turkey? The one sabotage attempt had been thwarted. Surely they would try again. A small missile and the whole thing would be up in smoke.

He should never have gone in search of such sacred treasures. He should have left them alone. They were God's business, not his.

The world would never forgive him. Could he ever forgive himself?

(2)

In despondency Adam landed at Gatwick. Somehow he made his way home. It was dark when he arrived.

Juliet and her aunt had been waiting anxiously for some word when the expected time of his arrival came and went, and then as several more hours passed.

When she heard the car drive up, Juliet ran outside, happy and relieved. One look at Adam's face, however, and she knew something was dreadfully wrong.

Adam collapsed in her arms. In the faint light coming from the house, Juliet could see the glistening of tears in his eyes. She had never seen Adam cry, never imagined him capable of crying. All she could do was hold him close as he wept and tried to tell her what had happened.

After a few minutes, they went inside. Juliet explained to her worried aunt that Adam had had a terrible shock, then helped him upstairs to begin getting ready for bed. Within thirty minutes Adam was sound asleep.

Juliet returned downstairs. Mrs. Graves said she had never seen him in such a state in her life.

(3)

Morning came. Juliet and Mrs. Graves arose and had tea together. But clearly their minds were elsewhere. Juliet was frantic for Adam. Her aunt was anticipating their guest.

Jen and Crystal came to work. Adam made no appearance all morning.

Half a dozen times Juliet crept to his door and listened for signs of wakefulness. Only silence met the straining of her ear.

Meanwhile, a little before eleven, Mrs. Graves waited in her parlor, hardly able to concentrate on the newspaper open on her lap.

The preparations had been effected. The sleepless night had been endured. Now she must just patiently—

An approaching automobile sounded out the front.

She started to her feet. The paper crumpled to the floor. A glance out the window . . . the next instant she was hurrying as quickly as propriety would allow toward the kitchen.

(4)

Downstairs Juliet ran from the front door and toward the parked automobile with most un-British lack of reserve.

She and Rocky shook hands, then embraced. Rocky wore a huge smile.

"It is great to see you again, Juliet!" he exclaimed. "You look well and content."

"Thank you, Rocky. So do you."

"You still planning to marry the aristocrat of this place?"

"What kind of question is that?"

"You Brits lead such tabloid lives," rejoined Rocky with a wink. "You can never be too sure what's going to happen next! Where's the man of the house?"

"Actually," replied Juliet in a serious tone, "still asleep."

"What! Adam Livingstone asleep at this hour!" exclaimed the American. Rocky saw from the change in Juliet's expression that something was wrong.

"Rocky . . . it's awful," said Juliet. "I don't know what to do."

He took her in his arms and gave her a reassuring hug.

"I am so glad you're here," she said, stepping back and trying to smile.

They walked slowly toward the front door. There stood the housekeeper.

"Mrs. Graves!" exclaimed Rocky, extending his hand. "How are you?"

"Well, thank you, Mr. McCondy," she replied.

A look of momentary question came across his face. He lifted his nose a few degrees into the air.

"That wouldn't be . . . surely my nose is playing a trick . . . that's not *coffee* I smell, is it, Mrs. Graves?" His tone was playfully serious.

"Knowing how you enjoy your coffee, Mr. McCondy," she replied, "and that you would probably be tired after your flight, I thought you might want a fresh-brewed cup when you arrived. I turned it on when you drove up."

"Mrs. Graves, you are amazing!" said Rocky with delight. "That stuff they serve on the plane has no business being called coffee at all."

As they continued across the entryway, Rocky spotted a figure standing at the top of the stairs as if he had just awakened, as indeed he had.

"Hey, what do you say, Livingstone!" boomed Rocky, springing toward the stairs. "What's this I hear about you sleeping the day away?"

Adam tried to smile. The effort was scarcely successful in producing more than a mordant grimace.

Rocky bounded the rest of the way up to the landing and gave Adam's lethargic hand a vigorous clasp.

"You're a sight, Livingstone," he exclaimed, thinking the lighthearted approach might work best under the circumstances. "I'm the one who's supposed to have jet lag, and there you are standing with a scruffy beard, bags under your eyes, and hair a mess."

Adam laughed thinly.

"I'm afraid I've got some bad news, Rocky, my friend," he said. "Let me finish getting dressed and try to do something so that my disheveled appearance doesn't offend you, then I'll tell you and the others all about it. Why don't you pop into the office and say hello to Crystal and Jen? I'll meet you downstairs in a few minutes."

(5)

After telling the others what had happened, over the course of the next day or two Adam recovered himself enough to return to something of a normal routine. However, he remained devastated at what had taken place, and had no idea what to do next.

Captain Thurlow and Inspector Saul of Scotland Yard paid a visit to Sevenoaks, as Adam had been expecting.

"Look, Livingstone," Thurlow said, "we know you had nothing to do with it. But there is the matter of the photographs and the Snow interview. The Ethiopians have the photos now, and they see them as proof of your involvement in the ark's disappearance. You see what we're up against—we need to release some kind of statement."

"Right, I understand," replied Adam. He had not yet told Scotland Yard about the incident outside Amsterdam. He probably should, he said to himself. But somehow he just couldn't bring himself to say it.

"It would really help, Livingstone," the captain continued, "if you would come down to the Yard yourself—you know, voluntarily coming in, making a full disclosure, giving us a set of the photos you took. I think that would go a long way to alleviating any suspicions in your direction."

"I understand," replied Adam. "How about this afternoon?"

"We'll be there," replied Thurlow, then rose to go.

"May I go into the city with you?" asked Juliet when the two detectives were gone.

"Sure," replied Adam.

"I've been wanting to get together with Erin's mother. I haven't seen her for a while. Maybe she and I can meet somewhere while you are at Scotland Yard."

(6)

"I don't know, Mrs. Wagner," Juliet was saying, "every once in a while I can't help doubts sweeping over me."

"What kind of doubts?" asked the mother of one of Adam's former assistants.

"I don't know," replied Juliet, "doubts that the changes will last, wondering if I'm going to sink back into depression again. Every once in a while I begin doubting that God *really* loves me. Pretty soon I'm doubting Adam too. I hate to think such thoughts. He's going through something difficult and I know he needs my support. But . . . sometimes I just can't help it."

The two women—the younger who had lost a father and brother, the older who had lost a daughter—had become close friends in the short time since their first meeting. While Adam concluded his business at Scotland Yard, Juliet and Mrs. Wagner sat visiting in a tea shop, where Adam had arranged to join them when his appointment was over.

"I try to have strength to overcome the doubts when they attack me rather than succumb to them," Juliet went on. "Sometimes it just seems so—"

Juliet stopped. Across the shop her eyes fell on a familiar figure walking toward them.

"Kimberly!" she said, giving a little wave.

Her friend approached the table, carrying a small tray with a single-serving teapot, cup, and milk.

"What a coincidence seeing you so far from Sevenoaks," exclaimed Juliet. "Are you meeting someone?"

"No, I only stopped in for some tea."

"Sit down and join us!" said Juliet. "Mrs. Wagner, this is Kimberly Banbrigge . . . Kimberly, Mrs. Katie Wagner."

The two women smiled at one another as the newcomer sat down.

"Kimberly and I met on some swings at a park," explained Juliet.

The three had scarcely chatted for another two minutes when Adam arrived. Juliet could see immediately that the interview had drained him even more. He served himself water and tea makings, then sat down, making the table a foursome. Again Juliet introduced Kimberly.

"You're *the* Adam Livingstone," she exclaimed.

"Guilty as charged," returned Adam, sighing.

"This is an honor. I've seen your photo in the paper."

"How did your meeting at the Yard go, Adam?" asked Juliet.

"As well as I'd hoped," he replied.

"You don't mean . . . *Scotland* Yard," said Kimberly.

Adam nodded. It was obvious he did not want to discuss the matter further.

"What's it all about?" she persisted.

"I'm sure you would find it very boring."

"I assure you I would never find it boring, Mr. Livingstone. Are you going on another expedition soon?"

"Trade secrets, I'm afraid, Miss Banbrigge," replied Adam. "I don't even tell Juliet half the schemes in this brain of mine. And we're engaged to be married!"

"Are you saying Juliet doesn't share in your work?"

"My, but you are inquisitive!" Adam laughed. "Of course Juliet shares my work. But sometimes the ideas my brain cooks up are so outrageous that I don't believe them myself. I don't tell her everything the minute I think of it. Sometimes I don't tell *anyone* for a while, till there is time to see what's going to become of it."

"So you're saying you *do* have something new up your sleeve, but no one knows about it?"

"I really think I've said enough, Miss Banbrigge," replied Adam, becoming a little annoyed by the questions posed by Juliet's friend.

On their way home half an hour later, Adam returned to the subject of the photographs.

"That reminds me, Juliet," he said, "we need to print up a new batch of prints from the negatives. The photographs may now be our only remaining link to the ark."

"I'll start on them first thing tomorrow morning," she replied.

✦ ✦ ✦

Then the Lord said to Moses, "I have chosen Bezalel son of Uri,
the son of Hur, of the tribe of Judah, and have filled him with the Spirit
of God, with wisdom and skill, and with knowledge in all manner
of craftsmanship, to devise cunning works in wood, gold, silver, and bronze,
in cutting and setting stones, to work with wood, and to carry out all other
kinds of craftsmanship. I have also chosen Oholiab son of Ahisamach,
of the tribe of Dan, to help him . . . to make everything I have commanded
you: the Tent of Meeting, the ark of the Testimony,
and the mercy seat that is to be upon it."

EXODUS 31:1-7 (AUTHOR'S PARAPHRASE)

✦ ✦ ✦

PROLOGUE

Bezalel, Cunning Craftsman of Metals

Mount Sinai, the Wilderness of Arabia, 1491 B.C.

Being summoned to the tent of their leader always sent a chill of fear into one's bones.

It was a fact hardly to be wondered at.

People had died, been struck with leprosy, and fallen mute when they crossed him. God's anger burned so hot following the incident of Aaron's calf that three thousand were killed and a plague had ravaged the camp.

Being sent for by the man of God was no light matter. He was not such a terrifying presence himself. But he had the Almighty's favor. When he spoke, it was best to listen carefully. And then do what he said.

Bezalel, son of Uri, grandson of Hur, of the tribe of Judah, made his way through the sleeping camp. Inside the tent ahead, Bezalel saw a faint light. Was it from a lamp or from the prophet's face? He bore a glow about him whenever he had been in the Almighty's presence. He had recently been away from the camp again and had just returned.

Fearfully Bezalel lifted the flap. A voice bid him enter. Slowly he came forward.

"You know I have been on the mountain," said the man of God. "I have spoken with Yahweh, the Lord."

Bezalel nodded. "I see his radiance upon your face."

"He gave me many commands for our people. He instructed me regarding what we are to make—that we might worship the Lord God as his holy nation."

Immediately Bezalel began to breathe easier. He was a craftsman. Talk of making things sounded less fearsome than being swallowed by a rift in the earth.

"He carved two new stone tablets," the holy man continued, "like the first, written in his own hand. These are the words of the covenant, the tablets of his commandments."

He pointed to the tablets on a table behind him.

"These stiff-necked people are so prone to evil that I must keep them in my own tent rather than the Tent of Meeting," he went on. "The Lord desires us to make an ark in which to preserve them. It will be a container of such beauty as has never been seen by the eyes of man. It must be a vessel worthy of Yahweh himself. The tablets will be contained in it forever after."

"Such a vessel will indeed be magnificent," said Bezalel.

"The people must look upon it with dread and awe. Otherwise, they may attempt to seize it and melt its gold for their wicked idols. It will be like nothing made by the hand of man, before or since."

"How will it be fashioned such as you describe?" asked the son of Uri.

"You will make it, Bezalel."

"But I am a mere craftsman in wood and gold and silver. I know nothing of the fabrication of dread and fear such as you speak of."

"He knows you, Bezalel. He knows your name."

"Who knows me?"

"Yahweh. He has chosen you *to make the ark and mercy seat."*

"How do you know he has chosen me?"

"He said, 'I have chosen Bezalel son of Uri, the son of Hur, of the tribe of Judah, and have filled him with my Spirit, with wisdom and skill, and with knowledge in all manner of craftsmanship, to devise cunning works of craftsmanship to make everything I have commanded.'*"*

"But . . . but why me?"

Well did the man of God understand the poor man's hesitation. He himself had resisted Yahweh's commands during the course of his own life at the site of the sacred bush that was not consumed.

He smiled at the humble craftsman. "He has given you wisdom and understanding," he said sincerely. "He knows you have the skill to make such as will emanate the power of his glory."

"What size will be this ark?"

"He gave me the dimensions. You shall have them before the night is out. It must be devised such that no man can destroy it. The Lord himself will give his holy vessel power to cause the peoples of the world to tremble. That is why I sought you tonight, Bezalel."

✦ ✦ ✦

Bezalel's heart had skipped a beat as Pharaoh's guards stopped him with whips raised to strike him. Quickly he showed them the pass given to him by Pharaoh. He remembered that long-ago visit so well, when Pharaoh had sent him as a slave to learn skills needed to repair the palace.

The man to whom he was sent was not difficult to find. Every man and woman in Memphis, near Cairo, knew the name Rashidi Amen-Ra. *In the garb of a Bedouin trader Bezalel had sought him whose name meant "wise one personifying the power of the universe."*

"I have come a great distance, honorable one," said Bezalel, bowing low to the ground. "I am told you possess secrets you might share with your humble servant."

"What secrets?" said the wise man, cautious that an apparent Israelite would make such an inquiry. The fellow before him did not bear the look of the wise men who travelled the earth seeking knowledge!

"Secrets of things that come out of the earth, secrets in the working of woods, precious metals, jewels, and gold."

The Egyptian eyed him warily. "Why do you want to know such things?"

"I, too, am a worker in metals," replied Bezalel. "But I have not your level of skill."

"What metals?"

"Gold, silver, bronze."

The Egyptian's eyes narrowed into an inquisitive squint.

"You know not of iron?"

"No, wise one."

"You do not appear a craftsman. And . . . your voice," he added reflectively. "Your Egyptian is clear. Yet . . . you have a peculiar tongue for a Bedouin. Where do you come from?"

"From the desert, wise one."

The Egyptian's eyes squinted still further. "You almost . . . ," he began. "No, that could not be," he mumbled, glancing away in brief reminiscence. His eyes came to rest again upon his peculiar visitor. "For a moment . . . you sounded like a Hebrew."

Bezalel's throat went dry. He struggled to maintain his composure. "Forgive my halting speech, wise one," he said. "He who sent me said you would look with favor upon your humble servant. He said you would open your mind concerning craftsmanship beyond my humble knowledge."

"What do you know of our craft?"

"Only that I have been sent to learn from you, wise one."

"What do you mean—he who sent you? Were you a trader or a craftsman? Who are you?"

"I have been sent, wise one, to learn from you."

"Sent—you say it again. By whom?"

Bezalel withdrew a small clay tablet, dried now to the hardness of granite. Upon it a message of request was inscribed. He handed it to the one known as Rashidi Amen-Ra.

The Egyptian took it. As he digested the figures upon it, his eyes widened. He shook his head in disbelief.

*"*Pharaoh himself!*" fell whispered from his lips. He turned and walked slowly away.*

Bezalel waited patiently. Rashidi Amen-Ra did not return for ten minutes. When he did, only these words were spoken: "Come to me tomorrow at this same time."

Bezalel bowed humbly, then departed.

✦ ✦ ✦

The scene four days hence was much different from that of their first meeting.

In an expansive work space, secluded behind massive stone walls outside the city, the Egyptian wise man and the Hebrew craftsman disguised as a Bedouin merchant were busily engaged over a flaming forge. From its heat no less than six different metals were being liquefied and combined in various stone basins and containers.

Equipment and devices, scales and maps and charts, pulleys and ropes and instruments of varying size and shape and purpose, such as the former slave had neither seen nor imagined, cluttered every corner of the building. Surrounding them were scattered sheets of papyrus as well as many clay tablets with unknown drawings and notations, some hanging, others spread over tables and benches. A wall of shelves held dozens of containers of herbs, chemicals, and other substances, some solid, some liquid.

The people of Memphis and of the rest of Egypt considered Rashidi Amen-Ra the greatest wizard in the land. He had been forced to transfer his laboratory here, away from prying eyes and superstitious gossip. Though they fea red him, however, it was to him they came when their physicians were unable to treat an unusual ailment they had not seen before. When they needed him, he was a man of genius. When they feared him, he was possessed of devils.

Even Pharaoh's personal attendants, who held the people in dread, stood in awe of Rashidi Amen-Ra.

His father, his grandfather, and his great-grandfather before him were likewise men of renown. They were of a select fraternity of Egyptian men of science and medicine who had learned much and had pooled their knowledge through the centuries. As a result of their brilliance, Egypt was the most advanced civilization on the earth.

In truth, Rashidi Amen-Ra was the most sensible man in Egypt and also the most intelligent and knowledgeable—not mere centuries but millennia ahead of his time. He was a scientist, not a master of wizardry, a physicist, not a metaphysicist. He cast no spells, only sought to understand the universe and its ways. He made things not by magic but according to mathematical laws of cause and effect. He was, as were those who had come before and taught him in their ways, capable of understanding his world far beyond the common peasant. These were men who had unlocked secrets those in civilizations to come would not discover for thirty or more centuries.

These early men of wisdom provided the engineering for the building of the great pyramids a thousand years before. The pharaohs gave the orders, and the masses provided the labor, but his predecessors provided the equations to make such wonders possible. Since then they had developed advanced methods of glassmaking, woodworking, shipbuilding, cloth making, and weaving. They had learned to make papyrus and pottery. Scrolls, even libraries, were coming into existence. They understood the stars and progression of planets, and they were even beginning to grasp what the heavens told them of the place of man in the universe.

The most remarkable area in which these men of genius were ahead of their time, however, lay in the metallurgical arts. Copper, tin, iron, zinc, and of course, gold and silver, lay at their disposal. By the labor of men could all these be quarried out of the ground. Only by insight, intuition, and intellect, however, could their manifold properties be harnessed.

Samples of these and many additional metals sat around the building in which the two men worked. Rashidi Amen-Ra found the Hebrew of like mind, capable of deep understanding, a man of extraordinary skill in spite of his humble demeanor.

And now did the Egyptian scientist divulge the skill of the metallurgical craft to the man who had come to him, sent by the Pharaoh.

✦ ✦ ✦

The morning after his terrifying and exhilarating visit to Moses, Bezalel set to work. He himself would see to the construction of the sacred ark, according to what God had told Moses on the mountain.

And so the ark was cunningly fashioned by Bezalel, son of Uri, son of Hur, of the tribe of Judah, in wood and by use of gold and various materials from out of the earth. Everything was done according to what the Lord had commanded Moses.

The ark of testimony and mercy seat were like nothing made by the hand of man, before or since. For indeed, as Yahweh intended, it was symbolic of holiness, obedience, and salvation.

When it was completed, God imbued it with the power of his presence, and all men were fearful of it.

Part Five

ENGLAND

✦ ✦ ✦

I will set his throne over these stones I have buried here;

he will spread his royal canopy above them.

JEREMIAH 43:10

✦ ✦ ✦

fifteen

Hidden Message from Antiquity

(1)

In pale blue suit, six-foot-three-inch self-proclaimed end-times expert and evangelical powerhouse Harry Standgood strode down a wide corridor flanked on both sides by reporters and aides. He was on his way to a television interview to cap off a three-day mini-convention in Atlanta, at which he had been signing copies of his newest best-seller on Revelation.

Even as they walked he was being pummelled by variations of the same question that had hounded him for a month or more, and which he knew would be the first posed when the cameras rolled an hour from now.

"What do you think of the sudden revival of interest in the Bible?"

To be honest, Harry Standgood was having a good deal of difficulty knowing what to think of it. That people were reading the Bible, of course, was to be applauded . . . and words generally to this effect rolled effortlessly from his lips as he gave what was intended to sound like a studied response. What he did not add was his confusion as to how the whole thing had exploded around the world without the least involvement on *his* part. He did not altogether relish being so thoroughly left out of the limelight. Hadn't he devoted a lifetime trying to turn people to the Word? Now everybody was coming unglued because an archaeologist who hadn't even been a Christian more than two years had made a couple of discoveries.

"But I would only caution," he continued solemnly as he walked, "that we must exercise restraint and care. The Word of God must never be taken lightly. I am concerned lest the Bible become *too* fashionable."

"But truth is truth, is it not?" asked another of those clustered about as they hurried along.

"Ah, but things are not always what they seem," answered Standgood. "What do we really know about this man Adam Livingstone? My point is simply that we must guard against allowing the secular world to dictate God's agenda by watering down the deeper truths of Scripture with this mass appeal approach. It is necessary that evangelical leaders and Bible teachers and theologians such as myself guard the gates of truth, as it were, so that God's purposes, rather than man's, are fulfilled."

"Then you will be speaking out publically on the Bible phenomenon?"

It was the question he had been hoping for.

"Indeed I will," replied Standgood. "I have a new book on the subject well under way."

Standgood, who could produce a book on whatever topic happened to strike public interest faster than any writer alive, had begun working on a response the day after the Livingstone-Snow interview. It was nearly completed, a fact he intended to disclose on television this morning.

He should have a half-dozen lucrative offers on the table by week's end.

(2)

Juliet sat in the darkroom of the basement lab, watching the first photograph of the ark develop.

Her mind wasn't on the work in front of her. She was worried about Adam. She had never seen him so despondent. It almost reminded her of how *she* used to be. He was lethargic, wasn't eating much, and had lost the energy, enthusiasm, and the zest that made him Adam Livingstone.

She knew what he was thinking—that the destruction of the ark was his fault. What could she say . . . what could anyone say? In a way it *had* been his research that had led to the horrible travesty.

And now, not only was he under suspicion himself, the worst of it was the fantastic discovery had been blown to bits before his very eyes.

She examined the shape emerging in the developer in front of her. As Adam had said, the pictures he had taken were now their only remaining link to it.

She continued to gaze at the first photograph. Something didn't look right. The lines and shadows were funny, with peculiar shapes to them. The image looked different than before. It seemed too dark.

Had she done something wrong, mixed the wrong recipe of chemicals?

She swished it around and took it out, puzzled, placed it into the tray of stop bath, and set another 8 x 10 sheet into the developer. She'd try one more and see if it turned out any better.

Her thoughts returned to Adam's current predicament. She knew there was probably little chance he would go to jail, though she couldn't help being nervous. But still it was—

A sound interruped her reflections.

Adam entered the darkened room.

"How's it going?" he said, placing a hand on her shoulder and peering over her at the print in the tray.

"I don't know . . . I think I may have done something wrong. Look at this picture—it seems different from the others. It's dark and odd looking."

Adam picked up the first print from the solution and held it up to the thin light.

"I see what you mean. It's nothing serious. The contrast is higher, that's all."

He set the print back in the tray and walked over to the developing machine.

"Ah, this explains it," he said. "The number-five filter is still on. I was using it for some of the pictures from Turkey."

"What does it do?" asked Juliet.

"Boosts up the contrast. Makes the lines and shadows jump off the page more graphically." Adam continued to glance about. "And did you use this paper?" he asked, pointing to a box of Kodabromide grade 5 sitting on the table beside her.

"Yes."

"That's it then. With the filter and super-high contrast paper, you got a higher range of darks and lights. Sort of turns the image into a bas-relief look."

"I'm sorry," said Juliet. "I guess I was being careless. I'll reprint them on normal paper and without the filter." She rose and walked back to the printer to begin reprinting the negatives. Adam started to leave. Juliet had gone but halfway when all at once she stopped in her tracks. Suddenly her brain registered what she thought she saw a moment ago. She quickly retraced her steps to the picture sitting in the solution.

"Adam . . . Adam, wait—look at this!" she cried.

Adam hurried back, squinting down where she was pointing toward the base of the image of the ark.

"Do you see what I think I see?" she said. "Down there . . . among the designs!"

"I think so!" he exclaimed, jolting to attention. He bent down for a closer look.

"How could we have missed it?" said Juliet.

"This is astonishing, if it is actually—"

Already Adam had turned and was swishing the second print about in the developer.

"We'll let this one get a little darker yet," he said. "It should raise the contrast even more."

He bent over again, gazing at it through the solution, and waited several more seconds. When it was ready, he removed the second print, doused it in stop bath, and held it up to the light. Then he ran from the room with the print dripping in his hand.

He returned a moment later.

"Never mind reprinting anything, Juliet," he said. "Develop everything you just printed! Your little accident may have succeeded in bringing out these images from the relief of the shapes on the bottom of the ark that we didn't see before."

"What do you think it is?" she asked.

"I can't be sure," he said. "We need to develop them all and get them under magnification before we'll know for certain. But I think there are letters intermingled with the design work of the gold, possibly words of some kind."

"That's what it looked like to me. Do you think they're what they appear to be?"

"I'm not sure . . . but don't they remind you strikingly of—"

"Hebrew!" they said together.

Adam continued to peruse the first of the pictures Juliet had developed.

"Something's going on here," said Adam. "I want to see the rest of those prints!"

(3)

That same afternoon, with the rest of his team scrutinizing various of the newly developed, high-contrast 8 x 10s, Adam leaned over the table, peering through a magnifying glass. They had been at it an hour, decoding one letter at a time, which without doubt they recognized as characters with linguistic rather than artistic basis.

Adam was doing his best to translate a short message in the Hebrew alphabet, circa 1000 B.C., which had been skillfully worked into the design of the bottom of the ark, intermingled with so many other shapes and designs that it was not readily visible at first glance.

He had several dictionaries, a Hebrew grammar, and two lexicons open in front of him.

Suddenly he leapt from his chair and half ran around the room in obvious elation.

The eyes of the others followed him through his outburst and dance.

"What is it?" queried Juliet, laughing. "You look like you've just stumbled on the discovery of the century."

He turned toward her with startled eyes. "I don't even want to say what I just found," replied Adam. "It's so unbelievable . . . if I'm right, it could change everything!"

"Everything . . . what do you mean?"

"Everything about our ark research. It all hinges on a single word. And Hebrew characters are so complex and confusing I may have mistranslated it. But—"

Adam paused.

"No, I don't even want to say it without confirmation. Crystal, get Dr. Bernstein at the Hebrew University on the phone. Tell him I have some characters to send him I need translated. See if you can fax this to him right away and ask him to call back as soon as he has it deciphered."

Crystal made the call. Adam followed it with a brief faxed message.

(4)

Anni d'Abernon rarely watched television news.

She was in the habit of *controlling* events, not hearing about them after the fact. But as she sat in front of the small screen in her office watching one more special on what was being called the Livingstone phenomenon, she could hardly believe her eyes.

Was this obsession with the enemy's book never going to end? It had been a week since she had destroyed the ark in Amsterdam. Of course nobody but those few present knew anything about it. The public didn't know.

But she was acquainted enough with how things operated in unseen spiritual realms to assume that its destruction would hinder the enemy's influence, at least temporarily. What Livingstone himself was doing, who could tell—little was being reported about his current movements other than that Ethiopian officials wanted to talk to him about the ark's disappearance, but that he had issued no statement.

Behind her the telephone rang. She turned off the set, then answered it.

"Yes, Ciano," she said.

"Rome—when was that?"

A brief answer.

"I see. No, he was in Amsterdam more recently. Unfortunately he turned up at a most inappropriate moment and there was nothing I could do. He disappeared just as suddenly."

She listened another moment.

"No—I would assume back to Baku, but he appeared different. He had a look in his eye I did not care for. Find him however you can, Ciano. He grows more dangerous the longer he is allowed to roam loose."

D'abernon put down the phone. Her reflections left Zorin and returned to Adam Livingstone. If blowing the thing up hadn't worked, perhaps it was time to let the public in on what had happened, and dump the thing right in Adam Livingstone's lap. Where was her file on that BBC journalist who had been showing such an inordinate fascination with the Livingstone group? It might be a way to handle this thing.

Discreetly of course.

(5)

Five or six minutes passed in the Livingstone office. At last the telephone rang. Adam sprang for it.

"Yes . . . hello, Dr. Bernstein. Thank you for calling back so quickly," he said. "Yes . . . right . . . can you understand the words . . . yes, I see–right, an old version of Hebrew. That's what I thought as well . . . right . . . hmm . . . wow . . . no, I'll let you know when I have more . . . great, thank you. I'll be in touch."

Adam put the phone down and turned back into the room.

"Dr. Bernstein's conclusion confirms my translation," he said excitedly. "According to him, the message which was apparently engraved into the side of the ark, or, perhaps I should say into the side of the particular object that I photographed in Aksum, *is* what I thought."

"What is it?" asked Scott.

"You're not going to believe it."

"Out with it!" said Rocky.

"Get this," said Adam. "The message reads: *This is a replica of the ark of testimony.*"

"A replica!" exclaimed Juliet, Rocky, and Jen all at once.

"You mean it wasn't the real ark in Aksum?" asked Scott.

"Apparently not."

"So it wasn't the ark of the covenant that was blown up!" exclaimed Juliet.

"More than that," added Adam. "It means that the *real* ark of the covenant still exists somewhere!"

Everyone was silent. The implications were huge.

"Well, gang," said Adam at length, "with this development, obviously our ark research is back on."

(6)

Alone in Los Angeles, a teenage girl glanced disinterestedly toward the television set.

It was sometime after midnight. Her friend had left it muted before leaving an hour before. Until a minute ago she'd scarcely noticed. Televisions were always on. Who paid any attention?

She'd been in the city for two months and still didn't have a job. She was about out of money and couldn't keep mooching forever.

She thought her luck might be about to change this afternoon. She'd met a guy who promised to help her get on her feet, maybe even get a place of her own after a month or two.

It sounded good. Maybe *too* good.

She'd agreed to go out with him later tonight and see what it was about.

But the rest of the day a queasy feeling had been churning in her stomach. She knew the guy was bad news. She hadn't wanted to admit it at first, especially when he turned on the charm and told her that he'd never met anyone like her. But he was a conniver. She could tell. If she got mixed up with him there'd be no turning back.

Nervously she began wandering about the room. She sat down and picked up a magazine, flipped through it absently, then tossed it aside. Her eyes fell on the book that had been sitting beneath it on the coffee table. She picked it up and opened it randomly.

Her eyes fell on the page and she began reading:

" . . . *this is how you are to build it: the ark is to be 450 feet long, 75 feet wide, and 45 feet high. Make a roof for it and finish the ark. . . .*"

It was a Bible. What was her friend doing with a Bible?

She glanced back at the TV, then stood, walked across the floor, and turned up the sound.

" . . . when last year the British archaeologist," the commentator was saying, "discovered the partially fossilized remnants of Noah's ark embedded in a glacier on the top of Mount Ararat in Turkey, who could have suspected that it would lead . . ."

It was a special on that archaeologist she'd heard about who claimed to have discovered Noah's ark. She drew nearer and continued to watch as video clips were shown of the recent activity in Turkey. And there it was–the huge ancient vessel . . . there on the TV in front of her.

She turned back to the open Bible on the table. A look of perplexity and wonder came over her face. She had just read about it . . . and there it was right on the television. What an incredible coincidence!

Or was it?

Mesmerized by the TV account, she stood watching for another several minutes. How could it be that she had just read about something four thousand years old, and then seen *that very thing* on TV?

She had always thought those old Bible stories were just fairy tales. But there it was! Like it was being reported in the newspaper.

A strange sense of conviction stole over her. With it came a new feeling of courage she hadn't felt in a long time. No, she thought to herself, she wasn't ready to give in to her circumstances quite yet.

In the midst of her thoughts, the knock she had been expecting sounded. She collected her resolve, then opened the door.

"Hey, babe, sorry I'm late. Let's go–got somebody waiting I want you to meet."

"I . . . I don't think so," she said. "I've changed my mind."

"You can't change your mind now, Brandi. Nobody goes back on me. Come on." He reached forward and tried to take hold of her arm.

She pulled back and began to close the door.

"I said I changed my mind." She shut the door the rest of the way and quickly locked it.

"Hey, babe, no second chances!" he yelled through the door.

Heart pounding, she stood still and did not reply. She heard him swear and leave. She drew in a deep breath, then sat down to watch the rest of the rerun about Adam Livingstone.

When it was over, she went out. She knew it was late. But she couldn't sleep. She reached the street and glanced about. She saw no one. It was a relief this wasn't the kind of neighborhood where people hung out on sidewalks at night.

Where she went after that, she paid little attention. Gradually she found herself in a residential area where there was little fear of running into anyone like the guy she had stood up. A few dogs barked from behind fences. Otherwise all was quiet.

Another forty minutes she walked. Finally her steps slowed. She looked up. She was standing in front of a darkened church. It was small and simply built. It reminded her of a country church that might have appeared on a Christmas card. A tall steeple extended into the emptiness above. A bright three-quarter moon shown to one side, outlining the thin silhouette against the black sky.

The thought came to her that maybe the vastness over her wasn't empty after all.

She stood staring for several minutes, then realized that without even knowing it she had begun to cry.

sixteen

The Quest Begins Anew

(1)

Adam Livingstone sat in his study with a dozen books open on his desk. An assortment of maps and atlases lay unfolded wherever he could find room for them. His research on this day was not archaeological but historical.

Finally he closed the book he had been reading and rose from his chair.

This investigation had taken so many confusing twists and turns. At this moment he felt further from his objective than ever. First he thought he'd found the ark, only to be denied sight of it. Then he actually did see it, and took photographs . . . or *thought* he'd seen it. Then the ark was destroyed. Now new evidence revealed that it hadn't been the ark at all!

So where was the *real* ark of the covenant?

After this whole last year, he was back to square one. If their Ethiopian research had been a red herring . . . where did they go from here? How could they possibly hope to pick up its trail again? He was peering for footprints laid down a thousand, two thousand, even three thousand years ago.

Adam turned, opened the door behind him, and stepped into the larger office. There sat Crystal, Juliet, Scott, and Jen at their desks.

"Anybody want to join me for tea?" said Adam as he walked in. "I feel the need of a brainstorming session. Where's Rocky?"

"Downstairs chatting with Auntie Andrea," answered Juliet.

(2)

"OK, Rocky," said Adam when they were all clustered several minutes later in the kitchen, pouring tea and coffee, "it's time you earned your keep as our resident sleuth. Let's get this investigation going."

"I've been waiting for you to say the word."

"I needed to get my thoughts organized and focused," said Adam. "Unfortunately, what I succeeded in doing was getting myself bewildered all over again. I mean . . . I really thought we'd found it. I suppose I was caught up in the moment, believing I had actually located something that has eluded fortune hunters for centuries. Then bam, the dream vanished before my eyes. I must admit it is difficult to pick back up and start over."

"That's why I'm here," said Rocky, "to get you jump-started again, to help you look at the thing through the eyes of an investigator. In my business you learn that clues aren't always what they first seem."

"What do you suggest?"

"I want to go through your complete research progression. We need to see if we can spot where you got off, and see if we can find clues leading to the real trail of the ark. So where does the mystery of the ark's movements begin?"

"Israel, Jerusalem . . . the temple of Solomon," replied Adam. "They placed the ark there after the temple's completion. That was its last known resting place."

"How did you attempt to trace it?" asked Rocky.

"We began with an exhaustive list of Scripture references concerning the ark."

"Do you have a copy?" said Rocky.

Crystal rose and within two minutes produced fresh sheets of the list and handed them around the room. Adam and the others, Rocky for the first time, spent several minutes perusing again the results of her earlier research.

God commands building of ark–Exodus 25:10-22 (1491 B.C.)
Ark and mercy seat built–Exodus 37:1-9 (1491 B.C.)
Ark placed in tabernacle–Exodus 40:20-21 (1490 B.C.)
Aaron's sons killed by offering "strange fire" before ark–Leviticus 10:1-2 (1490 B.C.)
Jordan River parts when ark is carried into it–Joshua 3:14-17 (1451 B.C.)
Israelites march around Jericho with ark to collapse the wall–Joshua 6 (1451 B.C.)
Ark in tabernacle with Eli–1 Samuel 3:3 (1165 B.C.)
Ark captured by Philistines–1 Samuel 4:1-11 (1141 B.C.)
Philistine god falls on face before ark, and affliction befalls Philistine cities–1 Samuel 5 (1141 B.C.)
Philistines return ark to Israel seven months after capture–1 Samuel 6 (1141 B.C.)
Seventy men die for looking into ark–1 Samuel 6:19 (1140 B.C.)
Ark brought to Jerusalem by David–2 Samuel 6 (1047 B.C.)
Uzzah killed for mishandling ark–2 Samuel 6:6-7 (1047 B.C.)
Ark placed in Holy of Holies–1 Kings 8:1-10 (1004 B.C.)
Josiah instructs priests to put the ark in Solomon's temple–2 Chronicles 35:3 (624 B.C.)
Lists of items in ark–Hebrews 9:4

(3)

San Quentin prison was no place to make friends.

For the cops and guards who pulled duty there, you couldn't let yourself develop a soft spot for a con. Show an ounce of sympathy and you were finished. It was a hard place, and you had to be hard to survive. On both sides of the bars.

When lifer Hank Scully heard the key in the lock to his cell, he didn't bother looking up. He had no friends. He deserved no sympathy. He'd been here twelve years, and would be here another thirty. He was as hard as they come.

He heard the door swing open, and became aware of someone standing facing him. Slowly he lifted his head from where he sat on the edge of his bunk.

"Scully," said his visitor with a nod.

"What do you want, Warden?" he replied irritably.

"To talk to you for a minute."

"Didn't think you suits dirtied yourselves coming all the way down here. So . . . what do you want?"

"I've been watching you, Hank," said the warden. "And praying for you."

"Save your prayers for someone who needs them. Won't do me no good."

"Maybe not, but I'm going to keep praying for you."

"What do I care?"

"I've been reading a book lately," the warden went on. "I'm looking at a lot of things differently than I once did. I've thought about you a lot—can't exactly say why. I thought it might help you too. So I brought you a copy. Here—I want you to have this."

He held out his hand. In it was a small book. Scully took it.

"A Bible! What do the likes of me want with a Bible, Warden?"

He threw it on the ground and it slid across the floor.

"Just the same, Hank, I want you to have it."

The warden turned and left the cell.

(4)

"This is excellent," said Rocky as he finished his scan of the sheet. "In addition to this list, what did you do?" asked Rocky.

"We conducted research on several fronts," Adam replied. "We studied all these biblical texts on the ark. We looked into the Jewish history and chronicles, as well as extrabiblical and non-Jewish sources. Somewhere in there, of course, we headed off toward Ethiopia with Solomon's son Menyelek."

"We also looked into contemporary writings and research," put in Crystal.

"The A.D. era," added Adam, "especially from the Crusades to the present. There are dozens of books on ark legends going back a thousand years. And, Scott, you read some of the current stuff."

"I stumbled onto one rumor," said Scott, "that the Israeli military has the ark under lock and key, waiting for the rebuilding of the temple in Jerusalem. There were interesting links to the Crusades and a group of crusaders called Templars. Although we dropped that line of inquiry when we got onto the Ethiopian trail."

Rocky took in the comment with obvious interest. Adam noted the expression on his face.

"What are you thinking?" he said.

"I am intrigued by Scott's comment," replied Rocky. "You say you dropped a particular line of inquiry. The instant I hear something like that, my investigator's nose starts to twitch. There might be a potential trail of clues that has not been followed to the end."

"I see what you mean," mused Adam. "Something I wondered about through our investigation," he went on thoughtfully, "has to do with the ark's power. It was the mightiest object in the Bible. How could something of such might just fade into insignificance?"

"Wouldn't it be explained by God's removing his presence," suggested Juliet. "The power itself was in God, not the ark, wasn't it? Maybe the ark is like Eden. It has been dormant . . . its power hidden from men's eyes."

"And like the garden," suggested Crystal, "awaiting a time for that power to reemerge."

"You do know," said Adam, "of the schools of thought, in both Judaism and Christianity, which says that the ark *will* be found, and that its discovery will trigger events leading to a new temple and the coming of the Messiah, the *first* coming according to the Jews, the *second* coming according to Christians."

"Pastor Mark has mentioned that," said Rocky, nodding. "But hasn't the common theory always been that the ark was destroyed by one of the invading armies who overran Israel?"

"When *was* Solomon's temple overrun?" now asked Jen.

"Anyone know?" said Adam glancing around. "Six or seven centuries before Christ, in that vicinity, wasn't it? Wait a minute . . . I've got an Old Testament archaeology book open on the table beside my desk," he added. "I'll get it. We'll nail down this chronology once and for all."

Already he was on his way. He returned a minute later flipping through its pages.

"Let's see . . . Jerusalem falls to Babylon in . . . here it is—586. Solomon's temple is destroyed, most of Judah taken into captivity."

(5)

Two anonymous communications were received on the same day by two individuals who had never met.

Only one knew of the other's existence. The brief messages would ultimately draw them together in an intricate plot destined to change both their lives, as well as perhaps alter the course of history itself.

As Kim Shayne opened the strange envelope that bore no return address, her fingers tingled in anticipation. What the feeling was exactly, she didn't know. Immediately she sensed something here that was important.

✦ ✦ ✦

At almost the same moment, Sir Gilbert Bowles opened an identical envelope which had arrived in a sealed courier pouch the morning after they had put in at Naples. He did not pause to reflect how or to whom his whereabouts was known so as to make him so easily accessible.

He read the enclosed typed message first, before examining the contents of the accompanying smaller envelope.

"*Major Livingstone revelation about to break,*" Bowles read, "*that could ruin his career and land him in prison. Photos you now hold are key. Suggest you break off cruise and fly home immediately. Someone of your stature must tell the world the truth about Adam Livingstone.*"

He had scarcely finished reading when his trembling fingers were tearing at the second envelope. Seconds later, fingers shaking, he half collapsed on the edge of the bed in his cabin, thumbing through the half-dozen small but sharp color photographs.

He could not believe what he was looking at!

It was the most astonishing evidence imaginable for what he had always suspected, that there was more to Adam Livingstone than the goody-two-shoes image.

At last he had proof! In his very own hands!

The ponderous bulk of Gilbert Bowles, rapidly regaining its former shape under the influence of the Norwegian master chef, began to chuckle, then laugh, and at last broke out in a great roar of delight.

"Ha, ha, ha . . . Adam Livingstone . . . ha, ha—you are finished at last!"

(6)

Rocky rose and walked to the large blackboard which hung on one wall of the large office.

"OK, then," he said, "what do we have? I'm going to go through this as if we're doing it for the first time."

He picked up a piece of chalk and started clacking down words as he spoke.

"We have the ark constructed by Bezalel in—"

"Around 1490 B.C.," said Juliet.

Rocky entered the date on the board.

" . . . and then placed in the Holy of Holies . . ."

"In approximately 959 B.C.," added Adam, completing his sentence.

Again Rocky entered the numbers.

"Let's continue it on," he said. He went on writing down the facts as Adam and his staff called out dates and ideas, filling in gaps as best they could, rehashing the data and brainstorming possibilities.

"David dies, Solomon becomes king in 970 B.C.," said Rocky as he wrote down the information the others gave him. "Temple completed in 959 . . . Queen of Sheba comes to visit probably five or ten years after that. Then, uh . . . let's see, Solomon dies in 930. The kingdom divides into Israel in the north and Judah in the south at that time, two kings replacing him, Jeroboam and Rehoboam. A couple of centuries pass . . . Israel invaded by Assyria in 743 . . . falls in 722. The northern kingdom ceases to exist . . . ten tribes lost. Various earthquakes throughout Israel. Judah continues on . . . but then is besieged by Nebuchadnezzar of Babylon around 600."

After fifteen minutes, Rocky stood back and gazed at the board.

"It looks to me like the most mystifying moment occurs at the Babylonian destruction of Jerusalem in 586 B.C. That's obviously a critical time. And when the Jews came back to Israel after the captivity . . . why do they never mention it again?"

"Because they thought it stolen or destroyed by the invading Babylonians," said Scott.

"Which is how that assumption has come down to us as the final chapter of the ark's history," added Adam.

"Fair enough," said Rocky. "But one thing an investigator might ask at this point is what if it had been *hidden* from the Babylonians . . . but none of the Jews knew of it when they returned?"

Silence followed, along with a few nods.

"Are you saying that it might have remained in Israel?" asked Adam.

"I'm only raising the possibility. It is an intriguing one, you have to admit."

"Something else we have to account for," said Adam, "concerns what we now know to be the Ethiopian replica. When was it made, and *why*? And was it made in Jerusalem and taken to Ethiopia, or made later after Menyelek got to Ethiopia?"

"The replica idea certainly would explain how the Ethiopians developed a fascination for replicas of the ark in every church in the country. It might explain a great deal."

"Except what happened to the *real* ark," said Rocky.

(7)

Angella Quinn knew she was lucky to have this job. To be working for a Christian publishing company among Christian people was more than she had ever hoped for. At eighteen, this was the first job she had ever had. She didn't want to lose it.

She couldn't keep her knees from shaking as she walked toward the office of the company president. What would he think? Would he fire her on the spot?

Yet she had to go through with it. The Lord had given her this idea, she was sure of it. She had to tell him.

The president's secretary took her into the office and introduced her to Mr. Williams. Her hand was sweating and clammy, but she shook his when he offered it. Anxiously she sat down, and the secretary left.

"Miss Quinn, how may I help you?" he asked.

"I . . . uh, have an idea, Mr. Williams, that I . . . that I want to share with you. I know I just work in the warehouse, and I don't know much about Bible publishing, and I hope you won't think it's too stupid . . . but I want to tell you how I became a Christian, and then tell you my idea . . . if that's all right."

"Of course, go on, Miss Quinn," said Mr. Williams, smiling.

"I never went to church or Sunday school," she continued. "My parents were divorced and we moved a lot, and neither of them ever took me to church. Then one day I found a New Testament. Really, I found it lying on a bench in the park when I was jogging. It was just a little paperback with one of the covers torn off. I didn't even know what it was when I picked it up. But I decided to take it home with me, and that night—I'm not even sure why—I started reading. I read through the story of Jesus, and then again, and then a third time. And when I was reading it that third time, and I got to the story of the man born blind when he said, *'Lord, I believe . . . ,'* something inside me wanted to say that same thing right along with him. And I realized from reading about Jesus, that I *had* come to believe. So I said to him, *'Lord, I believe in you.'*"

She paused.

"Well, I don't want to take too much of your time, Mr. Williams, telling you my whole life," she said, laughing nervously. "But I wanted you to see that I know the power the Bible can have to change someone's life, all by itself, without tracts, without sermons, without anyone witnessing to someone else . . . because that's how I gave my heart to the Lord, and I've never been the same since. I've grown and changed more than I could possibly tell you, and it began with a torn Bible sitting on a park bench.

"And with so much interest in the Bible lately, I thought that maybe you could print a small version of the New Testament or the Bible, and then tell people in advertisements that anyone who doesn't have a Bible can write in or call and get one—for free, I mean—or you could make them available to churches and Christian bookstores to give away, so that people will know that Christian publishers are not just trying to profit from God's Word, but truly care about people and want people's lives to be changed by what God has to tell them."

She stopped, her voice shaking.

"That is an excellent idea, Miss Quinn," said Mr. Williams after reflection. "I can see that it took courage for you to come here and tell me about it."

"And then I thought too," Angella went on, "that you could send the President a copy of it. He's supposed to give a speech on TV, you know, about the National Bible Day they're talking about. I'm sure he has a collection of expensive Bibles, but I think we ought to send him a small inexpensive one that is the very same Bible that is being distributed free all over the country, so that people know it is the Word of God, not the fancy cover, that is important. Do . . . do you understand what I mean, Mr. Williams?"

"Yes. Yes, I think I do, Angella. You just may be onto something. I appreciate your sharing this with me . . . I appreciate it very much."

Angella rose to go. Mr. Williams conducted her out of his office.

As soon as the young lady was gone, he said to his secretary, "Would you please tell the members of the executive committee that I want to see them right away?"

(8)

Juliet had been thumbing through her Bible, glancing back and forth at Crystal's list of passages. At last she spoke again.

"Look at this passage describing the Babylonian invasion . . . it's fascinating," she said. "It's in Jeremiah 52, in a description given of the final leveling of the city and of the booty taken from the temple by Nebuzaradan. *'He set fire to the temple of the Lord,'*" she began reading, "*'the royal palace and all the houses of Jerusalem. Every important building he burned down. . . . The Babylonians broke up the bronze pillars, the movable stands and the bronze Sea that were at the temple of the Lord and they carried all the bronze to Babylon. They also took away the pots, shovels, wick trimmers, sprinkling bowls, dishes and all the bronze articles used in the temple service. The commander of the imperial guard took away the basins, censers, sprinkling bowls, pots, lampstands, dishes and bowls used for drink offerings—all that were made of pure gold or silver.'*"

Juliet stopped to address the group. "Can you read between the lines?"

"I think I may see what you're getting at," said Adam. "What's *missing* from this description?"

"The ark!" exclaimed Jen. "How could it have been there and not be mentioned?"

"Precisely! If the ark was there, they would hardly overlook the most important item of all."

"Realistically, are they going to talk about wick trimmers and leave out the ark of the covenant?"

"Or shovels!" Jen laughed.

Everyone joined in. Now that Juliet called their attention to the omission, it was humorous.

"So the question is, *when* was the ark of the covenant removed from the Holy of Holies?" asked Adam. "And was it stolen or removed for the purpose of being hidden from the Babylonians? Originally," he added, turning to Rocky, "we assumed Menyelek had taken it. Now that doesn't seem to be the case."

"But how *could* anyone have taken it without dropping dead on the spot?" asked Scott.

"Unless the Levites or someone with God's protection were in on it."

"Maybe the most important question isn't when or why," suggested Adam, "but *where*?"

"One thing that struck me when I was reading about Israel's geography," said Juliet, "if someone *were* trying to hide the ark, there would be plenty of places to do it."

"How do you mean?"

"Israel is a land of a million caves. Jerusalem's history, the whole history of the country, is associated with caves. And then too," she went on, "I didn't realize how geologically active the region was."

"Earthquakes, you mean?"

Juliet nodded. "Palestine has an amazing earthquake history."

"It does sit on the great rift. I suppose we ought to have expected it."

"Hidden somewhere and then buried by an earthquake?" suggested Juliet.

Rocky scanned the blackboard again. "I want to go back to that trail you said you abandoned," he said. "The connection with the Crusades and that order—what did you say it was called?"

"The Templars."

"Right. Tell me more about that."

Adam and Scott briefed Rocky on what their research had turned up.

"The main point to this element of the story," said Adam, "is that we're not the first Europeans to make these connections between the ark and Ethiopia. We are only following in the tracks of other adventurers from long ago."

"You mean the crusaders?"

"I thought they were searching for the Holy Grail," said Crystal.

"Some say they are one and the same legend," put in Scott.

"Awhile back I thought about going to France to try to pick up the trail of the crusaders," said Adam. "Many legends say they were secretly attempting to find the ark of the covenant."

"I would say we need to study the Crusades in more detail," said Rocky. "I am very intrigued to learn if there is evidence about what the crusaders turned up. We may need to dust off your original plan. The crusaders may now be our only solid lead."

seventeen

Schemes

(1)

Gilbert Bowles had been back in London less than twenty-four hours when the knock he had halfway expected came on his door.

Ordinarily he might have been less than cordial under the circumstances. But in this case, notwithstanding the fatigue from his hastily arranged flight back from Italy, he opened the door almost eagerly.

There stood a young woman he had never seen in his life—attractive, twenty- or thirty-something, every inch a professional in dark gray suit with loose silky blouse tastefully complementing skirt and jacket. In his usual but rumpled khaki trousers and plain, ill-fitting white button shirt, the same he had worn home on the plane, the archaeologist was clearly the underattired half of the duo.

"Mr. Bowles," she said, "you do not know me, but I am a journalist with the BBC. My name is Kim Shayne."

"Uh, right . . . what can I do for you?" said Bowles. He had not expected a media interview.

"I understand you have a story for me."

"What kind of story?" replied Bowles.

"A new discovery concerning Adam Livingstone."

"Ah . . . yes." Bowles nodded. So this was connected to the Livingstone thing. "Why don't you come in, Miss, uh—"

"Shayne."

"Right—Miss Shayne . . . come in."

Bowles led her inside and offered her a chair. He took the one opposite.

"I must confess," he said as they sat down, "that I am a bit confused about your role in the affair."

"I am in the dark as well," said Shayne. "I was simply told that you had new photographs that would shock the world."

She extracted a typewritten note from her purse, unfolded it, and handed it to Bowles. He recognized both the paper and the script.

"*Sir Gilbert Bowles,*" he read, "*author and archaeologist and Livingstone rival, is in possession of photographic evidence of a major Livingstone cover-up concerning the ark of the covenant. Not only did Livingstone steal the ark from the Sanctuary in Aksum, he has since destroyed it to prevent its power from becoming known."*

Doing his best to hide his astonishment, Bowles handed the paper back and exhaled slowly. This was more than he dared dream would fall in his lap. But what could be this reporter's connection to the thing?

"Yes . . . I see," he said, guarding his words. "This certainly does put my dear friend Adam Livingstone in a pickle . . . *if* word of it was to leak out. I must confess, however, that I know nothing about it."

"Do you know about the photographs?"

"I was sent certain, shall we say, intriguing snapshots showing Adam and some object or other."

"May I see them?"

Bowles considered for a moment, then produced the envelope of pictures from his shirt pocket. He handed them to Shayne. Her reaction was far less guarded than his to the letter he had just read. She made no attempt to hide it.

"Unbelievable!" she exclaimed as her eyes lit up. "This is dynamite."

"That is exactly what it appears to be—a photograph of dynamite," quipped Bowles. "But what's it all about, Miss Shayne?"

"Someone wanted the story out but desired to remain in the background."

"But who?"

"I can't imagine," she said. "Maybe one of *your* fans. But what do we do? This is a huge story. It must be handled properly."

"What do you mean, what do we do," said Bowles. "We expose the fraud. Obviously that's why we were contacted."

"We must consider our options carefully, and do more research before we do anything."

"Research—what the devil for?" rejoined Bowles. "Put me on the telly live and I'll blow the lid off Livingstone's hoax."

"Not so fast, Mr. Bowles. The news business has a tradition of checking its sources."

"Bah! The photographs don't lie. Let's get the thing out to the public."

"Photographs can be digitally enhanced to tell any story you want. How do I know you didn't stage this whole thing and send me the letter yourself?"

"Don't be ridiculous, Shayne! Why would I do such a thing?"

"To ruin Adam Livingstone. Your feelings toward him are not exactly secret. I will do some checking. In the meantime, if I could borrow the photos for twenty-four hours in order to make copies for myself—"

"Tut, tut, Miss Shayne," said Bowles, chuckling. "What kind of fool do you take me for? You do whatever checking you want, but I will keep the photographs myself. And be quick about it. Otherwise I'll take the story public without you."

(2)

The Livingstone team continued to discuss the crusader connections to the ark of the covenant. After another few days, Scott flew back to Turkey.

"Where were you planning to go in France?" asked Rocky later that same week as he and Adam stood before the chalkboard.

"Chartres," replied Adam. "Many of the leaders of the first crusade came from that region. And the Chartres cathedral has heavy crusader connections."

"Then I think it may be time we took that trip," said Rocky.

Adam nodded. "Since the Ethiopian trail has cooled, the crusaders may hold the key after all. Well, Crystal," said Adam, turning toward his secretary, "flights to Paris. Actually, we'll fly to Turkey first to check in with Scott. Then you and Jen can meet us in France."

"Will do, Boss," replied Crystal. "Shall I make a reservation for Juliet too?"

But Adam's attention had been diverted back toward something on the chalkboard of clues he and Rocky had been discussing. He did not hear the question.

An awkward silence followed. Suddenly Juliet felt strange and out of place.

"Excuse me, Adam," said Crystal. "Who did you mean would fly to Turkey first? Shall I make a reservation for Juliet?"

"Oh, uh . . . right. Of course—just a slip of the tongue," said Adam, shaking loose from his reverie. "Juliet, you *do* want to go to France with us?" he added, addressing her.

A wave of perplexity swept over her. Juliet could find little reassurance in the nonchalant expression on Adam's face. She tried to speak, but could only stammer.

"Uh . . . I don't . . . perhaps I ought to go up to Bedford," she replied hesitantly.

"Hmm . . . well—whatever you think best."

"I need to get together with my mum about the wedding plans."

"Right," said Adam. "Maybe this is a good time."

Then, oblivious to the true reason for Juliet's hesitation, he began discussing something he had been in the midst of explaining to Rocky.

As the men went on talking, their voices faded into the background. A hundred thoughts flooded Juliet's mind.

Did Adam really care so little if she went along to France?

Why had Crystal singled *her* out to ask about tickets? She thought she was part of the team.

Juliet's former doubts swept over her in a wave. Again she felt very much an outsider, like when she had first arrived at Sevenoaks.

Struggling to keep from breaking into tears, she left the office.

(3)

A week passed since their first meeting. Gilbert Bowles and Kim Shayne had spoken several more times by telephone and now met again in person.

Bowles' importunity was making the reporter increasingly nervous about pursuing this story. Something smelled fishy. His insistence that they move quickly only heightened her suspicions.

Figuring it best not to beat around the bush, Kim said what was on her mind. "I am having second thoughts, Sir Gilbert."

"What in blazes for!" he replied, and none too happily. "I thought we were in this together. That's why you were contacted—to break the story."

Obviously their motives were different, Shayne thought to herself. She was an opportunist, she could admit that, but not totally without a scruple or two. She couldn't run into print without checking this out further. She had her future as a journalist to consider. How could she tell a man like Gilbert Bowles, though she had every intention of pursuing her other story, that she had developed almost a soft spot for Juliet Halsay and had no desire to see either her or the man she loved brought down?

"Hasn't it occurred to you," she said at length, "that this may all be a little too convenient?"

"What do you mean?"

"The photos showing up like they did."

"Who cares—we have the story."

"But what do we really know?"

"That Adam Livingstone stole the ark and then blew it up. I took you for a bright kid, Shayne. What's the problem—you going soft all of a sudden?"

"Journalists usually like to have something we call proof."

"Proof—we've got the pictures!"

"Pictures which you refuse to let me have subjected to analysis."

"Look, Shayne," said Bowles, finally growing irritated, "if you're not with me, then I go it alone."

"How?"

"I've got connections. Maybe I'll call Imre."

Shayne could not help bursting out in a laugh.

"The American scandalmonger?" she said. "That's a hilarious idea. *Eveningtalk* is hardly a serious news program."

"He's got a bigger audience than you'll ever have. He's one of the biggest names in the States."

"Sure, but you know Americans."

"I know that he would guarantee me an audience that would sink Livingstone for good."

"If you want people to take this seriously, Sir Gilbert, it ought to come from the BBC," rejoined Shayne. "And if you want me involved, you're going to have to let me take the pictures to an expert to confirm their legitimacy. I won't do it otherwise."

"You're not taking these photos to anyone. They're legit, I tell you, and I'm going public with them. Are you in or out?"

"If those are your terms, Sir Gilbert," replied Shayne, "then I guess I'm out."

She rose to leave, and they parted without further words.

When the door had closed behind her, Bowles went to his telephone as he peered at his watch. *Let's see,* he thought, *what time would it be in the States?*

Within a minute he was listening to the voice mail selections at Laurence Imre's network office in New York. When the prompts were finished, Bowles left his message.

"Mr. Imre," he said, "Sir Gilbert Bowles here, calling from London. I may have something for you that will repay many times over that favor you did for me three years ago. It's big . . . so huge I can't discuss it over the phone. All I will say is that I have proof positive—not rumor, but proof—that Adam Livingstone has been lying to the public, as I think you say, *big time.* You put me on your show, and this will be a bigger scoop than his so-called discoveries with Snow. I'll tell you this much—he's not an archaeologist, but a thief . . . and worse. Proof, Imre . . . I've got *proof.* It's eleven-thirty my time . . . give me a call. I'll be home most of the day."

(4)

The Livingstone household at Sevenoaks was bustling about in final preparation for Adam's and Rocky's departure. They would fly to Turkey today and rendezvous with Scott for several days before backtracking to Paris, where they would meet with Jen and Crystal. At eight o'clock, coffee, tea, and rolls were steaming and warm and set out on the breakfast table.

"This is the big day!" announced Adam as he walked in. "You set, Rocky?"

Only Juliet was quiet for the occasion. Though she would have hated for Adam to bring it up, it made it worse that he didn't even seem to notice.

An hour later, with luggage loaded into the car, Adam and Rocky climbed in. Juliet sat in the backseat. The lively conversation continued all the way to Heathrow, as it usually did prior to a trip when enthusiasm for a new project ran high. Adam had a way of making everything an adventure. Juliet, however, continued to be silent.

Once they were checked in and walking through the terminal toward their departure gate, Adam let Rocky get ahead, then drew close to Juliet and put his arm gently around her.

"I'll miss you," he said. "I wish you were going," he went on. "But I suppose if we're going to get married, someone has to plan the details, right?" He attempted a laugh, but it fell short. "You OK?" he said, glancing toward her. "You've hardly said a word."

"I'm fine," she replied, doing her best to keep a stiff upper lip.

"We'll be back before you know it," rejoined Adam. "If you change your mind, you can come over and meet us in France with Jen and Crystal."

Juliet nodded.

"Remember what I said. Go to Harrods and pick out some china and silver. I want us to start out with our own special things, not my mum's and dad's or anyone else's. You pick out the best. Nothing's too good for my wife-to-be!"

Juliet felt tears rising, but fought them back.

Sensing the cloudy atmosphere, Adam tried to alleviate it with reassuring conversation as they walked. "If anything big breaks," he concluded, "I'll send for you immediately."

"Thank you," Juliet replied softly. Her tone remained distant. She stared down at the floor.

They reached the gate where Rocky was waiting.

"Boarding in twenty minutes," said Rocky.

They found seats in the waiting area and sat down.

"Juliet," said Adam, "are you sure there's nothing the matter?"

"Nothing," she replied.

"If there is, I don't *have* to go. We can change our plans."

This was terrible, thought Juliet. She'd never been very good at hiding her emotions. The last thing she wanted was for Adam to start questioning her about what she was thinking!

"It's going to be different with you gone, that's all," she said. "I'm just being quiet because I'm going to miss you."

Adam stared probingly into her face. Juliet continued to look straight ahead. She was afraid to let his eyes find hers.

At last she forced a smile and turned jerkily toward him.

"You two have a great time," she said. Her attempt to sound upbeat was feeble at best.

The boarding announcement came. Juliet rose, a little too hastily. The others slowly stood. Genuinely concerned, Adam gazed toward Juliet's face. She would not return his look.

"I guess this is it!" said Juliet, forcing a smile. She gave Rocky a hug. He headed toward the line.

"Juliet . . . ," said Adam tenderly, but with obvious concern. He took her in his arms. They stood a moment, then Juliet pulled away.

"You'd better get going," she said. "Have a great time!"

She backed a step away, smiled again, but looked nervously away. Adam's probing eyes were like magnets!

Adam moved toward Rocky, smiling now himself, but with expression of bewilderment. Juliet gave a wave, then headed toward the large window that looked outside. She glanced back. The two waved one last time. Adam's hand lingered in the air. Rocky disappeared into the jetway. Finally Adam too disappeared from sight.

She drew in a great breath of air and sighed. She was glad that was over.

Juliet stood absently at the terminal window for five, ten, fifteen minutes, staring blankly at the nose of the airplane. Gradually the jetway pulled back. The plane inched away from the terminal.

She watched as it retreated, turned, and began taxiing out toward the runway. In another few minutes it was lost to her view.

Still she stood. Eight or nine minutes later the same plane sped back into view down the runway in the distance. The nose lifted off, then it rose in steep incline and banked away from the airport. In another thirty seconds it disappeared from sight into the clouds.

They were gone.

Juliet remained a minute longer, sniffed, drew in two or three shaky breaths, then walked away toward her car. It would be a long drive back to Sevenoaks.

What *was* Sevenoaks anyway, she asked herself. Surely not her home. How could she ever belong there? Even in her confusion as such thoughts went through her mind, Juliet hated herself for thinking them.

(5)

A bearded German student of archaeological engineering peered inside the darkened back room of a dingy coffeehouse in Istanbul. The time and place of the meeting had been set at the beginning of the clandestine transaction. None of his fellow students at the University in Hanover knew of his radical politics, or the conspiracy into which they had led him. They only knew he had done what many of them wished they could have done, volunteered his expertise during the summer past on the ark project. They envied him then. None would envy him when this day was done.

Given the outcome of his recent activity, he had considered not coming here at all. But in the end he judged it better to own up to what had happened. He had the feeling his employer was the kind who would be able to find him anywhere. And he had a new idea for blowing the thing up where it now sat at the base of the mountain. If he could just convince the man that his second attempt would be more successful than the first, everything would turn out in the end.

He ducked through the opening and squinted in the dim light.

✦ ✦ ✦

At the same time, Bonar and D'Abernon were speaking again. But as shrewd as Ciano Bonar may have been, it did not occur to her that perhaps her quarry had *let* himself be found. Even now she did not fully recognize her danger.

She called Zurich.

"I'm on him again."

"Where are you?"

"Istanbul."

"Do not let him see you, Ciano. He is a dangerous man."

"He has no idea I am here."

Zorin smiled to himself as he listened. Fausto Webbe was a genius in more ways than printing phony passports. This listening device was the best he had ever made use of. How could they think him so naive. But in the meantime he had a more pressing appointment.

✦ ✦ ✦

That Zorin's dubious lackey had expected to be paid after the failed sabotage of Noah's ark, showed he had seriously misjudged his employer. The student had been waiting some thirty minutes without sign of him when a grimy-looking fellow brought him a cup of coffee.

"But I didn't order–," began the German.

Already the Turk was gone, and the coffee left sitting on the table in front of him.

What was the harm, he thought, mistake or not. He picked up the cup and sipped at its edges.

Ugh–a foul brew! he thought. Bitter. Couldn't they make decent coffee here? Hadn't the Turks invented coffee, or something of the sort?

He took another swallow, then set the cup down in disgust.

Unfortunately, he would never have the opportunity to complete his studies in Hanover, or put into effect the plan for a new bomb. In less than five minutes his head slumped to the table with a crash, spilling across the table what remained of the cyanide-laced coffee that had killed him.

eighteen

Doubts

(1)

"Flying back to Turkey!" said Rocky enthusiastically once they were airborne. "I have indeed led an adventurous life since I ran into you!"

He picked up a magazine the stewardess had handed him and began absently flipping through it.

Adam remained subdued, regretting leaving Juliet. He tried to shake off the doldrums. It wouldn't do Juliet any good for him to remain downcast. He would call her when they landed.

✦ ✦ ✦

Below them as they banked steeply into the sky, Juliet drove out of the airport, her mind blank.

She reached the M25 and turned south. The great loop would take her gradually east and back in the direction of Sevenoaks. She recalled that other momentous afternoon when she had pulled off the motorway near Leatherhead to give her heart to the Lord.

How long ago that day seemed now. How much different she felt today. Then the fairy tale was just beginning. Today she felt as if it were coming to an end.

She tried to focus her thoughts on God, as if to do so might help her pray or think more positively. But she couldn't. She didn't know if she even *wanted* to pray.

She was afraid. But of what?

Her mood this morning brought to the surface the old doubts. She thought she was done with all that.

Did Adam *really* want her along? Over and over the brief conversation about reservations for France replayed itself in her mind. *She* could never really be part of Adam Livingstone's world. She ought to just do like Cinderella at the stroke of midnight and go back to where she belonged. Back to *her* life, not this high-society life she'd *thought* she was part of.

(2)

"Run it down for me again," Rocky was saying as they discussed their trip, "between the ark of the covenant, Ethiopia, Chartres, and the Templars."

"It was the Templars who discovered the Ethiopian connection with the ark," replied Adam.

"But now we know the ark wasn't in Ethiopia."

"Right. But there *was* a *replica* there, and a good one, probably of ancient date. So what I am thinking is that perhaps the Templars were substantially on the right track, but they didn't know that the Ethiopian legends concerned a *replica*, not the real thing. And if we managed to find the one . . . , " said Adam.

"Then why not the other," added Rocky, completing the thought for him.

"Exactly!"

Two stewardesses came by serving coffee and small rolls, bringing the conversation to a temporary halt.

✦ ✦ ✦

Meanwhile, Juliet continued to chastise herself.

Why had she withdrawn from Adam? She had positively been a limp noodle this morning!

If their relationship had cooled, it was her doing, not his. Or was it? Maybe he was looking for an excuse to get out of their engagement, and the trip to Turkey and France presented itself as the perfect opportunity to leave her behind.

Adam seemed so sure and confident and matter-of-fact. Did nothing ever ruffle him? Did *he* ever have doubts?

Maybe she always felt like a little girl tagging along beside him. What kind of marriage would that be! Why would Adam and the others even *want* her tagging along?

And now he was up there in the sky somewhere with Rocky, off on a new adventure, probably laughing and having a great time. And here she was down on the ground . . . alone.

Even if Adam weren't part of my life, Juliet thought—*even if all this fairy tale does come to an end, I have a new life in the Lord . . . that should be enough.*

Oh, this is all so confusing!

(3)

In his studio preparing for the taping of another telecast, Laurence Imre found himself thinking about Gilbert Bowles and his scheduled interview in five days.

He reflected on the hubbub recently over the Bible and all those religious things . . . what was it about anyway? What was Bowles' connection? Should he investigate before the interview?

Bowles had always been a character, even for someone like Laurence Imre, whom most of the media considered about as offbeat as they come.

But whatever Bowles had up his sleeve, he wouldn't let the interview get derailed by a bunch of religious nonsense. He'd had enough of that malarky from his grandmother when he was a boy. Yet . . . on the other hand, if people *were* interested in the stuff, maybe he should do something on it preparatory to Bowles.

Imre continued to debate with himself, but finally decided against it. Who cared about the Bible? He knew he didn't. It was news, image, spin, personality . . . what did ancient relics matter? He was in the image business. If the Bowles' program got high ratings, he'd follow it up with some Bible thumper. Let the two sides duke it out in public. A good argument between religious wackos—that always provided good theater. He'd use Bowles, the Bible, maybe some fundamentalist lunatic—he'd use them all if they would boost ratings.

But whether the Bible was true or not . . . personally, he didn't much care.

(4)

Juliet arrived back at Sevenoaks. She drove up in front of the house. She turned off the key but continued to sit motionless behind the wheel of the car. She had managed to hold off the tears until then. But at last they began to flow.

Lord, please help me not to worry and doubt so much. I thank you for all that has happened to me, she prayed. *I'll try to want whatever you want for me.*

Even as she said the words, her heart continued to sink. It had been an emotionless prayer. A prayer of obedience, it was true—always the best kind—yet without much vigor to back it up.

She sniffled, blew her nose, then got out and walked into the house.

The moment Juliet entered the kitchen, Mrs. Graves saw that something was wrong. She walked toward Juliet, wiping her hands on her apron. She wrapped her arms around the poor girl and drew her close.

"What is it, my dear?" asked Mrs. Graves in a voice of concern.

"I don't know, Auntie," replied Juliet in a moan. "I don't know what's wrong with me. Suddenly I'm filled with so many doubts."

"Doubts about what?"

"I don't know, maybe that I'm right for Adam."

"Why would you think that, dear?"

"I don't know—we're such different ages and from different backgrounds," replied Juliet, skirting the real thing that was plaguing her.

"That's never mattered to you two young people before."

"It seems to bother everyone else. It even bothers you, Auntie—you know it does."

Mrs. Graves did not reply. This was certainly no time to bring that up.

"And then—," Juliet continued, her voice catching, "he didn't seem to care if I went along," she burst out.

Juliet pulled away from her aunt's embrace and quickly left the kitchen. She ran upstairs to her room and threw herself on the bed.

Soon footsteps sounded behind her. Mrs. Graves approached and sat down on the edge of the bed. The loving aunt placed a reassuring hand of comfort on her niece's back, patting and stroking her gently while Juliet continued softly to cry.

(5)

Now at a thirty-seven-thousand-foot cruising altitude in a southeasterly course which would take them over the Mediterranean, the discussion resumed between Adam and Rocky.

"Tell me about the origins of the Templars," said Rocky.

"It is an ancient church order established during the twelfth century," said Adam. "It is no longer in existence in Catholicism, yet survives as one of the highest Masonic degrees. The first crusade began in 1096, and by the turn of the century Jerusalem was in the hands of so-called Christian troops. The Templars began eighteen years later as a group of nine young French knights, mostly from the region around the French town of Chartres."

"So that's the link between Chartres and the origins of the Crusades."

"But it remains a mystery of history why these nine young men decided to go to the Holy Land."

"You don't know?"

Adam shook his head.

"In any event," he went on, "these nine young Frenchmen journeyed to the Holy Land and presented themselves to the new European king, Baldwin, saying they had come to dedicate themselves to the service of the Holy Land. Moreover they committed themselves to the virtuous lifestyle common to monastic orders of the time—poverty, chastity, and obedience. Before long they had taken up residence in the king's own quarters, none other than the former Al-Aqsa Muslim Mosque on the very site of Solomon's former temple. They called themselves *Pauperes Commilitones Christi Templique Salomonis*—The Poor Fellow Soldiers of Christ and the Temple of Solomon. They were soon known throughout Jerusalem simply as the Knights of the Temple. Later this was shortened to the Knights Templar."

Adam paused.

"I have the feeling this is only the beginning," said Rocky.

"You're right there, my friend," replied Adam. "Trying to discover what the Templars found once they were in Jerusalem may be the key to everything."

(6)

Five minutes after Mrs. Graves' departure, Juliet also rose and left her bedroom. She avoided the office. She didn't want to see Crystal right now either.

The tears were spent for the present. She walked downstairs and out of the house. She needed to swing. Maybe her friend Kimberly would be at the park. It would be good to feel the wind on her face, to cool away the sting, and talk to someone not connected to Adam Livingstone.

Juliet walked slowly to the park, trying her best to fill her lungs with the chilly air, as if to somehow restore her emotional balance.

The park was empty. It looked so wet and wintry and uninviting. Vaguely disappointed, Juliet sat down and began to swing back and forth. Somehow the bare stark feel of the place suited her solitary mood. But even the swings couldn't set right what she was feeling inside.

She let the momentum of the swing gradually stop. For another minute Juliet sat motionless, then rose and walked back to the estate.

She found her aunt upstairs in her sitting room.

"I think I need to do something different for a while, Auntie," Juliet said as she entered. "I thought about it just now while I was out walking."

The housekeeper glanced up, noticing that Juliet had one of her old cardigans pulled tightly about her. "What kind of something?" she said.

"I think I would like to go to Bedford and see Mum."

"That's a wonderful idea, Juliet, dear," said Mrs. Graves, relieved at the sensible sound of it.

"It will feel good to get away from here, even if just for a little while."

"Why don't I go north with you, dear," said Mrs. Graves.

"I would like that, Auntie!"

"Then we'll go up together. We'll have a good time."

"Oh, I can't wait!" exclaimed Juliet, feeling better already. "I'll go call Mum right now."

nineteen

Traditions

(1)

After a five-hour flight, three time-zone changes, lunch, and an in-flight movie, Rocky and Adam at last began to feel the plane's descent. In another thirty minutes, they touched down in Yerevan, now with a very different future ahead of them than the triumph of a short time before.

It was late in the afternoon when Scott met them to drive south to the site.

"You'll be amazed at the progress," he said enthusiastically as they exited the city. "The final shape of the hangar is coming together. It's beautiful. And the climate control inside is functional."

"What about the hotel?" asked Rocky. "All I want to know is if we're still going to be living in tents."

Scott laughed. "Believe it or not, I moved in three days ago. I've got a nice big suite for us. A little spartan, but, hey—hot water, private bathroom, beds and sheets . . . who's complaining."

"What are the crowds like?" asked Adam.

"Most of the media and corporate types and half the students and hippies all left about the same time you did," answered Scott. "But tourists have been flocking in like crazy. Crowd control has been one of the major problems—*look but don't touch,* you know."

"Where do they all stay? There aren't that many hotels up and running yet."

"No, just the one, and they're only issuing rooms to VIP types. Many tourists come in for the day and drive back to Yerevan, or else they camp for a night—there are dozens of RVs always about. So far the Turkish government is remaining cooperative."

"Let's hold our breath it continues."

"How long are you two going to be here?"

"Six, maybe seven days—we'll see how it goes."

(2)

The following morning's *Daily Mail* came. Juliet sat with her aunt in the housekeeper's sitting room, enjoying a day's second cup of tea. She didn't feel like being alone this morning. They planned to leave for Bedford the day after tomorrow.

All at once Mrs. Graves gave an irritated *hmmph* and threw the paper down with disgust.

"What is it, Auntie?" asked Juliet, glancing toward her.

"Nothing, dear . . . ," replied her aunt. Her tone, however, said clearly enough that something had annoyed her.

"Let me see the paper, Auntie."

"You don't want to see it, dear," replied Mrs. Graves. She bent down to pick it up again before Juliet could reach for it.

But it was too late. Already Juliet had the newspaper in her hands. A few seconds later she saw what had prompted her aunt's outburst–another photo of her!

ADAM LIVINGSTONE ENGAGED IN SECRETIVE NEW QUEST read the caption. Underneath was the subtitle "Project So Hush-Hush, Even Fiancée Can't Be Told."

"I can't believe it!" exclaimed Juliet. "How did they get this picture?"

"What is the secretive new quest?" asked Mrs. Graves. "I didn't know Mr. Livingstone–"

"He's not, Auntie," interrupted Juliet. "I have no idea what they're talking about. This makes me so *furious!* Let me see what it says."

"*Matrimony seems not about to change Adam Livingstone,*" Juliet read. "*Communication is kept to a minimum for new and highly confidential endeavors. By his own admission marriage is unlikely to alter that pattern. Livingstone's present project is one not even fiancée Juliet Halsay knows about. Furthermore, Ms. Halsay will not be accompanying Livingstone on his upcoming trip out of the country. Is there already trouble in paradise, even before the vows are–*"

Juliet could read no more. This was the last straw! Her pent-up uncertainty over her future with Adam burst to the surface in anger.

"That does it!" she cried, jumping to her feet red-faced and throwing the paper across the room. "I'm going to put a stop to this!"

(3)

Juliet marched into the offices of the *Daily Mail* nearly as angrily as she had driven away from Sevenoaks, more steamed up than her aunt had ever seen her.

"I want to see your editor," she said to the receptionist.

"Which one, miss," the young lady replied, "city . . . world . . . sports?"

"I don't know," replied Juliet testily, "whoever's in charge of photographs."

"Are you a photographer? Do you have something you want to—"

"No, I'm not a photographer! I want to talk to your editor."

Juliet's tone was such that the young woman decided it best to buzz the paper's head editor, Tobias Tufts, known to everyone in London as Toby T.

He entered the lobby from an inner office somewhere two or three minutes later. Catching his eye, the receptionist nodded toward Juliet.

"Hello, Miss . . . uh—," the editor began with a smile and a handshake.

"Halsay . . . Juliet Halsay."

"Miss Halsay, I'm Toby Tufts. What may I do for you?"

"Your paper has been running photographs of me, Mr. Tufts," said Juliet in a tone which could hardly be mistaken for a friendly one. "I am here to personally demand that it stop."

"Photographs," repeated the editor, "I'm afraid I don't—"

He stopped as his eyes lit up.

"Halsay . . . of course! I knew there was something familiar about that name. You're the Livingstone mystery girl!" He spoke as if it were a label Juliet ought to be proud of.

"I am no mystery girl," she shot back. "I happen to be Adam Livingstone's fiancée, and my face is *not* public property."

"I'm sorry the publicity is disturbing to you, Miss Halsay," said Tufts, trying to sound pleasant, "but we of the press have the right to print news. Once you got involved with Adam Livingstone, you became news. That's hardly something I can help."

"Then let me talk to the photographer who's responsible. At least I ought to have the right to find out where I'm being spied on."

"It's freelance stuff," replied Tufts. "Nobody on our staff. We just pay for it."

"Who is it, then? Do I have the right to know?"

"I suppose. We get it from a BBC reporter who's moonlighting to make a few extra quid."

"Whose name is?"

"Kim Shayne."

"How can I find him?"

"*Her,* you mean. I don't know—talk to the BBC. Actually, she's supposed to drop by this afternoon."

Tufts' eyes wandered toward the front doors.

"Hey, here she comes now," he said. "You're in luck, Miss Halsay. Come and meet her face-to-face."

Juliet turned. Walking toward them was a familiar figure. When the newcomer saw Juliet, she stopped. Her face went white. At the same time Juliet's turned several brighter shades of red.

"Kimberly!" she exclaimed. "*You* . . . but . . ."

"You know each other?" said Tufts, laughing. "This gets better and better! Why didn't you tell me, Miss Halsay?"

"I *don't* know any Kim Shayne!" said Juliet. "I *thought* I knew Kimberly Banbrigge."

"Juliet, I'm sorry . . . I was going to tell you, really," said Kim, speaking for the first time. "There just never seemed a good—"

"A good time for what—betrayal?" interrupted Juliet. "You lied to me! You didn't even tell me your real name."

"I didn't lie about my name."

"You called yourself Kimberly Banbrigge."

"That's true. That wasn't a lie. My full name is Kimberly Banbrigge Shayne. I go by Kim Shayne, that's all."

"It's as good as a lie. You intentionally deceived me!"

"I really was going to tell you."

"When? After you'd gotten all the mileage out of my face you could?"

A brief awkwardness followed.

"Well, what's done is done," said Juliet. "But *don't* bring me or my private life into your paper again!"

"I'm sorry, Juliet," said Kim. "You've got to believe me."

"An apology doesn't mean much after it's too late."

"Maybe you're right, but Adam Livingstone is a public figure. He's fair game for the press. He knows that and plays along."

"I'm not Adam Livingstone."

"You're about to become his wife. That makes you fair game too."

"Fair game! I'm no public figure."

"Like it or not, Juliet, you are now," said Kim, quietly but definitively. "I can't make any promises."

The words hit Juliet with unexpected force and her brain went blank. She tried to make sense of what she'd heard. Her confusion only made it worse.

"Leave me out of it, I tell you!" she said. "Just leave me out of it!"

Juliet spun around and ran from the lobby. Already she felt the anger turning to tears. By the time she reached the car she was crying in earnest.

(4)

Brandi Corwin strolled leisurely along a wide flat beach at the point where the constant incoming flow finally gave up and gradually drifted back seaward to be swallowed in the next inrushing surge. Her bare feet moved in and out of the salty swirl without purpose, enjoying the eternal rhythmic interplay between sea and sand, earth and moon, hot and cold, feeling the chill of the sea, then moving up the beach a few yards where the sand was dry and warm, then back to the thin foamy tidal edge. She did not remember enjoying the simple pleasure of a walk on the beach so much ever in her life.

She had been out walking an hour or two. Hundreds of sun worshipers, children, joggers, and surfers were about. Solitude on the beaches of Southern California was not a luxury she expected. But her spirit was calm and she didn't mind the crowds. Something was happening inside her. As far as she was concerned, Brandi was alone in all the world. In her hand at her side she carried a tiny book. A book she hadn't read in years . . . until two nights ago.

What exactly she felt as she walked along, giving an occasional kick at a puff of ocean foam or chasing a retreating wave like she had as a child, she couldn't say. Free . . . lighthearted . . . almost—strange as it was to say it—happy.

Something had happened standing in front of that church the other night. She had been reminded of so many things out of a past she thought she wanted to forget—Sunday school and Bible verses among them. Suddenly the memories were fond ones . . . like rays of light into the middle of this awful life she had made for herself.

She returned the next day to the church that had made her cry. She hadn't expected it to be open in the middle of the week. She only wanted to see it in the daylight. Yet some impulse caused her to walk up and try the door. Surprised, she felt the latch turn and the door open. She walked inside.

It was not dead as she had expected. Lights were on and she heard voices, laughter, and activity. She followed the sounds. She found herself approaching an office area where several people were clustered about, adjacent to which a glass door stood open leading into a small room that looked like a tiny bookstore. A few of those present greeted her. She smiled, feeling conspicuous and out of place, then walked into the room with the books. As she entered she became aware of soft music playing in the background.

What was she doing here, she said to herself.

"Hello . . . anything I can help you with?" said a pleasant voice from somewhere in the room.

Startled, she turned toward it.

"Uh . . . no, not really," she said. "I'm kind of looking around. Actually, I didn't even bring my purse so I can't buy anything."

"No problem," rejoined the young man behind the counter. "We're happy to have you stay as long as you like. Selling is not primarily why we have the store here, but to provide a pleasant oasis for those who come in."

Strange words from a clerk, Brandi thought. Yet that was just what she felt as she continued to browse about the tiny shop and drink in the peaceful music—that she had discovered a refuge in the midst of the storms of her life.

She remained more than an hour, half of it spent talking to the friendly young man who couldn't have been more than nineteen or twenty himself. When she left she was carrying two small books he had given her, one called *Life at the Center,* which he said had helped him more than any book he had ever read, and a copy of the *Living New Testament*, which he said would make the Bible come alive as never before.

She had taken both gratefully, still not quite sure what was going on. It was the New Testament she had brought with her on today's walk.

She came to a portion of the beach where fewer people were about. After one final run into the water to cool her feet, Brandi walked up farther away from the water and sat down. She would not in a million years have anticipated opening a Bible again in her life. Yet here she was about to do exactly that. She was looking forward to what it might have to say. How could mere days make such a difference in outlook?

She'd made a mess of things, that was for sure. She'd nearly gotten in over her head. Had God perhaps kept that from happening?

She opened the New Testament and flipped through it, familiar with the names of the books, but with nothing particularly in mind to read. The easy style of the translation was so different than the verses she had been taught in Sunday school that she hardly knew some of it. She found herself reading in the middle of Luke's Gospel as if it were a story she had never heard before. When she came to the familiar story in the fifteenth chapter, she did not recognize it at first.

"*A few days later,*" she read, "*this younger son packed all his belongings and took a trip to a distant land, and there wasted all his money on wild living.*"

The words stung her. She realized that two nights ago she had come within an inch of heading down that very path. If it weren't for that program about Noah's ark she had seen, who knows what kind of further trouble she would have landed in.

She read on.

> *"About the time his money ran out a great famine swept over the land, and he began to starve. He persuaded a local farmer to hire him to feed his pigs. The boy became so hungry that even the pods he was feeding the swine looked good to him. But no one gave him anything. When he finally came to his senses, he said to himself, 'At home even the hired men have food enough to spare, and here I am, dying of hunger! I will go home to my father and say, "Father, I have sinned against both heaven and you, and I am no longer worthy of being called your son. Please take me on as a hired man."' So he returned home—"*

Brandi's eyes clouded with tears. She finally recognized the story. And she knew she was reading about herself. She tried to finish.

"*And while he was still a long distance away, his father saw him coming. Filled with love and compassion, he ran to his son and embraced him, and kissed him. His son said to him, 'Father, I have sinned—'*"

She broke down and wept. She could read no more. She too had sinned, and at last she knew it. She let the tears flow. They stung, yet somehow at the same time it felt good to cry.

When Brandi Corwin rose thirty minutes later, she knew it was time to go home.

(5)

Juliet gradually awoke. A chilly sun attempted to penetrate her aunt's small living room in Bedford, but without much warmth corresponding to the effort. She was surprised to find that morning had come so quickly.

She drew the blanket more tightly around her shoulders and rolled over on the couch where she'd spent the night. She heard voices, but they were distant. They came from the kitchen. Her two aunts and Mum were talking.

Juliet glanced sleepily about. Her suitcase lay open on the living-room floor. Mrs. Graves had squeezed into the bedroom with her mother and Aunt Betsy. In a contented way Juliet felt like a little girl again, hearing the three sisters chatting over their morning tea. Gradually the soft voices penetrated more distinctly into her consciousness.

It was a good feeling, she thought. She hadn't felt this peaceful since that awful day when her family–

Suddenly Juliet heard her own name. They weren't discussing sleeping arrangements at all. They were talking about *her!*

". . . dreadful to see poor Juliet's picture in the sheets," came Mrs. Graves' subdued voice from the kitchen.

"I can't but worry that something might go wrong and plunge her into despair again," whispered her mother.

"That mystery-girl thing was enough to make me sick," added Aunt Betsy, "as if Juliet were a celebrity whom they could . . ."

Her voice trailed off indistinctly.

"Then the announcement of the engagement," said her mother again.

". . . from having risen too far so fast."

". . . not as if we're not from good stock, mind you, but . . . well, Mr. Livingstone's a man of breeding."

". . . one of *us* ever really be part of *that* world . . ."

Juliet tried to prevent her ears hearing more. It was awful to eavesdrop when *she* was the subject of the conversation. But she couldn't help herself.

"What's he like, Andrea?"

". . . a good and honorable man, Lona. I couldn't love him more if he were my own son."

"Does he love her?"

"I truly believe he does, Betsy."

"But is love enough?" said Juliet's mother. "Perhaps that's the question my

Juliet ought to be asking . . . a body doesn't just step into a completely different world. . . ."

Juliet climbed out of her temporary bed and hurried to the bathroom. She didn't want to hear more.

(6)

By the time Juliet made an appearance in the kitchen, sounds of her waking had reached mother and aunts, and their conversation had moved into other channels. By lunchtime, however, talk between them made its way back to the subject on everyone's mind—Juliet's engagement to Adam.

Juliet told them of the incident with Kim Shayne.

"I don't know, Juliet," said Lona Halsay as the four sat nibbling on crackers and sipping their cups of tea. "It seems they're making sport of you."

"No, Mum," replied Juliet, "they're really good to me at Sevenoaks. Aren't they, Auntie Andrea?"

"Yes, of course, dear," said Mrs. Graves.

"I mean the press, dear," her mother went on. "They're using you. Do you really want that kind of life for yourself? You told us what that Shayne woman said—that *you* are a public figure now. And, dear, you must realize how very different the two of you are."

"But Adam's different," insisted Juliet. Even in the midst of her own doubts, she was quick to defend him. "None of that station business means anything to him."

"Is he the man you want as your husband?" asked her aunt Betsy.

"I can't think of anyone more perfect in all the world than Adam."

"But is he the man you want for *your* husband?"

Juliet could not answer immediately.

"I . . . think so," she replied at length.

"You don't sound very sure of yourself, dear," said Mrs. Graves. Though it went against everything she believed, Mrs. Graves dearly loved her master and could think of nothing more delightful than for Juliet to become his wife. But she could not keep from flitting back and forth in the matter.

"I'm just confused at the minute," replied Juliet. "But . . . of course I want to marry Adam. What woman wouldn't?"

"But is he right for you, dear?" asked Mrs. Halsay. "Our family's of the old school. We know our place. We cannot help but think about such things."

"Adam doesn't," said Juliet.

"Do you?"

The question, once again, caught Juliet off guard.

"Perhaps it is because you think about such things more than you realize," suggested Mrs. Graves, trying to reassure her, yet raising the specter of doubt still higher, "that you are so confused right now."

It grew quiet.

"Maybe I ought to try to go to University and try to get a higher degree," said Juliet after a minute. "Then I would feel more a part of Adam's team, and not so much an outsider."

No one replied.

"Have you and Adam . . . set a date for the wedding yet?" asked Aunt Betsy.

"No. But Adam told me to go to Harrods when he was gone and pick out some china and crystal. Will you go with me, Mum? I don't think I can do it alone."

"London is a long drive, dear."

"Come to Sevenoaks for a visit," suggested Mrs. Graves. "Come down with Juliet and me. We have the whole house nearly to ourselves."

"I suppose I could get away for a few days," replied Mrs. Halsay.

"You're all going to desert me!" said Aunt Betsy.

"Only for a while," replied Juliet's mother.

The conversation moved on to other topics. No one brought up the subject of Juliet's engagement again.

After two or three days in Bedford, Juliet, her mother, and Mrs. Graves left to return to Sevenoaks.

twenty

Unlikely Benefactress

(1)

Juliet and her mum walked through the famous doors of the Brompton Road entrance to Harrods. Neither had ever been into the world's most well-known store in their lives. They had dressed for the occasion as if going to church.

The two peered around to get their bearings.

"It's so much bigger than I imagined!" said Juliet. "We'll never find anything!"

After checking the directory and asking directions three or four times, they made their way to the second floor. China and porcelain, crystal and glass, and cutlery and silver were all located in close proximity.

After an hour of wandering, Juliet was more bewildered and overwhelmed than when they came in.

"Everything's far too dear!" Juliet's mum whispered. "You could never let Adam buy any of these sets for you."

"May I be of assistance?" said an approaching salesclerk.

"Well . . . I, uh," began Juliet. "I need to pick out a crystal and china set. I'm to be married."

"Ah . . . I see," said the man, concluding from their demeanor and accent that the two ladies before him had obviously taken a wrong turn somewhere. Juliet's mother's voice, in particular, grated on what he considered his refined ear.

"But everything's so expensive, and–," Juliet went on.

"I understand," said the clerk, his tone betraying the merest hint of that unmistakable patronizing effect with which individuals of his type are so gifted. As he was of the same background as Juliet and her mother, yet had successfully managed to climb the Harrods' ladder, he enjoyed exerting the phantom superiority he supposed lay with him.

"Perhaps," he went on, "I might be helpful in directing you–"

He paused briefly to clear his throat.

"–to our Homewares section. I am certain there you will be able to find something more suitable, shall we say, to your budget."

"My fiancé specifically said for me to come to the China and Porcelain, and Crystal and Glass departments," insisted Juliet. "He mentioned that perhaps I might find something in the Waterford, Spode, or Royal Doulton lines."

Another well-executed clearing of the throat followed mention of the exclusive names.

"Highly unlikely, I assure you, miss. You are far more—"

"Perhaps I might be of some help," said a silky voice from behind.

Juliet turned to see Candace Montreux approaching. Her heart leapt into her throat. Luckily the salesman, who in a mere few words recognized Candace's breeding as far above his own as he supposed his was above his two would-be customers, spoke first.

"I was explaining to these two ladies," he said, "that the items in my department here are quite distinguished. I thought that our less costly items, ma'am, which are to be found in Homewares, as I am sure you can understand, would no doubt be of more interest to them."

"Oh, but you must not know who this *is,*" said Candace, casting upon Juliet a smile which was intended to convey worlds of condescension though her words came enclosed in a shell of flattery. Then she addressed the clerk. "Why this, sir, is Mr. Adam Livingstone's future wife."

Candace's appearance, though seemingly coincidental, was in fact anything but. Indeed she had been more than a little curious about what sort of silver and china and crystal would be selected by the happy couple from Sevenoaks, though it galled her to even think of Adam marrying such a thing as the Halsay girl. She decided to pop in and see what she could learn from Harrods' wedding registry. But she had never expected this much good fortune to fall into her lap.

"Oh, well . . . I had no idea," the clerk replied, quickly backtracking into self-effacement. "I am pleased to know the fact, miss," he said toward Juliet, fumbling momentarily. He glanced back and forth between the two young women, not altogether able to make sense of the scene presented to his senses. "Has the bride-to-be filled out a Harrods' Gift and Bridal Registry form?"

Juliet shook her head.

"That department is also on this floor. Might I suggest—"

"Perhaps it would be best for us to come back another time," said Mrs. Halsay.

"Nonsense," said Candace. "We will get this straightened out in no time. You must be dear Juliet's mother?"

"Yes . . . yes, that's right."

"It is nice to meet you, Mrs. Halsay. My name is Candace Montreux. I have been a friend of Adam's for simply years."

Once the names *Livingstone* and *Montreux* reached the man's ears, he began to put two and two together with some things he had seen in the paper.

"But, I thought that *you*–," he began. Then he realized the hole he had created for himself.

"Yes, well . . ." Candace smiled toward him, then lowered her voice in a confidential manner. "Apparently our mutual friend prefers the young and inexperienced."

The man's eyes lit up. He had indeed stumbled into a juicy situation! Just wait till the missus heard this!

"In any event, perhaps you might show *me* some of your wares," Candace went on, slinking up to the man. "You see, I am on close terms with Mr. Livingstone and know his tastes intimately. I think I shall be able to help Miss Halsay understand."

"Yes, ma'am–it will be my pleasure," replied the clerk effusively, enjoying the private joke between himself and Miss Montreux.

They walked off, while Juliet and her mother followed like two puppies. Inwardly Juliet was dying of embarrassment to be trapped in such an awkward situation.

(2)

Hank Scully had no intention of leaving that Bible lying on the floor for someone else to see.

As soon as the warden was out of sight, he rose, took a couple of paces, and gave the thing a kick, sending it sliding across the floor again. It ricocheted off one of the walls and came to rest out of sight under his bunk.

Let it stay there and rot for all he cared.

But it didn't rot, it burned. Burned a hole in his brain all night. He couldn't forget that it was down there. All night he couldn't forget. And it kept him awake through every slow lonely minute.

He dozed off the next day. The light helped him forget. But as soon as night fell, again came the tormenting reminder of a foreign presence in his room, hidden in the blackness. He couldn't see it. But he could *feel* it under there.

Was he going crazy? What could that book have in it to freak him out like this?

He couldn't take many more nights like this . . . or he *would* go crazy!

(3)

Following the mortifying encounter in Harrods, Juliet began doubting herself even more. Even a clerk, a stranger, had been able to tell that *she* didn't belong with the name *Adam Livingstone.*

Was that sort of encounter going to be the story of her life, people hearing her uncultured voice, then wondering what a man of Adam's refinement was doing with the likes of *her?*

The next morning the knocker sounded outside the Livingstone home. Mrs. Graves opened the door. There she saw Candace Montreux staring her in the face.

"Hello, Mrs. Graves."

"Adam is not here, Miss Montreux," replied the housekeeper stiffly, her nose narrowing in spite of the flare of her nostrils.

"I didn't come to see Adam," she replied. "Is Miss Halsay in?"

"I will see if she is taking callers."

Mrs. Graves closed the door, leaving Candace to stew outside in the entryway. She went upstairs to her own sitting room where Juliet and her mother were seated together.

"You have a caller, Juliet," she said. Her tone conveyed clearly enough her annoyance.

"A caller? Me . . . who?"

"It's that Montreux woman."

"Candace Montreux!" exclaimed Juliet. "What could she possibly want with me?"

"No good, I'm sure."

Juliet rose and followed her aunt downstairs. Already her heart was beating twenty strokes faster! The very name Candace Montreux intimidated her. She did her best to hide the trembling of her knees.

"Miss, uh, Montreux," said Juliet in a tentative voice as she opened the door.

"Hello, Juliet," said Candace with smooth confidence and a bright red smile. "I hope you don't mind my barging in on you like this."

"Oh, no . . . would you, uh, like to come in?"

"Yes, thank you."

Candace followed Juliet inside, sweeping past the ever-vigilant Mrs. Graves and casting her a look of triumph, as if to say, *I'll take care of you later.*

The two young women walked into the guest sitting room. They sat down, Juliet obviously unaccustomed to the role of hostess in the house which would, as plans presently stood, one day be her own.

"I could not help notice when we met at Harrods yesterday," Candace began, "that you seemed nervous about your upcoming wedding."

"I've had a great deal on my mind," replied Juliet lamely.

"I can certainly understand that," Candace went on with tender sympathy. "I wanted to come by to offer my help in any way in which I might be able to serve you."

"That is kind, Miss Montreux."

"Please . . . call me Candace. After all, if you are going to marry Adam, you and I will have to be very good friends."

Juliet tried to smile. Awkwardness was written over her entire person. The fidgeting was not lost on her visitor.

"It is the least I can do," Candace went on. "Adam and I are such old and *dear* friends that the moment I read of your engagement I said to myself, 'Juliet and I simply must get to know one another better.'"

"Well," said Juliet hesitatingly, attempting a smile, "I suppose I am in a little bit over my head." Maybe she had misjudged Candace. "I decided," she added, "to wait on the china and crystal until Adam gets back."

"Oh, he's . . . out of the country again?" asked Candace innocently. She knew exactly when he'd left, though she had been unsuccessful in discovering his itinerary.

"Yes, on another research trip."

"Adam and his research!" She laughed. "If ever a man loved his work, it is Adam Livingstone. Where is he off to now?"

"Africa."

"Africa again . . . I see. Well—"

As Candace went on, she adopted the tone of confidante.

"—unless Adam has changed, he will have a difficult time leaving his work long enough to help you with the wedding plans. You'll never get *him* into Harrods."

"Why do you say that?"

"Oh, my dear, you can't be unaware that he is married to his dirt and fossils and maps and holes in the ground. He has never had time for anything else. I doubt he ever will. We were engaged for four years, you know. I had a dreadful time getting him to show the slightest interest in anything I considered important."

"You . . . were *engaged?*" said Juliet, her eyes widening.

"Oh yes, of course, Juliet dear."

"I didn't know."

"Adam didn't tell you? I don't suppose I'm surprised. Everyone always expected us to marry. We were the talk of London for the first couple years. But finally I couldn't take it any longer."

"Take what?"

"Oh, you know Adam," rejoined Candace with a knowing laugh, "the waiting, the uncertainty, his preoccupation with his work, his never noticing what I was wearing or if I had bought a new hat or dress. I finally had no choice but to break it off. Adam was crushed, of course. But I told him, 'Adam, you had your chance. If you ever find a woman who can endure what you put a woman through, then she'll be a better woman than I am.'"

Juliet listened with horrified fascination to Candace talk about Adam with such familiarity.

"I wish you every happiness, Juliet dear," Candace went on. "But speaking for myself, I couldn't live as second fiddle in Adam Livingstone's life any longer."

Juliet was putty in Candace's expert hands. The conversation continued, with Candace asking appropriate questions and then expanding on certain carefully selected subjects as Juliet's replies gave her opening.

By the time she left the Livingstone estate thirty minutes later, Juliet was more an emotional mess than before.

(4)

The first indication Juliet's mother and Mrs. Graves had that Candace Montreux was gone were Juliet's feet running up the stairs, down the hall, past where they sat in the housekeeper's parlor, and into her own room. Even from where they sat they heard her sobbing.

"That Montreux woman!" exclaimed Mrs. Graves. "I've a good mind–"

She broke off her thought. Actually, she didn't know what she had a good mind to do. She only knew she was angry, and that if Candace showed her face around her again, she might give her two cents of her mind.

"It's eleven. Perhaps we ought to go downstairs and have some tea," suggested Juliet's mother.

Her sister nodded. They rose and left the room. Mrs. Halsay turned toward Juliet's room. She walked inside.

"Juliet, my dear," she said with the sympathetic heart of a true mother as she sat down on the bed, "come down with Auntie Andrea and me and have some tea. It will help you feel better."

Juliet turned and gazed into her eyes with a more forlorn expression than her mother had ever seen. She sat up, and the next minute was in her mother's arms.

"Oh, Mummy," she wailed, "I just don't know what to do!"

twenty-one

Thief and Fraud!

(1)

Adam was up at dawn the morning after their arrival, walking the length and breadth of Ararat City in the cold wintry air, gazing up toward the mountain where he had helped make history. Blanketed again in snow, in the solemn quietness of the morning, the majestic peak gave no hint that such a short while ago it had been the center of the world's attention. It was a good thing they got the ark down when they did, thought Adam. Though snow had come to the mountains, the ground was dusty beneath his feet, the air chilly and dry. Except for what this place symbolized, and the construction around him, the sights and sounds and smells of the high desert terrain, the occasional sound of a far-off bird or wail of wind, it was not so very different than dozens of places he had arisen to walk in the early morning while on research trips through the years.

As Scott had said, progress on the hangar and facilities throughout the city had progressed at an unbelievable pace. Several petrol stations were fully functional, as well as two or three stores where food and camping supplies were plentiful. The one hotel would soon be followed by two or three others opening their doors. Not to be outdone by western efforts, the Turkish government had stepped up its own involvement, and was in the process of constructing several permanent buildings for official use. One, hastily constructed, already housed a number of offices connected specifically to the organizational and management necessities of Ararat City and its research facilities.

A half-dozen apartment buildings were under construction. Though the airport was crude, some regular traffic was beginning to be established between its new landing strip and Yerevan.

Adam could smell coffee coming from somewhere, and even—was his nose playing a trick on him!—the aroma of eggs and bacon! Civilization was indeed arriving at this outpost. It was becoming a real city.

He met Scott as he approached the hotel as he returned from his walk.

"Where's Rocky?" asked Adam.

"Still asleep."

Adam laughed. "Can't say as I blame him. But I had to get out, feel the air on my face, take the pulse of the morning."

"What do you think?" asked Scott, gesturing in a wide circle with his hand.

"It's fabulous," replied Adam. "I can hardly believe it. And there's the old ark of Noah in its glass house. Let the blizzards and wind and hail and snow come. It is remarkable to me that we actually did it."

"Let's go have breakfast," said Scott. "There are a million things to do today. Hundreds of people have been waiting for you to get here."

"Are you saying this peaceful morning isn't going to last?"

"Yep. You've got appointments with everyone in the place. It'll take you a week to see them. The Turks want to talk to you and the cartel people about establishing some kind of organizational structure as a temporary city government."

"Is that really necessary?"

"Things come up occasionally. With the National Guard gone, I think we need something like that, even a small police force. With this many people, stuff happens, you know."

"The cartel might request that the U.N. send in a limited contingent of troops for a while. But what does everyone need to see me for?"

"You're the man," said Scott, laughing. "Don't you know, this whole thing is built on your reputation. It's like the financial system. It rests on an idea—on trust . . . on trust in *you*. Just make sure you don't go getting into any scandals."

"I'll try to behave myself," Adam said, a twinkle in his eye.

"Good, just keep on your toes."

For the next forty-eight hours, as Scott had said, Adam was busier than he could have imagined. But his presence at the site reenergized everyone and enthusiasm ran high. It was reported that a team of scientists from Russia, heretofore cool toward the whole project in view of the official stance of communism toward the supernatural, was flying in to meet with Adam about possibly setting up a research office of their own once the facilities were complete.

(2)

Two days after Adam's arrival in Ararat City, in the New York studio of his network, scandalmonger Laurence Imre opened what would prove to be his highest-rated telecast of *Eveningtalk* to date.

"Ladies and gentlemen," began Imre, "my guest this evening for the full hour is noted British author and archaeologist Sir Gilbert Bowles. Later we will open the phone lines for your calls. But first we will hear from Mr. Bowles himself. Sir Gilbert," he went on, turning toward his guest, "you said you had startling news for the world, and proof to back up your words. The camera is yours."

"The astounding claim I have to make this evening," began Bowles, "is not a scientific one, although it certainly concerns the world's scientific community."

He paused briefly, doing his best to appear scholarly, which was not an easy task given his sandy gray ponytail and overall scruffy appearance.

"It has been all over the news for weeks," he continued, "that the Ethiopian government is seeking Adam Livingstone for questioning about the theft of the ark of the covenant from Aksum."

Bowles probed the eye of the camera with a solemn expression. It moved in more closely on his face, at just the angle necessary to keep visible the serpent dangling from his ear.

"Adam Livingstone is my dear friend," he went on, "or at least I should say he has been. But I have no alternative but to make public an extremely painful fact, one that I myself have had a difficult time believing. That is simply this—that Adam has in fact been lying about his involvement."

"You're not saying that he *did* steal it?"

Bowles nodded. "I'm afraid, Laurence, that that is exactly what I am saying. Adam Livingstone took the ark from Aksum."

✦ ✦ ✦

Kim Shayne had set her alarm for 5:00 A.M. to watch the program live on sky.

It would probably be re-run all over British television that same evening. But she wanted to know the instant the story broke.

She still didn't know why she had been contacted. She didn't like being secretly associated with a man like Bowles. She had no idea what he planned to say. But whatever this was about, she could not deny that she was part of it.

As Bowles continued, she shook her head.

Well, she thought, *he did it . . . just like he said he would.*

Her own story would pale into insignificance.

✦ ✦ ✦

"You are actually calling Adam Livingstone a thief!" said Imre. "I don't know what to make of it."

"It grieves me to do so," Bowles went on, preserving his somber countenance. "One hates to see a member of one's own profession fall like this, but what else could I do? Science is about truth if it is about anything. Therefore, how could one in my position remain quiet once I possessed the information I did?"

"You said there was proof."

"Yes, Laurence," replied Bowles. "But let me just say one more thing, and this is the most devastating statement of all. We are not only talking about a mere theft here."

"You mean there is more?"

"Far more I'm afraid. Something that elevates this incident to the level of a crime against history, against humanity, against the heritage of the people of Israel."

"What in the world are you talking about, Sir Gilbert?"

"Just this—Adam Livingstone not only stole the ark . . . after taking it from Ethiopia, he actually *destroyed* it."

"You can't be serious!" exclaimed Imre. Even one whose stock in trade was the outrageous found himself shocked at Bowles' charge.

"I am deadly serious, Laurence. Adam blew up the ark."

"I don't know how I can believe you." Imre was truly stunned by what he had heard, but inwardly delighted for news so juicy to break on his show. He loved this!

"It's true—unbelievable . . . but true."

"I am speechless . . . do you mean that this priceless object . . . is gone forever?"

"I am afraid so, Laurence," said Bowles. "Adam Livingstone has taken from the world one of its greatest treasures."

(3)

It was an hour or two after daybreak in the eastern highlands of Turkey.

In the middle of his morning shower, Adam was interrupted by violent knocking on the bathroom door.

"Adam . . . Adam!" Scott's voice called out.

Adam turned off the water. "What is it?" he called through the closed door.

"You gotta get out here. Now! Grab a towel . . . forget your shower."

Adam opened the door seconds later, still dripping, towel wrapped around his waist. The look on Scott's face was enough to tell him something serious was up. Scott paced. Rocky sat like a stone image of himself. In front of them the television set was on.

"Sit down, Adam," said Scott.

"What is it?"

"Just look," said Scott, nodding toward the screen. Beside him Rocky stared at the live satellite broadcast with an expression on his white face alternating between horror and fury. He did not even glance up as Adam approached.

(4)

"This is the most shocking claim imaginable," said Laurence Imre. "I am incredulous."

"Yes, and I have proof."

"You actually saw what happened!"

"No, but I have photos."

"You were there! You took them yourself?"

Bowles shook his head.

"How did you come by them?" asked Imre.

"That will have to remain confidential," replied Bowles. "Let me just say they came into my hands from a reliable source. Take it from me, they are legitimate. I have subjected them to careful analysis to verify that they are not composites. They have not been digitally enhanced or modified in any way. These are actual photographs that record an event exactly as it took place. In fact, I have Professor Klaus Schneider standing by from London University if you should want to confirm this by phone."

"We certainly shall," replied Imre. "May we see them?"

"Of course."

With a flourish, Bowles produced the photos from his pocket and laid them on the table where they sat. Instantly a camera zoomed in for close-ups of each one, gradually filling the screen with images of Adam, the ark, and the explosion exactly as it had taken place.

"I am afraid the entire interview with Sir Daniel Snow, for whom I have the utmost respect," said Bowles as the camera made its way from one photo to the next, "must be exposed as a sham. I don't know what to think except that Livingstone must have been using Snow for his own ends. As well as I thought I knew Adam," he went on, allowing sympathy and disappointment to penetrate his voice and face, "I must confess that I never expected something like this. I have no idea what it portends. If it was a publicity stunt it certainly has dark implications with respect to his reliability as a scientist."

"What are you suggesting? That Adam Livingstone's entire career has been a hoax?"

"I am drawing no conclusions," replied Bowles. "I am merely putting forth the evidence."

"He could not have faked something such as Noah's ark."

"The scientific community will have to decide these things," said Bowles seriously. "But it does make one wonder, now that this is known, how many other lies and forgeries might exist hidden in Adam's career? What if there is more to the Noah's ark situation than we have been told?"

"Such as?"

Bowles continued. "My point is only that we don't know. Once a man is exposed, once the door is open, as it were, to doubts of this magnitude, everything he says or does must come in for a new level of scrutiny. I mean . . . just when *do* we believe Adam Livingstone? How can we believe *anything* now?"

Imre continued to shake his head, then opened the program to calls from viewers.

(5)

The phone in their hotel room began ringing almost immediately. After six calls, Scott finally left it off the hook. They had to gather themselves for the day. Adam was still wrapped only in a towel.

The moment Adam, Scott, and Rocky appeared downstairs for breakfast forty minutes later, it seemed a thousand people were waiting for them.

The heads of every corporate sponsoring company, Turkish officials, and more men and women from the media than they realized were even in the area, all clamored forward in an uproar of questions. The place hadn't seen so much activity since the height of Operation Noah. By day's end this new flurry of activity would more resemble the exodus from a sinking ship.

When would Adam be releasing a statement was the question on everyone's lips.

"All I will say at this point," said Adam, doing his best to quiet the crowd in the lobby of the hotel, "is that I am as shocked by what I have seen and heard from my colleague Sir Gilbert Bowles as are the rest of you."

"What we want to know, Livingstone," called out a voice whose owner Adam could not even see in the sea of faces, "is whether the photographs are genuine?"

"I can honestly say that I know nothing about the photographs," replied Adam. "And I'm afraid that will have to be all for now. I haven't had time to sort anything out."

With Rocky's help, Adam escaped back in the direction of the stairway. A rising crescendo of shouts erupted behind him. With difficulty he tried to ignore them, and made his way back upstairs to the room.

Scott and Rocky went back down to find some breakfast for the three of them, negotiating through the crowd as if trying to wedge a football through a line of defenders fifty men thick, gradually making their way with trays of what fare they could quickly assemble back upstairs to the room.

(6)

At Sevenoaks, Juliet's face was white as she watched the interview that same afternoon. The replays had not waited for the evening news. By early afternoon, the shocking interview was spreading through Britain like a brush fire out of control. Every channel on the telly was running it over and over.

Juliet could not help herself. Devastated, she sat through it three times. Obviously she didn't believe a word of it. Nothing Bowles said could be true. Yet in some strange and irrational way, it only made her own doubts that much worse.

Meanwhile, in Los Angeles a mother of a wayward girl watched the broadcast and found herself praying, not for her daughter, but for Adam Livingstone. *God, be close to him at this time. I can't imagine what he must be going through, but remind him that he can trust in you.*

In Philadelphia, an eighty-eight-year-old prayer warrior sat in front of the television with a half-dozen of her friends at Bellevue. When the interview was over, the voice with which she spoke to the others was soft, but nonetheless determined. "We must all pray for Adam Livingstone," she said. "He has done the world much good, and I do not believe what they are saying is true. He needs our prayers more than ever."

In northern California, the manager of a small Christian bookstore prayed several times throughout the day, *Lord, keep Adam Livingstone in your care.*

In Oak Ridge, Tennessee, an invalid named Lucille Hutchins, whose own life could not be described as anything but miserable, watched the Imre interview and began to weep. She did not know why. She only sensed something very, very wrong. *Oh God,* she prayed, *this is not right. I pray that you will shine the light of truth into this controversy, and give Adam Livingstone an extra measure of your help . . . and continue to speak into my dear Fred's heart too, Lord. He needs you so desperately in his life.*

In Bryn Mawr, Pennsylvania, a first-year philosophy student by the name of Elizabeth, who had boldly spoken to her professor about the nature of truth, now turned that same love for truth inward. She did not believe what the man Bowles had said. She could not say why—she just didn't believe it. *Lord,* she prayed, *make your truth known. Reveal the truth about Adam Livingstone.*

In Chicago, a missionary lady who, upon her return from Addis Ababa some months before had had the good fortune to sit next to the man whose name was now on everyone's lips, saw the interview and was reminded of her conversation with the Englishman. "It cannot be true," she said to herself. "I know it cannot be true. I could tell that he was a man of truth." Quietly she began to pray. *Dear Father, vindicate Adam Livingstone in the public eye, and redeem his reputation before the world.*

In London, the assistant manager of a Christian bookstore instantly recognized the man who had come in looking for Romans 1:20. Whatever plans God might ultimately have, he knew that right now the man was not speaking the truth. He saw falsehood in his eyes. *Lord Jesus,* he prayed silently, *convict this man of the wrong he is doing. Show him who you are. Make him a man of truth. And give Adam Livingstone the strength and courage to endure these lies being told with dignity and faith.*

And all over the world, thousands of saints likewise offered up heartfelt prayers on behalf of their brother Adam Livingstone who was suddenly again in the public eye.

(7)

It took no more than a few hours before headlines in dozens of languages began to break.

In the United States all the major morning papers had enough lead time to get it onto their front pages. It was too late for the earliest U.K. dailies, but by noon the vendors in every tube station and on streets throughout London were shouting the news proclaimed by the headlines whose ink was scarcely dry: ADAM LIVINGSTONE EXPOSED AS THIEF AND FRAUD!

It was Inspector Saul who ran into his captain's office at the headquarters of Scotland Yard about 10:30 that morning.

"Did you hear about Adam?" he said in an urgent voice.

"Who . . . Livingstone? No—what?" said Thurlow.

"Turn on your radio. It's all over the BBC."

Five minutes later, Thurlow sat at his desk shaking his head. *Well, I guess I've seen it all,* he thought to himself. *Adam Livingstone lying to my face. I would never have believed it.*

He rose and sought Saul.

"We'd better bring him in," he said, "or we'll have an international situation on our hands."

"You don't believe it, Captain!"

"I don't know what to believe, Max. Sometimes you never know. Celebrities face pressures you and I will never know. Sometimes they get turned."

"But *Adam* . . ."

"We've got to bring him in. It's for his own good."

✦ ✦ ✦

That same afternoon Captain Thurlow inched his car through the growing crowd at the gate of the Livingstone estate at Sevenoaks and announced himself.

"Mr. Livingstone is out of the country, sir," said Mrs. Graves minutes later when she met him at the door.

"May I see Miss Halsay, then, ma'am?"

"I'm afraid she has taken to her bed," answered Mrs. Graves. "This has been quite a shock to her."

"Right—a shock to us all," said Thurlow, then turned to go.

(8)

The day following the Imre-Bowles bombshell, Ararat City was in complete disarray. If Bowles had intended to throw a nuclear device into the middle of Adam Livingstone's plans, he could not have succeeded more skillfully.

More than half the construction crew at the ark hangar did not report for work that morning. Scott and Adam scrambled from dawn to dusk, resembling politicians more than scientists, trying to reassure and alleviate concern. But without much to give in the way of answers, the pandemonium only increased as the hours wore on. Neither did irate calls from the Chairman of the Cartel and the Turkish Interior Minister help. Both were flying in the next day, and from their tones and threats, their presence on the scene was bound to be unpleasant.

Late in the afternoon Adam was approached by representatives from Rockwell, Raytheon, and NASA, who obviously intended to speak to him as a committee of three.

"You've got to understand, Livingstone," said Lou Jennings from NASA, "I've got nothing against you. But the Pentagon is all over me to pull our people out."

The other two nodded. They were obviously under similar orders.

"We can't get caught in the middle," said the Rockwell representative. "Not with international legal implications. This thing's a powder keg."

"I understand," said Adam. "But can't you give me twenty-four hours to get it cleared up?"

"Sorry, we've got our orders."

"When will you be leaving?"

"Immediately," replied one. The other two agreed that their timetables were no more lenient. "I'm afraid our work here is over."

Scott walked up at the end of the conversation, which mercifully did not last much longer, as the three men walked away.

"Same story everywhere," he said. "I'm sorry, man, but your name is mud around here."

"And everywhere, it would seem," sighed Adam.

"Suddenly Bowles is the expert."

"What could have possessed Sir Gilbert to do it?"

"I quit trying to figure Bowles out a long time ago."

"How in the world did he get those photos, that's what I want to know."

"Haven't a clue, Scott. I'm as stunned by this as everyone else."

"Except for one thing."

"What's that?"

"You were there."

"Yeah," said Adam. He exhaled slowly. "So however those pictures were taken," he mused, "it must have been a setup from the beginning."

"The photos are accurate, I take it?"

"From what I could see on TV," replied Adam. "I mean, they blew the thing up with me standing there looking on. But the implication that I did it . . ."

"I know that. I'm just trying to get a handle on what happened."

"I don't know what else to do but go public . . . you know, tell about what we found in *our* photos, and the replica theory."

"Let's wait and see how it plays out," said Scott. "Keep your options open awhile longer."

"But if we don't figure out a way to fend off this furor, we may not be able to save the project. Everyone's deserting the sinking Livingstone ship. This place will be—what do you call it?"

"A ghost town?"

"That's it—a ghost town within three days."

"We'll get through it," said Scott. "We've been on the wrong side of long odds before. Don't give up, man. Something will break our way."

(9)

Sir Gilbert Bowles flew home from the States feeling as good about life and his place in the order of things as he had in a long while.

He could not prevent a certain gloating sensation to attract the stares of the crowd wherever he went. In airports and restaurants, he was conscious of turning heads and whispered exclamations prompted by his presence. Radios and newspapers broadcast worldwide reports of the scandal, each after its own fashion, and he heard and saw his name wherever he went.

Yet there was a certain unnerving aspect to the whole thing. He continued to see evidence of undiminished interest in the Bible along at the same time. Right up there sharing the headlines with him was the U.S. President and his upcoming ridiculous National Bible Day.

No matter, thought Bowles to himself. He was back in the game!

✦ ✦ ✦

Meanwhile Anni D'Abernon thought to herself as she watched a replay of the interview that her scheme had gone off about as perfectly as she could have imagined. She had seen or heard nothing from the Shayne woman in the affair. But she must have been in touch with Bowles. And he had certainly handled *his* assignment with particular flair.

(10)

By 9:00 A.M. on the morning after the interview, cars and news vans were rolling up outside the Sevenoaks estate in a steady stream. By afternoon more than a hundred journalists and cameramen and women from every segment of the media were clamoring for a statement.

Crystal and Jen, who had been working on final preparations for their trip to France, were more and more distracted by the noise and activity.

"We've got to do something," said Crystal. "But I have the feeling to go out there now would be like facing a pack of wolves."

"The press is your department, Juliet," said Jen, laughing. "They all know you after Turkey."

"I don't think I could face them," replied Juliet.

The phone rang. Crystal looked at it, and let it ring three or four times, debating within herself whether to answer it at all. Finally she picked up the receiver.

"Adam!" she exclaimed. "What do we do? It's a circus here. The media's everywhere, and the phone is ringing off the hook."

"I take it then that the Bowles interview has been seen in England?" he said.

"*Seen!* It's all over every station and in every paper."

Jen and Juliet could hear Adam's loud groan where they stood at Crystal's side.

"OK," he said, "like they say in times of emergency—remain calm. It can't be any worse than it is here."

"Captain Thurlow came by yesterday."

"What did he want?"

"To talk to you."

"Surely he doesn't believe—"

"I don't know, but his voice was serious. I can never tell what he's thinking."

"I'll give Max a ring. In the meantime, let me talk to Juliet."

Crystal handed Juliet the phone.

"How's it going?" asked Adam.

"I don't know," answered Juliet. "Crystal and Jen want me to go talk to them outside. I don't think I can do it."

"You will do fine. Better a pretty face out there than mine."

"What if I see Kimberly Whatever her name is?"

"Punch her in the nose, then answer her questions."

Juliet chuckled.

"It's nice to hear you laugh," said Adam. "I tell you, I haven't been doing much laughing here lately! I really miss you."

"How could Gilbert Bowles do such a thing?" said Juliet. "*He's* the one we ought to punch in the nose!"

"I'm not sure I'd argue with you. But back to your immediate problem—for the time being, why don't you go out there and put on your smiling, confident face, and tell those reporters you don't know a thing, and that you're sure Adam will fill them in on the details as soon as he's back in the country."

"Oh, Adam!" wailed Juliet. "I can't!"

His words only exacerbated her doubts. If there was one thing Juliet possessed zero of inside right now, it was confidence. How long could she keep pretending?

"Besides," he added, "there's really no one else. After your performance at Ararat, if you *don't* appear, that will only add more to their questions."

"All right . . . I'll try."

(11)

Adam hung up the phone and turned back into the suite, where Scott and Rocky had flopped down in chairs to listen to Adam's end of the conversation. They were all beat after a long, exhausting, and frustrating day.

"You know, Adam," said Scott after a few minutes, "the only way for you to clear yourself is to get to the bottom of it."

"The bottom of what?"

"The whole thing—the ark situation. If that thing those people blew up really was a replica, the surest way you have to clear yourself, get your reputation back, and save this project, is to find the real one. That means continuing your research. You've got to go ahead with your plans to go to France."

"Scott's right," added Rocky. "Uncovering the truth is how to clear yourself. That's the only way you're going to get out from under this mountain Bowles has dropped on you. Otherwise, there will always be doubts."

"But we still have to address the immediate problem," said Adam. "Make some kind of public statement. I don't know what other option there is but to give a full disclosure. Tell what happened at Amsterdam, that *an* object was in fact destroyed. I've got to own up to the photos. Seems like I've got to say, 'Sir Gilbert is right—the object was stolen from Aksum and later destroyed, and I was there . . . but it isn't what he is making it out to be.' Then I should tell about our own photos, maybe even publish them, Hebrew inscription and all."

"It might be worth a try," said Scott. "And it may be all we've got."

"I think I'll set up a press conference for tomorrow. Then I'll call Juliet back. That will give her something to tell the media there too. Everybody in the world can get the story at once."

(12)

Gilbert Bowles was tired. The trip to the States had exhausted his weakened constitution more than was good for him.

He awoke sometime in early afternoon following his first night home in his own bed. Good heavens, he thought, looking at the clock. He had slept eleven hours and still felt like Wooster's irritable parrot that had been yanked through a hedge backwards.

He struggled out of bed and to the bathroom. He peered in the mirror. He looked like one too!

He dressed and staggered toward the kitchen to boil water, then sat down and tried to collect his wits. Now that he was home and felt so miserable, he realized he was not riding quite so high from the Imre show as he had hoped.

He went to the phone. He needed to keep the pressure on Livingstone.

"Shayne," he said when the familiar voice answered, "Bowles. I'm back. What's our next move?"

"What do you mean, *our* next move?" rejoined Kim testily. "I'm not part of your plan to ruin Adam Livingstone."

"You saw it, I take it," chuckled Bowles. "I was rather on my game, wasn't I?"

"I'm not sure that's how I would describe the performance."

"Come on, Shayne, wake up. The world's a cruel place. Survival of the fittest—don't you know your Darwin? Like it or not, you *are* part of it. Whoever took those pictures chose you and me together to break this story."

"Well, maybe I don't care for your style, Sir Gilbert. That was a pretty nasty drubbing you gave him."

"You doubt it's true?"

"I don't know what to think."

"We've got proof—the photos, remember?"

"Well, we in the press also like to check our sources, and give the object of our stories the chance to tell their side."

"Same chance you gave the Halsay kid, eh, Shayne?"

The words stung.

"That's different, Bowles."

"Not so very different. You reporters make your own rules. Heck, I don't mind. So do I. It's how you survive in this world. Darwin had it figured out. So don't come on to me with that holier-than-thou hypocrisy that makes journalism into a noble enterprise. You're out to get the goods on people just like I am."

"Well, I'm doing nothing more until I hear Adam Livingstone's side of it."

"And how do you intend to get that?"

"Maybe I'll talk to him. But until then, he's briefing the media from Turkey in a couple of hours. The BBC's carrying it live."

Bowles took in the news with interest.

"All right, Shayne, I'll be in touch later," he said. "But I don't intend to let this thing drop. Frankly, I don't think you do either. It's too big a story. It's opportunity, Shayne. I don't think you're one to let it pass you by. You know where you can find me when you're ready to join the team again."

(13)

Adam opened the following morning's press briefing at 11:00 A.M. If he thought coming clean about what he knew was going to make the doubts vanish, he had badly miscalculated the erosion of confidence that had already set in.

He began with a prepared statement that concisely revealed a basic outline of the facts:

Yes, as previously revealed, he had broken into the Sanctuary of the Ark at St. Mary's in Aksum. But only to photograph the object. When he made his escape it was there just as he found it. *Yes,* he was present at the later incident in question. *Yes,* the photos are genuine. He had been taken somewhere in the vicinity of Amsterdam by the people who stole the ark from Aksum after his visit, and they exploded it in front of him. He was shocked and stunned by what had happened, and had no idea photographs had been taken to implicate him. He did not know the identity of the people involved. *But . . .* he had good news for everyone! Further examination of his own photographs from Aksum revealed a message embedded in the design that indicated the Aksum ark *not* to be the true ark of the covenant at all, but a replica. So the thieves did not destroy the ark of the covenant as they thought. And he now possessed *new* evidence he hoped would lead him to the location of the real ark.

Even before he had finished reading the prepared text, a few snickers and a ripple of amused whispers began to circulate through the room.

American Don Samuelson, who had flown all night in order to get to the scene in time for the interview, was first to voice his jocular disbelief.

"Come on, Livingstone—are you serious?" he said, unable to prevent chuckling as he said it. "What do you take us for? We saw your photographs for ourselves when you were interviewed by Daniel Snow. There was no so-called *hidden message.* At the time you were proclaiming the thing as the long-lost ark of the covenant."

"I was mistaken," replied Adam. "The hidden message had not yet revealed itself."

"What—revealed itself! *Ha, ha!* Listen to yourself, Livingstone—would you believe me if I tried to pass off such a load of nonsense on you?"

✦ ✦ ✦

As he watched, Gilbert Bowles roared with laughter. This was brilliant!

Keep it up, Adam, old boy! he cried at his TV. *One nail in your coffin after another. Ha, ha, ha!*

✦ ✦ ✦

"I am truly sorry it sounds like nonsense to you, Mr. Samuelson," said Adam, trying to maintain his composure. "All I can do is tell you the truth. It was not until we redeveloped the exposures using high-contrast techniques that we first saw the Hebrew message embedded in the designs on the side of the container."

"And just what did this cryptic message *say?*" asked another reporter. His tone made it clear that he was asking as he might humor a child in the continuation of an imaginary experience.

"It said, *This is a replica of the ark of testimony.*"

Suppressed for the most part till that moment, laughter now spread in earnest throughout the press corps.

✦ ✦ ✦

Anni D'Abernon smiled to herself.

It was good to see Livingstone turning into a laughingstock. Deep inside, however, she remained uneasy. The minute he uttered the word *replica*, a shudder rippled through her body.

She refused to believe it. Yet on the other hand . . . it certainly *could* explain why there seemed to be no abating of this absurd spirituality everywhere.

Yes, she said to herself, it was premature to celebrate. Adam Livingstone was the kind of man who always managed to turn the tables on catastrophe.

They needed to find a way to rid themselves of him for good.

✦ ✦ ✦

"It gets better and better!" scoffed Samuelson. "A hidden message that no one else has seen, which you conveniently tell us about *now*, which miraculously absolves you of the theft . . . but *not* until the evidence is destroyed—come on!"

"Very convenient, Livingstone," called out another.

"Why did you wait till now to make this public?"

A flurry of similar questions abounded.

"I suppose you have photographs of this hidden message to show us," said Samuelson.

"Actually, I don't," replied Adam. "That will have to wait until I return to England."

More laughter.

"Again, very convenient. And we should be expected to take your word for it till then, I suppose."

"I had thought—"

"And where do these supposed *new* leads point?" interrupted another with humorous derision. "Somewhere in never-never land?"

"Actually, they point to France," replied Adam. "There I hope to find—"

"France! The ark of the covenant in France!"

"And how do we know there aren't a series of fakes, all with some kind of hidden message that will send you hopping all over the globe?"

"Please, you've got to believe that I—"

More laughter interrupted him. Scott could see that Adam was close to the edge. Anything more at this point was less than useless. He moved quickly to Adam's side, pulled him away, and led him from the room, which filled with a rising chorus of humorous and deriding comments behind him.

Within hours, headlines throughout the world featured Adam Livingstone again, and with conclusions that only exacerbated the charges from days earlier: PHANTOM NEW ARK proclaimed the *Washington Post.* LIVINGSTONE SQUIRMS WHILE PRESTIGE PLUMMETS blared the *Chicago Sun Times.* FABLED NEW ARK MESSAGE ONLY VISIBLE TO LIVINGSTONE declared the *Daily Mirror.* And others told a similar story, from SUDDEN COLLAPSE OF ARARAT CARTEL to ARARAT CITY DESERTED, ARK PROJECT SCRUBBED. And in the same tone as the headlines, editorialists were scathing in their ridicule and accusations.

Within another twenty-four hours it was more or less universally accepted that Adam Livingstone knew more than he was telling. Ethiopia was now joined by Israel in demanding the archaeologist's arrest. The assumption was that it was only a matter of time before Scotland Yard would be forced to take him into custody.

(14)

Although he relished in Adam's plight, Gilbert Bowles was astute enough to have picked up on the significance of the detail most of the journalists had let pass right by.

Ah, ha . . . my good friend, he thought, *France, eh! What do you have up your sleeve now?*

If what he had already given the public didn't ruin Livingstone, he would get more. He certainly had no intention of being left out at this stage. Although what France could have to do with anything, Bowles couldn't imagine.

Where he was going in France had not been divulged, and he doubted anyone in the Livingstone camp would give him the information.

But he'd track Adam down, thought Bowles. That part should be easy.

He sat a few more minutes contemplating what to do. Finally he rose.

Well, he said to himself, it appeared the game was back on. Time to pack his bags for the continent!

✦ ✦ ✦

How deserted lies the city. . . . All the splendor has departed from the Daughter of Zion. . . . In the days of her affliction and wandering Jerusalem remembers all the treasures that were hers in days of old. . . . How the gold has lost its luster, the fine gold become dull! . . . How the precious sons of Zion, once worth their weight in gold, are now considered as pots of clay. . . . It happened because of the sins of her prophets and the iniquities of her priests. . . . The Lord himself has scattered them. . . . Our inheritance has been turned over to aliens.

LAMENTATIONS 1:1, 6-7; 4: 1-2, 13, 16; 5:2

✦ ✦ ✦

PROLOGUE

Menyelek, Son of the Wise Man

Jerusalem, 937 B.C.

The night was black.

Menyelek, son of Solomon, king of Israel, stole quietly into the precincts of the temple that had been his grandfather David's vision, and for which his father would be known to posterity.

He glanced about. Azarius, son of Israel's high priest, Zadok, should have been here by now. There was no sign of the others.

Menyelek sat down to wait.

Their secret arrangements had been made. The feast had been concluded and most of Jerusalem's elite were asleep in their beds, half of them probably drunk. He and his companions had been careful not to allow much wine to pass their own lips. Their exodus would be like the exodus of old. It would occur at night and by stealth. He had left a message in his father's quarters explaining his reasons.

Lavish feasts with freely flowing wine were a favorite pastime with his father. He often used them to achieve his ends. On this particular night, his son had decided to use it to conceal his departure.

✦ ✦ ✦

Some twenty years earlier the king's palace in Jerusalem had witnessed another such celebration. It was on that occasion when Menyelek's own personal history had begun. On that night, the king's guest had drunk more than was good for her.

Solomon had instructed his cook to prepare the spiciest dishes and bring out the best wines. Makeda, the queen from the south who had come to Israel seeking wisdom, ate and drank her fill. Later that night, as she slept, Solomon satisfied his personal desire.

A dream that same night told the Hebrew king that God would give over his authority and blessing to a new dynasty which would begin with the child who had been conceived that night in Queen Makeda's womb. Solomon then sent her home to await the child's birth. A certain command was added: If she bore a son, she must send him back to Jerusalem to be trained in the religion, culture, and law of Israel.

Indeed did Queen Makeda give birth to a boy. She gave him the name Menyelek—"son of the wise man."

She raised him in her homeland until he came of age. Then Makeda sent him north to his father.

Solomon lavished riches and every comfort imaginable on the boy. He loved his dark-skinned son above all his other sons and daughters. Young Menyelek, however, never felt completely at home in Jerusalem, and the king sensed his divided heart. To keep him in Israel, Solomon offered to make him king after his own reign, even though he was not his eldest.

"Your reign shall outlast my own," vowed Solomon.

But Menyelek had his doubts. So did many of Israel's elders. Likewise did Solomon's other sons. And it was King Solomon's lavish promise that ultimately sealed Menyelek's fate and made this night inevitable.

Outside the king's hearing, jealous complaints were rife in the city. Priests, elders, and sons alike said that the king showed his Ethiopian son far too much favor.

Menyelek's older half-brother Rehoboam was especially livid. Already he eyed the future kingship as his by proprietary right.

Menyelek was well enough aware how tongues wagged of jealousy against him. He knew Israel could be no home for him if he desired to live long enough to enjoy a head of gray.

✦ ✦ ✦

King David's throne had been hotly contested. So likely would be that of Solomon's successor. Treachery and the sword played as great a role in this nation's history as its unique religion toward the one God.

Menyelek might lay legitimate claim to the kingship. His mother, after all, was a queen of stature equal to Solomon's. He had more distinctively royal blood than any of his half-brothers. But alas she was no Hebrew queen. Hers was the royal lineage of Ethiopia.

Thus would Menyelek remain in Hebrew eyes what Israel's elders had already proclaimed him—a foreigner, born to the prurient son of David by the beautiful queen of the land called Sheba.

It was only days ago when Menyelek had learned of Rehoboam's plot against his life.

"He has many supporters," said Menyelek's closest friend, Azarius. "Even if your blood stained his very hands, your father would not dare harm him."

"I have no choice but to return to the south," rejoined Menyelek.

"Let me go with you," said Azarius. "Like you, I will never rise above my brothers. Let me accompany you to your land where I may be high priest to those of us who worship the Lord our God there in that distant land."

Menyelek agreed. As their secret plan became known, three others of their closest companions begged to accompany them.

The time for departure at last arrived, and the feast just past gave Menyelek and his *friends the cover they needed to get far away before their exodus was known. His future lay in the land of his mother.*

Menyelek determined, however, not to leave the palace of his father empty-handed. Not only was his father considered the wisest man in the world, he was far and away the wealthiest.

For days he contemplated what to take—gold, other jewels, artifacts. He hinted at his thoughts to the son of the high priest.

"I have likewise considered such things," replied Azarius. "Why should we not also have such a treasure there to remind us of the God of our fathers, and to ensure that the blessings of the Most High follow us as we leave the land Yahweh gave to our fathers? If I am to be a priest of the lineage of Aaron in a foreign land, I would have a reminder of the holy Presence with me."

"Do you mean the ark?"

"Of course."

"It will be gold we need most of all if we are to fabricate the most sacred object of our heritage after our sojourn to the south."

More discussions over the next few days followed.

"To carry out your plan," said Menyelek, "would require that we enter the Holy of Holies. We will need the most precise of measurements."

Azarius nodded.

"I am willing to risk breaking the sacred Law. We must see it with our own eyes, and make drawings. What we fashion must be exact in every detail."

"Then we shall—"

Footsteps disturbed Menyelek's reverie.

✦ ✦ ✦

Azarius with several others approached. Two were carrying a box which, before the night was out, would contain as much weight as four of them could wield. A third carried parchments, measuring instruments, and writing instruments. Solomon's son rose to meet them.

Nods followed. This was solemn business. Not even the high priest's son was sure they would live to see the light of a new day. Dread of Yahweh had been instilled into them since birth. They were not certain how the Almighty with no name would react to their deed. The Holy of Holies was meant for no mortal but the high priest himself, and then only on the Day of Atonement.

Azarius led the way through the courtyard. The night was silent except for the occasional snort of bull or bleat of insomniac sheep in the animal pens behind the temple.

They ascended the steps, crossed the porch, and entered the Holy Place. A deeper quiet now possessed them. Their steps unconsciously slowed as they passed between the parallel rows of five golden lampstands, lit at all times. Toward the end of the room stood the altar of incense overlaid with gold. To its right sat the table for shewbread. Carefully they walked around the altar, and behind it at length arrived at their destination.

Azarius stopped. Menyelek, and another who held a hand lamp, paused beside him. A cedar-paneled wall marked the end of the Holy Place. In the center of it stood double doors of olivewood.

Azarius drew in his breath, glanced to his right and left, then stretched out his hands and drew the doors open.

Blackness, and the faintest aroma of mingled cedar and incense met their senses.

A moment they remained motionless. The high priest's son took the lamp from his companion, then crept tentatively forward into that holy sanctum where only his own father in all of Israel was allowed. A thick woven veil of blue, purple, and crimson hung down, barring his way. Gingerly he pushed it back and proceeded into the Holy of Holies.

His companions followed with pounding hearts.

Before them, even in the faint, flickering light from the oil lamp, the gold from the mercy seat and ark of the covenant sitting on the table at the rear of the cubical room seemed to radiate with a resplendent light of its own.

Azarius motioned to the two. They set their box on the floor. All approached the table with reverent step, gazing upon the two symbolic cherubim atop the mercy seat, which served as guardians to the presence of God, as well as the gold-plated reliquary underneath it. There was no sound. No bolt of lightning. No peal of thunder. No voice from on high.

It was time to be about their work. They could not take more than an hour. Azarius unrolled the parchments on the floor and began giving each his instructions. Every detail, down to the tiniest, must be noted, every measurement of length and width and height preserved with the utmost accuracy, every design artistically replicated. They began their work, with now and then a question to the son of the high priest, and soon settled into silence.

Slightly more than an hour passed. Soon the need for haste was borne anew upon their minds. Azarius examined what each had done, and at length was satisfied.

"It is time," said Menyelek. "Roll up the scrolls. Let us hasten to the temple treasury. We will fill the box with all the gold it is possible for us to carry. Thus our new ark will in truth be fashioned from the gold of Jerusalem's temple."

✦ ✦ ✦

Six hours later, he who would become the most famous king of his own land, and his devoted companions from among the noble of Israel's youth, were past Hebron and on their way, each with two servants, through the hills westward toward Gaza and the coast. Six camels, a wagon, several mules and horses, laden with food, water, and assorted goods of saleable appearance and value, disguised their precious cargo and their identities. They were garbed in the attire of Palestinian merchants.

Their route would take them southwest along the well-travelled Trunk Road connecting Egypt and the northern Sinai with the sea nations of the Middle East, Syria, and ultimately the rest of Asia.

In another hour it would be daylight. By the time their departure was known, they would *have at least an eight-hour lead on a route none would anticipate. Menyelek was not sure what his father would think, notwithstanding the message he had left him. When the youths were discovered gone, the king's mind would immediately ask why. And Rehoboam was certain to be suspicious.*

They would be lucky if it were only hours, hopefully a day or two, before it was discovered that the temple treasury had been looted. By then he hoped it would be too late for his half-brother to give chase. They would be in the Sinai and out of reach.

From Gaza, Menyelek's little band would make their way into Egypt, where they would abandon the wagon in favor of a barge capable of carrying the party what would eventually be eight hundred miles up the Nile, pausing for a season at Aswan on the east bank of the great river, moving ever closer to their ultimate destination.

They possessed documents of safe conduct for the regions through which they would pass. No ruler between Arabia and Egypt would dare harm the son of Solomon, king of Israel.

✦ ✦ ✦

It was months before the royal fugitive with sacred cargo entered the high country of his mother's domain with his companions. They left the main course of the river and moved upstream against the flow of the Atbara. Yet deeper into the highlands, the stiffening current of the Tekeze met them. When the way became unnavigable, their course again took them overland.

They were close to their destination now. Word of their coming went ahead. A great party, led by the queen herself, came to meet them as they neared the shores of Lake Tana.

During the celebration, Menyelek requested private words with his mother. He told her what he and his companions had done and what lay hidden among their possessions.

"Not even the servants suspect the treasure we have borne all this way," he said. "Only we six. We must keep it concealed and find a suitable resting place to keep it."

"You have done well, Menyelek," said Queen Makeda. "We must find a secluded place for the work to be carried out, and a safe home for it once it is completed."

"Why not the island in the middle of Tana, mother?"

"It could not be better," replied the queen. "I will gather my finest craftsmen immediately and put them at your disposal. The lake shall protect you. Upon my own mount here, just as upon the mount in Jerusalem, shall the ark's companion reside. May God look with favor upon what you have done, my son, that his people here may worship him as they do in the land of your father."

PART SIX

FRANCE

✦ ✦ ✦

The word of the Lord came to me, saying, . . .

I have put my words in your mouth.

See, today I appoint you over nations and kingdoms. . . .

For I am watching to see that my word is fulfilled.

JEREMIAH 1:4-12

✦ ✦ ✦

twenty-two

Defection in the Ranks

(1)

"Good evening, ladies and gentlemen, my fellow Americans," began the President. "I want to address you this evening about something that I believe concerns every citizen, nothing more nor less than truth itself.

"What is truth? Where is it to be found? These are questions that have plagued mankind since the beginning of time. And following on their heels comes perhaps the larger question—how should we live as a result of truth? Should it make a difference in our lives?

"These are questions perhaps we as a people have not considered in recent years as much as we should have. But circumstances are forcing them to the very forefront of discussion. That is why I have declared a National Bible Day tomorrow."

A pause followed so that the significance of his words would not be lost. Every U.S. network was carrying the broadcast live, juxtaposing in dissonant irony news of the exploding worldwide interest in the Bible with the corresponding collapse of Adam Livingstone's reputability.

"For years," he went on, "politicians and leaders have derided what they call our country's spiritual vacuum and the declining interest in spiritual things of our people. Many have called for a return to the ethical base and foundation of our nation. Yet nothing anyone said or did has affected the eroding moral and spiritual trend of our culture.

"But we *are* a nation of spiritual roots. Our heritage is a Judeo-Christian one. Now we find ourselves in the midst, if not of a revival, certainly an explosive renewal of interest in the Bible as a result of certain recent discoveries that seem to have no explanation other than that the biblical accounts are true. News magazines are full of astonishing accounts. Bible sales continue to soar. The unprecedented interest in the Bible spans the entire spectrum of race and society.

"It is almost as if the Almighty is saying to us, 'You are in spiritual decline and your own efforts have not been enough to stop it. So I will remind you of your roots by reminding you of my Word, and of the truth of my Word.' At least that is how I like to think of what we are presently witnessing. I am heartened and encouraged that though we as a nation have in many ways done our best to forget him, *God* has not forgotten *us*, and is determined to remind us of that spiritual foundation which sets this nation apart and has made it strong.

"The phenomenon that is sweeping the world must be viewed as wholely unexpected. It would seem to contradict almost every trend of modernism in this new millennial age.

"I want to read to you this evening, not from a fancy leather Bible—and the White House library is full of them, expensive gifts to presidents through the years—but from a simple, inexpensive paperback edition that was sent to me recently by a young lady representing the publishing house that printed it. I was touched by her simple letter, that said they were printing hundreds of thousands of this paperback edition to make available free for the asking, so that everyone who desires to read the Bible, even if penniless, will have that opportunity. So I read from this edition tonight, the same edition that many of you will be reading from in the coming months and years, to remind us that it is the *truths* found in this divinely inspired book that have the power to change individual lives, as well as influence nations and change history.

"Let me now read, and encourage you in the days and weeks to come, indeed throughout your lives, and especially during tomorrow's National Bible Day, to find a Bible and read it. Moreover, I challenge you to ask if it may not have relevance in your life in some new way that you had not considered before.

"Join with me as I read from John's Gospel."

The President took a breath, then began reading from the paperback in his hand.

"*In the beginning was the Word, and the Word was with God, and the Word was God. He was with God in the beginning. Through him all things were made; without him nothing was made that has been made. In him was life, and that life was the light of men. The light shines in the darkness, but the darkness has not understood it.*

There came a man who was sent from God; his name was John. He came as a witness to testify concerning that light, so that through him all men might believe. He himself was not the light; he came only as a witness to the light. The true light that gives light to every man was coming into the world.

"*He was in the world, and though the world was made through him, the world did not recognize him. He came to that which was his own, but his own did not receive him. Yet to all who received him, to those who believed in his name, he gave the right to become children of God—children born not of natural descent, nor of human decision or a husband's will, but born of God.*

The Word became flesh and made his dwelling among us. We have seen his glory, the glory of the One and Only, who came from the Father, full of grace and truth."

(2)

Anni D'Abernon and Rupert Vaughan-Maier were speaking together in the latter's high-rise office complex in Amsterdam.

"How can this societal impact of the book be so strong?"

"Livingstone is the key to all this," rejoined the Swisswoman. The frustration in her ordinarily calm demeanor was evident. "He must be neutralized. Obviously nothing we have done thus far has worked. He is lower in public esteem than ever, yet this idiocy about their sacred book continues."

"We should have blown him up with the ark."

"And make a martyr of him? No, it must be more subtle."

"All I know is that he grows more and more dangerous by the day."

A crystal sat on the table before them. They had already attempted to coax information from it, but the Dimension was still. Therefore they were resorting to more commonplace stratagems.

"Has Zorin been located yet?" the Dutchman asked at length.

"You mean after his disappearance following the incident in Amsterdam?"

Vaughan-Maier nodded.

"Soon," lied D'Abernon. In truth she hadn't the foggiest notion where Zorin was.

"My contact had him recently in Istanbul," she said, not adding that Bonar had lost him almost as soon as she had found him.

"The Montreux girl may be an avenue we should revisit," said Vaughan-Maier.

D'Abernon realized the Dutchman's thinking was sound. Besides, they were running out of options. Candace Montreux was better than nothing, and they had to find some way to take Livingstone out of the game.

"Perhaps we should get the Baron on the phone," she said.

"Exactly my thought," rejoined Vaughan-Maier.

Two minutes later the three were speaking in conference. Lord Montreux had just explained to his two colleagues that the relationship between his daughter and Livingstone had cooled.

"Does she still have feelings for the man?" asked D'Abernon.

"I believe so. But he—"

"For the moment, Baron, my concern is only with your daughter," interrupted the Swisswoman. "We must speak with her."

"I seriously doubt that Candace will be amenable to assisting us with Livingstone."

"That is hardly of concern. *Bring* your daughter, Lord Montreux," insisted D'Abernon in tone of command. "We will *compel* her to obey our wishes."

(3)

Halder Zorin's private jet banked up and out of Istanbul and set a course toward Baku. It was time to consider what to do next.

How could he best bring D'Abernon and the rest of them down?

His thoughts turned toward the English archaeologist. Perhaps there was another way to preserve the power they thought they could take away from him.

He mused further. The Council wanted Livingstone. But if he could get to him first, perhaps—

Zorin's brain exploded with insight.

Of course! he thought. How could he not have seen it sooner? Livingstone was the key to everything, the ultimate bargaining chip, the perfect way to bring down the Council. Livingstone was a man of influence. He was just temporarily on the wrong side of the fence. Why should he not take advantage of what he realized had been the right idea all along? Power was his goal, total power. Adam Livingstone was the most powerful individual on the other side. If he could get to Livingstone first . . .

Why couldn't *he* harness the power Livingstone possessed?

If he could nab Livingstone, it would put him in a powerful position. The Englishman would place D'Abernon in the palm of his hand!

Would it be possible to turn the man?

He reflected a few more minutes. He could turn anyone, Zorin thought to himself. Livingstone's present predicament gave him the perfect opportunity. He needed help to reestablish himself, to get his power and reputation back. And he would give it to him! Livingstone would not refuse . . . he *could* not refuse. He would lavish upon Livingstone anything he wanted, anything in the world—wealth, power, women, fame. And he, Halder Zorin, could place it all in the archaeologist's hands.

And was it possible that what Livingstone had announced could be true, that the real ark of the covenant still existed? That was just like D'Abernon, to have bungled the whole thing! Even getting the wrong ark!

Ha, ha, ha! Zorin laughed aloud. *The fool, the positive idiot! She was an amateur and bungler.*

He would get his hands on Livingstone *and* the real ark!

The very thought of such a union filled Zorin with anticipation. No one could stand against them! The two would make the most powerful alliance in the world.

But where was Livingstone? He would use D'Abernon to locate him. She would no doubt be on his trail already. Or perhaps the fool Montreux might be useful.

A smile spread across Zorin's thick lips. *It was too delicious to contemplate,* he thought. He only wished he could be there to see D'Abernon's face when she realized she'd been had. Unfortunately, by then he'd be gone, and Livingstone and the ark of the covenant with him.

(4)

Two days passed since the telephone conversation between Harriman Montreux, Rupert Vaughan-Maier, and Anni D'Abernon.

The Swisswoman remained in Amsterdam. Their English colleague was expected any moment, bringing his daughter for her assignment.

Swisswoman and Dutchman were awaiting them.

Lord Montreux arrived with his daughter.

As they entered, Candace caught the fragmentary ending of the conversation which had been in progress.

". . . Livingstone must pay for his meddling . . . can't learn of Templar roots . . ."

The words meant nothing in her ears. As soon as Montreux and his daughter appeared, the two immediately stopped talking. Though she was intimidated, even terrified, Candace was shrewd enough to realize she'd overheard something she wasn't supposed to. Something was up that meant no good for Adam . . . probably not for her either.

"Miss Montreux," D'Abernon began, without expending time in superficial pleasantries, "we must find what your friend Adam Livingstone is working on. We know he is out of the country. We understand he has left Turkey for France after his unpleasantness in the media."

"I don't know where he is," Candace answered guardedly.

"Come, Miss Montreux, surely your fiancé—"

"He's not my fiancé," interrupted Candace.

"Nevertheless," persisted D'Abernon, "as I said, we are certain he is on his way to France, and all we ask is that you help us with a little information. I am certain you could find out."

"I could do no such thing. Adam no longer confides in me."

"We need to know, Miss Montreux. We *must* know."

D'Abernon drew close to Candace's face as she spoke. Even Candace's hair stood on end in the presence of this woman. "You cannot refuse . . . you *must* not refuse us."

"Get away from me," said Candace irritably, squirming where she sat. "Even if I knew, I wouldn't tell you anything."

"Don't force us to coerce you, Miss Montreux. Our means can be anything but pleasant."

As if caught in a trap, Candace turned helplessly to her father with forlorn and scared expression, which yet had a little of Candace's hot temper mixed in with it. "Daddy?" she said.

"Please, Candace," he said, "just cooperate. It will make it easier for all of us."

"Easier . . . what do you mean easier? Are you going to let them treat me like this?"

Tense silence followed.

"I won't," she cried. "Even though I've got no more use for Adam, I *won't* do anything to harm him."

"You *must,* Miss Montreux," said the Swisswoman, bending close to Candace's face again.

"You can't make me," said Candace in the tone of a child. "I'll tell him. I'll tell him everything!" She tried to rise.

"Sit down, Miss Montreux."

"I won't! I'm going to warn Adam. I'll tell him everything," she burst out, jumping from the chair. "I'll tell him about the Templars and you people and that you're after him!" she yelled, hardly realizing what had come out of her mouth.

A heavy stillness instantly descended.

"A word that means nothing," said Vaughan-Maier. "You have no idea what it is."

"Maybe I don't," Candace shot back. "But Adam might. I'll warn him, I tell you. I'll tell him about the Templars, whatever it is!"

She fled from the room.

The three watched her go, not knowing how to react to her childish outburst. They stood, stunned that their collective wills had not been sufficient to coerce her to their bidding.

Within seconds D'Abernon came to herself.

"Lord Montreux, go get your daughter," she commanded.

He turned and went after her. But already Candace was speeding down the elevator. By the time Lord Montreux reached the ground in the other elevator and ran laboring through the lobby out of the building, his daughter was climbing into his car, for which she had a key in her purse.

"Candace, come here," he called after her.

"No, Daddy, I won't! Those are bad people. I will not do what they say."

He approached. But down here in the parking lot he was a mere father, not a member of the Council. He was powerless to compel her beyond the limits of her own will.

Candace turned on the ignition. Her father continued to walk toward the car.

The tires squealed backwards across the pavement. The next moment Candace was speeding away. Lord Montreux gazed after his own BMW retreating in the distance in disbelief that she had so flagrantly defied him.

Not only that, she had taken his automobile!

Watching from the window above, Anni D'Abernon pondered the situation. Slowly her vexation moderated. Actually, she thought to herself, this development might prove fortuitous. The foolish Montreux girl would go straight to Livingstone.

She'd follow the vixen . . . and then kill Livingstone herself. That appeared to be the only way to be done with this whole troublesome episode.

twenty-three

Clues in Chartres

(1)

In the famous French capital of Paris, which Rocky had never seen, they left their hotel to walk the half mile to the great French museum and art gallery.

"If we can just get there, and in and out without being noticed," said Adam as he glanced along the street in front of them.

"We've blended in anonymously so far," said Rocky. "I haven't noticed anyone even looking twice."

"We've been lucky," rejoined Adam. "I should never have told the press we were going to France. It just slipped out. One false move and the Judiciaire will arrest me and ship me off to some Ethiopian jail."

"We'll be okay. We just have to solve the case before the authorities or press discover your whereabouts."

"Have you heard from Scott?" asked Crystal.

"Talked to him this morning," replied Adam.

"How are things in Turkey?"

"We only left him yesterday. But he said it's still bleak, and that everybody continues to pull out. He's desperately negotiating with the Turks to keep some sense of continuity going, assuring them that we'll turn this around."

"Juliet has sure been quiet lately," said Jen. "I can't get her to talk about anything. When was the last time you talked to her?"

"Last night, from the hotel, after we got in," said Adam, sighing. "She's having a hard time. I'm not sure what the problem is."

"At least the press crowd at the house eased up before Jen and I left," added Crystal.

"Nobody told them where I was, or where you were going?"

Crystal shook her head.

Adam continued to think about Juliet. He wished he knew what she was thinking. But sight of the Louvre a block ahead soon moved the discussion in other directions.

"By the way," asked Rocky, "why are we going to the Louvre?"

"Believe it or not," said Adam, "the *art* of the Renaissance is one of the significant points of interest in our quest."

"Art . . . why–in connection with the ark?" asked Rocky. "What does art have to do with it?"

"Gothic architecture in particular," said Adam. "Pre-Renaissance actually. We'll see links to the crusaders, as we were talking about before. I want you to see the entry to the church of Saint-Germain-l'Auxerrois. It is one of two Gothic doorways in Paris, and bears a striking resemblance to the entry of the Al-Aqsa Mosque in Jerusalem. You're going to see a similar one in a couple of days in Chartres. It's all about Gothic architecture, and the Templars are the link."

They continued along the bank of the Seine, enjoying the crisp sunny Parisian morning and the sights of the world's most beautiful city. Suddenly Adam disappeared. He returned a few minutes later carrying a small bag.

"What did you get?" asked Crystal.

"Some postcards to send to Juliet and a scarf I saw at that stand back there. Can you believe it–here I am walking along the Seine . . . *without* my fiancée. No offense to the rest of you, but something about that doesn't seem right!"

Jen and Crystal flanked their boss and the American investigator as they made their way along the sidewalk, listening to the conversation between them.

As they spoke, Jen continued to glance about. It gradually became obvious she was not looking at the scenery.

"What is it, Jen?" asked Adam.

"I don't know," she replied. "I've just had the feeling that someone's following us."

"We'll lose them in the Louvre," said Adam, not feeling her anxiety and trying to set her mind at ease with a laugh. "The place is a maze. Once we're inside they'll never be able to follow us!"

(2)

Managing again to convince Beeves to let her through the gate, Candace Montreux flew up the Sevenoaks driveway still in the BMW she had taken across the channel by ferry. She screeched the tires to a stop on the entryway pavement. From upstairs the housekeeper heard her coming well enough. Mrs. Graves was already on her way downstairs in a mounting huff as Candace jumped out of the car and ran for the front door. It opened as she raised her hand to the knocker.

"Mrs. Graves," she said immediately, "where's Adam?"

"Really, Miss Montreux, after driving up in such–"

"Mrs. Graves, *please!*" interrupted Candace. "Where is he?"

The Montreux girl sounded different. Mrs. Graves could tell something was wrong. "Please, Mrs. Graves," Candace repeated with urgency, "I know you don't like me. I can't even blame you for that. I know I've been positively horrid to you. Hate me if you want to. I don't even care anymore. But you've got to believe me–Adam is in danger. I must warn him."

"What kind of danger?" asked Mrs. Graves, finally growing concerned.

"They're trying to kill him, Mrs. Graves! Please . . . I've *got* to find him!"

For the merest instant the housekeeper felt a strange sympathy, as if they were two women who, each in her own way, cared for Adam and must help him.

"They–Mr. Livingstone and the others–they went first to Turkey," Mrs. Graves finally said.

"Yes . . . yes, I know, but then–what about France? Are they there?"

"They were to fly to Paris."

"*Paris!* I'll never find him there!"

"Wait, Miss Montreux, I think . . . wait just a moment."

Mrs. Graves hurried back inside. She returned two or three minutes later.

"I'm taking a dreadful chance telling you this," she said. "You must assure me no one else will know."

"Yes, of course . . . I promise, Mrs. Graves! What is it?"

"Juliet said she spoke with Adam yesterday evening. They were in Paris. She said Adam called from the Hotel des Tuileries."

"Where is it?"

"Near the Louvre," she said, "on the *Rue Hyacinthe.*"

Already Candace was running back toward her car.

(3)

Some sixty miles southwest of Paris, Adam and Rocky led Jen and Crystal into the famous and magnificent cathedral of Chartres. They had left Paris early that afternoon.

Approaching, they observed the two immense and distinctive steeples toward the west, Gothic in design. They entered through the central of the three highly sculpted doorways at the west end, whose arches, as Adam had explained, bore the same reminder of Templar influence they had seen in Paris and as existed on the Temple Mount in Jerusalem.

They made their way inside, walking slowly through the nave, then up and down the aisles on each side. In hushed tones Adam continued to explain about the Templars.

"The Knights of the Temple became a fixture in Jerusalem," Adam was saying. "Gradually the story began to go around that they had discovered something of great value."

"What did Bernard of Clairvaux have to do with them?" asked Jen.

"By the way, still think we're being followed?"

"No," said Jen, laughing. "That feeling left me as soon as we got out of Paris."

"To answer your question, with Bernard's help, the Templars received the official sanction of the pope. Recruits flocked in from all over Europe. In less than eighty years the Templars had accumulated astonishing wealth, and had even ventured into international banking."

(4)

Candace Montreux flew into Paris late in the day, rented a car, and drove to the Hotel des Tuileries. As soon as she walked in she didn't like the place. She felt an unfriendly presence, as though eyes were focused on her. But she hadn't told a soul of her plans.

She walked straight to the reception desk and asked the clerk to call Adam's room. His reply was not what Candace expected.

"But I don't understand," she said, "he was supposed to be here."

"*Je regrette,* mademoiselle. Mr. Livingstone and his colleagues checked out—how you say . . . *au matin.*"

"This morning!" exclaimed Candace. "Where did they go? Are they still in Paris?"

"I am sorry. Mr. Livingstone did not inform us of his plans."

"I *must* find him. It's a matter of life and—"

Candace stopped. Something caused her to look about nervously.

"I don't know what to do," she went on, more to herself than to the patient Frenchman. "Well, I've got to have a room for tonight. I presume you have something?" she asked.

"*Oui,* mademoiselle."

"Then I'll take a room . . . for one night. I'll decide what to do later."

Candace signed the registry. The clerk gave her a key.

"Fourth floor, mademoiselle. The elevator is there across the lobby—it is slow but reliable."

"Thank you," said Candace distractedly, then headed toward it.

(5)

Adam and his team continued to walk about inside the cathedral at Chartres, examining its various rooms, trying to take in every detail. As they went, Adam pored through the guidebook he had purchased.

"This is considered," explained Adam, "the most thorough example of Gothic architecture in the world, begun shortly after 1130."

"Right after the Templars returned from Jerusalem!" said Rocky with interest. "That is a coincidence no self-respecting investigator can ignore."

"The dates I'm sure are *not* coincidental," rejoined Adam. "We're in the middle of the region that Bernard of Clairvaux, Hughes de Payns, André de Montbard, and the rest of the original nine came from. The north tower was completed in 1134."

By now they were coming out of the southern end of the main part of the cathedral. "This is one of the most interesting features of the place," said Adam as he led the way outside onto the south porch.

He paused, then pointed across the street. "Do you see that cafe there?" he said. "It's called *La Reine de Saba*–The Queen of Sheba."

"The Ethiopian connection!" said Rocky.

"There's supposed to be a small sculpture of the Queen of Sheba," answered Adam, "in this porch. Look around–hundreds of statuettes and larger statues of the kings and queens of the Old Testament."

Adam read for a moment. "It's supposed to be over here," he said, moving toward a statue of David holding a harp. The others followed.

"This whole south porch was built some years after the main cathedral," Adam went on, "to commemorate the story of Queen Makeda and her son Menyelek, and the legend that he had taken the ark."

"How would the builders have known of it?" asked Crystal.

"Legend has it that the Templars followed the trail of the ark to Ethiopia just as we did," replied Adam. "While not finding the ark, they learned of the Ethiopian legend."

"So what the Templars discovered was the *Kebre Negast* epic," said Jen. "Then they brought the story with them back to France."

"That's how it seems to connect. Then around the same time came the German epic *Parzival,* in which the ark became the grail. Before long, the legends and secrets were blending into mysteries that have never been unraveled. Even the Ethiopians themselves lost track eventually of the fact that Menyelek hadn't actually stolen the ark itself, but had probably stolen the gold to fashion a second ark, the replica to be used by the Jews of Ethiopia. That's my guess, anyway. The legends got jumbled together. How else do we explain the replica turning into the real ark in the *Kebre Negast*? Eventually the story became that he had actually taken the ark itself. That story found its way into the epic, and then into Templar tradition. Meanwhile the real ark just faded out of sight. Ah–here it is."

✦ ✦ ✦

None of the four had noticed the shadow of a large man following their movements most of the day.

Under normal circumstances, he would have been impossible to miss. But dressed in a priest's robe, his bulk was well disguised, and the loose-fitting hood kept the distinguishing ponytail and serpent concealed. If he did not exactly blend in with the scenery, he did not attract too much attention to himself, especially in a cathedral sprinkled here and there with other silent clerics.

It would have struck him as enormously humorous to know, at a moment when he turned away and bowed his head down so as to remain out of sight, that a little boy who happened to be watching thought that he was praying.

(6)

Anni D'Abernon did not like the feeling of losing control.

The Dimension was growing far too quiet. The Spirit Guides were mute. Her Wise One offered no counsel. What was this clouding of the Dimensional Eye?

Where was the fool Montreux's daughter? She had to be stopped before she got to Livingstone. Her efforts to locate the girl thus far had proved unsuccessful.

D'Abernon rose and walked toward the far wall of her office. It was time she enlisted more help. If her father would not speak from the other world, she would bring out the object he had given her. Despite its mystic power, she was actually a little afraid of it. Her father's death had come before her training in its use was complete. She always sensed strange powers emanating from it that she was not confident of being able to control.

Five minutes later she sat with the object on the table before her. She turned out the lights and drew the blinds. This was something not even her closest colleagues on the Council knew of.

"Candace Montreux," she chanted in an otherworldly voice, "I command you to make yourself known. You *must* reveal your presence to me," she said, drawing out the word as an incantation against the woman. "I command it by the power of the Dimension. *Candace . . . Candace . . . Candace . . .* You must hear my voice . . . you must bend yourself to my will . . . *Candace . . . Candace . . .*"

(7)

Rocky, Jen, and Scott stared at the statue of the Queen of Sheba that Adam had just pointed out.

"Nothing so remarkable about it that I can see," observed Jen.

"Except when you stop to think that it's here at all," said Rocky. "Why is the Queen of Sheba included among the kings and queens of Israel?"

"By the time this portion of the cathedral was constructed," said Adam, "the Templars were obviously familiar with the legend of Solomon and the Queen of Sheba and Menyelek. They built clues of what they'd learned into its architecture. Those nine crusaders returned from Jerusalem, and from what they had learned constructed a cathedral that changed European architecture forever."

✦ ✦ ✦

After her arrival in the French capital and an uninteresting walk along the Seine and an uneventful early dinner, Candace Montreux returned to the Tuileries.

She still had no plan, though the need to warn Adam had not lessened in urgency. She was not accustomed to the desire to *help* someone, and her inexperience rendered her helpless. But the longer she delayed, the more afraid she became.

When Candace walked into the hotel, she was overcome with the same sensation of skin-crawling fear she had felt earlier. She shivered.

The figure of a man caught her eye, a goateed Frenchman with wool cap pulled down at an angle over his forehead. Something about him arrested her gaze.

She trembled involuntarily and continued across the lobby. She waited a few moments for the elevator. Its doors opened. She stepped inside, turned, pushed the button for the fourth floor, then raised her eyes out into the lobby as the doors began to close.

The man she had noted stood and now stared straight toward her. Her eyes widened in terror.

Zorin! she breathed.

He took a step forward. The elevator doors closed. Candace collapsed against one elevator wall in close to a faint.

Jerkily the outdated lift began its slow ascent.

(8)

Adam and his team stood in the north porch of the cathedral gazing about at the carved stone statues while Adam read the descriptions in the guidebook.

"OK," he said, pointing to one of the figures, "that fellow there—with the cup in his hand—he's supposed to be the ancient priest-king Melchizedek."

"Is that the Holy Grail he's holding?" asked Jen.

"I would say it's a good possibility. Right, and . . . let's see, over there in that bay . . . see those three statues, the two bearded men on either side? That's the Queen of Sheba in the middle."

They moved toward the figure, gazing with wonder upon these clues from so far in the past, yet which had been standing in plain view for eight hundred years.

As Adam continued to read, the other three wandered about the room on their own. Two or three minutes later Rocky's voice boomed out. Several of the other tourist groups stopped at the sound. Heads turned. Rocky quieted in embarrassment. The others were at his side within seconds.

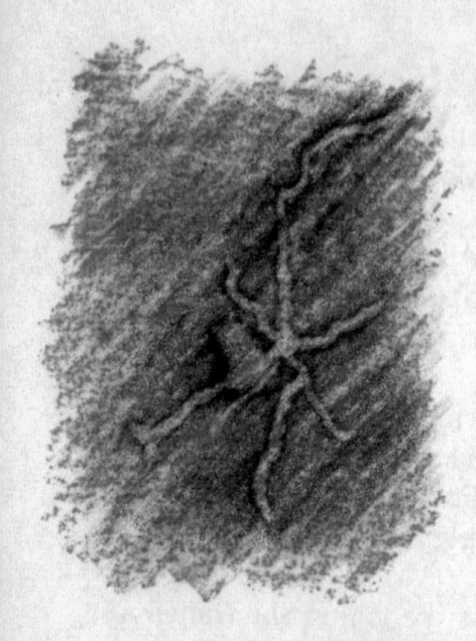

"Get a load of this!" he whispered, pointing to some miniaturized sculptures carved on a great column between two of the large statue-bays. "If that isn't supposed to be the ark of the covenant, I don't know what is!" he said.

The others bent forward, peering at a box atop a cart with wheels.

"You're exactly right, Rocky," said Adam. "This is an exciting find! And there's writing underneath it," he added, "but not Hebrew this time. My guess is Latin, but I'm not sure I can decipher it."

"Look over here," said Jen. She had located an altogether odd design on the opposite side of the same column. Four sets of eyes bent down to peer at it. Beneath several words in Hebrew was the border of a square box, in which had been scrawled what looked like a random and meaningless conglomeration of lines.

"What in the world can it be?" said Jen.

"More cryptic Templar clues?" suggested Rocky.

"But meaning what?"

"Anybody have a piece of paper . . . blank paper?" asked Adam.

Ever the efficient secretary, Crystal produced a sheet from the notebook always in her hand.

"Now a pencil, my dear," said Adam. "Ah . . . thank you."

"What are you doing?" asked Rocky.

"If these *are* clues," replied Adam, laying the sheet over the strange engraving and beginning to rub across it with the pencil, "I don't want us to have to trust our memories."

Five minutes later he stood, holding in his hand a crude but accurate rendition of the designs and words.

"If these things have any meaning," said Adam, "now we can take our time finding out. I think it's time we headed to our hotel. The cathedral is about to close for the night."

They began walking toward the exit, talking excitedly about what they had found and the possibilities to which they pointed.

"You know," said Rocky, "I can't help wondering if there's a Middle Eastern connection we're missing."

"Do you mean Jerusalem?"

"Israel is where it was fashioned, and where it disappeared. And I haven't been able to get that peculiar reference made to the ark in the book of Jeremiah out of my mind. What if the old prophet knew more than he divulged on the surface?"

"You might be onto something indeed," rejoined Adam.

✦ ✦ ✦

As they left the cathedral, none noticed the hurried gait of a lumbering priestly clad figure behind them, who had just overheard the clue he had been waiting for. It was time to blow this burg. He had what he'd come for.

(9)

In weak terror Candace watched the numbered lights of the elevator illuminate as they passed each floor with painful tedium.

She couldn't believe it. But Zorin's eyes had found hers. In that mere instant they bored into her with sinister intent. There could be no doubt about those eyes!

"Oh, oh . . . can't it go any faster!" she said to herself in half-whimpering agony, urging the old lift along. "Oh . . . oh, God . . . help me!"

She could almost imagine Zorin's footsteps racing up the stairs. He would be there when the doors opened, staring at her from less than two feet away, ready to put a bullet through her heart! She had seen him kill and knew he would not think twice to do so again.

Unconsciously Candace shrank as far back into the lift as possible, as if somehow distancing herself from her inevitable fate. The light on floor four went on. The elevator began to slow.

Oh . . . God . . . what am I going to do?

With agony she watched the doors part.

Whimpering to herself in relief to see the corridor empty, Candace squeezed through the doors and ran down the hall toward room 43. She fumbled madly in her purse for the key. With shaking fingers, she rattled it toward the lock.

The faint echo of footsteps sounded down the hall.

Frantically Candace turned the key. It clanked in the lock. She grabbed at the handle, threw the door open, dashed inside, then relocked and bolted the door behind her.

She fell on the bed, trembling in every muscle of her body.

Then she began to do something she hadn't done in years. Candace Montreux began to cry.

(10)

It took Candace not long to realize that she had only succeeded in making her situation worse. The flow of tears began to halt.

It had been stupid to come back to the room.

She sat up and took two deep breaths. She had to compose herself. This was no time to fall apart. Quickly she considered her options.

Zorin had her trapped. He could kill her at his leisure. She should *never* have gotten into the elevator!

She had to get out of here.

If she remained where she was, Zorin would know where to find her. This was too dreadful. She wasn't ready to die!

She'd telephone the police . . . she'd telephone the man down at the desk!

No. Zorin would expect that. He was probably listening beside the desk right now for the clerk's phone to ring, all the time watching the stairs and the elevator to make sure she didn't make a run for it.

Sighing to herself, Candace lay back down on the bed. Oh, what could she do!

Gradually she began to cry again. With confused and terrified thoughts racing through her brain, at length Candace fell into a sleep which, though fitful, was far better than wakefulness.

(11)

It took some time for Larry Slate to locate the man who had given him the Bible. And it took a little doing, given his own high profile, to arrange for a private discussion with the man. That would be all he needed, for someone like Laurence Imre to get wind of his meeting with a pastor. But here he was.

"I'm sure you wonder why I wanted to see you," Slate began somewhat nervously. "So I'll tell you straight out—I read some in that Bible you gave me a month or two ago. And to tell you the truth, it got into me."

He went on to recount his mental quandary after reading the story of Zacchaeus, and the promise to repay fourfold anyone he had cheated.

"So that's about it," he concluded. "I'm not sure quite what to make of it. How could I possibly ever do such a thing?"

"Do you *want* to, Mr. Slate? Is that what you're asking?" said the pastor, a simple man by the name of Archer. He was no flashy orator or noted evangelist. But when the Lord had led him to pray for Larry Slate after seeing him briefly on a television interview, he had taken the charge seriously and had sent him a Bible. "Do *you* also want to repay four times over to those people whose lives you feel you have cheated by your magazine?"

"I don't know exactly. The words hit me hard. I haven't been able to get them out of my brain. I think maybe I'm *supposed* to do something."

"Why do you think so?"

"Well . . . look at me, Reverend—my life hasn't done anyone much good. Why did you send me a Bible with that note saying you were praying for me and that God loved me, if you thought I was filled with virtue? That Zacchaeus story got me thinking maybe it's time I thought about changing that."

"I see," said the pastor, nodding as he took in the information. Then he opened the Bible that had been sitting on his lap.

"I respect what you are trying to do, Mr. Slate," said Rev. Archer. "I honestly do. It took guts for you to seek me out and come here. I appreciate that fact. So I feel I owe you my complete honesty. In that light, let me say that there is an important aspect of the story of Zacchaeus that you haven't mentioned—and it's the most vital of all. Without it, nothing else you do will matter much."

"What's that?"

"Salvation, Mr. Slate. Jesus came to bring Zacchaeus *salvation.*"

Rev. Archer read the account in Luke 19 through aloud.

"You see, Zacchaeus was a sinner, and he knew it. Do you consider *yourself* a sinner?"

"Uh . . . I don't suppose I would have thought so two months ago . . . but now that you put it like that, I think that's what's made me so uncomfortable recently, that for the first time maybe I *do* feel like a sinner."

"And something else Zacchaeus did—he called Jesus *Lord.* That's a big step for a sinner to take. Do you know what it means?"

"No, I don't suppose I do."

"To make Jesus one's Lord means turning away from a life of sin. It means starting a whole new way of living, a new lifestyle, with someone *else* in charge, not yourself."

He looked into Slate's eyes. "Do you want to make Jesus your Lord, Mr. Slate?" he asked.

"You do get blunt, don't you, Pastor?"

"I've been accused of that," Archer said, laughing lightly. "But you came to me for help," he went on. "For all I know, we may never meet again. I'm not going to do you any good by beating around the bush. The only way I can help you is to tell it like it is. Then it's up to you what you want to do with it. Salvation is a serious business, and I think we need to look it in the face."

"I get your point," said Slate. "I suppose I ought to be man enough to handle it."

"I said that salvation is a serious business," Rev. Archer continued, "but salvation is also an *exciting* business. There's nothing so wonderful as making Jesus your Lord. We're not talking about a ball-and-chain life, but a new life of freedom and purpose. We're talking about a life in fellowship with a God who loves us. *Loves* us, Mr. Slate! And who wants nothing but the best for us. When I asked if you want to make Jesus your Lord, it's like handing you a check for ten billion dollars and saying, 'Would you like to have this? It's free for the taking.'"

"Come on, Pastor—that's a bit of an exaggeration."

"Eternal life is priceless, Mr. Slate. So is the love of God. That's why I hope you don't think my being blunt is in any way to criticize you. I'm a sinner too. I had to go through a difficult time of facing my sin too and deciding whether I was going to make Jesus Lord or not. It's a time that comes to everyone sometime in life. But the rewards last forever—eternal life with the God who made us. What could be better than that!"

"And that is the salvation you're talking about?"

"Exactly. Zacchaeus recognized he was a sinner and he said to Jesus, 'I'm going to turn away from my life of sin and make you my Lord.' Once he had gotten right with God in his life, he could set about to make restitution—the fourfold repayment."

"I guess I see what you mean," said Slate, "that there's an order to the thing. You need to do the one before the other."

"That's how I see it," replied Archer. "That's why I asked, 'Do you want to make Jesus your Lord?' That's the question everything depends on—your life, your past, your future, your eternal destiny. So what do you think, Mr. Slate—*do* you want to make Jesus your Lord?"

The office hushed for several long minutes. Larry Slate had never been spoken to in his life like this. He was one of the most powerful men in the publishing industry, whose face was as well known as many television and media personalities. And yet now in the quietness of a small study, with a pastor no one had ever heard of, who would never write a book or preach on TV, Larry Slate was alone in the universe, alone with his thoughts . . . and with God.

"It would probably change everything," he said at length. His voice was soft.

"I'm sure it would," replied the pastor tenderly. "But all for the good."

"I . . . I don't even know how to do such a thing."

"If you truly want for it to be said of you, Mr. Slate, as Jesus said about Zacchaeus so long ago, 'Today salvation has come to this house, because this man, too, is a son'—if you want that to be said about *you,* there is no easier thing in all the world. I can help you."

"Yes . . . yes I think I do," said Larry Slate after reflection.

"Then I suggest we go to our knees and pray . . . will you join me? There's nothing to be timid or afraid about. It's the most natural thing in the world."

Rev. Archer slipped to his knees beside his chair. Awkwardly, for he had never done such a thing in his life, and yet given courage by the new humility that had already begun to infect his character, Larry Slate eased out of his chair and joined him on the floor.

"I'm going to lead you in a simple prayer," said the pastor. "You can say the words after me, or change them into your own words if you like. There are no formulas with God. He cares what our hearts say, not our lips. Feel free to say whatever you're comfortable with and use whatever words that express your feelings. If you have questions as we go, say so. The Lord is here with us right now. We're not doing this for show, but so that you can talk to him—as naturally as you are talking to me. All right?"

Slate nodded. "Do I need to close my eyes?" he asked.

"It doesn't matter," replied Archer. "However you're comfortable. The Lord is listening to your heart."

The pastor began. "Dear Father and Lord Jesus . . ."

Haltingly Slate repeated the words. They were scarcely audible. They were the first words of prayer his lips had ever uttered, and he could not prevent a slight quiver in his voice.

" . . . I realize, just like old Zacchaeus, that I am a sinner and that I haven't lived a life to make you proud. . . ."

"*I know I'm a sinner and haven't lived a very respectable life,*" Slate went on, his voice gathering more strength as he went, "*and I'm sorry about it now.*"

" . . . but I want to change that. I want to make you my Lord," Pastor Archer said.

"But I want to change that, and make you my Lord."

"So I ask you to forgive my sins . . . "

"I ask you to forgive my sins."

" . . . and even more than that, to forgive me for the sinner I have been. . . ."

"And forgive me for the sinner I've been."

" . . . to forgive me for living my whole life apart from you."

"And forgive me for living my life apart from you."

"I thank you, Jesus, for making salvation possible by your death on the cross."

"*Thank you, Jesus, for making salvation possible–*" He paused. "I guess I've got a question about that, Pastor," said Slate, looking up from where his head was bowed toward the floor, "if that's all right."

"Of course," said Rev. Archer.

"I'm not sure I understand what Jesus' dying on the cross has to do with it. We didn't talk about that before."

"The Bible says that the penalty for sin is death. And since all men are sinners, we are all under that penalty. But Jesus was sinless, so he took that penalty on himself, for the whole world–for you and me–when he died on the cross. I'm sure you are familiar with the words of John 3:16–*For God so loved the world that he gave his one and only Son, that whoever believes in him shall not perish but have eternal life.* That is how salvation comes to us."

"I see what you're saying," said Slate, "but Zacchaeus couldn't have known anything about all that, since Jesus hadn't died yet. So Jesus' death on the cross didn't get him saved. Yet he said salvation came to him anyway."

"I admit it is confusing," said Archer. "The Atonement has puzzled theologians through the ages."

"What in the world is the Atonement?"

"The fact that by his crucifixion, Christ *atoned* for our sins. It is a great theological mystery. But the fact of the matter is that the Bible says that Jesus died for our sins. So even if we don't *understand* it, we can still accept that salvation through faith. That's what putting one's trust in Jesus for salvation means."

"Oh . . . I see. I suppose I can go along with that. All right, I'm ready to go on."

"Then shall we continue to pray . . . thank you Lord, for making salvation possible by your death on the cross. . . ."

"*Thank you Lord, for making salvation possible by your death on the cross.*"

"I accept that salvation into my own life personally."

"*I accept that salvation into my life. . . .*"

"Even though I don't understand it, I accept it by faith."

"*I accept it by faith.*"

"And I now ask you and invite you to come into my heart. . . ."

"*I ask—*" Briefly his voice caught, but he continued, "*And invite you to come into my heart. . . .*"

". . . and live with me and help me to become God's child in all the ways you taught when you were on earth. . . ."

"*And to live with me and help me become God's child—I forgot the rest, Pastor.*"

" . . . help me live as you taught when you were on the earth."

"*Help me live like you taught on earth.*"

"I thank you for your salvation."

"*I thank you for your salvation.*"

"I thank you for the Bible and for leading me to this story of Zacchaeus."

"*I thank you for the Bible and for leading me to this story of Zacchaeus.*"

"Now, God, my heavenly Father, I ask that you will help me and teach me to live as one of your sons. Amen."

"*And now, God, uh . . . heavenly Father, help me learn to live as one of your sons. Amen.*"

Rev. Archer rose and took his chair again. Larry Slate stood up, then smiled, an awkward, childlike smile.

"It's funny," he said, "the only thing I can think to say is that I feel . . . clean."

"Believe me," said the pastor, extending his hand and giving Slate's a vigorous shake, "that is the *first* of many changes you are going to feel."

"But . . . but what do I do now?" asked Slate.

"What you have been doing—keep reading the New Testament. Your life is no longer your own. You're a businessman—it is like you've brought in a new management team to run things, with Jesus as CEO. You've made him your Lord. So you have to find out what he said to do . . . and then do it. The Bible is your Training Manual."

"That's it?" said Slate.

"That's really all there is to being a Christian," replied Rev. Archer. "It's no big mystery. Just making Jesus Lord, then doing what he says."

(12)

In her hotel room in Paris Candace Montreux suddenly awoke. She was cold.

The room was black. It took several minutes for her senses to fully return. Then she remembered her last waking moments. The eyes of Zorin haunted her brain. She started up on the bed with a return of terror.

She calmed herself with two or three deep breaths. It wasn't as bad as it might be, she thought. At least she wasn't dead.

Why hadn't he come to find her . . . or broken in without benefit of an invitation?

Sitting on the edge of her bed, Candace considered her options. She had to get away. But how?

If she tried to leave now, that would put her out on the streets of Paris all night. True, that might be better than facing Zorin . . . *if* she could escape.

What time was it?

She groped her way to the nightstand and pulled the chain on the bedside lamp. Ten-fifteen. Zorin was probably still hanging around. If he hadn't harmed her yet, she would probably be safe till morning. *Unless* . . . he was waiting till everyone in the hotel was asleep!

Candace's fright returned full force with a reminder of Dr. Cissna's face, the man she had personally witnessed Zorin murder in Egypt. After that horrible episode, nothing Zorin did would shock her.

No, she couldn't afford to wait–she had to get out of here . . . now!

(13)

If Zorin was still watching . . . she couldn't worry about that, thought Candace. She only hoped she could sneak downstairs without being seen. But the stairs were hardwood, without carpet, and creaked. At this hour the entire hotel would hear someone creeping down four floors!

It would have to be the elevator.

Candace turned out the light in her room. She opened the door a crack and peered out. The coast looked clear. Cautiously she pushed the door further open until she was able to see up and down the hall.

Empty!

She crept out with tentative step, then began making her way down the hall. It was deathly quiet.

She reached the elevator and pushed the button. Anxiously she waited as it ascended from the lobby.

Half expecting to find her enemy waiting inside when the doors opened, Candace breathed a sigh of relief when the elevator was passenger-less. She stepped in and pushed *L*.

Candace slunk to one side of the front corner beside the control panel, hoping it would keep her from being seen when the doors opened. Gradually it slowed, then came to a halt. The doors opened.

Candace craned her neck sideways from her hiding place until one eye could peek toward the lobby. If she saw Zorin waiting, her finger was poised on the Close Door button to make an escape back upstairs.

The lobby was deserted!

She dashed from her nest of safety and across the floor toward the front door.

"Oh . . . mademoiselle!" called a voice.

Candace nearly jumped out of her skin.

She spun half around. "You frightened me!" she said to the desk clerk behind her. "I can't talk now," she added, trying to keep her voice low and continuing on toward the front door.

"But the man you were inquiring about . . . Monsieur Livingstone–"

Candace stopped. "What about him?" she said, turning toward the reception counter.

"I asked some of the staff if anyone knew his plans."

"Yes . . . ?" said Candace.

"One of our bellboys heard two of Livingstone's associates talking about the cathedral."

"Which one?"

"Notre-Dame."

"But that is in Paris," said Candace, glancing nervously about.

"There is another by the same name, even older."

"Where . . . not in Paris?"

"*Non,* mademoiselle . . . in the town of Chartres."

(14)

Candace left the hotel, ran along the *Rue Hyacinthe,* down several side streets, then stopped to catch her breath in the shadow of Saint-Germain-l'Auxerrois.

She listened intently. This section of Paris was mostly asleep. She heard no footsteps.

She had to get to her car, but it was still at the hotel parking lot. For the moment she was safe. She would wait another twenty or thirty minutes, to see if Zorin had followed her. Then she would carefully make her way back to the hotel.

She realized she was cold. How stupid of her–she had left the room without a coat! She'd left her suitcase and personal belongings too! She'd come away with nothing but her purse. What a nincompoop! There was no going back now. She'd telephone the hotel tomorrow and arrange for something.

Adam, where are you when I need you! she said to herself. She felt like crying again. But she couldn't afford that luxury . . . not yet.

Good at it or not, Candace's makeshift plan worked. She retrieved her car and drove away without incident. Several blocks from the hotel she began turning corners randomly until she was lost herself. Finally, under the shadow of the Eiffel Tower, she pulled over, parked, had the cry she had postponed from earlier, and fell asleep.

Candace awoke at four-thirty—hungry, thirsty, and freezing, but glad to be alive. More sleep was out of the question. She'd rather drive toward her destination and put as much distance between herself and Zorin as possible. If she got sleepy, she'd stop. She still had to find Adam, if she had to go to every hotel in Chartres.

By five Candace Montreux was speeding through the outskirts of Paris in her tiny rented Citroën, hoping she had finally managed to elude her onetime, as she thought, friend and now dreaded enemy, Halder Zorin.

If only she could keep from getting distracted and wandering over to the left side of the street! Fortunately the Citroën's heater worked. Gradually she warmed up.

Once she was on her way toward Chartres, Candace began to relax.

However Zorin had managed to show up at the Hotel des Tuileries, she hoped she had seen the last of him.

twenty-four

Shocker!

(1)

Adam Livingstone awoke early and was out walking as the French city of Chartres came to life.

He was not exactly praying as he went. The continuous uplifting of the heart into the heavenly realms was still developing as an aspect of Adam's spiritual journey. But he was on the pathway toward deepening intimacy with his heavenly Father, which is the one and true good that ought to be said about every man and woman.

He had been out now for an hour or more. It was somewhere between seven and seven-thirty. Their hotel, *Le Relais Bastille,* was located in a quiet region of parks and old gray-stone homes and buildings, none of which appeared younger than two hundred years in age. The only shops open at this hour were bakeries, one on every block, it seemed. Most of the other pedestrians were either on their way to one of these establishments—whose morning wares gave pleasant fragrance to the morning—or were walking away from one with a thin, golden, crusty loaf sticking out of a bag or clutched under an arm. A few rode about on bicycles, with long slender loaves strapped behind them.

To his right, the Eure River snaked its way northward, where it would be joined by two or three others, and eventually empty into the Seine. Adam ambled along the uneven cobbled sidewalk, taking in every detail of the aged stone buildings with relish. As he walked, the walkways and streets filled. Noises of the day increased. Old women, always in black, cloaked about in the same sweaters and scarves seemingly whatever the weather, made their way carefully along the stone path, chattering in groups. Old men, more colorful in their garb but always with characteristic wool mustang cap, walked along sidewalks and occasional dirt pathway, clustering especially wherever a park or canal or a few trees afforded a more country setting, every one with a cane or walking stick, out for their daily stroll.

And ever and always from everywhere in Chartres, the great cathedral loomed as a silent presence over men and women, over the town and nation.

All through the night one word had reverberated through his brain from Rocky's comment as they were leaving the cathedral the previous evening.

Jeremiah!

The ancient prophet was the last biblical writer to mention the ark of the covenant, and Adam could not think that reference accidental. More clues *must* exist in the book bearing his name.

One way or another—even if he had to pick apart the book verse by verse until something jumped out at him—Adam was determined to find it!

(2)

Adam arrived back at hotel *Le Relais Bastille* at quarter till eight. Everyone else was ready for coffee and croissants.

Thirty minutes later, as they sat around the table in the breakfast room, Adam was telling the others about his thoughts from earlier.

"I felt God perhaps saying that Jeremiah could be the key," he said. "I wondered if he hadn't left clues behind in the records he wrote down, just like the clues to Eden that we discovered in your grandfather Harry's journal, Rocky."

"Sounds like we need to read the book of Jeremiah again," said the investigator.

A waiter approached the table.

"Mr. Livingstone," he said, "you have a telephone call."

Adam glanced at the others, then rose and followed the man to the nearest phone.

"This is Adam Livingstone," he said.

"Hello, Adam . . . it's Juliet."

"Juliet!" exclaimed Adam.

Half those in the breakfast room turned toward him, including his own three companions.

"I'm sorry for calling so early in the day, but I could hardly sleep all night," said Juliet. "Over and over I felt the Lord impressing upon me something about the prophet Jeremiah, and it seemed important that I tell you."

"That is too incredible," said Adam softly. "I woke up with Jeremiah on my mind too."

A hesitation followed the initial exchange.

"I know it's been . . . uh, you know . . . awkward between us lately," fumbled Juliet. "I know I was horrible at the airport when you left—I'm sorry . . . I'm just . . ."

"I know, it's all right," said Adam. "Please, don't worry about it."

"I'm just going through a tough patch . . . if you can just give me some time, I'll be OK. I'm sorry for being so stupid."

"Don't say that, Juliet—it's all right, really. But how did you think of Jeremiah," he said, trying to get her talking about something else.

"I've been so depressed lately that I tried to read the Bible. At first I tried the Psalms, but it didn't work. A lot of times when I get depressed I read Jeremiah—he makes me feel like I'm not the only one who gets gloomy and down. But no matter what happens, I'll always respect you and appreciate all you've done for me . . . we'll always be friends. I just need time."

"I understand. I love you, Juliet—don't forget that."

She did not reply.

"And, Juliet," added Adam, "I appreciate your calling—it has been great to hear your voice."

"Good-bye, Adam."

Adam returned to the table. He did not like the sound of what she had said at the end of the call. It seemed so final.

(3)

Adam again went out walking in Chartres in the descending dusk of early evening.

Jeremiah and the Templars, his legal and reputational difficulties, and even the ark of the covenant . . . seemed so remote now. Throughout the day he had been thinking about Juliet's call. If there was some way to reassure her and help her see and understand how much she meant to him. If only—

Adam had no chance to complete the thought.

Suddenly in the distance, from out of the quiet evening, he heard his name.

"Adam . . . Adam, wait!" cried a voice.

What! he thought, recognizing the sound. He peered through the dusk.

A solitary figure a block away hurried toward him.

It couldn't be . . . yet he would know that face anywhere!

"Adam . . . oh Adam . . . it *is* you!" came the frightened cry again, mingled with the echo of footsteps on the cobbled walkway.

"Candace?" Adam called in shock. He began walking toward her.

In her frantic exhaustion Candace ran forward in a delirium of relief.

✦ ✦ ✦

Forty yards away, the slender black barrel of a specially tooled Walther PPK bore straight toward the forehead of Adam Livingstone.

The index finger pressing lightly against the trigger in readiness was thin. It did not appear to be the finger of a murderer. The eye squinting at Livingstone from behind the barrel, however, was steely and without conscience.

Dressed from head to foot in black and concealed in the deepening shadows of a deserted onetime office building, the assassin waited for the perfect moment. At last they would be through with Livingstone forever. The Montreux girl had played her role to perfection.

The quarry began walking forward as Candace ran toward him. A second later he came into perfect sight beneath a pale streetlamp.

✦ ✦ ✦

"Adam . . . Adam!" Candace cried out as she ran, "I've been looking for you all day . . . oh, I'm so glad to find you!"

"But, Candace—what are you doing here!" said Adam, dumfounded. "How did you find me?"

Candace wavered and slowed. Even as she drew within twenty feet, under the streetlight Adam could see her physical condition and the terror in her eyes. He had never seen her look such a mess.

"Adam . . . Adam . . . I came to warn you! Adam . . . you're in danger . . . Daddy's people are—"

✦ ✦ ✦

At the final instant, the eye flinched. The barrel wavered. The hand trembled.

Suddenly it was not Livingstone's face along the barrel of the PPK. The girl's back came into view. The murderess cursed, and tried to force the pistol back to Livingstone.

Her hand quivered as she squeezed the trigger.

✦ ✦ ✦

Candace opened her arms, crying for joy. She didn't care that he was engaged to someone else. He was still *Adam* . . . he would make it right again . . . just as soon as he got out of danger! She ran toward his waiting embrace.

" . . . Daddy's people are—"

The sharp report of a single shot shattered the peaceful air.

"Candace!" howled a great cry. The sound of both shout and shot echoed away through the night.

The bullet angled through her shoulder blades and out the other side just above her left breast. Hardly aware of the warm explosion of red splattering over his chest and face, all Adam could do was allow Candace's limp body to collapse, blood-drenched, into his arms.

(4)

The Voice sounded in the Swiss murderer's ear.

Involuntarily Anni D'Abernon shuddered again. It was a voice she knew only too well. Was she surrounded everywhere by a conspiracy against her?

"So . . . you couldn't pull the trigger on him?" it said. "I watched with fascination the battle you had with yourself."

"What battle—she's dead, isn't she?" returned D'Abernon, staring upon the pathetic scene of Livingstone kneeling slowly to the ground holding the body. A few onlookers from a block away were already running toward the scene. D'Abernon began backing away.

"*If* she had been your target . . . which you and I both know was not the case," said the Voice. "Why don't you shoot him now?"

D'Abernon hesitated but a moment.

"You can stick around if you want, Zorin," she said, "but I'm getting out of here."

She pivoted and began walking quickly but noiselessly away from the scene into the shadows. Zorin hastened after her.

"I never took you for a coward," he chided.

"I *always* took you for a fool, Zorin!" she shot back.

"Easy, Miss Holy Grail. It would not do to anger me."

The words stunned the Swisswoman. Her knees buckled slightly, and she struggled to hide her discomposure. "What did you call me?"

"You heard me clearly enough."

"How do you know about . . . that?"

Zorin laughed, throaty and evil. "I know much more than you give me credit for. Do you think you are the only one to whom the Dimension makes revelations? Do not forget, I was to be the Chosen One."

"You were *never* chosen, Zorin," spat D'Abernon with scorn.

"I too am of ancient lineage," Zorin said, ignoring her petty display of power. "My ancestors were at Bern along with yours. There have been rumors in my family for generations about the object. Fortunately you have confirmed what I long suspected. I wonder how your colleagues on the Council—"

"On which you will soon be replaced, Zorin."

"All the worse for the Council. You will all go down. Then only I shall remain. You should have considered your moves more carefully. But as I was saying, I wonder how your colleagues would take the news that you possess the secret of ancient Templar power, and have kept knowledge of it from them."

"They will never know."

"How can you be sure?"

"They would never believe *you,* Zorin."

"Don't be too certain. It may be *I* who will replace *you.*"

Another evil laugh followed. D'Abernon again shuddered at the sound of it. When it ceased, she turned in the direction of the Voice she hated.

But she was alone in the night.

[illegible] natural. [illegible]

[illegible]

[illegible]

[illegible] said [illegible]

[illegible]

[illegible]

[illegible] Zack [illegible]

[illegible]

[illegible]

twenty-five

Letter Bomb

(1)

In his Chartres hotel room Adam Livingstone sat, stunned, as the uniformed French policeman made notes on his pad. Jen, Rocky, and Crystal stood somberly, knowing all they could really do was offer Adam moral support.

"Tell me again, monsieur," said the agent at length, "when was the last time you saw Mademoiselle Montreux?"

"I don't even remember . . . weeks—probably months, actually," replied Adam. He stared blankly ahead, oblivious to the blood drying on his shirt, hands, and face. He knew there could be no other explanation than that the bullet which killed Candace had been meant for him.

"Did you contact her in that time?" came the policeman's voice into his thoughts.

"No . . . not at all," he replied.

"How did she know you were in Chartres, monsieur?"

"I have no idea," replied Adam.

A few more notes followed. The policeman now addressed Rocky, thinking perhaps it would be best to conclude matters with him.

"You will have to remain in Chartres for now, of course," he said. "And once this becomes public, no doubt Scotland Yard and the Ethiopian authorities will be interested," he added in none too sympathetic a tone. "Be sure we are able to reach you, monsieur. We may have more questions."

(2)

"Lord Montreux," said Anni D'Abernon, "I am afraid I have some bad news."

"Yes . . . what is it?" he said into the telephone.

"Your daughter is dead."

"What!" he said, shaking his head as if he had not heard her correctly.

"Your daughter Candace is dead, Baron," she repeated without emotion.

"But . . . how?" he said, weakening under the obvious truth conveyed by the

Swisswoman's tone. Her countenance was as chilly as if she had been in the room with him.

"She tried to warn Livingstone," answered D'Abernon. "I am sorry to be the bearer of such tidings, Baron. But her reckless defiance of our wishes put her directly in harm's way."

"I . . . I don't understand. What could Livingstone have had to do—"

"It turns out that Zorin was tracking Livingstone, Baron," she replied. "Your daughter got in his way, and he shot her."

"The blackguard!" cursed Montreux, though his voice was soft and did not carry much conviction. He was struggling to prevent his voice from cracking in the hearing of the stoic D'Abernon. "I'll kill him myself."

"He *will* be attended to, Baron. But it will be best for your hands not to be sullied in the affair."

(3)

In her bedroom at Sevenoaks, Juliet Halsay had just opened her suitcase on the bed. Her mother would be taking the train back north to Bedford tomorrow.

The phone call had helped . . . but it *hadn't* helped.

Hearing Adam's voice and reassurances had nearly torn her apart. In one way it had only made it worse. She still felt that she did not really belong. Was she just afraid, afraid of being in love with someone like Adam Livingstone? Obviously she loved him. Deep down she knew he loved her. Then why was she doing this? Why was she being such an idiot?

Tears formed in her eyes as she began placing clothes and personal items inside it. Then the tears began to flow in earnest. She forced herself to continue, though her heart was breaking.

Obviously the suitcase would not be nearly enough. She left the room and went downstairs. Perhaps her aunt had some boxes.

She heard her mother and Mrs. Graves speaking in the kitchen in hushed tones. She paused, wiping back and forth at her eyes and nose, although anyone could see well enough that she had been crying, then entered.

"Auntie Andrea," she said, sniffling, "do you have some boxes?"

"What kind of boxes, dear?"

"Any kind—for packing, you know."

"How about some tea, dear?" said Mrs. Halsay, trying to sound cheerful. "We just brewed a fresh pot."

"I don't want any tea, Mum," replied Juliet. "I only want some boxes."

Again the two women looked at one another, concerned. Mrs. Graves rose.

"I'll see what I can find downstairs, Juliet dear."

Juliet left the kitchen and went back up to her room. The moment she was inside, the tears came anew. The bed looked so inviting! Tears like these needed a pillow and bed!

But she could not give in to the urge. Something else must be done first. Juliet walked to the desk, sat down, then took out paper and pen from the top drawer. Slowly she began to write the most painful words she had ever written.

(4)

The following day's bombshell was not a telephone call but the express-letter that came to Adam Livingstone, addressed to him at *Le Relais Bastille* in Chartres. He recognized the handwriting on the envelope immediately.

He grabbed eagerly at the envelope and nearly tore it in half to get at the contents. It read:

> *Dear Adam,*
>
> *It was good to talk to you yesterday on the telephone. I am sorry I have been so stupid. I've been so confused. Forgive me for that. I guess in many ways I am a little girl after all. During this last month I have come to realize more than ever what a great difference there is between us—the age is just one part of it. You seem so mature and strong. I feel like such a child. I am even crying as I write these words to you. See—I am a little girl!*

Adam's heart nearly broke to read Juliet's words. His eyes were already misty, but he struggled to continue.

> *You have been so good to me. I want you to know how much I appreciate everything. I will never forget any of it. These have been the happiest days of my life.*
>
> *But I have too many doubts . . . about myself, about us, about our ages, about our future, and about whether I am truly the right person to be your wife. I suppose I'm confused about God right now too. He seemed so real such a short time ago. I'm sorry I'm not stronger. As long as I have these doubts, I don't see how I can go on.*
>
> *I especially can't stand myself for doing this now, right after that terrible interview by Mr. Bowles and all the problems in Turkey and with so many bad things happening to you. But I don't know what else to do. To wait will only make it harder for both of us.*
>
> *So I am writing to tell you that I have packed up my things, and think it best that I return to Bedford with my mum who has been at Sevenoaks visiting. She and Auntie Andrea are blaming themselves, but I keep telling them it has nothing to do with them, or you, but only me.*
>
> *What I must tell you is that I think it best that we break off the engagement. I am sorry to have to tell you in a letter like this. But*

I don't think I could face you. One look in your eyes and I would turn into a positive puddle! Then you would try to talk me out of it, and you might. But I can't let that happen because I think this is best.

Please don't call me. I know you will want to, but I don't think I could handle it right now.

Dear Adam. I am sorry I am not stronger and more mature. I am so sorry! I guess if you want to do anything, you can pray for me. I sure need it. You have been so good to me, and I hope we can remain friends. I will always love you.

Cordially,
Juliet

Already Adam was stumbling from the room, Juliet's letter crumpled in his hand, tears of devastation flowing liberally down his cheeks.

God, he prayed, *I do pray for Juliet like she said. But this can't be your will—surely this is a mistake!*

He wouldn't wait for a plane, thought Adam. They had received clearance to leave France about an hour before. He would leave for the coast immediately. He would be to Calais in six hours.

The Chunnel, hovercraft . . . he would swim if he had to!

He had to get back to Sevenoaks before Juliet left.

(5)

Adam arrived back at his estate in scarcely less emotional turbulence than when he had left Chartres.

He ran into the house shouting, "Mrs. Graves . . . Juliet . . . is anyone home?"

Footsteps sounded from somewhere. Mrs. Graves came hurrying down the hall from her sitting room.

Adam flew up the stairs toward her two at a time.

"Where's Juliet?" he said. "Is she still here?"

Mrs. Graves' long face told Adam what he had feared most—that he was too late.

"I'm sorry, sir," said the housekeeper. "She is in Bedford with her mum. I . . . we understood she had written you, Mr. Livingstone."

"She did . . . she did," said Adam, slowing as he approached. "Dash it all! I hoped I could get here before she left. Well . . . I'll have to go to Bedford then." He headed back down the stairs.

Timidly Mrs. Graves followed him.

"I think . . . that is, sir," she began hesitantly.

Adam detected in her voice a tone that made him stop and turn to face her.

"Yes—what is it, Mrs. Graves?"

"Meaning no disrespect, sir, but . . . I don't think that would be best at the minute. Juliet, you see, sir . . . that is, she asked me to tell you that she'd rather you didn't."

"Didn't what, for heaven's sake, Mrs. Graves?"

"Go to Bedford, sir. She said she needed some time alone."

✦ ✦ ✦

And when midnight came Jeremiah and Baruch went up together onto the city walls in accordance with the Lord's instructions to Jeremiah. . . .

And the Lord said, Speak, Jeremiah, my chosen one. And Jeremiah said, Behold, Lord, now we know that thou art delivering thy city into the hands of its enemies, and they will carry off the people to Babylon.

What should we do with the sacred things in thy temple, and the vessels used in thy service? What wouldest thou hae us do with them?

And the Lord said to him,

vTake them and consign them to the earth.

THE PARALIPOMENA OF JEREMIAH 3:1, 5, 7-8

✦ ✦ ✦

PROLOGUE

Lineage of Darkness

Bern, Switzerland, A.D. 1467

In a room, dimly lit, nine men sat in solemn counsel.

They represented the most powerful families on the European continent. Their names, however, were not so widely known as the Habsburgs, Wittelsbachs, Viscontis, and Luxembourgs, who contested for the crowns of their fragmented nations. The secret bonds which drew this alliance together originated in another realm than earthly thrones. Ultimately, however, their influence in world affairs had proved, and would continue to do so, more pervasive and permanent than that of all princes and queens, kings and popes, put together.

They had come together on this day to widen the scope of their mutual and clandestine heritage. They had just sealed a bond yet deeper and more mysterious than that which had been sworn beneath Solomon's temple mount, and from which their high standing in the world had come.

The pact begun with their predecessors and now deepened between themselves would dominate the politics and religion of the world in the five centuries that followed in more widespread ways than even any of the nine could imagine. The murkiness of the age overspread their schemes for the future exploitation of nations not yet in existence. A druidic occultism had grown to dominate the concealment of many branches and offshoots, which extended outward from their beginnings in a web of hidden vows, pledges, and rites.

The Renaissance had come to Italy. The Templar antecedents of these nine had in no small measure been responsible. A similar awakening showed signs of spreading northward into the German states. Rightly had they divined that great change was about to sweep across the continent, from England to Moscow. They could use it to either strengthen their grip on European affairs or watch that power gradually diminish.

They had chosen the former.

The number of the highly secretive Templar Grand Council had not increased in more than three hundred years. Their forebears had discovered in Jerusalem's temple vault the mysteries of the ancients which imbued them with tremendous power. Several from that group were included in this new and even more select fraternity. The line of Hughes de Payns' lineage remained at the core of its powerful leadership, possessing the greatest among many Templar secrets, and passing it down through the generations from father to son. There were also represented Freemasons, Rosicrucians, and members of various other guilds, orders, and brotherhoods—every one cloaked in secrecy.

From Templar roots these nine had gathered to give birth to an even more powerful organization, gaining potency from the mystical Egyptian and Babylonian secrets that de Payns and his eight comrades had discovered. In time they would spread out to surpass the achievements of the original Templars, and eventually encompass the whole of society.

Now these most influential men of their generation, all with Templar pedigree, had come together to form an alliance linking financial empires. This loose and undercover society would be known as the Illuminare, *for they spoke of illumination from higher sources.*

The true Light of Life, however, was their enemy.

✦ ✦ ✦

The genesis for this new Templar tributary, destined to become its most powerful, came from the Illuminated Ones founded by Joachim of Floris in the eleventh century, who, like the Templars, disguised illuminism behind a thin veil of Christianity. The Alumbrados of Spain, and societies of enlightenment in other countries, grew out of these beginnings, claiming mystic knowledge from secret sources. Gradually had the similar movements—templarism and illuminism—fused.

One force alone held the potential to threaten their objectives. That was a reawakening of the spiritual vitality of the true religion out of which they had come, to which only faded memory linked them. Yet curiously—a dichotomy to which deception is prone—they claimed the very attributes that were in fact their opposites. Rooted in darkness, they took unto themselves the label of illumination. *How could anything but blindness result, for they had chosen to look away from truth. Their very name exposed the falsehood ensnaring them. Their master was the eternal enemy of Light. Mysticism and secrecy remained the cornerstones of their creed.*

Where shadows reign, Light is barred entrance. Private revelation is the soil which breeds witchcraft and sorcery. Cults, at root, originate as nothing more than closed societies where confidential disclosures, presumably from "higher powers," are the binding force of relationship.

The Power of Light, on the other hand, never works to hide and exclude, but always to reveal and draw all men and women, regardless of station, toward the truth of universal, not private, revelation.

✦ ✦ ✦

The nine were discussing their future.

"We should be twelve in number," said their leader, eighty-nine-year-old Christian Rosenkreuz, founder of the Society of Rosicrucians forty-five years earlier. He had journeyed to Damascus, Arabia, and Egypt early in life, where the mysterious wisdom of alchemy and an-

cient metallurgical arts had been revealed to him. Returning to Germany and imparting his findings to others, the society of the Rose and the Cross was born.

"Why not nine?" asked one. "We here present are nine."

"The number nine has always been sacred to Templar foundations," rejoined Rosenkreuz. "It is the perfect number, the number of mystery, of wonderfully symmetric divisibility. I propose, however, in sealing this new pact, which will add to and strengthen what our fathers began, that the time has come for an expansion of those threefold threes, to four."

"On what grounds?"

"That our number will be yet more highly symbolic. It will represent the conveying of our power to the uttermost ends of the earth."

"Twelve," repeated another with a smile. "It is indeed fitting."

"A Council of Twelve."

"Twofold sixes? Why not threefold, as has been prophesied?" queried another.

The question hung heavy in the air.

"That number is not for this time," replied Rosenkreuz. His voice was soft and sounded from another realm. "The season for that number of power shall indeed come. But such a time lies outside our hands."

Every man among them knew well enough to what he referred. A yet lengthier silence followed.

"Then a Council of Twelve it shall be," said an Englishman at length, a Plantagenet, whose distant cousin was King Edward IV of England, and whose ancestor Comte d'Anjou was among the first Templar recruits beyond the original nine.

"And it shall not be increased again," added Rosenkreuz, "until that new age which has been foretold, the age when the completion of our domination shall be at hand."

✦ ✦ ✦

Like their predecessors of the temple in Jerusalem, these nine, soon to be increased to twelve, were driven by temporal motives. Spiritual awakening was their enemy. If true belief ever took hold among the masses, or in society in general, their power in politics and finances would necessarily diminish. Faith, therefore, must be kept distant, impersonal, and knotted in tradition rather than personal vibrancy. They could not, at this early point in their history, foresee the approaching Reformation.

The discussion among them spread to the ancient relics of their common religion. Knowing the formidability of such artifacts to stimulate the hearts and minds of common men, they were concerned lest their power be broken.

One of their number spoke. "At all costs we must prevent Messiah myths from springing up."

"The ancient legends are mere fancies."

"Perhaps, but containing potency. The religious myths of our past are full of substance. There is the sacred book, the temple, and other artifacts. The people hold them in high honor."

"The temple is no more."

"Prophecies say it will be rebuilt."

"Where? Jerusalem is again in the hands of infidels. The Crusades which gave rise to our power failed in their larger design."

"There are other artifacts, perhaps yet more powerful."

A hush came over them.

"Such as?"

"You know to what I refer. The ark, and the tablets it contains. Our forebears found neither."

At the words, a shudder ran through each of the men's frames. Of nothing were they more afraid than that mysterious vessel of Exodus 25, lost to the eyes of history from the days of Jeremiah. Intuitively they knew that when the receptacle of the commandments was found, the day of the Messiah would be at hand.

"I do not believe such a thing exists," said one. "Our ancestors discovered what was far more valuable—the secrets of the knowledge and wisdom of Egypt and Babylon."

"There are rumors that the original nine learned something of the ark's whereabouts."

"We have heard such rumors. There are no facts to substantiate them."

"The ark exists," repeated another, "however lost to history it may be. Whether they discovered clues of its movements, I cannot say. But I tell you, it holds a key more important than the temple itself."

"Then it must not be found. On the day the ark is discovered, came the prophecy, will the veil be lifted. Then will the people of the covenant recognize their Anointed One."

"Which covenant?"

"All the covenants. Then will the time be fulfilled. Our age of power will be at an end."

"Then indeed . . . it must not be found—not now . . . not ever."

PART SEVEN

BELGRADE

✦ ✦ ✦

Flee from Babylon! Run for your lives! . . .

It is time for the Lord's vengeance . . . the wall of Babylon will fall.

Come out of her, my people! Run for your lives!

Run from the fierce anger of the Lord.

Do not lose heart or be afraid when rumors are heard in the land;

one rumor comes this year, another the next.

JEREMIAH 51:6, 44-46

✦ ✦ ✦

twenty-six

Confusion

(1)

Two weeks passed since Adam's hasty return from Chartres to Sevenoaks.

Little work had been accomplished during that time. Adam was despondent and confused over Juliet's decision. He glanced toward the phone at least six times a day. Each time he recalled the words of her letter. If she wanted time to herself, the least he could do was respect her wishes. Several letters sat in the top drawer of his desk. He had sent none of them.

He loved her . . . he wanted to marry her . . . he missed her. They should be together during this difficult time. But he was leery of chasing her away—of pursuing her too much—for fear of preempting this interlude for her to think. He would give her the time she asked for.

Rocky flew home to New Hampshire. When they would get together again was undetermined. The case was still dangling and Adam's legal and reputational troubles were no better than they had been when he left Turkey. Pressure mounted by Israeli and Ethiopian authorities for action in the matter of the ark. Meanwhile, Adam gave Crystal and Jen some much needed R and R, while Scott and Figg remained in Ararat City doing what they could to hold together at least a skeleton crew at the hangar site.

One morning the telephone rang. A moment later the buzzer on Adam's office phone sounded. He answered. "It's Mrs. Livingstone, sir."

"Thank you, Mrs. Graves," replied Adam. "Hello, Mum," he said as he answered the other line.

"Adam," said his mother, "I hear you're back in the country. I thought I'd call and see how you were."

"Not so good at the minute actually."

"What's the matter?"

"Juliet left, Mum."

"Left—what did you do?"

"What makes you think I did anything?"

"Oh, Adam, you were probably so involved in your work, you didn't even notice what you did."

"I've been racking my brain and I can't think—"

Adam hesitated.

"What am I saying?" he added. "You're probably right, Mum. I'm sure that's part of it."

"Part? What do you mean?"

"I don't know, Mum. Juliet has doubts about herself."

"I can't imagine why—she's a lovely girl."

"But she has to discover that for herself. I think she worries about being younger, and . . . you know, whether she's suitable for me and all that."

"Suitable—heavens, Adam. Of course she's suitable!"

"I know that. But as long as she has doubts, what can I do?"

"Have you told her?"

"Told her what?"

"That she is suitable, that you love her, that none of those old-fashioned things matter?"

"Of course, Mum."

"Well, these kinds of things are good," said Mrs. Livingstone with sudden optimism. "That's something I learned in Tibet, Adam, that doubts are stepping-stones to finding truth. I like your Juliet. I'm glad she had the courage to do what she did. It shows she's a thinker, and that she's got integrity and guts. She had enough courage to take a stand in the face of difficulties."

"I see what you mean, Mum. But I don't want to lose her."

"You won't. You must have faith, Adam. It's best Juliet work through this now rather than later."

"Well, it's not best for me!"

"Tut, tut, Adam . . . you've been a bachelor too long. If you're going to be married, you can't think only of yourself. If you're not meant for each other, better to find out at this stage than after you're married."

Adam wasn't sure how far down that road he wanted the conversation to go. "But you know how sometimes women want men to be strong and come after them," he said, "and say, 'Hey, you're marrying me, and that's that and be dashed with your doubts!'"

"That's ridiculous, Adam. What you know about women would fit in a thimble. Where did you ever hear such nonsense?"

"I've seen it in the movies."

"There you are!" said Mrs. Livingstone, laughing. "I rest my case."

"But what if Juliet is waiting and expecting me to go to *her*?"

"You've got to let her work it out in her own way."

"I'll try to remember. You're a trouper, Mum. Keep in touch. Thanks for the call."

(2)

The letter that arrived at Bellevue Retirement Home produced tears of thankfulness before the eyes for whom it was intended had read a fourth of it.

Dear Grandma,

I'm afraid I find myself embarrassed by the last letter I sent, and the article that went with it. Down inside I suppose I knew you would not be proud of my accomplishments in the feminist world. I don't know why I sent it to you—certainly not to hurt you, because I love you deeply. Maybe just to get one more dig in at the Christian faith, which, until a short while ago I thought I despised.

But recently I have found myself looking at many things in unexpected ways. I don't suppose there's much point in going into great detail about what caused it. I'm not sure I know myself. It has to do with Adam Livingstone and Noah's ark and the Bible . . . and you too, Grandma, I imagine. And one of my students, a young lady who is enthusiastic about her faith who challenged me in ways I wasn't prepared for.

What it boils down to is that I am beginning to see that I have committed my life to what is called the search for truth, yet I have vigorously made sure I kept my eyes closed in one direction where millions of people throughout history claim to have discovered truth. I never investigated it for myself. Not a very open-minded position for someone to take who is supposed to teach others how to find truth. Once I began to realize this, I was shocked at my own blindness. If I'm going to be really honest about it, I would have to draw the conclusion that I have been more in love with my own intellect, and what I thought was my modern and liberated way of looking at things, than I have been in love with truth itself. That is a difficult admission to make. It stings my pride.

So I've been reading and thinking—even reading some in the Bible, believe it or not. I wanted to tell you this because I have a favor to ask. If you could send me a list of passages in the Bible that might help me be able to know whether the Bible is true, I would appreciate it. And if there are any books you think would help me in this new quest. I know you have a lot of books that you've read over the years—would you mind if I borrowed a few of the more significant ones? I've talked to a couple of people, one young lady in a Christian bookstore. The names Francis Schaeffer and C. S. Lewis have been recommended to me, as Christian writers with a philosophical bent.

I've not heard of the one, although the name Lewis *sounds vaguely familiar. Have you read either of their books?*

I'll write again, but I have a class to teach in twenty minutes, and I'd like to get this in the mail.

I don't know where this search will lead me. For all I know I may come out of it still not believing in Christianity. But at least I feel I am willing to keep my mind open to the possibilities, and that can't help but be a step in the right direction.

Thank you for listening, Grandma. I love you.

Oriel

(3)

From certain important meetings with the Council's political operatives in the States, Anni D'Abernon flew by private jet to New York, by Concorde to Paris, and was soon back in Zurich.

The trip had filled her with uncanny premonitions. She had not completely recovered from the unnerving experience of being unable to pull the trigger on Livingstone. A fresh snow had fallen over Switzerland in her absence, and the temperature was subzero centigrade, which only increased the chill she felt in her marrow.

She went straight to her office, closed and locked the door after her, got out her favorite assortment of crystals and two candles, lit the latter, then sat staring into the former. But the Dimension was quieter than ever.

She sat back in the candlelit darkness. Though she was glad to have inherited his power at such a young age, there were times she missed her father. She needed him now. Why would he not answer her summons?

The memory of their last conversation together sent her gaze across the room in the direction of her private safe.

"What I am about to show you," he had said, "has given our family preeminence over others in the Council throughout the centuries. No one can ever know what we possess. It has the power to destroy as well as compel. You must use it with extreme caution, for the enemy's hands once held it. Never take its otherworldly energy lightly. It is no magical icon. Do not let it become an obsession. The more you succumb to its lure, the more it will possess you. If abused, it will consume."

As he spoke, her father's voice had taken on a quality she had never heard from him before. She trembled to recall it.

"You will only use it when—" he had continued, then stopped as a fit of coughing seized him. He had never been able to complete his instructions.

Had he had a premonition . . . had his own Guides informed him that he was on his way to their world? Was that his reason for bringing out the sacred, dreaded object on that particular day?

The conversation had never been resumed. A week later Arnaud D'Abernon was dead. His mantle passed to his thirty-nine-year-old daughter, adding to what she knew . . . and what she didn't know.

Anni D'Abernon forced her thoughts back to the present. If ever there was a time when she needed help in discerning the Dimensional Eye, that time was now.

She rose and walked to the safe. She spun the dial to the right, left, right again, and finally left, and opened the steel door. Reaching in, she removed the plate of the false back wall, then unlatched the hidden inner compartment.

With shaking hand she reached in yet farther and clutched hold of the only object inside. A slight tingle surged through her hand and arm at the touch. Carefully she removed it.

With deliberate step she returned to her chair, then set the silver chalice between the crystals and candles. The flickering yellow light danced upon the lines of pure gold crisscrossing around the cup. What ancient craftsman in old Jerusalem, she wondered, had fashioned such a thing of exquisite beauty? How had he imbued it with such great power?

A soft chant of incantation began to flow from her lips—the crooning mantra her Spirit Guides had taught her.

A gradual warmth began to replace the chill as she chanted, eyes closed, rocking back and forth. The sense of a Presence began to fill her and she chanted yet more loudly.

At last . . . after such a long silence . . . she had been heard! They were coming to her . . . she could feel that she was not alone.

She reached out and again took hold of the chalice, continuing to gently move back and forth, bringing it slowly toward her. The warmth of the Presence was all about her now. She drew the cup closer . . . closer . . . until it touched her chanting mouth.

Suddenly a jolt as of a stinging electric charge bit into her lip with a lightning stab of pain.

"Aaagh!" she cried in terror.

She flung the goblet from her. It clanked across the floor with metallic dissonance. The spell of sorcerous incantation was broken instantly. Though it had been in evil hands for centuries, the purpose of this sacred cup still pointed toward righteousness.

(4)

Electronic wizard and corporate tycoon Lee-Hia Kiang glanced down from the glass window of his office high above the bustling city of Singapore. It was like no place on earth, he thought, probably the most prosperous and vibrant metropolis in the world.

On his desk sat a letter from Adam Livingstone, the Englishman. He had received it months ago but had never responded. It was a request for financial help with the Noah's ark project in Turkey.

Why he had taken out the letter again this morning, he wasn't sure. But it had prompted an unexpected twenty minutes of thoughtful reminiscing.

Why had Livingstone contacted him? Was it purely financial?

He was a Buddhist. He was not interested in Christian artifacts. He was not interested in archaeology or history either. His world was the present—Internet, lasers, computer networking, medical research, global distribution, commercial aspects of private space exploration.

There had been a time. . . .

His thoughts drifted back to his student days in Calgary, Alberta, and the enthusiastic Christian pastor he and some of his Chinese friends had become involved with. Back then, for a brief period, he had considered the Christian alternative to his Buddhist upbringing. He had even taken a trip to California packed in a van with thirteen other students. The pastor had taught from the Bible every day.

But once leaving Calgary, he had scarcely thought of all that again. His rise in the high-tech world of lasers and infrared scanning devices had been so rapid he had never looked back. With wealth, his company had expanded in more directions than he could keep track of. Kiang Enterprises was known as a corporation that could do anything.

Why on this day were memories of the past flooding back upon him for no apparent reason?

He turned and walked to the bookcase across his office where he kept a few momentos. There was the Bible the Canadian pastor had given him. He hadn't even noticed it in years. He'd forgotten it was even here.

Slowly he took it out and read the inscription.

To my good friend Lee-Hia. You are one whom God has gifted in many ways—may you use that gift for him. I pray that God's Word will always be powerful and real in your life. Your Canadian friend, David.

The words and familiar handwriting brought a nostalgic smile to his lips.

He sat down and began randomly to thumb through it. Forty minutes later Kiang still sat, now engrossed in a certain gospel story and feeling inexplicable sensations in his heart, tugging him in directions he could not explain, yet which he knew he could not ignore.

twenty-seven

Friends and Foes

(1)

The cloaked figure of a man in strange attire had been watching the Livingstone home for several days. Sophisticated electronic equipment allowed him to track most of the comings and goings about the place, though with the staff gone there weren't many.

This morning the opportunity he had been waiting for at last arrived. Soon after he saw the master of the house leave in his car for downtown London, he decided it was time to make his move.

✦ ✦ ✦

At nearly the same time, the telephone on Kim Shayne's desk rang. She answered it.

"Shayne, it's Bowles," said the familiar voice. "I'm back in England, but not for long. I may have it now."

"Have what?"

"I think I know where the ark is."

"So does everyone—in Turkey."

"I mean the ark of the covenant. Can you meet me for lunch?"

"I suppose—but no guarantees, Sir Gilbert. Nothing has changed since we last spoke."

"That may be. But this thing's about to blow wide open, and I don't intend to be left out. This time *I'm* going to be the one breaking the story. It could be you in front of the camera with the scoop of all time. You've got to decide whether you're in or out."

Shayne paused. "All right, Sir Gilbert," she finally said. "I'll listen to what you have to say."

(2)

Anni D'Abernon had not been in such a state since her father's death. But even the funeral of Arnaud D'Abernon, which half of Zurich's financial community had attended, had not unnerved his daughter. Everyone said she possessed nerves of steel and a heart of stone. She had displayed both on that day.

But now things were different. Something was wrong. The steel and stone had gone mushy.

Never before in her life had she felt such emotions as were becoming a daily occurrence . . . jittery, anxious . . .

What did this thick silence portend?

The whole Council was nervous. They looked to her for stability, leadership, strength. Rupert may have been the spokesman. She knew well enough that several Council members bitterly resented the stature he afforded her. Yet those with wisdom in the Dimension recognized that she possessed inroads into those mystic realms beyond their own powers. They looked to her for illumination.

Yet she had none to give them.

Behind her, the telephone rang. She started at the interruption to her thoughts. It was her private line.

"D'Abernon," she said softly.

"It is Bonar."

"Ciano—you have . . . news?"

"Zorin has resurfaced," said the Italian in perfect French, the preferred language between the two whenever they were alone. "I am back on his trail. I can see him at this moment."

"Excellent. Does he suspect your presence?"

"No. He is cleverly disguised. But then, so am I."

"Where are you, Ciano?"

"England."

"Zorin is in England! What could he possibly be doing there!"

"Only for a short time."

"What do you mean?"

"When I next speak with you, he will be dead. I will deliver that news to you in person."

(3)

"Look, Livingstone," said Captain Thurlow, "personally I doubt you had anything to do with this thing, but I'm getting heat from upstairs."

"I understand."

"There's international pressure building. I don't know why the Ethiopians have so much clout all of a sudden, but the squeeze is on."

"I don't know what more I can tell you," replied Adam, shaking his head. "I've given a complete accounting of what happened in Amsterdam."

"The trouble is, there's no proof to back up your story. And the fact is, you did break into the church in Aksum."

"I know it looks bad, but–"

"Look, why don't you get Jordan back here. Being an American, and black . . . who knows–maybe his word will count more heavily than yours at this point. He was with you the whole time?"

"Almost. He didn't go all the way in with me. But he can certainly attest to the fact that I didn't come out carrying anything resembling the ark."

"Then I would like to question him. For the record. We'll put it all over the news–JORDAN EXONERATES LIVINGSTONE."

"I appreciate it, Captain. I'll call Scott immediately."

"How are things going on your ark project in Turkey, by the way?"

"A disaster." Adam laughed sardonically. "They could hardly be worse. Funding and human resources have about dried up entirely."

"I'm sorry to hear that. But is the ark safe? You know, all that climate control and everything?"

Adam nodded. "For now," he said. "But we need continuous funding to maintain it. Imported electricity to such a remote spot is our greatest expense, and then there's security and all the rest."

"Keep a stiff upper lip."

"Thanks. I'll let you know as soon as Scott's back in the country."

(4)

Forty minutes after Adam's departure for his morning interview at Scotland Yard, his housekeeper answered the intercom from the outside gate.

"British Telecom, ma'am," said a voice.

"Yes?"

"The telephone repair you requested."

"What telephone repair?" answered Mrs. Graves.

"Got it right here . . . let me see, complaint from a bloke named Jordan on the sixteenth, then another call from, who was it–right . . . fellow called Livingstone on the twenty-second, asking us to come out and check the wiring and connections of the office phones."

"I didn't hear anything about it."

"Don't matter to me, lady. Bloke said it was urgent. I'll go back to the office if you like. You tell the chap to reschedule, and to tell you about it this time."

"No . . . no, wait–I suppose it would be best to do it now, if there's really trouble. It's just that I didn't know. Here–I'll open the gate. Come up to the front door. I'll show you to the offices."

(5)

Several days later, Adam Livingstone and Scott Jordan, who had flown in the previous evening, walked into Granby's where an initial informal meeting with Captain Thurlow had been scheduled. They took seats, ordered tea, and waited.

"Oh no, don't look now," said Scott, who was facing toward the door and had just seen a huge man enter with a petite and attractive young woman at his side. "You're not going to believe who just walked in and is headed this way!"

Adam turned around, then closed his eyes in disgust. But it was already too late to avoid a meeting. He sighed inwardly, summoning what strength he could, then rose.

"Sir Gilbert," said Adam, extending his hand.

Bowles shook it, even more surprised than Adam at suddenly finding himself in the presence of his adversary.

"Quite a trouncing you gave me on that American program, Sir Gilbert," said Adam.

"Yes, well, uh . . . I call it like I see it," said Bowles a little awkwardly. "But, Jordan, Livingstone," he added, "please meet—"

"Kimberly, isn't it?" preempted Adam. "Kimberly Ban—"

"You two know each other?" said Bowles before Adam could get the word out.

"We've met."

"Well then, Jordan, I'll just have to introduce you. Say hello to Kim Shayne, of the BBC."

"Kim . . . *Shayne*—of the BBC," repeated Adam in surprise. "I didn't know you were a journalist. Would the two of you like to join us?"

The newcomers sat down, although Scott had the look of a man about ready to tear Sir Gilbert Bowles' head off.

"I thought you were a friend of Juliet's," said Adam.

"I, uh . . . I am," Shayne replied. "How is she, by the way?"

The expression on Adam's face indicated that something was amiss. "I'm afraid she's in Bedford at the minute," he said. "She's broken off our engagement."

"I'm sorry to hear that," said Shayne. "Any particular reason?"

"A number of things, I suppose," replied Adam as they prepared their cups. "There were difficult pressures for Juliet."

"Such as?"

"Mostly a series of stories in the tabloids. Someone managed to sneak photos of Juliet, calling her Adam Livingstone's mysterious houseguest, and nonsense like that."

Adam glanced up from a sip of his tea at the instant his unexpected words registered shock over the reporter's face. She recovered herself quickly. But he noted the expression. And she could not hide the crimson that flooded neck and cheeks a moment later.

"It was crude journalism, of course," Adam went on, continuing to eye her carefully, "but it hurt Juliet. She wasn't prepared for that sort of thing when she became involved with me. We could never figure out where the photos came from. Juliet said it was almost as if someone close to her had been–"

He stopped, realizing that his suspicions were on target. The recurrence of red in the cheeks of the woman at Bowles' side, and the darting away of her eyes, confirmed clearly that she was guilty.

"I see . . . ," he said with altered tone. "It would appear, Miss Shayne, that you have been closer to Juliet than even she realizes."

"She realizes it now, Mr. Livingstone. I have already apologized to her, which I would like also to do to you."

"I appreciate that. Unfortunately, it would appear the damage is already done. When did you speak to her?"

"We saw one another at the *Mail*."

"What was Juliet doing there?"

"She came to demand that they stop making her a news item. She was angry. Honestly, I tried to apologize. But I also explained that she's fair game if she's associated with you."

"What day was that?" asked Adam.

She told him. Adam nodded thoughtfully. Things were starting to make sense.

"I'm genuinely sorry, Mr. Livingstone," she said. "I really hope the incident had no bearing on–"

"Forget it," said Adam. "The deed is done. Let's forget it for now, shall we? And I suppose you'll have to excuse us anyway. I see Captain Thurlow over there."

Only too glad for an excuse to end the unpleasantness, Bowles and Shayne rose and left as Thurlow approached.

A moment later a waiter appeared to take their luncheon order. As the conversation began between the captain and Scott, Adam's mind was on Juliet. But by the end of the meeting he found himself wondering what connection could possibly exist between Shayne and Bowles. He wasn't sure he liked it.

(6)

After learning what he had concerning Kim Shayne's–or Kimberly Banbrigge's–stormy relationship with Juliet, all Adam could think of during the drive back to Sevenoaks was what Juliet must have been going through after he left for Turkey.

If only he'd paid more attention to the stresses she had been under. When he arrived home Adam went straight to the telephone. He didn't care what she'd said about not calling. This had gone on long enough.

Mrs. Halsay answered the phone in Bedford.

"This is Adam Livingstone calling," said Adam. "May I please speak with Juliet?"

"Oh . . . uh, yes, Mr. Livingstone. Wait a moment please . . . I'll see."

A long silence of two or three minutes followed.

"Mr. Livingstone," at length came the same voice on the line. "This is Lona Halsay—I'm Juliet's mother."

A brief pause.

"Juliet . . . she's lying down right now, Mr. Livingstone. She asked me to give you her regards, but to say that she cannot take your call. She said she hopes you will understand."

"I see . . . hmm—well . . . tell her, then, would you please, that I just learned about the Kim Shayne incident at the paper, and I'm very sorry. And, Mrs. Halsay," Adam added, "would you also please tell her that I love her?"

Adam put down the phone, thought for a minute, then ran downstairs and made straight for the garage. Twenty-five minutes later he was on the M25 en route north to Bedford.

Outside St. Albans, he pulled off the motorway. He had been thinking the whole way about what he would say to Juliet. But at last the one glaring question replaced all his best-laid arguments: Was this the right thing to do?

Was this the time to fight for Juliet . . . or respect her wishes and stay away? It was one of the hardest dilemmas Adam had ever faced in his life. Certainly the most personal.

For ten minutes he sat in his car wrestling between the two sides of his self. The emotional side said, *Continue on—tell her how you feel even if she doesn't want to hear!* The rational side said, *You have to give her time and space to make up her own mind.*

After half an hour, Adam started his car, drove to the roundabout, and headed out of the service area toward the south, back in the direction of Sevenoaks.

He trusted Juliet. He trusted her enough to know what she was doing. He knew she would be praying even now for God's guidance. Though he wanted desperately to continue on to Bedford, he would respect her wishes.

If she was going to be his wife someday, he had to trust her to do what she thought was best.

twenty-eight

Disappearance

(1)

Rocky McCondy managed only about five hours sleep.

Sometime before dawn weird images of a white-robed and gray-bearded prophet striding through ancient Jerusalem had intruded into his dreams, perhaps inspired by Adam's words during their time at Chartres about Jeremiah. At first the fiery figure was carrying a police bullhorn, broadcasting out doomful messages of invasion and destruction.

Then the dream changed.

Now the fellow stood before a bevy of television cameras, microphone in hand, stroking his beard as he awaited the cue that the broadcast was about to go live.

"All right, Jeremiah," said a voice somewhere, "we're on in five . . . four . . . three . . . two . . . one . . ."

"Good morning," boomed the prophet's voice, "this is Jeremiah Hilkiah reporting live from Jerusalem for the JPN. Behind me you can see the Hebrew capital in relative calm after a peaceful night. In the distance, however, over those city walls to my right, reports are already coming in of a great Babylonian army, led by King Nebuchadnezzar himself, marching steadily toward us. A massive war the likes of which this city has never seen appears to this reporter inevitable. Even now there is concern in some quarters about the disposition of the valuable contents of the temple, should the worst come to pass and Jerusalem be overrun. Judah's King Zedekiah, having ignored repeated warnings from this reporter, is unprepared to meet the onslaught. At the same time, most of the city's citizens go about their lives unconcerned. What will the future bring to this proud city? We can only wait and watch. This reporter will remain on the scene to bring you up-to-date, breaking reports as events unfold. For now, this is Jeremiah Hilkiah, reporting for the Jewish Prophetic Net–"

Suddenly Rocky awoke.

He half expected to see his television on! But the morning was black and his house silent.

He was wide awake. The book of Jeremiah was on his mind more strongly than ever. An impulse told him he needed to get up and go out for a walk.

He climbed out of bed, walked more awake than was usual to the bathroom for his fifteen-second shivering wake-up ritual beneath the icy blast of the showerhead, then dressed warmly and went outside into the chilly morning.

He would save the day's first cup of Starbucks for his return.

(2)

A knock sounded on the door of Betsy Attwell's flat in Bedford.

Juliet was nearest the door. She opened it. There stood a familiar face, though the last person in the world she expected *here*, right in front of her eyes.

"Mrs. . . . Livingstone!" she said in astonishment.

"Yes, it's me, Juliet," said Frances Livingstone. "Hello—how are you?"

"Uh . . . fine," stammered Juliet. "Please . . . come in," she added, taken aback by the appearance of Adam's mother at their front door.

Juliet's mother and aunt appeared.

"Mum, Aunt Betsy," said Juliet, "I would like you to meet Mrs. Livingstone—Adam's mother."

Awkward and uncertain introductions followed. No one but Mrs. Livingstone knew what to do with themselves. She, however, had been in numerous situations far more ticklish than this, and immediately took charge.

"What's all this I hear about you and Adam?" she said when they were seated and water for tea was on the stove. "Mrs. Graves told me there was some trouble."

"You spoke with Mrs. Graves?"

"Yes, my dear, I did. She says you've called the engagement off."

Juliet looked down, embarrassed. Mrs. Livingstone's abruptness went like a knife straight to the wounds the rest of them had been trying to soothe over by avoidance.

"I . . . I thought it was best under the circumstances," Juliet replied softly.

"Under what circumstances?" asked Mrs. Livingstone, intent on boring straight forward.

"That . . . Adam and I are so different."

"Different, nonsense . . . what do you mean?"

"From different social stations."

"Pshaw! Nonsense again," remarked Mrs. Livingstone. "What century are you living in, my dear—the eighteenth?"

Juliet fidgeted nervously with the laced edge of the tablecloth. Her mother and aunt were speechless. They had no idea how to reply to this well-dressed society lady who was as much in the news as her son and Juliet, yet who seemed to be throwing custom and caution to the wind.

"Ladies," said their guest, addressing all three, "Juliet, Mrs. Halsay, Mrs. Attwell—if I didn't know better I would think *you* the problem, with snobbery toward such as us."

The straightforward lady meant no criticism. Her blunt remark, however, stirred things up around the table. Shifts and uneasy glances and throat clearings followed.

"Come, my dear . . . Juliet," she said in the tender tone of a would-be mother-in-law, "Nobody cares about that station business nowadays, least of all the Livingstone family."

At last Juliet tried to speak again.

"It's just . . . that I'm so . . . ill-suited for him," she said. "How can I be a help to him? How can I—"

She stopped and glanced away, fighting tears again.

"I will answer your question, dear," said Mrs. Livingstone, reaching over and placing her hand upon Juliet's. "But you must look at me."

Juliet turned her face toward Adam's mother.

"You can be a help to him," said Mrs. Livingstone, "by being *you*. That's the one thing you can do better than anyone else in the world. No one else but you can be that to him—you're the only one who can be . . . *Juliet Livingstone*."

Juliet's eyes were glistening.

"My dear, Adam cares for you deeply," insisted Mrs. Livingstone. "Anyone with eyes can see it. Why, you should see him moping about the estate. He's like a boy again—sent all of his staff on holiday, sent the big American fellow home. He's worthless without you. And I'm going to keep telling you he loves you until you let me go back to London and tell him he can call you and tell you himself."

(3)

It was a little after seven o'clock in the morning in Peterborough, New Hampshire.

Under the yellow light of the town's sparsely placed streetlights, Rocky made his way along the sidewalk with no particular destination in mind.

In the distance, already the lights of the cafe shone brightly through its windows. Maybe he'd stop in and see Darci after a bit. It was too early for ham and eggs, but maybe some toast and a cup of her notoriously bad coffee.

Rocky's mood was expectant. He sensed that something was about to break. It happened with every case he worked on, that moment—and usually he could sense it coming just before it actually hit—when the pieces of the puzzle came together.

He loved it! Sometimes it was a long time coming. Sometimes he thought the breakthrough would never happen. But it always did. If he kept stirring up the clues, revolving them over and over and over, mixing them up, looking at the facts from different angles . . . if he kept everything alive in his subconscious . . . *eventually* the pieces aligned themselves . . . until that breakthrough when he at last *saw* the picture they'd been trying to reveal to him.

The incessant bark of Mrs. Hanks' irritating little dog down the side street from the cafe alerted the whole town that the paperboy was out on his bike making his morning rounds.

"Bugsy," said Rocky, "I'm not going to give you a chance at *my* ankles this morning."

Gradually the high-pitched yaps of the terrier faded.

This case was about to shake loose, he was sure of it. And somehow it had to do with Jeremiah. He would telephone Adam. Maybe it was time he returned to England.

(4)

Meanwhile in Bedford, the discussion continued around the kitchen table.

"Do you . . . you really want me to be part of your family?" Juliet said. The thought that this lady, whom all of England knew, would actually want *her* to be her son's wife, was almost more than Juliet could comprehend.

"Of course I do," replied Mrs. Livingstone. "Why else would I have browbeat poor Mrs. Graves into telling me where you were and come all this way?"

Juliet's mother and aunt looked at one another. Neither could prevent a slight smile at the thought of their sister being interrogated by Mrs. Livingstone.

Juliet's Aunt Betsy spoke up.

"May I say something about all this?" she said. "That is, if anyone wants to know what I think."

"Of course," replied Mrs. Livingstone.

Juliet's aunt glanced toward her niece, as if awaiting her approval. Juliet nodded.

"In one thing you are mistaken, Mrs. Livingstone," she said, looking back toward Adam's mother. "You called me Mrs. Attwell a bit ago. Actually . . . I am *Miss* Attwell. You see, I am the only one of my family who never married."

She turned again toward Juliet and began speaking to both her sister and her niece.

"I didn't say much when you and Andrea were talking about Juliet's situation before," she said. "And the reason is this–I think Mrs. Livingstone is exactly right."

Juliet and her mother glanced up in surprise.

"Look at me," Betsy went on. "I never married. But you know, Lona–you were still at home at the time. It was one of the happiest years of my life. . . ."

Her voice drifted poignantly away as tears filled her eyes.

"I said no when my young man asked me to marry him," she went on. "Now . . . I don't even know why. I had high hopes about so many things, and I suppose I was afraid. But I was already twenty-eight, and . . . well, there's no sense going into all that again. I kept waiting . . . I thought perhaps he'd come back and try again . . . and my chance never came again."

She stopped, took a deep breath to put the painful memory behind her. The others waited.

"So all I have to ask, Juliet," she said, "is this—do you love him?"

"Yes . . . yes, of course I love him, Aunt Betsy."

"Do you love him enough to marry him?"

"I think so."

"Enough to spend the rest of your life with him?"

"Yes."

"Then if my vote counts for anything . . . marry him!"

(5)

Brandi Corwin got off the Greyhound bus and stood looking at the familiar main street through town.

The ride north into the valley from L.A. had been quietly full of memories—family trips south to Disneyland and Knotts Berry Farm, arguments with her father while driving, visiting relatives—some good, some bad. During the first hour or two of the ride she'd done quite a bit of reading in the book and the New Testament the bookstore clerk had given her. But then her thoughts had drifted into the byroads of the past.

She didn't know what the future held for her here. But it didn't matter so much now. She knew she was home. And for the first time in her life . . . she wanted to be.

After a minute or two, she picked up her suitcase and began walking the half mile toward home. Ten minutes later she rounded the corner of the last block.

There were the birds chirping around the bird feeder next to the kitchen window. The sight sent a pang of nostalgic longing into her heart. The big sycamore in front of the house looked the same . . . the bark of the neighbor's dog . . . and there was her mother on her knees weeding in her patch of roses.

Brandi continued on slowly.

Her mother looked up and saw her.

An exclamation burst from the woman's lips as she stood, wiped her hands quickly on her faded jeans, and began hurrying toward the street.

Brandi's suitcase was already on the ground . . . and she ran toward the waiting embrace.

(6)

"Adam, it's Rocky," said an excited voice when Adam came on the line.

"Rocky—where are you?"

"I'm at home. Listen—I think you were right about where the clues are hidden that may tell where the ark is."

"You have new information?"

"No, I'm just convinced you were on the right track about the book of Jeremiah."

"I'm all ears."

"Nothing specific. What I'm saying is that we have to find the clues."

"You're the investigator—what do you suggest?"

"That I book a flight, and that we reopen this case."

"Great! We'll be waiting!"

"Any news from Juliet?" asked Rocky after a brief pause.

"No, nothing," answered Adam. "It's a hard time. I really don't understand what's going on."

"Well, being without my own wife for several years . . . my advice is not to give up. Juliet's worth fighting for."

"Thanks, Rocky. I appreciate it."

"Any other developments?"

"Scott had a long session with Captain Thurlow. I think his account of our Aksum break-in may help a little."

"How long will he be in England?"

"He's back off to Turkey tomorrow."

(7)

The next morning Adam left the house to drive Scott to Heathrow for his return flight to Yerevan.

"How long will you be gone, sir?" asked his housekeeper as the two men approached the door.

"I don't know, Mrs. Graves. Most of the morning."

"Shall I plan lunch, Mr. Livingstone?"

"Something light and cold. I may not be back till one, perhaps two."

Strangely, however, twelve hours passed and Adam did not return.

When her master had not come home by the time she retired for the night, Mrs. Graves had grown concerned. When she awoke to a silent house in the morning, two days after the call from Mr. McCondy, with no sign that Mr. Livingstone had come home during the night, her concern grew to outright worry.

Adam made no appearance all day. Another evening came, with still no word.

This wasn't like him at all. Feeling more than just a little nervous, the faithful housekeeper went to bed for a second night in a row in a quieter and yet more lonely house.

In the morning, worried about doing so—she had never called anywhere out of England in her life—she went up to Mr. Livingstone's office and found the New Hampshire number. After two or three attempts, at last she heard the telephone ringing.

"This is McCondy," answered the familiar voice.

"Mr. . . . Mr. McCondy," she said. "Hello, it's Andrea Graves."

"Mrs. Graves! How are you?"

"I'm a bit concerned, actually, Mr. McCondy. I haven't seen Mr. Livingstone for two days. I believe you were the last one to speak with him before he left. I wondered if he mentioned anything to you of his plans."

"No, Mrs. Graves," replied Rocky, "not a word. That doesn't sound like Adam. Where was he going when he left?"

"To take Mr. Jordan to the airport."

"Hmm . . . well, I'm sure he'll turn up."

The housekeeper hung up the telephone, still more concerned. She had so hoped that Mr. Livingstone had said something to the American investigator. She would call Crystal.

"Crystal, this is Andrea Graves. Do you know where Adam is?"

"Why, no, Mrs. Graves . . . why?"

The housekeeper explained.

"I'll be right in," said Crystal.

Thirty minutes later Adam's secretary arrived. Jen was not far behind. Within the hour Crystal had Scott on the phone in Ararat City.

"When he left me at Heathrow he was planning to drive straight back to Sevenoaks," said Scott. "I'm starting to feel like I live in an airplane! But if he doesn't show up in another twelve or eighteen hours, I'll catch another flight back."

(8)

Crystal and Jen remained at the office on the second floor of the Livingstone estate for the rest of the day. Their holiday was instantly over.

They put their heads together for the rest of the day, telephoning dozens of people whom they thought might have heard from Adam. No one had. Mrs. Graves even called her sister in Bedford to see if he'd been there.

Late in the afternoon Crystal finally contacted Inspector Saul at Scotland Yard. It took no more than the briefest of explanations before the inspector was on his way from the Yard's headquarters to Sevenoaks.

He arrived fifty minutes later. Crystal met Adam's longtime friend at the front door.

"I know it's probably nothing, Inspector Saul," said Mrs. Graves, inviting him inside. "But we can't help being anxious. You know Mr. Livingstone. This is not like him."

Saul nodded in obvious concern, then proceeded to go over with the others present what they had gone over a dozen times already amongst themselves.

This time, however, the facts were being gathered for a missing persons report.

Midway through the following morning, Captain Thurlow and Inspector Saul arrived at the Livingstone door. They asked Mrs. Graves if they could speak with Mrs. Johnson.

Crystal and Jen were downstairs within seconds.

"We found Livingstone's car," said Thurlow to the three women as they gathered around to listen.

"Where?" asked Crystal.

"Couple miles from here."

"And?"

"No sign of him," answered Thurlow. "Not a trace."

"What are you going to do?" said Jen, nosing her way forward to Crystal's side.

"We don't know exactly, Miss Swaner," replied Saul. "We're concerned. We'll file the report, get an all points out right away. Then I suppose . . . we wait."

"It'll take top priority," added Thurlow. "Despite everything that's been going on recently, Livingstone's a favorite around the Yard. In the meantime, I think it's time we sit down with you, Mrs. Graves, and see if there might be *something* else you can remember about what Livingstone said about where he might be going . . . anything."

But already Mrs. Graves had slumped into a nearby chair, her face white as a sheet.

"I think she's going to faint," said Crystal. "Just give me a few minutes with her before you start with questions. I'll run upstairs and get a couple things," she added, hurrying for the stairs. "Jen, why don't you start some tea?"

twenty-nine

Flight

(1)

The drone of a single jet engine gradually intruded into Adam Livingstone's ear. Slowly his senses returned to consciousness.

From the events just before he passed out, he knew well enough that he had been abducted. His head throbbed. Obviously he had been drugged.

He tried to clear his foggy brain.

Where were they going? Knowing their heading would be a start to getting his bearings. How long had it been? He opened his eyes a slit.

Daylight. Judging from the angle of the sun, which still seemed high in the sky, they hadn't been in the air more than an hour or two. If he could sneak a glance at his watch. But that would be impossible—his hands were tied behind his back.

Suddenly a deep voice interrupted Adam's thoughts.

"Open your eyes, Livingstone," it commanded. "I know you're awake. The stuff should have worn off two minutes ago. So don't be cute. You're awake and we both know it."

Adam opened his eyes and tried to take stock of his surroundings.

It was a small, private jet, as he had suspected, expensively appointed. The sun had a waning look. He'd spoken with Rocky on the phone, dropped off Scott at the airport, and had been on his way back to the estate when he'd been pulled over. That would have made it sometime around one. If they'd flown *west* for two hours, then the sun would still be bright . . . and they would be out over the Atlantic somewhere. They must be going north or east.

Two men sat at the plane's controls. Seating in the cabin, with deluxe swivel chairs each with its own table and minibar, could accommodate six. Adam was the only passenger.

Several minutes later Adam sensed an imperceptible slowing in the engine and the slight feel of descent. If they were heading down now, obviously their direction had to be *east*.

The continent, no doubt . . . probably eastern Europe.

(2)

They were on the ground within twenty minutes.

As they taxied to a stop, one of the men rose and walked back toward his guest. Adam recognized him immediately from the incident outside Amsterdam.

"On your feet, Livingstone," he said. The authoritative voice, penetrating eyes, black hair, and carriage of command were not easily forgotten. "I'm not going to blindfold you or secure your hands," the man added. "I don't need the nuisance of staring eyes. I think you're smart enough not to try anything. You have no friends here. You're in my part of the world."

They had landed at a corner of the airport from which no signs of location were visible. A car awaited them. Adam was shoved into the passenger seat. The Voice took the wheel himself, giving no indication of being worried that his guest would try to escape. Glimpses of the city before they headed east along the Drina River indicated to Adam that they had landed in Belgrade. He scarcely recognized it from the reminders of the recent bombing.

A drive of approximately thirty minutes followed. Their course abandoned the river halfway through the journey in favor of a southerly route into the hilly region south of Belgrade's Danube plain. How close they were to the new Bosnia-Herzegovina border Adam didn't know. He was reasonably sure they were in Serbian Yugoslavia.

Eventually a huge stone mansion or castle loomed through the trees ahead, after the fashion of eastern European austerity. It was imposing in height and sprawl, though without the decoration or fanciness or bright-colored gardens which would have been added to an English or French castle of the same period. Adam guessed it was from the seventeenth or eighteenth century. Singularly out of place in such a setting were what appeared to be the tips of a helicopter's wings protruding from above one of the flat roofs. All Adam could think of as they ascended the hill upon which the intimidating structure sat, was a Bach organ fugue in permanently minor key. If it were true that vampires came from Bulgaria, it would not surprise him to learn that a stray one had wandered over the border and set up shop in this place.

Adam was escorted to a room high on the fourth floor of one of the wings, unceremoniously shoved inside, and the door locked behind him. There were a chair, a bed, a writing table, an adjacent bathroom, and a window overlooking the woods. For a dungeon it wasn't really so bad, thought Adam. His watch was still on his wrist, though wallet, with money, credit cards, and ID, was gone.

Had he been kidnapped or what? Whom would they extort ransom from? None of his staff had unrestricted access to his accounts.

Within an hour it was dark. Dinner was delivered by a servant. Adam tried to engage her in conversation but it was clear the woman understood no English. The night passed without further human contact.

With morning came an adequate breakfast considering the locale, with coffee rather than tea.

Sometime shortly before noon, his host reappeared. He strode into the room and got straight to the point.

"You have something I want, Livingstone," he said. "At least you know where it is. Do as I say, and you will be released unharmed."

"I will help however I can," said Adam.

"Yes," rejoined the Voice with a smile, "I am sure you will. You English are all alike—anything to save your own skin."

"What is it you think I have?"

"The ark . . . the ark of the covenant. As you and I both know, the little box we had in Amsterdam was not the real thing."

"But I don't have it. You must know that."

"Don't toy with me, Livingstone. You and your American friend have located it—the real one this time. I heard you and the American talking about it on the phone."

"So that's what this is about. You bugged my estate."

"Yes, and I heard everything clearly. Where is it?"

"I honestly don't know. My friend called to tell me he thought he had figured out the location of clues only."

"Yes, and he said you knew where they pointed to."

"Who are you?" asked Adam, returning the man's gaze. "And where am I?"

"Where you'll rot if you don't come straight with me, Livingstone!" the man shot back. His commanding demeanor was steadily giving way to something decidedly psychopathic.

Adam tried to think where he had seen him prior to that terrible day in Amsterdam. He had seen him in the Buckingham Palace gardens. In fact, he thought he remembered seeing him speaking briefly with Candace. Come to think of it, now came also a faint reminder of the Nile Gardens Hotel, a glimpse down a hallway, the sound of a man with his back turned speaking with—

Adam's reflections were cut short. His head was jerked to the side by the slap of a powerful hand.

"It's mine, Livingstone!" said the deranged Voice. "I have a right to it. All I want is the ark. I have no interest in murdering you like I did that girlfriend of yours."

"You shot Candace!" exclaimed Adam angrily. The man's cruel laugh and the evil glint in his eye brought his Egyptian colleague Dr. Cissna and his former employee Erin Wagner—both now dead—to Adam's mind. The man was a madman as well as a murderer, and probably responsible for their deaths two years earlier.

"Actually I didn't," replied Zorin. "But I watched the whole thing. The bullet was meant for you, you know. I'll think nothing of finishing that job right here if you don't cooperate."

"They say the ark is in Ethiopia," said Adam, calming. Maybe it would be better to play along. This guy obviously had a few screws loose in his malfunctioning mental elevator.

"I've heard the old legends," he snapped back. "My ancestors thought so too. But they found nothing. The box my friends stole recently was a fake. Everybody knows that."

"What ancestors?"

"The Templars, you fool."

"The Templars—that was centuries ago!"

"You think we aren't still active! Ha—you're a fool, Livingstone. You and this whole modern culture. I'm a Templar, Livingstone, don't you understand! A Knight Templar. Haven't you heard of the Masons? Don't you know who we are? What do you think it's all about—fun and games? I tell you, it's my heritage, my destiny . . . I have a *right* to the ark!"

Zorin's eyes glowed as he strode in wrath from the room.

(3)

Zorin returned ten minutes later.

His rage had cooled, but the diabolic glare of his eyes continued to burn. That he had once considered himself the leading candidate to become the Council's Man of Peace would have seemed incredible given his present fiendish condition. He had fallen like the morning star, from one of the world's most powerful men to little more than a murderer.

Adam hadn't exactly arrived at a plan during Zorin's absence. But there was no doubt that he had to do *something*. There wasn't a ghost of a chance the fellow intended to let him loose.

Zorin walked in, carrying an automatic pistol. The natural way his fingers and palm molded themselves to the contour of its steel handle evidenced clearly enough that he was well familiar with its use.

"All right, Livingstone," he said.

Adam returned Zorin's gaze. The next words out of Adam's mouth surprised even him, for he had not planned them. Yet when they came from his mouth, they seemed the most natural thing he could have said. "Tell me," Adam said, "Mr.—"

"Zorin!" Zorin spat back. "But don't think knowing my name will do you any good!"

"It wasn't *your* name I was thinking of," replied Adam calmly. "There is another name which I wonder if you know. Tell me, Mr. Zorin," Adam repeated, "what do the words *Jesus Christ* mean to you?"

The words seemed to strike Zorin a physical blow and rendered him incapable of speech. He shook his head, as if to wake himself from the trance.

"*Mean to me?*" he said. "What kind of question is that? They mean nothing to me!"

"They mean something to me, Mr. Zorin."

"I care nothing about this . . . this supposed person to whom you refer!"

"He is no supposed person, Mr. Zorin. He is the most real individual who ever walked the earth. Jesus Christ is my Lord. He died for me, Mr. Zorin—and you."

"Shut up . . . quiet!" cried Zorin, "or I swear I will pull this trigger!"

Adam stood and approached his adversary. Zorin watched with eyes wide, powerless to stop the flow of events in which *he* had become the weak, and this man before him the fearless and the strong.

Adam stopped two feet in front of him and stared with a penetrating gaze of command into Zorin's twitching eyes.

"Mr. Zorin," said Adam calmly, "give me the gun."

Without awaiting an answer, Adam reached forward and took firm hold of the pistol, loosening it from Zorin's grip. He stepped to the window, opened it, and threw the gun as far as he could out toward the trees below. The motion brought Zorin momentarily to his senses.

"How dare—" he began.

Adam turned back toward him, raising his hand, beckoning silence.

"Easy, Mr. Zorin," he said. "You are no longer giving me orders. Now sit down in that chair."

In disbelief himself, Zorin obeyed.

Adam backed toward the door, keeping his eyes locked on Zorin's. He opened the door, backed through it, then bolted it behind him. Almost immediately he heard furious movement and cursing inside.

There was no time to lose. The lion was already awake!

(4)

With no idea where he was or where Zorin's own quarters might be, Adam sprinted down the corridor in a general direction that might lead him to the center of the house, then down the first flight of stairs that presented itself.

Whatever sort of staff Zorin had at this place, at least there didn't seem too many of them about.

Adam dashed this way and that, taking several false starts and wrong turns, then retreating, ever working his way down more stairways and toward the central portions of the sprawling complex. Most doors were closed, though unlocked. As he hurried along, he glanced into whatever rooms looked likely.

At last, near the landing of what appeared the main staircase he saw two large double doors slightly ajar. He crept toward them and peeked inside. The room was empty. Quickly he opened the doors and entered.

The leather sport jacket Zorin had worn earlier was draped over a chair. This was obviously his personal headquarters, with sleeping quarters in an adjacent room to the right.

Hastily Adam scanned the room. He ran toward a bureau with a few personal items on top.

Keys! Adam grabbed them. A leather hand wallet. Adam opened it.

This was more than he had hoped for—three separate passports issued from different countries, all in the name of Halder Zorin, and plenty of cash in several currencies! He'd rather have his own ID, but Zorin's would have to do.

Adam pocketed the wallet, grabbed Zorin's leather jacket and the black leather cap on the chair beside it, and headed for the door. He threw the coat on and stuffed the cap into his back pocket.

Then he tore from the room, flew down the stairs and outside to the Mercedes, which was parked where they had left it the day before.

(5)

Frantically Adam drove down the hill away from the eerie mansion. He had not gone more than three or four miles when he heard a great *whishing* above him.

The helicopter! How had Zorin escaped from the locked room so fast?

Adam wheeled along the narrow road at breakneck speed. It was obvious, however, that nothing he did would shake Zorin, who had a clear view from overhead.

Suddenly a crash sounded above. A fiery blast exploded to the right of the roadway.

What kind of artillery did he have up there? Some kind of small missile, a Stinger or an RPG?

If Adam didn't ditch the car in a hurry, he would go up in a plume of smoke!

Another missile landed with deafening blast forty feet in front of him. A chunk of road exploded. Adam yanked the wheel hard. The tires screeched. He careened to the right. Barely missing the crater, the car blasted through the fire and smoke. Swerving, Adam righted himself, grinding down yet harder on the accelerator.

A straight stretch lasted another hundred or one hundred and fifty yards. At its end the road bent out of sight. That's where he would make his move.

Adam swerved the black Mercedes around the bend. For an instant he moved out of Zorin's range of sight.

He hit the brake hard, slowed for a second or two, yanked the door latch, steadied himself, then shoved the door open and flung himself out.

He tumbled over and over, rolled off the roadway, and fell down over the embankment into the brush. He came to a stop and crouched under the overgrowth.

The abandoned Mercedes careened to the side of the curve, then over, into the air briefly, hitting once, twice, then bounced and crashed down into the gorge below.

An explosion followed. In the sky above, the helicopter bent down, swooping directly above Adam to follow the crash.

Adam scrambled up and away from the site. Pain from numerous scrapes and bruises shouted to him. But he hadn't broken anything and was able to walk. Zorin's jacket had prevented at least a few scratches.

He only had a minute or two. Above his head the helicopter returned. Adam dove into a dense thicket. The screaming blades came nearer. Zorin paused above him, scanning the terrain beside the road for trace of a survivor. Breathing heavily, Adam felt the wind from the giant blades. Back and forth the sky spider crawled, then gradually moved away.

Adam remained where he was until the giant rotary blades retreated up the hill toward the mansion.

Zorin would be back, he was sure of that, to investigate the site thoroughly. He was not the sort of man to leave loose ends.

Exhausted from the harrowing leap out of the car, Adam tried to clear his head. It was still midday. He would either have to wait until dark, hoping to elude Zorin for the rest of the day, or get going now, keeping to the wooded area beside the road.

Fatigue and pain notwithstanding, Adam chose the latter. He wanted to hang around Zorin's compound no longer than he had to. The man was likely to have a small army at his disposal, of either mercenaries or German shepherds. Either way, Adam had to get out of here!

Besides Zorin, there were the Serbian nationals and Kosovars to consider. That's all he'd need—to stumble into the middle of a minefield left over from the war!

He'd seen a track on the drive up. If he could get to a train, maybe he could find a way to get aboard. He climbed to his feet and began the trudge along the side of the winding roadway.

He would prefer a train bound northwest toward Hungary. But at this point he wouldn't be choosy.

(6)

The scene outside the Livingstone estate was hectic.

News teams from both BBC stations and four major American networks had rolled in all morning and were setting up outside the main gate. Every pass through by one of the Livingstone staff or someone from Scotland Yard sent cameras, microphones, lights, and eager journalists into instant action.

News of the Livingstone disappearance was spreading through the U.K.'s newswires as rapidly as had his ruin at the hand of Sir Gilbert Bowles on United States TV. By this evening's telecasts it was sure to dominate every station in the country, and would probably make front-page headlines in tomorrow's London *Times*. No one was calling it an abduction or kidnapping . . . *yet*. But obviously those were the words on everyone's minds. The theory was already being advanced that Ethiopian fanatics had tired of waiting for results through official channels, and had decided to take matters into their own hands.

Poor Mrs. Graves was beside herself. Everything was happening so fast. The moment Adam's car had been found, it seemed the whole world knew.

But the whole world *didn't* know!

Suddenly Adam's housekeeper realized there were two people who probably hadn't yet heard. Heaven forbid they should hear it on the telly! She turned from the entryway where she had been standing watching the commotion outside, and immediately went upstairs to her apartment.

There were two important phone calls she needed to make at once.

The first was to her sister's flat in Bedford.

"Betsy, I need to talk to Juliet," she said as soon as her sister answered.

Juliet came to the phone several seconds later. "I know you wanted time to yourself, dear," said her aunt, "but I have to know if you have heard about Adam."

"Heard what, Auntie? I did get a call from Crystal asking if he'd been here."

"I am afraid there is distressing news."

"What do you mean, Auntie Andrea?"

"Adam is missing, dear," replied her aunt. "No one has seen him in several days. Scotland Yard's here now."

Juliet felt herself going faint. She made her way to the nearest kitchen chair while doing her best to hang onto the phone.

"I'm sorry, Juliet dear," said her aunt. "But I need to ring off. I have to try to contact Mrs. Livingstone as well."

"She's here, Auntie," said Juliet. "In Bedford, I mean."

"You saw her!" rejoined a surprised Mrs. Graves.

"She came for a visit several days ago. She's staying at some convent or other for a few days of retreat, she calls it."

"Will you see her again?"

"She's coming for supper this evening."

Swallowing her continued astonishment, Mrs. Graves merely replied, "Then, dear, tell her what's happened and have her call me the minute she gets there."

(7)

In New Hampshire, Rocky McCondy had just settled into his chair with the morning edition of the *Globe* and fresh Yukon Blend when the telephone rang.

"Rocky . . . Scott Jordan."

"Hey, Scott—how's it going?"

"I've had better days. I've been logging more air time than sleep time. I just arrived back at Sevenoaks."

"Why—what's up?"

"Brace yourself, man. Adam's disappeared."

"What! You serious?"

"Afraid so. Been gone three days. Scotland Yard found Adam's car this morning, not far from here. But no trace of him."

"I should have tried to get over there the minute Mrs. Graves called."

"Don't worry about it. You couldn't have done anything by then anyway."

"Are there no leads?"

"Nothing. The press has been rolling in ever since. Thought I'd better call before you heard it on the radio or something."

"Yeah . . . yeah right—thanks, Scott. I'll be there as soon as I can. I'm not sure whether you want to tell Thurlow that," he added with a chuckle. "I doubt he'll want me around. But I'm coming whether he likes it or not."

(8)

Kim Shayne was torn.

Suddenly she had more opportunities than she knew what to do with. A huge, breaking Livingstone story . . . and Sir Gilbert Bowles telling her he was about to scoop the world and locate the ark of the covenant!

She looked at her watch as she approached the exchange for the M25. Bowles' flight for Jerusalem left in two and a half hours. She could still make it. Her packed suitcase lay on the backseat behind her. Her ticket was in her purse. She had spoken with Bowles just an hour ago. He was going with or without her.

Would she take the Motorway east to Heathrow, or west to Sevenoaks?

She realized she had already made up her mind some time before. She entered the roundabout without hesitation and eased into the flow of traffic . . . westbound.

Forty minutes later, Kim Shayne was inching along the country lane toward the Livingstone estate, already choked with hundreds just like her.

It had been a reflective, in some ways melancholy drive. The decision not to chase the big exclusive with Gilbert Bowles went deep within her, deeper than she had expected. She couldn't say why, but it had set off a chain of thoughts she hadn't seen coming. The face she had determined to make into a media star with her "mystery girl" photographs was a face whose eyes were probing most piercingly of all . . . into *her.*

Ever since he had uttered them, she had not been able to get Bowles' words out of her mind: *Same chance you gave the Halsay kid, eh, Shayne?*

She had tried to pretend the case was different. But it wasn't. She had used Juliet for her own ends. And the memory of Juliet's eyes, from one of her own photographs, haunted her. She was a hypocrite, pure and simple. She pretended to hold up one standard, but made exceptions for herself when it suited her. What else was a hypocrite than that?

The uncomfortable sensation of having her conscience nipping at her heels had triggered other thoughts and sensations. Being around this whole Livingstone business was forcing her to look at herself, her priorities, her past, even her future, through different eyes than ever before.

She dabbed at her eyes. Good heavens, what was that about? Where had the tears come from?

She pulled over and parked alongside the road. She would walk the rest of the way. The fresh air and exercise would do her good.

She started to get out, then paused and opened her purse to take out the airline ticket and rip it in half. The action would strengthen her resolve to behave differently as a journalist from now on.

Her hand fell upon a tiny book. She glanced down. It was the Gideon New Testament she had been given at the fund-raiser in Washington. Had it been kicking around in her purse ever since, without her noticing? She'd forgotten it was even there. Why had she kept it?

She dealt with the ticket, then took out the New Testament and put it in her pocket. Maybe it was time she had a look at it after all.

thirty

Vigil at Sevenoaks

(1)

For the moment Adam was glad to be in this unsettled region of the world. In England he would have been stared off the train in such a smelly, disheveled state. In Serbian Yugoslavia he had hardly been looked at twice.

It was good he'd thought to take Zorin's coat and cap. He'd practically frozen waiting overnight in the woods outside Sabac.

The first train of the morning was an outdated commuter into Belgrade pulled by an ancient, chugging steam locomotive. From there he'd get something north into Vojvodina, hoping he didn't encounter any unfriendly troops. His Slavic wasn't the best. But again, in this part of the world no one cared. It wasn't exactly Nazi Germany, and no Gestapo were prowling about. He knew the *Simplon Orient* went all the way from Belgrade to Paris. That would be his best chance. North to Budapest would be the other option. One of Zorin's passports should get him over the Hungarian border. From there it would be a hop, skip, and a jump westward to Austria. Thanks to Zorin's fat wallet, at least money was not a problem.

Across the dirty aisle a man who appeared on his way into the city for a day at some factory munched solemnly on a crust of bread. The train clacked rhythmically along, mesmerizing Adam as he stared at the man. Suddenly he realized that he was very, very hungry.

He forcibly took his eyes off the stale loaf. Maybe he could get something to eat in the station in Belgrade.

Fifteen or twenty minutes passed, including another two stops in small villages. This had to be the slowest train he had ever been on. Again they built up speed, which amounted to perhaps twenty miles an hour.

Another sound intruded into the midst of the *clackety-clack* reverie. As it grew louder, he awoke to its terrifying familiarity.

He leapt to the window. Outside a helicopter approached rapidly. It bore toward the train with frightening speed, as if homing in directly on *him*. Did that beastly machine have X-ray vision?

He glanced about. Maybe that guy with the bread was Zorin's spy. He probably had a microphone stuck in the end of the loaf, through which he was whispering–

Stop, Adam, you idiot! he said to himself. *You can't go crazy now!*

The chopper screamed to the side of the train, then hovered beside it. It glided back and forth parallel to the rows of windows with uncannily precise movement, seeming to possess eyes of its own, probing every car.

Adam shrank away from the window.

The helicopter disappeared, raced ahead, and swept dangerously in front of the train. The engine lurched and a jerk of brakes followed. But the engineer wasn't about to be so easily intimidated.

Adam pressed his face to the glass to look forward. The helicopter rose again, soaring high in a wide arc, then swooping back toward them.

Adam saw a white plume of smoke leave the chopper from beside one of the skids.

Another missile! The man was a lunatic!

"Get down!" Adam cried, jumping across to the bewildered man with the bread across from him, yanking him from his seat to the floor. "Get down, all of you!" he shouted, gesturing wildly to the ten or twelve other men and women.

An explosion erupted beside the train, rocking it dangerously from side to side, sending Adam sprawling into the aisle half on top of the man he had tried to help.

Now the passengers understood Adam's warnings well enough! They scrambled and dove for cover. Adam was back on his feet and running over and through people to the rear of the coach. With hope vaguely mingling in his brain of getting away from Zorin at the same time as saving the train by removing himself from it, Adam threw open the door and stepped onto the landing. Already another missile had been launched from above.

Sucking in a breath, Adam leapt into the air in the opposite direction from Zorin's attack.

Even as he landed, an explosion sounded. Adam spun and rolled away from the track. When he came to a stop, he jumped to his feet and crept up the embankment to gain a view.

The helicopter still hovered in the air above the train. A third missile fired, this time finding its mark.

It exploded against a front wheel of the old locomotive, blowing a hole in the steel frame. The screeching of brakes was too late this time. The explosion tore apart a great section of track.

The engine careened dangerously to the side, then crashed violently to its side, its weight and momentum carrying it sliding another thirty or forty feet down the embankment. The tremendous sound of the crash sent shock waves rippling through the earth toward Adam, who watched in horror.

A freight car derailed and toppled on its side, luckily disengaging from those behind it. The first passenger car behind it derailed and came to a stop tilted sideways but upright. The coach from which Adam had jumped managed to remain standing, with its two leading wheels off the track.

Smoke and steam, shouts and screams all mingled with the descending whir of Zorin's machine of death setting itself down beside the scene.

From his vantage point a hundred yards away, Adam stood helpless. The screams struck anguish into his heart. His first impulse was to run forward to help. But he realized there was nothing he could do. The moment he appeared, Zorin would kill him.

It was probably another ten or twelve miles. He would have to make it into Belgrade on foot. He'd keep to the woods and back roads. It was going to be yet a long time before breakfast!

(2)

Near the gate of the Livingstone estate at Sevenoaks, two men approached one another.

"How did you get here so fast, McCondy?"

"Connections, Thurlow," Rocky answered, laughing.

"You Americans!"

"This time it was a guy with connections high up in United," added Rocky. "Course, no doubt you Brits don't know anything about favors and greasing the wheels."

"Don't have an inkling what you're talking about, McCondy," replied the captain. "You Yankee investigators are way ahead of us."

Rocky glanced over at Inspector Saul, who smiled where he stood next to Scott. Rocky threw Jordan a quick wink, then turned his attention more seriously to the Scotland Yard captain.

"So . . . what do you have, Thurlow—anything new?"

"I'm afraid not. No ransom demands. No contact at all."

"No clues or leads?"

"We found Adam's car about two miles from here, that's it. Nothing was disturbed, no sign of a struggle . . . nothing. We dusted the car for prints, of course."

"And?"

"No one's but Livingstone's. We went over every inch of the surrounding area with a fine-tooth comb. Not a tire track, not a footprint—zero. That was a week ago."

"So what are you doing?"

"The usual. Computer tracking of possible enemies, known associates—people like you, McCondy."

"Very funny!"

"We're trying to get a line on that bunch in Scotland from last time," Thurlow went on, "but I doubt we'll find much. There's not much to do but wait."

(3)

How long had he been running?

It seemed he'd been on his feet for as long as he could remember. He needed to sleep. He needed food, shelter . . . someplace safe . . . out of the sight of . . .

Then Adam remembered. Was he cracking up? He'd only left the Belgrade train an hour ago. He couldn't lose it now. Leave the lunacy to psychopaths like Zorin. He had to keep his wits inside his head.

Why had he left the train? Oh yes—to cross the Hungarian border by foot. As they'd approached he'd realized that to show any of the passports would give Zorin that much clearer a trail to follow. He left his second train of the day at the next village of Sombor.

And just in time too. Ten minutes after it pulled out toward Bezdan, in the sky came the evil whirring sound of Zorin's helicopter again.

How could the man track him so incessantly! Would he blow up this train too? Would he track *every* train Adam tried to take?

Adam jumped into a culvert and waited until the sound retreated. Thankfully no sound of explosions followed.

Adam dragged himself to his feet and crept back into the light. An open field lay between him and the wooded area in the distance. He hoped he could make a dash for it without Zorin appearing again.

Adam took off in what he could manage of a run, though it could certainly not be called a sprint.

His legs couldn't keep going forever. He was *so* tired.

(4)

A blustery wind whipped around the metal equipment, slides, bars, rings, and swings of a neighborhood park in Bedford. A hint of spring was in the air.

It was as chilly as it might have been a similar day four or five months earlier when the year was winding to an end. But today's was a brighter chilly, and thus more hopeful. The eternal seasonal battle for sunlight was being won. The sun gained strength with each passing day. There were also scents in the air, borne on the breezes, which spoke of green and newness and life, rather than brown and decay. They were subtle fragrances of mystical hope and optimism. If the earth could burst again into life after a cold, frozen winter, why might not also the human spirit likewise renew itself? Why might not spring come to the soul as well as to the grass and trees and fields?

Alas, thought Juliet as she swung back and forth on one of the park's three swings, the awakening spring in her own heart had come too late.

What a fool she had been to leave Sevenoaks, to write that letter to Adam, to become so upset over such trivial things.

And now . . .

Tears glistened in Juliet's eyes at the reminder. What if . . .

She couldn't think it!

She let herself swing down to a stop, sat a minute or two more, then stood and began walking back to her aunt's flat.

✦ ✦ ✦

At nearly the same time, Kim Shayne sat slowly swinging at the little park near Sevenoaks. She had taken a break from the endless waiting at the Livingstone estate for some news, and walked the several blocks to the park where she had first met the young lady who unknowingly was now exercising such an impact upon her.

The circumstances of this situation were doing strange things to her. Even in the midst of her anger that day at the paper, Kim had noticed something indescribable about Juliet that drew her. Adam Livingstone was the same way. Could it possibly have anything to do with their being Christians?

It was not the kind of thing she had ever considered. But Kim Shayne was thinking of many new things these days.

She took from her pocket the New Testament that had been her constant companion for the past forty-eight hours. She had certainly never expected to be reading a Bible. Now she found herself picking it up and snatching every chance she had. Already its pages were getting bent and rumpled.

She began reading:

I have come that they may have life, and have it abundantly. . . .

Twelve simple words. But they plunged straight to the core of her heart, a heart that for the first time in Kim Shayne's life realized that it was lonely.

How, she wondered, did one find and experience that kind of *abundant* life? In the midst of her active, modern, sophisticated life . . . it sounded almost too good to be true.

✦ ✦ ✦

These had been the hardest two days of Juliet's life. Between tears of despondency, sighs, silences as they waited for the phone to ring, prayers, and her own self-recriminations, Juliet had searched her own soul more than at any other time in her life. She had to figure out what it really meant to be a Christian, even when things didn't go well, when God seemed distant, when guilt and self-doubts were overpowering.

She had also searched her soul in regard to her own future . . . and where Adam fit into it. What did she really want in life? A week ago she hadn't known.

Now at last she did.

When Juliet reached the house fifteen minutes later, the car of a visitor was parked in front. She recognized it immediately.

She walked inside. Her mother, aunt, and Frances Livingstone were seated at the kitchen table. The conversation ceased when Juliet walked in. The heads of the three women turned.

"Hello, Juliet," said Mrs. Livingstone as she stood. "I came to say good-bye. I'm driving back to London. With Adam's disappearance going on so long, I think I should be there."

Her words hung in the air. It was obvious to the three older women that Juliet had been crying. But when she spoke, none of them expected the words they heard.

"Would you mind waiting, Mrs. Livingstone," Juliet asked, "while I gather up my things? I'd like to go with you."

(5)

When word came later that same afternoon that a car was trying to get through the crowd around the gate, a buzz immediately spread through the house. Ever watchful Mrs. Graves was the first through the front door of the house. Two minutes later she was welcoming her niece home amid tears and hugs and a flurry of questions.

Unfortunately, the joy of Juliet's return was short-lived. It only accentuated Adam's absence more. By evening's tea the mood again grew subdued. The vigil resumed.

Every ring of the phone sent hearts into throats. Anything would be better than endless waiting. Yet any call might equally bring the news everyone feared.

The only calls, however, were for one of Scotland Yard's agents, or from a newsman or newswoman hoping for an impromptu interview from one of the staff.

The next day came. Though it rejuvenated everyone's spirits to have Juliet back, time continued to drag. Every hour or two, Mrs. Graves somberly returned to the kitchen to fix tea. When all else failed, there was always tea.

Frances Livingstone had not spent a night at Sevenoaks for years. But she decided to stay in her old rooms. Not wanting to leave the estate for a second, Scott and Jen took up temporary residence in two of the guest rooms. Crystal returned home to her family every evening. Adam's field assistant, Figg, was expected back from Turkey any day.

The nights grew increasingly restless. Even Frances Livingstone was less than her normally ebullient self.

(6)

A few more days passed. Still there were no developments.

The number of reporters outside gradually dwindled, evidence that it grew less and less likely that the affair would have a happy ending. Eventually the networks and papers reduced to skeleton crews.

After a week and a half, Captain Thurlow came to the door about midday and asked to see Scott.

"Get your people together, Jordan," he said when Scott appeared. "I think it's time we had a talk."

"Who do you want?"

"Everyone—staff, family, the whole household."

Ten minutes later, Adam's friend, Inspector Max Saul, and Captain Thurlow stood before the assembly of men and women who were Adam Livingstone's closest friends and associates.

"Look," began Thurlow, getting straight to the point, "there's no sense in us beating around the bush here . . . it's not looking good. We all know that. I hate to be the one to have to say it, but that's my job."

He hadn't actually said the word, but Thurlow was obviously trying to prepare them for the likelihood that by now Adam Livingstone was probably dead.

"What exactly *are* you trying to say, Captain?" asked Scott.

"What I'm saying, Jordan, is that in 99 percent of these cases, when you don't hear within seventy-two hours, you *never* hear . . . and the body is never found."

"*The body* . . . gracious!" exclaimed Mrs. Graves, her face drawing up in pale shock, her lower lip quivering.

"We don't want to hear that, Thurlow. He's OK, I tell you," said Rocky, as if speaking confidently might somehow help the situation.

"I'm sorry," said Thurlow in as compassionate a voice as he could muster. "I know how you feel. I've known Adam Livingstone longer than some of you."

Even as the captain spoke, Juliet, Jen, and Mrs. Beeves began to cry softly. Poor Mrs. Graves wasn't far behind. Adam's mother sat, stoic. Crystal's face was sober.

"Adam's been a friend of Max's here for twenty years," Thurlow went on. "It's my job to make sure everyone involved is realistic. I don't know any other way to say it than to just say it—the chances are . . . we're not going to see him again—"

Mrs. Graves burst into a wail.

"Perhaps you, his mother, Mrs. Livingstone," said Thurlow, nodding in her direction, "and the rest of you, his friends and coworkers, might need to start thinking of what to do next, what kind of memorial—"

Mrs. Graves could take no more. She rose to leave the room. Jen, Juliet, and

Crystal, crying freely, went after her. Mrs. Beeves followed a moment later. Mrs. Livingstone and the butler sat and both began dabbing at their eyes. Rocky, Figg, and Scott remained motionless.

Thurlow sighed with obvious feeling. This wasn't exactly the way he'd envisioned this.

"Livingstone is the kind of guy who had enemies," said the captain, speaking to the men and Adam's mother. "There was that attempt on his life last year, and then the Montreux girl getting killed in France. I don't know, Jordan, McCondy . . . it's not looking good."

"We're going to keep praying," said Rocky, to the vigorous agreement of Beeves and Adam's mother.

(7)

Thick fog blanketed the wide river mouth at the waterfront.

Muted sounds of a harbor sounded dully in the night. Wavelets slapped against the cobbled quay. A few late fishing boats putted homeward toward their slips. The water was black and frigid.

A foghorn sounded in the distance. Seagoing vessels, though they could not be seen from here, bumped with occasional thuds against ancient wooden moorings.

The night was cold. Most of the city was asleep. Nefarious designs, however, yet lurked in shadows as thick as the mist. Evil never slept.

A thin lone figure, obviously looking for someone, walked out across a stone bridge. So heavily did fog cling to the coastline that its center tower could not be seen. The trail had again been lost.

Fifty yards away two gleaming eyes watched. He had detected his prey stalking him several days ago, and now by night would end this little game of cat and mouse.

The end to this long pursuit had come in a port city. A chill like this rarely came to the Mediterranean, however. The journey had been long and arduous and had covered an entire continent. This was a northern port, far from Baku, Belgrade, Budapest, Vienna, Prague, Dresden, and those numerous cities and hamlets across Europe which had, in the end, led these two here to this climax. It had been a circuitous trek. Who was hunter and who was hunted had been a question occasionally in doubt, for numerous shadowy schemes were involved.

"So, my friend," whispered the watcher's resonant Voice, "at last we end this chase which has brought us so far. You thought you could outwit me. But it is I who triumph in the end."

He raised the Makarov pistol, stretched out a muscular arm, squinted down the barrel, then fired. The report was crisp and quick. No echo sounded in the soupy mist.

A third of the way across the bridge, the walker fell and lay motionless.

Out of the shadows stepped the Voice. He walked forward onto the bridge, his heels striking the pavement with dull precise cadence. Had another been watching, it would not be good to think of encountering such a man in his present mood in so desolate a place.

The murderer reached the body. One shot had been sufficient. He turned the corpse over with his foot. A yellow bridge light shown from above. He gazed into the dead face, a smile twisting his thick lips.

He stooped down and took hold of the familiar beret which had fallen and now lay beside the head. He rose, holding it, the smile widening, then flung it over the railing into the murky water below.

Gradually a laugh began to sound through the fog . . . a cunning, remorseless laugh that would stir trembling in any who chanced to hear it.

(8)

Andrea Graves was the first of the household to wake.

She peered outside into the dawn. The fog was as thick as she had ever seen it. She gathered her robe more tightly around her shoulders, and headed downstairs to put the water on to boil. She felt strangely that this was going to be unlike the other previous days of waiting.

Throughout the morning, as the sun climbed higher in the sky, burning the fog away, the sense of gloom in the Livingstone camp also began to lift. If anything, the tension grew yet more acute.

By midmorning the sense grew upon Mrs. Graves that the vigil was drawing to a close. News would come today, she was certain of it. Her heart feared for what those tidings might be. As the day progressed, she grew more jittery and pale than she had been throughout the entire ordeal.

Her peculiar mood infected Juliet, then slowly spread to the others. Conversations were minimal. Heaviness descended over the estate. Solitary walks in the garden and long gazings through windows comprised the day. Everyone expected the phone to ring.

Captain Thurlow and Inspector Saul held close and private counsel. It was obvious they were accomplishing nothing. A change was imperative. They feared the household was about to crack.

The telephone remained silent.

(9)

In her Zurich office, Anni D'Abernon stared blankly at the sheet of paper she had been handed from her private fax machine.

Her face remained dispassionate as the messenger disappeared from the room. A moment more she stood, then walked to her secure telephone line.

It took a minute for the connection to be made to the source.

"Is the identification certain?" she asked.

The answer was in the affirmative.

"I see," said D'Abernon.

A few more questions followed. The Swisswoman hung up the phone.

(10)

"Look, I'm willing to pay, and pay handsomely," said a low voice in the shadows of a filthy Jerusalem coffeehouse located in one of the most ancient parts of the Arab sector.

"Money is not the only consideration. The precincts are holy."

"Bah! What you people care about religion could fit on the head of a pin. You'd kill for five shekels—you know it as well as I. Hatred, not holiness, is the ruling creed of you Arabs. So don't play your religious games with me—they won't work. For a price you would spit on Mohammed's grave."

The blasphemous words brought the listener's hands momentarily to the hilt of the long blade tucked out of sight among several layers of grimy clothes. It would almost be worth killing this fat western pig just for the pleasure of it. But he knew the man was rich. Chances like this didn't come often.

The two men speaking in low tones each despised the other. But both were opportunists, and were willing to lay aside such feelings for the sake of gain. The one was a large Englishman, the other a slightly built Palestinian native of this city who, despite his appearance, had grown very powerful and was acquainted with many of influence. He probably knew more about the hidden, inner workings of this city and the complex interplay between politics, religion, and greed, than any man alive. He also knew a great deal about the history of its subterranean network of archaeological passageways.

"I've already spent a small fortune and more time than I can afford getting to you," the Englishman added. "Your identity is closely guarded. But believe me, if you are not interested, I will take my business elsewhere. I am confident others know what you know, and many would be only too glad for my money."

The Arab's fingers released their grip on the knife. Unfortunately, the fool was right. He took a sip of his thick coffee and nodded cryptically.

"So what I want to know is," Bowles asked, "*can* you get me into the old Templar tunnels?"

The Arab again lifted his cup to his lips. "They are well guarded," he said at length.

"Yes, and every guard has his price."

"There are sanctions and legalities, and, as I say, the holiness of the ground."

Exasperated, Bowles began to rise from the table. He would take his business elsewhere!

"For the right price," said the Arab's voice to his back, "what you speak of *may* be possible. . . ."

Bowles relaxed and eased his huge frame back down onto the rickety chair.

" . . . but I warn you, the way is treacherous."

"You have been down there?"

"I know one who has."

"And?"

"There are many perils."

"I will take my chances."

(11)

About ten-thirty Mrs. Graves appeared at the front door, walked outside a step or two, and peered into the distance. She stood a few moments with hand to forehead, shielding her eyes from the sun.

Juliet wandered through the open door. "What are you looking at, Auntie?" she asked.

"Oh . . . nothing, dear," replied Mrs. Graves.

All day in Sevenoaks the sense of impending closure mounted.

The journalistic coterie outside the Livingstone gate began again to enlarge. Word had gone out that Captain Thurlow had called a press conference for 3:00 P.M.

Rumors circulated that he would announce an end to Scotland Yard's active investigation until some word was received from the archaeologist's abductors.

(12)

Anni D'Abernon flew immediately north upon receiving the startling news.

She took the elevator to the highly private, windowless suite on the twelfth floor, gaining entry with the secret, coded chip implanted in her right palm.

Rupert Vaughan-Maier awaited her. Formalities of greeting were brief. The Dutchman's Swiss colleague handed him the faxed sheet which had prompted the hasty rendezvous.

(13)

"Ladies and gentlemen . . . ," began Captain Thurlow outside the open front gate of the Livingstone estate. Listening to him from inside the fence stood the Livingstone family, household, and staff.

". . . I am here with Adam Livingstone's mother, Mrs. Frances Livingstone, along with his staff and coworkers, to announce what I wish I could say was happier news. That is simply that there is *no* news. We have exhausted the Yard's efforts in trying to piece together any leads or clues, but without success. There has been no word from any kidnapper or terrorist organization. We simply find ourselves at this juncture. . . ."

(14)

Vaughan-Maier scanned the paper and took in its message with equal lack of emotion as had D'Abernon a few hours earlier:

> Bonar found dead on bridge in Vlaardingen. Shot to death. One bullet, untraceable.

He glanced up from the sheet.

"Had you heard from her recently?" he asked.

"Yes. She had recovered Zorin's trail and was following his movements across the continent in this direction."

"When?"

"That was three days ago."

"Why in this direction, did she know?"

"She said Zorin was following someone," replied D'Abernon.

"Do we know who? Do we have any idea what happened to him after the shooting?"

D'Abernon shook her head.

(15)

Meanwhile, Captain Thurlow continued with his prepared statement to the press.

". . . which cannot help but necessitate a reevaluation of the investigation," he was saying. "I have been in consultation with the good people of Mr. Livingstone's household here behind me. They are . . ."

(16)

"Could it be that Zorin was following one of the Council?" said Vaughan-Maier. "He has made threats against us."

"Ciano did not know. When she discovered whom he was following, she was to notify me."

"And then?"

"She was to kill Zorin . . . both if necessary."

Vaughan-Maier pondered the developments.

"I don't like it," he said at length. "If Zorin's hand is in this, he could be in Amsterdam even now."

"Precisely my thoughts."

"We must summon the Council."

"He must be eliminated."

"A madman like Zorin must be allowed to interfere no longer."

(17)

As Thurlow spoke, a few heads of the journalists on the outer edge of the gathered reporters began to turn. A sound intruded upon the captain's remarks.

". . . understanding of our position and have been completely cooperative . . ."

More heads turned. The noise began to interfere noticeably. An automobile was coming up the road toward the gate. And fast.

". . . realize that we sympathize with their grief," said Thurlow, himself unconsciously glancing up over the heads of his listeners toward the interruption. He did his best to continue. "And of course the moment . . ."

A buzz filtered through the crowd of journalists as a black taxi bore toward them. Cameras began to turn. Thurlow's voice went silent. The hubbub grew.

The taxi stopped. The passenger door opened.

A clamor of movement and noise erupted. Behind them, the gate began to swing open.

A figure stepped out of the car. A healthy head of blond whipped up from a gust of wind. Shouting, the crowd surged toward him.

"It's Livingstone!" came a shout. It was joined by a sudden chorus.

Bedlam broke out.

"Livingstone . . . it's Livingstone!" cried dozens of voices.

Rocky and Scott forced their way through the tumult. On their heels the household and family struggled forward.

"Let them through!" shouted Thurlow through his microphone. "Let the family pass!"

Like a sea parting, the journalistic tide swept back to create a path through its midst.

Pushing frantically through the bodies, sobbing and crying in laughing hysteria, Juliet burst through and ran past the others.

Behind her came Scott, Crystal, Figg, and Jen, with Beeves and his wife puffing their way behind them. Rocky lumbered beside them, and Mrs. Graves trundled along to the extent she was able, forgetting propriety, tears streaming down her happy face.

Adam broke into a labored sprint toward the throng bearing down upon him. There was Juliet out in front, crying as she ran toward him. A weary grin spread over his face.

He ran toward her, then slowed as Juliet collapsed bawling into his arms. Adam spread his arms and hugged her close to his chest.

All the shouts and cheers retreated far, far away. For a minute or two they were alone in the world, just the two of them, together again where they belonged, in one another's arms.

"Oh, Adam . . . I'm so sorry." Juliet sobbed. "It's all my fault . . . I was such a ninny. I'm so sorry!"

"All's forgiven," he said, stroking her hair tenderly. "I'm sorry, too, that I wasn't more sensitive. I love you, Juliet."

"I know," she whispered in his ear. "I finally know it's true. I'm sorry I didn't believe you before. Oh, Adam, I love you too."

The tender reunion lasted but a moment.

Already others were running up and clustering about, grabbing and shouting and clinging to Adam. Only Scott's eyes were dry, but barely. Rocky's cheeks were as wet as any of the women's.

"Mr. Livingstone . . . Oh, Mr. Livingstone, we were so dreadfully worried!"

"I'm sorry to have put you through it, Mrs. Graves. Hey, Rocky . . . you made it back to England!" exclaimed Adam, grasping with his left hand toward Rocky while he kept Juliet securely at his side with his right.

"I had to see if I could help these people find you," replied Rocky through a wet smile.

"I can always count on you when there's trouble!" Adam laughed.

Rocky took out his handkerchief and blew his nose and wiped at his eyes.

"Mrs. Beeves, how are you?" said Adam, addressing the little circle surrounding him. "Jen . . . Scott . . . hey, Figg, buddy . . . Crystal—it's so great to see you all! You can't imagine how good it is to be home . . . and, Mum—what are you doing here?"

Behind them clustered eager newsmen and newswomen, thrusting microphones in the air above the heads, trying to catch every word spoken in the inner circle, while camera personnel caught the incredible scene live.

In the middle of the crowd of journalists was one who had yanked her camera out feverishly when Adam had stepped out of the taxi, but now put it back in its case. This was one occasion she was not going to try to capitalize on, no matter how many other photographs of the event might be taken. She couldn't change the entire journalistic world, but maybe it was time she thought about changing herself.

Back at the gate, Captain Thurlow and Inspector Saul watched with incredulity.

"You know, Max," said the captain at length, a wry smile spreading over his face, "I think that's the worst response to any speech I've given in my life. They weren't listening to a word I said."

Saul looked over at the captain, then gave out with an uncharacteristic roar of laughter.

"Considering that it was beginning to sound like a eulogy," he said, chuckling, "I have to say I'm glad you didn't have a chance to finish it!"

(18)

That same evening in front of their television in Bedford, Juliet's mother and Aunt Betsy watched the same scene as it had been replayed nationwide already dozens of times. Both sat quietly weeping.

"This is one time I don't mind seeing Juliet in the news," said Mrs. Halsay.

"I suppose this means the wedding is back on," said her sister.

"I would say it has that look," replied Juliet's mother, then laughed lightly.

They watched awhile longer.

"I'm so happy for her," said Aunt Betsy.

Juliet's mother reflected on all that had happened.

"So am I," said Mrs. Halsay softly. "Now that I'm used to the idea, I see what a fuddy-duddy I've been. I'm happy for Juliet too. It is obvious she and Adam love one another."

"I don't think there'll be any doubt of that again," said Juliet's aunt. "Not with the whole world watching!"

✦ ✦ ✦

Christ loved the church and gave himself up for her to make her holy,

cleansing her . . . to present her to himself as a radiant church,

without stain or wrinkle or any other blemish, but holy and blameless.

Then I heard what sounded like a great multitude . . . shouting:

"Hallelujah! For our Lord God Almighty reigns.

Let us rejoice and be glad and give him glory!

For the wedding of the Lamb has come, and his bride has made herself ready.

Fine linen, bright and clean, was given her to wear." . . .

Then the angel said to me, "Write:

'Blessed are those who are invited to the wedding supper of the Lamb!'"

And he added, "These are the true words of God."

EPHESIANS 5:25-27; REVELATION 19:6-9

✦ ✦ ✦

PROLOGUE

Anticipated Feast

A lavishly appointed table spread to the right and left beyond sight.

In the region of which the invited guests had once been a part, it would be said that it stretched in both directions as far as the eye could see.

But that was a place of finiteness. Here words like beginnings *and* endings, length *and* breadth *and* duration, *even* time *itself, had no meaning. Nothing here had endings.*

This was the kingdom of the infinite, the eternal, the everlasting. Everything here was now. Everything here had always been. Everything here was limitless. Everything here was of the Divine Will.

Though preparations were complete for what was obviously a celebration unmatched in all the universe, the hall without end was quiet.

The table sat ready . . . but empty.

✦ ✦ ✦

Two stood gazing out upon the expanse.

Both were of timeless countenance. Though they were two, they were One. Before the table existed, they had been One . . . only One . . . eternally One. Before the realm of existence with which their hearts were occupied, they had been One. Even when he whom finite eyes would call the younger of the two—in truth, neither was possessed of age at all, for they had always been together, always been One—had left this, the domain of his home, for a season's sojourn in the other which they had made . . . even then they had been One. It was a region to which he would shortly return.

"When will you send me for them?" asked the younger who was not younger.

"When the time is fulfilled and they are ready," replied the older who was not older.

It was silent for what may have been a second or a millennium. Time did not exist here. Another instant in the timeless eternity of love passed between them.

"My prayer must be answered," said the Son.

"All must be fulfilled," said the Father.

"They must be one, as we are One, that they may wear the garment."

"Otherwise there can be no marriage, or wedding supper."

✦ ✦ ✦

Outside the infinite hall, ten thousand, or it may have been ten million, were gathered in expectant celebration.

They had preceded those they awaited. Upon their faces too were signs of timelessness, for they were now of eternity. They had arrived here through that portal greatly feared on the other side, greatly marveled at the instant it closed behind them on this. The table had eternally been set. Yet expectation mounted that the hour of the feast was nearly at hand.

The Son appeared among them. He knew every man, woman, and child intimately—though each was ageless here. They were sons and daughters of his Father. He knew their hearts with the knowing of infinite love. They knew his with the trust of worshipful adoration. All had come here to dwell with him forever. They too awaited the day of completion, the day of restoration, the day of reconciliation . . . the day of the feast.

A man of white beard and white robe approached, eyes full of love for his friend. He was of a chosen few who had been privileged to know his Savior on both sides of that door separating the domains of time and eternity.

"Where is your bride?" asked his bearded friend.

Tears rose in the Son's eyes. The questioner waited. He had been impatient in the other world. He could wait forever in this.

"My marriage proposal has been given," replied the Son at length. "Now I wait."

A century passed . . . or a moment.

"But surely there must be something you can do to hasten the day of obedience?" said the bearded one.

"I have done all I can do. My Father sent me to her. I died for her. I instructed and warned. I sent my Spirit as my Father sent his prophets. With clear command I offered her my hand, to be my pure bride forever. Again we wait."

"Is there nothing *you can do?" repeated the fisherman.*

"All that can be done has been done and is being done. My Father's will must be fulfilled and will be fulfilled. The time of culmination approaches."

"Everyone here says the day is nigh."

"Everyone there is saying it likewise. But only the Father knows the day and hour."

PART EIGHT

JERUSALEM

✦ ✦ ✦

"And I saw four angels standing at the four corners of the city, each of them holding a fiery torch in his hands. And another angel began to descend from heaven, and he said to them, 'Keep hold of your lamps and do not light them until I tell you. For I am sent first to speak a word to the earth and to put in it what the Lord, the Most High, has commanded me.' And I saw him descend into the Holy of Holies, and take from it the veil, and the holy ark, and its cover . . . And he cried to the earth in a loud voice, 'Earth, earth, earth, hear the word of the mighty God, and receive what I commit to you. And guard them until the last times, so that, when you are ordered, you may restore them, and strangers will not get possession of them.'"

THE APOCALYPSE OF BARUCH

✦ ✦ ✦

thirty-one

Prophet or Angel?

(1)

About five o'clock on the afternoon of Adam's return, after more joyous visiting, some obligatory time with the press, an initial briefing with Thurlow and Saul, all followed by a delicious shower and clean clothes for Adam, the entire household and staff gathered for a high tea more wonderful than Adam had imagined even during the lowest points of his harrowing flight across Europe.

"Mrs. Graves!" he exclaimed, walking into the dining room with Juliet on his arm, "you don't know how I have dreamed of your spreads! Seeing it laid out, the aroma of tea rising from the pot . . . surely I have died and gone to heaven."

The housekeeper smiled. Her master's were words of praise to cherish a lifetime. All the more that she had considered the possibility that he actually *had* died and gone to heaven!

The others arrived in equally high spirits. Tea and coffee were poured, then several of the number offered thankful expressions of prayer for Adam's safe return.

As they began to eat, questions flowed rapidly. Before anyone realized it, two hours had passed and darkness had closed in. Yet Adam had recounted his harrowing escape only as far as the Hungarian border.

Fresh coffee and tea were made. They retired to the first-floor sitting room, where Adam's tales continued, his escape gradually taking him across the continent and eventually to Rotterdam.

"I still didn't know how he kept track of me all that way. I could not shake him. It wasn't until I was nearly to Holland that I found the computer chip sewn into his wallet. It must have been some kind of a device he was able to track. I got rid of it, but he kept after me. And when I saw him shoot whoever it was last night in Vlaardingen, I said to myself, 'I'm getting home tomorrow if I have to *swim* the channel!'"

A serious expression spread over Adam's face.

"That laugh I heard through the night," he added, "as I watched him stand over the dead body on the bridge sent chills through me. It was the sound, if you can imagine such a thing, of evil incarnate."

"Once you were out of that mansion or castle or whatever it was, why didn't you call and let us know you were safe?" asked Juliet.

"I *wasn't* safe!"

"You know what I mean."

"Actually," replied Adam thoughtfully, "I did try to call—a half-dozen or more times. I knew you'd all be worried about me. But every time the connection began I heard snaps and buzzes on the line—faintly, but I could tell something wasn't right. If they had the incoming lines here bugged, not only might that mean they were watching or listening in on the house, which I didn't like, they would also have been able to trace my movements too."

"That was the police listening in, waiting for a ransom call!"

"I thought about that, but I couldn't take the chance. I didn't want to endanger any of you. And," Adam went on, "I was afraid of being watched every second. I got so paranoid by how he kept finding me, I suppose I figured every phone in Europe was bugged. When you're exhausted like that, your brain quits working."

A lull fell over the room. It was the first break in the conversation in hours.

"Who was he?" asked Rocky.

Adam did not answer immediately. The question brought to mind reminders of his captor's face, eyes, and voice. The very memory of that face brought a chill to his bones.

"He called himself *Zorin*."

Even the name had a chilling sound.

"Whether the Yard will be able to track him down with the passports I took," added Adam, "I have my doubts. But I hope the information will eventually lead them to his cohorts who blew up the Ethiopian ark. Thurlow said he's not going to make anything public yet, but at least there are some good solid leads for them to explore."

Again it was quiet. Mrs. Livingstone had remained uncharacteristically silent most of the time. In fact, Adam's abduction had shaken her Tibetan optimism more than she would have expected. She found herself near tears most of the day just to look upon her son and realize how much she loved him.

"That reminds me," said Adam, "Rocky, now that you're here, we're going to have to check the phones thoroughly again. Zorin must have managed to plant a bug. He knew about your call. Speaking of which—we've got to talk about why you called—the ark and the book of Jeremiah, remember?"

"Haven't you had enough adventure for one day?" Rocky laughed.

"Actually, you're right," said Adam. "Suddenly I'm very tired. It will feel so good to sleep in my own bed!"

(2)

Hank Scully, murderer, walked alone in the yard at San Quentin prison, reading from the book that had become his constant companion during the last month.

The other inmates saw the signs almost immediately and kept away from him. They knew that when men got religion in this place, it was best to give them their space.

High above, two men stood at a window overlooking the compound.

"Scully's up to something," said one suspiciously. "I think we had better keep a close watch on him."

Beside him, Warden Ruben smiled. "I don't think so, Lamont. He'll be OK."

They stood a few moments longer, then the assistant warden turned to go.

"Just a minute, Lamont," said Ruben.

The warden walked to his bookshelf, removed a book, opened and flipped through its pages, then sat down at his desk, took out a sheet of paper, and began to write. Several minutes later, he set down his pen, folded the paper, and handed it to his assistant.

"Give this to Scully," he said.

Half an hour later, Scully looked up from his solitary walk to see the assistant warden approaching. Without a word, he handed him a sheet of paper, then walked back across the yard.

Scully stopped, put the book under his arm, unfolded the paper, and read it. He turned and glanced up. There stood the warden in the window of his office looking down.

Scully nodded, then continued his walk, reading the words again:

> *Scully—these are the words of the great Russian novelist Fyodor Dostoyevsky, written during his horrible years of imprisonment in Siberia, after he had discovered the love of God from a New Testament he had been given. "One sees the truth more clearly when one is unhappy. And yet God gives me moments of perfect peace. In such moments I love and believe that I am loved. In such moments I have formulated my creed. This creed is extremely simple. Here it is—I believe that there is nothing lovelier, deeper, more rational, more manly, and more perfect than the Savior. There is no one else like Him." Believe it or not, on his knees while he was in prison, Dostoyevsky thanked God in prayer for those who had condemned him to Siberia, for it was there that he discovered God's love for him. I hope this quote might be an encouragement to you.—Ruben*

He folded the paper, slipped it into the back of the book, then continued reading where he had been before the interruption:

> *"Do not let your hearts be troubled. Trust in God; trust also in me. In*

> *my Father's house are many rooms; if it were not so, I would have told you. I am going there to prepare a place for you. And if I go and prepare a place for you, I will come back and take you to be with me that you also may be where I am."*

He paused to let the words sink in, then returned to the page.

> *"I am the way and the truth and the life. No one comes to the Father except through me. . . ."*

(3)

The joyous mood of celebration at the Livingstone estate continued through the following day. Journalists and photographers were everywhere. The phone rang off the hook.

About eleven Adam went out, with Juliet at his side, to submit to the inevitable round of questions. They saw Kim Shayne, who, with curious expression on her face, said nothing but watched the two intently.

The next day Adam had recovered sufficiently that his investigative juices were flowing through his veins again.

"Sit down, sit down, everyone," he said when he had gathered everyone together. "I am still waiting to hear why Rocky called me."

"Actually, it started with a rather silly dream," Rocky said lightly. "Then I became convinced that the book of Jeremiah contained clues, confirming what the two of you, Adam and Juliet, felt earlier. So we have to dig for those clues."

"Like biblical archaeologists," put in Adam.

"What I found myself thinking," Rocky went on, "is that perhaps there are other clues, more subtle, that don't mention the ark by name. Jeremiah was in Jerusalem when the Babylonians invaded—God's man on the scene, like in my dream—an ancient journalist in Jerusalem at a critical time in Israel's history. So it makes sense that he might have known something."

Intrigued nods went around the room, as if to say, *Why not? We've tried everything else.*

"So what do you suggest, Rocky?" asked Adam.

"I thought maybe we ought to sit and literally read through the whole book together and brainstorm ideas . . . anything that pops out at us."

"I like it! What do we have to lose? Let's break out the Bibles, the tea, and the coffee, and get out our scriptural picks and shovels, and go to work!"

(4)

"All right, Rocky," said Adam when they were situated and ready to go twenty minutes later, "what exactly are we looking for?"

"I'm not sure . . . some word or phrase or hint that Jeremiah might have put in his writings to indicate what he knew about the ark."

"You heard him, everyone–creative thinking!"

Eight or ten minutes later, within seconds of one another, everyone in the room began to glance up from their Bibles with smiles on their faces.

"I take it we have all arrived at Jeremiah 3:16?" said Adam.

The other heads nodded.

"The last specific mention of the ark in the Old Testament," said Crystal.

"The curious sound of this passage makes me think Jeremiah might have known more than he was telling," said Rocky. "The more I've considered it, I realize we may never have asked the most obvious question of all. *Why* does he even bring it up?"

"What if he not only knew what happened to it," said Juliet excitedly, "what if he's the one who hid it? Can't you read it between the lines–*the ark of the covenant will never enter their minds or be missed.* That is a very peculiar thing to say unless there is a hidden meaning. I think Jeremiah himself was involved!"

"Good point!" said Adam. "With that in mind, let's continue on."

Crystal paused the discussion again at Jeremiah 13:5.

"Look, he's talking here about hiding something."

"A linen belt," said Jen. "What can that have to do with it?"

"Could it be a veiled reference to the ark?" asked Rocky.

"I suppose," mused Adam. "Gold, like linen, is a symbol of purity."

Over the next couple of hours, dozens of such ideas were thrown out.

Juliet was the first of the group to reach Jeremiah 32:9.

"Here Jeremiah is told to buy a field," she said. "And look, in verse 14 he hides the deed. Here he is *hiding* something again. Has anyone noticed how often this seems to come up? It sounds suspicious to me."

"The general trend throughout the book of hiding things *is* beginning to be a pattern," remarked Figg.

Once more the discussion continued, though without any breakthroughs. After a while they gradually broke from reading. The women headed for the kitchen to warm up water for tea and coffee and put together snacks, while the men fell to talking casually.

"Why *was* Jeremiah always hiding things?" said Scott, half to himself. "It is like Juliet and Figg said before–linen belts . . . jars, of all things . . . deeds, bricks, stones. And Pharaoh's palace, what could that have to do with–"

"What did you just say!" exclaimed Adam, spinning around. "About Pharaoh's palace."

"The forty-third chapter," replied Scott. "I just finished reading it."

"Right, I remember that too, but it didn't strike me. But . . . palace . . . palace . . . hmm, what if–"

Adam stopped dead in his tracks. His brain was whirling with possibilities.

"Of course—*palace!*" he repeated again. "Maybe he wasn't writing about Pharaoh's at all! That was only symbolic. What if he was writing about the future . . . the canopy of the palace . . . the canopy of Babylon—"

"Get back in here, everyone," Rocky shouted. "Adam's onto something!"

Adam was pacing excitedly around the room and trying to keep up with the flow of ideas. "Juliet's point from earlier," he was saying, "was that things are constantly being hidden underground throughout the book. Jeremiah is thrown into a cistern—*underground.* He buys a field and hides the documents in clay jars. Where . . . *underground.*"

"Still no mention of the ark," said Rocky.

"Maybe by this point in the book he is talking about it in symbolic terms. What if all these are clues to what Jeremiah may have done to something of far *more* value?"

"For the sake of argument, even if he did hide the ark in crevices or caves," put in Jen, "how could anyone discover where? People have been digging in Palestine for two thousand years."

"But they didn't have modern technology," said Scott. "Or Adam Livingstone!" he added. "If it's there, I'll put my money on some invention of Adam's to find it!"

"But there is another astonishing clue," Adam went on. "There in the forty-third chapter, again the Lord tells Jeremiah to *bury* something, this time some large stones. The reason I call it astonishing is that perhaps this time Jeremiah *does* tell us something about the location."

Most of the group had wandered back to their seats and picked up their Bibles again and were looking at the ninth verse.

"Here's where you have to get creative with the interpretation," Adam went on. "But God's clues are sometimes deeply embedded in the Scriptures, like the whole Bible code thing that's being discovered with computers. So let me get creative with Jeremiah 43. You have to look for both the primary and the secondary meanings. So in anticipation of *the future,* the Lord divinely inspired Jeremiah to implant a clue to the ark's location . . . right here!"

"I'm sorry, Adam," said Juliet, "I'm reading the words, but I don't see it."

"Jeremiah buries the large stones at the entrance to the palace. The *literal* meaning, of course, is Pharaoh's palace. But as I read I was reminded of King Baldwin's conversion of the Al-Aqsa Mosque to his own palace after the first crusade."

"The site of Solomon's former temple," said Rocky, getting that look on his face that indicated he was gradually laying hold of what Adam had in mind. "The Templars' first home."

Adam nodded. "What if the mosque is the *secondary* meaning—a hidden meaning, a prophetic interpretation to the word *palace.* Jeremiah himself wouldn't have even known toward what his words pointed. But what if, by God's inspiration, he was referring to the sacred mount where Solomon's temple, or palace, was located in his own day, but where later the Al-Aqsa Mosque, or palace, would be built? And then, what does Jeremiah say will occur at a later date," asked Adam, "at the very place where he buried the large stones?"

Adam waited for his question to sink in.

"Do you see it?" he said. "Jeremiah says that the king of Babylon would come and set his throne above them, spreading his royal canopy *above* them—above the buried stones, above the rocks . . . a *canopy* above the *rock*. Now do you see it?"

He looked around the room, eyes wildly enthusiastic.

"The *canopy*," he repeated, "above the *rock*."

"Canopy . . . arch . . . the canopy above the rock . . . *the Dome of the Rock!*" exclaimed Scott.

"Adam, that's fantastic!" said Rocky.

"But that's not all," Adam went on. "We don't only have the word *canopy* here. We have a canopy that is spread over the hidden stones by whom?"

"The king of Babylon," suggested Crystal.

"Islam," said Jen.

"Exactly! Babylon, the very seat of the Muslim faith."

"And right over the top of the former temple," said Adam, "sits the Muslim canopy, the Dome of the Rock. In other words, according to the Livingstone translation," he went on, "Jeremiah buried some *stones* at the site of a *palace* where later a *canopy* would be erected by *Babylon*. To me, that makes the road map as clear as day."

"Adam, you are incredible!" Juliet said appreciatively.

"Isn't it possible that Jeremiah buried his enigmatic large stones," Adam concluded, "which could symbolically represent the ark of the covenant, somewhere in the depths, in the *crevices in the rocks* below the temple that was about to be destroyed by Nebuchadnezzar's army?"

After their initial amazement, everyone now took in the implications of Adam's analysis thoughtfully.

"It makes as much sense as my Eden theory when we started on that," added Adam. "I have the feeling this search might end where it all began several thousand years ago—at the site of the threshing floor of Araunah the Jebusite, where David built his altar to the Lord."

(5)

Downstairs the telephone rang. A few moments later Mrs. Graves interrupted the discussion.

"Juliet," she said, "you have a telephone call."

Juliet went to the phone and answered the incoming line.

"Juliet, it's Kimberly," said the familiar voice. "Please, don't hang up—"

Juliet recalled the expression on her face she had seen yesterday.

"Could I talk to you?" asked Kim.

"What about?" she said.

"Something . . . personal," replied Kim. "I promise—no camera, no tape recorder, no pen and notepad."

Her voice sounded different too. "Where are you?" Juliet asked.

"Actually, I'm outside your gate," replied Kim. "I'm calling from my mobile phone."

"All right," said Juliet, "I'll be out in two or three minutes."

(6)

Juliet Halsay and Kim Shayne walked slowly along the lane leading to the estate. They were about a half mile from the house.

"I know I apologized before," the journalist was saying, "that day you came down to the paper—"

"Stormed down, don't you mean?" asked Juliet, smiling

"Well, maybe you were justified in what you said. But what I wanted to say was that I want to apologize again—I mean *really* apologize. It was sort of a formality before. I meant what I said, but in a way my words were cheap since you had caught me red-handed. What else was I going to do? But now I find a much deeper sense of having tried to take advantage of you that I very much regret. I am *truly* sorry."

"Thank you," replied Juliet. "It's OK. I survived. Maybe I even grew through it too. And I need to ask your forgiveness for lashing out like I did at you. Justified or not, it was hardly a Christian response on my part. But I do appreciate what you say. All is forgiven."

"On my side too," rejoined Kim.

They walked on in silence for a while.

"Do you mind if I ask you something?" asked Kim at length.

"Of course not."

"How long have you, you know . . . been a Christian?"

The question took Juliet off guard. It was the last subject she would have expected someone like Kim Shayne to bring up. No one had ever asked her about her faith before in quite this way.

"I grew up, I suppose," she began, "*believing* most of the things about Christianity. We went to church semi-regularly. I mean, we're all taught Christianity more or less, right? It's part of the culture. But about two years ago I gave my heart to the Lord in a new way."

"What does that mean really?" asked Kim, "that you gave your heart to the Lord?"

"Hmm . . . I guess it's the difference between believing religious doctrines or ideas in your head—you know, intellectually—and actually saying to Jesus, 'I make you Lord of my life. I invite your Spirit to come into my heart and live inside me. I want to be your follower—doing what you tell me, living as you taught your disciples.'"

"So you consider yourself . . . a disciple of Jesus?"

"I guess I do," replied Juliet, "though I've never thought of it in exactly those words before. That doesn't mean I think I'm any better than anyone else, just that I have decided to be a follower of Jesus, to make him Lord of my life."

By now they were some distance down the lane and had left all sounds of the estate behind them.

"Thank you for sharing that," said Kim after a while. "I've never heard it explained quite so simply. Most people make religion into such a complicated thing. The way you describe it, it's really just a matter of deciding how you want to live."

"And deciding who you want ruling your affairs," added Juliet, "yourself . . . or the Lord."

"Yes . . . yes, I see. But that brings up another question. Do you mind? I mean, I don't want to pry or get too personal, but I am very interested."

"I understand," replied Juliet. "What did you want to ask?"

"How does one set about, like you say, to have someone else—the . . . uh, the Lord, rule your affairs? The very idea sounds so foreign to my whole way of thinking."

"It takes some getting used to," said Juliet. "You have to train yourself to think differently."

They continued to talk freely, and did not return to the estate for another hour. It was a conversation neither of them would ever forget.

(7)

Adam embraced Juliet warmly when she reentered the house.

"What was all that about?" he asked.

"A most interesting discussion. Our friend Kim Shayne is thinking seriously about some things."

"In any event," said Adam, "I am so glad to have you back from Bedford."

"Not half as glad as I am to have *you* back!" Juliet replied.

It was not until later in the day that the team gathered again to continue their discussion of Jeremiah.

"That was a good bit of work we did earlier," said Adam. "Let's see what else we can find."

"Since we last talked," said Jen, "I've been thinking. Remember how I was reading in Josephus and seeing what I could find in other extrabiblical Old Testament sources?"

They nodded.

"There are also some writings by a friend of Jeremiah's by the name of Baruch, and—"

"Baruch!" exclaimed Adam. "Of course!" he exclaimed. "Why didn't I think of it sooner!"

Everyone turned. A lightbulb had obviously gone on.

"What . . . what?" clamored several voices excitedly. Even Jen was surprised at Adam's reaction.

"Baruch!" he said. "Do you want to tell them, Jen?"

"I didn't find anything yet." She laughed.

"What is a Baruch?" asked Rocky.

"A member of an influential Jerusalem family," said Jen. "He lived in the years prior to and after the Babylonian invasion. He was Jeremiah's close friend and Jeremiah's disciple and secretary. He wrote down what Jeremiah dictated, and probably most of the book of Jeremiah, and there is a book by him in the Apocrypha. Beyond that, I don't know anything about his writings. I was starting in that direction when we went to Ethiopia the second time. I never picked it back up."

Adam dashed from the room, leaving everyone looking at each other perplexed. They heard his feet racing up the stairs to his office. He came back a couple of minutes later holding two or three books, his eyes aglow.

"This may be what we've been waiting for!" he said, sitting down again. "As Jen said, one of the books in the Apocrypha is attributed to Baruch," replied Adam. "I studied some of those old sources years ago for an Old Testament history course. I'd forgotten about it. Here, Jen, look up Baruch," he said, handing her one of the books. He sat down and began hurriedly flipping through another thick old volume.

"I recall some connection between Baruch and the ark," he was saying, almost to himself. "Let's see. . . ."

A minute or two later, Jen had located one of the passages and handed the open book back to Adam.

"Actually there are two books said to be authored by Baruch," he began. "The second is not included in the apocryphal canon but has circulated among Jewish rabbis for a couple thousand years. It's called the *Apocalypse of Baruch.*"

"What is so significant about Baruch?" asked Juliet.

"His apocalypse describes the destruction of the temple and the city. On the basis of Baruch's writings the legend was carried down through the centuries that right before the destruction of the temple by Nebuchadnezzar's army, the ark of the covenant was hidden in a secret vault somewhere below the temple, supposedly by angels."

"Just like we thought of this morning!" exclaimed Juliet.

"Yes, and this account confirms that we may be on the right track."

"Here it is," said Adam, holding up the book in his hand. "Listen—"

Adam found his place and then began to read aloud:

> *"And it came to pass in the twenty-fifth year of Jeconiah, king of Judah, that the word of the Lord came to Baruch, the son of Neriah. . . .*

> "Well, I'll skip ahead a bit to where he gets to the Babylonian invasion." Again Adam began to read.

> *. . . and on the next day the Chaldaean army surrounded the city. And when evening came, I, Baruch, left the people, and I went and stood by the oak. And I was grieving over Zion and lamenting over the captivity that had come upon the people. And suddenly a powerful spirit lifted me up and carried me over the wall of Jerusalem. And I saw four angels standing at the four corners of the city, each of them holding a fiery torch in his hands. And another angel began to descend from heaven, and he said to them, 'Keep hold of your lamps and do not light them until I tell you. For I am sent first to speak a word to the earth and to put in it what the Lord, the Most High, has commanded me.' And I saw him descend into the Holy of Holies, and take from it the veil, and the holy ark, and its cover. . . . And he cried to the earth in a loud voice, 'Earth, earth, earth, hear the word of the mighty God, and receive what I commit to you. And guard them until the last times, so that, when you are ordered, you may restore them, and strangers will not get possession of them. . . .' And the earth opened its mouth and swallowed them up. . . . And after this the Chaldaean army entered and took possession of the house and all that was round about it. And they carried the people off as captives. . . . And I, Baruch, came, together with Jeremiah, whose heart was found pure from sins, and who had not been captured when the city was taken. And we rent our clothes and wept, and we mourned and fasted seven days."*

Adam set the book down.

"That is remarkable," said Juliet.

"It's symbolic, yet it reads like an eyewitness account, don't you think?" said Adam. "And there is another apocryphal account well known among the Jews called the *Paralipomena of Jeremiah.*"

"The what!" said Jen.

"The *Paralipomena of Jeremiah*. It means the 'things left out' of the book of Jeremiah."

"No kidding!" exclaimed Rocky. "Does it mention the ark?"

"Not just a mention—the whole story is repeated, similar to that described by Baruch. Listen."

Adam flipped through the volume and again began to read:

"It came to pass, when the Israelites were taken captive by the king of the Chaldaeans, God spoke to Jeremiah, saying, 'Jeremiah, my chosen one, get up and leave this city, you and Baruch, for I am about to destroy it because of the many sins of those who live in it. For your prayers are like a solid pillar in the middle of it, and like a wall of adamant around it. Get up now, both of you, and leave it, before the army of the Chaldaeans surrounds it . . . neither the king nor his army will be able to enter it, unless I first open its gates. So get up, and go to Baruch, and tell him what I have said. And then, get up both of you at midnight, and go onto the city walls. . . .'"

"Let me skip on . . . uh . . . here we are–

"And when midnight came Jeremiah and Baruch went up together onto the city walls in accordance with the Lord's instructions to Jeremiah. And behold, a trumpet blast sounded, and angels came forth from heaven with torches in their hands; and they stood on the city walls. . . . And the Lord said, 'Speak, Jeremiah, my chosen one.' And Jeremiah said, 'Behold, Lord . . . what should we do with the sacred things in thy temple and the vessels used in thy service? . . .' And the Lord said to him, 'Take them and consign them to the earth, saying, Listen, O Earth, to the voice of him who created you.'"

"What strikes me immediately," said Rocky, "is that if this legend was circulating among the Jews, the Templars had to know of it. It would easily explain why they spent so much time digging under the mosque. They had heard the stories too."

"Yet there we are back at the question which has bewildered me throughout this investigation–*why* didn't they find it?" he said at length.

"I'll come back to what I said earlier," replied Scott. "They didn't have modern technology . . . *or* Adam Livingstone! If it's still there, Adam, you'll come up with something that will help us find it."

Adam glanced around the room from where he and Juliet were sitting on the sofa, then turned back to Crystal.

"I think it is time to start investigating some travel arrangements," he said. "Book us all–"

He paused and put his arm around Juliet, then added, "especially Juliet!–to Jerusalem!"

thirty-two

Technology from the East

(1)

It turned out to be far easier for Adam's secretary to book air passage to Israel and hotel accommodations in Jerusalem than it was for him to gain access to any of the politically sensitive and secretive excavation sites in the vicinity of the Temple Mount.

Reports had circulated through the archaeological community for years of top-secret excavations carried out by the Israeli government deep beneath Mount Moriah. They had freely sponsored digs to the south and west in the Jewish sector of the old city. But everyone knew discovery of unauthorized activity extending eastward directly beneath the Muslim-controlled Temple Mount—where two of the most sacred sites in all Islam had stood for more than a millennium—could precipitate a full-scale Middle Eastern war.

In the summer of 1988, a major incident had erupted over Israeli excavations of the ancient canal near the western wall of Herod's temple discovered by British explorer Charles Warren in 1867. It had remained mud-filled and mostly forgotten for decades until the Ministry of Religious Affairs for Israel decided in 1988 to dig out and drain the Hasmonaean cistern and link it to the western wall tunnel. Thinking the Israelis were attempting to dig under the Al-Aqsa Mosque, outraged Palestinian leaders sent an urgent summons over the loudspeakers of the mosque's minaret, which was answered by hundreds of Arabs, who attacked the Jewish workers with stones and bottles. Israeli police stepped in with tear gas and rubber bullets in an attempt to stop the rioting, which eventually encompassed the entire old city. Once the hostilities quieted, and with many assurances that Muslim holy sites would not be disturbed, the draining and cleanup of the tunnel proceeded more slowly and discreetly.

That project and related digs in recent years had exposed much of the original stonework from the western foundation of the temple northward from the Wailing Wall. In spite of public denials to the contrary, rumors persisted that secretive excavations fingered off the main tunnel passageway in many directions, even extending under the Temple Mount itself.

Visitation permits were not difficult to obtain for the western wall tunnel. Yet Adam hoped to find a way to penetrate the yet more hidden vaults and passageways whose existence he suspected might lead them closer to the object of their historic quest.

Going through official channels, however, proved less than useless. After several days Adam realized their departure would have to be postponed.

(2)

Crystal was going through the morning's mail as Adam got off the phone after a round of calls that had proved generally discouraging.

As he entered the room from his private office, she handed him an envelope.

"Here's an interesting letter that just arrived today," she said.

Adam opened and unfolded the single sheet.

Dear Mr. Livingstone,

You contacted me awhile ago when you were raising support for your project with Noah's ark in Turkey. I am embarrassed to say that I was uninterested at the time. However, recently I found myself contemplating your request again. Curiously, this reflection has also prompted me to begin reading the Bible for the first time since I was a student many years ago.

I realize your project in Turkey has advanced to a new stage, and that you may no longer be seeking help. However, I felt prompted to write and lend my support and the services of my company in whatever way they may be useful.

To be honest, however, our specialty, and the area to which Kiang Enterprises devotes most of its research, involves laser technology, mostly in the medical field. We are in the process of developing a new generation CAT scanning system. We have, however, recently been in contact with the American space agency about the development of a laser probe to be utilized on future missions to Mars to map the interior of the planetary crust by scanning the density variations of its materials. So I do not readily see how the facilities of my company could help you. But I nevertheless wanted to establish contact with you.

Yours sincerely,

Lee-Hia Kiang,
Kiang Enterprises, Singapore

(3)

"You're right, an interesting letter," said Adam, setting it down and walking in the direction of Scott and Rocky where they sat talking.

"I'm still confident we'll be able to get to the northern foundation of the western wall," he went on, his thoughts returning to the proposed Israel trip. "Guides watch that area like hawks. If we're right about an underground network, it's more top secret and sensitive than we can imagine. I've got a number of additional people to see. In the meantime, we'll continue with what research we can."

"What can we do from here?" asked Scott.

"Come on, Scott," said Adam, chuckling. "You've been with me long enough! This ought to be a piece of cake compared to finding Noah's ark and getting it off the mountain."

"That was purely technological. Once we had the science, it was only a matter of time before we found the thing. The scanning technology—"

Scott stopped.

"Wait a minute!" he exclaimed. "Do you realize what I just said—scanning technology!"

It took Adam several seconds more to realize what Scott was thinking. Then his face lit up.

"Scanning technology!" he repeated.

"Are you thinking what I think you're thinking?" Scott asked incredulously.

"If technology allowed us to look inside a glacier," said Scott, "then why couldn't it likewise enable us to look inside a mountain, even under Jerusalem itself."

"Of course—some kind of laser scan!"

"I'm afraid you've lost me," said Rocky, who had been listening intently to the whole exchange. "Are you talking about some kind of laser Geiger counter that would lock onto the gold of the ark?"

"That would be nice," Adam responded, "but I don't think we have that technology yet or gold miners would be roaming every inch of the planet with it. But, Rocky, what about some kind of three-dimensional scanning system? Although I don't know how we could ever—"

He stopped and again his face lit up.

"Wow!" he cried, already hurrying back to where he had set down the letter. He grabbed it up and hastily read through it again.

"It's exactly this man's specialty!"

"But what are you talking about trying to scan?" asked Rocky, still puzzled.

"Like Scott said, if we can look inside glaciers, and this fellow's talking about looking beneath the surface of Mars, then why couldn't we scan the tunnels and excavations *beneath Jerusalem!* Look at this—"

Adam excitedly opened several books and atlases and spread them out on a corner of one of the desks, shoving papers and files and others books aside to make more room.

"There is a vast underground network under the Temple Mount and throughout Jerusalem," he was saying. "If you look at old maps and atlases of Jerusalem—these are just a few I have—evidence exists of digging and passageways, tunnels, shafts, cisterns, aqueducts, secret chambers . . . it's everywhere, from the Cave of the Kings up near the Damascus Gate to Solomon's quarries and the tombs outside the old walls at the Gordon Calvary site, all the way southward under and around Moriah to Hezekiah's Tunnel and the Siloam Tunnel and Jeremiah's Grotto. There's evidence scattered underground over every foot of ground . . . Warren's Shaft near the Gihon Spring, and Conder's work following Warren's. Just look at it all! If we could produce a three-dimensional scan of every such passageway, we might discover some that have never been excavated and are not known—dating, for example, say . . . from the time of Jeremiah."

"Now I see where you are going with it! What a fabulous idea. But to get under the old temple and find whatever tunnels Jeremiah might have had access to, like you're talking about . . . ," said Rocky.

"What do you think, Scott?"

"We've tackled no less daunting hurdles in our time. The technology would be cutting edge, no doubt about that. But with what computers are capable of today . . ."

"And if we could enlist this Lee-Hia Kiang's help," replied Adam.

"How would you actually scan *beneath* the city?"

"I don't know, Rocky," replied Adam. "But I *do* know that I want to talk to this Mr. Kiang! Crystal, I have another trip I need to make before we go to Jerusalem. Where's Juliet?" he said, glancing around. "Juliet!" he called again, running from the room and toward the stairs. "How would you like to see Singapore?"

(4)

Four days later, Adam and Juliet approached the imposing Kiang Enterprises Building in the heart of Singapore. They had landed thirty-six hours before, booked rooms in the closest hotel, and met again the next morning to spend the day sightseeing. On the following morning they had arranged to meet with the president of one of Singapore's largest multinational corporations. Still in awe at how different this part of the world seemed, yet at the same time how modern, Juliet followed at Adam's side, looking at the buildings and people and bustle, hardly able to take it all in.

Five minutes later they began zooming up the glass-enclosed elevator outside the building.

"Oh, my!" Juliet exclaimed. "My stomach and throat just changed places!"

"It is a spectacular city," said Adam. "What a view."

"I had no idea it was so huge and modern and sophisticated."

"The New York City of the Orient."

Within seconds they had arrived on the forty-third floor and were immediately shown into Lee-Hia Kiang's office. He greeted them warmly, as if they were old friends. His English was flawless, flitting somewhere between American and Australian for accent.

"I cannot tell you what a privilege it is that you called and asked for my help," said Kiang, as they sat down to tea served by his secretary.

"We are equally appreciative that you made time for us," said Adam. "I know your schedule must be extremely busy."

"Of course. But a technological challenge, with a history and intrigue, and perhaps a little daring thrown in—that is not an opportunity that comes to one in my position every day."

Adam laid out his plan, which was still only a dream—some might call it a harebrained one at that—unless his host could turn it into reality.

Kiang listened intently, now and then interrupting with a question, then at one point lifting a hand, and abruptly stopped Adam in midsentence.

"Excuse me, Mr. Livingstone," he said, "but do you mind if I bring in one of my top engineers to listen to this? He is a creative thinker, loves a challenge, and is head of the Mars probe research. I think he will be able to help us get quickly to the crux of the matter."

"Not at all."

They poured more tea and chatted informally while they waited. In less than ten minutes, after more introductions and a brief recap for Kiang's associate, Adam continued.

"As I was saying," Adam went on, "another thing that fascinates me about it is that obviously this underground network of tunnels and passageways, if it exists as we think, is irrespective of walls and borders and buildings above. It is as though there is an entire subterranean city down there that could tell the most unbelievable stories of the history of the city, but no one is able to thoroughly explore it because of the ethnic and political conflicts which control the ground above. . . ."

The discussion continued for another hour or two, eventually involving five more men and two women, and a trip to the Kiang lab and research center where the prototype for the Mars probe was already under way.

(5)

The following afternoon Adam and Juliet were on their way back to London.

"Do you think he will be able to help?" asked Juliet.

"He seemed excited," replied Adam. "And the way their whole engineering team started brainstorming when we were in the lab–"

"In Singaporean Malay no less!" exclaimed Juliet.

"That was something to hear!" Adam exclaimed, laughing. "I only wish I could have understood everything!"

The following week was full for everyone connected with the Livingstone estate. Once again Adam was off into the city.

When he returned that afternoon, manila envelope in hand, he was obviously excited.

"What this file reveals," he said, "–and it's highly classified stuff–is that there *are* indeed explorations going on right now. But everything's being done in the dead of night and underground. Apparently the Israelis have excavated some tunnels and dug some new ones, extending a great distance west, which enable them to come and go freely without being seen. There's a government building–unidentified in this report–whose basement provides the entry into an elaborate network of archaeological sites, exactly as we were talking about."

"Can you get in?" asked Rocky.

"No way!" rejoined Adam. "They would deny that such a building and tunnels existed at all. This is a more highly guarded secret than the Israeli defense systems."

"What does the report show?" asked Scott.

"Not much, really. No details. Just confirmation that our suspicions about underground explorations are on the right track."

"Did you find anything that specifically helps?" asked Juliet.

"Oh, right, I almost forgot," said Adam, flashing one of his boyish smiles. "I don't suppose it helps much, but it dovetails exactly into all our research. A few years ago, in the early eighties I think it was, it seems that Israeli archaeologists found a tunnel thought to be–get this–of twelfth-century Templar origins."

"Did they explore it?"

"Only to the point of the Jewish-Muslim boundary above. It led in the direction of the mosque."

"I wonder why the Arabs haven't investigated those caverns under the mosque attributed to the Templars to see where they might lead. You'd think they would be anxious to explore too."

"Not really," replied Adam. "The impetus for exploration comes from the Israelis, the Americans, and the British. I think the Muslims realize that anything found will strengthen the Jewish claim to the Temple Mount. The Muslims are latecomers to the region. All the history which might be uncovered would be Jewish. The Muslims don't *want* anything found. Especially they don't want anyone to locate the actual site of Solomon's or Herod's temple, or anything that might be hidden underneath it."

(6)

Five days later the call came to Sevenoaks that Adam had been waiting for. The instant Crystal announced who was on the other end, Adam jumped across the room to grab the phone.

The others watched Adam's face as it went through a range of expressions as he listened intently, obviously becoming more and more enthusiastic and animated as the conversation progressed. After several minutes and final salutations, he put down the phone.

"As I'm sure Crystal told you," he said to the others, "that was Lee-Hia Kiang. . . ."

Adam paused to draw out the suspense. "Do we have any fresh tea made?" he asked casually.

"Adam!" exclaimed Juliet. "What did he say?"

"He thinks we can do it. His engineering team dropped work on the Mars project and has been spending every minute on this since we left. He thinks they've cracked it. They're assembling a laser density scanner designed for earth, not Mars. He said to think of it as a gigantic geologic CAT scan. And they've already tested it on a region near Singapore known for its caves."

"Tested it . . . how? Where did they position it?"

"From the air. And he said it worked. The only glitch was that the images came out a little two-dimensional. But he thinks that was because they didn't scan a wide enough sector from enough variation of angles and elevations to achieve thorough triangulation of the cross section. But they're developing a computer program to help with that, and to translate the data into an actual three-dimensional map."

"And . . . what next?" asked Scott.

"He also thinks he can rig up a relay system to enable us to make use of a global positioning scanner underground. He is pretty sure he can better the standard accuracy of one hundred meters down to twenty or thirty. He said that he and his team will meet us in Jerusalem the minute we give the word."

(7)

Already Adam was pacing the room, his brain sifting through possibilities and necessities like a coin sorter. "I'll talk to Kiang again," he said. "Scott, I may want to send you down to Singapore immediately to get yourself up to speed with his people on the scanning equipment."

"Do they speak English?"

"I'm sure most do," Adam replied. "You'll have no problems. But you're my own personal Inspector Gadget and I want you to know every inch of what's going on. I don't trust myself in any high-tech operation without you at the controls.

"I'll continue to work on exploration permits. Juliet and Rocky, I might have you two help me on that. A pretty face and American accent might go down easier with the Israelis than an Englishman they're already mad at. Kiang says we'll need a helicopter. He could bring his own in, but would rather arrange for something locally. I'll have to see about that. Then we need somehow to get authorization to take pictures of Jerusalem."

"How about another documentary?" suggested Crystal.

"Perfect! That's it–set it up, just like what we did in Ethiopia. Our request will be completely above board. We'll just do laser scanning along with it."

"Sure, no problem! And no one will be the least bit curious!" said Rocky.

"We'll have to keep a few things to ourselves," Adam explained. "We'll just be photographing the city. We don't have to tell anyone that we've got a state-of-the-art Mars scanner aboard."

Rocky roared.

"Shall I contact Jim Lindberg?" asked Crystal.

"Right–let's get him down there if he's free. And besides hotel and other arrangements, you're going to have to find us the software we need to be able to download our images to give us a detailed and specifically accurate three-dimensional computer image of the whole."

Adam paused.

"We'll have to interface their systems with ours. So, Crystal, you be in touch with their computer people to make sure the software is compatible. We don't want to get to Jerusalem and have a bug we can't fix. Jen, you'll go into the city and get your hands on every scrap of information you can find of old maps of archaeological digs and any kind of ancient maps of the city. You know how to get that kind of information. Go up to Oxford and Cambridge if you need to. Oh, and Scott, get in touch with Figg and see what's up in Turkey, and if he can continue to hold it together another few weeks without you."

The room quieted briefly. Then Juliet said, "I hate to throw a wet blanket over all this enthusiasm, but even if we do have machinery to detect passageways and all the rest, how will that tell you where the ark–"

Suddenly Juliet stopped.

"Oh . . . Oh . . . I just had an incredible thought!" she exclaimed. It was obvious from one look at her face that a high-wattage lightbulb had gone off in her brain. Now she scurried about the room, obviously looking for something.

"Where is that rubbing from the cathedral in Chartres?" she asked.

"Right over there, on the bulletin board," pointed Adam.

She ran to it and took it down.

"As I was listening," she said excitedly, "before we went to Singapore, remember, you were looking through those old atlases of Jerusalem showing some of the tunnels. . . ."

Adam nodded.

"I remember staring at the etching then, but it didn't register. But I just looked at it again and wondered—what if it is a map? A tiny portion of a map? Something made by de Payns and left as a clue at Chartres?"

"Yes!" exclaimed Adam. "That may be exactly the connection we've been looking for!"

"Except that the Templars never found the ark," put in Rocky.

"But who knows, Rocky—what if somehow they knew more than the world ever found out about? Juliet's suggestion is worth a try. With the laser scan of the underground network of passages and tunnels . . . *if* we can find a match with the shapes and angles of this engraving, then that will be where we will concentrate our search!"

thirty-three

High Tech to Solve an Ancient Mystery

(1)

As their Alitalia Boeing 757 touched down at the Ben Gurion Airport outside Tel Aviv, Juliet and Jen's hearts were pounding with a sense of mystery and antiquity. They were landing in *Israel!* This was the land of the prophets, the land of Jesus . . . and the land of the future!

They checked into Jerusalem's Renaissance Hotel an hour later, settled into their rooms, and met again at three for an initial drive about the city, with Adam as tour guide. Everyone was anxious to see the old city walls and some of Jerusalem's eight famous gates.

The following morning, as they partook of a bountiful Israeli breakfast downstairs in the dining room, Adam explained the plan for the day.

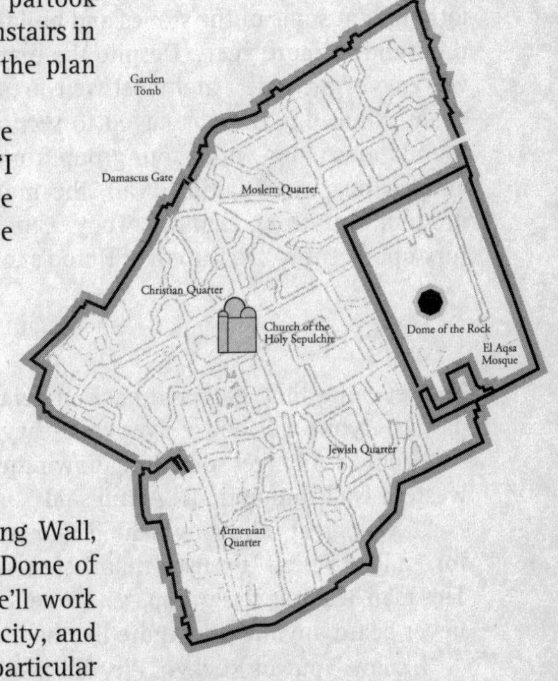

"We'll do a walking tour of the old city this morning," he said. "I know you're anxious to get into the heart of it. I'll take you through the Dung Gate—"

"Dung Gate! What on earth is that?" asked Juliet.

"In Nehemiah's day there were eleven gates in Jerusalem. Near the southwest corner of the wall was the Dung Gate, used when disposing of refuse and other waste. From there we'll walk to the Wailing Wall, then to the Temple Mount and the Dome of the Rock and the Mosque. Then we'll work our way through the rest of the old city, and I'll show you some of the sites of particular interest—the Via Dolorosa, St. Anne's, the pool of Bethesda, the Church of the Holy Sepulchre—"

"It's so exciting," interrupted Juliet, unable to contain herself.

Adam laughed. "Then this afternoon—see what you think about this—if I can get passes for us, I thought we could take the walk through the western wall tunnel to get a first impression of some of the underground regions."

Within the hour they were off again, arriving first at the Dung Gate. They walked through the inspection point into the old city with eyes full of wonder. Even being questioned and having bags examined by soldiers with guns couldn't dampen their enthusiasm.

Two hundred feet ahead rose the famous Wailing Wall. The large, open, paved plaza was already filled with tourists and praying Jewish faithful.

"There's the entrance to the foundation tunnel where we'll go later," said Adam, pointing to a nondescript door in one of the stone buildings bordering the plaza, where a half-dozen or so guards stood. "But first let's walk up to the Temple Mount," he went on, pointing to the walkway leading around to the right of the plaza. He led the way and the others followed.

"Remember," said Adam as they went, "both the Dome of the Rock and the Al-Aqsa Mosque have stood for more than a thousand years. It was in this very mosque that the Templars established their headquarters. That's where their explorations began."

Antiquity surrounded them everywhere they walked. It was difficult to fathom that some of the stones and buildings and walls had not changed in a thousand or more years. Despite the many wars that had raged over it, this was one of the oldest and most well-preserved cities on earth.

Later that day they managed to secure permits to walk the western wall foundations along with a tour group from the United States. From where they entered near the Wailing Wall, the moment they made their way underground, everything changed. They seemed literally to be walking back century upon century, to the era of Herod's temple when Jesus walked the earth.

(2)

That evening they gathered back in Adam's room to compare notes on the day. Everyone was abuzz over what they had seen.

"I could really feel something down there when we were walking along the western wall foundation," Adam said.

"It was great following behind that small group led by the American pastor," added Juliet. "I sensed that there was more involved than mere tourism. The man leading the group, as I listened, seemed unusually dynamic. I've never heard anyone pray quite like he did."

"I know," put in Rocky. "We will probably never see any of those people again. Yet I could not help feeling that our presence with them was not accidental, that in some way they were helping prepare the way for us."

"And those intriguing passageways leading off into the blackness on both sides," said Jen. "Is that where we'll be going later?"

"Who knows," replied Adam. "We have to wait to see what—"

The telephone rang. Adam answered it. The message was brief.

"That was the lobby," he said excitedly. "Scott and Lee-Hia Kiang's team just arrived. They are checking in now downstairs!"

Everyone was on their feet in an instant and flying down the hall toward the elevators.

From the reunion that took place a few minutes later, an observer would have assumed the parties involved lifetime friends who had been separated for years. In fact, half of those involved among the two Americans, one Swede, three Brits, and five Singaporeans had never met, and Scott had been gone from the rest of his team less than two weeks. The jubilation of the western welcoming committee was heightened more by Scott's enthusiastic report.

"Lee-Hia Kiang is really something!" he said as he and Adam shook hands. "He's got the thing sussed out. I have a feeling I'm out of a job as your technical expert."

"Not a chance!" Adam said, laughing. "But I'm glad for his help along with yours. Lee-Hia Kiang!" he said, now greeting their new Singaporean colleague who approached from the hotel desk. "How good to see you again."

"And you, Adam. Hello again, Miss Halsay," he added to Juliet. "So . . . when do we start?"

Adam laughed once more. "You are eager. But I want you to meet the rest of my team."

Introductions all around followed, with interpretations, smiles, and multiple handshakes.

"Where is the equipment?" asked Adam. "Did everything arrive intact?"

"We airfreighted it to arrive a day ahead of us," replied Kiang. "It was waiting at Ben Gurion. Everything is outside in our vans."

"Good—Scott, Rocky, shall we begin unloading and getting everything upstairs?"

"What's the room situation?" asked Scott.

"We have two large adjoining suites, as well as private accommodations for everyone. We've been unloading our equipment and computers in one of the large rooms. We'll have to coordinate everything. First let's get your boxes up there. I think we should handle that ourselves and not involve the hotel staff."

As soon as check-in was complete and the Singaporean contingent had taken their own bags and belongings to their room, the men met downstairs with hand trucks and carts borrowed from the hotel. Within forty minutes all the boxes were safely up in the two suites.

✦ ✦ ✦

The next day they began setting up command headquarters in the two large suites in the hotel, getting computers ready and software for the two systems interfaced and running smoothly. Scott, Rocky, Adam, and Lee-Hia Kiang's four colleagues unpackaged the largest and most delicate of the laser equipment. By day's end, the computers were operational and the place had taken on the look of an Adam Livingstone research base with a decidedly Far East flavor.

The three women, however, were especially glad for the deluxe accommodations rather than tents in the bush! This was the sort of field work they could deal with.

Anticipation began to mount.

(3)

Anni D'Abernon had never felt so disturbed and anxious in her life.

Something big was up!

She sat before the crystal that had never failed her before, chanting low incantations and summonings, rocking back and forth in the candlelit semidarkness of her private chamber. These were desperate times, but never had the Dimension been so quiet.

She had removed her clothes so as to strip away from herself the slightest earthly hindrance to that ancient communion she sought. She now sat upright before the eerie light, eyes closed, softly crooning weird cadences from another time, another world.

Something caused her to open her eyes. An unconscious glance darted toward her safe. A chill swept through her. She would *not* consult that object again! With determination she forced her face back toward the crystal. She must not allow her focus to divert from that world from which she gained her power.

Again chanting flowed from her mouth.

Several minutes passed.

Suddenly her body trembled, shook for several seconds, then warmed. A smile came to her lips, though her eyes remained closed. The welcome Presence had returned! Heat surged through her legs and arms and neck, then through her entire body. Her lips began to quiver.

"J . . . Je . . ."

The Presence was attempting to speak. She relaxed, yielding to its Dimensional influence.

"Je . . . Jer . . ."

A single jolting word exploded from her mouth in a masculine voice of antiquity.

Jerusalem!

D'Abernon's flesh trembled from head to foot. Again a chill swept through her. Then her body went limp and she collapsed back in her chair, breathing in and out heavily.

She sat a few minutes in darkness. Gradually she calmed.

She rose, dressed, then turned on the light and went to her desk.

The Dimension had spoken. But she hated all thought of the place. But it had been given her, no doubt by her very ancestors who had been there. Was some evil design of the enemy's about to break? Was she being given instructions about completion of the quest in which her forebears had failed?

She contemplated this for some time.

This was a definite warning. The enemy was active. Something was about to happen in the ancient city where the war had culminated between her master and his enemy.

She reached for her private telephone. The connection took but a matter of seconds.

"Rupert," she said, "the enemy is on the move. We must summon the Eleven. Meet me in Jerusalem. A climax approaches."

A response followed, then a question.

"No longer can there be any doubt," she replied. "I will be at the Renaissance."

(4)

Sir Gilbert Bowles, meanwhile, had been beneath Jerusalem's holy mountain twice, with a sleazy Arab so-called *guide* to the secret excavations. Bowles had been forced to pay him twenty times more than he was worth.

He had a good mind to try slipping into the entrance on his own. Now that the guards were used to him, he might be able to pull it off. But he would accompany the fool called *Sarsour* once more first, thought Bowles. The man did possess a wealth of information, and *said* he knew the whereabouts of the Jewish ark.

Why hadn't he taken him there then, barked Bowles.

Because it was a long and treacherous way underground. If they were gone too long the guards would become suspicious.

"Then draw me a map, you idiot," rejoined Bowles in exasperation, "and I'll go myself. I don't care what the guards think."

Sarsour chuckled a low, evil laugh.

"You would be dead if you tried it, my foolish English friend," he said. "I am the only reason you are able to move freely in the Arab sector and in these highly secret tunnels. Even if you did manage to get in, you would disappear down some hidden cavern and never be heard from again. I tell you, the way is perilous."

"Bah, I don't know whether to believe anything you tell me!"

"Do you believe the rumors of other western adventurers who have come to Jerusalem and never been seen again?"

Bowles did not reply. In truth, he *had* heard the reports. He had better play along with this scum a little longer. But if he saw an opportunity to go it alone without getting his throat slit, he would take it.

(5)

After her talk with Juliet, Kim Shayne's life had not been the same. Feelings and thoughts she had never before experienced rose and fell in her heart and brain, causing occasional discomfort as well as unexplained outbursts of happiness. She didn't know what to make of it.

One of the effects of the former was the growing conviction that Adam Livingstone and Juliet should know about Gilbert Bowles and the photographs. And she needed to tell them of her own involvement in the mysterious affair and that Bowles had gone to Jerusalem.

She drove out to the Livingstone estate with the intent of telling them, only to discover that the whole team had left the country again. Their destination, however, she was not able to determine.

It was by a stroke of luck that she heard about Jim Lindberg's hastily arranged flight to Jerusalem, and its purpose. She went straight to Lindberg's office on the sixth floor.

"Mr. Lindberg," she said, introducing herself to her BBC colleague. "I want to know if you would like an assistant for the new Livingstone Jerusalem documentary."

"How did you hear about it?"

"I overheard Glendenning and Prentiss in my office—one of them mentioned it."

"I haven't spoken to either of them," replied Lindberg.

"I honestly didn't know there was anything secretive about it," Kim went on. "And I know about the project. I would like to be part of it."

"What's your interest, Shayne?" asked Lindberg.

"I suppose partially it's personal. I am interested in Jerusalem, and I know Livingstone and his fiancée."

"So do I."

"I have a strong personal interest. I don't have any credentials. I am just asking you, please, if you would let me be part of your team."

"I don't really need anyone else."

"I'll carry your bags and equipment if you want. I'll even pay my own way if I have to."

"You *do* want to go, don't you?"

Kim nodded.

Lindberg thought a moment.

"Well, I don't see any reason why not. You've done some good stuff. Maybe I can find a way to make use of an extra person. Sure, Shayne . . . I'll bring you aboard."

(6)

The following two days in Jerusalem were spent checking and testing the equipment, both in the hotel and out, and poring over every map and atlas of Jerusalem Jen had been able to get her hands on to determine the most likely regions of exploration. Adam and Scott divided the city into a network of grids four hundred meters square, each of whose latitudinal and longitudinal corner coordinates were entered into the computer program to provide base reference points for the later entry of information from the scanners. If everything worked as Lee-Hia Kiang hoped, every piece of data would be linked with pinpoint precision to the grid coordinates, thus allowing the complex program they had designed to produce a three-dimensional underground map of whatever hollows, cavities, tunnels, or other irregularities existed in the geologic structure of each grid, down to a depth of one thousand feet, far deeper than anyone felt they would need.

Pending final approval of the excursion into the highly sensitive airspace above the city, Adam made arrangements for a helicopter at a private Jerusalem helipad. If the government authorized the project to film the city, it would be according to a very strict flight plan whose every move, he knew, would be monitored.

The first tests were run with the Kiang Enterprises equipment by van. With Scott and Lee-Hia Kiang at the controls, they drove randomly about the city, pointing the invisible beam of the laser scanner out open side windows. It was admittedly a crude bit of work, but proved enough to tell whether the scheme had a chance of succeeding.

Back at the hotel, Adam, Juliet, Rocky, Crystal, and Jen clustered around excitedly watching the computer. As images began to come through on the screen, a collective shout went up from the group.

"What was that?" came Scott's voice over the mobile radio.

"We're cheering your success," replied Adam.

"Is it actually working?"

"Seems to be," replied Adam. "We're not really seeing that much. We were just excited to see anything. But the lines and squiggles are jerking all over the screen."

"We're in traffic, man!" said Scott, laughing. "I'm holding the scanner by hand like a radar gun. I wanted to make sure we were connected and coming through. We'll mount it on a tripod and stop every half mile, or wherever we can, and scan back and forth. We'll see if that gives us a decent reading."

✦ ✦ ✦

Twenty minutes later, the image on the computer screen came dramatically into clearer focus.

"Whoa, Scott–what's happening?" exclaimed Adam. "All at once you're looking great!"

"We pulled over and parked. The scanner's mounted on the tripod. How's it look?"

"Fantastic!"

"As long as we can keep from arousing too much suspicion with these police and military types."

"The image is two-dimensional," said Adam. "But I can make out definite patterns."

"Tunnels and excavations?"

"Hard to tell. But the data is definitely of save quality. I would say from here on we ought to record everything digitally into the system while you start a grid-by-grid scan."

"What do you think, drive around the perimeter of the old city?"

"Probably the best place to start. Try to stop if you can somewhere in each grid and take a reading with the GPS. We'll enter the coordinates into the computer, and you scan from that position all around you, trying to cover the whole grid as best you can, then move on to the next."

"Even the two-dimensional images may help, Adam," broke in Kiang's voice over the radio. "I'll have to take a look when we get back to the hotel. I'm especially curious because this will provide me the most thorough test for our Mars probe to date. So save all this data."

"Will do. I'm not sure about the readings in the middle of the old city you won't be able to reach with the van. But scan toward the central portions as thoroughly as possible. Pay special attention to the old burial sites and Solomon's mines out by the Damascus Gate–what is that, grids fourteen and fifteen–"

"Right–I know where you mean."

"–as well as the Kidron Valley on the other side. From the Derekh Ha Ofel you can get the valley to one side and should be close enough to get the Temple Mount in the other. Scott, you got all the maps you need?"

"Think so. If not, I'll let you know and you can bring them out to us. Come to think of it, we might be able to get a more accurate reading of that whole east side and the Temple area from up on the Mount of Olives."

"That's a great idea. You'd be less disturbed. Park across the valley at the Church of the Tears. That's a perfect panorama."

✦ ✦ ✦

By evening they had accumulated a thorough two-dimensional reading of density variations under about two-thirds of the city. Scott and Kiang were already discussing their plans for the next day to complete the grid patterns, as well as retrace their route to pick up a few gaps missed the first time around.

The next afternoon while the team in the van was still out, Adam bounded exuberantly into the command suite at the hotel.

"Hey, everybody—look!" he exclaimed, triumphantly waving a piece of paper. "The final permit came through. Scott," he said, taking the headset from Crystal and speaking into the microphone, "we got it!"

"What?"

"The permit to film the documentary. You're in the air day after tomorrow!"

thirty-four

Scanning for Clues beneath the Temple Mount

(1)

Jim Lindberg, Kim Shayne, and their BBC cameraman arrived at the Renaissance Hotel in Jerusalem.

After checking in, Kim walked toward the bank of elevators, while the two men began loading onto a cart the photographic equipment they did not want to trust to a bellboy. Kim waited absently as one of the two elevators descended from above to the lobby. As the doors began to open she heard lively talk and laughter from inside.

Suddenly there stood Adam Livingstone, Juliet Halsay, and a large man she did not recognize staring her in the face. Immediately their conversation came to an abrupt halt.

A stab went through Kim's heart to realize she was an outsider. No reporter's urge rose within her to know what they had been talking about, only the personal realization that the three were enjoying a friendship she could not share.

"Kimberly!" exclaimed Juliet, walking out ahead of Adam and Rocky. "What . . . a surprise!"

"Miss Shayne," Adam said, nodding.

"Hello, Juliet . . . Mr. Livingstone," said Kim, backing away into the lobby. "I know it is unexpected seeing me here like this, but I—"

"Jim—you made it!" exclaimed Adam, glancing behind Kim as Lindberg approached.

"All in one piece," replied Lindberg, shaking Adam's hand. More greetings and introductions followed. "I see you've already met the latest addition to my team," he added.

"Ah, so that explains it," Adam said, looking back in Shayne's direction.

"I was just trying to explain it to them," said Kim. "I would really like to talk to you, Juliet," she went on. "And you too, Mr. Livingstone, if you don't mind. That's one of the reasons I asked Mr. Lindberg if I could come along and help with the documentary. I have something to tell you that I think may be important."

"We came down for coffee and tea," said Adam. "Why don't you get settled in your room, then join us if you like? We'll be in the coffee shop."

"Thank you . . . I will."

✦ ✦ ✦

An hour later, the four sat with empty cups around the table where they had been talking for some time. Adam's initial caution at seeing her again had been moderated by Kim Shayne's openness. He could tell, as Juliet had earlier, that a change had taken place in the journalist. It was impossible to hold against her what had happened previously, though neither was he inclined to reveal the complete nature of their business in Jerusalem. All Kim knew about their intentions at this point was the plan to film the city by air. They would have to take Lindberg into their confidence before tomorrow, but Adam was not ready to go quite so far yet with Kim Shayne.

"Well, Miss Shayne," he said, "I am certainly appreciative that you have told us this, although it is puzzling, as you said, what it could be about. As far as Sir Gilbert being here in Jerusalem—I don't suppose there is much we can do about it. He said nothing about where he would be staying?"

"Nothing. Except that he thought he knew where the ark of the covenant was."

As they had when she had first told them of Bowles' objective, Adam, Juliet, and Rocky took in Kim's words calmly, with only subtle glances back and forth between them.

"And you have no idea why he would think such a thing, when everyone else seems to think I destroyed it?"

"No, Mr. Livingstone," replied Kim. "Apparently he believes you about it not being the real ark."

Adam smiled. "If you're right," he said, "it would be the first time Sir Gilbert paid attention to anything I said. And it would make him about the only one in the world who does believe me! If I know Sir Gilbert, he's got something up his sleeve."

Adam looked at his watch, then rose.

"I think we had better be getting back upstairs. We've got a few things to do. Tomorrow's the big day, and it's an hour till dinner. We will see you then, Miss Shayne. I spoke to Jim—you and he and Bridges will be joining us down in the dining room."

(2)

The day for the great experiment came. The sun rose bright and clear. It looked to be a spectacular day for filming—they might turn this search into a decent aboveground documentary after all!

Everyone woke at the crack of dawn.

Will it work? was the question on everyone's minds.

Scott, Rocky, and Adam, along with Lindberg and Bridges from the BBC, and the entire Kiang Enterprises team, were on the way to the airfield by eight. Juliet, Jen, and Crystal bustled about the suite, making sure everything was ready.

Three of Kiang's men set up in a van with a second scanner to follow the helicopter roughly from below, simultaneously feeding in additional ground data. Three separate computers would receive and record the information back at the hotel, by radio signal from the two scanners and matched to the detailed GPS map of Jerusalem in the computer, producing multiplicity and cross-checking accuracy with the previous ground scans.

Rocky and Adam saw the team aloft in the large helicopter they had rented for the occasion.

"Good luck!" shouted Adam to Scott and Kiang as they waved from the chopper.

"Radio the minute you're back and we'll start the—" called Scott.

His voice was drowned out in the roar of the huge blades accelerating to speed. A second or two later the skids lifted off the tarmac.

"Let's go, Rocky!" cried Adam.

The two ran for their waiting car and sped back to the hotel.

(3)

Kim Shayne had also risen early.

She knew more was going on than they had told her. She had been told by Jim Lindberg to "stand by in case he needed her," which he didn't yet, and she felt useless. It was a new and unpleasant sensation to one who liked to be in the center of things.

She was now walking along the wide Eliezar H. Kapian Boulevard away from the hotel. The morning was both quiet and full of activity. The bustling city was awakening to life all around her. But in her heart resided a strange calm. On the hill to her left, she looked up to see the entrance to the Knesset, Israel's Parliament building. She continued on, then wandered off down a pathway sloping to her right away from the sidewalk down into a large undeveloped area of trees and pathways.

Soon she found herself lost among rocky paths and olive trees, an oasis in the middle of the city. Her thoughts still revolved around the people with whom she had suddenly become involved. Ten months ago Adam Livingstone and Juliet Halsay—she didn't even know her name then—had only represented a story, objects to be made use of. Now they were people, real people . . . quality people, she realized, the kind of people she wanted to know on a different basis than for what she could get out of them . . . maybe even the kind of people she wished she might herself become.

A gnarled old olive tree caught her attention. She walked off the path toward it, felt its rough bark with her hand, and pondered its significance. How could these trees, which grew almost like weeds in this region, not remind her of the gospel stories that vaguely rose into memory from the undefined past?

Jerusalem had an effect on you, she thought. She had not even been here twenty-four hours. But here she was already thinking about the spiritual heritage of this place . . . and the One who had once walked here, and what Juliet had said about what she called her relationship with him.

Jesus, she found herself thinking softly, *did you really live and walk these streets and paths? Is everything they say about you true?*

She paused, turned away from the tree, began walking away, then added, *If you are real . . . please show me.*

(4)

As Adam and Rocky drove back to the Renaissance Hotel, they saw the huge helicopter arcing up above them toward the old city. Ten minutes later they ran into the suite–Rocky puffing, Adam's face aglow with anticipation.

"Hurry!" exclaimed Juliet the moment they burst in. "Images from the scanner are already coming through."

Adam ran to the computer, Rocky on his heels.

"Scott's on the phone," said Crystal, handing Adam the headset.

"Hey, it's looking good from here, Scott!" said Adam. "Where are you?"

"Just crossing about, getting the equipment working. How's it look?"

"Great. A little jittery every once in a while."

"We'll smooth it out. Kiang's pilot says he can go into a hold that will allow us to scan a grid area, and then move on."

"They won't be able to do that on Mars!" exclaimed Adam.

"I think they've got a slightly different arrangement planned for that application," rejoined Scott. "Have you superimposed any of these airborne images with the ground data?"

Adam questioned Crystal. She shook her head.

"Not yet," he said into the mike. "You just proceed to scan the grids. We'll juxtapose the coordinates later."

"Will do. We'll start with the Mount of Olives and Kidron Valley and work our way west, over the Temple Mount, the Mosque, the Dome. If the Arabs give us any trouble, at least we'll have that sensitive area done."

"If there is trouble, get back over Israeli airspace. I want you taking no chances."

"You got it, Boss!"

"How are Lindberg and Bridges doing?"

"Filming away out the other side of the chopper like they were doing a documentary of Jerusalem or something."

Adam laughed. "Two documentaries for the price of one!"

✦ ✦ ✦

For two hours there was nothing for Adam and the others in the hotel to do other than watch as the computers gathered the data. With every change in grid radioed in by Scott, Crystal opened a new data file to correspond to the change in coordinate location.

Finally Scott radioed in another message.

"We're going to land and take a break and fill up with petrol."

"You've got about two-thirds of the grids completed," said Adam.

"We ought to be able to finish it up in another hour or two."

"You want us to bring you anything?"

"No, we'll get a cup of coffee and sandwich someplace and get back up. It's going so well, I want to get it done before anyone gets too curious."

(5)

Fred Hutchins walked out of the IRS audit and exhaled deeply. It could not exactly be called a sigh of relief, but at least it was over. It wasn't as bad as his waking nightmares had led him to expect. They hadn't treated him like a criminal or put handcuffs on him.

The news wasn't good, but they would work out some kind of payment plan, they said. There would be no charges filed as long as he demonstrated a good faith effort to clear up the debt in a reasonable manner.

He walked back to his car, got in, sat down at the wheel, then stared straight ahead for several minutes. It was time he took care of the other item of pressing business in his life. Maybe with the audit behind him, at last he could face it. In a way it would even be harder.

But he knew it was time. He had to tell Lucille.

The drive home was slow. He was not looking forward to this. If anything had ever taken courage in his life, this was it—owning up to his own sin. Did any man, any woman ever enjoy that? Realizing what you were—and that it was ugly—was never a pleasant experience.

He walked into the house half an hour later. Lucille was in her chair in the living room. He greeted her and tried to smile.

"How did it go?" she asked.

"I don't know, not so bad, I suppose," he replied with a shrug. "I mean, they hammered me pretty good, but at least I'm not in jail."

Fred put his jacket away in the hall closet, then shuffled back into the living room.

"Would you like some supper?" asked Lucille. "I made a pot of soup."

"Uh . . . no, maybe after a while."

He sat down opposite her. "There's, uh . . . something I've got to tell you," Fred began. Lucille was looking him straight in the eye, but he couldn't hold her gaze. He brought his eyes back down to his lap.

"I'm afraid it's not . . . not pleasant," he went on, groping for words. "It's about something I've done that I'm not proud of. But it's happened, and it's over . . . and I can't live with myself anymore until I tell you."

"If it's the other woman, Fred," said Lucille, "I know about it."

The words jolted Fred like a fist between his eyes. Again he looked up, this time with an expression of bewilderment on his face.

"But . . . what . . . did Sally—"

"No. She said nothing. Although I knew she knew too."

"Then . . . how . . . ?"

"Wives can tell, Fred. They always know. Women have a sense when they are violated. They just know."

Fred began to shake his head.

"Lucille," he said, "I'm . . . I don't know what to say. I am so sorry. I didn't mean for it to happen. I would never try to hurt you."

"I know, Fred."

"It just . . . I don't know—*happened.* It's over, but I feel like such a heel. I never thought I'd be in a position like this. It's the kind of mess other guys get into, not me. But here I am."

It was silent a few moments. Fred was the first to break it.

"But then . . . if you . . . if you knew—why didn't you," he began again, "I mean . . . why didn't you say something, why didn't you leave me? Why did you put up with it?"

"Where was I going to go? We're man and wife, Fred. No unpleasantness changes that, not even an affair."

"But what are we going to do now . . . I mean—do you want me to leave?"

"We'll go on, Fred."

"But doesn't this change everything . . . for you? I mean, how can you—"

"What does it change? We knew we had problems and we're human like everyone else. Like I said, we're still husband and wife. Maybe a little more bruised. But God loves us just like we are, even in the mess we're in . . . we'll get through it."

"You'd stay with me, even if we lose everything? The bank may take the house, you know."

"I made a vow, remember—through thick and thin, for better or worse, richer or poorer? I can live without this house."

"The situation's really bad, Lucille. I don't want to put you through anymore. I think maybe you'd be better off—"

"Don't even say it, Fred. I will never leave you. And besides, we won't lose everything."

"What do you mean? It looks like the audit's going to cost sixty-five hundred in taxes. Then with the charge cards and the house payments, it's up close to thirty grand. I've really messed us up, Lucille—we're tapped out. There's nothing left. I've blown it big time. If the bank doesn't take the house, the IRS will."

Lucille rose, wincing as she stood, then walked across the room. Puzzled, Fred rose to follow her, giving her his hand as she made her way to the bedroom. He watched as she opened her dresser and took an envelope out of the back of one of the drawers. She led the way back into the living room, then handed him the envelope and sat down again.

"What . . . what is it?" he asked.

"Savings bonds," she replied. "My mother and father bought them for me when I was in college. I know it's not supposed to be a very good investment. But they matured four years ago. I've been saving them for the right time."

Still baffled, he looked inside the envelope. There was a thick clump of what appeared twenty or more certificates.

"I think they're worth twenty or thirty thousand dollars," said Lucille.

Fred drew in a gasp of astonishment. He began thumbing through the notes. Most had a face value of one thousand dollars, although a few were higher.

"But . . . you would do this . . . for me . . . after all—?"

"Of course, Fred. I love you. I didn't marry you because you were perfect, but because I loved you. Everybody has hard times, Fred. We're no different. We're in this together, and we'll get through it together."

"But even after what I've done?"

Fred still held the notes and envelope, incredulous not only at the sudden turnaround but at Lucille's forgiving spirit.

"I know it hasn't been easy for you, with this sickness of mine," she said, "and the financial pressure. I don't hold it against you, Fred. You're the man I love."

Finally Fred could take no more.

His eyes swam with tears. The notes dropped to the floor. Lucille rose again from her chair and took him in her arms as he came toward her. He began to weep as he had never wept in his life.

"I am so sorry, Lucille," said Fred. "If I could only make you know how sorry I am. I can't believe how stupid I was. I'm sorrier than I can possibly tell you. I just . . . lost my perspective."

"Like I said, we'll get through it."

"I feel so horrible to have deserted you when you needed me most. I know I don't have the right to expect it, but can you ever forgive me?"

"Fred, I forgave you when it was happening."

"Weren't you hurt?"

"Of course it hurt. But there are worse things in life than that. I knew you were hurting too. Sometimes I was angry with you. But that didn't keep me from forgiving you."

"But . . . why?"

"I made a commitment to you. It wasn't based on how you might or might not treat me."

They stepped back and again sat down. Slowly Fred's tears subsided.

"I'm going to the doctor tomorrow, you know," said Lucille, trying to help ease the conversation in another direction. "I really think this new medication is helping. I'm sure I'm feeling better."

"You seemed to be walking a little easier."

"I felt pretty good today."

"You know something else," said Fred after a minute, "I'd like to ask if you'd go with me . . . I think we ought to go to church this Sunday. Maybe start reading the Bible too."

"I'd like that, Fred, especially if we were doing it together. I think it really might help."

"Whatever time we've got left together, I want us to make the most of it. I know I can never make up for what I've done. But with God's help, and yours, I want to turn my life around and start doing things right for a change."

(6)

While the helicopter was on the ground, Juliet, Jen, and Rocky went out to get lunch to bring back to the suite. Crystal and Adam remained behind. Crystal immediately began downloading the new information into the external hard drive where the backup data was being kept.

"All right if I try to start putting some of the samples together?" she asked.

"You bet," replied Adam. "Let's see what happens."

"Kiang's guy is the sharpest computer whiz I've ever met," she said as she sat down at the third computer and began to open some of the previous files. "If they are successful with this Mars probe they're working on, it will be amazing. It's thanks to the program he's developed that this plan of yours may work."

"*May* work!" said Adam, chuckling. "Don't you have any more confidence in me than that?"

"I'll ignore that. OK, we need to feed in the coordinates. Each of the preset grids is in a separate file. Let's put in all the information for one grid and I'll show you what happens."

She punched in a series of commands, waited for the downloading from the morning's input to be completed, then turned toward Adam.

"All right," she said. "In here, grid by grid, we've got all of the ground read-

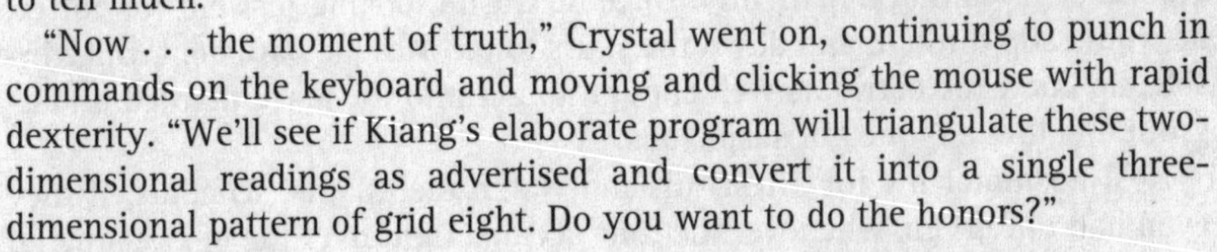

ings Scott took by van. I've just added the recent scans. I'll pull up one of the grids—any requests?"

"Number eight," replied Adam without hesitation. "The Al-Aqsa Mosque."

Crystal's fingers flew over the keyboard.

"I'll bring up the information from both scans out of the two data files . . . side by side in separate boxes . . . and—there we are."

"Yeah! I see what you mean. It's still hard to tell much."

"Now . . . the moment of truth," Crystal went on, continuing to punch in commands on the keyboard and moving and clicking the mouse with rapid dexterity. "We'll see if Kiang's elaborate program will triangulate these two-dimensional readings as advertised and convert it into a single three-dimensional pattern of grid eight. Do you want to do the honors?"

"Let me at it!"

"Press Command M."

Adam reached forward from Crystal's side and set his fingers on the two keys.

"All right, here we go . . . *Merge*!"

On the screen, the two separate images began coming together, slowing superimposing, then steadily merging into one. After three or four seconds, exclamations broke forth from the two witnesses to the transformation as a three-dimensional image came into focus before their eyes on the screen.

"Wow—I don't believe it!" said Adam. "It did it! A three-dimensional underground map. Where was archaeology before computers?"

"Wait till the rest of them see this!" chimed in Crystal.

"Just look at those tunnels and passageways, and—what do you suppose that is?" he added, pointing to one corner of the screen. "It's huge."

"An empty cistern, a storage room of some kind?" suggested Crystal.

"We'll have to analyze it later. But whatever these shapes and apparent corridors and open vaults actually represent, we now know that it is just as we suspected—an underground labyrinth that seems to extend everywhere beneath the city!"

(7)

That same afternoon, Gilbert Bowles made his decision. This was now twice that Sarsour hadn't shown up at the agreed-upon time.

His patience had run out. Didn't the fool realize what was at stake?

From here on, he would go it alone.

He would have to devise a means to gain access to the tunnels under the Mosque. But for all their security, these Arabs ran a pretty loose ship. Half the guards in this city seemed to be nothing but old shepherds with scruffy beards sitting on rickety chairs at various gates and entrances to holy or secure sites, most of them nearly asleep. He could slip by the idiots. That was the least of his problems.

He would appear at the usual place at the Mosque, ask if Sarsour had gone inside yet, tell the sleepy moron he was supposed to meet him here, then hang around as if waiting impatiently. Once he wasn't looking or went for coffee, he would slip through and down the stairs to the Mosque basement. Once inside, he knew the corridors well enough to get into the maze that led underground before anyone got suspicious.

He'd go tomorrow for a test run and watch the guards' schedule, if they even had one. Then, whenever the time seemed right over the next couple of days, he'd make his move.

He'd take food and water in case he had to stay underground all night. He'd roughed it out in the wilds many times under worse conditions. This would be a piece of cake.

He'd also better conceal a gun somewhere on him, just in case there was trouble.

(8)

The scene at the Renaissance Hotel in the Livingstone-Kiang suites late in the afternoon after completion of the scanning was one of exuberant semipandemonium. One might think they had discovered, not just tunnels under Jerusalem, but life buried in the interior of the planet Mars!

Crystal and Kiang's computer expert, Lek—whose English was fortunately as good as Kiang's—had their heads together at one of the computers. Everyone else was talking excitedly, hovering about and drifting between computers and printer, waiting for each successive scan, as they arrived about five to eight minutes apart, to come out of the printer. As each new image appeared, a half-dozen or more hands grabbed at it, anxious to see if the day's scanning would continue to produce images as spectacular as it had for grid eight.

To one side of the room, apparently heedless of the noise and hubbub around her, Juliet was poring over a printout Crystal had prepared of that initial three-dimensional merged image for the mosque area. Beside her on the couch sat an atlas open to a nineteenth-century archaeological map.

"Find anything interesting?" asked Adam as he approached and sat down beside her.

"I'm just checking our printout with this old map. As much as I can tell, the scanned image verifies most of what I can make out from the atlas. Some of the images are almost exact matches. But you have to go over every inch and compare the two. And them not being to the same scale makes it difficult."

"Ours seems more detailed," said Adam, taking the printout from Juliet and scrutinizing it carefully.

"And extends deeper below the surface."

"This really is amazing," said Adam as he continued to look at the newly created map. "Some of these things we try are so far out there that even I am astonished when they actually work."

"Am I visualizing it correctly," said Juliet, pointing to several places on the printout. "Doesn't it show tunnels and passages and caves that aren't in this atlas at all?"

"That's the way it appears."

"But how are we going to find the ark?" asked Juliet. "Even if we map every inch beneath the city."

"That's still the big question about this whole gambit," replied Adam. "Like you said, we'll have to go over every detail and hope we spot something."

(9)

Once the images were complete and dozens of copies had been printed covering all thirty-two grids of central Jerusalem, then the real investigative work began.

Every plot now had to be examined from various angles to get the full effect of the three-dimensionality. Adam realized they possessed the most thorough mapping ever produced of an underground maze even more vast than he had anticipated. Miles and miles of man-made and natural tunnels, burial caves, or what might be mere anomalies and air pockets within a very porous geologic strata, along with dozens of cisterns and larger cavities and caves—everything had to be analyzed.

Spread out over a half-dozen counters and tables throughout both suites, and hanging from walls and tacked to windows and mirrors, enlargements of all the maps, magnifying glasses, notepads and papers and more than two dozen different maps of Jerusalem of every conceivable kind, created a research scene unlike any Adam Livingstone had sponsored in his life. This was an archaeological "dig" that had to take place, for the moment at least, on paper and in the command center. Lee-Hia Kiang's team had been scheduled to return to Singapore by now. But Kiang and Lek were so caught up in the project that they remained on at the Renaissance with the Livingstone team after seeing their other three colleagues back to Ben Gurion.

"I am not about to miss the climax!" said Kiang. "I am part of this. The Mars probe research can wait another few days."

And indeed, he and Lek pored over the images, magnifying glasses in hand, along with everyone else. Every extra set of eyes increased the possibility of finding *something* that might tell them how to proceed and where to concentrate their efforts. In the meantime, Jim Lindberg, who had not been brought quite *this* far into their confidence because of the danger of potential media leaks, worked on the documentary footage with Shayne and Bridges in another suite in the hotel.

On the second day, Rocky set down his magnifying glass with a groan and a sigh, then rose to stretch his shoulders. "I know it's an investigation," he said, "and that's supposed to be my field. But I must say it would help to know what I'm looking for."

"You always tell me," replied Adam, "that sometimes you just have to keep at it, and wait for a clue to pop up in front of you. Haven't you told me that half the time it's not what you expect?"

"True," Rocky exclaimed, "but usually I have some idea where I'm headed!"

"This is archaeology, man!" said Scott, glancing up from across the room. "The science of the unknown!"

"Come on, Scott!" Adam said wryly. "You're making our profession sound like a guessing game!"

"And all this time I thought that's what it was!"

On the third day, there were more than a hundred printouts scattered about the room, representing the thirty-two grids enlarged further and divided into quarters. With everybody weary and bleary-eyed, the group began to rise and stretch and walk about the room. Rocky was thinking to himself that the time for a breakthrough in the case had better come soon.

"I need a break," said Adam. "Let's go downstairs and get some coffee and tea and something to eat. My eyes can't take any more."

No one was inclined to argue. The rest set down maps and pencils and magnifying glasses and began heading for the door.

"Come on, Juliet," said Adam, poking his head back into the room where Juliet still sat squinting over one of the tables. "We've put in enough for one afternoon."

"I want to finish this one up," she replied. "It's grid twenty-seven, the Damascus Gate area just outside the old city wall. I don't want to leave it unfinished. Go on ahead."

"You sure?"

"I'll be down in a few minutes."

Adam followed the others out of the room. They did not get more than halfway along the corridor toward the elevator, however, when a great shriek sounded from the room behind them.

Adam spun around and raced back toward the suite, half expecting to see Juliet facing either an Arab terrorist or a mouse scampering across the floor. Instead he found her flying through the room in an unexplained frenzy.

"Where's that drawing, the engraving . . . the one you took from Chartres?" she cried the instant Adam entered.

"In my papers," replied Crystal, running two steps behind Adam.

"Get it. Get it now!"

Crystal hurried toward the box of papers and notes.

Ten minutes later every head was squeezed together as they placed the two images side by side, the emblem they had scratched from the pillar in the Chartres cathedral, and the underground images of a maze of tunnels somewhere outside and deep underground below the Damascus Gate.

"I think it is a perfect match," said Juliet. "I'm sure of it. Can't you see it—look!"

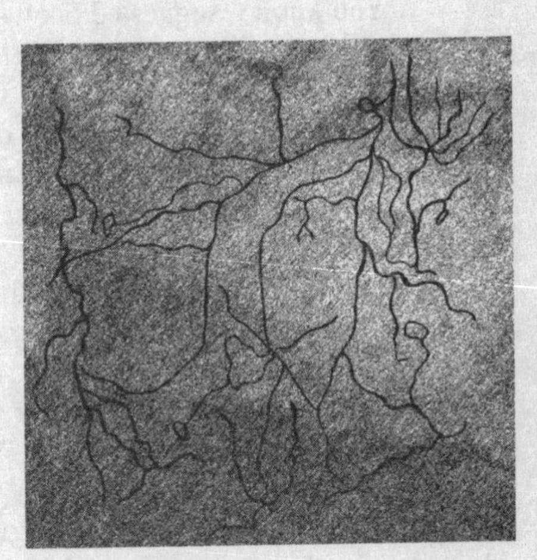

Adam took the two images in his hand, held them up toward the light of the window, superimposing one over the other.

"It's hard to tell," he said. "They're different sizes and slightly different angles . . . but it certainly could be."

"Let's enlarge the Chartres drawing to the same size," suggested Scott.

"Give it to me," said Jen. "I'll go enlarge it on the copier."

"And I can probably alter the angle of the computer image," said Crystal, "to correlate it to the same angle as the drawing."

"Let's do it!" said Adam. "Coffee break officially postponed!"

(10)

Thirty-five minutes later, everyone in the room—newly energized as they hadn't been since the day of the laser scan—was satisfied that there could be no chance of mere coincidence. The correlation was too precise for the Chartres drawing to be anything other than intentional.

"The shapes exactly correspond to these tunnels at the point where they connect," said Rocky.

"Do you really think de Payns made the engraving?" asked Crystal.

"Do you think," added Jen, "that he was leaving a message for those who came after him and knew what to look for?"

"I do think so," replied Juliet. "Can't you just feel it?"

"But what's the connection with *our* scan?" asked Kiang.

"Obviously, if Juliet is right," replied Adam, "then it means that de Payns found something in Jerusalem after all, and left a clue at Chartres as to its—"

"Who is de Payns?" asked Lek.

Two or three of the others laughed.

"A long and involved story," said Adam. "We'll tell you about it . . . sometime when you have four or five hours! In brief, he was a pilgrim here to Jerusalem in the twelfth century that we suspect might have been on the trail of the ark of the covenant."

"And you think he left you this drawing as a clue?"

"That's what we hope—and that we may just have discovered the location he was pointing to with his engraving."

"Like a treasure map that no one knows how to decipher," added Rocky.

"Exactly."

"You know," suggested Scott, "we could drive back out there and do a more detailed scan of this area. It might not give us any more than we have here. But it's a possibility."

"What's that tiny little image down there?" said Jen, pointing to the spot they had been examining on the quarter-grid map.

Adam grabbed a magnifying glass and bent down to the table for a closer look.

"Is it just my imagination," he said half to himself, "or . . . ?"

He stood away momentarily, his face registering the question, then bent down quickly again.

"No, it's too incredible! There's no way we could actually *see*—"

"Give me that," exclaimed Rocky. "Let an investigator analyze the evidence!"

Adam handed him the magnifying glass, standing back from the table shaking his head, not believing what had just entered his brain. By now everyone else was clamoring around Rocky for a closer look.

Finally Rocky brought his big frame back up from the table and looked at Adam.

"I don't know, Adam," he said. "I see what you mean . . . you can *almost* see something."

Adam nodded. "Something that the imagination says *might* be an object buried deep in the middle of that chamber or air pocket or whatever it is."

"You know," rejoined Rocky, "now that we've come this far, there's only one way to find out for certain."

"Are you thinking what I think you're thinking?" said Adam.

"Yep—it's time this investigation went back out into the field!" said Rocky exuberantly. "And this time, I mean a true *dig*."

"Yes!" exclaimed Jen. "When do we leave?"

"You women don't think *you're* going," said Scott jovially.

"Of course!"

"It's too dangerous. This is Israel we're talking about. We could get into serious trouble."

"Don't even think it, Scott Jordan!" replied the Swede. "If you think for a second that you're leaving me behind—"

"Or me!" added Juliet."

"Are you part of this feminine insurrection too, Crystal?" Adam said jokingly, smiling at his secretary.

"I'm not sure," she answered. "I'm a little too old to be crawling around tunnels on my hands and knees. Maybe I'll keep the home fires burning back here."

"I'm glad to hear I don't have a total mutiny on my hands!"

"Well, Jen and I *are* going," insisted Juliet, "and nothing you can do will stop us. Besides, if we get caught, having women along will make a more convincing case that we're just tourists who got lost."

"No one will buy that for a second!" Adam said. "Tourists . . . lost beneath Jerusalem? No way!"

"Then we just can't get caught," added Juliet. "We're going!"

"We're getting ahead of ourselves anyway," put in Scott, who had picked up the map and was scouring it again. "Look, Adam," he went on, "if we're going to pull this off, we've got to find a way *into* the underground maze. Then we need to chart a course through this labyrinth that will actually get us to this location. That may be easier said than done."

"If *he* got there, and got back out again, then obviously such a route exists," rejoined Adam. "Unless I miss my guess, his point of entry would have been from the Templar headquarters beneath the Mosque."

"We obviously can't get in there."

"Then we'll have to find somewhere else to get in that will link us up with the same tunnel."

"With these maps from the laser scans," said Jen, "it's a matter of finding a continuous pathway through the labyrinth."

"Like one of those children's maze games with a start and a finish," added Juliet. "We have to connect the two."

"Looks like it's back to the maps!" said Rocky.

Lek was already ahead of them. He had gone back to the original stack of thirty-two maps and now began pulling out several of the perimeter grids and arranging them alongside one another on the floor.

"You've got something in your head, Lek, I can see that," said Adam. "But what?"

"You must get in from a low spot," replied the Singaporian. "Some location in one of the surrounding valleys."

He completed the arrangement, then stood and stepped back.

"Look—the Tyropoeon Valley, the Transversal Valley, and the Citadel Valley are all too central. They run straight through the middle of the city. And the Citadel is too far from your objective over here."

As he spoke he was pointing with animation to the various locations, showing that he had already gained a remarkable grasp of Jerusalem's topography.

"What about the Beth Zertha Valley?" suggested Scott. "That's exactly where we want to be."

"Too central and congested," replied Lek. "Don't you remember what it was like when we drove through there?"

"*And* in the very middle of the Muslim quarter," added Adam.

"And everywhere else in the old city sits atop the ridges," Lek went on. "Therefore, we must examine the perimeters, especially the Kidron Valley."

"Good thinking, Lek!" exclaimed Adam.

"But the Kidron is on the opposite side entirely from the Damascus Gate," now said Scott, who had been following Lek's reasoning carefully.

"Yes, but it is the lowest point in Jerusalem, and reasonably undeveloped and deserted."

The room quieted as they considered Lek's proposal.

"I like it," said Adam at length.

"And look," Lek went on, "many of these tunnels appear to approach close to the steep slope of the hillside. If we could find a spot far enough north that took you under the Beth Zetha Valley and avoided the Temple Mount area—"

"Perfect," said Adam, bending to his knees and beginning to peruse the maps of that area more closely. "Away from the public eye."

"I don't like to dampen your enthusiasm," said Scott, "but we're still talking about the Arab quarter."

"That can't be helped," rejoined Adam. "Our objective is in the Muslim sector too. We will just have to be very, very careful, and plan our clandestine little excursion for a time when no people are around."

"First we've got to find your means of entry," said Kiang.

"Crystal," said Adam, "print up another batch of the enlarged quarter-grid maps for the Kidron Valley between the Temple Mount and the Mount of Olives. OK, everyone, let's solve this puzzle and plot a course through this maze."

thirty-five

In the Steps of the Prophet

(1)

Thirty-six hours later, alarms rang almost simultaneously in eight rooms of the Renaissance Hotel. They all read 2:00 A.M.

The members of the Livingstone team had made use of their own clocks rather than the hotel's wake-up service so as to arouse no suspicion. A brief meeting followed in the command suite, where already Crystal and Lek were warming up the computers and Rocky had three pots of coffee and hot water brewing, and several thermoses standing by.

As they talked they proceeded to consume as much coffee and tea as possible. Despite only five or six hours of sleep, everyone was keyed up and excited for what the day might hold.

"We'll track your movements," said Crystal, "and try to keep you on course. But what if our radio contact breaks up once you're underground?"

"Then the maps will have to be enough."

"You've all got your torches, extra batteries, water—"

"Yes, Mum, we've got everything," replied Jen in fun. "Don't worry, Crystal—we'll be fine."

"I don't want any of you getting lost down there," replied the secretary. She had been part of dozens of Livingstonian adventures. But she couldn't help being nervous. There had never been one in the heart of such a politically explosive area. "And the cameras?"

"Yes, we have the cameras, *and* food, *and* warm clothes."

"Just be careful."

"We promise," said Juliet, giving Crystal a hug for reassurance.

They made their way downstairs and out to the waiting van one at a time—separated by several minutes and using several different of the hotel's doors—out into the cool night air. When all were present and accounted for, Lee-Hia Kiang climbed into the driver's seat. Slowly they pulled out of the parking lot and toward the old city and their immediate objective, the Kidron Valley.

The previous day's efforts poring over the maps had paid off.

They had located what looked to be the end of a disused, and hopefully dry, drain that had apparently at one time emptied into the Kidron from one of the northern branches of Hezekiah's water system, but in the intervening centuries had been covered and blocked up by dirt and rocks and lost to view. If they were successful in gaining entry, they would follow the drain into the hillside west where it connected with a network of larger tunnels. There they would turn right, and from that point their route would take them roughly northeast in the direction of the Damascus Gate. The entry drain was located away from the main Hezekian discoveries, roughly down the Kidron slope approximately halfway between St. Stephen's and the former Golden Gate. According to their scan, the tunnel ended a mere two or three feet from the surface, and appeared on none of the archaeological maps of Jerusalem.

Adam's conclusion was that it was probably among those of Hezekiah's tunnels completely forgotten and never rediscovered as was the rest of the system in the Middle Ages, when the Gihon Spring was once more brought into use.

Armed with the picks and shovels they had stowed in the van the day before, and guided by pinpoint accuracy with Crystal monitoring their position at the computer in relation to the hidden drain, they hoped it would be but a few minutes' work to break through the surface, clear away the surface dirt and rock, connect with the opening of the drain, and crawl inside. From there they would make their way on hands and knees to the larger tunnel with which it appeared to connect. Thus they hoped to gain entry to the labyrinth that would give them access to the invisible foundations of David's City.

(2)

All Jerusalem slept and the night was black when Kiang slowed along Derekh Ha Ofel, flicked off the headlights, pulled over, and stopped.

The van emptied noiselessly. Jen and Juliet carried food, water, and other equipment. Everyone was wearing loose-fitting trousers. All were bundled warm, knowing it would be cool underground. The three men lugged two picks and two shovels. All five wore backpacks. Adam and Scott each had headsets and microphones, as well as miner's lamps, built into their hard hats, linking them verbally to Crystal and to one another. Both also had the small transmitters of Kiang's design strapped to their bodies, linked to satellite relay GPS with Kiang in the van. His information would be relayed to Crystal, by which she would monitor their position on the grid on her screen. Juliet,

Rocky, and Jen also wore compact helmets with built-in lights. Several handheld halogen flashlights were in the packs.

Kiang sped off. He would wait about a quarter mile away in case the expedition had to be aborted quickly. Adam led the way and the others hurried from the roadside and down the slope toward the valley.

"We're alone in the Arab sector," whispered Scott. "No turning back now."

"Let's go," Adam replied.

They crept down the rocky incline, doing their best to prevent pebbles and rocks from tumbling down in front of them.

"Crystal . . . can you hear me," said Adam softly into the microphone attached to his headset.

"Loud and clear," she replied.

"What do you make of our position?"

"Looking good. You seem to be moving straight toward the end of the drain . . . it's about a hundred feet ahead of you and slightly north."

"Scott, go on ahead. Guide him in, Crystal. We'll follow."

✦ ✦ ✦

Within ten minutes they had the site located, as close as GPS technology would allow. Juliet and Jen stood with their handheld lights encircling the three men as they shoveled and picked at the stubborn ground. They worked as quietly as possible, but their watchfulness revealed concern about the noise they were making.

After twelve or fifteen minutes, Scott's shovel broke through into a void. He was on his knees in an instant.

"Juliet, hand me the large flashlight!"

She did so. He probed the opening, grabbed for the shovel again, and frantically continued digging. After two or three minutes more, he scrambled down into the side of the hill, burrowing headfirst like a mole, and disappeared. The others waited. A minute later the thin beam from his helmet light appeared, then his head popped out of the opening with a big white-toothed grin.

"Come on," he said. "What are you waiting for?"

Jen needed no further encouragement. She took off her pack, shoved it in to Scott's waiting hands, then dove in after him.

"I don't know, Adam," said Rocky. "It looks pretty tight. Maybe you ought to radio Kiang and I should go back to the hotel with him."

"No way, Rocky," said Scott, reappearing again. "We'll clear out enough from the opening to get you in. Once inside, you'll have room. The tunnel's three feet all around, and shows signs of enlarging in the distance. You're part of the team, man."

As he spoke, Scott was banging and chipping away at the opening to make room for his American compatriot. After a minute or two of more digging he stopped and cleared away the debris he had created.

"Come on, Juliet," he said, "you're next."

Juliet took off her pack and handed it to Adam, then got on her knees, reached down, took Scott's waiting hand, and eased into the opening.

Rocky and Adam heard the two women's voices, muffled and distant, greeting with whispered shrieks of delight.

"I think you're up, Rocky," said Adam.

"Don't forget, I'm older than you kids. I'm not so sure about this. . . ."

"Go on, you'll make it. You can always change your mind if it doesn't work."

Again Scott reappeared.

"Get down on your belly, Rocky," he said. "Just crawl in. Nothing to it."

Rocky labored to the ground, then tentatively crouched and wriggled forward. The opening was barely wide enough, but slowly his body disappeared. The moment he had room in the hole to maneuver, Adam followed, pulling the last pick and shovel in with him.

The next voice Crystal heard where she sat in the hotel room was Adam's.

"We're in," he said. "We've managed to close up the opening as much as we can behind us. We'll leave the shovels here to get out with later. Scott's doing a little advance work up front–"

"Yes, I can see that his transmitter has separated from yours on my screen."

"It would seem the system is working so far, then. How about my voice–can you hear me all right?"

"The signal weakened a bit when you got underground. But I can hear you clearly."

"So can I on this end," rejoined Adam. "I suppose we'd better get to work."

(3)

The press conference had been called for 7:30 P.M. at the Knoxville Hilton, Larry Slate's hometown.

The peculiar time was in keeping with one known for activities generally associated with the night. He had scheduled it thus in hopes that many of his former colleagues would be there in person or else watching on television.

"I have a statement to make," began the publishing mogul when the cameras were rolling, "after which I will answer your questions. As most of you know, I have made my reputation and established my publishing business on the principle of taking advantage of other people's weakness–specifically their lusts and sexual appetites."

At the blunt words, already ripples of astonishment began to spread around the room. In less than a minute, several of the local stations, who had not decided to carry the press conference live but sensing a major breaking story in the wind, interrupted their regular broadcasts and switched over to the event as it was unfolding.

"For most of my life," Slate continued, "I thought there was nothing wrong with this. It was the American way, after all. I was not *responsible* for lust, lewdness, and exploitation of women. My publication was a mere reflection of our culture. Why should I not profit from it like others were? And by many such arguments I justified to myself that what I did was not wrong."

He paused reflectively, drew in a deep breath, then continued.

"But it *was* wrong," he said. "Our culture isn't wrong. *People* are wrong, because they take no personal account for integrity. I was the worst of the lot. Nothing in life was ever *my* fault. Our culture is sinking because too few are willing to take a stand for integrity anymore. So as I say, what I was doing was, plain and simple, wrong. And I would like to tell you how I came to realize it. A courageous man I had never met, a pastor from Oak Ridge, sent me a Bible. Enclosed was a short note that challenged me to take a hard look at my life, and encouraged me to read the book."

Slate went on to explain his initial negative reaction, which was inexplicably followed by a strange compulsion to read the New Testament account, which he did. He told of his encounter with Zacchaeus, how the story had shaken him, how he had contacted the pastor, of their talk, and then of their time of prayer together in which he had invited Jesus into his heart and made the decision to dedicate the rest of his life to God.

By now the room was abuzz with suppressed reaction, and a half-dozen or so of the listeners had already bolted for telephones to alert the major national networks, most of which, thinking it mostly a local event, had passed on live coverage.

"So the conclusion," Slate was saying, "is that I am announcing a change of direction for my magazine. I have turned over complete control of my company and its assets to the Christian organization known as the *Institute for Integrity in Journalism*. I have kept my home and fifty thousand dollars. Other than that, I have divested myself of all links to my company. The Institute may decide to continue publishing the magazine, with a different emphasis, or discontinue its publication altogether after its next issue.

"Furthermore, as is explained in the story of Zacchaeus, I am announcing my intent, so far as is possible, to repay fourfold those I have taken advantage of through my magazine all these years. Clearly I have not actually 'stolen' from anyone in a strict sense. But if we do not begin taking account for our motives with the same severity as perhaps we take account for our actions, it seems we are never going to get this country on the right track. That is one of the lessons I learned from my reading of the gospel account—that motives and attitudes of the heart count for more than we want to admit. I have been lying to myself about so many things since I was a young man, and I intend to put a stop to it. I must take account for what I have done. I *have* been taking advantage of people. Reparations need to be made. The example of Zacchaeus is one I feel I must follow. If the Bible is true, as I believe it is, then its precepts and instructions and examples cannot be ignored. I am well enough aware that tomorrow's papers will be full of accounts calling me looney and saying I have flipped my lid or that I 'got religion.' They can say what they want. But I assure you I am sane and feeling more alive and mentally vigorous than at any time in my life.

"Therefore, from the proceeds of my company, and working in conjunction with the Institute, I will initiate what I call *Operation Zacchaeus: Repentance and Restitution.* The plan is simple enough, and involves sending four items free upon request to anyone who has purchased a copy of my magazine at any time. A brief questionnaire will be included in the final issue of the magazine in its present format, which appears on newsstands tomorrow. Though there has not been time to change the entire format for this issue, it will obviously be much different than all former issues. A statement of my personal testimony will be included, and there will be no photographs. Those responding to the questionnaire will be sent, to begin with, a personal letter from me telling my story in somewhat more detail than I have told it to you this evening, a paperback edition of *The New Living Bible,* a copy of a book which has helped me understand this new road on which I have embarked entitled, *A God to Call Father,* and a pamphlet telling about the Bible and giving a Bible reading plan, entitled *Guide to the Book.*

"Beyond what I have outlined tonight, I have no future plans. What I will do, what direction my life and career will take, and to what I will devote my efforts, I do not know.

"That concludes my prepared remarks. I will now be happy to respond to your questions."

Two dozen hands shot into the air, accompanied by a clamor of voices shouting to be heard.

(4)

In a passageway deep below Mount Moriah, otherwise known as the Temple Mount, shadows from several flashlights cast eerie glows on the stones that had once led laborers into Solomon's quarries. Only six sets of human feet had trod this path since the ancient prophet's the night of the Babylonian invasion. That had been in the year A.D. 1121, and only one of those had lived to tell about it, and that cryptically.

They had been underground for three hours, penetrating ever deeper below the sacred mount, moving slowly and prayerfully, gradually growing more and more conscious of the historical import of their mission. Whether they were what would be called "lost" they did not pause to ask. It seemed an insignificant point. If they had made it this far, surely finding their way out of this labyrinth would not be a serious matter.

Only Rocky, the eldest and largest of the group, showed signs of fatigue. But nothing could dampen his optimism. Their clothes were covered from head to foot, especially around the knees, with dirt and scuffs.

Their way led in a generally northwestern direction, covering a distance, not as the crow flies but as a rock-burrowing mole might dig, of about a mile. In all, with curves and twists and ups and downs, they had walked probably a total of two or three times that distance.

Within the first hour they had passed evidence of excavation here and there. Then had come what appeared to be rooms or vaults. The precise angles and evenly lined walls raised the question whether they were of temple origins. But as they moved on these disappeared and again the walls and ceilings of the rocks lowered and enclosed around them.

Whenever an intersection or junction or other uncertainty presented itself, Crystal and Lek managed to keep them generally on the course they had planned. A few times their hoped-for route proved too tight for human passage, but thus far improvisation had conquered such obstacles and, with Lek and Crystal plotting their progress, they continued inching in the direction of the destination, down occasional stairs and steep inclines, now and then on hands and knees, descending deeper into the earth. Without realizing it, they were in fact following an approximate line directly under the original north-south ridge of Mount Moriah, and had passed under both Antonia's Fortress and the Via Dolorosa.

Then came again a wide tunnel of skillfully hewn stones. It led for perhaps a hundred and fifty yards, then gave way again to more rugged and natural surroundings. Walls and ceilings narrowed even more. Progress slowed. Nothing for some distance appeared man-made, although the tunnel appeared to have been dug by hand.

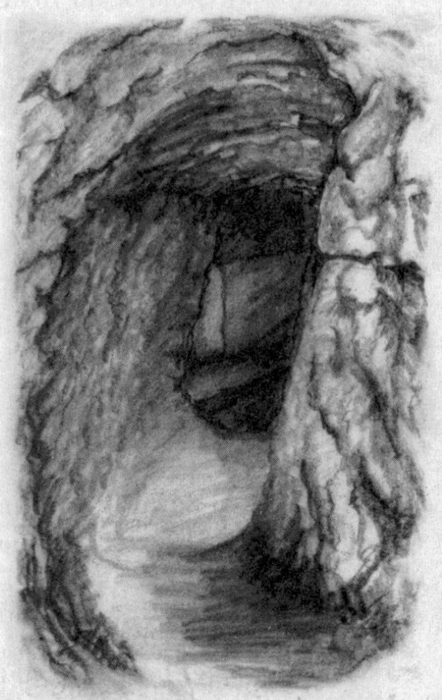

Then came evidence of quarrying—several large chambers off which led wider tunnels that had obviously been used at one time for moving great stones up and out of the earth. But this too eventually gave way again to cramped, stooping passageways.

"Solomon's quarries, would you say?" observed Scott, as they stood glancing around.

"Looks like it to me," rejoined Adam.

"According to the monitor, that is exactly right," said Crystal into the two earpieces.

"The Damascus Gate is now almost exactly west of you, I'd guess four hundred meters, Zedekiah's Cave north of you only about a hundred meters, and the Gordon Calvary site about five hundred meters northwest. You're also not far from Jeremiah's Grotto—"

The words sent chills through Adam's body as he recalled the writings of Baruch.

"The de Payn region is about between them," Crystal went on, "toward the Garden Tomb."

"All right, then," said Adam, "we'll keep on."

They began walking again in the same direction.

(5)

In the lead, Scott froze.

"Did you hear that?" he said.

"I heard something too," said Jen. "What was it?"

"I thought—"

He was interrupted by the sound again. This time all recognized the shout of a human voice.

They went dead silent, straining to listen.

"Could we have come up near the surface," whispered Juliet. "Could somebody have heard us?"

"It sounded like a cry for help," said Rocky.

"*Nobody* could be down here," said Scott, "unless . . . Adam, you don't suppose we've stumbled into some Arab archaeological dig!"

"That would be great! They'd bury us where they find us!"

"Shh—there it is again!" exclaimed Juliet. "At least I thought I—"

"Help . . . hey, whoever you are," echoed a frantic cry in English from somewhere ahead in the blackness, " . . . can you hear me . . . hey—I need help!" The sound was dim and muffled, but distinct.

Scott ran toward the sound. Following on his heels, Adam could not believe it—but he had almost recognized the voice, though the terror of its cry, and the dull underground reverberations made it difficult to be sure.

Scott had disappeared. The others heard him calling out and tracked his voice ahead in the passage.

"Hey . . . hey, keep talking so I can hear you," yelled Scott as he hurried ahead. "Where are you?"

"Here . . . down here," came the voice. "Hurry . . . down here!"

A minute or two later Adam saw Scott's light ahead. He crouched under a low arch.

"Careful!" exclaimed Scott, extending a hand toward him. "The path gives way. There's a treacherous drop-off. I almost tumbled down myself. Whoever's down there must not have seen it in time."

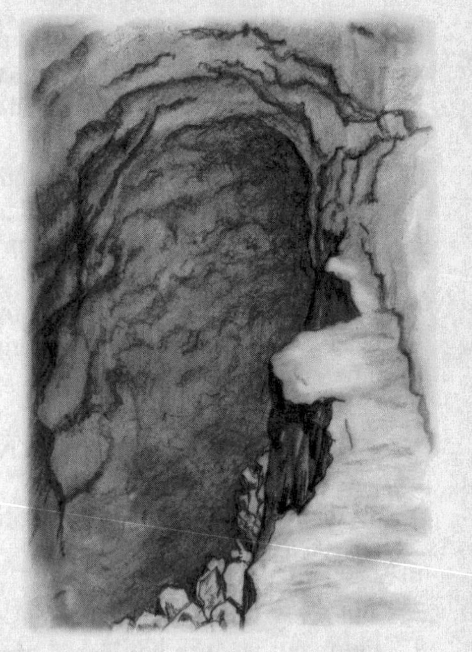

"Easy," said Adam, turning to Juliet as she, then Rocky and Jen, approached behind him.

"Jen, get me one of those halogen lights out of your pack," said Scott.

She squeezed forward and handed it to Scott. He quickly sent the beam panning and probing down into the chasm.

"Hey, quit fooling around up there!" cried a voice from somewhere below, clear and unmuffled. The next second Scott's light located its owner.

"I don't believe it!" he exclaimed.

"It's Gilbert Bowles!" exclaimed Jen.

By now several more flashlights had discovered the huge bulk of a figure half-dangling from a jagged ledge.

"Sir Gilbert!" cried Adam. "What in the world—"

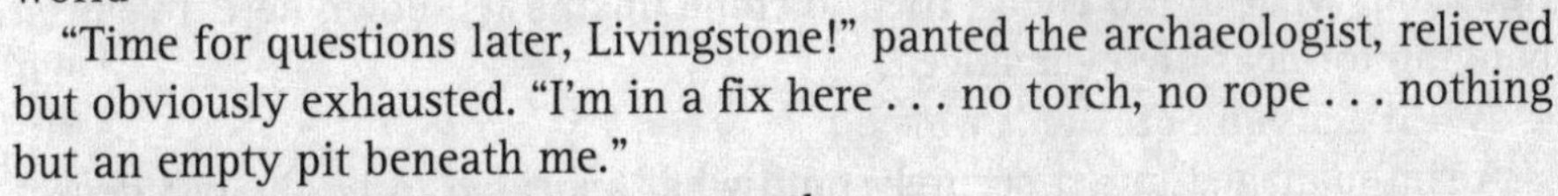

"Time for questions later, Livingstone!" panted the archaeologist, relieved but obviously exhausted. "I'm in a fix here . . . no torch, no rope . . . nothing but an empty pit beneath me."

Adam and Scott glanced at one another.

"We've got no rope either," said Scott. "Below him . . . there's nothing. He falls, it's over. I can't even see the bottom. It's a bad situation."

"We're going to have to go down after him," said Adam.

"And do what? The man weighs three hundred pounds. We'd need a hoist."

"What are you fools jabbering about!" growled Bowles. "I can't hang on much longer. I've already slipped from where I first fell."

"Hold on, Sir Gilbert. I'll get you," said Adam. He threw off his pack, helmet, and headset, and scrambled down over the side of the treacherous ledge.

"Adam!" cried Juliet.

But he was already on his way.

"Watch yourself, Adam," said Scott after him. "Remember how dangerous a drowning man is. If he grabs at you and you both fall, we'll never get you out of there!"

(6)

Adam slipped and crawled down the cliff-face, accompanied only by the lights from above. The voices of his comrades were silent. They watched his progress in terror lest the same fate would befall him as had Bowles.

How Sir Gilbert had ever stopped himself once toppling over the side,

Adam didn't know. There were precious few handholds, and the rock itself was prone to crack and crumble under pressure. He had never been much of a mountaineer and now wished he had paid more attention to some of its finer points.

Below him, his feet probed and felt their way in blackness, tentatively trying one, then another jut or indentation in the surface to see if it would hold him, then easing his weight onto it before shifting hand grips and inching down another foot or two.

After about five minutes, his feet reached the approximate level of Bowles' head. Slowly he tried to lower himself beside the big man so as not to come down right on top of him.

"How's it going, Sir Gilbert?" he said as he drew near.

"Not so good at the minute, Livingstone. I have to admit, I'm more glad to see you than ever in my life."

Adam could not help smiling to himself. "How long have you been here?" he asked.

"Don't know . . . hour or two," replied Bowles. "I fell awhile back. My torch and everything else disappeared down there. I sat for quite a while trying to figure out what to do. Then I tried to climb up and fell down here. I've been hanging for dear life ever since."

"We'll get you out. Don't worry."

Adam managed to get securely onto what appeared to be the last decent ledge before the sheer drop-off. One of Bowles' knees, bleeding slightly through his torn khakis, was managing to keep hold of it.

"Scott," Adam called up, "shine your light around—can you see anything below this ledge?"

"Looks pretty empty down there."

"I've got to get beneath him."

"You've also got to keep your footing!" rejoined Scott. "This is no time for foolish heroics, man."

"Sir Gilbert," said Adam, glancing about as best he could, "I'm going to inch down and get below you. When I'm in position, you put your loose foot on my shoulder and step up. You've got to get both your feet on that ledge your right knee's on. From there, you can climb back up the way I came. Scott will guide you with his light."

"Right—I appreciate the chivalry, Livingstone," said Bowles. "But don't be an idiot. You know as well as I do that I'm a heavy man. What if you can't support my weight?"

"You let me worry about that, Sir Gilbert. You just get up on that ledge. From there you'll be safe."

Another few minutes of silence followed. Very carefully Adam continued to descend around Bowles' body, gripping bits of stone with his fingers and one foot at a time, feeling about in the darkness below, his feet probing the surface like tentacles.

"There . . . good, Sir Gilbert," he said at length. "I think I'm solid, for the moment at least. Now put your foot on my shoulder. . . ."

Though he could no longer see Adam below him, Sir Gilbert moved his dangling boot about, feeling for Adam's shoulder.

"Ouch!" cried Adam. "A little more to your left, Sir Gilbert—that was the side of my head!"

"Oops, sorry, Livingstone."

"No problem, just . . . good, right—there you are . . . now you're on my shoulder."

"You sure about this?"

"No, but what else can we do . . . now ease down your weight."

Gradually Bowles' foot crunched onto Adam's shoulder.

"Aargh—Sir Gilbert," groaned Adam, "have you ever thought of going on a diet?"

"Sorry, Livingstone."

"Can't be helped. When you're steady, give one hard lunge upward. Give me a three-count so I'll be ready, then step hard and I'll shove while you hoist yourself up on that ledge. Got it?"

"Yeah . . . you ready?"

"Ready, Sir Gilbert."

"OK . . . one . . . two . . . three!"

Huge grunts of terrific effort echoed throughout the subterranean cavern.

With a lunge and push, Adam shoved down hard with his foot and up on his shoulder with every ounce of strength he possessed. At the same time, the again three hundred-pound booted foot of Sir Gilbert Bowles ground down into the flesh of his shoulder. Bowles pulled upward with what little strength was left in his arms.

But just as Bowles managed to scramble and claw his way onto the ledge, the thin piece of protruding rock under Adam's left foot gave way under the force of their combined weight. The four observers above heard a voice cry out.

"Adam!" Juliet screamed in terror.

The sounds of Adam's body sliding and bouncing off rocks and boulders mingled with the echoes of Juliet's voice, ending in a tumbling heap some fifteen feet below in utter blackness.

The sounds faded. The cave fell deathly silent. No one uttered a word. Several long seconds passed.

"Adam . . . Adam!" called Juliet again.

A faint groan of pain drifted up from far below. At least he was alive, they knew that much. But no words followed the dull moan.

"All right, Sir Gilbert," said Scott, "before we do anything else, you've got to climb back up here. Do you think you can do that?"

"Uh, I don't . . . yeah, probably—what about Livingstone?" said Bowles, peering down into the yawning abyss below him, obviously shaken.

"Just get up here, Bowles. You can't do anything for him there. Look—here's where Adam climbed down . . . I'll direct you with the flashlight. Just make sure your feet are steady, then pull yourself a little at a time."

Slowly Bowles began the upward climb out of his predicament, with Scott guiding him and talking him up to each new point of safety. In six or eight minutes he was sitting up on the pathway with the others. Juliet quickly got him water and something to eat. Bowles sat in a stupor, receiving her ministrations as a child, seemingly confused at the outpouring of compassion and care. His foot had just sent the young woman's fiancé down into the ravine and none of them knew whether they would ever see him again, and here she was taking care of him and tending to his wounds.

They could all see that Bowles' face was white as a sheet, from exhaustion but also in shock from the terrifying sound of Adam's fall. That he and his arch rival had so suddenly changed places had rocked Sir Gilbert Bowles' brain. No one had ever put himself so directly in harm's way for him before. He didn't know what to make of it.

Meanwhile, Scott had begun the precipitous descent up which Bowles had just come, guided as much as possible from above by light from Rocky's hand. Suddenly he stopped.

"Rocky, see if Bowles is wearing a belt," he said. "If so, get it. Take yours off too. Dangle them down to me. With three belts together, I can make a five- or six-foot rope. That might help."

Quickly Rocky obeyed, and Scott continued the descent.

He reached the ledge that had stopped Bowles' fall, paused to free one hand for use of a flashlight, then sent the beam of his light downward.

"Hey, Scott old buddy," said a faint voice from below. "I knew you wouldn't leave me to the rats."

"You OK, man?"

"My arm and one leg are banged up pretty good," replied Adam. "And I whacked my head on something coming down. I just had to sit for a few minutes and get my breath back and see if I could remember my postal code."

"You in pain?"

"Yeah, but nothing's broken."

"I've got three belts' worth of line. If you can climb up halfway, I think I can pull you up from there."

"Piece of cake. Just give me some time."

"Take all day, man."

"Keep talking to me—tell me a joke or something. You know . . . that one about the lady and her cat."

"Shut up, man. Let me do the talking—you save your strength."

(7)

It didn't take all day for Adam, bruised and bleeding in several places, and with a welt on the opposite side of his head from where Sir Gilbert's boot had kicked him, to work his way up to a point where Scott could begin helping him. Together and with the aid of the belts, Adam at last struggled up twenty-five minutes later to rejoin the rest of the team, where Juliet lavished him with kisses and hugs and tears of relief.

"Hey, how's it going Rocky, Sir Gilbert?" panted Adam, sitting down on the path, closing his eyes, and letting out a long breath of air.

"That's what we should be asking you," rejoined Rocky. "We're glad to see you back in one piece."

"Whew . . . I will admit that that was some bit of work."

"Oh, Adam," exclaimed Juliet, "your head and arm are bleeding."

"Women always notice the details, eh, Rocky?" said Adam, forcing a grin.

"Just let me put something on them," insisted Juliet.

They rested another thirty minutes, providing what limited first aid their supplies made possible to Adam's scrapes and cuts.

"I'm afraid if we sit any longer," said Adam at length, "I will get too stiff and sore to continue. We obviously can't turn back now. What do you say we get this show on the road?"

With a few groans Scott hoisted him to his feet. Adam hobbled to the front of the line and began leading back the way they had come, followed by Juliet, Jen, Rocky, then Sir Gilbert Bowles tagging along like a silent puppy, beginning to feel refreshed by the water and food yet awestruck at the sudden reversal of his fortune, with Scott bringing up the rear.

"Crystal, are you still there?" said Adam once they were under way.

"I'm here, Boss," she answered in his earpiece, "and relieved to hear that you are as well."

"Then get us back on the route, ma'am, if you please."

The party resumed its underground trek, Crystal guiding Adam to the right and left and forward, through many more intersections and junctions, more or less on the course they had plotted.

Then came an apparent impasse. The six stopped. The way was blocked in all directions, ending in a wall of stone. They looked about, on all sides and above. Scott retreated twenty or thirty yards backward to see if they might have missed an opening off to the right or left. Soon he returned, shaking his head.

"If we missed something," he said, "it must be a good way back."

"Crystal, have we taken a wrong turn?" asked Adam. "We seem to have reached a dead end."

"I don't understand," replied Crystal. "According to the screen, the passage continues."

"No way. It's blocked in every direction but behind us."

"Wait a minute, Adam–Lek is trying something with the other computer."

Adam's headset went silent.

"He's adjusting the angle of the image," said Crystal. "Hang on . . . he's got something for me to look at."

Crystal returned a moment later. "Adam," she said, "you're not going to believe this, but when we rotated the image around, we discovered a slight jutting to the passageway, a ninety-degree turn exactly where you are standing–but ninety degrees *downward*."

"Down!" repeated Adam, then addressed the others. "Any of you see anywhere the path could lead downward?"

They all looked at one another with confusion.

"Hold it!" Rocky said. "This rock under my foot is loose."

Instantly Adam and Scott were on their knees. Rocky stepped back off the large flat slab, which the back-and-forth movement of his feet as they stood waiting had imperceptibly loosened. Scraping away dirt and dust and smaller pebbles, they managed to free one edge enough to get their fingers beside it, then tried to pry it up.

"Come on, Bowles, Rocky," said Scott, "squeeze in here if you can. We need all the hands we can get. This thing's heavy."

Several minutes later, with the slab pulled aside, their flashlights probed straight down into a shaft which revealed a narrow stone stairway into yet a lower level of passageway. A gentle breeze of cool air, dank but seemingly dry, wafted up into their faces.

"That's it, Crystal–good work!" said Adam. "A ninety-degree change of course, straight downward! We would be lost without you up there at the controls."

Adam immediately began the descent, followed one at a time by his companions.

A few minutes later they were walking on the rocky floor–obviously manmade and well hewn–of the passage to which the stairway had led.

(8)

It was silent for some time as they went. Fatigue was overtaking them in earnest. It was clear that Adam's injuries were finally taking their toll. They now entered a region of ancient tombs.

"You know what these spaces are for, dug into the walls?" said Adam.

A few shakes of heads met his look, although Jen and Scott recognized them easily enough.

"This is an ancient crypt," he said in answer to his own question. "We're out beyond the city walls."

"Adam . . . Scott . . . ," said Crystal.

"We're here," answered Adam.

"According to our computer image and your locater, I think you're getting close. You appear to be moving straight along the passageway from the south, leading north. Unless you reach some obstruction, you should encounter de Payns' intersection in the next hundred or hundred and twenty-five meters."

"Hey, everyone, Crystal says we're close," said Adam behind him. "Get out your copies of the de Payns' engraving and keep your eyes open for anything you see that resembles those shapes!"

"We're getting a lot of rocks in the path," said Scott. "I hope these walls and the ceiling are stable. Looks to me like the effect of an earthquake."

"This is definitely earthquake country," said Juliet.

"Who's de Payns?" asked Bowles.

"Sorry, Sir Gilbert," replied Jen. "That story will have to wait. Let's just say he is the key to this expedition."

On they continued, anticipation mounted. Juliet inched forward, passed Scott, and wriggled alongside Adam in the tunnel.

"How are you feeling?" she asked.

"I'm pretty worn out. But I'll make it."

"Look—it's widening ahead!"

Juliet dashed forward, unable to keep from breaking into a run. Jen squeezed by the others and was after her.

"Careful," Adam called after them. "We don't want you falling down any more hidden chasms. One rescue a day is enough!"

As Juliet had said, the passage widened as they walked. Eagerly flashlights probed the floors and walls as the others hurried to keep up.

Suddenly Juliet's shrieks echoed in the tunnel.

"Here it is . . . here it is! Jen, look . . . Adam, Scott—we've found it!"

Even Adam now managed to break into a painful, hobbling run. In less than a minute they all stood at the conflux where several tunnels met.

"Look, Adam," said Juliet excitedly, running to meet him. "It's just like the Chartres map. There is the passage angling back to the right, and the other one going left right where this tunnel widens—"

"And does another veer off right a little ways beyond?"

"Oh, I forgot to check that!"

She turned and dashed off again.

"Don't trip over those stones on the floor."

Jen was already running back to meet them from farther ahead.

"Yes—the third passage is here too!" she exclaimed. "They all match the engraving!"

"So *that's* what you were doing in Chartres," said Bowles. "Finding a clue to this place in the cathedral."

"You were in Chartres too?" said Adam, startled.

"I confess—sorry, Livingstone. I overheard you talking about Jerusalem, but didn't know any of the details. That's why I came."

"Ah, well, no harm done. But if Hughes de Payns was leaving us a map," Adam went on, "then we ought to see a break through the wall just opposite the corridor to the left . . . right about—here."

"Yes!" exclaimed Scott and Jen at once.

The attention of the explorers now focused toward the wall on their right, which was partially broken through.

"It was obviously sealed up at one time," said Rocky, examining the wall around the opening. "This is some kind of crude mortar."

"And then broken through later."

"By Hughes de Payns?" suggested Scott.

"That would be my guess," replied Adam.

"Why are we standing around—let's get somebody through that opening!" said Rocky. His adrenaline was pumping at full throttle.

As they all spoke, Gilbert Bowles stood silently back, taking it all in, scarcely understanding a word they were talking about, still in a daze that *he* was actually a part of this Livingstone team. For the first time in his life, the thought of scooping Adam was the last thing on his mind.

"Come on, Sir Gilbert," said Adam, gesturing him forward to join the rest of them. "You're part of the team now. We're about to break the case wide open."

Scott was already in the process of hoisting Jen through the opening in the wall. Juliet followed.

"We'll have to knock more of these rocks loose," said Scott.

"Sir Gilbert and I can wait here," said Rocky. "You two go on through."

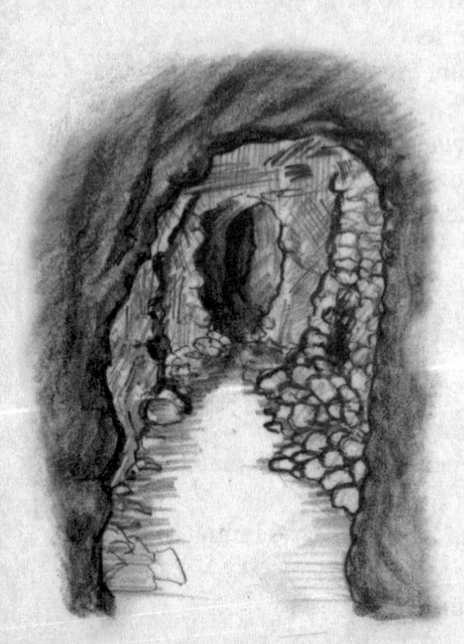

"No way," rejoined Adam. "Girls, stand back inside there, we're going to enlarge the opening. By the way—do you see anything in there?"

"Just rocks and debris," Jen called through the opening. "It looks like an empty cave."

Within a few minutes the opening was double its size, and with a little work even Bowles was able to squeeze through.

A short time later all six stood in the cave that had been sealed up by the prophet Jeremiah and discovered by Hughes de Payns and his ill-fated colleagues.

"This place was definitely hammered by an earthquake," said Adam. "Half the ceiling is on the floor."

"Look at these rectangular cavities dug

out of the rock," said Scott as they all glanced around. "This was definitely a burial tomb at one time. Unless I miss my guess, the tunnels out in the main passage lead to more of the same. I would say this was probably the mausoleum of a wealthy family."

Juliet shivered at the direction the discussion had taken.

"This gives me the creeps," she said.

"Don't worry," said Adam. "It doesn't look like many of them were ever put to use."

"We need to explore this cave thoroughly," said Adam.

"We'll leave that to you men," said Juliet, shuddering. "I don't want to stumble over any dead bodies."

"Even if you did," laughed Adam good-naturedly, "there'd be only bones by now."

Scott and Adam smiled at each other. Bones and crypts—that's what they liked best. They wandered about the cave, peering into its corners, making their way to the far end.

"Look!" said Adam, stepping over some large stones and shining his flashlight ahead. "There is a passage leading straight away from the opposite end."

"Let's go!" said Scott.

Adam led the way out of the cave and into the passage leading out of it. Gradually the slope of the path steepened downward. Ahead he saw the opening into another small cave. But the way to it was blocked by a pile of stones and rocks.

Adam glanced overhead.

"There must have been an earthquake," he said. "The ceiling gave way and obstructed this passage. We'll just climb—"

"Adam," interrupted Juliet. "Adam, look—what's that?"

Juliet pointed her flashlight toward an object protruding a few inches out of the pile of rubble.

"It . . . it looks like a wooden pole," she said. Even as she said the word, her voice began to tremble.

Adam was scampering up over the pile of rocks instantly, climbing on hands and knees, heedless of his injuries, and disappeared down the other side. The others stood in silence for several seconds.

"Can the rest of you hear me?" came a muffled voice. "I think you'd all better come see this . . . but very, very carefully."

Juliet now hastened after him, followed by Jen and Scott. Gasps of astonishment escaped several lips as they crawled over the stones and rubble.

Within a minute the four were squeezed inside a cramped room some five feet by nine feet, and no more than six feet high. Sir Gilbert and Rocky had satisfied themselves to observe from atop the pile of stones, but had not climbed down the other side. The two young women were on their knees, Scott and Adam ducking down.

The light from the flashlights reflected off the brilliant object partially buried in stones, and the tip of the acacia pole that Juliet had seen extended up and through the debris.

For several long minutes they stood and then knelt, staring in shock. Surrounding the ark, with the bony remains of their fingers around the two poles, were five human skeletons.

"Look," said Scott, stooping down and clasping something from near one of the skulls. "A crusader cross."

"They've all got them," said Adam.

"Is one of these Hughes de Payns?" asked Juliet, still unnerved at the sight of the skeletons.

"I don't think so," replied Adam. "He lived many years after leaving Jerusalem."

"He was obviously here," added Scott. "And left the engraved clue of the location at Chartres."

"The mystery solved," said Rocky.

"Not completely," rejoined Juliet. "If he discovered the ark, why didn't he tell about it?"

"That may be one mystery he took with him to the grave."

"Let's try to free the ark from this debris," said Adam after a moment, "and drag it back into this chamber."

"Be careful!" said Juliet. "Look at these crusaders!"

"Yes, we'll use the poles. You two stand back over there. Scott, give me a hand. We'll move some of these stones out of the way. Rocky, can you and Sir Gilbert pull down the pile of rocks a bit in your direction and try to dislodge that pole?"

(9)

Twenty minutes later, Adam and Scott had freed the ark and dragged it away from the pile of rocks and the five skeletons—careful neither to touch the ark nor disturb the bones of the crusaders—and back to the tiny crypt where de Payns and his companions had discovered it. The photographs had been taken. Now it was time to rest and simply contemplate the wonder of this day.

In awe, the six explorers sat around the sacred object in the middle of its twenty-five hundred-year-old grave.

"I know we're gazing upon it," said Adam at length, "but I can hardly make myself believe it." He shook his head in continued wonder. "I'm thinking to myself this must be a dream . . . that I'll wake up any minute and find myself in bed at Sevenoaks."

"If so," said Scott, "then we're all having the *same* dream."

"Do you suppose we're near Jeremiah's Grotto?" asked Scott.

"Very near it," answered Crystal, who had heard the question.

"We may even be in an offshoot of it," mused Adam. "The place may have been more aptly named than anyone realized."

They all recalled their research about Jeremiah's hiding things that had led them here.

"It is a priceless treasure," said Rocky, "though not because of the gold itself. This is truly a significant moment. Just think what this represents! Along with your discovery of Noah's ark, Adam, this validates the biblical account. The ark of the covenant is the most sought-after and treasured object in the history of the world. And here it is . . . right in front of us—or the most important part of it, at least."

"Truly remarkable!" said Juliet. "Adam . . . you did it."

"But consider the practical implications," added Adam. "We're surely under Palestinian land. Neither the Israelis nor the Arabs will believe us if we go public."

"They wouldn't believe us. Yet if we revealed the location," said Scott, "you can bet that the Arabs would instantly seal off the area."

"You're right," replied Adam. "Any statement would cause a great deal of trouble."

"Those are hardly obstacles to God," said Juliet. "This is *his* land, *his* city. He will reveal it when he wants to. But for some reason he has purposed for us to find it prior to that revealing."

"Obviously God wants to reveal it," said Rocky. "He *has* revealed it by leading us here."

Adam glanced up at Sir Gilbert. His expression was one of stunned disbelief. Slowly he began shaking his head, then spoke, half to himself. "You mean . . . it's all true," he mumbled, unable to comprehend the implications of the find. "The stories . . . the Bible—all of it . . . it's actually true!"

"It's true, Sir Gilbert," replied Adam. "The Bible is true."

"But . . . but all this time . . . I always thought . . . I mean, I've dedicated my whole life to disproving what I knew beyond a doubt was a complete load of nonsense. And now . . ."

"I was once a skeptic myself, just like you, Sir Gilbert, until the reality of Noah's ark upset my world and I knew God was alive and real and personal. This may be that moment for you."

"But the very thought . . . of such a being . . . I don't know what to think of it all . . . this . . . your saving my life . . . all that's happened."

"He has had you in his sights all along, Sir Gilbert."

For the moment Sir Gilbert's questions and confusions were silenced.

"I am feeling that we are to leave this place," said Adam after a few minutes, "and leave the ark here for the present at least. There is much to consider."

"What will you do?" asked Rocky.

"We may need to notify Israeli sources, whether they believe us or not," replied Adam. "Though it is spiritual in its significance, it is also a priceless historical treasure to which Israel naturally has undisputed right of possession. In any event, we will certainly have to pray concerning our next steps. I have to admit, I never thought once about what we would do if we actually *found* the ark. I think we should retrace our way as quickly as possible, and trust the Lord to tell us when and how we are to return."

Adam rose with a groan.

"I am stiff and sore! How are you doing, Sir Gilbert?"

"I've felt better. My body aches and I am hungry and tired. But I'll make it."

The others climbed to their feet.

"Scott, why don't you leave your transmitter there beside it? That way we'll keep a pinpoint on the location. Crystal," said Adam into his microphone, "do you think you can guide us out of here the way we came?"

(10)

Two hours later, Adam led his exhausted team to the end of the narrow tunnel into the Kidron Valley. Crawling the final thirty meters on sore hands and bruised knees was arduous for the two injured archaeologists, and especially for Sir Gilbert Bowles, whose size and physical condition nearly rendered the operation impossible.

Scott reopened the hole at the end of the drain with one of the shovels that was lying where he had left it, widening it as much as was practical in consideration of Sir Gilbert.

"I'll go first," he said as he crawled out. "If the coast is clear and Kiang is up on the road, I'll bring you out one at a time. If I'm not back in five minutes, close up the hole and wait until dark."

Carefully Scott poked his head out, then shoulders, looked about, then jumped up and back into the brightness of daylight, squinted to regain his bearings, then hurried up the hill.

He was back in three minutes. He jumped to his knees and called down into the hole.

"All clear!" he said. "But hurry—Jen, Juliet, you first—come on . . . get up to the van as fast as you can . . . Rocky, you're next—women and civilians first."

"Shall I bring one of the shovels?" asked Rocky as he crawled out.

"No, we'll leave them inside," replied Scott. "We can't go walking up onto that busy street there carrying a load of excavation tools. Adam and I will seal up the hole as best we can by hand with some rocks."

"Up the hill, Rocky. The van is waiting. Next!" called Scott into the hole as soon as Rocky was on his way. "Come on, Sir Gilbert."

✦ ✦ ✦

Thirty minutes later, the six weary pilgrims walked into the lobby of the Renaissance Hotel, appearing noticeably out of place in the high-class surroundings, their clothes grungy, some torn, and two of the men limping and with dried splotches of blood on arms and legs.

When they walked in, Jen shivered. "Suddenly I'm very cold."

"I noticed it too," said Juliet.

"Something's wrong—something's changed here since this morning," said Rocky.

"Let's get showered and changed," said Adam, trying to ignore the heads turning their way. "I'm going to try to put a call in to Jim Lindberg immediately and see if he's in his room. Then we'll have dinner and try to put this into some kind of perspective. Sir Gilbert," he said, turning to Bowles as they approached the elevators, "why don't you come up to my room and clean up a bit while I talk to Lindberg? Then I'll grab a quick shower and take you back to your hotel. You can shower, change clothes, and I'll bring you back and you can join us for dinner. Sound all right with you?"

"That's kind of you, Livingstone," replied Bowles. "But I can take a cab. You don't have to—"

"Nonsense, Sir Gilbert. You're one of the team now."

Bowles nodded appreciatively, making a game attempt at what passed for a smile.

"Yes . . . then yes," he said, "I think I would like to join you."

Across the lobby a tall stately woman of European roots, in a suit of very dark green with a gold brooch on one lapel, watched the proceedings. She knew all the principal players in this drama, though they knew nothing of her presence. She was astonished to see Gilbert Bowles with them, and had no idea what it could signify.

Had his eyes been drawn in the woman's direction, Adam would have recognized her from Amsterdam. But as they were not, she remained unseen. Her presence, however, accounted for the chill.

The moment they were in the elevator, she went to a phone and called her Dutch colleague's room.

"The enemy's people are here," she said. "Have you been in contact with the others?"

"They are on their way. Everyone should be to Jerusalem within two or three days."

"There is agitation in the Dimension," she said. "The enemy is at work. Something serious is at hand."

thirty-six

The Archaeologist Who Cried Ark

(1)

Adam set up a meeting with Jim Lindberg for ninety minutes later.

"I think we've scooped our own documentary," said Adam on the phone. "We obviously can't film what we found, so I'd like to go public with it right away. That's what we need to talk over. This is the biggest yet. It will answer the questions that have been rampant, and I hope clear my name with the Ethiopians and everyone else too."

"What about Shayne and Bridges?" asked his BBC friend. "You want them involved?"

Adam thought a moment.

"Could I get back to you, Jim?" he replied. "I'd like to talk to Juliet about Kim. I would trust her read on it better than my own."

Ninety minutes later, a knock came on the door of the Livingstone suite. The whole team was present, including Gilbert Bowles, tired but clean and feeling better, and the two Singaporeans.

Adam went to answer it.

There stood Kim Shayne with Jim Lindberg.

"Jim . . . Miss Shayne," said Adam, shaking both their hands. "Come in."

The look of astonishment on Kim's face the instant she saw Sir Gilbert Bowles in Adam Livingstone's room was more than evident.

"*What are you doing here?*" sprang noiselessly to both their lips. The words that came out, however, were more subdued.

"I believe you already know Sir Gilbert Bowles," said Adam to Kim.

"Indeed," said Kim. "But, Sir Gilbert, this is . . . well, a surprise to put it mildly."

"It would seem that perhaps both you and I have had a change of heart recently," replied Bowles.

"What have you told her, Jim?" asked Adam as they all took seats.

"Actually, nothing," replied Lindberg. "I thought I'd let you break the news."

"What news?" said Kim.

"The biggest," answered Adam, "the story you've been trying to get hold of all this time. But you have to promise that what you hear will not leave this room except on my timetable. Otherwise—"

"You don't even need to say it, Mr. Livingstone," interrupted Kim. "As I told you earlier, I've been changing my mind on many things lately. You have no worry about confidentiality. I give you my word."

"That's good enough for me."

"But . . . what about . . . uh—"

She glanced back and forth between the two rival archaeologists.

"What about Sir Gilbert," she went on, speaking to Adam, but cocking her head toward Bowles. "Surely he hasn't given you . . ."

"Sir Gilbert and I are on the same team now," replied Adam. "Right, Sir Gilbert?"

The big man nodded.

"So, let's get down to it, shall we," said Adam. "We need to plan an interview in order to make this news public. Jim, I will depend on you to figure out the best way to go about it."

Lindberg assented.

"And the first thing I want to establish," Adam continued, "on both your parts, Jim, Miss Shayne, is that you must conduct the interview not as my friend or acquaintance, but as you would any other such interview. Otherwise it will look phony. In a sense, you will have to give it to me with both barrels. Your job will be to voice the skepticism people will naturally feel. I will let you ask your own questions without any advance knowledge on my part."

"You still haven't told me what the news is," said Kim. "I have the odd sensation that I am the only person in the entire room who doesn't know."

"Ah, yes—sorry. I forgot," said Adam. "It's quite simple, Miss Shayne. We have at last located the real ark of the covenant."

(2)

Word of the hastily arranged televised interview spread quickly through Jerusalem, somehow making its way onto CNN's telecasts the following day.

When time came that afternoon, therefore, the Renaissance Hotel was packed with journalists and camera personnel from every media organization within hundreds of miles. Adam's own reputation, and his recent troubles, ensured that no one in either Great Britain or Israel took the event lightly. The BBC had arranged for an additional highly visible personality to participate in the live discussion.

Jim Lindberg had decided that he and Kim Shayne would coanchor the interview. He feared that one more "Livingstone interview" with yet one more so-called "breaking story" could be greeted with more skepticism than would be good for either his or Adam's questionable present reputation. He hoped adding the interest of an attractive new journalistic face to the broadcast would moderate any negative reaction.

Adam, Lindberg, and Kim Shayne took seats in front of the cameras and spotlights, while Juliet, Rocky, Scott, Crystal, Jen, and Gilbert Bowles sat in the front row of those gathered to watch. Kiang and Lek needed to return to Singapore and had departed that morning.

Lindberg began the interview with a recap of Adam's recent disasters and legal troubles, including the flap over the Bowles' interview with Laurence Imre.

Adam sat calmly as every eye and camera awaited his words. When they came, none considered the buildup exaggerated.

"I am fully aware that the public must be tiring of these interviews and breaking stories and discoveries of mine," Adam began. "But I am reasonably certain what I have to share today will not be a disappointment and will put much of the trouble of recent months to rest. I hope I will be able to give a plausible account of myself and the efforts of my team which will set the skepticism to rest once and for all. What I have to tell you about is no mere scientific or archaeological discovery. Actually it is not a discovery. It is, in the full sense of the word, a *revelation*. There is great meaning and significance attached to this find—spiritual meaning which I believe reveals much about the future, not only for this sacred land and this city, but indeed for all mankind."

He drew in a breath and continued.

"I know these words will be difficult for many to believe," he said, "but here they are: Two days ago, in a cavern deep below this sacred city, my research team and I located a priceless sacred treasure, placed there, we believe, by the prophet Jeremiah on the eve of Jerusalem's destruction by the Babylonians in the year 586 B.C. I am speaking of the ancient ark of the covenant—the *true* ark as distinguished from what we now know to have been a replica of the ark fashioned in Ethiopia and recently destroyed by forces which have as yet to be identified."

At Adam's words, instead of the sounds of astonishment and incredulity as might have been expected, the room of journalists broke into whispered chuckles and comments.

"Was it as portrayed—angels on top, and made of gold?" asked Lindberg, trying to keep the interview on track.

"As far as the gold," replied Adam, "that will have to be determined. It appears so—plated gold, of course, as described in the Bible. And as for the design, it is an exact match with the replica I saw in Ethiopia and which was later destroyed. The photographs I made public earlier could have been of the actual ark of the covenant which is now resting beneath Jerusalem."

"Was anything inside?" now asked Kim Shayne.

"We did not touch it."

"Why?"

"According to the Old Testament Scriptures, if anyone not authorized by God touches the ark, he or she will die."

"Who can safely touch it?"

"Only designated Levites of Israel."

"Do you actually believe you would be dead now had you accidently touched it?"

"I don't know what would have happened, Miss Shayne," replied Adam. "It was not so much fear of being struck by lightning that prevented us, as reverence for and obedience to the Scriptures."

"You say the ark is still below the city—why did you not bring it up to substantiate this incredible claim?"

"We felt for the time that we should leave it where we found it. Obviously it belongs to the people of Israel and they will ultimately have to decide what is to be done with it."

"Upon what do you base the conjecture that it was the prophet Jeremiah who placed it there?"

"What might be called extrabiblical writings which describe the Babylonian invasion."

"Where exactly is the ark at this moment?"

"Just where we found it, very near a section of the present wall of the old city."

"Where *exactly?* Can you show us the location on a map?"

"Not at this time, I'm afraid."

"How did you get there? How did you come to find it? How did you get down there in the first place?"

"I'm sorry. I'm afraid I cannot divulge that yet either. To do so could have political repercussions. There will have to be some agreements made among the powers that rule in Jerusalem in order to ensure that this artifact will be used and preserved peaceably. As for *how* . . . we made use of a new laser technology to fix the ark's location, then made our way to it."

"In what sort of place was it found, then?"

"In what we judge to be a burial crypt—a small cave carved out of rock, and set into a recess. It was partially obscured by rubble, we believe from an ancient earthquake. There was also compelling evidence that we were not the first visitors to the site after Jeremiah. I will explain all that in the written account of our search, which is a long and complex story. The carrying poles, somewhat decayed but mostly intact, were there as well. I have made this sketch."

The camera zoomed in as Adam held up what he had drawn.

"But as far as where this crypt was, under what part of Jerusalem, you have nothing further to say?"

"That is correct."

"Surely you do not plan to make such an astounding claim and leave it at that. When *will* you reveal the location?"

"I really am not sure," replied Adam. "After all that has happened recently, I must be very careful to do what is best, and what is right. I hope to speak with Israel's prime minister about it. As I said, the nation of Israel, I feel, must make the decision what is to be done now."

(3)

"I mean no disrespect, Mr. Livingstone," said Kim after a brief pause, "but you of all people must know what this will look like to many viewers."

"What is it you think they will think?" asked Adam.

"The story about the boy who cried wolf comes to mind," she replied. "Why should they believe you this time? What would you say to such skeptics? I mean, I think many of those present would say that their initial reaction is that you are attempting to wriggle out of your troubles with the Ethiopians with one more publicity stunt."

Adam had told the two journalists to keep no punches back, and they were certainly proving up to the assignment!

"I suppose I can give no good reason why people ought to believe me this time," replied Adam. "All I can say is that the discovery *will* come out in time. So in a way, perhaps skepticism at first is to be expected. Maybe I deserve the boy who cried wolf charge. But I assure you, this is the genuine article."

"Then you will not mind if we bring into the discussion what might be called an impartial observer and expert?" asked Lindberg.

"Of course not," replied Adam. He had suspected something like this, but Lindberg had not divulged his plans.

"We have arranged for someone else to join the discussion, whom you just said you wanted to speak with Kim."

"I have Israel's prime minister standing by in his office," said Shayne, glancing toward a large television screen to her left. "Mr. Prime Minister, can you hear me?"

Immediately the picture came on.

"Yes, I'm here, Miss Shayne."

"What is your reaction to this amazing claim Adam Livingstone has made?"

"I am astounded," replied the prime minister, "as I am sure everyone is. However, I must confess more than a small amount of suspicion. I have been made aware that Mr. Livingstone has made numerous inquiries and applications over the past month for permission to participate in Israeli excavations in and around Jerusalem. As I understand it, these applications have all been denied—and of course we have no active digs in progress anywhere in the vicinity of sensitive places in the city. This has the sound to me, as you yourself suggested, of a stunt to gain publicity for himself, to perhaps gain access to explorations which he has been unable to obtain through other channels. It might be conjectured that all this is but an attempt to bolster his sagging reputation and somehow make up for his apparent involvement in what my country as well as Ethiopia is still looking into as a serious crime against history. His reluctance to divulge specifics certainly diminishes the credibility of this claim."

"What do you have to say, Adam, to the prime minister's charge that this is a publicity stunt?" asked Jim Lindberg.

"I am sorry he feels that way," replied Adam. "I can assure you, however, that such is not the case."

"Why then will you not reveal the location of the site?" now asked the prime minister.

"It is beneath a sensitive area, Mr. Prime Minister. We ourselves arrived at it underground. It is my hope that you yourself, along with Palestinian and Christian leaders, will be able to come to agreement ahead of time concerning the disposition of the ark, to prevent hostilities over the find. At that time, we will welcome the opportunity to sit down with you and make a more specific disclosure to you all jointly."

"And who is *we?*"

"My research team."

"And of course you came and went undetected?"

"Not exactly. I would say we were protected by the Lord."

The prime minister could not keep himself from chuckling at how ridiculous the whole thing sounded. A few of those in the live audience began again to snicker along with him.

"As Israel's prime minister, what do you intend to do about Mr. Livingstone's claim?" asked Shayne.

"Do?" repeated the prime minister. "I don't see that there is much to do at all. I don't see what else to call this but another Livingstone ploy. We will look into it further, of course. We will question Mr. Livingstone's people. But truthfully, this is not the first time, nor will it be the last, when publicity has falsely raised the hopes of our people."

"You say *falsely*. Do you use that word intentionally, Mr. Prime Minister?"

"I use it very intentionally, Miss Shayne. If there was some *proof* Mr. Livingstone could offer, some *evidence* of this high-tech method he says he used, or if he was willing to divulge the exact location so that we could look into it ourselves, obviously then it might be different. As things stand, what else can I do but consider it a hoax? There have been others, an American recently, who claim to have discovered the ark. But there is never any proof."

"Getting back to the discovery itself," interjected Lindberg, "would you perhaps like to enlighten our viewers how this present find ties in with that supposed ark you photographed in Aksum?"

"The ark of the covenant was conjectured by many to have been removed many centuries before Christ to Ethiopia," replied Adam. The prime minister's tone of ridicule had stung his optimism, but he tried to sound positive and upbeat. "I feel my own research corroborates that conclusion. Now we know that the so-called ark I made public earlier with Sir Daniel Snow was a replica, I believe fashioned by Menyelek, son of Solomon, ancient king of Ethiopia, for use in worship by himself and those of his nation who had converted to the religion of his father and grandfather, King David of Israel."

(4)

Watching the broadcast in her room in the same hotel, Anni D'Abernon trembled as she listened. She picked up the telephone. In another moment she was speaking with Vaughan-Maier.

"This is not good," she said. "There is danger to us here. How many of the others have arrived?"

"I have spoken with several of them," said Vaughan-Maier.

"We must meet tonight."

"There is an agitation among them."

"I am not surprised. They sense the enemy's presence."

"But our Master is at work," said Vaughan-Maier. "Did you not see how Livingstone was mocked before the watching world?"

"The enemy is close as well," replied D'Abernon. "Yet you are right—our Master is also here. He will divert the eyes of the enemy's people so as to render the Livingstone threat impotent. Whatever Livingstone is up to, I am confident in the powers of the Dimension."

(5)

There was more laughter and ridicule at Adam's attempted explanation.

Suddenly Jim Lindberg and Kim Shayne saw the ponderous form of Sir Gilbert Bowles rise from where he had been sitting in the front row and approach. He walked straight toward the front of the camera.

"It seems we have a surprise guest," said Lindberg, trying to maintain his poise. "Adam Livingstone's chief antagonist and sometime rival, Sir Gilbert Bowles."

Lindberg rose from his chair, signalling to one of the production crew beside Bridges at the camera to bring another, offering Bowles his own in the meantime.

"I presume, Sir Gilbert," he continued as the impromptu arrangements were attended to, "that you have something to add to this discussion."

Bowles nodded as he sat down. The camera zoomed in for a close-up of his face.

"I can corroborate everything," said Bowles.

The listening audience began to buzz with astonishment.

"Have you and the Livingstone team joined forces?" said Lindberg. "I thought you were rivals."

"At one time perhaps, but no longer."

"And *how*, Sir Gilbert . . . how exactly can you corroborate Mr. Livingstone's claim?"

"Simple. I was with Adam when he made the discovery," replied Bowles calmly. "I saw the ark with my own eyes. It is exactly as he has said. Adam Livingstone is telling the truth."

Now at last the crowd erupted with exclamations and questions. But it did not take long for laughter to be heard throughout the room. Gradually chairs began moving back and reporters rose to leave. They were through with this. Most would probably not even file stories, except as comic relief pieces. The thing was a farce.

One thing everyone in the scientific community knew for a fact was that Sir Gilbert Bowles could not be bought off. There must be some other explanation.

That alternate explanation did not wait long in coming, and ran in headline type in several of Great Britain's dailies, ranging from BOWLES JOINS LIVINGSTONE IN FUNNY FARM to BOWLES FLIPS LID to LIVINGSTONE AND BOWLES TEAM UP IN ARK HOAX to TWO MAJOR ENGLISH SCIENTISTS DISCREDITED. Even a guest editorial in the London *Times* by Jim Lindberg, who flew back to London immediately after the broadcast, substantiating at least the credibility of the science behind the Livingstone claim, did not stem the tide of response against it.

Now *both* of Great Britain's leading archaeologists were being ridiculed. Adam and Sir Gilbert had indeed joined the same team. According to the world's news media, they had gone over the edge together and were virtually through as reputable scientists.

thirty-seven

Cataclysm

(1)

The world's largest rift—extending from the Sea of Galilee southward through the valley of the Jordan River to the Dead Sea, then to the Red Sea and the Great Rift of Africa—was one of the most geologically active regions on the earth. The Great Rift region had had more than its share of massive seismic events, though not so frequent as the earthquakes of the Pacific Rim and California, as excavations throughout Israel documented clearly enough.

At precisely 5:37 A.M. two mornings after the interview, every guest in Jerusalem's Renaissance Hotel was jolted violently out of whatever level of slumber they happened to be enjoying. A massive earthquake struck the northernmost section of the great rift. Veering off violently in a newly created fault line westward into the Judean mountains, it rocked the central portions of Palestine for forty-three seconds.

As the cataclysm subsided, sirens and alarms began blaring throughout the city. Gas lines broke. Smoke from at least two dozen fires rose into the pale light of the dawn sky. Power lines were down everywhere. Spouts of water gushed into the air. Power throughout the city was immediately slashed 90 percent. Destruction was everywhere.

Whether this unprecedented shifting of the earth's crust was a symbol of God's judgment or the mere result of natural forces, scientists and theologians would argue for years. One thing was sure: The history of Jerusalem had been forever altered in the twinkling of an eye. Never in recorded history had the epicenter of so massive a quake occurred so close to the Holy City itself.

The wonder of the modern world, the Dome of the Rock, lay in a heap of rubble, smashed to pieces upon the very *shetiyyah* stone it had been erected to protect. The altar of Isaac's salvation had survived without so much as a crack, while the sacred canopy of Babylon had been splintered upon it. Likewise, the Al-Aqsa Mosque, onetime home of the Knights Templar, was in ruins.

Neither disaster could the Arabs blame on the Jews. If anyone was to blame, Jews, Muslims, and Christians alike would have to look to their mutual God.

Even as the quake subsided, Juliet, Jen, and Crystal met in the darkened hall, trembling. Screams came from throughout the hotel. Almost immediately others of the team, as well as dozens of other hotel guests, groped in semiblackness into the hall.

"Is everyone in one piece?" asked Adam.

"Shaken is all," replied Jen.

"This is one of Jerusalem's newer hotels," said Adam. "It's solid, though we may be without power for a while. Let's get dressed—then meet back here. We'll see what we can do to help."

"Power!" Crystal exclaimed. "Adam—what about the computer, and all our data?"

"You backed up everything?"

"Of course. But even backup hard drives can be damaged by something like this. I'll have to get working on a full recovery the minute power is restored."

(2)

Throughout the day of the quake, Jerusalem stood at a standstill.

Emergency teams, police, firefighters, and ambulance crews were operating at peak capacity. Hospitals were clogged with the dead and the dying. Power had not been restored. A dozen major fires burned out of control. Many hundreds were dead, thousands missing.

While maintaining military forces at key border installations on alert throughout the rest of the country, what Israeli troops could be made available were summoned to Jerusalem. Quickly they began setting up barriers and makeshift fencing around endangered historic sites as well as areas deemed especially hazardous. No incidents or skirmishes had been reported. From radios and loudspeakers blared the edict that driving on major thoroughfares was curtailed until further notice so that emergency and rescue vehicles might pass unrestricted. Shrill sirens blared everywhere.

About one o'clock came a minor aftershock, insignificant by Richter standards—a mere 3.7. Yet apparent fissures and cavities below the precise location of the aftershock somehow combined to shake open a huge yawning cavern extending seventy-five or a hundred feet straight down from the corner of the Gordon Calvary site just north of the Damascus Gate. It was judged so dangerous that two truckloads of Israeli troops moved in instantly to fence off the perimeter.

(3)

"This is Kim Shayne reporting live for the BBC from Jerusalem, where behind me you can see the rescue operations which are in progress here around the clock. I am standing at the edge of the largest chasm of all created by the quake, just outside the Damascus Gate, which seismologists and geologists warn is still highly unstable and dangerous.

"Humanitarian aid is pouring into Israel from all corners of the globe, with offers from thousands of agencies, missionary groups, and relief organizations to send teams of volunteers. Emergency sessions of several UN committees have been called. The prime minister has been in touch with the U.S. president, the pope, the prime minister of Great Britain, as well as dozens of other world leaders.

"In the thirty-two hours since the Jerusalem quake, estimated at between 7.9 and 8.2 on the Richter scale—making it the fifth strongest earthquake of the past century—the death toll is presently estimated at something over twenty-seven hundred, although with communications so severely cut between the city and outlying regions such as Bethlehem, and with power still not functional in many areas, fears are that figure, which is but a preliminary guess by government sources, could climb higher.

"As you can see, much of central Jerusalem is in ruins or badly damaged. Large segments of the old city wall have fallen, though foundations remain intact around most of the perimeter. Jewish faithful the world over are lamenting the toppling of the upper portion of the Wailing Wall, which killed four men and two women. If any consolation is to be found amid the heartbreak, it is that the quake occurred in the early morning hours when praying pilgrims were few.

"All three of Jerusalem's major religions suffered devastating losses to their holiest shrines, although preliminary reports place the epicenter in the Muslim quarter. Besides the damage to the Wailing Wall, the demolition of the Dome of the Rock and the Al-Aqsa Mosque has sent shock waves throughout the Muslim world. In the Christian sector, the Church of the Holy Sepulchre has been damaged beyond repair.

"Human suffering at this hour is obviously great, but at the back of everyone's minds is the question: What will be the political implications of this tragedy? Israeli troops were quickly ordered throughout the city. Palestinian leaders have publically decried this unilateral action."

Kim stopped, interrupted by a sound behind her. "Oh, my goodness—did you hear that? Another portion of the wall has collapsed!"

Cameras swung around to zoom in on the site, not far away, where an unsteady portion of wall had given way.

"Other Arab nations are predictably weighing in on the side of the Palestinians," Shayne went on after a few moments. "Iraq and Iran and the rest of the Arab world have expressed what could be alarming anxiety, apparently fearing that an attempt may be coming by Israel to seize the Temple Mount area, which has been in Arab hands since the Crusades. Israel denies such motive. Yet the more radical Hasidic faction is already proclaiming a divine hand in the quake for the purpose of driving Islam from the Temple area and making possible the building of a new temple which, according to devout Jews, will bring their long-awaited Messiah.

"Such sentiment resonates with Christian evangelical leaders, who maintain that this event signals the return to earth of Jesus Christ. Thus many Christian and Jewish groups are in a frenzy of anticipation. Many Protestant Christian leaders are booking flights to the Holy Land. And while not making such bold proclamations, it can hardly be denied that many Israelis hope the Temple Mount will return to Jewish hands.

"Meanwhile, Israeli troops continue to surround Jerusalem's key areas, keeping especially close watch on the massive pit created near the Damascus Gate. Archaeologists and geologists and historians the world over are already clamoring for exploration permits to this as well as the many other caverns which have been opened in and around Jerusalem, revealing tombs, previously unknown sections of Solomon's temple, and some say the site of the Holy of Holies itself.

"The Israeli government, obviously with its hands full with rescue operations, is making no comment on its plans. A special session of the Knesset is being convened this afternoon.

"We have reports that Israel's prime minister will be personally visiting the site after the session. And American evangelical leader and spokesman Harry Standgood is reportedly enroute to Tel Aviv even as we speak."

(4)

Services throughout Jerusalem were gradually being restored. The Renaissance Hotel was operating at 75 percent strength with the aid of backup generators. It would be many days before visitors to the area managed to get home, although Ben Gurion had not been severely hit and was already gearing back up to full operations.

In one of the two suites they retained as their Jerusalem office, Adam was frantically glancing back and forth over Crystal's shoulder at the computer screen, then to Kim Shayne on the television set.

He had a bad feeling about the location of that huge pit the earthquake had created, and the danger it could pose to hopes of recovering the ark. One thing was certain, no one would ever be able to retrace the route *they* had taken to find it. The quake had destroyed any chance of that. And before he could do anything further, he had to know for certain where they had been. Any dispute over jurisdiction now could cause a war!

"The recovery's nearly complete, Adam," said Crystal.

"Anything lost?"

"I think we'll be OK. All the data from the scan and my recording of your movements seems intact . . . right, there it is—recovery complete. What do you want me to bring up on the screen?"

"I need to look at exactly what you saw when we were in the ark crypt," said Adam.

Crystal moused in the information.

"There it is."

"Yes!" exclaimed Adam. "And there's the signal from Scott's transmitter still going strong!"

"If it is still with the ark at all," said Scott, walking up behind them.

Adam turned. "Thanks for that pessimistic idea! As if I needed to hear that!"

"Just trying to help," said Scott with a grin.

"No matter. It's all we've got to go on at the minute," said Adam. "What I need you to do, Crystal, is change that entire grid back into a two-dimensional image, then transfer it straight vertically up to ground level. I have to see precisely where the ark is . . . on the surface."

It took Crystal about three minutes to effect the change.

Adam saw the information come up onto the screen, then nodded to himself.

"That confirms it," he said. "It's exactly as I thought. I've got a very important telephone call to make."

(5)

"Prime Minister," said Adam into the telephone back to his homeland, "I appreciate your taking my call. I know I'm not the most reputable Englishman in the world right now."

"I was told that you are still in Jerusalem and that the matter was extreme, possibly even involving national security interests," replied the prime minister. "They had to trace me over half of London–I'm in my car on the way to the houses of Parliament right now, so I hope this is as important as they say. With all respect, Livingstone, I do not want to be dragged into one of your–"

"I am sorry for how it looks, Prime Minister. But believe me, I do not overstate the seriousness of the matter. You knew that my team and I located the ark of the covenant?"

"I heard of the *claim* that you had, yes. The reports here are not, as it were, particularly keen on the reputability of the so-called find."

"Despite what you may have heard or seen in the papers, sir, the claim is accurate. I saw the ark, and so did five others. We left a transmitter at the site. That is one fact I did not divulge in the interview."

"An underground transmitter! Do you mean–"

"Yes, we have a computer image–I am looking at it even as we speak across the room–that is giving us a signal from beside the ark at this very moment. We know exactly where it is, sir."

"Hmm . . . I see–all right. You've got my attention."

"The reason this involves you, sir," Adam went on, "is this: We have just confirmed that the crypt lies directly below the Gordon Calvary site."

"I'm . . . I'm not sure I follow you, Livingstone," said the prime minister hesitantly.

"The plot of ground known as the Garden Tomb," explained Adam, "discovered by General Gordon in 1882 and purchased by him."

"I'm afraid I'm not familiar with that portion of Jerusalem's history."

"Many Protestants do not believe the Church of the Holy Sepulchre, or what is left of it now, I should say, is the true site of Christ's crucifixion," explained Adam. "They believe that the crucifixion and burial of Jesus took place on the small plot of ground discovered by General Gordon."

"I wasn't aware of the dispute."

"There is compelling evidence for the Protestant claim, especially when you visit the two sites. The point is, Prime Minister, for the last hundred years, England has owned this tiny parcel of land in Jerusalem. It is literally an oasis within the city under British jurisdiction. And that is the rub, sir—if the ark is excavated, though it lies within the Muslim quarter of Jerusalem, I believe it would legally be the rightful property of the United Kingdom."

"I *see*!" replied the prime minister significantly. "Yes, if you're right, this *would* have major repercussions, and land us right into the middle of a dispute between the Israelis and Palestinians."

"That is why I called, sir," said Adam.

"What do you suggest, Livingstone?"

"First, one of us must get in touch with Israel's prime minister," replied Adam.

"Yes, I spoke with him less than an hour ago."

"The situation is truly dangerous," Adam went on. "The area is geologically very unstable. One more aftershock could destroy any hope of recovering the ark, if it hasn't been damaged already. Since our transmitter is still functioning we hope the ark remains safe. But we must mount an excavation down into the pit immediately to try to recover it."

"I understand. I will get on the phone to Israel the moment you and I are through."

"But, sir," Adam went on, "the other matter is one of jurisdiction. You need to decide, or Commons or whomever has authority in such matters, whether the United Kingdom would press a claim to ownership. That factor would enter heavily into how to proceed. If we can convince the Israelis to mount a recovery operation, it would, technically speaking, be on *English* soil."

"A sticky situation, indeed. However, I cannot see us pressing a claim, as you say. If the ark is there, and is genuine, surely no MP in the British House of Commons would say anything but that it belonged to the nation of Israel. But as you say, the situation is urgent. I shall get in touch with the prime minister immediately. How can I reach you back, Livingstone?"

Adam gave him the number. "I'll await your call here, sir," said Adam, then hung up.

(6)

It was an hour and ten minutes before the telephone in the Livingstone suite rang again. Adam leapt for it.

"Hello . . . yes, Prime Minister, good of you to ring me back."

"I'm afraid I don't have good news, Livingstone," said the voice on the line. "I spoke with the prime minister. It was a job getting through. They are just going in for a special session at the Knesset over this earthquake business. When I explained the reason for my calling back, he told me in no uncertain terms that he doesn't believe your story. Apparently you and he have already exchanged words about the affair."

"He was linked into the interview I did with Lindberg."

"Well, he hasn't changed his mind. He was irate at me for interrupting him with what he considers a publicity stunt."

"What are we going to do then, sir?"

"I don't see that there's much we can do, Livingstone," replied the prime minister. "Even if, as you say, the area is technically British, what can I do? It would take weeks for us to get a team of engineers there."

"I am here, sir."

"Right, and your name is mud with the Israelis, besides which you have no equipment, as I understand it. You would have to depend on local authorities, and they are angry about your claim to have been snooping around without their permission. They're not going to help you on what they consider a wild-goose chase. Especially with their city in ruins. I'm afraid there's nothing I can do."

"But the ark, sir . . . surely–"

"Even if the ark is there, Livingstone, I wouldn't touch this one with a ten-foot pole. It's too potentially explosive. Let me know if there are developments. Otherwise, I'm afraid you are going to have to let events take their course."

Adam hung up and turned back into the room. The faces of his friends were staring at him, waiting for a report of the call. Briefly he relayed the gist of the conversation.

He began pacing the room, obviously in thought.

Suddenly he spun around.

"Crystal," he said, "get me a printout of the images showing the signal and location of the ark. I want two-dimensional, three-dimensional, and any other dimensional you can think of. And I want them now!"

Already Crystal was on the way over to her chair in front of the computer.

Three minutes later the images came out of the printer. Adam grabbed them and headed for the door.

"Where are you going!" exclaimed Juliet.

"To see a skeptic," answered Adam, and was gone.

He flew down the corridor, took the elevator to the ground floor, ran outside the hotel, and hailed a cab.

"The Knesset!" he said urgently.

(7)

Talking his way through initial security at the outer gates and onto the grounds was as adroit a feat as Adam Livingstone had ever pulled off. Israeli security was legendary, and this was one of the most highly secure buildings in the world. He could never have done it had the entire city not been in a state of emergency, and most of the building's electronic security measures been rendered inoperable.

He ordered the cab to stop, then jumped out and ran to the guards at the entrance to the building, waving the papers in his hand and stretching the truth a bit as he cried, "The prime minister is waiting for these. They're images of the damage site at the Damascus Gate!"

The prime minister was waiting for them, thought Adam. He just didn't know it yet!

He flew through the doors, ignoring questions from the guards behind him. He was determined not to be stopped, even if it landed him in jail by day's end.

He slowed, got his bearings, located his objective, then broke into a run, hoping his apparent haste and the emergency status of the Knesset would work as well with the guards stationed at the large double doors into the parliamentary hall.

He ran shouting toward them.

"I'm Adam Livingstone," he cried imperatively. "I've got information of the quake site for the prime minister!"

Calmly the guards began with their questions.

But again Adam did not pause. Taken by surprise, the guards now began yelling behind him.

"Hey . . . stop–you can't–"

It was too late.

Adam shoved the large doors open with his shoulder, and ran inside.

The moment he burst into the assembly, with voices raised behind him in pursuit, Adam stopped in his tracks. Every eye of the Israeli parliament turned toward the sounds of commotion. Adam saw the prime minister–who had paused in midsentence at the interruption–in front. As the guards came through the doors behind him, Adam again broke into a run down the wide aisle.

"Livingstone, what is the meaning of this outrage?"

"I am sorry for barging in like this, Prime Minister," yelled Adam as he ran, "but you *have* to listen to me!"

"Come here—hey . . . stop!" cried one of the guards, pulling the gun from his waist and raising it toward Adam.

"Guard—hold your fire!" cried the prime minister. "The man is no threat. Just call security, then take him away and have him arrested!"

"Wait!" said Adam, spinning around frantically and addressing the Knesset. "I know the earthquake has caused dreadful chaos. But I tell you, the ark of the covenant is also in danger. For the sake of your nation and your history, please listen to me!"

"I listened to all I needed to the other day," said the prime minister. "Guards, get him out of here!"

"Look—here is the proof you wanted," cried Adam, turning back to face him, "the evidence you said would make you look into it. Please—just examine it."

His words seemed to jolt the prime minister momentarily. All around, the Knesset buzzed with reaction.

Three guards ran forward down the aisle after him and grabbed Adam from behind and stopped him.

"There is a transmitter beside the ark of the covenant," Adam went on. "We left it there. It is giving off signals of the location. Here is the printout, Prime Minister—all the proof you should need."

The guards yanked Adam back and pulled him away. The two sheets fell from his hand to the floor. One of the members sitting next to the aisle jumped out of his chair and retrieved the papers. He looked at them a moment, then ran forward and handed them to the prime minister.

"I think you ought to look at these," he said. "It's near Jeremiah's Grotto—there may be something to it."

The prime minister took them and studied the computer images for several seconds.

"Just a minute," he said, glancing up. "Guard . . . wait."

Halfway to the doors, the guards stopped.

"All right, Livingstone, you have two minutes," said the prime minister. "Have your say. We're listening."

The guard released him and Adam came forward to the front of the Knesset.

"It is very simple, sir," he began. "There is nothing more to say than what I have already. I assure you, I am no kook. The ark of the covenant *is* down there, and we must get equipment and a team to the Damascus site without delay and excavate that pit opened by the earthquake. We have to recover the ark before another aftershock rips the earth apart and we lose any chance of finding it again."

"Whom do you suggest to do this?"

"I can lead the team," replied Adam. "But I will need equipment. And you will need to provide for transport of the ark."

"Transport . . . what exactly do you—"

"Levites!" came a cry from the floor. "We will need a team of Levites!"

A flurry of calls and suggestions broke out, and within seconds the Knesset became a hubbub of frenzied reaction.

thirty-eight

Hidden in Time

(1)

Harry Standgood and his fundamentalist entourage entered Jerusalem with a triumphant flourish. Every news camera in the city would be upon him to put the story into a pre-Trib imminent Rapture end-times perspective. A new book about the event was already hatching in his brain.

He instructed the fleet of three limousines to drive straight to the site of the most dramatic quake damage, where his PR man had already been in touch with the journalist on hand. The broadcast would be live via satellite. It would be the lead story on tonight's newscasts in the States. His name would be everywhere. What an opportunity!

Standgood reached the site and sought the reporter. Kim Shayne—pressed into hurried service by the BBC following Lindberg's departure—was waiting for him.

"We've had a makeshift platform built here," said Shayne, as they shook hands and began walking toward the roped-off cavern. "You will be able to speak from the edge of the cavity. Our cameras will get both close-ups as well as wide-angle shots to show the Damascus Gate in the distance behind you."

"Good, good," said Standgood, noting the positions of the cameras in relation to the site and what there was to be seen of the city in the background. "Yes, this is perfect."

He leaned over slightly and peered, squinting, into the pit.

"Careful, Mr. Standgood, it is a treacherous drop-off into the chasm."

"Yes . . . yes, I can see that."

"We'll begin with a close-up of you," Kim went on, "then pan back to the city as backdrop. All right, let's get some makeup on you. We're planning to go live in . . ."

Shayne checked her watch.

". . . about fifteen minutes."

(2)

Cameras rolled as Harry Standgood stepped forward, microphone in hand, and began to speak in sober tones about the devastation to the world's most holy city.

"But in the midst of pain perhaps we may discover blessing," he went on after two or three minutes of introductory remarks. "In an exciting and special way, this is also a great day. Why do I say that? Because I believe this earthquake was sent to give the world an unmistakable sign of the soon coming of the Lord Jesus Christ, the Messiah of God's chosen nation of Israel."

He paused for a moment, glancing up at some noise in the distance. Trying to ignore it, he went on.

"This truly represents an extraordinary day in the history of mankind," the evangelical leader continued, "when the Christians and Jews and Muslims alike who inhabit this historic city have the opportunity—"

Again he stopped. The noises had grown too loud to ignore. It was the rumble of approaching trucks, jeeps, heavy equipment, and military vehicles.

What could be the meaning of this? thought Standgood. *This is no time for—*

Within seconds the crowd began to scatter with the arrival of the first vehicles of the convoy. The lead jeep parted the crowd with horn blaring, pushing its way through the throng straight to the edge of the pit. Adam Livingstone leapt out and ran forward. From the backseat Juliet climbed out and quickly followed.

"You know what to do?" said Adam.

Juliet nodded.

Adam jumped onto the makeshift platform.

Behind Adam the other vehicles lumbered to the scene. Rocky and Jen jumped to the ground and hurried forward. Their large companion followed, but was soon lost in the crowd. A line of huge construction cranes now came into view. The interview was clearly over. Having no clue what was going on, Standgood backed awkwardly away.

Trying to recover herself and knowing the cameras were still rolling, Kim stepped toward Adam, where he stood peering over the brink of the chasm.

"Adam . . . Adam Livingstone," she said, trying to work the microphone in front of him, "can you tell our viewers what—"

"Sorry, Miss Shayne," said Adam, "there's no time just now."

He turned away. "Scott! Over there," he cried to his assistant riding atop the control booth of the lead crane. "I think that's the best spot!" he continued, pointing around the edge of the crater. He ran off the platform in the same direction, leaving Kim staring bewildered after him.

Suddenly behind her, she heard a familiar voice.

"I'm sorry, Kimberly," said Juliet, approaching, "but if I could just borrow the microphone for a minute or two, I will explain everything."

As she spoke, Juliet calmly took the microphone from Kim's hand, then turned to face Bridges.

"This is Juliet Halsay," she said into the camera. "The chasm behind me is directly above where the ark of the covenant, discovered by the Livingstone team several days ago, now rests. A transmitter is beside it with a live signal. With permission from the Knesset, we are going to try to save it before the earthquake claims any more ground. . . ."

Astonished exclamations filtered through the crowd. Like a wildfire, news spread of the announcement. It did not take long before all that was left of Jerusalem began pouring—on foot, on bicycle, by car, by bus—toward the scene in a human flood. Around the world, the moment they heard the news, every station and network interrupted their regular programing. Within five minutes, half the television sets in the world were tuned in to the remarkable broadcast from the edge of the Damascus Gate pit.

" . . . being guided by computer link," Juliet was saying, "back in our control center at the Renaissance Hotel. The electronic transmitter placed beside the ark is emitting a signal, which is displayed on the computer grid at the hotel, where Mr. Livingstone's assistant is relaying information into the headsets of both Mr. Livingstone and Mr. Jordan.

"Mr. Livingstone will be strapped—"

Juliet looked quickly away from the camera.

"—there! Scott Jordan is fastening Adam to the cable now, by which he will be lowered by crane into the pit. Several Israeli seismic engineers and geologic experts, a half-dozen construction workers, along with the equipment they need, will also be lowered. As they are guided to the spot where the ark rests, hopefully they will be able to excavate away the rubble, and then exhume the precious treasure . . . I think that will give a quick idea of Mr. Livingstone's plan. Now I will turn the microphone back over to Kimberly Shayne. Kimberly."

Juliet handed Kim the microphone with a smile.

"Thank you, Juliet," said Kim, "that was extremely helpful. Do you mind if I ask you a few questions?"

"I will remain here," replied Juliet, now placing on her head the set of earphones and mike she was holding. "I will also be linked by headset to the others."

"So Mr. Livingstone will let you know what he is seeing down there?"

"I hope so," replied Juliet.

"You must be very excited."

"Of course. I saw the ark a few days ago. But I know the world remains skeptical. So for Adam's sake, I hope everyone will soon see it for themselves."

"But once they locate it," said Kim, "how will they actually be able to bring it up? I mean, if the stories—"

Kim stopped abruptly.

"What is this! I see—"

Already Bridges was panning around with the camera as another vehicle bounded to the scene. Seconds later a military van emptied of five robed and bearded Hasidic Levites.

"There is your answer, Kimberly," said Juliet. "Only Levites are allowed by Mosaic law to touch the ark of the covenant. These Levites you see will be lowered with the workers. It is they who will actually be able to bring it out from its resting place."

(3)

Meanwhile, Adam was strapped in place. Scott ran back and climbed aboard the crane. Immediately he barked out instructions to the lift operator.

Within seconds Adam's frame jerked off the ground.

"Whoa!" he exclaimed. "Hey, Scott—make sure he knows I'm a human being, not a wrecking ball!"

"Just hang on, Adam!" Scott said, laughing. "I think he is aware of that fact. You're on your own for a while—I'm going to get the others strapped in."

As Scott climbed down and ran toward where the convoy of cranes was lining up in a circular pattern around the pit, the arm of the lead crane carefully extended outward, carrying Adam straight over the yawning gulf.

One by one, Scott cinched and strapped and hooked workers and engineers in place, while others attached lines to a four-foot-square steel construction platform to carry picks, shovels, seismic testing devices, straps, ropes, lights, and other equipment. One by one, with yells from workers and exclamations from the crowd, the men were raised off the ground, then extended out over the hole after Adam.

Adam and Crystal maintained voice contact as Adam slowly descended into the cavity.

"How are we doing, Crystal?"

"I'm still shifting and rotating the scan," she replied. "I'm trying to get a direct vertical image for the best angle to display your transmitter above the ark's. Right now it looks like you're forty or fifty meters too far . . . let me see—it would be northeast. *Very* close to the Golgotha site according to the Gordon theory. The way it appears to me, the ark is resting directly under the scene of the crucifixion. How large is the pit?"

"A hundred and fifty, maybe two hundred meters across," replied Adam. "Scott, are you getting this?"

"Yeah. As soon as everyone's clamped in, I'll get back on the crane and get you targeted more accurately."

Adam tried to swing himself around, then gave a slicing motion across his neck to the crane operator. Instantly his downward motion stopped.

On the platform as the operation continued, Juliet spotted Gilbert Bowles at the front of the crowd standing between Jen and Rocky, watching the developments with unusual placidity. She indicated to Kim that she had something to say. Kim put the microphone in front of her again.

"I see our friend Sir Gilbert Bowles," said Juliet into the camera. "Sir Gilbert was with us down there when we found the ark. Sir Gilbert, would you mind coming up onto the platform," she said, gesturing toward Bowles with an outstretched hand. "I'm sure the viewers would like your expert commentary on the proceedings from an archaeological perspective. Please, Sir Gilbert . . ."

She handed the microphone back to Kim, then stepped down and went to lead Bowles forward. The big man seemed remarkably bashful for what had always been his bread and butter—a live television camera. But he complied, and was soon chatting freely with Kim Shayne, answering questions as they watched the workers and engineers being lowered behind them.

Scott had moved on to the contingent of black-robed Levites, some of whom did not seem altogether to relish the idea now that they actually saw what was planned for them. But one by one they too were lifted into the air, with long black coats and earlocks, tzitzits and phylacteries, all flying about in the breeze. The sight as they were craned out over the chasm presented what surely had to be one of the most unusual spectacles in the history of archaeological excavation.

In the Knesset, where the members remained in session to decide on urgent matters of earthquake cleanup and response, a large-screen television monitor had been brought in.

Discussions ceased as soon as the operation began. Though there were not many strong Hasidic sympathizers among them, a cheer now went up, and a great deal of laughter along with it, to see their robed religious countrymen dangling on the ends of crane lines.

"I'm going to the site!" declared the prime minister, caught up in the excitement of the event. "Carry on without me."

Meanwhile, Scott had again taken up his position on the crane and Adam was nearly out of sight below. The other crane operators followed Scott's instructions visually, keeping their lines far enough apart to prevent tangling or bumping, but lowering the players in the drama toward the same section of the cavern.

As of one accord the watching crowd, enlarging by the minute, quieted. Soon the only sounds to be heard were the crane engines, and an occasional shout in frantic Hebrew from the normally calm and spiritually minded Hasidics, flailing about in the air and trying desperately to keep their hats upon their heads.

Adam disappeared. One by one the workers lowered into the ground. The platform of tools was lost to view. Slowly the Levites followed into the blackness of the earthquake pit.

(4)

Now came the wait, as the real work of prophetic archaeology began underground, lost from view to those above. Dozens of television cameras were focused down into the hole into which eighteen or twenty lines stretched taut and out of sight. For several long minutes, the conversation between Adam, Scott, Crystal, and Juliet remained private. Though more than a billion eyes were watching on television, Crystal, alone at the Renaissance Hotel, was guiding the entire operation.

At last Juliet indicated to Kim that she was ready for a report. Kim signaled Bridges, and the camera panned back and zoomed in upon the faces of the two young women.

"Mr. Livingstone has reached a point," began Juliet, "where the ground appears stable. He is removing himself from the line and will explore the area to be sure it is safe."

"Where are they in relation to the ark?" asked Kim.

"According to Mrs. Johnson, some fifty or sixty meters."

"Above it?"

"Above and north—at an angle."

"How will they reach it?"

"Adam is able to see several passages and tunnels. He doesn't know yet where they—wait just a minute . . . "

Juliet paused. Kim waited. Bridges waited. The crowd waited.

Cameras swung back to a view of the pit, where one line could be seen to have released its weight and was dangling loose. The others still stretched tight and straight down.

"Adam is walking down a sloping incline," said Juliet after about a minute, "trying to see if—"

Another pause.

"He says it is definitely a passage of human construction," Juliet went on, "not caused by the earthquake."

"Is that good?" asked Kim.

"Yes, very good—it means that the underground maze of tunnels and passageways may be sufficiently intact for him to get to the ark.

"He is seeing evidence of tombs and burial sites . . . much debris and fallen rock . . . the passage is tight . . . portions of wall are fragile, pebbles falling here and there . . . a few deep new fissures . . . cracks from the quake evident around him . . . he is exploring further along the passage. . . ."

Juliet was quiet a moment.

"Sir Gilbert, tell us—" asked Kim while she waited, "what is it probably like down there right now for Adam Livingstone?" She extended the microphone toward Bowles.

"For one like me," said Bowles with a wry grin, "a very tight squeeze! But seriously, everything depends on what damage the quake did down at that level. The passages were really quite passable when we were—"

Juliet's raised hand and the look of excitement on her face brought a sudden end to the brief Bowles interview.

"Adam has come to an intersection of three tunnels . . . much damage . . . can't tell if . . . ," she began again. "Adam, Adam!" she cried, grabbing the tiny microphone attached to her blouse and speaking into it. "Adam, what did you just say?"

She listened intently—and forgot that she was being watched on televisions the world over.

"Jen, Rocky!" she exclaimed down toward the crowd. "Sir Gilbert!" she added, spinning around to Bowles, "Adam says he's just walked out of the tunnel that came from the opposite direction in the de Payns engraving! He's at the same place we were! He's crawling through the hole into the cave right now!"

Frantically Kim tried to get an interpretation, but to no avail. Calmly Bowles attempted to explain the situation, but was interrupted again by Juliet.

"Adam has gone back for the workers and Levites!" said Juliet. "The passage between the cave and the crypt is blocked with debris from the quake . . . he thinks they can clear it . . . he's sending the engineers into the three segments of tunnel to check for potential cracks that might signal danger . . . otherwise they will begin clearing it out. . . ."

(5)

Another interruption caused television cameras to swing away from the pit and toward the nearest street.

A limousine was approaching at great speed. It screeched to a stop. Out stepped the familiar form of Israel's prime minister. He hurried forward through the crowd, then jumped up onto the platform with Juliet, Bowles, and Kim.

Kim briefed him on the latest announcement from below.

"So what is next?" he asked.

"We don't know," answered Juliet. "We are waiting for more news."

The next minutes were interminably long. There was nothing to see, nothing to do. The messages into Juliet's headset from Adam had ceased. All eyes glued themselves down to the crane lines, dangling free since their human weights had been released.

A long anxious period of silence and inactivity set in. No sounds could be heard from below. No messages were sent back.

After perhaps seventy or eighty minutes, one, then another of the lines went taut again, signalling that something had been attached and was ready to be raised out of the earthquake grave.

Up came one line with one of the Army's chief engineers attached. Now up came several workers and another engineer, then workers and equipment.

Another tense minute passed.

There again appeared to be activity at the end of one of the crane lines. Juliet again heard Adam's voice.

"Scott, old buddy," said Adam as Juliet listened. "It seems we're going to need to use my cable for something else. So I am staying behind. Send another line down after me as soon as you can."

"Will do," replied Scott.

Kim knew from the look on Juliet's face that she had heard something in her headset. But she only grinned from ear to ear. She motioned for Jen and Rocky to join her on the news platform.

All around the cavern, thousands of eyes peered down.

"Pull them up!" shouted Scott. His voice echoed across the sea of heads.

Instantly the remaining six cables went taut again, then began to move upward. Overhead the afternoon sun shone down into the cavern.

An object at the end of one line began to come into view.

The glint of the sun flashed the brilliant color of gold!

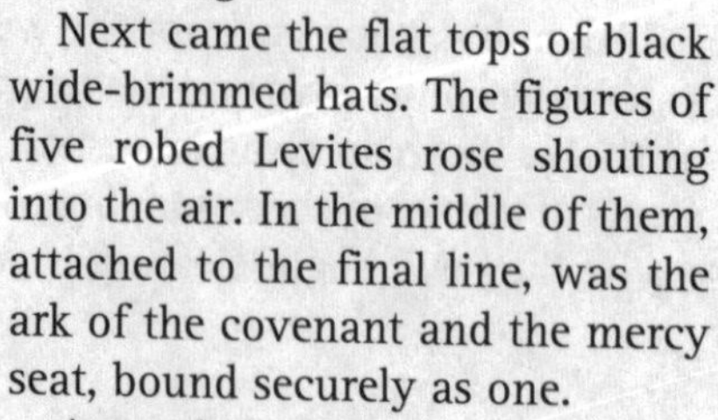

Next came the flat tops of black wide-brimmed hats. The figures of five robed Levites rose shouting into the air. In the middle of them, attached to the final line, was the ark of the covenant and the mercy seat, bound securely as one.

Around the edge of the cavern shouts and exclamations burst out.

"There it is!"

"The ark!"

"It's the ark of the covenant!"

A deafening roar went up from the

crowd. Television cameras zoomed down toward the historic discovery. Around it even the dangling Levites were shouting and waving to the crowd and praising the God of Abraham, Isaac, and Jacob.

(6)

Watching from the edge of the pit some hundred meters west of the news platform, sufficiently surrounded by the throng to avoid any chance of being recognized, a rush of terror seized the heart of Anni D'Abernon, inheritor of the Templar mantle of her family, one of the secret Illuminated Ones, and powerful member of the worldwide Council of Twelve, which was now a Council of Eleven, at the sight of the object before her.

A physical sensation of nausea consumed her as gold flashed off the angels' wings like a searing arrow of truth into her eyes. She felt power instantly drain out of her.

She had failed utterly to stop Livingstone. She knew there would be consequences.

Slowly she turned and stumbled through the crowd and away. For one of the first times in her life, she had no idea what to do. Ever confident, ever in control, it was an utterly unfamiliar and horrifying sensation.

She was not used to this bewilderment and confusion. Perhaps they had misread the signs and this was not the prophesied time. That would explain the silence.

Even by the time Anni D'Abernon reached her car, her self-assurance began to return. Perhaps it was time to withdraw from active participation in spiritual matters for a season, and return their focus to the financial and political aspects of the Dimension, as their founders had done.

(7)

Scott was unfastening workers from their straps, and now sent one of the cables back down into the chasm for Adam.

The ark rose, then the crane arm swung toward the edge of the pit. With exclamations of awe and terror, the crowd parted below it as if an unexploded neutron bomb were swinging above and toward them. Very gently the historic cargo came down . . . down . . . down, and finally rested on the ground. Not a soul moved toward it.

Slowly the Levites descended and landed nearby. Quickly a hundred eager hands rushed to help unlock them from the crane lines.

A minute or two later up rose Adam from the chasm, a true world's hero now. The crowd burst into a roaring cheer of congratulatory shouts and applause.

Liv - ing - stone! one section of the crowd began to chant. Soon thousands had joined in the cadence.

Liv - ing - STONE! LIV - ING - STONE! LIV - ING - STONE!

The moment he was on the ground near the ark, Adam turned, hurried to the platform, embraced Juliet, shook the prime minister's, then Rocky's, Jen's, and Bowles' hands, then turned to Kim Shayne.

"I'm sorry for giving you the brush off earlier, Miss Shayne," he said with a smile. "I was worried about the potential of another aftershock. If you have any questions for me now, I would be happy to attempt to answer them."

"It would certainly seem that you have vindicated yourself for all the world to see," said Kim.

"I can assure you," began Adam, "vindicating myself was not—"

Adam was interrupted by shouts and commotion from near the ark.

"Stop . . . no!" cried a voice.

More yells, shouts, warnings.

"You fool . . . don't—"

A terrible cry sounded, followed by a huge collective gasp from the crowd close by.

Then silence.

"He's dead!" came a shout.

"He touched it and fell over dead!" called out another.

The hush of awe gave way to a crescendo of exclamation and wonder.

Adam jumped from the platform and ran toward the scene. Cameras attempted to follow him. Beside the ark lay the body of a young Jordanian radical who had thought to prove the silly thing a hoax.

Now truly did awe strike into the hearts of the crowd. Even the Levites who had safely brought the ark out of the crypt and prepared it for its rise out of Jeremiah's grave were sobered. The crowd backed further away. The Levites approached, gathered around, and waited. They had touched and carried the ark safely a few minutes earlier, but now seemed hesitant, as if they had not even quite themselves believed the ancient sacred tradition of Uzzah until this moment.

The prime minister approached to discuss with the Levites what should be done. As they talked over practicalities, the body of the dead youth was carried away.

Presently the Levites gathered around it, picked up the ark and mercy seat, set it atop planks of wood for safety, then lifted it and carried it to a waiting military truck. Accompanied by Adam and his team, and an entourage of Israeli officials, it was transported to the Israel Museum, where it would be temporarily housed under strict guard until permanent plans were made.

By evening troops had been brought in and the Damascus Gate site cordoned off.

As Adam had said, the area of the find was under British jurisdiction. But since it was surrounded by the Muslim quarter of the city, a dispute was certain to arise. Following hasty talks by telephone, the prime ministers of the

United Kingdom and Israel issued a joint statement later that afternoon emphasizing the fact that the ark represented Israel's heritage, with the assurance that no British claim would be pursued. If the Palestinians objected, or anyone else in the Arab world, the two leaders said privately to one another, they could take the matter up in the world court. For now it belonged indisputably to Israel.

Newspapers the world over broadcast the find in three- and four-inch headlines.

Adam Livingstone, whom the media had been ridiculing for months, was suddenly the most sought after man in Palestine. Second to Livingstone, Sir Gilbert Bowles was also a sudden star. Most appearances over the next several weeks, however, in Jerusalem and after their return to England at week's end, Adam made with his entire team present, including Sir Gilbert Bowles. They had *all* contributed to the effort, he said, and would share the spotlight together.

thirty-nine

Truth to Change a World

(1)

Over the course of the following months, cleanup and rebuilding operations in Jerusalem were carried out at three or four times the pace normally possible in such circumstances. Truly this was one of the world's most beloved cities. Never had a natural disaster prompted such a worldwide volunteer effort. More people flocked to Israel to help than the country could handle.

Remarkably, as rebuilding efforts began, it was discovered that by far the majority of the damage had occurred in the Muslim sector and to Muslim sites. Much of Jewish Jerusalem would apparently be preserved.

Politically the event was still charged with tension. Privately, the Israelis were determined to use the opportunity to regain control of the Temple Mount area despite the risk of Palestinian outrage or reprisals. The United States and United Kingdom both backed the effort and the U.N. did not appear likely to oppose it. With both sacred Muslim mosques in ruin beyond any hope of repair, Arab claims to the sacred land had been significantly weakened.

Discussions began almost immediately to plan construction adjacent to the Wailing Wall of a permanent repository to house the ark, with a whole new highway system in and out of the city, through the Kidron and Hinnom valleys, in order to handle the huge flow of tourism expected. Many were already predicting that it would become the single most visited site on earth. At its temporary home in the Israel Museum, hundreds of thousands had already come to see the incredible discovery for themselves. Miracles had begun to be reported and were becoming a regular occurrence.

It could truthfully be said that the nation of Israel had never witnessed anything like this. Reports of a massive revival of Messianic Christianity were spreading through the land from northern Galilee to the Dead Sea. Though the ark was an Old Testament find, its effect had prompted a huge outbreak of belief in Jesus Christ as Israel's Messiah. Massive revival seemed to affect Jews the world over, especially among the younger generation. There were reports, unsubstantiated, of a New Testament study group meeting weekly in a conference room in the Knesset.

Statistics showed a marked decrease in the influence of Islam and Buddhism in China, India, and the Middle East. Interest in Christianity and Judaism in these regions was so great that books and Bibles could not be printed fast enough in the necessary languages and dialects to supply a hundredth of the demand.

Thousands of articles and television specials on the Bible were broadcast worldwide in more than a hundred languages. Some new documentary or book on one of the two arks, the Garden of Eden, or Adam Livingstone appeared, it seemed, weekly.

The phenomenon reported a year before on the broadcast of *Sixty/Twenty* of thousands carrying Bibles not just to church, but to work and school and reading them at every opportunity, had become such a commonplace sight that nobody thought twice of it. The only difference was that the thousands had become millions, and the Bibles they carried no longer looked new. The hunger to know the Bible's principles, and the desire to apply them in daily living, had become the unexpected passion of the new millennium. Men, women, and children were accepting Jesus into their hearts by the tens of thousands daily.

(2)

Sunday morning dawned as a bright reminder of resurrection truth to the congregation of Oak Ridge Community Fellowship north of Knoxville. A vibrancy had been growing for some time in the church family, due in no small part to the simple boldness of its pastor in his conviction that the Word of God truly possessed power in this new millennium to work miracles in the hardest of lives and most impossible of circumstances.

As the service broke up, as was his custom, rather than stand facing a solemn exit processional at the door, Rev. Archer moved freely through the crowd, visiting, shaking hands, and laughing informally with these people he loved so dearly.

"Fred and Lucille," he said, warmly embracing the two who were relatively new to the church. "It is good to see you. How is that new job working out, Fred?"

"I'm enjoying it very much," replied Hutchins. "It is an unexpected change in direction for me, but—well, let's just say that with the opportunities it may afford me, and with our financial situation, I am very thankful."

"And, Lucille—you're looking very well."

"I am feeling better every day."

"I've been praying."

"I know you have, Rev. Archer. Fred and I can't tell you how much that means to us."

"I've been planning to call you," said the pastor. "I want to invite you to a Bible study we're going to be starting—nothing fancy. Just going through the Gospels to see what they might have to say—"

He paused as a man approached.

"Mr. Slate—good morning!" Rev. Archer said, shaking the newcomer's hand. "Meet my new friends, Fred and Lucille Hutchins—Fred and Lucille, this is Larry Slate."

More handshakes followed.

"I was telling them, Larry, about the Bible study I spoke with you about yesterday. I hope all three of you will be able to come."

"We don't know much about the Bible, I'm afraid," said Fred.

"Believe me," Slate said, laughing, "neither do I. I doubt if there's a man in this church as ignorant about spiritual things as me. But I'm trying to learn."

"We're all seekers of truth together," said Archer. "I will be there trying to learn just like the rest of you. The Lord isn't looking for perfect people, but for *growing* people."

"Then I think we would very much like to come," said Fred.

"Great!" rejoined the pastor, then moved away to greet more of the worshipers.

The new acquaintances continued to chat, with the result that within twenty minutes Larry Slate was on his way to the Hutchins' home to share Sunday afternoon dinner.

forty

Nothing Is Hid That Shall Not Be Revealed

(1)

The third interview with Sir Daniel Snow was taped in Adam's study several months after the discovery and earthquake. It was scheduled to be aired during prime time three evenings later.

"I see in the papers that matrimony is the next adventure in the Livingstone career," said Snow, after a few minutes of introductory talk had eased both men into the discussion. "The newspapers are full of your wedding plans these days. I think I've seen more photographs of Miss Halsay recently than of you."

"Please don't say that in Juliet's hearing," said Adam, chuckling. "She has had some difficulty with the public aspect of her life with me. But she is handling it bravely. We're both learning to laugh at it."

"When is the happy day?"

"Next week, actually," replied Adam. "We will be married in the gardens of my estate in Sevenoaks."

"Who will perform the ceremony?" asked Snow.

"An American clergyman by the name of Mark Stafford."

"And your best man?"

"I shall have two men beside me—my assistant, Scott Jordan, and my friend, also from the United States, Mr. Rocky McCondy."

"And Miss Halsay?"

"She will be accompanied by her mother and one of my assistants, Jennifer Swaner. A small gathering of family and friends will be in attendance. We would be delighted for you to come, Sir Daniel."

"Thank you. That is most kind of you. I would consider it a great honor."

"But *without* a film crew!"

"Understood," said Snow.

✦ ✦ ✦

As Adam Livingstone's close circle of friends watched the broadcast in Adam's private sitting room three evenings after the taping, including Rocky and the Staffords, just arrived in preparation for the wedding, shufflings of proud embarrassment went around the room as they heard themselves spoken of before the nation. Juliet especially was relieved as the interview moved in other directions.

"I feel I must offer an apology, not only for myself but for many in the media," said the journalist, "for much of our skepticism concerning your activities and claims during the past year."

"Thank you," replied Adam simply. "I was in no way offended. And honestly, it was a difficult time, what with the Ethiopian theft and suspicion of my involvement. How could I blame you for not being hard on me?"

Snow nodded appreciatively.

"Have there been any further developments," he asked, "in identifying those individuals who stole the ark replica from the Sanctuary in Aksum and later destroyed it?"

"Nothing more," replied Adam, shaking his head. "It seems whoever it was has vanished. My attempts, as well as Scotland Yard's, to pinpoint the exact location have been unsuccessful."

"These three astonishing discoveries you have made—they prove the veracity of the Bible beyond doubt, wouldn't you say?" said Snow.

"They certainly do," replied Adam.

"Additionally, it would seem that events have vindicated you far better than anything I could say at this point," Snow went on. "That is why I wanted to contact you for another interview, to put these remarkable finds into perspective. You have been gracious in allowing me to put forward some of the questions people would naturally be curious about, such as your plans with the future Mrs. Livingstone. So now it is your turn. Tell our viewers what is on your mind. What do you think the ark of the covenant signifies, and why has it been revealed at this moment in time? In other words, what does all this *mean*, Adam—these astonishing biblical discoveries?"

"Two things, I believe, Sir Daniel," replied Adam. "One, that the Bible is true, not merely as a historical document, but as a book with power to change lives."

"Why is that so? Why do you consider it so unique among the world's religious documents?"

"Because it is *God's* book, not an invention of man's to explain him. It is *God* who changes lives, Sir Daniel."

"What is the second thing?"

"Many have proven the Bible true long before I came along," replied Adam. "But the world has a way of refuting even the most obvious proofs and will probably find a way to explain away these recent revelations. That is why we mustn't get distracted from their true import. Proving the Bible won't bring people to a saving relationship with Christ. That can only happen as each person decides for himself whether to make Jesus his or her *own* personal Messiah. It's all about why Jesus came . . . and how he will come again, to the hearts of those who are waiting for him. That is the second thing I believe these discoveries signify, that the Messiah, Jesus Christ himself, is soon to return to the earth, and that the revelation of these things that have been hidden in time until now points to that coming."

"And this Messiah—the man Jesus . . . Jesus Christ, who lived in Palestine two thousand years ago—you say he is about to return to the earth?"

"He is."

"How will we know when that time is? Will we see him? He will not be wearing white robes and look like the pictures painted of him, will he? How will we know it is truly him?"

"Jesus will return as a thief in the night," replied Adam. "That is the only information about it he gave, other than telling us to be vigilant and watchful . . . and ready."

"But how do people get *ready*, as you say? Surely you don't mean looking up into the sky as some suggest?"

"No, Sir Daniel. Readiness is born in obedience and in heeding the signs of the times, which he said would precede his coming."

"What are these signs of the times?"

"Earthquakes and rumors of war are two. And great deception throughout the world concerning spiritual things, to name a third."

"What kind of deception?"

"Calling white black and black white. Righteousness being slandered as evil, and evil masking itself as good."

"And you believe the Garden and the two arks are also involved?"

"These revelations God has made, occurring nearly simultaneously in conjunction with the beginning of another millennium, and the massive earthquake—these are all important signs. As I said before, the countdown has begun."

"What countdown," said Snow. "Toward what are we counting, Adam?"

"To the culmination of history. To the building of the new temple as a home for the Messiah."

"Are plans for the rebuilding of the temple actually under way?" replied Snow excitedly. "This is a major news development! I've heard nothing about it. When is it scheduled to begin?"

"It has already begun, Sir Daniel," said Adam with a mysterious smile.

"But . . . but when did all this take place?"

Adam returned the journalist's astonished expression calmly, then replied. "It is a different sort of temple than you mean, Sir Daniel. It has been in progress in hearts for some time."

(2)

Meanwhile . . .

All charges and extradition requests by Ethiopian authorities against Adam Livingstone were dropped.

Funding and support for Operation Noah in Turkey again turned into a flood. Construction on the Noah's ark hangar and other facilities in Ararat City was back in full operation.

In northern California, the manager of the small Christian bookstore continued to see a gratifying number of Bibles leave her shelves. She had noticed increased interest in other Christian products as well. In a slump only a year before, sales were now up 30 percent.

Rev. Archer expanded his Practical Gospels Bible study to three groups weekly. Response was so overwhelming among visitors that Oak Ridge Community Fellowship added an assistant pastor to its staff, whose job was devoted entirely to the training of new Christians in the basic tenets of the faith.

Senator Duke Quinby initiated a political action committee in Washington D.C. called "Restoring Biblical Truth in American Politics." He was praying seriously whether to run again when his present term was up.

Brandi Corwin was attending the local junior college and had become active in the college group at her church. She and her mother had never been closer.

Harry Standgood released a book entitled *Recomputing the Prophetic Calendar: Why 2000 Was Not Really the Year 2000.* In its first month it topped two best-seller lists.

Dr. Oriel Tornay had visited her grandmother twice. They had talked about many things. The young professor was coming to realize what a limited perspective she had held on the depth and scope of the feminine character. Her students at Bryn Mawr College had noticed a distinct shift in the emphasis and tone of her lectures. She did *not* have any future books planned.

Hank Scully had been put in charge of the San Quentin library and was leading a weekly Bible study for inmates.

Warden Ruben was still reading the works of Dostoyevsky.

Angella Quinn was promoted to the head of her publishing group, whose responsibility once a month was to brainstorm creative concepts for getting the Bible—even in the midst of its worldwide revival—read by still more people.

Singapore's Kiang Enterprises continued to perfect its laser scanner and Mars probe. The company's president, Lee-Hia Kiang, however, returned to Calgary to pay a long overdue visit to his pastor-friend from college days. While there, Pastor David led him in a profession of faith in Christ. Most of Kiang's personal energies were now devoted to importing vast quantities of Christian literature and Bibles for distribution throughout Malaysia and the Far East.

Kimberly Shayne's Jerusalem prayer had been answered. She knew that Jesus was real indeed, and had prayed with the new Juliet Livingstone to accept him as her Savior and Lord. She had been promoted to assistant producer in the Documentaries division of the BBC. She and Juliet were the best of friends and saw one another every several weeks.

As for Sir Gilbert Bowles . . . he gave his housekeeper a substantial raise the day he returned from Jerusalem. The moment she was alone, the good lady broke down and wept from the kind words he had spoken and the smile with which he had greeted her. The next morning Bowles removed the serpent from his ear, though he continued to sport his sandy gray ponytail.

He was rarely to be found these days without the Bible Adam had given him. He was growing in the direction of truth, which is the best thing that can be said of any man.

Though he tried to pretend he was keeping his options open, he believed more than he was ready to admit.

(3)

Two women in their early forties, the closest of friends except in the area of relationship that matters most, walked into the same bookstore where Brandi Corwin had found a warm and friendly reception in her season of aloneness.

As on that day, pleasant music was playing from the Christian radio station. The young man behind the counter greeted them with the same smile that had gone into Brandi's heart like an arrow of spiritual sunshine.

"Hello, Jacob," said one of the two women, a member of the church and frequent customer. "I need to get a Bible."

"You know where they are, Mrs. Cameron. Let me know if I can be of any—"

He stopped. The attention of both had been arrested by an announcement over the radio preempting the music.

"—repeating the breaking news," said the broadcaster, "word has just come over the wire services from Jerusalem . . . the prime minister of Israel announced today that the long-awaited plans for rebuilding the temple upon the former site of the Dome of the Rock and the Al-Aqsa Mosque will get under way sometime next year."

"Did you hear that!" said Mrs. Cameron.

"Wow!" was the only word Jacob could immediately find at his disposal.

✦ ✦ ✦

When the two women walked out together ten minutes later, the heart of the one still beat more rapidly than usual for excitement at what she had heard.

"I know we've never really spoken about spiritual things," she said to her friend. "But I really want to share this Bible with you. This is a translation that makes it so easy to understand. I hope you will read it. Everything happening in the world is so significant, and the Bible puts it all into perspective. This book is true. It has the power to change your life."

She handed the other woman the book.

"Thank you," said her friend. "To tell you the truth, I have thought lately that maybe I should read the Bible. I don't really know much about it, but suddenly I want to. I have had the feeling that something is missing in my life, and that the answer might be here. I appreciate this very much. I will read it, I promise."

> *The hour has come for you to wake up from your slumber, because our salvation is nearer now than when we first believed. The night is nearly over; the day is almost here.* ROMANS 13:11-12

About the Author

Michael Phillips has authored nearly fifty fiction and nonfiction books with total sales of more than 5 million copies. These include his best-selling series The Secret of the Rose, The Journals of Corrie Belle Hollister, Caledonia, and The Secrets of Heathersleigh Hall. He is also the editor of twenty-eight best-selling editions of the works of George Macdonald. Phillips and his wife, Judy, live in Eureka, California.